SAY
NOTHING

ELLY MAGDALUYO

Say Nothing
Copyright © 2023 Melissa Magdaluyo
All rights reserved.

www.ellymagdaluyo.com

Paperback ISBN-13: 979-8-9876854-2-6
Hard Cover ISBN-13: 979-8-9876854-3-3

Cover design & Format by: Melissa Magdaluyo
Edited by: Leilani Dewindt

Trigger Warning: This book depicts scenes of abuse and neglect of minors in deplorable situations.

For those who say nothing...

Every year 6.3 million people are victims of human trafficking. If I were to fill a book with all the names of those people, this book you're holding would be 13.6 times the size. Each one of those 6.3 million has a different story, but 6.2 million never make it home to tell it... The 1% that make it home will never live down their memories, and they might just...

Chapter 1

Bexley

"I want my money back for the week, minus last night," I said, trying to hold a firm voice. "It's two-hundred fifty-seven."

My slumlord, Roy, was on his way to bed. He was always on his way to bed when I was leaving for the restaurant at four-thirty in the morning. The night before, he'd raised the rent a hundred dollars a week for the one bedroom I rented in his dilapidating house. Preparing for my personal apocalypse didn't leave me extra funds for higher rent, and I didn't want to lose money I could use for a deposit somewhere else just to have a place to sleep for the week.

"No refunds," he grumbled, not bothering to stop.

"I wasn't asking." I grabbed the metal can with everyone's rent money, ripped it open, and pulled out the cash I'd given him. My stuff was already packed in a bag and slung over my shoulder.

"Uh-uh!" Roy reached into his bathrobe. "Put it

back," he warned as he showed his gun.

"No." The gun should have scared me, but it didn't. My childhood had given me more experience than a person should.

I closed the can, leaving everyone else's money, and turned to the front door.

"I said, 'Put it back.'" The gun cocked behind me.

I turned around again and walked right up to the gun he had pointed at me. "Go ahead." I looked at his ugly, yellowish-brown eyes. "Please... kill me. I've been waiting to die since I was eight. So, do it."

Roy's angry eyes continued to stare down at me.

"Aim here for an effective kill." I wrapped my hand around his, pointing the gun up under my chin, angled to hit my amygdala. "I've never been brave enough, so do me a favor."

"You're sick. Get the hell out of my house." He threw his hand to the side and stepped back to get away from me.

I didn't understand why it always worked. Every time I asked someone to kill me they'd never do it. I might've gotten beat, but I was still painfully alive.

———※※———

"Moving again?" Carol asked when she saw me come in the back door, putting the black bag in the corner. Her fading strawberry-blonde hair had the small glow of a halo from the fluorescent lights above us. She ever so slightly reminded me of my mom, with her softly pointed features and hair pulled in a French twist. Like my mom, she was tough but fair, smiled at everyone until they gave her a reason not to, and was decently kind to me.

"He raised the rent again, and I'm tired of the parties." I grabbed my apron and wrapped it around my waist.

"Oh..." Carol stood in the small area where the CO_2 tanks and soda syrups were, continuing to look at me.

"You know, we have a perfectly good room at our house. Rent's so cheap, some would say it's free." Joe, Carol's husband, put his arms up in the hallway where the door to the walk-in fridge was. He wore a small kind smile.

I shook my head. "I appreciate it, but I'll get it worked out."

"We won't bother ya, hun. We're a couple of old farts that work all day, go home, and go straight to bed. It'd help you get ahead and save up, and we'd feel better knowing you're not bouncin' place to place." Carol spoke almost sympathetically.

I pulled back the corner of my mouth and shook my head. "Thank you, but no." The could never understand how much I wanted to say yes. It would be quieter but it could put them in danger. They were too kind to bring my mess to their door. I also wouldn't be able to lie about where big chunks of my money went. I was paying for several getaway cars in different locations. The cars weren't usable to me except for their intended purpose. If I had to go off-grid, I needed cars I'd never been seen in before.

"Well... offer's always on the table, kiddo. Just a night, or a year, it don't matter. The room's yours. Alright?" Joe looked disappointed but took it as kindly as he always did.

I nodded. "Thanks."

"Yep." He gave one of his cheerier smiles and dropped his hand from the wall.

I waited for him to go back behind the grill before I walked through the kitchen and out to the dining room to get started putting the chairs down and setting the tables. Fridays were always busy.

———————※◈※———————

"Honey, I'm worried about you. Where are you gonna stay tonight?" Linda asked quietly as I refilled the salt and pepper shakers.

"You can stay with me," one of the other servers, Ann, suggested. She was likely the closest thing I had to a friend, but I still maintained my distance from her as much as I could. She just had her son when I first moved to Monterey, California two years ago, and I didn't want to put either of them in harm's way by being around them too much. Our interactions were typically only at work or when she needed a babysitter and had no one else.

I shook my head, keeping my eyes focused on my work. "I found a listing in the paper this morning. It's taken care of, and no one needs to worry."

"Do you wanna leave a little early? I mean, I know it's already late, but if you call them now, explain to them that you need something for tonight, then at least you could have a roof over your head." Carol's voice was still full of concern.

"Or she could take the free room we offered," Joe called from behind the window to the kitchen.

I shook my head and looked at Carol. "I'm alright, I still have a customer, and thank you, but no." I looked back at Joe so he'd know I was speaking to him too.

She let out a sigh. "Okay. Well, you know where we are, and the back door will be open if you change your mind."

It was nice that Carol and Joe were sweet enough to care, unlike most, but I had to minimize my impact on any one place or person. Part of me was already considering finding a new job and place to live because two years was a long time to stay, but moving wasn't so easy. The cars I had stashed would have to move with me, and I'd have to plan new escape routes again.

"I'll cash you out. It looks like your last table is leaving." Carol held out her hand for my book of receipts.

I gave it to her and watched as the old guy who'd come in alone put cash on the table after he got up. He used to come in with his wife every Friday, but now it was just him. She'd passed away less than a year ago.

"Have a good night," I told him on his way out the door, picking up the plate and glass from the table.

He gave a polite nod. "You too."

"I've got this," Ann picked up the tip money and gave it to me before she took the dishes from me. "I've still got a guy just sitting and drinking coffee and you did most of the side work."

"I don't mind." I liked staying busy, and if she had less side work, she could go home to her son earlier. "And I'll wait out your customer and leave the money with Carol." I took the dishes back. "Go home and see Rowen." She had someone waiting for her and I didn't, so it only seemed fair.

"Bex." Ann gave me a pouting look.

I shook my head. "Go."

"You're too good of a friend." She was going to touch my arm then remembered she shouldn't. I couldn't stand being touched. It sent painful shocks of electricity through my nervous system.

"Goodnight." I forced a kind smile and walked back to the cart with the tubs for the dishes, then went to the guy sitting with the single cup of coffee and his laptop. He had a stubble beard, dark hair, and dark eyes. While he looked like he could knock someone out, he seemed calm and quiet by nature. "Can I get you another cup of coffee or a slice of pie?" I asked quietly.

He looked up from a screen, seeming like he was taking a moment to bring himself back to reality. "Uh," he looked down, "no thanks. Just the check."

I nodded. "I'll be right back with it."

Chapter 2

Ryan

Idiot. Grey Maslen was a goddamn idiot, and I didn't know why I kept putting up with his annoying ass. It was nice having my classes paid for, but at a certain point, he was annoying enough that it wasn't worth it; and he was closely approaching that point. He considered us friends, but really, I'd never been able to shake him. Grey was like a conspicuous tattoo I couldn't scrub off. Apparently, his parents taking me and my brother in as kids meant he was glued to me for life.

I barely landed in Monterey before Grey's impatient ass was calling about the girl we found information on from an external hard drive. She was definitely pretty, but he'd gone all stupid at the sight of her... Whatever. I was getting paid.

It wasn't challenging to go to the restaurant she worked at, sit at a table, and observe while I worked on my term paper. She was goddamn scared of everything, always keeping a careful eye on the door and the people in the dining room. When someone got too close to her, she automatically moved to put an acceptable amount of distance between herself and that person. The two things that stood out to me most were her voice and her calm nature—past the serious anxiety. She waited on the table behind mine, and her voice had an eloquent charm. I hadn't meant to stay so long that my waitress left and she took over.

When she'd been waiting for customers to clear out, I watched as she sat in a corner booth, rolling silverware, and she seemed perfectly content completing the monotonous task. I certainly wasn't as obsessed as Grey, but after watching her for a couple hours, I had a mild curiosity in meeting her. After I texted Grey, I smoked a cigarette in my truck and waited across the street. It was only thirty minutes or so until she walked out with a black garbage bag slung over her shoulder. I thought she was going to throw it in the dumpster on her way out, but she didn't. She carried it with her down the alley. I waited until I could hardly see her before I started my truck and followed her. Something told me if she suspected she was being followed she'd make a run for it. There was a hypervigilance about her, and I understood it because I was the same way.

"So? Do you know anything yet?" Grey asked me.

I frowned and lit up another cigarette. "If you're so damn concerned, why aren't you down here stalking her?"

"Because I have board meetings. Have you found anything out, or talked to her?"

I took in a breath and wondered if I should say anything at all. "She's staying in a motel. I've been following her for the last hour and a half. No car, it looks like she's carrying everything she's got in a trash bag, and I went inside one of the motels she stopped at and they said she left because she couldn't afford the rate." The girl had a name listed on the hard drive, Bexley Nelson, but I had done enough digging to know it was a fake.

"But she found one she could afford?"

"Mm-hm."

Grey's response was automatic, and almost like he was upset. "Go inside, pay for the room, and tell them to give her money back. Use my card."

I rolled my eyes. "If I'm supposed to stalk from a distance, then I have to keep the distance. This girl's jumpy, man. I don't think she wants anyone to find or notice her."

"Too bad. I noticed, and I wanna help."

"Then help her when you get down here. I'm not gonna freak her out." I took a drag from my cigarette and watched as the girl came out of the room she rented.

"Okay..." The inflection in Grey's voice displayed he was pissed, but he knew it was pointless to argue with me. Once I decided something, I was stubborn to move. "I gotta go to bed. Check in on her in the morning."

"Mm-hm. Bye." I hung up and put my phone in the cup holder, watching as the girl looked around before she went dumpster diving behind the gas station next to the motel. It took a few minutes for me to realize she was looking for food. Obviously, she wasn't slinging drugs anymore, or she wouldn't have been in such poor financial shape. She found a premade sandwich still in the plastic container, opened it, inspected the sandwich, then looked around her. Her face changed to hopeless-ness, and she threw the sandwich back in the trash and walked back to her room.

Dammit...

I started my truck, went to the gas station, bought a bunch of food and shit, then went and rented the room next to hers. I wouldn't look too suspicious because my suitcase was still in the back of my truck from Seattle. The girl was sitting in the chair outside the door to her room, reading a book. It honestly looked like she was struggling though, which gave me enough to try to be social and strike up a conversation.

"*Trigonometry for Dummies*, that must be a real page-turner," I said casually as I put my key in the door.

The girl looked over at me, partially closed the book to look at the cover, then at me again. "It might be if they dumbed it down a little more."

I opened my door and put my suitcase inside. "Yeah, that book probably isn't the best guide if you're honestly trying to learn. It works better to apply the problem to something you can remember." I looked at her and the unsure posture of her body.

Her shoulders pulled up in a nervous shrug. "It's the only book I could mildly understand from the library, and I don't know how to apply a cotangent to anything because I can't even understand the definition."

"Can I see?" I held out my hand for the book.

She bit her bottom lip for a second and shook her head. "It's okay. I can ask a friend tomorrow. I don't wanna take up your night."

"You're not, and I happen to be good at math." I continued to hold out my hand.

She shook her head again, closing the book. "Thanks, but I really have to get to bed."

I took in a deep breath and gritted my teeth for a second as she got up and turned to her door.

"Okay. Fine. Here." I set down the bag of food from the gas station. "I saw you digging in the dumpster when I drove by to get a pack of smokes. If you change your mind about the help with your math problem, you know where to find me. I'm here all night."

She stopped with her hand on the door, looking confused, embarrassed, and maybe scared. Her eyes glanced at the bag for a moment—seeming almost desperate—before she looked at me again, then went inside her room.

I was mentally growling. As stubborn as I was, I was irritated by other people's stubbornness when there wasn't a good reason behind it. So, I went into my room, scribbled a triangle on a piece of paper, picked up the bag of food, and knocked on her door. It took a second or two, but she cracked open the door with a scared look on her face.

"Maybe it was pride, but you forgot this." I held the bag out so she'd have to take it, and hesitantly, she did. Before she could speak a word of protest, I held up the paper with the triangle. "This is a right triangle. What makes it a right triangle is that in this corner," I pointed on the paper, "the angle is ninety degrees. The objective is to find the angle of this part of the triangle." I pointed to the opposite angle. "To do that, you measure this side. We'll call it side O because it's on the opposite side of this angle. And we'll say that the measurement is ten inches." I put the paper against the door and wrote the number ten. "Then we'll call this side A because it's adjacent to this angle. Meaning, it's 'next to' the angle. And side A's measurement is fifty inches." I wrote out the number again. "Now, you take the number from side O and divide it by side A. So, ten divided by fifty is point two, which is twenty degrees. That would be your tangent. Now, with triangles, all points have to add up to a hundred eighty degrees, so if you need to find the other angle, you'd add ninety and twenty, which gives you one-ten. One-ten minus one-eighty is seventy." I wrote out everything as I explained it and handed her the paper. "You shouldn't be embarrassed to accept help when it's offered. The majority of the time, people have good intentions. Have a good night." I turned to go back to my room, leaving the girl with a miffed expression.

I stopped when she said, "Wait," and turned around.

She held out the bag of food timidly. "I ha-have money to buy food. I'm just trying to save right now."

I nodded toward the bag. "Then save up."

She looked away for a moment, and her face was so sad I almost felt like I should apologize for being an asshole and find the nearest bridge to jump off of. When she looked at me again, the corner of her mouth pulled back and a deep-set dimple showed. "Thanks."

"Anytime. Knock on my door if you need more help understanding that book. I'm not usually asleep until two or three." That wasn't true. It was far past my normal bedtime. I went to bed at ten, I didn't party, didn't stay out late with friends. Ten. I went to bed at ten, and I was up at six.

"Okay." She nodded and went back into her room, quietly closing the door.

I let out a huff. What a pain in the ass...

A quiet knock on the door interrupted my train of thought. I was trying to finish the last paper I had due. All my other homework had been finished before the start of Spring break, but I wanted to put some actual thought and effort into this paper, so I mulled over my ideas all week long.

I checked my watch before walking to the door and opening it. It was just after one.

"I'm sorry to bother you. I saw your lights were still on, and I was wondering if you could help me with more of this?" The girl looked at me almost like she was in trouble for something.

"Yeah... One sec." I walked back and grabbed my phone off the dresser, then went out on the balcony. She probably wouldn't want to sit in a room with a stranger, so I didn't bother to ask. "What've you got?"

She opened her book, already sitting in the crappy plastic chairs provided by the hotel. "I'm supposed to put these into a graph, but I don't know how." She itched under the hair pinned to the back of her head. It was interesting that her hairstyle had never changed through

the years of pictures Grey and I found, and it looked the same in person.

"Easy enough," I muttered, pulling over another chair, then sat down. She handed me the papers she was working on. I looked them over, realizing they weren't normal homework papers like I thought. "GED prep test?" I looked at her.

She bit the inside of her cheek as she looked at the papers with embarrassment, then nodded. "Yeah. Um... I didn't get to go to school as a child, so I'm trying to learn all this stuff and take the test." Her voice was smooth and quiet, but she looked humiliated.

"At least you're doing it. A lot of people wouldn't bother." I rewrote a couple of numbers she had wrong as I spoke.

She held up her shoulders. "I can't go to college without it."

"Nope." I pointed at the paper. "You had the right idea here, but the wrong answer. Since these numbers are in increments of ten, you can set up your graph the same way. These ones are for Y, and these are for X." I handed her the pencil.

She looked down at the paper with a slight frown. "I guess that was my problem." She started writing increments of ten up the side, then out for Y. "Are these supposed to go in any particular order on the graph? I've never done this before."

"Not this one. I'd just go in the order you solved the problems."

She put dots down on the graph, then drew a line to connect them.

"Any others you need help with?"

"Not for math. Are you any good with chemical compounds?"

"Show me what you've got."

The girl pulled out a paper from behind the book on her lap.

"So, what do you mean you didn't go to school?" I asked as she flipped through a packet of papers. "Like, at all?"

She shook her head. "Just until I was eight, otherwise, nothing after..."

"Did your parents try to homeschool you?" How was it possible she had no schooling? She'd hardly be able to read, or even add up the basic numbers to do the math she was working on.

"No... There was a set of encyclopedias in the house, but I didn't really learn to read until I was fourteen."

I raised an eyebrow, slightly disgusted at the thought. "Did you grow up in a cult or something?"

"Or something," she responded quietly, pointing to the packet. "I don't understand what I'm supposed to do here."

I took it and started reading. It was hard to focus because I wanted to keep prying about why she hadn't been allowed to go to school. What was her reading comprehension like? She was twenty-two, had no more than eight years of self-education, and was trying to pass the GED so she could... do what? College wasn't all that difficult for people who'd gone to school, but what about for her? Did she know how to cite a paper, take notes, or anything common in college; things a GED wouldn't test on?

"This one's gonna take a while to complete. Any chance you have time tomorrow to do this? We can meet up at a coffee shop or something."

"No, I have the test tomorrow, but it's okay. I can try to figure it out. I don't want to keep you up." She closed up the packet. "Thank you for the help with the graph."

"Sit your tiny ass down," I said when she started to stand.

She looked at me like she wasn't sure what to do and slowly sat. I held out my hand for the paper.

"Really, it's okay. You've helped me enough."

"Zip it. We're doing it." I opened the packet to the right page. "Do you have the periodic table in your book?"

It took me about an hour to show her what she was supposed to do, explain it, and help her work it out. I tossed in the occasional question, but she wasn't very forthcoming with information about herself. I had a good laugh when she was able to keep up a conversation about string theory, though. Basic math eluded her, but string theory didn't. Apparently, she liked to read anything she could get her hands on. It was her way of learning outside of a classroom. I was fairly fascinated by her, wondering where she came from, and what in the world Roger Maslen's association with her could've been. He was Grey's asshole father, and worth many more billions than Grey. I was grateful he'd taken me and my brother in as kids, but he was still a dick.

"What's she like?" Grey sounded like he was about to lose his mind with curiosity.

"Scared of her own shadow... I don't know. She's nice, and smart—sort of." I stuffed a folder into my laptop bag, holding the phone up with my shoulder.

"What do you mean?"

"Her ability to learn, retain, and apply is exceedingly high, but she's delayed in knowledge because she only had a couple years of schooling until she was eight. Her parents kept her on a tight leash from the sounds of it." I slung my bag over my shoulder and grabbed my keys.

"Did she say where she grew up?"

"I didn't ask. She got squirrely every time I asked too personal of a question."

There was a quiet clicking of keys in the background. "Mad jumpy, or scared jumpy?"

"I said she was scared of her own shadow, what do you think?" Stupid questions pissed me off.

"Did you mention anything about my family name

or business?"

I walked through the glass door of the basement in the Maslen's Pebble Beach house. I stayed in the house with Grey's little brother, Sam, to make sure he didn't do anything stupid. "In a roundabout way. I mentioned I worked for MWM, but she didn't know what it was, showed no signs of lying, so then I threw out your dad's name casually, and still nothing."

"Weird... You'd think there'd be something, just based on the detail of records kept on her over the years."

I shrugged as I walked into the garage. "Yeah. I don't know. I could try putting a picture of you, me, and your dad on my phone. The one from the Hampton's when we went fishing."

"Do you have an excuse to see her again?"

"Yeah. Coffee after class. She's taking the GED on campus, so we're meeting up after."

"Then try it. It can't hurt, right?"

"Nope. I'll talk to you later. I'm running late." I got in my truck and closed the door.

Grey laughed a little. "No, you're not, but bye."

I hung up and tossed my phone on the dash.

Chapter 3

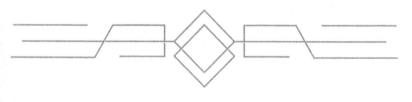

Grey

"Really? This is where we're going?" My brother, Sam, gave the diner a twisted look as we pulled into the parking lot.

"Yeah. Ryan said the food is good." I turned into a parking space, trying not to let my nerves get the better of me. Bexley Nelson's face was burned into my mind the moment I saw the first picture of her. Ryan had spent the last couple weeks hanging out with her and getting to know her; now it was my turn.

"I can't even picture Ryan eating here, but I'm down. Burgers sound good." Sam unbuckled himself and got out.

I smiled a little at how easy Sam was to please and got out of the car. He was a good kid, but our parents didn't make time for him, so I did. Every two weeks, I flew to Monterey, where Sam went to school, to spend the weekend with him. He went to a private school away from Seattle because the baseball program was better, and Ryan lived with him in my parents' house in Pebble Beach. In exchange, I paid for Ryan's college classes and looked after *his* little brother, Tim. Unlike Sam, he was an adult, but also a severe agoraphobic who never left the basement of Ryan's house in Seattle.

"Hi there, I'll be right with you," a red-headed lady said as she walked by with a tray full of food.

I gave her a nod with a polite smile, then looked around for Bexley. My heart stopped and restarted when I spotted her at a table around the side of the diner. She was far more beautiful in person. Her doe eyes were dark brown with long lashes, and she had the slightest of a saddened resting face. The hard drive didn't explain what had happened to her or why my dad had been having her followed for the last seven years. Usually, he only kept tabs on people he was worried about getting sued by, but her records were different. There were seven years of medical history, financial records, pictures of weird buildings that weren't really warehouses but were supposed to be, and pictures of a creepy house that had dolls hanging from their necks in the basement.

Bex had undergone thousands of dollars worth in cosmetic surgeries down in Mexico to remove scars, got a full mouth of dental implants, and corrected broken bones that'd gone untreated. She used to run drugs across the border for a cartel out of LA but quit after the last of her surgeries. The financial records for her were strange and incomplete. It had her taxes, a list of her known debts, but there was money that was completely unaccounted for. Whoever my father had hired to track her couldn't find where the missing sums of money went. She didn't have a bank account, or at least not one they could find.

"Damn, she's hot."

I looked at Sam to see where he was looking, and he had his sight set on Bex too. "Don't be disrespectful," I responded quietly.

"Who's being disrespectful? She's a knockout."

My eyebrows raised. "And it's not okay to talk about women like that. Knock it off and act like you know what manners are."

Sam gave me a wry expression. "What's with you? Are you pissed at me or something?"

I took a deep breath and let it out in a sigh. "No. Sorry, I'm stressed out. But still, you shouldn't talk about women that way. It's rude."

"Just the two of you?" the redheaded lady asked as she grabbed two menus.

I nodded with a smile. "Yes, please."

"Right this way." She led us to a corner booth. "Your server will be right with you."

"Can we get that girl over there?" Sam asked as he pointed to Bexley.

My heart jumped a little. I wasn't going to ask, and it wasn't bad that Sam *did,* I just wasn't expecting him to.

The lady turned to look. "Bex? Sure. I'll send her right over."

I could've kissed Sam but continued to appear indifferent.

"Hey, a hundred bucks says I can get her to go out on a date with me." Sam smiled at me with an excited smile.

"She's too old for you."

"So? Older chicks are—"

"Don't even say it," I warned.

"Pretty?"

I raised my eyebrows at him. "And you're jailbait. Don't." I looked over toward Bex again, watching as she forced herself to smile at the customers who were taking forever to order. None of the pictures I'd seen of her had her smiling. Granted, most were for medical purposes, but even the candid ones, she was never smiling. She was a complete mystery to me. There was no real record of where she came from, what she'd survived, or why she didn't smile. Everything about her screamed that she was a victim of abuse, but I couldn't see how my dad would fit into that. He'd laundered money for all kinds of illicit businesses, which was the whole reason I was out to take him down. My grandpa had prided himself on honest business, and I wanted to pinch my dad out and restore honesty into MWM.

I looked down at the menu when Bex turned around so she wouldn't catch me staring at her.

"Hundred bucks. Take it or leave it."

"Leave it. Don't bother her."

"Hi, welcome to Joe's Place. Can I get you started with something to drink, we have fresh lemonade or sweet tea?" She looked up from the notepad in her hand.

Her voice was just as stunning as she was. It killed me that I didn't already know her. I wanted to listen to everything she ever had to say, but I also wanted to find a way to make her smile.

Sam gave his most charming smile. "Which one's better?"

"Sweet tea." She seemed unphased by Sam's million-dollar grin. Ryan was right, she was the quiet type, which meant Sam wouldn't stand a chance.

"I'll have sweet tea then." He held his brilliant and perfect smile, looking relaxed but slightly cocky.

"And I'll have two lemonades because he doesn't like tea and he'll drink all of mine." I handed her my menu with a gentler smile. "I'll also have the Great Dane sandwich with no mustard seed, please."

She nodded once and took the menu. Something in her eyes had changed when she looked at me, so I had a small chance. Reading people was a skill of mine. I could pick up on the most subtle of changes on a person's face.

"And I'll have The Whip, with everything on it, since I probably won't get another suggestion from you." Sam held up his menu with another big smile.

"I'll be back with your drinks." She forced a smile

before she turned to go turn the ticket in.

"Dude, you just tanked me. I had a chance until you told her I wouldn't drink the damn tea," Sam complained quietly.

"Then I guess you owe me a hundred bucks." I looked at him and smiled. "Pay up."

He rolled his eyes. "I'm not done yet."

"You are, you just haven't figured it out yet. Did you retake the test you missed?" I cared about his test, but not enough to really pay attention. Keeping my eyes on Sam meant I could keep my peripheral on Bex. The redhead was ogling at me as she talked to Bex. I could only assume it was because she knew who I was. Not everyone did, but a better population of the US. I was the grandson of Willum Maslen who started up Maslen Wealth Management, most commonly referred to as MWM. My family and I were all billionaires, but like my Pops, I'd earned my billions myself. My arrogant father had just walked into Pops' business and was handed his fortune. And from what I'd found, what he had earned was mostly dirty money.

"Has anyone taken care of you guys yet?" a different waitress with faded purple hair asked as she approached the table.

"Yeah." Sam glanced back at Bex, then looked at the girl. "What's her story? She's gorgeous, and I wanna ask her out."

The girl looked over at Bex. "Uh, I don't know, but I wouldn't. She's super weird. Like a stray dog or something." She looked at Sam flirtatiously. "I'll go out with you, though. I'm off at eight."

Sam's expression had changed to mild disgust the minute the girl called Bex weird. "Pass. I don't date mean girls. And why settle for a five when I could go for ten." He looked at me. "Did you hear about Ryan and Sarah?"

I shook my head, waiting for the purple-haired girl to walk away. "Nice one." I chuckled a little.

"Dude, for real?" He glanced over in disgust. "Who says shit like that right off the cuff?"

"Someone could say the same about you." I pretended not to notice right away that Bex was coming back.

"So, who would we have to talk to, to have you sit and eat with us?" Sam asked as Bex set two lemonades on the table.

I smacked the back of Sam's head. "Manners." I looked at her apologetically. "Sorry. He doesn't get out much, we try to keep him locked up from society."

She frowned and walked away from the table without a word, like I'd called her something hurtful. It was a strange response, then I sat there wondering why she might look at me that way.

"What the hell, man?" Sam smoothed his hair forward. "I wasn't being a pig."

I looked at him. "You need to learn to read the room. She's not interested. Girls like her don't respond to aggressive passes. Look at her, right now." I kept my voice quiet as I snapped at him.

Sam glanced over, then looked at me. "What?"

"Do you see how her hands are shaking just talking to those old guys over there? Or how she's keeping her distance from every table she has to stand at? She's *afraid*, Sam. Women aren't your property, you don't get to treat them how you want. Quit acting like you're excited to jump in someone's pants and observe your audience before you start acting like a jackass."

"Sorry... Seriously, what is up with you? Did dad piss you off or something?" He looked at me like I was an alien, likely because it wasn't often that I chastised him.

"No. I don't like that you think that behavior is okay. If you're so desperate to have a girlfriend and keep one, then man up."

Sam and I ate without him making any more passes

at Bex. I tried to focus on him a little more and her a little less, but I kept stealing glances. It was interesting the way people interacted with her. Customers were either desperate to get her to like them or acted like she didn't exist in the world. She paid more attention to the ones who paid her no mind, so when she brought our food, I thanked her but tried to pay no mind.

After a table of teenagers got up, I noticed them swiping another girl's tips off the table on their way out, but so did Bex. She didn't say anything to the kids, and for a moment, I thought she was going to tell her boss, but she was just looking around to see if anyone else noticed. Bex picked up the check on each table, then pulled cash out of her apron and left it in place of the money that'd been stolen. When the blonde girl finally noticed that her tables were empty, Bex quickly started grabbing dishes and didn't say a word to the other waitress. I knew from the records on the hard drive that she didn't really have money to give. Her beauty was radiant, and not just because of her appearance... I had to know her. It had nothing to do with finding out her connection to my dad, I just wanted to know a person who was so quietly humble.

As soon as Sam was done with his food, I got up from the table to go ask her for the check. Bex was standing against a counter with her back to the front of the diner munching on ice cubes. I don't know how a person made it look so good, but she did. Her ankles were crossed as she stared thoughtfully at the counter across from her. The pale blue t-shirt complimented her complexion, and the way her hair was pinned up could've fit any occasion.

"Miss?" I wore a small smile, looking forward to seeing her soft eyes again, but she didn't hear me. "Miss?" I reached forward to carefully touch her arm but didn't expect that she'd jump so hard and drop the glass in her hand.

28

"Opa!" the redhead called from the back at the sound of glass shattering.

Bex held her arm as if I'd truly hurt her. Her eyes were sad and afraid when she looked to see me standing there. I felt like an asshole for scaring her because I knew better than to touch someone without them expecting it.

"I'm sorry. I didn't mean to startle you." I glanced down at her arm because she was massaging it like it was still hurting her.

"No. I, um... I-I." She swallowed hard and tried again. "Is there something I can get for you?" Her eyelashes fluttered as she tried to maintain eye contact.

"Just the check." I gave a hopeful and kind smile as I held out my credit card to her.

"Of course. I'm sorry." She took the card and walked behind the half wall to grab a caution sign for the mess of broken glass.

"No apology necessary. We ate fast." I kept my tone kind as I walked toward the front counter where the cash register was. "Do you go to school around here?" I looked at her with the same small smile, hoping she'd talk to me now that Sam wasn't there to be a pest.

"No." She put the receipt in front of me with a pen.

"Are you from around here?"

"No."

I laughed a little, smiling at the paper. "Where are you from?"

"Illinois."

"Oh yeah?" I looked up at her with a smile. "What part?" From what Tim and Ryan could find, there was nothing but a weak paper trail in Illinois.

She shook her head. "Small town. No one's ever heard of it."

"Well, if it's an actual town, someone's had to have heard of it before." I smiled a little more because she seemed to be easing up a bit.

"Galena."

I laughed. "I haven't heard of it."

She smiled a little but didn't seem entirely comfortable.

"What's your name?" I put the pen down.

"Bexley."

"Bexley... I haven't heard of that either. I like it. I'm Grey." I reached my hand over with a continued smile.

She clenched her hand closed for just a brief moment—looking nervous—then shook my hand. "Nice to meet you."

"You too. Have a good night." I turned and walked back to the table because I was going to get on my knees and beg her to go out with me if I didn't leave.

"Well?" Sam asked. "Did you ask her out?"

I shook my head and put my credit card in my pocket. "No. Put that hundred you owe me on the table and let's go."

He gave a wry smile. "Trying to win her over with money? That's not your style."

I shook my head. "No, she gave up some of her tip money when those loudmouths from your school swiped them from the other girl's tables. Put it on the table and let's go."

"Okay. Did you at least get her number?"

I shook my head and laughed a little. "Just shut up and let's go."

Sam slid out of the booth and we left.

"Damn it, man. Go back in there and ask her out. You were staring at her the whole time. You're in love, just do it. It's been years since you've had a girlfriend," Sam said when we were halfway to the car.

"I don't have to go back in. I left my wallet behind." I looked at him with a smile. "She'll call."

"You're asking to get ripped off."

I shook my head, smiling as I walked on my light cloud. "She won't. I told you, she replaced that other girl's money with her own. She'll call, I'll come back tomorrow, and I'll ask her out."

"Yeah, good luck with that."

I didn't need luck. If it didn't work, I still had Ryan as a resource.

Chapter 4

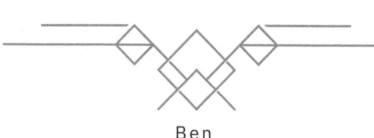

Ben

"Okay, let's work on our trust exercise before time's up today." I gave a kind smile.

My patient, Ethan, had been locked in a shed for a little over a year. His evil and adolescent parents had drawn inspiration from a book they'd read. The things people did to children made me want to puke, but I had to listen, and I had to help. I couldn't help my sweet baby sister who'd been taken when I was sixteen, so I had to help other kids.

Ethan got up from the couch and walked over to the white shag rug under the window. I got up too, slipped my shoes off, sat directly in front of him, and held out my hands. Ethan had severe PTSD and a form of Sensory Processing Disorder from the abuse he'd sustained. So, every session, we'd sit down on the floor facing each other. He'd put his hands on top of mine, and I'd ask simple questions.

"What's your number today?" I asked.

"Three." Ethan's blue eyes were focused on our hands.

"Not bad. Can you look at me and tell me if it gets better or worse?"

He carefully looked up and trembled a little as he did.

I gave a reassuring smile. "It's okay if you need to take a break and count," I reminded.

Ethan shook his head. "Five." His face was honest, but he was also trying to be brave. I appreciated how much he tried to push past his fears. A lot of kids I saw didn't have the ambition Ethan had, but I attributed some of that to Ethan's grandma. She was nothing like her daughter. She supported Ethan and continued to encourage him. He was only seven years old but tried to act a little older.

"Five isn't bad. How was your day at school today?" I kept eye contact with him, making sure to keep a light smile.

"I got an A plus on my art project. I made a clay dragon, and Mrs. Elmer said she's gonna show it in the glass case." Ethan glanced down at our hands.

"Congratulations. Are you happy about that?"

He nodded. "Yeah."

"Good. Did you tell your Grandma?"

He nodded again. "She bought me an ice cream cone on the way here."

"Yeah? What flavor did you get?"

"Chocolate."

Ice cream made me think of my sister. She was obsessed. Vanilla and strawberry swirl. She'd want the same thing every time. I'd always get rocky road, and halfway through, she'd get sick of hers and take mine. My other sister would have never gotten away with it, but Hannah was different... I'd let her get away with anything.

"Your turn." Ethan pulled back his hands, then held

them palms up.

I put my hands on top of his.

"Did you ever get anything put in the display case at school?" Ethan asked earnestly.

"I did, but not until high school. I broke a record for baseball, so my trophy went in the display case."

"Wow. Um... What's your favorite kind of ice cream?"

"Strawberry swirl." I gave an adoring smile at the question.

"Weird. I don't think they have that kind at McDonald's."

"No. Probably not." I laughed a little.

"Am I your favorite patient?"

I scoffed like it was a silly question. "Are you kidding? Of course you are." At least I didn't have to lie.

Ethan smiled just a little. "Good, 'cause you're my favorite doctor."

"Well, thank you, Sir." I picked up my hands and held out a fist. "That's it for today. You're doin' good."

Ethan bumped my fist, said, "Thanks," and got up from the rug.

I got up and walked behind Ethan. As soon as I opened the door, he ran quickly down the hall to his grandma—a massive improvement from eleven months ago when he first came to see me. He used to cry when it was time for him to go home.

"How'd it go?" Gretchen, Ethan's grandma, asked him.

Ethan looked up at her. "Good. Can I go play at Aden's house now?"

Gretchen looked at me for confirmation. There were times when Ethan wouldn't want to answer my questions or engage, but it hadn't been that way for a few months now, so I nodded.

Gretchen smiled down at him. "I guess, but I need to call Aden's mother first." She looked at me. "Thanks,

Doctor Lawrence."

I gave a smile and nodded. "No problem. You two have a good evening and I'll see you next week."

"Say goodbye," Gretchen reminded Ethan.

Unexpectedly, Ethan stepped toward me, hugged my side briefly, and said a quick "bye." Gretchen and I looked at each other half surprised as Ethan went to the door.

"Well, all right then," she laughed. "Have a good evening."

I laughed a little. "You too." I watched as Gretchen left behind Ethan. It felt good to have one more kid on the path to improvement. I didn't know if I'd ever have that chance with Hannah. I knew she was out there somewhere, but I'd never been able to find her.

"Any plans tonight, Doctor Lawrence?" Amy, the girl who manned the front desk, asked.

"Yeah," I sighed. "Dinner with the family."

"That sounds like fun," Amy smiled.

"Sounds like chaos. Is anyone else still in session, or am I the last one?" I pulled the mail from the basket on the end of the desk.

"No, Dr. Beasley has one more."

"Alright. Have a good night then." I tapped the counter with the side of my fist and went back toward my office to get my stuff.

"You too."

<hr>

"Daddy!" Ella, my five-year-old daughter, ran to me at full speed.

"Squeaker!" I mimicked her tone and bent down to catch her. She didn't deserve my fake enthusiasm, but I was in a shit mood and tired.

Ella wrapped her arms around my neck and hugged me tightly. "I missed you."

"I missed you too." I kissed her cheek and put her down to greet my waiting niece and nephews. "Happy birthday, Little Lady." I ruffled a lock of Gracie's hair and smiled at her.

"Thanks." She hugged my side lightly.

"How've you been? I haven't seen ya in a while."

"Good," she answered simply with a shrug. Hannah was the same way when she was little, quiet and gentle, but Ella was the one who looked like Hannah. Gracie looked more like Toby, except for her dark brown eyes and dimples.

"Yeah? Just good? Nothin' special?" I gave a small laugh.

She nodded, looking at Ella who was pulling on her hand.

"Alright. I'll believe ya this time."

Austin, my sister Emily's youngest, held onto my pant leg, looking up at me. He was a mellow two-year-old. It was beyond me how he could possibly be that way, being the spawn of my spastic sister, and related to his terror of an older brother.

"Oh," I bent down and picked Austin up. "Who left you out here without an adult? Huh?" I smiled at him.

"I'm watching him," Kylan, his older brother, said in offense.

"Yeah? Who's watching you?" You'd think after having been through a child abduction, my family would be more cautious than to let the kids run wild in the front yard. "Girls, come on. Let's take it to the backyard," I called as I turned Kylan by the shoulder.

"Mom said we could play out front," he protested.

"And I said you can't. I'm older, so I win." He'd argue breathing if I let him.

Gracie led Ella up the steps to the porch, then inside. Kylan went in behind them, and I followed with Austin. Emily was coming down the stairs, putting her hair up as she went.

"You're early," Emily commented. Meaning she just got busted for leaving the kids alone in the front yard.

"And you're asking for someone to rip off a kid." I passed Austin to her. "He was just sitting by the edge of the sidewalk. You realize he's two, right?"

She widened her eyes with a shit expression. "Oh my god, and he lived?"

I rolled my eyes. "You're irresponsible."

"I went to the bathroom, jackass. Chill out." She put Austin down. "I don't put my kids on a leash and suffocate them."

"Maybe you should be suffocated," I muttered as I walked through the dining room to the kitchen.

My mom, Millie, had the mixer going and was pouring something in.

"The kids were out front without anyone watching them," I said to her, pulling Ella's greedy hand back from the candy bowl.

"Well hi to you too," my mom smiled.

I raised my eyebrows. "I'm not gonna allow Ella over here if my rules aren't respected."

"Oh, pull the stick out of your ass," Emily chided. "She was fine. Kylan and Gracie were watching the little ones."

I shot her an angry stare. "Yeah, and I was sixteen and you were twelve, and we were watching Hannah. How did that work out?"

"Alright," our mom put her hands up, "don't start you two. Ben, honey, I'm sorry. I was finishing up dinner, I didn't know she was out front without an adult."

"Gramma, can I have a popsicle?" Ella asked.

Mom looked down at her. "No, sweetie. We're gonna have dinner in a minute. Go play out back."

"Kylan, that means you too." Emily took the popsicle he'd already pulled out and tossed it back in the freezer. "All kids outside." She followed them out, and my glare followed her.

There was a little body stuck to my leg again. I looked down and Austin was looking up at me with

37

his big eyes. He was another one that reminded me too much of Hannah.

I bent down and picked him up again. "You're like a suction cup, ya know that?"

My mom gave a pouting smile. "You love your uncle, huh?"

Austin nodded, with his head resting against the front of my shoulder.

"I'd stick to someone sane if Emily was my mom too." I tugged on the puppy security blanket he always carried.

"Don't say that to him," my mom rebuked.

I scoffed, going to the fridge for a bottle of water. "Don't think I haven't heard the things Emily says about me to Ella. She's a parrot."

"You two need to stop." My mom sighed. "How was work?"

"Same as it always is. Where's Dad and Toby?" I wrapped an arm around my mom's shoulders and kissed the top of her head. "Hi."

She put an arm around me. "Hi. They're out in the garage, working on Gracie's present from Dad and I."

"Didn't you guys get her a bike?" I cracked open the water bottle.

"Yeah, but Dad's adjusting the pedals and putting streamers on the handles." My mom looked up from the mixer and gave me one of her warm smiles. "You can go join them. I'll get ya later."

I gave her a small smile. My mom was the sweetest, red-headed firecracker there ever was. I passed her in height by fourteen, but I still looked up to her. Losing Hannah had devastated all of us, but it was my mom who kept everyone going. She was tough, and she'd make sure everyone was as happy as they could be. I loved her for it. My dad was a good man, but sometimes his expectations were a lot. He didn't like that I'd left the church, that I'd had a child out of wedlock, or that I continued not to find Ella a mother—amongst other things. Suffice it to say, we locked horns on occasion.

I opened the garage door and stepped down. Toby and my dad were by the workbench in front of the cars.

"Good timin', Son. Can ya get that basket off the top shelf?" My dad gave me a light-eyed smile.

"Sure." I pulled Austin away from me and handed him to my dad. "Go see your Papa."

I signed a greeting to Toby. He was an extremely nice person, and deaf. He had cochlear implants, but his brain didn't always recognize the things he heard. When he was with Hannah, the batteries were dead most of the time, and he'd taught her sign language. He could read lips, but certain words looked similar to others when spoken. Toby had taught her to read and write as well. He'd been her only source of education, and the only reason she'd gotten out. So, while I hated him for impregnating my sister, I also appreciated how much he'd tried to help her. Of course, all of it was on the assumption he was telling the truth, but I saw nothing in him to make me think he'd lie.

I reached up on the top storage shelf and grabbed the small basket that went on the front of a bike. It used to be on Hannah's bike, but Emily stole it once Hannah was gone, and it got put on the shelf when I took it off Emily's bike in a heat of anger. I wouldn't say it to my dad, but I didn't like that he was giving it to Grace. It wasn't that she didn't deserve it, or wouldn't take care of it, because she would, it was Hannah's... People didn't understand how much she meant to me, even still.

Gracie was the only reason we knew Hannah was alive and escaped our Uncle Patty, the person who'd kidnapped her. Hannah had fled to Nebraska and left her baby in the bathroom of a feed store that Toby's parents owned. Toby had been captured, taken to the house where Hannah was kept, forced to procreate with her, and they tried to escape, but only Toby made it out. Hannah didn't escape until a day later, just a day before the FBI stormed the house she'd been kept in. Our Uncle

Patty was apprehended in a raid in Minnesota a few days after Hannah got away, but there were other monsters out there that'd be after her. My parents still prayed for her to come home, but I knew she couldn't.

18 Years Prior

Hannah's sweet little face lit up like Christmas. It was her first bike without training wheels. She'd asked my dad to have a bike like mine yesterday evening, and today he came home with a brand new one.

"Here ya go, Sweet Girl. Your very own bike without training wheels," he said proudly as he lifted it out from the back of the truck. "And I made sure to get one with a basket for your little rock collection."

"How come she gets a new bike?" Emily whined.

"Shut up. You got one for your birthday." I shoved her shoulder to make her back away from Hannah. Emily was terrible to her and perpetually jealous.

"So!? She's supposed to get mine and I get a new one."

"Ben, stop pushing her, and Emily, go inside if you're gonna whine," our dad sighed.

I held the handlebars for Hannah so she could get on. She had the happiest little face as she climbed on.

"Ready?" I asked her with a smile.

She nodded, her curled pigtails bobbing in response. She had to be the cutest kid on earth.

"Okay." I grabbed the back of the seat and guided her to the sidewalk just behind the truck. "Start pedaling."

Hannah started pedaling and I ran beside her until she was balanced enough for me to let go. Her pigtails blew back in the breeze, and her little legs pumped the pedals to keep going.

"Keep up with her, Son," my dad called from behind.

I continued to run behind Hannah. "You're doin' it, Bean! Keep going."

She smiled, staying focused on what was in front of her. At the end of the block, she stopped and put her feet down.

"What are you doing? You can go around the block, I'll follow you."

"I can't turn," she said as she waddled, trying to turn the bike around.

I laughed. "Just turn the handlebars like you do with the training wheels."

"I can't." She straightened out the bike to go back toward the house.

I reached forward, ready to help her get going again, but she started off all on her own. She went in a constant line until Emily threw out a large stick in front of her. I was already running, and my dad leaped forward as soon as he saw what Emily was about to do, but neither of us could get to her in time. The front tire hit the large stick, the wheel twisted, and Hannah went down.

"What the hell's the matter with you!" my dad yelled at Emily.

Hannah's sweet little face pinched up as my dad picked her up from the pavement.

"Mom said I could have a new bike! Not Hannah!" Emily yelled in her raging tantrum, then took off in a run down the sidewalk.

My dad handed Hannah to me without thought and ran after Emily like a pissed-off dog. Our mom was already coming out with worry on her face.

"It's okay, Sissy. We'll fix it," I said to Hannah as I carried her toward the house. She held on to me as she bawled.

"Oh baby, what happened?" my mom asked Hannah as she ran down the steps.

"Stupid Emily threw a stick out in front of her because she wanted the new bike." I held onto Hannah as I walked toward our mom.

"Dear lord, that girl needs her butt swatted." My

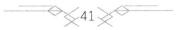

mom reached to take Hannah.

"He's probably doin' it now."

"No! I want Ben," Hannah screeched when my mom pulled her away from me.

"Okay, honey, I know. He's coming. Just let me carry you inside."

"I'm right here, Bean." I reached up and took her hand. It was default for Hannah to always want me or Dad when she was upset, but mostly me. Even when she was a baby. I held her all the time, because the second I saw her for the first time, I just loved her. Emily I could do without.

My mom carried Hannah inside to the downstairs bathroom and set her on the counter. She'd stopped crying, but I wouldn't have blamed her if she'd kept on. The side of her knee was scraped badly enough to make me cringe, a tough feat.

"Here." My mom handed me the antiseptic spray.

"No. I'll hold her. You do it." I put the toilet seat down so I could sit.

"Good idea." My mom moved Hannah to my lap.

Hannah would sit through anything or take any medicine she was asked to take if I was holding her. My parents found it annoying, but I loved it because I loved Hannah.

"Alright, this will sting, but if you blow on it, it goes away fast." My mom sprayed the antiseptic before Hannah could even fight or say anything. She didn't though. She just sat there like a tough little cookie and watched as our mom cleaned up the wound.

"I love that you're so good. Your sister would be howling," Mom muttered quietly as she washed the scrape.

I kissed Hannah's head and hugged her a little tighter. "Emily should be the one howling."

"No. No one should." My mom let out a loud sigh. "I don't know what's wrong with that girl."

"She's evil," I responded bitterly.

My mom gave me a dirty look. "No, she's jealous because you only make time for Hannah."

"Because she's not a pain in the ass."

My mom smacked the side of my knee. "Don't talk like that." She grabbed a large bandage and taped it on Hannah's knee. "Okay, let me see that forehead." She reached up and brushed Hannah's hair back.

After Hannah was all bandaged and cleaned up, I sat on the couch with her. My mom was making her stay put with an ice pack for the lump on the side of her forehead. She fell asleep holding it, so I held it for her.

Present

I wiggled the basket to make sure it was secure. "That'll do it." The memories the basket brought were a little too much and I had to walk away without another word.

I went out to my truck to get Grace's presents. If I'd gone back to the backyard, I probably would've throat-punched Emily for being an asshole eighteen years ago. A van drove down the street while I pulled out the painting easel from the back of my truck and I made a mental note of the license plate. I'd done it ever since Hannah was taken. I'd been able to tell the police the make and model, even the year of the van, but I forgot to look at the license plate.

I put the easel down on the ground for a minute and rested my elbows on the edge of the truck bed to rub my forehead. Hannah didn't usually consume my thoughts so much, but it was that time of year again. Gracie's birthday and the day Hannah had been craftily snatched from the doctor's office were dark days for me, and every year it just got harder to take. I understood why she felt like she couldn't come home, and maybe she didn't want to, but I just wanted to see her and know she was okay.

A few times, I'd followed up on a few leads, but none of them ever turned up anything. After I graduated high school, I'd spent an entire year searching for her. What was so damn infuriating was, I'd been right there. Bell Buckle, Tennessee. I was within a few mile radius of her at the end of my searching, and I gave up—thinking it was a dead end like everywhere else I'd been.

In the moment, I wanted to find her so badly I felt like I should just allow the mental snap, get in my truck, and go. The only thing stopping me was Ella, but my parents would take good care of her. There were other doctors in my practice to take over my patients. I had more than enough savings to pay bills and be on the road. Hannah was the reason I always made sure to have a large nest egg in the bank. What if she found me and needed it? What if she was spotted and in trouble? What if there was a ransom? What if my parents finally gave up and rescinded their offer of a reward?

"Are you okay?" Toby's voice was quiet, but he was always quiet.

I took my hand away from my forehead and looked at him but didn't move my elbows from the truck. "Yeah... Just can't stop thinking about her."

Toby nodded, walking closer. "Me too." He signed as he spoke because his speech wasn't always clear.

I looked out at the street. "She got out seven years ago, and she still hasn't turned up, or even tried to reach out to anyone... I can't help but wonder if they caught her again." I rubbed my forehead after signing.

"No... She's too smart for that."

I took in a deep breath and let it out before shaking my head. "I feel stuck. I wanna go look for her, but I don't know where to start... and I could be leading someone right to her if I do find her."

"She'll come back... She just has to know she's safe enough."

I looked at Toby, his sandy blonde hair tufted up

from the wind. "Why doesn't she know I'd keep her safe? I spent the first eight years of her life protecting her."

Toby shook his head. "I don't think it's her safety she's ever been worried about. Henry wouldn't kill her if he found her. He'd go after everyone she loves and make her live with it."

I let out a huff of irony. "What's to stop him from doing it now? To draw her out."

Toby chewed on his lip for a second, then shrugged. "He wants his money more than catching some girl who got away. But he'd go after her if she started making waves, threatening his business and money. If she comes home, she'll have a bunch of cameras in her face."

"So? So did you. You still do. You've written books, signed movie rights—he's never even tried to go after you." It didn't make sense.

He pulled back the corner of his mouth. "Because I don't know his inner workings. I only know what happened in that house—to Hannah. She knows things that could get him caught, and—"

"Then she should use them," I snapped out of irritation, but not at Toby.

"She wants peace. She always did. It was never about getting out or revenge. She just wanted the quiet... And I think if we haven't heard from her, it's because she found it..."

"And what do you tell Grace? 'Mommy doesn't love you enough'?" I rolled my eyes.

"No. I tell her to be happy that her mom is out there and free..." Toby looked like he might cry, and his voice was straining a little. "She's gonna wish for her mom to come back before she blows out the candles, and tonight before she goes to bed, I'll tell her a happy story about Hannah to try to make it as real as I know how... I tell *myself* Hannah knows how to find me if she needs help, and if she doesn't, then I don't need to worry."

I shook my head. "I can't tell myself that... It was

one minute... I wasn't paying attention, and she paid the price. She could still be paying, and I'd be sitting here trying to fool myself into thinking she's happy and living a normal life."

"If she's not yet, she will. I only spent a year and a half with her, but I know her better than anyone. She has the strongest will I've ever seen."

The screen door to the house opened with a loud creak and we both looked back.

"You boys comin'? Dinner's ready," my mom called.

"Yeah," I called back, then let out a sigh before grabbing the easel from the ground and the paint set from the back of the truck.

Chapter 5

Bexley

For the first time in seven years, I had a person in my life I mildly trusted. Ryan didn't usually ask questions I didn't want to answer, and while he was a little sharp, I didn't feel as threatened by him as other people. Possibly because he didn't seem to have an ulterior interest in me. He'd helped me study for my GED test, had coffee with me afterward, then told me two days later he'd help me study again when I didn't pass the writing and science portions. It'd crushed me that I'd worked so hard to study just to fail again. This would be my third time. I couldn't have a high school diploma like other people, so I wanted this one thing that gave me some kind of hope and normalcy. Having Ryan around gave me a little hope for the future too.

It was hard to afford a motel room and save up enough for a deposit to rent something, so I'd been trying to only get a motel room every other night. The rain had made things difficult last night. I'd taken a couple trash bags from the restaurant to help stay dry, but they didn't keep the cold from seeping in. I'd fall asleep for only an hour or so at a time, then wake up from the aches that came with being cold. I should have been used to it, and I used to be, but not anymore. I was wishing I'd kept that hundred-dollar tip from the blonde guy and his brother, but I couldn't. A hundred dollars on a thirty dollar tab was ridiculous.

The sun started to come through the many windows of the diner on the east side. I stood in the light and enjoyed it for a few minutes. The quiet wouldn't last long. I was only working until two today because Carol had insisted I get rest after seeing me sneak into the bathroom to fix myself up before the restaurant opened. She told Joe, and he had another conversation with me about staying with them. This time he wouldn't take no for an answer. I was trying not to see it as a step back and focused on the sunshine.

The bell on the door jingled and I turned my head to look. It was Grey, the smiley customer that'd forgotten his wallet. Carol had called him last night using the phone number in his wallet to let him know it was here. He hadn't answered, but apparently got her message.

"Good morning." He smiled and his eyes crinkled at the corners. He was still dressed in clothes that looked like they'd just had the tags pulled off.

"Morning." I walked over to the cash register and opened it. I handed him the wallet and got stuck on the intense blue color of his eyes. They looked different in the natural light from the sun than they had the night before. After talking to him for a minute before he left, I knew I'd initially misjudged him.

"Thank you. I didn't even realize it was gone until I saw I had a message."

I nodded.

"I'm sorry about my comment last night."

I frowned a little, then recalled what he was talking about. I cleared the frown and shook my head. "No. I'm not always good at understanding when people are joking."

"Well, my brother has horrible manners anyway," he laughed a little. "That's what school teaches you I guess, right?"

I shook my head. "I don't know. I was homeschooled." Another lie. I hated lying, yet it was all I did. The only reason I hadn't lied to Ryan was because I desperately needed his help.

I looked past him at the incoming customers.

"Lucky you. I would have killed to have that kind of time with my parents." He tapped his wallet on the counter. "Thanks again." He held up his wallet.

I nodded and watched him walk toward the door for a moment. He seemed so different than I would have thought... genuine, maybe, and it seemed so rare.

I picked up the menus to seat the people that'd just come in, but Carol took them from me and greeted the newcomers. I didn't understand why until I saw Grey walking back with a funny smile on his face.

I frowned a little and looked back to see if maybe he'd forgotten his keys or something. He hadn't.

He laughed and shook his head a little. "So, this is a problem I never expected to have." He opened his wallet. "I have extra money that I'm not supposed to."

"There was a hundred on the table. I assumed it was yours."

His eyes crinkled a little more, but his smile didn't grow anymore. "That was for you."

I shook my head. "That's too much."

He took in a breath and let it out in a huff. "Alright... How about dinner then? What time do you get off?"

I shook my head again. "It's okay. Really."

His smile was perfect and charming. "Come on. What time do you get off? I'm buying you dinner."

"She gets off at two, but you can pick her up at five. I'll make sure she's ready for you," Carol answered from behind me.

I looked at her feeling mortified and shocked. She knew better, yet insisted he'd be perfect for me last night after Grey and his brother had come in. Ann had chimed in, saying we'd make the cutest babies.

Grey chuckled a little. "I'll be here at five."

"Have a good day, honey." Carol gave him one of her sweet smiles.

I wanted my mouth to work. I wanted to say no, but he was out the door so fast I didn't have a chance. I chewed on the inside of my lip while Carol squealed with excitement.

"Joe! She just got asked out on a date!"

"What? Who did?"

"Bex. Who do you think?"

"Good for you, kid! I get to meet him, right?"

I turned around and looked at both of them. How did they think this was okay? I didn't want to date anyone. I wanted to be alone.

"Don't give me that look. This is good. New experiences." Carol nodded once. "Now, go help that table."

I walked over to the table and took their drink orders. I was irritated with what had just happened, but I knew better than to say anything. Carol was trying to help me be normal, but it wasn't possible. I would never be normal. I didn't fit in with people, I didn't know when they were joking or harmless... I saw everyone as a threat.

Because of my dread of the pending dinner, two o'clock came too quickly. Joe drove me home, chattering the entire way about how proud he was of me, and that I wouldn't have come close to this two years ago. It made me feel all the more pressured not to let him down. He and Carol didn't have children of their own, so they treated their staff as such.

I sat in the room at Carol and Joe's, at the end of my bed, and looked at my clothes in the bag. I didn't have much that didn't have the restaurant logo stamped on it. I worked six days a week and would have worked seven if it were open. I pulled out a white scoop neck shirt with sleeves that went just past the elbows and a pair of jeans Ann had given me. She dressed well, so I decided to wear something she would. I dug out a pair of white sneakers and called it good. After I laid them on the bed, I put my stuff away properly. Letting it sit in a bag would bother me, even if I was going to move out as soon as humanly possible.

Hair and make-up were something I was good at. Since I was fifteen, I had to look like I was twenty. I kept my make-up on the natural side to match my face and dark brown eyes. Wearing my hair down made me look significantly younger, so I avoided it. I always swept back my long brown hair in a pile of curls and pinned them. Keeping my hair up served another purpose too. If someone grabbed me by the hair, the pins would come out and give me a chance to get away.

At four-thirty, I changed into my clothes and walked to the diner. I got to the restaurant early and was going to roll silverware, but Carol had the girls fixing subtle things on me to make me look better. Chelsea rolled up the bottom of my jeans, so they were somewhere between capris and full-length. Ann added a scarf from her car and switched out my purse for one of her more fashionable ones.

"Seriously, you're not even that dressed up, and I could be in a ballgown and not look that good." Ann tilted her head, looking at me with a longing smile.

"That's not true." I twisted my hands because I was done with being touched.

Ann was extremely pretty. She had bright blonde hair that was wispy and always curled. She always dressed nicely outside of work.

"Come back to the office with me, honey." Carol wiggled her fingers as she held out her hand toward me.

I forced a smile at Ann. "Thanks for the help."

"Of course. And keep the bag and the scarf. They look better on you." She turned as I passed her.

"Come on. Hurry up. I have tables waiting."

I followed Carol back to the office, and she waited for me to step in. She put a chair in front of the doorway instead of closing the door, for my benefit. I couldn't take being shut in rooms that didn't have windows, especially with another person. Everyone knew to steer clear of the office if the chair was in the doorway.

"Are you gonna be okay tonight? This is kind of a big deal for you. I don't want any mishaps like when you first came here."

I shook my head. "There won't be."

"Are you sure?"

I gave a small shrug. "He seems nice and it's just dinner." That's what I'd been telling myself for the last couple hours.

She smiled. "Right."

I was still nervous about the whole thing, but I'd been oddly calm talking to him before, which was something I hadn't experienced with someone on the outside. Even Ryan made me fairly nervous because of his sharpness, but he reminded me of my brother, which was why I'd bothered to talk to him at all.

"Are ya ready? He's here." Joe stood in the doorway, breaking the rules of the chair.

"You should put your hair down. It's so pretty when you have it down." Carol spoke quickly.

"She looks beautiful. Leave her be." Joe reached out a hand to me.

I shook my head, refusing his hand as always, and he moved the chair out of the way.

"Have a good night, pumpkin. Stay out late." Carol

had her hands pressed together in front of her mouth as she smiled like a proud mom.

I smiled a little. "I'll try."

I walked out of the kitchen and Grey stood at the counter looking out the windows at the ocean. Monterey was most beautiful in the evening, and the diner had a front-seat view of the ocean and the incredible long sunsets.

Grey looked at me the moment I passed through his peripheral vision. He smiled beautifully, mostly around the corners of his eyes. "Are you ready?"

I nodded.

He lifted his chin toward the door. "Come on."

I walked with him to the door, and he opened it for me. I stepped out and to the side so he wasn't behind me. He didn't seem to notice my awkwardness as much as I expected. It made my back hurt to have someone so close behind me.

"Do you like fish?" He looked at me as we walked down the stairs.

"As long as it's cooked." Usually, I tried to avoid speaking as much as possible, but I didn't want to be rude.

"What? No sushi?" His eyes were vibrant as he smiled.

"Afraid not."

"Meh. That's okay. There's nothing good around here for that anyway. Personally, I'm picky over sushi. I went to Japan a few years ago and ever since, I can't find anything stateside that's good enough."

"One of the other waitresses goes to a place in San Francisco. She says it's fairly close, but not the same."

"You'll have to ask her what it's called. The eleven-hour flight to Japan isn't worth it." He walked up to a BMW SUV, opened the door with a smile, and closed it after I got in. The inside was immaculate. It looked and smelled like he'd just driven it off the lot, but the dash-

board showed a fair number of miles on the car.

"Are you opposed to a long trip for food, or would you rather stay close to home?" He got in and pushed the button to start the car.

I thought quickly. Joe and Carol would have a fit if we came back too soon, but at the same time, I didn't want to stray far. "How long of a road trip?"

"San Fran?" He gave an impish smile.

Be brave Bex. You can do this. "Okay."

"Yeah?" He looked genuinely surprised.

I nodded and tried to keep from laughing at his child-like enthusiasm.

"Sweet. Much better food options, and I love the drive." He backed up out of the parking space and pulled out to the street. I caught a wiff of his cologne. It had hints of citron and pepper, making it smell differently than most men's cologne.

"What were you in Japan for?" I twisted my bracelet and started picking at one of the charms.

"Work." He shrugged and looked unamused.

"What do you do?"

"Ever heard of Maslen Wealth Management?" He looked at me and somehow seemed a little timid.

I shook my head. "Someone mentioned it to me a couple weeks ago, but otherwise, no."

"Really?" He raised his eyebrows, seemingly surprised.

I shook my head again.

"Well, that's refreshing." He let out a breath and looked relieved.

"I'm a high-risk day trader slash next in line to run the family business which is a little more than I want to take on. MWM is a massive wealth management company that my grandpa started back in his younger days when the stock market was a new thing."

"Oh... Do you know Ryan Brae?" I asked because Ryan had mentioned knowing the CEO.

Grey gave a gentle rye laugh. "Actually, I do. He's a very good friend of mine, and he looks after my brother Sam when I'm not in town. How do you know him?"

How was I supposed to answer that without sounding pathetic? "Um, he helped me study for a test I had."

"I thought you didn't go to school here?" He looked at me, but without judgment.

"I don't, but I'm trying to." I suddenly realized I'd told Grey a different lie about being homeschooled. I'd told Ryan that I hadn't gone to school, which was the truth.

He nodded once, looking back at the road. "Gotcha."

"What's a day trader do?" I asked to get him to start talking about something else. I'd read in a book that people mostly liked to talk about themselves, so if you wanted to lift a conversation, you should inquire about someone.

Grey went on to explain what he did and talked about his dad pushing him up to the top of the pyramid. He loved the stock market and doing the actual trading and research that went into it. Grey said his business was a little different because he helped his clients make substantial amounts of money in a short amount of time. It gave them the capitol they needed for bigger investments so they didn't have to resort to shareholders or business loans. I knew very little about the stock market but formed a better grasp as he continued to speak. I asked him questions now and then when I was lost, but for the most part, was able to keep up.

When we got to the restaurant, he told me about some of the different countries he'd been to and his experiences there. He was twenty-seven and more interesting than a book. He'd been to places I'd only read about. Grey told me about a trip to Cambodia that he'd taken and how poor the country was.

"I was driving down the road—which was terrify-

ing because no one there knows how to drive—and on the side of the road was this little boy, maybe seven or eight years old, and he was crying. I don't know why I stopped, but I pulled over and got out of the car with my translator. I asked him to ask the little boy what was wrong, and why he was standing over a dead cow."

"Are cows sacred there?" I poked at the green ball on my plate. It looked like a miniature head of lettuce, but I honestly didn't know what it was. I'd never seen one before.

"White ones are. But this kid said it was his family's only cow and his father would never forgive him for letting it get hit by a truck. I felt so bad for him and I asked the translator how I could help the kid out. It killed me that something so seemingly small was the world to him. I'm forever going to all these poverty-stricken places because I'm humbled. My dad is always wrapped up in his money, and I don't like it. I don't see a point in having it if I can't share and help people out, ya know?"

I nodded. I didn't know, but I could understand. "Did you help the little boy?"

He gave a cringing expression. "I bought him a herd of cattle... and a house."

I raised my eyebrows.

"Yeah, I know, it's over the top, but you didn't see this kid." Grey automatically looked sympathetic. "He brought me to his family's house; there were twenty-three of them. Grandparents, aunts and uncles, the whole family shared this shack made out of half a shipping container and a bunch of rusted-out metal siding..." He shook his head looking slightly upset at the memory. "I have everything, and they had half a shipping container and a dead cow that was hit by a truck."

I gave a sympathetic smile. "You changed their lives." It was nice to hear how much he cared about others who were less fortunate. Even when I was homeless, I'd still spare a few dollars for another homeless person

56

who asked.

He forced a smile and picked up his fork. "Yeah. So, you're from Illinois, what's that like?"

I shrugged. "Like being raised in a place that's a couple thousand miles in either direction from the ocean."

He laughed. "That bad, huh?"

I nodded, but he didn't know it had nothing to do with a state that I'd never lived in.

"What do your parents do?"

I shook my head and looked down at my plate. "They're gone." Another lie.

"Both of them?"

I nodded and looked at him again. I admired the way he held such confidence and I wanted to learn to do the same.

"That's rough. Do you mind if I ask what happened?"

"An accident."

"How old were you?" He took a bite of the flounder on his plate.

"Fifteen."

"That's terrible." He shook his head and looked genuinely upset by the news. "Did you go live with other family or something?"

I pressed my lips together. Why did I want to tell him more than I told anyone else? Only one person in the world knew the truth, and that was because, for a short time, he'd lived it with me. Maybe I could tell Grey just a little more than I told others. Worst thing that would happen was we'd never see each other again and it would affect absolutely no one.

"No. I've been on my own since then," I answered quietly.

He raised his eyebrows. "Wow..." He opened his mouth to say something, but I interrupted him, knowing that it would be another question.

"Have you been anywhere in South America? I've been reading a book about this tribe of people that live in caves in the Andes mountains."

"Only to Ecuador once. I'm hoping to see a little more of it soon, but I haven't had the chance for a lot of travel lately."

"What was Ecuador like?"

Grey started to talk about his experience and I listened intently. He'd witnessed a massive mudslide while he was there.

After dinner, Grey and I walked down a street filled with small shops and he talked about his family. I smiled a little as I listened. I remembered a lot about my own family, but I could never see them after what happened, which made it nice to hear stories from someone who had a family they could enjoy.

We stopped at a park against the bay and aimlessly walked through the grass barefoot. The moon was hanging brightly over the water.

"So, how long have you worked at the diner?" Grey looked at me with the light smile he'd held all night.

"Two years yesterday. Joe and Carol thought they needed to celebrate it for some reason." My cheeks felt a little warm. I knew being a waitress wasn't considered a good job.

"That's cool. You seem like you're pretty close to them. Did you know them before you started working there?"

I shook my head. "They sort of adopted me when I started—at least in their own mind. They don't have any kids, so..." I shrugged a little.

"That's awesome, though." He laughed a little. "Joe seems pretty nice, aside from the death threat." He looked at me with a smile.

I frowned a little, looking at him questioningly.

He laughed again. "When I came in, Joe came out from the kitchen. I was warned to behave, or he'd chop me into pieces and feed me to the seagulls."

I held my frown. "I'm sorry. I'm sure he was kidding."

Grey laughed. "Maybe about feeding me to the seagulls." He looked at me with another beautiful smile. "It's great, though—that they care so much."

I nodded. "Overwhelming at times."

"So, do you wanna go to college in Monterey or somewhere else?" He stopped at a park bench and sat down to put his shoes back on. We'd reached the end of the long park.

"I don't know," I shrugged and sat down, leaving nearly a three-foot gap between us. My short answer seemed rude, so I added, "California is kind of expensive, so I might find somewhere else to go."

"Yeah. What would you want to study?"

I shook my head. "I don't know. I haven't thought about it."

"You said you read a lot, is there anything that stands out to you? There's a billion things out there. You could be a doctor or something."

My heart pounded a little at the thought of being a doctor. There wasn't anything more terrifying to me as a profession. My uncle had been a doctor and the thought of him made it difficult to breathe.

"No? Maybe a teacher?" He filled my lack of response with another suggestion and a smile.

"I haven't thought about it," I said again, hoping he would drop the subject. I didn't even have a basic education, there was no way I could teach children what I had yet to learn.

We started back for the car after a lighter conversation about a book I'd read, and he drove back to Monterey. I asked him about his college experience and opened another conversation for the ride home. I didn't want any more prying questions.

"Thank you for dinner. I had a great time." I smiled kindly and kept my hands on the handles of the bag Ann

had given me.

"Of course." He nodded and pointed over his shoulder at the restaurant with his thumb. "Can I walk you inside?"

I shook my head. "Not unless you plan on being stuffed with cobbler and stay to answer questions until three in the morning. Joe and Carol are full of them."

He nodded once with a crinkly-eyed smile. "Well... have a good night." His ocean-colored eyes were still an incredible blue in the darkness of the parking lot.

"You too." I gave another small smile and started toward the restaurant. "Thanks again."

Joe and Carol were both pretending not to notice me but sat in a booth with a clear view. I shook my head as I went up the steps.

"Midnight. Not bad for a first-timer," Joe teased with a smile as he looked at his watch.

"We went to San Francisco for dinner."

"What?" Carol's jaw dropped a little. I didn't understand if she was giving me a bad look or a good one. "He must be some kind of guy. How did it go?" She slid over, patting the spot next to her.

"He talks a lot, but he's nice." I sat next to Carol in the booth and Joe pushed a half-eaten plate of cobbler in front of me.

"Tell us everything." Carol leaned forward, looking excited.

I smiled and started to tell them about my night. I could only think of a couple other times in my life when I had enjoyed myself as much. And none of them had happened since I ran at fifteen.

Chapter 6

Bexley

The bell on the door jingled and I turned, ready to greet the next customers. I paused when I saw it was Grey. I'd had fun last night, but I'd hoped this would fall through the cracks and just be a good memory. It was a lot of work to pretend I was a normal person or close to good enough to be around anyone, let alone him.

"So, I'm an ass." He wore an apologetic expression mixed with his usual smile.

I frowned and shook my head. "I don't understand what you're alluding to."

"Sam, my brother, asked me how it went last night, and I realized I talked almost the entire time."

I blinked and waited to understand the problem.

"I didn't let you get more than a few words in."

I shook my head. "I didn't have much to say."

"Maybe, but how would either of us know? I didn't shut up." He smiled a little more, but still had a slight bit of sympathy on his brow. "I'd like a chance to do better. I'll be back in two weeks and I want to take you out again." He held up his hand to stop me from speaking too soon. "And I promise I won't talk your ear off this time, or be a huge ass and make it sound like I'm bragging about myself."

I looked back toward the kitchen window. Joe and Carol were standing there, pretending to talk to each other. I wanted to say no, but I didn't know how to do it nicely and Carol would be completely disappointed. I looked at Grey. He had a hopeful and pleading look, making it even harder.

"Please? One more chance?"

I picked at my nails with one hand at my side. "I'm not a good conversationalist."

"That's okay."

I let out a breath. There was a strong likelihood he'd forget in two weeks. He was extremely busy with his job in Seattle, and it would most likely slip his mind.

"Come back here to the diner when you're in town again."

He smiled brilliantly. "I'll see you in two weeks then."

I nodded once.

He looked relieved of something as he turned around and left. I didn't understand why it was such a big deal to him. If anything, I had been the most boring date he'd ever been on. I had no idea what I was doing, and I knew this wouldn't go anywhere... It couldn't.

"What did he say? Tell me what he said." Carol was beside me the moment the door was closed.

Ann stood next to her. "He is gorgeous. Blonde hair, strong jaw, and that smile. How is he so perfect?"

"I know. He's beautiful," Carol agreed.

I looked at both of them. They were staring at Grey through the windows longingly. I shook my head and walked back to the corner booth to roll silverware for tonight.

"Hey. You didn't tell us what he said." Carol and

Ann followed me.

"He apologized for talking too much last night." I picked up the tray of silverware from the kitchen window and set it on the table.

"And?" Ann sat in the booth and Carol sat next to her.

"And that's it. He wants a chance to make up for it in two weeks when he comes back, and two things will happen. He'll either forget or I have two weeks to think of a nice way to say no."

"What? Why? You said you had a good time last night." Carol stopped laying out napkins and looked at me almost horrified-like.

"I didn't actually wanna go. You're the one who said yes." I sat down in the booth and grabbed a stack of napkins.

"You had no good reason to say no."

I had plenty of good reasons, but she didn't know that.

I didn't understand why, but Grey had been stuck in my head. He'd sat so confidently last night over dinner but shared humbling experiences. He'd been able to talk about things in his life, without really mentioning himself too much. He'd focused more on the people he'd helped or his family. He drew no real attention to himself. I wanted to learn how to do that.

"Bexley, come here, honey," Carol called from out front.

I walked through the kitchen, wiping my hands on a towel, and pushed through the door. A man stood at the counter with a smile and a large arrangement of peonies.

"They're for you," Carol smiled.

I frowned, feeling confused.

"Bexley Nelson?" the man asked.

I nodded.

"Sign here for me." He handed me his clipboard

and a pen.

I took them and signed my name. Carol and Ann stood there, quietly squealing with excitement.

"Read the card. What's it say?"

I turned the vase, pulled out the small card, and handed it to Carol.

"You read it." She nodded at the card.

I took in a breath and opened it. "'Beautiful Bexley, thank you for giving me another chance. Hopefully, these flowers last until I get back. Grey.'"

"Oh my gosh! That is so sweet!" Ann made a terrible squeal.

"Sh." I looked around to see if people were staring, then set the vase down below the counter.

"He called you beautiful." Carol held up her hands with a smile, like she was going to hold my cheeks, but didn't make contact. "I agree."

"I need to work. I'm busy." I shook my head and walked back into the kitchen to finish what I was doing.

Beautiful Bexley. Seriously? I didn't know this guy and he was sending flowers, making promises to return, and calling me beautiful? And what did he really expect to happen? I had nothing to offer him. I could barely afford to rent a bedroom, worked six days a week in a diner, and didn't know how to be around people. I didn't know how to be around him. *I'd* kept him talking last night.

"Something on your mind, kiddo? There's not gonna be much salad left if you keep chopping."

I dropped the knife and stepped back, putting my hands up like the lettuce had just pulled a gun on me.

"Hey now. Come take a break with me." Joe stood next to me and leaned forward a little to look at my face.

I stood there for a moment and forced my mind to clear, and my heart to stop jackhammering.

"Come on."

I blinked quickly and turned to follow him outside. He lit up a cigarette and handed it to me.

"What's got ya bothered?" he asked before he lit up another cigarette for himself.

I shook my head.

"Come on now. It's not nothing."

"Have you ever heard of Maslen Wealth Management?"

He laughed. "Of course I have. That'd be like saying you don't know Wells Fargo or Meryl Lynch."

"I don't know what Meryl Lynch is." I shook my head with a frown and took a drag of the cigarette.

Joe let out a chuckle and shook his head. "Jeez, kid. What about Maslen Wealth?"

"That guy, Grey, he's the grandson of the man who started the company."

Joe raised his eyebrows and let out a low whistle.

"What does someone with all that money want with me?"

Joe knew it was a loaded question, but to my surprise, answered anyway. "Well, I suppose he wants to date ya. Is there a problem with that?"

"Yes. He's worth billions of dollars. I looked him up last night after we got home—his whole family. Why is he bothering with some diner waitress that can't function?"

"You function just fine." Joe gave me a flat look. "Maybe he sees somethin' you don't. I think ya'd do just fine to find out what that is."

"You're not telling me what I want to hear."

He laughed. "That's not how life works. All I can say is, there's somethin' pretty special about you, and you caught his attention."

I shook my head and looked at the fence around us.

"And there's nothing wrong with my little diner waitress. She's sweet and she deserves everything good." He took in a long drag from his cigarette before he bent over and put it out in the pot of sand.

I stepped away from the door to let him inside so

he didn't move behind me. I put my cigarette out and went inside to wash my hands. I'd quit smoking, but now and then I'd have one with Joe.

⎯⎯⟨⟩⎯⎯

A few days later, on a Tuesday when the restaurant was closed, I went around town to look at rooms that were for rent. Carol had offered to drive me around, but I didn't let her. I had just enough money for a deposit and rent, so I was able to get a room just a few square feet bigger than the last, but in an even crappier house. Drug deals went on twenty-four-seven, and I knew that because my former dealer, Jose, lived there. Because of that, I knew it'd be a no questions asked kind of place. Jose was definitely a thug but loved me like a little sister, and someone far above him in the hierarchy knew me, so I had a little protection from the unfavorable clientele going in and out. My room also had its own door from the outside, so I didn't have to go through the house all the time.

I got through the next week taking as many tables as I could handle. It was hard to save when everything coming in was immediately going out, so I needed to work more. I couldn't even afford the pills I needed to make sure I didn't end up with broken bones from something as simple as a fall. I'd been starved or only allowed small portions since I was eight, then from fifteen on, managed how I ate because I often didn't have enough money. When I'd been running drugs up from Mexico, I had more money than I ever had, but it all went to medical procedures, then to the pill habit I formed from pain meds.

Chapter 7

Ryan

"Yeah," Tim answered on the first ring.

"Find anything yet?"

Tim was my brother, so it wasn't a hard ask for him to withhold information from Grey and feed it to me first.

"So far, her identity is complete bullshit. The guy who did it left a trail the size of the Colorado River, but I fixed it—"

"Grey already told me that. Tell me what I don't know." I was sure her identity was bullshit before I met her, which was why I didn't call her by her first name. She didn't look like a Bexley to me. Nelson was more bland, so that's what I'd chosen to call her.

"She's a ghost, man. Before six years ago in LA, she doesn't exist. Later today, I'm gonna try running that folder through an A.I. program and see if it can put something together..." There was an annoying munching as Tim spoke, likely him eating carrots. He ate carrots when he was overthinking something.

"What are you not telling me?" I rolled my eyes out of irritation, knowing him too well.

"I found the connection between the warehouses and houses on the hard drive to Roger. He was funneling money through a dummy corp. called IG Holdings for a man named Troy Granger. It was quickly sold seven years ago to another guy named Terry Hawkins. I searched for Troy Granger and it was flagged as an 'also known as' for Henry Greer."

"Why does that name sound familiar?"

"Look him up online. I gotta go. Another call."

"Okay. Bye." I pulled the phone away, hung up, then searched the name online. As soon as the results came up, certain things started to fall in place.

Henry Greer was on the FBI's most wanted list for a multitude of things, namely sex trafficking. If Nelson had been a part of that, it would explain her fearful ticks. It also meant I had to make sure Grey didn't get the information. He'd start digging and he wouldn't be careful about it. It was rare that anyone ever got away from Henry and lived, so much so that there was a book about one known person who had. It was written by a guy named Toby Anderson. So, if she had escaped Henry, she was likely trying to stay hidden. I'd keep her secret, but I couldn't say the same for Grey. He'd never do anything to hurt her, but he'd leap to her defense without thinking it through.

"'The Basement Child'?" A familiar voice sounded from behind me. "An interesting choice of read. Even for you."

I didn't look, knowing who was behind me and not giving a shit enough to fully acknowledge her.

"I know you heard me," Sarah sighed in another attempt to get my attention.

"The irritation of your voice could be recognized by

a corpse. Go away." I flipped to the next page in the book about Toby Anderson's account of being groomed by Patrick Lawrence, a doctor who worked for Henry Greer. Two chapters in and it was revolting.

She sat down next to me. "You're the one who didn't call. I don't know why you're mad at me."

"Not my fault you lack the brain power to figure it out. Go away."

"All I know is I went to a party, and that was suddenly a problem for you." Sarah crossed her legs and leaned forward to look at my face.

"Parties aren't a problem for me unless I'm on the attendance list. Go away."

"And you weren't, so I don't get it."

I took in a deep breath and let it out, doing my best not to have an immediate explosion. I looked at her. "I wasn't, however, Jordan was. The same Jordan you used to be engaged to. The one who was seen escorting you around *during* said party. And if I'm not mistaken—and I rarely am—it would be the same Jordan that texted me saying he was really sorry about what happened at the party. I didn't even text him back, but he's a dipshit that doesn't know when to stop and continued to explain exactly what happened. I don't do cheating—any kind of it." I pointed up and down at her legs. "Crossing those was what you should have been doing at the party. And did you? No. So, if you really can't figure it out, then go have a head CT and let the doctor explain how you don't have the slightest ounce of matter resembling a brain inside your very thick skull." I gave her a deadening stare of hatred as I spoke calmly. We were in a library and I didn't need to be the one to draw attention.

She sat there looking at me as if I'd told her that *I* cheated and didn't know what to say.

"Do you need me to call someone to drive you?" I raised an eyebrow. Why the hell was she still sitting there?

"I was really drunk, and—"

"I don't give a shit what your excuses are. Go. Away. Now."

She looked out toward the front windows of the library, took in a deep breath, then left. I opened my book and returned to reading without another thought about it.

I'd chosen to come to the library to find the book on Toby Anderson, so there'd be no chance it'd be found by Grey, and there would be no proof of purchase. It wasn't all that thick, so I could easily finish it in an afternoon, though I felt like I'd need a break from the heavy gore soon. Usually, I wouldn't be so bothered, but the girl Toby spoke of—whose disappearance was made famous years before—Hannah Lawrence, bore the resemblance of Nelson in my mind. Thinking she may have been treated only half as badly put a pit in my stomach.

After another hour of reading, I had to stop. I couldn't stop seeing Nelson as the one being brutalized. Hannah Lawrence had endured egregious amounts of torture and abuse, and reading about it was sickening. The part that made me stop reading was when Toby described how the skin on the bottom of her legs stuck to the floor after she sat because she'd been hanged by her wrists and ankles from a clothesline outside. She'd been badly burned by the sun, having rarely spent time outdoors. The only time she was allowed outside was when she was forced to carry a body from the house to bury out in the woods. The way she grew up was completely out of the norm for a sex trade operation. Patrick Lawrence, Hannah's uncle, was just an odd, but necessary, cog in the machine. The house he lived in was either a starting point for children going out or an endpoint for kids they were done with. Patrick was a doctor who was used for all medical needs within the operation. He had an onslaught of mental conditions, so it was easy for Henry to leverage Hannah as a pawn to persuade Patrick.

I raised an eyebrow with an otherwise flat expression. "Are you a drug dealer?"

Nelson looked back at the shit box of a house behind her and back at me before shaking her head. "No." Her eyes looked me up and down. "Why are you asking?"

"Because you're living in a drug den." She wasn't stupid. She'd seen enough to know what she was living in.

Nelson held up her shoulders nervously, like I was going to hit her. "It's just a place to live."

"An apartment is a place to live too."

"I can't afford an apartment." She pulled her worn-out backpack up higher on her shoulder, keeping her eyes toward the ground, and walked toward my truck.

I took in a breath, mentally reprimanding myself for being a judgmental dick, and turned to my truck. Nelson looked more tired than she usually did but still well-kept. It was amazing to me that she'd spent a couple weeks homeless but never looked it. I'd been about to ask one of my friends to let her stay with them, but she moved in with the diner owners. Now, I was considering asking again. Nelson was afraid of everything, and she had to have some kind of fight in her if she'd survived Henry, but it wouldn't be enough to help her if she got caught up with anyone in the house she was living in.

"You want a coffee on the way? My treat." I closed the truck door and pulled my seatbelt on.

"No thanks." She put the backpack on the floor but held onto the top like someone might take it from her.

I rolled my eyes at her continuing stubbornness. "You realize it's considered impolite to continuously reject offers of generosity, right?"

"You've already driven out of your way to give me a ride to the school." She rubbed her thumb over the side of her middle finger, something she did when she was irritated.

"My god, three streets over from my normal route. Shit, just shoot a hole through my gas tank. Do you wanna steal my wallet, social security number, and cut my arm off on principal too?" I shook my head. "I'm getting coffee, and you can either take it black or choose what you want." I realized I sounded like an asshole, so I tried to sound friendlier by reeling it back to the offer of coffee.

"I don't like coffee." Her voice was so quiet I barely heard her.

"What? What human on this planet doesn't like coffee?"

She pointed to the corner of the block. "Can you stop at the gas station?"

"That one's crappy. There's one up ahead that's nicer."

"Please pull over so I can get out."

I looked over at her as she pulled her backpack onto her lap. I let out another breath, forcing it upon my brain to understand she didn't understand sarcasm very well. "It was a joke. I'm not attacking you. Coffee is life for most people, and it's rare when someone doesn't like it."

She looked at me with stubbornness and upset. "And you weren't ridiculing me because of where I live, or the gesture of being considerate of your time and money by giving me a ride?"

"No. I'm a bitter asshole with no filter. If I was pissed about giving you a ride, or at all inconvenienced by it, I'd say no. Trust me. And as far as your living arrangement, it's dangerous. Nothing to do with your ability to afford anything else. So again, not an attack, and I didn't mean to piss you off." I slowed down to round the corner.

"I'm well aware of my living situation, but if I stretch myself thin trying to pay for something nicer, then I have nothing left to save for other things. Things that get me ahead permanently instead of temporarily. I don't need your opinion, criticism, or judgment. I work hard for what little I have, and there'll be more, but I have to get there first." Her voice was a near whisper toward the end and her eyes were open a little wider, which likely meant she was staving off more emotion.

"You're right. I'm sorry. I wasn't trying to criticize you." Normally, I didn't apologize, but Nelson's face had a way of making me feel like I constantly owed her one.

She looked out the windshield, then down at her backpack, picking at the handle. "No. I'm sorry... Carol spent twenty minutes telling me how irresponsible I am... I'm responsible for myself, and that's all I can do right now."

My stomach physically felt clenched again. It'd taken me two hours to get rid of it after I left the library yesterday, and now the feeling was back.

"Don't worry about what anyone else has to say about your life, Nelson." My voice was quieter, in an attempt to sound empathetic. "As long as you're good, it doesn't matter what anyone else has to say. Me included."

"And what the hell does your friend, Grey, want with me?" She looked at me, appearing tired again. "He's the richest man in the US under the age of thirty, and I..." She shook her head and looked forward again.

"Mm, I wouldn't bring that up to him. He doesn't like people throwing his financial situation in his face any more than you do."

"That's not an explanation," she said quietly.

"You're nice." And genuinely pretty enough to make every head turn within a ten-mile radius. I wasn't immune, I just didn't feel the need to jump like a dog.

She shook her head. "He sent me more flowers at the diner and a note saying he'll be in town tomorrow... I don't want to go out with him, but I don't know what to say without being mean."

I smirked. "Yeah. He's not the guy that takes no for

an answer." I turned into the drive-thru of my preferred coffee shop.

"What does he want from me? I can barely function as a person, how am I expected to navigate a relation-ship?"

I stopped behind the car ordering and took in a breath. "That's the nice part about Grey," I looked at her, "he doesn't have expectations other than not being a shit person. As long as you're well-intentioned, you can be who or whatever you want, and he'll just be nice. Like you, I read people because I don't trust anyone. Grey has been glued to me since we were six. Do you think I'd let him if he was a shitbag?" While it was true, the only reason I was trying to convince her was because Grey would help her. Even if it didn't end up being some long-term thing with them, he'd find a way to help. "Do you like tea? They have the world's best Earl Gray here."

"I don't know what that is." She let out a slight tired sigh.

"Tea or Earl Gray?" I raised an eyebrow, slightly teasing.

She frowned. "I know what tea is. I work in a diner."

I let out a short laugh. "I don't know. You didn't know what brussels sprouts were. Earl Gray is a type of tea. Are you willing to try it?"

"As long as it's not fruity. I don't like fruity teas."

"It's not." I pulled up toward the speaker to order.

I took Nelson to retake the two parts of the GED she'd failed, went to my two classes for the day, then took her to the diner after we were done. Somehow, I'd managed to convince her to come with me to a low-key party at my friend's house. I'd called between classes and asked them if they'd be willing to let Nelson rent their open room for cheap. They wanted to meet her first.

"Hey, Ry!" Megan, my friend's sister, smiled flirtatiously. Too over the top for me, but it didn't stop her from trying.

"What's up?" I gave an upwards nod in acknowledgment.

"Not much. You?" She looked at Nelson.

I shrugged, blowing off the question. "This is Bex. Nelson, this is Megan."

Nelson gave a small smile. "Hi."

"Oh my god, I'm jealous of your face! Can I please look like you?" Megan stepped toward us because a group of people were squeezing through behind her. So much for low-key.

Nelson looked nervous as to how to respond.

"Dial it back." I took the blue cup from Megan. "Good god, are your insides sterilized?" Without even bringing the cup up to my nose, it reeked of booze.

Megan laughed. "They should be close. Drew's back in the kitchen." She pointed over her shoulder with her thumb, then went quickly past me to squeal at more of her friends walking in.

"Come on," I told Nelson, who was too busy looking around like there was an imminent threat she couldn't spot.

We walked back toward the kitchen and Nelson followed closely behind me. I picked up a couple beers from the cooler on the counter and handed one to Nelson before we found Andrew. He was someone I'd met in class. We weren't all that close of friends, but he thought so.

"Hey man, you made it." Andrew tipped his beer bottle toward me.

"Thought this was supposed to be just a few people?" I knocked my bottle against his.

"Yeah, well, you know my sister." He looked at Nelson with a bigger smile. "You must be Ryan's new girl. I'm Andrew, nice to meet you."

Nelson shook her head and clenched her hand be-

fore she reached out. "No, I'm just a friend. Bex."

"Bex? Cool name. This is Josh, Mark, and Jake." Andrew pointed to the rest of the guys grouped around.

She pulled back the corner of her mouth in a forced attempt of friendliness and gave a small wave.

"You and Sarah split up?" Jake asked with a slight frown.

"Like three weeks ago, man," Andrew frowned at Jake.

"Shit. Really?" Josh looked surprised. "What happened?"

I shrugged, displaying that I didn't care because I didn't. "She's back with her ex."

"Eh, she's psycho anyway," Jake dismissed.

My eyebrow twitched upwards quickly. He wasn't wrong.

Andrew smiled at someone behind me in a quick flash. "Damn, I haven't seen you in forever, man!"

Nelson and I both turned and took a small step back. I frowned when I saw Grey and his regular brilliant grin. Sam was with him.

"I know. It's been a while," Grey responded easily. The guy was a social chameleon. This wasn't his crowd of people, but he'd never show it, and everyone loved him.

"How the hell have you been?" Andrew extended a hand.

"Not too bad. You?" Grey shook his hand.

"Can't complain. Sam, you've grown like a foot."

Sam shrugged. "Got sick of being short."

"You're still short." I bumped his arm lightly with my elbow.

Sam looked at me. "Who isn't compared to you?"

"How'd you get suckered into coming here?" Grey asked Nelson with an adoring smile. Honestly, I'd never seen him so outright star-struck over someone. It was so genuine it felt wrong to even take a shot at him about it.

She held up her shoulders, with a small attempt at a smile. "Nothing else better to do. I thought you weren't coming until tomorrow."

"I didn't have anything scheduled for tomorrow morning, so I decided to come early."

"Code for he couldn't wait to see you," Sam laughed.

Grey's smile grew a little and he didn't look away from Nelson. "Not afraid to admit it."

Nelson started to smile, but someone from behind me threw their drink in Nelson's face.

"What the hell?" I turned around. Son of a bitch. "God dammit, Sarah! What the hell's wrong with you?"

"You're barking up the wrong tree, bitch!" Sarah yelled at Nelson as I pushed her back.

"Shut the hell up. What's your fricken problem?" I snapped darkly.

Chapter 8

Bexley

I should have been humiliated, but at best, I was slightly embarrassed. It didn't even scrape the surface of "worst" things in my life. Some people laughed, others were quiet and just watching, but it still didn't affect me. What was terrible about getting a drink thrown in my face was the fact that I'd been paying too much attention to Grey and hadn't seen it coming, so my skin reacted with a hard shock. Being touched unexpectedly, even by a liquid substance, felt like being electrocuted so intensely my bones hurt.

"Shit. Here. Are you okay?" Grey's voice was sympathetic.

I opened my eyes to see him grabbing a wad of napkins from the kitchen island. My eyes were burning, and I felt like another attack could hit me from any direction, but I nodded.

"The bathroom is down the hall on the left." Andrew held out a hand towel to me.

"Thanks." My voice didn't actually make a sound. It happened when I was upset. My vocal cords would pinch and just stop working. I could whisper, but that would be it.

I found my way to the bathroom and locked myself in. Wiping the sticky alcohol off me wasn't a priority, my mind was too filled with the burn on my nerve endings, and I couldn't stop shaking. If it'd been seven years ago, I wouldn't have been phased in the slightest, but I'd been living comfortably for too long. Most wouldn't count my situation comfortable, but it was comparable to heaven from where I was seven years ago.

It took me a few minutes to just stand there and get over the worst of the shaking, but after, I cleaned myself up as much as could be expected. When I opened the door, Grey was standing there with a kind but sympathetic expression. He held out a hoodie to me.

"It's Sam's. He said you can return it later."

I shook my head. "That's okay. I'm just gonna go home."

He smiled a little more genuinely. "I figured as much, but you can still take the hoodie and I'll drive you."

I took the hoodie but hoped he'd accept my rejection to let him drive me. All I needed was another conversation about my living conditions. "Thanks, but I'd rather walk."

"Ten miles back to Monterey?" His eyebrows raised, but the smile didn't disappear. I wondered if he knew how beautiful his smile was. It was strange how he made me feel calm and almost comfortable, similar to the way I'd felt around Toby.

"What do you want with me, Grey?" The words fell out of my mouth before I thought about them. "I have nothing to offer. No money, hardly a basic understanding of social situations, no education. I work six days a week and barely afford to live. We couldn't be from more opposite sides of life, so I really can't understand. I can't be in a relationship—I wouldn't know what to do with one. So, unless there's something I'm completely missing, I don't know what someone like you could want with me."

Grey took in a breath and held it for a second, but he still held a friendly appearance. "'Someone like you?'" He quoted as his eyebrows raised, making him look hurt.

"You have money, went to prestigious private schools and college, drive cars I couldn't dream about owning. You asked for a second date because you think you were talking too much on the first, but it was on purpose. I asked you questions so I wouldn't have to talk. I have nothing I can say, nothing in common, and no stories from the past I can share. I don't want to tell them, and who wants to sit there with someone who doesn't talk?"

"Okay, I understand what you're saying," he nodded. His smile had left.

I held Sam's hoodie out to him. "I appreciate the date and the flowers. Despite your reflection on the date, I *did* have a really great time."

He took the hoodie. "Then go out with me one more time."

I shook my head, not even knowing what to say. Didn't he hear anything I'd said?

Part of his smile returned. "I get it. My life experiences and your life experiences are completely different, but it doesn't mean we don't have anything in common."

I raised my eyebrows. "No?"

His smile grew a little more. "No. You breathe air, I breathe air. We live on planet Earth, we're both human, we eat food..."

I frowned. He was making light of something while I was trying to have a serious conversation.

His joking smile relaxed into a kind expression. "One more date. *Please.* We don't have to talk about past things, we can find things we have in common now and talk about those things. Eat cotton candy and decide it's gross and gritty, tour a museum and come up with a list of ways to make a painting funny, eat ice cream. No judgment of financial status or anecdotes, just you and me doing whatever sounds like a good time."

I pressed my lips together and looked away. Just as Ryan had said, Grey wasn't taking no for an answer. For his sake, and because there was a bigger part of me that liked him, I wanted him to. No one understood that knowing me on any level was a risk. It was already disgusting of me that I'd decided to be friends with Ryan. Despite his bitter way of speaking, he was a good person.

"Based on what you said, you're afraid of being judged. But I think maybe you overlooked the fact that you're judging *me*. Call me petty, but I don't think it's fair."

I looked at Grey with a slight frown, wondering how he could think I was judging *him*.

He gave a shy kind of smile. "You don't deserve to be judged just because you don't have money, but I don't think I deserve to be judged because I *do*." He held up his shoulders. "I'm still just a person. Ten fingers, ten toes, came into this world the same way as everyone else..."

Never in a million years would I expect a person like him to look embarrassed, but it put into perspective that I was the one passing judgment, not him. I took in a breath, wanting more than anything to apologize and go out with him again, but also knowing better.

His smile changed again. "I promise, if you go out with me a second time, and you have a terrible time or you discover signs of me being an extraterrestrial, I'll let you rip my heart out and say no to a third date."

Something about the way he spoke nearly made me laugh, but it came out in a small huff with a near smile. I could remember the last time I'd laughed and smiled for real, and both were more distant than the last time I'd cried—seven years ago.

"Okay," I nodded.

His eyes crinkled at the corners as his perfect smile grew. "Are you saying yes so you can say no and be left alone later?" He held out Sam's hoodie to me again, but this time in a position for me to put it on.

"There's a good chance." I pulled the hoodie over my head.

"Good. I like a challenge. Will you let me drive you home?"

"Mm... You can drive me to the diner." I turned out of the doorway of the bathroom.

"Can I take the long way and buy myself some extra time with you? Maybe stop at a drive-thru because I'm starving, stop for a caffeine fix, convince you to take a short walk on the beach?" He walked down the hallway with me as he spoke.

"You wanna do the second date tonight?"

"No, I was just hoping to cure my hunger, headache, and hankering for fresh air in one shot. Your attendance would be a bonus."

"No chance of you grabbing a handful of chips here, an aspirin, and rolling down the windows?" I looked at him.

Grey let out a sigh. "Alright, I'll take you back to the diner."

"Suit yourself. I didn't say no, I just asked if there was an alternative." I *did* want to spend more time with him. It was strange and unlike me, but he made me feel different. His lightness was like stepping out into the sunshine from years in a dark basement.

He laughed. "Just when I think you're going to zig, you zag."

"Sometimes, it's better to have no expectations."

Grey and I walked out the back door of the house and Ryan was standing outside, leaning against the side of the detached garage smoking a cigarette. I envied his ability to so plainly hide emotion from people. I was decent at it, years of pain and suffering aided my learning, but I didn't detach from things as completely as he seemed to.

"Hold on a second," I told Grey quietly before walking over to Ryan. "Are you okay?"

Ryan blew out a line of smoke and frowned like he smelled something rotten. "I didn't get a cup of shit thrown in my face. I'm fine. You?"

I held up my shoulders. "Worse things happen."

His eyebrows raised and dropped quickly. "I guess... Not the one who owes you an apology, but I'm sorry you got caught in the middle."

"It happens... I think I'm gonna head home though, if that's okay?"

He looked behind me in Grey's direction. "Try not to crush Blondie. He's a pain in my ass, but he's a good guy."

I looked back at Grey, then at Ryan again. "I think I have to be nice. He pointed out something I didn't think about. I was being judgmental because of his money."

Ryan nodded. "He usually gets the shit end of the deal. People either think he's a rich snob, or they're standing in line holding their hand out for a freebie. Nobody takes him at face value as a person."

"You don't have to keep talking him up. I already agreed to a second date."

Ryan shook his head. "I'm not talking him up." He dropped his cigarette and stepped on it. "Have a good night. I'll see you Monday night at the coffee shop."

"Okay, and you too."

Ryan pushed off the side of the garage and stopped beside me, holding out a fist at elbow level. I smiled just a little and bumped the side of his fist with the side of mine. He gave a slight smile that almost matched mine and went back in the house.

"You're one of a rare kind," Grey said when I walked back to him.

"What do you mean?"

Grey shook his head. "He doesn't like anybody."

"He likes *you*," I pointed out.

He laughed lightly. "No. He works for me, and he tolerates me. You might be the first person he's genuinely befriended."

I frowned. "What is it with you two and the need to talk each other up?"

Grey gave another quiet chuckle and pulled his keys out of his pocket. "We like you. We're trying to keep you around."

"I think that's beyond me too. I haven't done anything."

"You have. You just don't know what it is." He opened the passenger door for me.

I got in, wondering what that meant, and contemplated if it was important enough for me to ask. When he got in and started the car, I did ask. Grey told me he'd watched me take my own tip money and put it on Ann's tables at the diner. I'd only thought to look for Carol when I'd done it, not check to see if a customer might see. Apparently, the thing that made me stand out to Ryan was the fact that I'd chosen to swallow my pride and ask him for help that night at the motel. He also appreciated I wasn't academically lazy.

Grey stopped at a drive-thru for food, then drove to the diner and parked in the parking lot facing the beach. We ate our burgers and talked about how exceedingly un-profound Shakespeare was after he mentioned a test Sam failed. It wasn't everyone's opinion, but Grey was the first person I'd met who agreed. I'd first read about Shakespeare in the encyclopedias available to me growing up. Toby had told me how great the plays were, so when I'd escaped, I read some of them. I didn't carry Toby's opinion.

When the burgers and fries were gone, Grey and I walked out to the ocean. There were more people at the beach than usual because there was bioluminescent algae in the water. I'd never seen anything like it, and I didn't even know the water could light up the way it did. I was glad I'd chosen to wear shorts because I wanted to stand in the water for a closer look. Grey and I stood at the edge of the tide, up to mid-calf level, and watched the incredible blue glow. People were surfing the waves as they came in, and it was all beautiful. Moments like the one I was in were ones I never took for granted. I absorbed the calm every time it visited me.

It took a good thirty minutes before we walked back to dry sand and sat down just to watch from a short distance.

"We can go back if you want. You look bored."

I looked at Grey and shook my head. "The opposite. I'm fascinated, but we can go if you want to." I'd likely come right back once he was gone.

Grey smiled and shook his head. "You're hard to read, you know that?"

"I know. Carol says I have two expressions, scared shit-less and pathetically sad."

Grey laughed a little. "She might be right, but I think I may have caught a couple of tiny smiles—ones you weren't faking."

It wasn't out of stubbornness that I didn't smile, I just didn't feel it. Things that other people found funny were monotonous to me.

"Would I be breaking the rules if I asked you what your single happiest memory was?"

I looked at Grey for a moment, deciding if it was breaking the rules, and looked back out at the water. "Last year the diner was closed for a week when Carol and Joe went to Georgia to see their family. I had some extra money, so I rented a moped and drove down highway one. People mention the Bixby Bridge all the time, but they never mention the cliffs that look like the edge of the earth... Big Sur felt like a warm canopy of green.

Then I stopped at this little pull-off that had a public bathroom, and the ocean water had that teal crystal blue color because there wasn't any sand stirred up. I kept going, all the way to Cambria, and the lady at the bed and breakfast told me about this back road that wound for miles and ended in Morro Bay. The road was only wide enough for a single car, but not a single second of the three-hour drive was disappointing. There were secluded farms, small vineyards, and hills so steep the dumb moped could hardly make it, but it was breathtaking. For that entire day, I didn't think about myself once. I didn't worry about the money spent, anything in the past, or what I was supposed to do when I got back. Nothing outside that day existed. Maybe it's an exaggeration, but I felt like I'd died and gone to heaven."

"It doesn't sound like an exaggeration, it sounds peaceful... but I can't picture you on a moped." He chuckled.

I smiled a little, but it was mostly at the sound of his laugh. "It was all I could afford, but it ended up being really nice because I didn't have the restricted view of a car."

"No, I'm not mocking." He shook his head with his beautiful smile in place. "I just can't picture it."

I nodded. "I know. I don't fit the type."

"Not even a little bit... Would you do it again? Retrace your steps just to see the scenery, or would that put a damper on your good memory?"

"I'd do it again in a heartbeat, but maybe not on a moped. I had to walk that thing up one of the hills on that back road and it was exhausting."

Grey laughed again. "Maybe a nice convertible would do the trick. Top down, still gives you that open sky feeling."

"Maybe..." If I could ever be in a position to rent a convertible.

"There's a road in Rainier National Park I like to

drive. Sometimes Seattle feels like a constant foghorn and I have to get away. So, I go for a drive through the park, roll the windows down and just drive through every bend in the road and smell the trees... It drives my dad through the roof because he can't call me with a hundred stupid questions or force his expectations on me. No cell phone reception."

"Carol harasses me to get a cell phone all the time, but I see no point. There's only one day a week I'm not at the diner." I looked down at my toes in the sand.

"That partly sounds blissful, and partly painful. I like the convenience of my phone, I just wish it didn't ring so much."

I shook my head. "You shouldn't wish that. Isolation is only nice for so long. You have your family, and I'm sure you have a lot of friends." I would have given anything to be like anyone else and have the privilege of my family calling me.

"That's true. You don't have any relatives out there?"

I could feel Grey stealing glances at me as I continued to watch my feet move in the sand. I shook my head. "No... It's just me."

"That must be hard. Were you close with your parents?"

It was a tough question to answer, with a wildly different answer, depending on who one was referring to. There were the people I was born to, then the person who raised me.

"No... I was adopted and they weren't good people. It all ended, and it was honestly just a blessing for everyone." I'd just told him more than anyone else, and while it felt all too easy, I also hoped it wouldn't pose questions I couldn't answer. Grey's easy nature made me want to tell him more than I should. I wouldn't, but I wanted to.

"Then it sounds like you deserved the blessing."

I looked at Grey. His response wasn't what I expected.

He gave me a gentle smile. "Have you ever tried to find your biological parents?"

"No... I don't have much, but I have quiet... and I like the quiet." Mostly, that was the truth. The only thing that drew me to want to see my parents again was curiosity, but it had been fourteen years. People could change a lot in fourteen years. Also, they'd have questions I'd never answer. No matter how much I'd like to dream and think I could go back, and everything would fall beautifully into place, it would never be the truth.

Grey's smile grew, and he was looking at me in a way that seemed to only exist in movies. "I know it's forward as hell, but you're unexpectedly beautiful. And I don't mean that in terms of physical appearance." He laughed a little. "Though you're not hard on the eyes either."

I shook my head with a sigh and looked back out at the ocean. "The dimples, the cheekbones, the eyelashes... I've heard it all, and a thousand times."

"Yeah? Have you ever thought about taking the compliment?" He laughed.

"Nope. I've met all kinds of people, pretty and ugly, and they come in all forms. Physical form isn't something achieved, it's something a person is born with. Being a good person, on the other hand, is something people choose and work for, therefore being worthy of a compliment."

"And you realize I complimented your mentality and you *still* didn't accept it." The smile Grey had affected the tone of his voice.

"I don't know what to do with compliments. They make me nervous." I looked at him with no associated emotion.

"Nervous? You should be confident with who you are. I'm sure you've heard the saying, 'Opinions are like assholes, everybody has one.' So, if someone admires something about you, thank them for the compliment.

If they don't, what do you care? As long as you're good with you, the rest doesn't matter."

I shrugged, already looking at the sand. "Compliment or criticism, nothing changes... I'm still who I am." I looked at Grey. "But thank you, the kindness is appreciated."

Grey smiled a perfect smile with his dimples showing. "There you go again. I expected a zag and you zigged. You're welcome."

I took in a breath and looked at my watch. The time was wrong. It said it was just after ten, but I'd gotten to the party with Ryan around that time. "My watch stopped. What time is it?"

Grey twisted his wrist to make his watch light up. "Ten after two."

"Geez. I need to get home." I rubbed my face. By the time I walked from the diner to the house, took a shower, and got ready, I'd have to walk straight back.

"How far do you live from here?" Grey got up and offered a hand.

I hesitated, wondering if my hand would burn by taking his, but did it anyway. My hand only tingled mildly. "A few miles. Over in Seaside."

We started toward the diner parking lot.

"Let me drive you. I promise I won't turn into some creepy stalker and show up at your house unannounced. If I want to find you, I'll come to the diner."

I shook my head. "It's not that... Thanks though." Me getting out of an expensive ass car in my neighborhood wouldn't be good for either of us. Jose's goons would find a way to extort money from me or Grey. I couldn't afford it. Ryan was okay because he had an old pick-up and didn't look like he was loaded to the walls.

When we got to Grey's car, he stopped and faced me. "You don't have to be embarrassed about where you live. I'm not judging."

I shook my head again. "It's not that either. Really. The people I live with suck and I don't want to start anything. Thank you for tonight though, I enjoyed the conversation." I forced a small smile, but I *did* mean my words.

Grey had that same look from the movies again, like he truly appreciated being near me. "Good. I'm still getting that next date then?"

I nodded. "Yeah. I'm working all day tomorrow—or today, I guess—but I'm off Sunday."

"How early is too early on Sunday?"

I shrugged a little. "I get up at four every morning, so it's up to you."

"I'm usually up around then too. Do you wanna meet here at six, we'll grab an early breakfast, then carry out my plan to make it so you can't say no to a third date?" He flashed a wide, but beautiful grin.

I nodded once. "I'll be here at six."

Chapter 9

Ryan

"How'd it go last night?" I asked when I set my keys down on the counter.

Grey stopped typing and looked over from his spot at the kitchen island. "Good. I need to find her a different place to live, but good."

I frowned. "She let you take her home?"

"No. I kept a distant tail on her. That place is a shit hole."

I nodded. "I told you."

"Any luck getting Andrew to agree to let her rent a room?"

I shrugged. "I don't think it'd work for her. He was too interested."

Grey went toward the fridge. "Because living with a bunch of drug dealers is better?"

"No, but Andrew can be as persistent as you and they'd be living in the same house. I think the wiser move would be to wait and find her something else."

"Yeah, well, I'm working on it. I found a small condo I can rent. If she agrees, then I'll just make the people an offer they can't refuse so she can stay."

I rolled my eyes. "Okay, I get that she's nice and she lives in shit, but you realize it's weird to buy her a condo? Just outright spend hundreds of thousands of dollars on someone you don't know?"

Grey turned around, looked surprised, and like I'd hurt his feelings somehow. "I have more than I'll ever use in a lifetime. Why is it such a big deal to try and share it with someone who has a need and might actually deserve it? She has nothing and no one. There's no way she did something to deserve that."

"I'm just saying. Two hundred K is a lot for someone you've gone out with twice. Give her a job or something, then help her get an apartment. I don't know." Grey was forever getting ahead of himself when it came to his humanitarian projects. Nelson probably *did* deserve the generosity, but she wasn't the kind of person to take handouts. I'd barely been allowed to pay for her tea the other day, and she'd left ten dollars in my truck for the gas station run when I first met her.

"It's *my* money and not your business. What did you find out about where she's living?"

I took a deep breath, knowing I wouldn't get any further on the previous subject. "I did some asking around. She used to deal for the guy who owns the house, Jose Chavez. The people I talked to seem to like him. Obviously, his choice of profession is deranged, but I didn't hear anything too crazy." I reached in my pocket, pulled out a dime bag, and tossed it to Grey. "I paid a kid to ask one of the dealers about her and they told him she's out of the game. I had him pretend to be a pig and be after her or something, and basically, he was told if he went near her, Jose would come kill him in his sleep. So, she's probably safe for now."

He raised an eyebrow. "I'd rather not leave it to

chance for that long... I don't get it. What is someone like her doing living in a place like that? She's smart. And for someone who claims to have no prior education growing up, she's well-spoken."

I shrugged. "She works hard at it. She reads a ton. I don't know. Maybe she's lying and covering up something else." If I could steer Grey away from anything that might lead to the truth about Nelson, I would. At least until I knew the truth.

Grey seemed to think for a minute before he responded, "She admitted she was adopted, which we already knew. Have you found anything out about her adoption yet?" He grabbed a knife from the block and cut into the apple he'd retrieved from the fridge.

"Not yet. Tim's gonna poke around in the FBI database, but I doubt anything will turn up." Tim had already poked around and found a fake biological mother. I'd have him give the information to Grey when the time was right. I needed to know Nelson's real identity and past before I sent Grey on a wild goose chase. "Also, her credit has been officially cleared up, debts paid, and I've got a few interviews set up to find someone to keep an eye on her when we're not. I'm meeting them at the library." Roger didn't appear to know we were talking to her yet, but we had to keep her safe when and if he found out.

Grey nodded. "Thanks. You need to figure out where her missing lumps of money are going too. The diner is consistently packed, so either they're stiffing her or it's going somewhere else."

I felt badly about betraying Nelson's trust and hiring more people to follow her, but I was doing my job. Right now, my job was to protect her.

I had a couple hours to read before the first of my interviews, so I worked on finishing the book. At chapter nine, I had to pause, go outside, smoke a cigarette, take a small walk around the parking lot, smoke again, then just stood against my truck. In the previous chapters, Toby Anderson hadn't mentioned the dolls hanging by their neck from the basement rafters because it wasn't relevant. But when Hannah had told him that they were hung there to mark the children she'd seen killed, it became very relevant. Not just to the book, but to the pictures Tim had pulled off the external drive.

I found Hannah Lawrence... At thirteen years old, I remembered the entire country was in an uproar searching for her. Every news station and paper across the country picked up the story. Her face still appeared on the fake news tabloids every year or two, saying she'd been spotted in a grocery store or something...

The more I thought about it, the more I didn't know what to do with the information. Roger had obviously been keeping tabs on her because if it came out that he was in any way affiliated with Hannah, her disappearance, or the people who'd harmed her, his money would never be enough to buy his way out of jail. This was more than enough leverage for Grey to use against Roger to shove him out of the company, but at what cost to Hannah? Would it stop at quiet and simple blackmail? I'd have to keep Grey away from any kind of "Hannah Lawrence" topics, books, and movies. He didn't have cause to look into it as of now, but if he were given the wrong piece of information, it'd send him down the rabbit hole.

My fourth cigarette was about done, so I used it to light another while I contemplated how to handle the situation at hand. First, I was going to go back into the library to find the best damn person I could to keep a close eye on her. I had school and Sam to look after— both very time consuming without the whale of a mess Nelson brought to the table. Second thing would be finishing that book. After that, I needed to get my hands on the movie. Sure, it'd have its Hollywood spin, but I needed to know everything I could know about Nelson and where she'd come from. It was the only real way to help her.

After my fifth cigarette was burned out, I went back inside to start chipping at my to-do list.

I walked into the living room from the hallway and frowned when I saw Grey on the couch with his laptop. He'd texted me to come upstairs when I woke up, but I'd been awake for a while.

"What's up?" I yawned, making my way to the kitchen for food.

"She's gone," Grey answered.

"What?" I stopped and looked at him.

"She took off and no one knows where."

"What do you mean 'took off'?" I walked around the side of the couch.

Grey handed me his laptop. "I went to the diner this morning and waited for a few minutes until one of the owners came out and told me Bex was gone. They said she called in yesterday morning, quit her job, and they don't know where she went. The house is all taped off with police tape, cops going in and out, and reporters standing around with cameras. So, I came home and looked online." He pointed at his laptop in my hand. "It says a young woman came home in the early hours of the morning, someone tried to sexually assault her out on the front lawn, the guy was shot by someone living in the house, cops were called, the house was raided... I called the police station and pretended to be her brother, they said they interviewed her, and she took off after that. She's gone."

I stared at the pictures on the screen as Grey told me what the article read. My face felt numb and my stomach was hollow. The words of the book were circling in my head, and I wondered why she couldn't just have a break from the shit in life. Hannah had been raped nearly every day for seven years. If not by her uncle, then other people. How much more could life beat her down before she gave in? I wanted to give up after chapter two.

I gave Grey his laptop back and went straight for the garage door.

"Where are you going?" he asked.

"To find her." On my way, I reached over to the fruit basket for an orange.

"I'll come with you."

"No. If she sees you, she won't say anything, and she might run. She trusts me. Just do your thing and I'll text you when I find her." I stepped into my shoes at the door. "I'm taking the Range Rover." I grabbed the keys and went into the garage. It was a vehicle she wouldn't recognize.

I knew her patterns. For a month, I'd been watching her like a hawk at all times of the day and night. She had places she went to think, places she deemed safe enough to sleep—I knew all of them. The ocean seemed to be a magnet for her. That first night I'd watched her at the diner, she must have looked out the windows a dozen times to see the water. It surprised me that she'd agreed to go to the beach with Grey because it seemed to be an almost private place for her. She'd mentioned how Carol would ask her to go for a walk down the beach during the two hours the restaurant was closed every day, and Nelson would refuse because it was something she liked to do alone.

It was two hours before I spotted her, but once I did, I watched her for a while. She was sitting in the sand with her arms wrapped around her legs, just staring out at the waves. I almost didn't recognize her because her hair was down. It was surprisingly longer than I would have thought, just four or five inches from the ground as she sat, and full of large curls. She had the same clothes on from the other day, but not Sam's hoodie. When I got closer, I could see her cheek was bruised. Her eyes were bloodshot, and I'd never seen her look so run down.

Nelson jumped and looked up at me when I came up to her from the side, but she was already looking back out at the water before I was fully seated. I hated sitting in sand, but I didn't want to stand there towering over her, and it was unlikely that she'd follow me back to the car if I asked. There had to be a million terrible things rolling around in her head, so I'd take the irritation of sitting on the ocean's litter box.

While looking for her, I'd tried to think of how to start a conversation. Asking her if she was okay could pose to be a dangerous question. I wasn't good with other people's emotions—I wasn't good with my own either, but I really wasn't good with other people's. Telling her I heard what happened would close off a conversation before it had a chance to start. Why would she feel the need to talk about something if I proclaimed to already know of it?

"How'd you find me?" she asked quietly.

"Lucky guess... Ever read Moby Dick?"

She looked at me with a deep frown. Her cheek looked worse up close. I'd also noticed her knees were scraped too, and blood stains on the front of her shirt.

"It's a book with the world's longest run-on sentences. The main character talks about growing 'grim about the mouth', wanting to knock 'people's hats off,' and whatever. And when that happens, he says he knows it's time to 'take to the seas'... You mentioned once you like coming here... I saw the police tape around your house..." I looked out at the water. Sand I hated, but the view wasn't wasted on me.

"Whatever shit remark you're about to make, I'm not really up for hearing it." Her voice was barely audible over the wind.

I hated that she thought I'd ridicule her, but it wasn't all that unfair of her to think so. "No shit remarks," I said quietly. "I just wanted to make sure you're okay."

She shook her head. "I'm never okay... Even when *things* are 'okay', I'm not... No matter where I go, how hard I work or try to get ahead, I end up in the same place. Different chains, but always the same place."

If I hadn't learned who she was, her words wouldn't have made so much sense.

I nodded a little. "I can understand that."

She gave a humorless laugh. "Really?" She looked at me. "How's that?"

I pulled back the corner of my mouth. "At the risk of preaching, everybody has shit they can't scrub away. Obviously, no two people have the same shit, but everybody's got it... The worst thing in my life is my little brother dying when I was sixteen, but there's someone out there who lost their entire family, and another person who lost everything they knew. The list goes on, but it doesn't mean losing my brother is less than someone who lost everything. It's just different."

She looked at me for a moment, seeming angrier and more hurt than she could really express. Her eyes went back to the crashing waves.

"You don't deserve it." I stayed careful of my words. "Whatever it is that keeps you from being okay... you don't deserve it... I can help you find another place to stay. I've got friends who rent out rooms, I'm sure I can haggle someone on price. At least until you find something else."

She shook her head. "I don't know if I can stay in town... I'd be gone already, but the police said I had to stay until the investigation is over. *I* get attacked, and now I'm a suspect in drug dealing because I lived in that house. The only thing I've got going for me is the room I was renting has its own outside entrance, giving me plausible deniability."

I let out a breath. She'd put herself in a bad position by living there, but it didn't mean she deserved what happened. Ultimately, everything that happened to her was just a trickle effect of her childhood, and she couldn't be held accountable for that.

"Do you need a lawyer? I know plenty of people who'd take you pro-bono." Pro-bono meant Grey would flip the bill behind the scenes.

She shook her head. "They can't make anything stick. I was too careful to make sure I knew nothing about what went on in that house for the whole two weeks I was there."

"The offer stands if something changes. Same goes for helping you try to find a place too."

"It's okay. I'll figure it out."

"Are you allowed to get your stuff out of the house? I can drive you and help out." She didn't have so much as her purse with her.

For a moment she didn't show a sign that she'd even heard me, but then she reached up and pinched her forehead, closing her eyes. "I don't know... I didn't ask."

I reached into my pocket, pulled out my phone, and called the police department.

"How is she?" Grey asked when I came in the house.

I nodded. "She's alright. It took me forty minutes to convince her to let me pay for a hotel room. The police station wouldn't give her purse back because it's evidence, so she has no money. And we met an officer at the house so she could get her stuff. I bought her some food and left her a hundred bucks." I handed him the receipts from the hotel and food, purchased on the company card I had.

"Okay." He picked up the receipts and looked at them.

I opened the fridge and grabbed a jerky stick and a bottle of water. "I've got the guy I hired keeping an eye on her. He'll call if she leaves the room."

Grey pulled back the corner of his mouth. "I hate spying on her, but I'm worried."

I let out a huff. "After yesterday morning, I don't feel bad at all."

"Did she say anything about it?"

"No, and she was too upset for me to ask. And when you see her next, don't say anything. I told her I wouldn't say anything to you. I'm supposed to tell you she overslept."

"I wasn't planning on it anyway. I'm letting you handle the heavy." Grey frowned at his watch as it rang with a call. He tapped the screen to answer. "Hello?"

"Hey, it's Bex." Nelson's voice was even and calm.

Grey smiled instantly. "Hey. You pulled a disappearing act on me. Everything okay?" He closed his laptop and reached into his pocket for his phone.

"Yeah. Sorry. Lack of sleep caught up to me and I over-slept. We can still do something if you want."

Grey raised his eyebrows in surprise. "Yeah, sure. I don't think we have enough time for my original plan, but I've got a couple ideas. What time did you want to meet up?"

Chapter 10

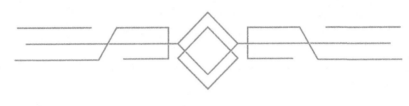

Grey

I couldn't believe Bex had called. When she didn't show up at the diner, not only was I worried, but I was crushed. I was still bummed there wasn't enough time for the day I'd originally planned, but I was happy for whatever time I got with her. After asking her if she minded horses, I picked my first backup option of taking her trail riding through Big Basin Redwoods. When we got to the stables, her eyes had a sort of liveliness. Some friends of my parents lived in the area, so I texted them and they had their stable workers get two horses ready.

"Well, you've got Admiral, and Judge here," Randy, the horse trainer, said as he tightened the saddle on Judge. "They're both our best behaved. And if you get lost out on the trails, just tell them to go home and they'll bring you back."

"Thanks for having them ready for us. I appreciate it." I gave a friendly smile.

"No problem. I'm glad someone's getting them out. They're no good for racing anymore, so they're not getting as much riding time as they're used to."

"You should tell Bart to call my mom then. She's on the hunt for a few horses to keep out in Martha's Vineyard." I smoothed my hand over Judge's nose.

"I just might do that. These boys aren't done yet, just done racing." Randy stood up straight and looked over Judge's back. "Looks like someone found a kindred spirit."

I looked over and smiled when I saw Admiral with his head hung over Bex's shoulder. She looked just as happy as the horse did.

"He's sweet," she responded, itching behind the horse's ears.

"Must be you. He usually nips at people. If I'd had a say in it, I would've named him Dog."

I laughed a little, wanting to take my phone out and get a picture of Bex with the horse, but the timing seemed off. She looked beautiful though. The sunlight showed the natural highlights in her hair, and while she wasn't actually smiling, there was happiness in her eyes.

"You ready to go?" I couldn't keep the smile from my face.

Bex nodded and walked around to the side of the horse. "I got it," she said before my hand touched her arm to help her up.

"I'll take it this isn't your first time on a horse?"

She shook her head. "I rode some when I was little... It's been a long time though."

I grabbed the horn on the saddle that sat on Judge. "It's been a few years for me." I pulled myself up and swung my leg over. "My mom's an East coaster at heart, so I played polo every summer when we went to the Hamptons."

"Looks like you need those stirrups adjusted." Randy reached toward Bex's foot, and his hand didn't make it there before the horse stepped to the side and started talking back while bobbing its head.

"It's okay. They're fine." Bex looked afraid, but not because of the horse's reaction. She glanced at me, almost like she was making sure she hadn't done something wrong, or like she needed help.

"It's all good. If she changes her mind later, I know how to adjust them." I didn't know why she was so scared, but I figured I'd give her a way out of it. "You ready?" I smiled at her like I hadn't noticed anything at all.

Her eyebrows gave a micro-twitch while giving me a slightly unsure expression, but then she nodded and forced a smile. Even if it was forced, it was beautiful, but I was still holding out for a real one.

"You kids have fun." Randy gave a small wave.

Bex slightly nudged her horse's sides and started forward.

"So, basic questions." I made my horse match pace with hers. We weren't quite to the road yet, and there was a looming silence. "What's your favorite color?"

"Um, I don't know. I haven't thought about it... Maybe sea glass? The sort of translucent bluish-green kind."

It was interesting that it wasn't something she knew. "We should go up to Fort Bragg sometime. They have an entire beach of sea glass."

"I'd probably come back with a few jars full."

"If you could go anywhere in the world, on vacation, where would you go?" She didn't know I was making plans for future dates.

"Probably Switzerland... I've seen pictures of the Alps. It looks breathtaking. You?"

"I'd like to go back to Iceland. Favorite meal?"

"Don't have one."

"What? No Thanksgiving dinner, or like a spread of Chinese or something?"

"I've never had Chinese, so I don't know. I like strawberry swirl ice cream and chocolate chip cookies, but otherwise, food is just food."

I looked at her like she was crazy, and she might have been. "You've *never* had Chinese food?" I asked skeptically.

She shook her head. "No. I usually have something at the diner or pick up one of those frozen meals at the store."

I didn't know what to think, so I just kinda laughed a little. "Guess I know what we're having for dinner tonight. What did your family do for Thanksgiving?" There was a chance I was touching on a forbidden subject.

She shook her head. "We didn't celebrate holidays. What about you? What's your favorite meal?"

I turned my face completely serious. "I'm surprised you have to ask. Any meal with you."

She frowned.

I laughed. "No? Not even a tiny smile?"

The corner of her mouth pulled back as she shook her head. "No."

"Why not?"

"Because I think part of you was serious."

I laughed again. "My favorite meal is the barbeque ribs my parents' chef makes for the fourth of July." I shook my head with a slight chuckle. "Okay. What's something you do well? Better than most people."

"I can't tell you that." She pressed her lips together and the corner of her mouth pulled up. "And I already know your answer, so, what's a hidden talent you have?"

I had to think about that. "Uh... I'm an excellent cook. I hardly have the time to do it, so few people know. And the only person who can outcook me is probably Ryan."

She raised an eyebrow. "I can't picture him cooking. And especially not liking it."

I laughed. "Actually, he loves it. It's probably the *only* thing he loves. How about you?"

She sighed. "Can't answer that one either. If you weren't in the stock market, what would you do?"

"No. Hold on." I laughed. "First, you're turning everything on me again, and second, you only get one free skip. So, you either have to answer the last question or this one."

"Mm." She made a face like she was thinking. "I really don't."

"If you don't, then you're cheating."

"Okay."

I laughed quietly because of her simple nature. "Okay," I agreed. She might not have been hinting that she didn't like being questioned, but I was taking it as that.

I hung back just enough to be able to watch her without her noticing. The trees towered around us, and the sun was coming through in beams. Bex looked more comfortable than she normally did, but she still looked like she was ready to dive off the horse and run if she had to.

"I know it's none of my business, but I have to put it out there because I feel like I'm keeping something from you." I had to get her to tell me about what happened when she went home. "Carol said you quit your job when I talked to her this morning. I'm not trying to call you out on a lie, I just don't get why you felt like you needed to." I really did hate lying. It was fine if she didn't want to tell me something but lying would eventually piss me off.

Bex stopped her horse and looked at me. "Ryan told you what happened?"

"No. I asked if he knew anything, and he said he didn't, but I know when he's lying." And now I was lying to try to make her clear her lie. Great...

She bit the inside of her lip for a second, took a breath, then it was like any visible fear left her body. "I didn't quit, Carol fired me. When I first moved to Monterey, I had a drug problem, and I was selling them. She and Joe helped me clean up, and I've been sober and out of the game for two years. The other night when I went home, some things happened, cops were called, and the house I was renting a room in, was raided. The guy who owns the house is a dealer I used to work for. I wasn't dealing, and I've been sober, but she doesn't believe me." She held up her shoulders. "If she told you I quit, it's probably because she's too nice to smear someone's name."

I nodded. "Okay... You're not in any trouble over the house being raided, are you?"

She shook her head, still looking as if she were afraid of nothing. "No. They can't tie me to anything, because I didn't do anything, and my room had a separate entrance."

"The guy you rented from won't throw you under the bus?"

"Not unless he wants to get tied to a murder charge. I know plenty. Yesterday morning was deemed as self-defense, but I know of another time it wasn't. I know it's not right, but I have to do what I have to, to protect myself. He'll be quiet."

Geez. Who was she? It was off-putting that she could shut off any sign of emotion, but now I understood why she and Ryan got along.

"I didn't realize it was you they were talking about on the news... Are you okay?" I tried not to appear overly concerned, but not uncaring either.

She nodded. "Yeah... This morning, not so much, but now I'm better."

"Okay... I know you don't know me that well, but if you need anything—and I do mean *anything*—I'll be happy to help."

"Thanks. I've got it handled."

I gave her a smile because I knew she had to want out of the conversation. "Feel like making these horses do some work?"

"The poor things are carrying us on their backs.

How much more do you want to make them do?" She gave a small twisted smile.

I laughed. "Honestly, none. I'm ready to go back whenever you are."

"I'm ready."

"Thank god. This was a better idea in theory than practice." I turned the horse around.

"Yeah. It's beautiful out here, but it's been the same for the last thirty minutes."

"Yup," I agreed simply. "Let's shorten this. Go home." I pressed my heels into Judge's sides.

He cut off the trail and went for a straight shot back to the stables. Bex kept up, and we got back in ten minutes.

Since we were halfway to San Francisco, we went there instead of back to Monterey. What better place to have Chinese food for the first time than China Town? Instead of taking her to one place to eat, we went to several, then found a place to sit and people-watch. She actually did some of the talking this time.

"What time are you going back to Seattle tomorrow?" Bex scraped the surface of the red bean ice cream she'd gotten.

"Not until late. Maybe ten or eleven? Sam has a baseball game tomorrow at five. If he wins, then he'll probably have a small party after, and if not, I'll take him out for dinner to cheer him up. I was gonna ask if you wanted to tag along."

"Um, I would, but I need to find another job and a place to live." She looked down at her ice cream.

"What if I could help with the job?" I hoped she'd accept my proposal of her own volition. If she didn't, Ryan and I had a backup plan.

Bex looked at me. "How so?"

I flashed a smile. "Promise you'll hear me out before you say no?"

"Okay."

"I have a position at my office I've been trying to fill. It's just data entry, taking numbers from my trades and putting them into a spreadsheet. I use them to watch my trends and also to explain to clients what I'm doing with their money. My assistant, Erin, used to do them, but she doesn't have the time anymore. Me taking on more responsibilities in the company means she is too. The nice part is, you can do it whenever you have time, or until something better comes along. So, if you want to go to school, or want a second job or something, you can work when you have time, as long as it's done on time."

Bex shook her head, looking at her ice cream again. "That's really nice of you, but I don't think it's a good idea. Mostly because it feels like something you pulled from thin air, but also because I'd feel terrible if I made a mistake and put you in an unfortunate position of feeling like you couldn't fire me or something."

"I promise, it's not something I pulled out of thin air." I reached into my pocket and pulled out my phone. "And short of just not doing the job, there's no way you could make a mistake big enough with this to cause a problem. Here." I handed her my phone with the email from Erin. It was written three weeks ago. "See the date? It was before we even met."

Bex looked at it briefly and gave my phone back. "It still sounds like a bad idea."

"Okay. I don't want to be a pushy asshole, but at least consider it for a little bit. I'd really like to see you have the time to go to school like you want. Also, as with all jobs at MWM, it comes with paid health, dental, and vision insurance. The pay is a thousand a week, minus taxes." I held up my hands. "That's it. I won't bring it up again unless you do. All I ask is that you think about it."

Just as I suspected, she wouldn't be easy to sway into my offers of assistance. I genuinely wanted to see her get ahead, which was why I'd find a way to help her.

Even if I had to set up the situations to make it happen. It was a horrible form of manipulation, and she didn't deserve to be manipulated, but I felt desperate to help her get ahead. She was smart, hardworking, and a good person. I was also madly in love with her for reasons I wasn't sure I could even name.

She nodded. "If nothing else turns up, I'll consider it."

I smiled, liking that she was at least willing to consider something better for herself. "Alright. What's the deal with the ice cream? Not a fan of the red bean?"

She shook her head. "Not so much."

"Try the green tea. It sounds like it shouldn't be good in ice cream, but it is." I handed her my cup of ice cream, keeping my spoon.

She smiled just a little and traded ice creams. I wondered what about trading ice cream would make her smile when little else seemed to.

"A random smile. What are you thinking about?"

She shook her head and the smile didn't leave. "My brother... I used to get sick of my ice cream halfway through and he always traded with me."

Brother? "I didn't know you *had* a brother. What's his name?"

She shook her head and the smile left. "It doesn't matter. He's gone." She looked at me and tried to smile, but it wasn't real. "Just a brief memory. Do you have any other siblings besides Sam?"

"Nope. He's the one and only." I gave a smile for her sake, but I didn't want to. She was alone, and she'd been alone for years. I knew she kept it that way, but it was heartbreaking to me. So much so that I wanted to hug her and make promises she might not let me keep... "Alright, you ready to go find frivolous Asian things to buy?" I got up and grabbed the bag of empty food containers.

"If it's frivolous, why buy them?"

"Because it's fun and part of the experience." I held

out my hand. "Come on."

She seemed to hesitate less this time than when I'd offered my hand the other night. The first time I'd startled her at the restaurant by touching her arm, I thought it was because she wasn't expecting it. Now, I'd realized she didn't like being touched in general. Things as simple as a handshake made her nervous. She'd clench her hand closed at her side, shake a person's hand as quickly as she could without being rude, then her hand would clench at her side again.

To test boundaries, I kept her hand as we walked, just to see if she'd allow it, or if it would bother her. She let me keep her hand, but I could almost feel the extreme nervousness radiating off her. I didn't want her to feel that way, so I found something interesting to point out and let go of her hand. She didn't need to feel trapped or afraid. It was obvious something in her past *had*, I only wished I knew what it was.

At the end of the night, when we were back in Monterey, I dropped her off at the hotel she was staying at. It surprised me that she didn't seem to be in a hurry to get out of the car. We sat for a while, finishing the conversation we were in the middle of. It could have been a vain hope, but maybe she was warming up to the idea of being around me. When she *did* get ready to leave the car, she thanked me and had the most beautiful smile. I felt like I was going to explode, but contained myself. At least until I got home.

Bex had previously made plans with Ryan to go job hunting. Before I went to bed, I made Ryan sit down with me to hash out a plan. I needed Bex to work for *me* so MWM could pay for her college classes and it wouldn't look like it was coming from me. My first motive was to help her get ahead and be in a position to guide her there, but I still needed to have her in the inner circle to see if it would catch my dad's attention. The more time she spent with Ryan or me, the safer she'd be. I'd never let anything happen to Bex, but I needed to find out what her position with my father was.

The next morning, right after Ryan left, I got to work on my end of the plan. First thing was calling Carol at the diner. Bex would be picking up her final check at some point, and I needed the visit to contain a little more.

"Thank you for calling Joe's Place, how can I help you?" A woman, whom I was pretty sure was Carol, answered.

"Hi, this is Grey Maslen. Is this Carol?"

"Oh, hi, hun. What can I do for ya?"

"I was wondering if you could help me with something. I'm sure you already know, but Bex is between living situations at the moment and I want to help her. I can't directly offer, because I don't want her to feel embarrassed and refuse the offer. A neighbor to one of the properties I own, Fran, asked if my brother would house-sit her place for the summer, but I thought it might be a good offer for Bex. I talked to Fran, and she's fine with it, but I was wondering if you might tell Bex that Fran is your friend, then give her the name and address? I'll take care of the rest." I traced my finger on the edge of my laptop as I spoke.

"Oh, well..." Carol sounded hesitant, "I'm sure your heart's in the right place, but I'm not so sure you should recommend Bex to your friend. She can be... flighty. Don't get me wrong, she's a sweetheart, but she's got baggage and I'd hate for something to happen."

"I'm not worried about it. Worse case, my brother ends up house-sitting, but right now, I just want to give Bex a leg up without making her feel like she's taking handouts. She works too hard to have as hard of a time as she does. I'm already helping her get enrolled in college and lining up a job that can accommodate her schedule. She's got it, she just needs to see for herself."

Carol saw herself as a sort of mother figure to Bex, which was the only reason I was throwing so many words in. Normally, I'd just use money to do the talking.

"What is it you're after with her?"

I expected the question, so I already had the answer. "Right now, just being the friend that makes her smile... She works hard to be unseen, and I don't know why, but maybe she won't be so afraid if she finds out someone can see her with good intentions."

Carol took in a deep breath and let it out. "Alright. What's that address?"

I smiled. "Eight ten Lighthouse Avenue, Pacific Grove. The lady's name is Fran Bennett."

"Phone number?"

I read the phone number off to her, then got off the phone, but not before she told me she'd break my neck if I did anything to hurt Bex. If I hurt her, I think I'd have to break my own neck. She was too kind and too beautiful from the inside out.

After I was off the phone with Carol, I started formulating the rest of my plan. I wasn't going to be coming to Monterey in a few months because Sam would be out of school, but I couldn't ask her to move to Seattle so soon, so I'd give her until the end of summer before asking. I'd make sure she'd get an acceptance letter from a college in Seattle, point out that MWM would pay for certain classes, and make her position more convenient from Seattle too. It was horribly manipulative, and I hated that part of my plan, but I couldn't stand the thought of her burning herself away at a dead-end job, a less-than-deserved college, in a town where the rent would just keep jumping to a number she couldn't afford. Also, Ryan would be coming back to Seattle, and I felt like he needed her as much as she needed him. If he'd convinced her to stay, it meant she really did trust him, and I wanted that for her.

I wanted to give Bex every opportunity to stand up

from whatever lingered in her past and never look back on it. I didn't care about thanks, I couldn't care less about how much it would cost me, I just wanted her to be happy. Even if she'd eventually decide she didn't want anything to do with me, I would do everything to help her.

Chapter 11

Bexley

I walked into the diner with Ryan, who'd insisted on coming in for a slice of pie, but I was pretty sure it was just an excuse to keep an eye on me. We'd had a long talk when we got to the hotel yesterday, and I'd said I was tired of fighting with life. He'd taken it as a suicidal flag, and while I always kept it as an option, I was still willing to take what came; I wasn't there yet. Our talk had refocused a few things though, and one of our conversations today wasn't falling on deaf ears either.

Carol handed off a couple plates to Ann when she saw me. "Hold on a second. It's in back."

I nodded and found somewhere else to look. Even though I hadn't done what I'd been accused of—though I'd come extremely close—I still felt embarrassed.

"Little lady, come here for a second."

I looked over and saw Joe standing in the doorway of the swinging door to the kitchen. He looked angry, and it immediately made me shake. If I could have grabbed

Ryan's arm and dragged him with me, I would have. He reminded me so much of my brother, Ben, that by default, I felt like I could trust him. If Ben had been there, I was sure he would have protected me.

My stomach churned, my chest felt heavy, and my blood felt cold as I walked behind the counter.

"Come on," Joe said when I stopped outside the door.

I shook my head because I couldn't. There was no way I could stand in a kitchen feeling as terrified as I did. Ryan being close by was the only reason I was able to move behind the counter.

Joe took in a deep breath, clearly not happy that I wouldn't go back to the kitchen. "You sure you want other people overhearin'?"

My mouth opened and I struggled to speak. "I-I don't have anything to hide." It wasn't true, but unless Joe magically knew my life's secrets, I wasn't concerned.

"Alright." He took a deep breath. "I want you to look me in the eye and tell me you didn't slip up the other night, or any other night."

I looked him in the eye, but it felt like it was causing me physical pain to do it. "I di-didn't." I was shaking so badly it made my lungs jerk.

"What were you doin' livin' in that house then? You had a perfectly good room at our house, free of charge. There was no reason for you to be livin' there unless you were doing what I think you were."

I didn't look at him as he spoke because I couldn't, my back was burning. One unexpected touch would have sent me through the ceiling.

"Kid, ya can't take a step forward if you're putting yourself back in old places."

Even though I wasn't looking at Joe, I could see from the corner of my eye that Carol had slipped past him in the doorway.

"Here. You pee in this and it's clean, you can have

115

your job back." She held out a white cup with a latex glove draped over the top.

I felt incredibly small, and it brought a burst of anger forward, so I took the cup, went to the bathroom, peed in the damn cup, and came back out.

"I want my check." My voice had little sound because of the pinch in my vocal cords.

Carol took the cup and turned it upside down to activate the test strips built into the lid. "You can wait a second." She stared at the lid, waiting for the strips to change color. When they didn't, she checked her watch, then looked at it again.

"She asked for her check," Ryan reminded Carol from the other side of the counter. "You legally can't withhold it."

Carol looked at him, then me. "I'll still give you your check today, and time to go cash it, if you'd like to pick up your normal shift tonight."

I shook my head. "No. Just the check."

"Carol, that's not an apology, and we owe her one." Joe looked at me with sincerity. "Kid, we're sorry for not believing you. You've been lookin' more and more tired, skinny as a starved weed, and jumpy as ever."

I held up my shoulder and pulled back the corner of my mouth because I didn't know what to do with apologies when they came.

"Honey, I'm sorry I overreacted. We want you to come back and work for us." Carol sounded completely sincere. She reached out to touch my arm and I stepped back and held my arm as if she'd already touched me and made my skin burn.

I shook my head. "I don't want to work for people who don't trust me. Thi-this will happen again. I passed my GED, and the only time I have to study is after work. I have to go to school because I can't afford to eat outside of my one meal a day here."

Carol held out my check. "You didn't tell us, hun.

Why don't we make it two meals a day, and you're welcome to study here any time it's slow. We want you to do well, so we'll help you out however we can. Alright?"

I bit the inside of my cheek, weighing if it was worth it, but then I figured if it wasn't, I'd just quit. "I can't work tonight. Tomorrow?"

"That's alright. I just figured you might like the hours. Tomorrow is just fine." Carol smiled and held out my check.

I nodded and took the check. "I'll be here at five."

"Okay. You have a good day, hun. We love ya."

I nodded once and turned around to leave. My stomach was still in knots and I wanted to puke. Ryan walked out with me, apparently forgetting about his craving for pie.

"You okay? You look like you're about to shed a layer of skin." Ryan held out a cigarette to me.

I took the cigarette and nodded.

"Bex! Wait up!" Ann called.

Ryan and I both turned around. She ran up and pulled out a piece of paper from her apron.

"Hey, I have a place for you. At least for the summer. One of the ladies in my mom's sewing group is going to Florida to stay with her daughter. She needs someone to look after her condo and cat while she's gone. No rent, just utilities. Her name is Fran. I already told her about you, and she's expecting you at three o'clock." Ann handed me the piece of paper, smiling brightly.

"You didn't have to do that," I said quietly as I took the paper.

"I didn't do anything. My mom asked if I knew anyone who'd be willing, and I figured it'd be a nice chance for you to get caught up on money and have a place to yourself." Her smile stayed. "I gotta get back. I'll see you tomorrow." Ann turned quickly and ran back inside the restaurant.

"If we're gonna meet this lady, we better go now.

It's two-thirty." Ryan's voice was low and quiet. "After you finish your cigarette and stop shaking. You're giving me anxiety watching you."

"Do you think I should do it? It seems kinda weird that someone would offer up their house like that." I held out the piece of paper to him.

"There's an expression, 'Don't look a gift horse in the mouth.' Go check it out, say yes, and take the good fortune. You can work at the diner, take the job with Grey on the side, and get something in your pocket before school starts. Books aren't cheap." He took the cigarette from me and took a drag.

I nodded. It was a good idea. Ryan had pointed out that Grey wasn't a bad person to know. He had connections in more places than could be counted, and connections meant potential opportunities at something better. It was also a good idea to have more than a pack of criminals in my arsenal if I was found.

———※———

Grey's face lit up with a bright smile. "Hey," he laughed, "what are you doing here?"

"I figured I accomplished what I needed to today, so I thought I'd come and see Sam play." I gave the smallest of a smile. If I was being honest, I wanted to see Grey one more time before he went back to Seattle. Yesterday with Grey had been fun, and I hadn't had actual fun since I was a small child. There'd been days I enjoyed, like my mini trip down highway one, but none that were "fun."

"Yeah? You found a job then?" He stood up from the bleacher, moved down a little, and let Ryan by, but didn't look away from me.

"I got my job at the diner back and found a place to live. The living situation is just for the summer, but it's nice, and I don't have to pay anything more than utilities."

He raised his eyebrows, looking a little surprised. "How'd you manage that?"

"One of the girls I work with at the diner set it up.

118

The lady is leaving for the summer and needs someone to house-sit. She was super nice."

"That's great. I'm glad you got your job at the diner back too, I know you like it there."

I pressed my lips together and nodded, glancing out at the field. The last time I'd watched a baseball game was when I'd gone to my brother's game. I wondered if he still played, or if he'd grown out of it.

I looked at Grey again, trying to be brave. "I was wondering if maybe I could take you up on your job offer too?"

His smile grew, if that was even possible. "Of course. Job's yours as long as you want it. We'll hash out the details before I leave tonight."

I nodded. "Okay."

"Pickle chip?" He held out his chip bag to me.

"Pickle?" I raised an eyebrow out of confusion.

"The best kind. Try one."

I reached into the bag, pulled out a single chip to try, and liked it more than I thought I should. Pickle-flavored chips sounded weird, but they might have been my favorite. "I think I agree. That's really good," I nodded.

"Ha. I knew you were good people." He handed the bag to me.

Ryan leaned forward. "I'm gonna get drinks. What do you guys want?"

"I'll take a beer," Grey answered.

Ryan looked at me and I shook my head. "I'm okay, thanks."

He raised an eyebrow out of irritation. "Bullshit. They have beer or soda, and if you say you don't want anything, I'm gonna get you nasty diet crap. So, tell me what you *actually* want."

"Coke is fine."

"I'll be back." Ryan stood up and went the other way.

Grey was texting someone, so I looked out to

watch the game and try to understand it. Even though I'd watched Ben, I'd forgotten how it worked.

"Here. Erin needs this information from you." Grey handed me his phone. "It's so she can get you put in the system for payroll."

I took the phone and looked at the screen before I started typing. As long as I was doing actual work, I wasn't taking advantage of him. I had to keep telling myself that. Ryan had already tried pounding it into my head, but for whatever reason, I felt like a thief.

I stopped texting and looked at Grey. "Why me?"

"What?" He looked at me with a partial smile, from watching the game.

"Why me, for the job?"

He shrugged. "Why not you? You're looking for something to put you ahead, you need other experience than restaurants, and I desperately need the help and someone I can trust. It's flexible hours, steady pay, full benefits, and after ninety days you can apply for college financial assistance toward any classes that benefit MWM. Win, win." He flashed a beautiful smile.

I frowned. "You made that last part up. You can't pay for my school."

He laughed. "I didn't make it up. Lots of companies do it. Here, let me show you." He held his hand out for his phone, so I gave it back and watched as he pulled up the website for MWM. "Okay, right here on the careers page." He handed the phone back and pointed at the screen.

It was there, all of it. Full benefits, opportunities for paid college courses, and something called a four-zero-one-K.

"What's this?" I pointed to the screen.

"A four-O-one-K? It's a retirement fund. You can choose to set aside money from every check and MWM will match it. Then after so long, you can borrow against it, or roll it over to another company that offers a four-O-one-K."

"Oh... Do I have to put money into it?"

He shook his head. "No. Not if you don't want to. MWM will still contribute, though. I don't remember how much. I'd have to ask Erin. She's my know-it-all."

I nodded. "How do I get back to the text message?"

Grey reached over and swiped up on the screen, then tapped another window with the text message. I finished typing the information Erin asked for, then gave the phone back to Grey. He sent it, and we watched Sam play. There was nothing particularly special about watching the game, but I enjoyed it.

Afterward, Grey took me to the apartment I was staying at and showed me what he needed me to do. The job came with a new laptop, cell phone, and printer. We sat in the dining room while he showed me what to do, and I took notes. It was simple work, but there was a lot of it. I knew I could get through it faster by doing it a different way, but I'd do it the way I was shown to start with. There'd been many times when Carol had teased me about the way I did things at the diner, but when put to the test, I was faster by minutes.

"That's it," Grey said with a light smile as he closed the laptop. "And feel free to use the laptop and phone as you please. School work, watching movies, whatever."

I held up my shoulders. "I don't have much of a need, but thanks."

He nodded and looked around the dining room and kitchen. "I like this place. It's homey."

"I know. I tried to offer her something for staying here, but she wouldn't accept."

"Nah, I'm sure she's just happy to have someone here taking care of the place... and that cat." He laughed a little. "Little guy loves you."

I looked down at my lap and the sleeping kitten on it. Fran had told me he was a seal point Himalayan, he was three months old, and his name was Holland. "He's cute, considering I don't like house pets."

"Really? Not even dogs?" Grey looked a little surprised.

I shook my head. "Especially not dogs. I'm terrified of them."

"Wow. I wouldn't have guessed." Grey reached over and pet the cat's head with the side of his finger. "It's a good thing you're not a dog, Sir. You would have been a 'no-go'."

"When do you need the rest of these reports done?"

"I need the first section no later than Friday, and the rest by Monday. After that, every Friday before the end of day. If you can't get the second half by Monday, just text Erin and you guys can divide them out."

I shook my head. "I'll make sure they're done on time." He was paying me more than I'd ever been paid legally, so I'd stay up all night if I had to.

"Awe crap, I forgot. Do you have a blank check I can bring back to Erin? She needs it for direct deposit."

I shook my head. "I don't have a bank account."

He pulled back the corner of his mouth. "Can you get one? We don't do paper checks."

"I don't know. I've never tried." I only did things in cash because it was safest.

"I'll see if Ryan has time to take you on your break tomorrow."

I shook my head. "It's okay. I've bothered him enough."

"You're not bothering him. He works for me, and this is company business."

"Okay..."

Grey had another one of those made-for-movies kind of smiles. "You know, you surprise me... most people usually only talk about doing something to change their situation, but when the opportunity comes, they pass it up because it's too intimidating or too much work."

I held up my shoulders. "I was about to... not because it's hard, just... I don't know. I still feel like you're handing me something I didn't earn."

He shook his head with the same content smile. "That's the thing about jobs, they're handed to you but you do the work and earn the right to keep them... I know you're still not entirely convinced the position isn't made up, but once you see how everything comes into play, you'll see it's not. Erin really is overloaded and it's not something I have time for, so... it's there for the taking. And in terms of pay, I do things a little differently. I decide what I think a task is worth and pay a flat rate per week. So, if you end up taking on more, you get more money. Once a year, I go through and raise the task rates because I don't give people raises. So, if you ever want more to do, even just for a week to make some extra cash, just ask Erin and she'll help you find something."

I nodded. "Just... please don't do me any favors. If it's not working out, or I'm doing something wrong, treat me like you would anyone else."

He smiled and breathed like he was about to let out a laugh. "I am... I didn't build my business or network of good people by being greedy."

"You know what I mean."

He nodded. "I do. No favors, you earn everything fair and square, and Erin will bust your chops if you mess something up because that's what I pay her for." He took in a deep breath and looked around at the dining room walls. "I really like the color in here."

I looked at the faint sea-glass colored walls and nodded. "Yeah. It's calm." It was funny that I'd mentioned the same color to Grey and now it was on the walls of someone else's house that I happened to be staying in. I liked everything about the condo. It was decorated beautifully. Outside of the sliding glass doors were beautiful green vines growing on the wall, and so far the neighbors all seemed to be quiet. The best part was I didn't have to share it with anyone.

"There it is." Grey's voice was smooth.

I looked at him questioningly. "What?"

"There was a small smile on your face." He laughed a little. "Guess I blew that one."

I shook my head. "I wasn't paying attention."

Grey grabbed the empty beer bottles from the table and stood up. "That's the point of a smile. You shouldn't have to pay attention to it."

I stood, gathering the papers and laptop into one neat pile. "When will you be back?"

"Uh, I don't know. Sam's wrapping up with school and going back to Seattle for the summer, so it just kinda depends on what I've got going on. I'll see if I can swing this weekend, if not, for sure next weekend."

I turned to look at him. "If he's not gonna be down here, then why come back?"

Grey smiled at me. "Because I have another date with you. The one we were *supposed* to have." He laughed a little. "After that, I'll just have to keep finding excuses."

I honestly didn't know what to think, but I felt like I wasn't a good enough reason for him to come back if he wasn't already here for Sam.

He looked at his watch. "I gotta run. I'll text you tomorrow."

I nodded. "Okay... Thank you... for everything."

"It's just a job, Beautiful. Don't sweat it." He picked up his keys from the counter. "And don't be too afraid to ask for help if you get stuck. No one's expecting perfection right off the bat."

I nodded once.

"Goodnight." He gave a charming smile and flipped his keys around his finger before turning to leave.

"Grey?" I spoke quietly. As much as I was looking forward to being alone in my own apartment, I didn't want him to leave. I missed him before he was even

124

gone. "Is there anyway you could stay and fly out in the morning?" I gave an impish and hopeful smile. "A drive sounds nice, or we could stay and watch a movie."

Grey smiled like I'd said the most kind thing he'd ever heard. "You got it, Beautiful. Grab your purse and let's go."

I tried not to over smile. "I'll be right back." As I turned down that hall, I remembered that my teeth had been fixed over three years ago and smiled.

Grey and I spent the night driving all over the area. By the time the sun was ready to rise, we were parked at the Bixby Bridge to watch. We'd had calm conversations, heated debates over hypatheticals, and too much caffeine. On the way back to Monterey, I drove—initially with caution—and Grey told me to speed up. I averaged over a hundred miles an hour up Highway One until we got to the outskirts of the city. I still missed him before I dropped him off at the airport, and even more as I drove to work. He told me I was free to use his car anytime he was gone or take it back to his parents' house where Sam and Ryan lived. When I got to the diner, a bouquet of peonies waited for me on the counter.

Chapter 12

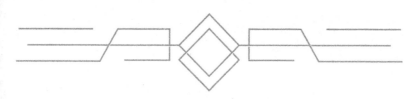

Grey

The more time I spent with Bex, the more she became an essential part of my life. Instead of flying to Monterey every other week, I was there every chance I had. I still couldn't find the link between her and my dad, even after asking her carefully crafted questions. Before, it only mattered in the interest of taking him down, but now it mattered because of Bex. She was this beautiful and kind person who fought so hard to be like anyone else. Every touch, every unfamiliar place, an out-of-place noise—soft or loud—scared her. She'd do her best to hide her fear the moment she realized there was no threat, but it was hard to watch her be rattled to her core over the simplest of things. It put me on edge being near her, and normally that would irritate me, but with Bex, it humbled me enough to be empathetic.

Bex had been in overdrive, taking advantage of the opportunities provided to her. She worked at the diner three days a week, passed her GED, applied to a few colleges, took on more work for me, and saved as much money as she could. I about threw a party when she asked me how to invest a portion of her savings. There'd been a couple of hiccups in the short four months, but she was actively working toward a better life, which was all I wanted for her. While she'd made a great amount of progress, there was more to make. It wasn't that she wasn't good enough for me or that I felt the need to control her life, I felt badly she'd never had anyone in her life to encourage her or help her along. Joe and Carol were the only people she had, but her relationship with them was strained because Carol was too harsh with Bex. She was hungry to get ahead, but no one actually helped her do it in a way she was willing to receive.

"You're quiet tonight... Are you okay?" Bex's gentle voice pulled me from my thoughts as we walked along the beach. The sun had sunk behind the ocean but left a dusk light behind.

I rubbed the back of her hand with my thumb. "I'm good. Just... nervous, I guess."

"Nervous?" She stopped and turned just enough to look at me with undivided attention.

I smiled a little, both at her instant concern and the beauty of her kind face. "Yeah. I have something I want to talk to you about, but I'm not sure what you'll think." I gave an inaudible nervous chuckle and rubbed the back of her hand with my thumb again to dispel some of my nervousness. She'd become more comfortable with harmless touches, but only by me or Ryan. "It's nothing bad, but I'm hoping you'll hear me out before you shut me down." I let my smile take on an impish quality so she'd take pity on me and agree. It was rare for me to feel genuinely nervous about something. I dealt with high-stress situations on a near daily basis, which allowed me to be calm in almost all situations, but my hopes were up, and my chances were slim in this instance. She had become exceptionally helpful with my business the past few months, but I also wanted to feed her eagerness to learn and achieve greater advances in life.

"Okay..." The word had the inflection of a question in it and her eyes studied me with a light amount of worry.

"I'd like to ask if you'd be willing to move to Seattle..." I had more words—a lot of them—but the small frown of disapproval on her face made me stop in my tracks.

"Um... Why?"

I took a breath, trying to reset myself, and let it out slowly. "A few reasons. The first one is entirely selfish. Flying down here on a near weekly basis is becoming tough." I smiled at her because I couldn't help it. I would have flown a hell of a lot further to be near her, but I couldn't say that. "I don't mind, but it's hard trying to balance my time." I gave a light shrug. "The next reason is I need Ryan in Seattle, but I don't want to steal him from you. I can and will continue to work with him over the phone and via video calls, but it'd be easier if he were physically present in Seattle again. I'd also like to give you a different position in the company because you have a talent I desperately need that's being wasted on my tracking logs." I took in a breath and pointed ahead of us to signal that I wanted to continue walking back to the house.

"What kind of position?" Bex walked forward and looked out at the sand in front of us as if it would give her the answer.

"I'd like you to do what you did a few weeks ago at dinner with Dan and Mary, explaining parts of my contract or what I do in terms clients can understand. When I said you sealed the deal that night, I meant it. I know what I'm talking about, but my clients don't always. I'd like you to come to meetings with me and essentially be my translator for people who have no idea what I'm saying. Also, you're incredibly good with contracts, so I'd like you to help with those as well. Just like any additional task, it comes with more money. We can set client meetings around your school schedule. I'll make sure it's still a priority for you, but I think it'd be a better fit for both of us." I stopped to face her, even though I'd been the one to get her to keep walking.

"I know you love Carol and Joe, so I'll throw in the perk of a private jet to go see them when you want. I can easily pull a few strings to get you a late admittance into WSU, you can stay with me or Ryan until you find a place to live, and you're locked in for a better job..." I held up my shoulders, watching her dark eyes stare at me with no visible answer in them. "I want you closer, B... I don't think it's too forward to say, you and I both know you would have kicked me to the curb a long time ago if you knew there was nothing between us. I don't want to push you into something you're not ready for, so if you want to stay here, we'll make it work, but... I want you closer. You've more than earned a promotion job-wise, and Ryan and I are more than happy to help with whatever you need, but mostly... I just want you closer."

Bex bit the inside of her cheek for a moment, looking behind me at the ocean as she seemed to think about it. I realized I was holding her hand a little too tightly out of nervousness, so I relaxed it and took her hand between both of mine.

"You don't have to give me an answer right now. I know you're tired from being at work all day and we have a busy couple of days coming up. I'm just hoping you'll consider it." I moved one hand to touch her cheek with the back of my fingers because I couldn't help myself. Her face was mesmerizingly beautiful and I constantly felt drawn to touch her.

Bex's eyes set on me the instant my fingers touched her skin; there was a small amount of fear in her eyes, but it wasn't a prominent expression as she shook her head. "I don't need to think about it..." Her thin shoulders raised. "I like Seattle, WSU is a better school, and... being closer would be nice, so my answer is yes."

What!?

My eyebrows raised immediately. "Yes?"

She appeared slightly confused as she nodded.

I couldn't help the oversized grin on my face. Not only was I relieved, but I felt like I'd just landed the biggest account of my life. "Yes," I repeated quietly. "I can't help it, I'm hugging you. Squirm if you will." If she were anyone else and unafraid, I would have picked her up in a hug and kissed her, but I knew I had to be careful. I'd only hugged her a few times, but it was hard when I could feel the anxiety it caused her.

Bex had a quiet laugh as she wrapped her arms around me, seeming less rigid this time. "I think you've squirmed enough for the both of us, and you can hug me whenever you'd like."

I laughed a little. "Because I'm afraid of coming across as a controlling jack-ass trying to manipulate you into something you wouldn't want."

She shook her head, then moved her chin from my shoulder to rest her cheek against the front of my shoulder. "I don't think that... You wouldn't spend so many words trying to be careful if you meant otherwise. And Ryan has made it a point to let me know how stubborn I can be. I'm also really tired of saying goodbye after just two days or a few hours."

I chuckled again and hugged her just a little tighter—out of pure happiness and relief. I was surprised to feel her body so relaxed because she never did. Even when I was simply holding her hand, she never relaxed. For a moment I had to question if it'd really happened—making me loosen my arms briefly—but then I just hugged her. She'd pull away if she felt the need.

I dropped my keys on the counter on the way to the fridge. "You're going back to Seattle."

Ryan kept his eyes on his laptop, tapping away at the keys viciously. "We'll see. She has a month to overthink it and back out." His tone was flat as if it were an automatic gut response.

I shook my head and opened the fridge. "I don't think she will. She didn't even put up a fight." I grabbed a bottle of water out and closed the door. "I told her to think about it, and it took her a whole three seconds to say yes."

"Mm..." Ryan continued to type like he was in a texting war with someone, then stopped abruptly with a last thud of a key and closed his laptop before looking at me. "Hundred bucks says she backs out." He looked at me as if he was irritated.

I raised my eyebrows. "If she doesn't, you can't go back to Seattle."

He rolled his eyes. "If your dad hasn't come after her yet, I don't think he's going to."

I held up a shoulder. "Not a chance I'm willing to take. You're responsible for making sure no one goes after her for anything. I'm less interested in what her history is, and more focused on helping her achieve the life she wants. On Monday, I want you to call the Volvo dealership and order that car she likes." I grabbed an orange out of the fruit bowl.

"She's gonna shit a brick if you buy her a car."

"If I'm going to help her, I don't want to do it behind her back. I'll take the blowback on the car if it means I don't have to lie to her." I'd told her the truth about the condo she was living in out of sheer guilt. Tricking her wasn't something I was at all proud of, it put a pit in my stomach.

Ryan's nose turned up. "You know she's going to find the shittiest place in Seattle, right?"

I held up a shoulder again, peeling back the rind on the orange. "She's not. We already talked about it. She's gonna take the master on the second floor at my house. She insisted on paying rent, so I negotiated with her. That reminds me, send Erin a text and have a

locksmith change out the handle for one that locks with a key. Anyway, we've taught her how to better manage money, she's finally got decent savings, so the ball is in her court to do better this time. She can't be expected to make better moves without the opportunity. If the car situation is taken care of, she has the opportunity to make a better choice. I want to see what she does with it."

"Take your saint hat off, she's gonna be pissed." He pulled out his phone and started texting.

I shook my head. "There's no hat. She's being exposed to my dad and we don't know what that means yet." I glanced up from my orange to look at Ryan.

He let out a huff and stood with his laptop and a raised eyebrow. "You better have a backup plan if this doesn't work. She teeters on a fine line between moving forward and straight up running. I won't help you find her if she takes off because you made a stupid move." Ryan walked toward the hall.

I took in a breath and let it out. It wasn't fair of me to bring Bex into the bullring, but I felt like I didn't have much of a choice. It was the only way I could trigger my dad to make a move. I needed to catch him amid his dirty dealings so I could remove him from the equation. Bex deserved to be free of whatever my dad had over her and he deserved to be in jail.

I paused on my way through the living room, spotting Bex out on the back deck with Joe and Carol. Bex looked like she was taking a verbal beating from Carol, and Joe didn't look too happy either. My blood boiled under my skin. Carol and Joe were nice people with good intentions, but Carol was too much when it came to Bex. I hated how she spoke to Bex. A point could easily be made without making her feel half an inch tall.

"Hey." I caught Sam's arm. "What's that about?" I nodded toward the deck.

Sam looked to see what I was talking about. "Uh, I don't know. Want me to go out and break the tension?"

I was hoping Sam might've overheard something so I wasn't walking into a conversation blindly. "No. I got it." I let out a breath and went outside.

Carol was chiding quietly while Bex stared at the floor of the deck. I still couldn't make out the subject of the conversation over the chatter of others and the music playing in the background. It was the fourth of July and I'd decided to have a small party. It was Bex's favorite holiday and mine, so we went to the parade downtown, then went out on the yacht with Ryan, Sam, Ann, Ann's son, and Joe and Carol. After a few hours out on the water, we'd come back to the house for a small party that included a few of my best employees, some of Sam's friends, and Bex's friends from the diner. As soon as it was dark enough, I had a fireworks display planned out over the ocean.

Joe looked from Bex to me as soon as I was close enough to spot. He lightly bumped Carol's arm and her harsh stare turned to me.

I ignored her expression with a small smile but didn't pretend to be oblivious. "Everything okay?" Bex's body cringed away from my hand as I reached toward her back, so I went for the back of her forearm. Having her cringe away from me made me want to take a verbal shot at Carol and Joe, but I wouldn't lose my composure in front of Bex.

"No, it's not, Grey." Carol's tone was sharp as she crossed her arms. "Asking Bexley to move to Seattle with you is hardly appropriate. You've only known each other four months." Her glare turned back to Bex.

"I'm going for college," Bex said quietly with her eyes still on the floor.

I took in another deep breath, reminding myself not to explode on Carol. "I understand why you're concerned, but Bex *is* going to Seattle for a better college opportunity and a job that can take her somewhere. My dad is really impressed with the work Bex has been doing and he offered her a better position." The last part was bullshit, but Bex would go along with it if it meant getting Carol off her back.

Carol shook her head. "No. The college here is perfectly suitable. Honey, running off with some boy is not going to fix anything. What happens if the two of you break up? You're trying to plan your life around someone who might not be there tomorrow."

I felt like I was on the brink of a mental snap because I was so angry. "She's not planning anything around me. She's accepting a better position in a company that has far more to offer her than the diner, and choosing to go to a better college with more class options and opportunities. Bex, I'm sorry for speaking on your behalf but this is insane. You're an adult, you have your reasons, and you don't owe anyone an explanation." I kept a cool tone, but I was raging inside.

"Excuse me, what's wrong with working at a diner?" Carol's eyebrows were in a full arch.

I shook my head. "Nothing, but there's no opportunity for growth for her. You and Joe already overpay her, she's not gonna learn anything new, you can't accommodate her school schedule without hurting your business or cutting her hours—it's a dead end for everyone. If it doesn't work out, if she hates Seattle for whatever reason, nothing is stopping her from coming back. No one's keeping her from visiting. This is a necessary step to something better, it's her step to take, and no one's forcing her. I told her she could stay here and keep the same job if that's what she wanted—and neither you and Joe or I get to decide where she should be. Nor should anyone be badgering her about it." I understood how it looked from the outside; it looked like Bex was blindly following a guy she barely knew, and partially, she was, but there was a much bigger picture. Bex knew that or she wouldn't have chosen to go.

Joe scratched the top of his head. "You can always come home, kid... We'll be here." He put a hand on Carol's back, then the other on Bex's shoulder as they passed by. She cringed with her entire body at the touch. "We'll see ya tomorrow."

As soon as Joe took his hand away and he couldn't see, Bex shuddered as she rubbed her shoulder. She looked like she might cry but took a deep breath to re-compose herself.

"I need a minute. I'll be back." Her voice was quiet and as shaky as her hand, when she touched my arm before walking away.

Immediately, I felt sick to my stomach. I didn't know if sticking up for her against Carol and Joe was the right thing to do, but I couldn't stand by and watch as they made her stand there and cower in front of others. It was heartbreaking.

"What was that about?" Ryan's voice was a low rumble from behind me.

I shook my head. "Seattle. I was hoping she'd wait to tell them."

"They'll get over it." He took a sip from his beer. "Want me to go talk to her?"

"No, she wanted a minute. I'll go find her if she doesn't come back after a few." I looked at my watch so I'd have a point of reference.

"Hey, any chance we can get on the boat and help with setting the fireworks off?" Sam pulled his hat off, combed his fingers through his hair, and put it back on. Two of his friends were standing there waiting for an answer.

I gave a short laugh. "Not after last year. You three are spectators this year."

Sam laughed. "How are we supposed to get proper training if we don't get the chance, man?"

Ryan let out a snort. "There's only one technique,

don't be a dumbass."

I frowned at Ryan. Sam *had* acted like a dumbass last year, but I didn't like Ryan calling him that. I looked at Sam again. "The answer is no. And you guys better not set off anything more than sparklers in front of the house."

Sam let out a huff as his hopeful shoulders dropped. "It's official, you're old." He turned and walked away with his friends.

Ryan let out a laugh. "I take it you didn't tell him about your dad's car?"

I laughed at the memory. "And give him another bright idea? He'd go for the house."

When I was nine, I was sick of being ignored for my dad's clients. We had thousands of dollars worth of fireworks and I gave my parents' guests a show no one forgot. I loaded my dad's Bentley with all the fireworks, lit a few, quickly closed the door, and watched the show from the front stoop. My dad couldn't kill me because there were too many witnesses. But he was so angry I spent the rest of the summer at my grandpa's house.

I went into the house for a minute to check on Ann and her son, then went outside with a peace offering for Bex. I'd already apologized for speaking on her behalf, but I'd apologize again. She was probably just as upset with me as she was with Joe and Carol.

Bex was sitting on a rock on the edge of the cliffside to the ocean. She was wearing a sheer powder-blue blouse, white shorts, and brown leather strapped sandals. Her hair was perfectly pinned as usual, making her appear warm and approachable despite the lost expression on her face. The last of the setting sun made her skin glow, and some of her remaining scars were visible. I tried never to notice when she might see, but there were so many. Most of them were only visible in a certain light and still faint at that. I didn't know who'd put them there or what happened to her, but I wished all of it could be erased. To think of anyone—not only Bex—going through so much pain, to have that many scars, was heartbreaking.

"Can I raise the white flag?" I wore an apologetic smile before she turned her head to look at me.

"I don't know what you mean." Her dark eyes surveyed me, noticing the jar of Nutella in my hand.

I held the jar and a spoon out to her before sitting beside her. "I think I overstepped with Carol and Joe. I know I should've stopped and let you handle it but watching Carol rail into you got to me. I'm sorry."

Bex took the jar and spoon, looking at them as she shook her head. "I'm glad you stepped in... You're brave enough to say it like it is and not look like a coward."

Her words felt like a barb directed at me instead of herself. "Coward? You looked hurt—rightfully so."

She shook her head again while tracing her nail over the edge of the lid. "I love them, but... I'm never allowed to decide for myself when they're around... Where I live, who I choose to be around, what I should or shouldn't do... Carol always has something to say about it. That's why I try not to tell her anything unless I don't have an option."

"I've noticed..." I wondered if she felt that way about me. "I think she cares though."

Bex nodded. "I know she does... but I wish she trusted me more." She took in a slow deep breath and looked at the sunset. "I know there's a lot I don't understand, and I make mistakes, but this isn't a mistake. I never intended to stay here as long as I have, and everything has changed... When we were filling out college applications, I was hoping to be accepted anywhere but here so I'd have a reason to leave, then the acceptance letters came, and I felt like I couldn't leave because I have something here I wasn't willing to lose."

"You don't have to leave if you don't want to, B. I can still fly down here, just maybe not as often." I'd always loved working, but I was resenting it because I never had enough time with Bex. I had more than enough money to never work another day in my life and spend like crazy, but it seemed lazy.

She shook her head and looked at me. "It's you..." Her shoulder raised a little. "You and Ryan push me forward, Carol and Joe want me to stay in place because they think I can't do things."

I had to keep myself from dying of an exploding heart.

"I think they want to keep you close so they know you're safe, but I understand what you mean. My grandpa drilled into my head at an early age to never keep company that doesn't enrich my life, and enrich people's lives if their company is worth keeping. I only see a small portion of your relationship with them, but it seems like with Carol and Joe, it's turned into a one-way street. You're giving more than you get back."

She pulled back the corner of her mouth. "It's felt that way for a while..." She looked down at the Nutella jar again. "What do you get back from me?"

I smiled at the question as much as the beautiful look of innocence on her face. "More than you think."

"That sounds more like a deflection than an answer." She looked at me almost as if I'd said something hurtful.

I shook my head, letting my smile soften. "No. You give me your time without condition, something I don't get from most people in my life. You make me nervous as hell—which sounds like a bad thing but isn't—"

She let out a quiet huff as she smiled and looked at me. "I make you nervous?"

I laughed. "Yeah. You're jumpy as hell. One wrong move and you're gone—and I know it."

One of her eyebrows pulled down in skepticism. "How is that good?"

"Because it reminds me to have humility. I make my

money on inflated confidence. You knock me back a few pegs and I like that." I took a breath because thinking about my nervousness around her made me nervous. "You also give me a good reason to slow down with work. If it weren't for you and Sam, I'd inevitably be worse than my dad as far as hours at the office. Then there's the fact that you could care less about my money." I smiled a little. "I think you'd like me better if I was broke."

She pressed her lips together to hide a beginning smile. "You couldn't handle it."

I laughed. "Probably not." I didn't know what it was like to have nothing. "I know you won't, but take my word for it, you enrich my life *plenty*. Don't think you're on the receiving end of a one-way street."

She held up her shoulders, looking at the sunless horizon. "I think you give a lot more than you get back."

I reached over and took her hand. "I have what I need, and I'd say something if I didn't." I kissed the back of her hand. "Bust open that Nutella so we can get back to our guests and watch the fireworks."

A small smile pulled up the corners of her mouth and her dimples deepened. "I don't know why you think Nutella is the cure for everything."

I laughed. "Because it is." I gave her hand a few light squeezes. "It makes you smile, which makes me smile."

Her cheeks pinkened as she looked at me with a slightly raised eyebrow. "You'd smile anyway."

"But you wouldn't." I let go of her hand to take the Nutella jar and opened it. "Come on. I promise you won't break. Nutella and smile."

"I think you need to learn I'm not the smiley type."

"And you wanna be. I know you do," I taunted lightly as I held a spoonful of Nutella in front of her with a smile.

Bex rolled her eyes with the smallest of a smile and took the spoon. I laughed and wrapped an arm around the back of her shoulders to pull her closer. "Hearing you say you don't want to lose me, and knowing you care more about *me* than the things I have to offer... that's all I've ever hoped for. Just last week, you flew to Seattle on a whim because Ryan told you my favorite client—who was like a dad to me—died and you didn't want me to be alone... I'm terrified of losing you. I love all the thoughtfulness, joy, and caring you bring into my life... and I love you." I felt terrified to say the words, not because they weren't true, but because I didn't know how she'd feel about them.

Bex looked at me, no readable expression on her face, but then a small and very beautiful smile touched the corners of her eyes. "I don't want to be anywhere without you. I love you too."

I desperately wanted to kiss her, but knew I couldn't without terrifying her, so a loving smile and touching her velvet cheek had to suffice. If touching her cheek in place of kissing her would keep her next to me and feel safe, then it was better than a simple kiss.

Chapter 13

Ryan

I'd flown to Mobile, Alabama, drove to New Orleans on back roads, then flew to Dallas. If someone had been following me, I'd know. Tim was also keeping an eye out for any cell phones following my pattern and erasing any data my phone might leave behind. Grey could never know what I was about to do, and Nelson would probably kill me. For someone so timid, she still had some fight in her. Something I found out when I let Grey plan a surprise birthday party for her and didn't give any type of warning. She put on a good face for the party, but she ignored me for almost a week after and exploded when I cornered her at the diner.

My first day in Dallas, I just observed from a distance. The Lawrence's house was large but modest. Kids were playing out in the front yard while Nelson's mother, Millie Lawrence, did a cross stitch on the porch. There were two boys and two girls. Both girls looked like Nelson, but especially the youngest. She had Nelson's dark brown curls, soft pointed nose, and big brown eyes. She was too young to be Nelson's kid though, and the other girl, who looked to be about the right age, just didn't look enough like Nelson to be hers. I didn't care enough to keep guessing, and no one else seemed to be at the house, so I moved on.

Don Lawrence was a federal judge, so he was easy to find. I walked in the courtroom between hearings and sat down to watch. It was amazing to me that Nelson could be so much like him without having been raised by him. He was mild-mannered, fair, and never really got riled about anything. While Nelson looked a lot like her mom, she had Don's dark-colored eyes. He looked just as worn down as Nelson did, and I wondered if that was just a trait, or if it was the past that made them look that way. Just like Nelson, he'd itch the back of his head when he had to make a decision he didn't like. Normally, I didn't take a real interest in people, but I felt like I wanted to know him as much as I did his daughter.

Emily was next. I found her Facebook, and she kept nothing private, so it was easy to find out what she did, and where to find her. She was a professional barrel racer, Miss Texas from ten years ago, and she'd also written a couple of children's books. I drove to the arena where she trained, slipped around unnoticed, and watched her for a few minutes. Emily was identical to Nelson in looks, but she was blonde and had a normal weight on her. Nelson was so damn skinny it was almost gross. Even Grey, who couldn't say a negative thing against her, agreed on that. After watching Emily race a few circles, I was bored with her.

Toby was next, and he'd been much harder to find. Tim had pulled his address from the DMV because there was basically no other way to find him. He wasn't home when I arrived, so I called Tim and had him hack the three cameras that were posted outside the house. If there was anyone, besides Nelson, who might know where

Henry could be, it'd be Toby. Thankfully, Toby's backyard was matched up to an alleyway of tall wooden fences, and there was no view from anyone's house. I slipped into the backyard undetected, tried a couple windows, then picked the lock on the backdoor.

The inside of the house was fairly barren. The kitchen had a simple wooden table with two chairs, a coffee maker on the counter, and a few matching decorations. It was enough to keep it from looking sterile. I imagined that *he*—like Nelson—was afraid of kitchens and basements, so I didn't bother to see if there was anything to find. My best chance was going to be the bathroom. I noticed that Nelson kept a pathetic stash of money taped to the back underside of the sink, a small backpack of necessities hidden behind the towels in the linen closet, and an unregistered gun in what was supposed to be a large-sized bottle of shampoo.

On my way to the bathroom, I stopped in the living room to look around. It was strange that there were no pictures, and it looked even less lived in than the kitchen. Down the hall, I opened the first door, and it was clearly a little girl's room. There was a picture this time, and the only way I knew it was Nelson was because of the dated clothes. The frame was decorated with seashells, silver glitter, and small pebbles. Someone had spent some time making it. Hanging on the light purple walls were many canvases with various animals painted on them. I looked at one of a cow, closest to me, and saw the initials GA in the corner. Grace Anderson... If she'd been the one to do all the paintings, she had a God-given talent at an incredibly young age. They honestly looked like they could be something purchased in a store.

Toby's room was nearly empty. There was a full-size bed made up like it'd never been slept in, a nightstand with only a lamp and clock, a wooden chair in the corner, and nothing else. I slowly opened the closet door to see a few articles of clothes hanging and a dresser.

Out of curiosity, I opened a drawer. Clothes sat in neat stacks, but there was nothing special about it. Before I shut the door to the closet, I looked up out of habit and saw an entrance to the attic. It wouldn't have caught my attention, other than the fact that the dangling string looked to be very well used, along with the hinges that showed metal dust on the surrounding trim.

The house didn't look lived in, because it wasn't. Everything was in the attic. A couch, TV, blankets, pictures, a large rug, TV trays, and various other things that appeared to be regularly used. I looked back at the floor near the attic opening, and there was a lock on the inside. This is where they spent their time when they were home. There were skylights, but garage-door-like shades that could retract over them. The two windows at the front and back of the attic had been closed up and boarded off. Toby seemed to be every bit as paranoid and scared as Nelson, so much so that he hid in the attic of his own house.

I looked around the attic on the off chance I might find something but didn't. The other girl I'd seen at the Lawrence's house was Nelson's daughter, but that's the only information I gathered from the attic. The single bathroom was a treasure trove, once I figured out that the cabinet under the sink had a false back. Toby had money, bags of clothes and other necessities, passports, and two guns ready to go. There was a small cabinet in the corner of the bathroom that looked like a linen closet but was really a laundry shoot converted to a small elevator. Toby was well prepared, I had to hand it to him.

Ben was really the person I'd come to see, at least for now. He was a specialized psychologist who worked with adults and children who'd been through substantial amounts of trauma. He'd written books of his own, solely for educational purposes. I'd read two of them at the library, but they weren't enough to help with Nelson. One was about a little boy who believed with every fiber of his being that he could turn himself into a mouse, there-fore able to hide from people and things that hurt him. The other was about a woman with split personalities. Nelson obviously didn't fit into either of those categories.

"How can I help you?" The woman behind the desk smiled at me sincerely.

"I have a consultation with Dr. Lawrence at four-thirty." I didn't smile or give any inkling of kindness. Her fake sincerity irritated me.

"And your name?"

"Brae Thompson."

"Okay." She held her smile and handed me a clip-board. "Just fill this out for Dr. Lawrence, and he should be done in just a few minutes."

"The point of a consultation is to discuss whether or not there's a point in doing business or other such actions. I'm not wasting my time with papers until I've established a decision on the continuation of business." I wanted to stump her.

"Um. Okay. Sure."

I let out a breath, feeling better that I'd asserted some form of control. No, it wasn't necessary, and had no benefit other than amusement, but I felt better. Most people would go sit after they'd been told to wait, but to continue my sick game of manipulation, I walked around as I observed, then stood as I waited. Watching the girl behind the desk grow more uncomfortable by the min-ute was enjoyable.

Once Ben came out to the waiting area, saying goodbye to the client he'd been with, the girl almost crawled out of her skin to tell him his "four-thirty" was waiting. He reached out for the clipboard; she shook her head quickly and opened her mouth to speak.

"I didn't fill out any papers, because I'd rather talk first and see if you can even help," I said before she could utter a word.

Ben looked at me. He looked a little worn, like Don and Nelson, but friendly enough as he forced a small smile. "Sure. Come on back."

I followed him down the hall to a room on the right.

"Have a seat," he said as he opened the door and went through. It was interesting that he didn't wait like most doctors would have. Nelson would have loved that. She almost had to be scraped off the wall if someone walked in a door behind her.

The room was a decent size with two leather chairs, a matching couch, a rug off to the side in front of the windows, and a desk in the back with another set of windows behind it.

"How can I help?" Ben asked easily as he sat in one of the leather chairs.

"Mm." I turned and sat. "It's a little bit of a complicated situation, I guess. I know you can't treat someone who isn't your patient, but I'm hoping maybe you can help coach me on ways I can help my friend. I'll pay cash—once a month... But I really need to be able to help her because she's not in a position to be able to help herself." I had to be careful of my words, but I also wanted to see how he'd react.

Ben nodded a little. "Okay. I'm following, but can you explain to me a little more about why and how you're looking to help her?"

"Yeah... She spent a good part of her childhood cut off from the outside world, and her parents were a few notches past evil. She does pretty well, considering. She holds down a job well, and tries to interact with people normally when they talk to her. Her living situation can be messy, but she works hard to make sure it's as stable as she can manage... She's afraid of everything, though. By some magical stretch, she seems to trust me more than anyone else, but even that only goes so far. She can't be touched, and I'm not looking to, but it'd be nice if I didn't have to peel her off the ceiling every time some dipshit

146

shakes her hand, or accidentally bumps her arm. And it'd be really nice if the seats in my truck didn't vibrate from her shaking all the time. I'm sure you can tell I'm not the most nurturing of people, and I struggle to have an emotion called giving-a-shit."

Ben gave a slight laugh but didn't have one of those overly bright smiles. He had Nelson's minimalist way of smiling, but still appeared friendly and approachable. "Well, you must have some kind of 'give-a-shit' if you're here. Can I ask why it's important for you to help her instead of having her come see me herself, or just leaving it alone?"

I pressed my lips together for a moment. I had to tread carefully. "Yeah... First, she doesn't know I know what she's been through. If she did, I'd never see her again. Her parents are the worst kind of scum alive, she ran away, and they're still looking for her. She's an adult, but that wouldn't stop them from kidnapping her and dragging her back. She can't go to the police or anything because her parents have friends, almost like a cult kind of thing..." I took in a deep breath, shaking my head and internally kicking myself for lying to this guy about his sister. I was doing this for two reasons, to help Nelson, and make it so that if she ever did return to her family, Ben would already have the know-how and knowledge of how to help her.

"Why's it so important that you help her?" Ben asked after my thoughts paused for too long.

"Because she's the only person I'd truly consider a friend... I have other people I call friends, but I don't feel the same way about them as they do me. Nelson, on the other hand... she's not bothered that I don't smile at things I don't think are funny. She's not offended when I'm pissed off, or annoyingly trying to fix shit that isn't hers to fix. She doesn't smile either, she feels free to be pissed when she feels it, and the only thing she's worried about fixing is her own life. But... she'll make time to listen. Every time. She's got this overgrown mound of shit on her shoulders—I truly don't know how she doesn't put a fricken gun to her head—but it's the least important thing to her when someone needs an ear to bend." I would've held back on the details normally, but I needed to convince him to help me.

Ben nodded. "Sounds like you two are pretty close."

"Yeah," I nodded. "Platonically, I love her more than I've ever loved another person since I lost my little brother years ago." I hated mentioning Remy, but Ben knew something about losing a sibling, so it made me relatable.

"I realize this might be a personal question, but I'm wondering just in the way of trying to help you help her, is it only platonic?"

"Yep. Not my type, have no real attraction to her—I mean she's pretty, but I just don't feel that way about her. It'd be like trying to date my little sister." I scrunched my nose at the thought. "That's kinda that category she's in, I guess. That favorite little sister thing... Also, she's seeing one of those other friends of mine, and he's probably the best thing to ever happen to her. He's more annoying than a body covered in mosquito bites, but he loves the hell out of her, and he's done more for me than I can repay, so there's that if there ever wasn't the 'little sister' view."

He nodded again. "I get it. Can you tell me a little about the abuse she's sustained?"

"All of it. Everything you can think of, imagine, things you can't imagine, and don't want to. All of it."

"Okay. So, sexual, verbal, physical, psychological, the works?"

I nodded. "Yeah, in every extreme way imaginable. Greg, the chipper mosquito friend, can hardly hold her hand. She says it feels like someone is shocking her with a car battery, not so much with him because she trusts him okay, but with other people. I'm not the kind of guy that flinches at other people's pain, but there comes a point where I can see how very real her pain is. When someone so much as grazes her arm, she's got a look like someone pinned her arm to the table and sawed it off. I'm constantly having to scrape her off the ceiling."

Ben's eyebrows raised. "That's a pretty strong reaction, even for someone with sensory issues. How does she react when someone's in proximity to her? Say at ten, then six feet, then three." He watched me carefully, but it seemed to only be out of professional curiosity.

"Ten foot, she's got her eye on you and she's very aware. Six foot, she'll watch you like a hawk. And the only people I've ever seen her allow in a three-foot or less proximity would be me, Greg, and possibly her ditsy co-worker friend who has boundary issues when she gets too excited. Even then, she'll take a couple steps back pretty quick. Greg and I are the only ones in the three-foot range without her trying to melt into the floor or sneak away."

"If someone were within three feet and she was uncomfortable or unfamiliar with them, what would she do besides step away?"

"She'll start shaking, lose her voice, start to lose control of basic motor skills, throw up if she's gone too long without food, find the nearest small space and cram herself in it. In the most severe case, I've seen her just stop functioning altogether. It was like a switch got flipped, no more shaking, nothing. She was highly functional and went right back to working. By the next day, when she finally snapped out of it, she had no recollection of what happened, or that anything had even gotten to the point of triggering something like that. Complete dissociation."

Ben nodded with his eyebrows raised. "Yeah... Sounds like she's got some pretty strong symptoms and effects. What have you been doing to try to help her before now?"

"I try to keep people away from her. And it sounds

like shit, but I usually bitch at her to knock it off. It's effective most times. I always end up apologizing to her because I feel like a dick, but... Greg's worked hard to change what and who's in her life to try to help her. When we first met her, she was homeless, then living in a house with a bunch of drug dealers, so Greg found a condo to rent and duped her into living there. Her job at the diner has been a problem because the owners are overbearing weirdos who think she's their kid, so Greg gave her a job with his company, and has slowly been giving her more responsibilities. She's been cutting her hours at the diner more, and now with school starting up and the lease on the condo being over, she's quitting the diner and moving... Wow. All of this sounds really bad without knowing us and the entire story." I rubbed my forehead with a finger and thumb. "We're not a pair of controlling assholes. We're legitimately doing what we can to help her without her feeling like a charity case. It was her choice to quit the diner and move to a different city for school. She didn't have an education growing up, she's busted her ass to get accepted to college, and Greg pulled some strings to make sure it was a good one. His entire goal is to help her get to a point where she doesn't need to rely on anyone for anything. Mine is to make sure she doesn't get a blast from the past to screw it up."

Ben smiled a little. "I'm glad you clarified. It *did* sound pretty bad..." He took in a deep breath and let it out evenly. "Well, like you said, I can't treat someone who isn't my patient. The best I can do for you is give you pointers on how to help her through episodes brought on by various stressors."

"That's all I need. I can be here once a month, but it might be easier to just call since I don't actually live here and it's a pain in the ass to try to find time to come here without anyone knowing. That's another thing, Greg doesn't know what I know about her. I'm the only one who knows it. I work for him, making sure *she's* looked after, amongst other things. I'll pay cash in advance, no bullshit, I just need a person to call because I'm out of my element."

Ben nodded. "I think that'd be fine. I'd like to help however I can."

Thank god! Mostly, I'd expected him to tell me to piss off since I wasn't actually a patient.

"Thank you." I nodded once.

"You mentioned your brother passed. Can I ask what happened?"

"No." The mere suggestion of the question pissed me off, not to mention the actual question. "I'm off limits. This is only to help my friend so she has a shot at a normal life. She's my favorite person, and Greg and I are all she has. No one tries to understand her, they bully her into submission. She trusts us not to do that to her. I'm abrasive and I see that she needs help, so I need less abrasive ways to do it."

"I understand. Are you able to come back tomorrow and we can start?"

I nodded. "As long as it's before two. I have to get back."

"How about eight in the morning?"

"I'll be here."

Convincing Ben to help me had been easier than I expected, and liking him was also easier than expected. I understood why Nelson trusted me so easily; I reminded her of her brother. The only thing that bothered me about what I was doing was that Nelson didn't know. I could only imagine how hurt she'd be that I could so easily waltz in to see her family, and she couldn't.

I waited down the street for a while to watch Ben leave, then followed him. He was a big fan of speed limits and traffic laws. Once he was in the neighborhood of his parent's house, I went to the next street over and parked where I could see through the yards to the front of the house. Toby was out front with Grace, walking to a perfectly plain silver car. When Ben got out of his truck, Grace hugged him. I didn't know how I felt about the whole Toby and Grace situation. I knew Toby's side of it, but I didn't know Nelson's. He claimed they'd been forced to have a child together, but if it were me, I'd rather take a bullet than hurt someone that way. Nelson may not have known the difference at that age, but Toby did.

My phone vibrated in the cupholder and I debated on whether or not to answer.

I let out a breath and picked up the phone. "What's up?"

"Hey," Bex's voice was calm. "The mechanic finished with your truck early. I'm here and the guy is saying more than he told you because he's charging for parts. I told him you supplied the parts."

Ben took his daughter home and didn't leave the rest of the night. After she was in bed, he went outside and sat on the porch with his laptop. I'd been waiting for him to check his email, and he did. He'd given me his business card before I left, and I would have taken one even if he didn't offer. With one email Tim would have his IP address, and I'd be able to see everything he did on his computer. He went through a few more emails, then did as I predicted. While I'd been careful about what I said earlier, I knew I'd stirred the pot.

Chapter 14

Ben

The metal door buzzed loudly and slid back. It wasn't the first time I'd been here, and if I didn't get what I was coming for, it wouldn't be the last. It'd been several years though, and now I was running out of time because an execution date had been set.

I sat in front of Patty, a man who hardly looked like he was related to my father.

"I told ya last time, I don't know where she ran off to." Patty sat and let the CO chain his cuffed hands to the top of the table.

I shook my head, sitting down. "That's not why I'm here."

"Well, you're tryin' to find her again, and I told ya, I wouldn't know where to start."

"I won't need to find her if I find Henry." Every time, it took every ounce of me not to lunge across the table and kill the bastard with my bare hands. "And you should want me to find him before *he* finds *her*, because you and I both know he'll kill her."

Patty sighed and shook his head. "I can't tell ya that neither."

"You can, and you will if you don't want the death penalty taken off the table." He wanted to die rather than sit in prison.

"Yeah? How you figure you're gonna make that happen?"

I gave the slightest of a pompous smile. "It'll happen if I don't get what I need, and that's all you need to know."

Patty let out another loud sigh. "Well, I'd tell ya anyway, but I don't know. And ya shouldn't be lookin' for him anyhow. He'll kill you then he'll go out and kill Hannah too. Ya best just leave it alone. She's outta his sights, just leave her be."

I shook my head. "I'll find him with or without you. Either you can make the process easier, or you can sit here. I'll appeal your death penalty sentence and make you sit in solitary the rest of your life. You thought you were crazy before?" I gave another asshole smile. "I'll make you live in a special kind of hell because the real thing isn't good enough for you."

Patty's jaw tightened and he looked away. I knew I would strike a chord.

"There's a lotta people out there, sicker than me... You wanna take Henry down, you gotta start with the people givin' him business..." He looked at me again.

"I need names."

"And I need a goddamn cigarette and shower slippers. I got fungus so bad I gotta piss on my toes every time I gotta use the john. I ain't allowed to work and I don't got money for commissary."

"You'll have it before I leave. Names." I'd honor my word, only because I needed the information.

Patty looked at me for a moment, took a breath and let it out. "You gotta be careful. He ain't gonna hesitate to kill ya if he catches ya."

"I'll be the one to worry about it."

He nodded, then sniffed and wiped his nose on the side of his upper arm. "Ya gotta go to the house. The post at the bottom of the stairs there, the top comes off if ya pull it straight up. It's a snug fit, but it'll jiggle up. Inside, you'll find what you're lookin' for."

"How do I know you're not setting a trap?" I watched his face for any micro twitches, anything that might tell me he was lying.

"Cause I'm still tryin' to get Donny to come talk to me, and he ain't ever gonna if somethin' happens to ya... And it'd hurt Hannah. I can't hurt her no more."

I wanted to cut him from the center up just for mentioning her name, or showing that he cared about her at all. He had an obsessive psychosis over my sister, and he truly believed in his mind that he cared about her above all else. It'd caused him a severe mental snap to let her escape, but he did it because he knew Henry was getting ready to kill her.

I stood up without another word and walked to the door.

"Please don't forget about those slippers. I don't give a shit about the smokes." Patty almost sounded like a worried child.

I sat in my truck for almost an hour, just trying to get myself back to a functioning point. My mom thought I was working late, and I needed to get Ella, but I didn't want Ella subjected to me while I was in a "Hannah" mood. I also needed to figure out what I was going to tell my parents. If I told them I was searching for Hannah again, my mom would try too hard to be understanding, and my dad would tell me I was walking a dangerous line. It wasn't that he didn't want to find her, he was just afraid of what it would mean for her. Also, the man believed in "God's time," and I believed God was a scare tactic to make people stop acting like jackasses.

"Hey Son," my dad gripped my shoulder from behind, on his way to the kitchen, "you're just in time."

"Actually, I can't stay. I brought Ella a bag and I'm leaving my house key. I got a call from a family in Kansas City, and they need help with their fourteen-year-old. She's seen seven psychologists, been committed a few times, and no one seems to be able to get through to her. It's pretty serious and they can't wait, so I agreed to fly out there tonight."

"Oh..." My dad looked at me with slight disappointment. "Don't ya have time for dinner? I smoked some ribs, your mom's got potato salad, maple beans, and frog-eye salad."

Probably one of my favorite meals.

"My plane leaves in two and a half hours. Sorry." I scratched the back of my head.

He nodded. "It's alright... We're worried about ya though... You've been working an awful lot and it seems like things haven't been quite right with you for a while now."

I pushed my hand through my hair, thinking that it might be easier if my parents didn't care so much. They had the biggest hearts out of anybody I knew, and I hated disappointing them as much as I hated lying.

"Yeah... I don't know. They've got that damn movie coming out, and..." I shook my head, losing words.

"I know. We're not happy about it either, but maybe something good will come of it."

And there it was! Something *always* had to have a bright side. What the hell was bright about a girl being raped and tortured for seven years? What good could possibly be worth Hannah suffering? Could there ever be anything in her life where she'd stop and think that she was glad for all she'd gone through?

I let out a huff. "I gotta get going. Can you tell mom

I'll call her tonight when I land?"

"Aren't you gonna say bye to Ella first?"

"No. She'll start screaming her head off if she knows I'm leaving." I pulled the bag off my shoulder and put it on the bench that sat next to the door. Hannah and I had helped my dad build it, and it was one of those items that would make the house feel empty if it disappeared. "Can you give this to Mom? Ask her not to lose it this time." I handed my dad the house key.

"I will. Be safe, alright? And make sure you call or you'll make your mama crazy and I'll have to hear about it all night."

I nodded. "I will."

"Love ya, Son. Be safe."

"Love you too." I turned and left the house. Mostly, I felt like a dirtbag for lying to my parents, but I had to do this. If I failed, they'd never know, and if I succeeded, we'd have Hannah back and it wouldn't matter.

I stood in front of the two-story white house with the sagging white porch, and I—at six foot four—felt small. Thick green trees lined the property in all directions, and the clearing of grass around the house was as tall as it could get. My stomach felt like a hollow void of space in my body and my heart was pounding so loudly that the wind and birds were almost inaudible. The entire drive I'd convinced myself I wouldn't look through any other part of the house, but I knew I had to. Movies, books, and Toby's account would never give me a real picture of the house Hannah had been locked in.

After several minutes of standing there, I finally braved my way up to the front door. It was busted and just set in the doorway, so I had to lift it and move it out of the way. The wood floor inside was covered in a thick layer of dust with leaves scattered mostly in the entryway. My back tickled with the worst sensation that someone or something might jump out at me, so I put my hand on my gun, ready for a quick draw.

The living room was off to the right, and exactly as Toby had described. It was lined with windows from halfway up the floor, and metal rods ran horizontally outside of them. When Hannah was here, an electrical current ran through the rods to keep anyone in the house from escaping. She'd burned her hands trying a few times. To the right of the large doorway into the living room, there was an old baby grand with nails hammered through the lid. Helen, the woman who'd played "mommy dearest" for a short time, had forced Hannah to play, and would slam the nail-spiked lid down on Hannah's hands when she fumbled too many times. She's started playing at three years old because she loved it so much, and now she probably hated it. Toby told me Hannah had played more beautifully than anyone he'd ever seen, but I couldn't picture her wanting to ever again.

I looked to the left of the piano, and on the wooden wainscoting it read, "My name is Stupid," repeatedly. Hannah had been forced to write it. My chest ached at the thought of her sitting on the floor while Helen screamed and called her worthless.

I backed out of the living room, looked at the banister post I was supposed to open, but went past it to go upstairs. The door at the top had been Patty's room he shared with Helen until she went missing. All that was left in the room was empty dresser drawers and an old metal bed frame. Several floorboards were missing because Patty had a knack for hiding things in all kinds of places and the FBI had torn the house apart in the raid.

On the left wall of the bedroom was a two-way mirror, but the mirrored side faced Hannah's "playroom". It was frilly and looked like it should have been any girl's dream, but it was her nightmare. Men would watch her play, while jerking off, when she was seven through ten, but after Helen was gone, they did more than watch while Patty watched. Seeing the rooms made me want to go straight back to Texas and kill him in his cell at all costs.

I couldn't continue going into the "playroom," or the "theater" room. My stomach was on the verge of losing its contents as it was, and my eyes were burning as I held back tears. I went back downstairs, around the banister and back to the room that Patty had deemed as his office, and everything in me just felt cold. Toby had described it to me, it'd been portrayed a certain way in one of the movies, but it was a very different thing to see it. Hannah's blood had really spilled out on that laminate floor, her little body had really been strapped to that table, and she'd really been hanged by her wrists from the chain that dangled down from a beam across the ceiling.

The very thought... I couldn't handle it.

With a stiff lip and blurred vision, I walked to the banister and started pulling on the top of the square post. It was on there so snug I almost thought Patty had lied, but then it started to give. Inside there was a piece of paper and it was new. All it read was, "Go home."

A fast burst of anger hit me and I kicked the post, punched the wall, then went through the house, throwing any furniture the FBI hadn't taken as evidence. That stupid house had been my sister's prison in hell, and the least she deserved was to have it destroyed! I raged like a wild beast, breaking chairs from the kitchen table where Helen had stabbed a fork through Hannah's hand for asking for a piece of cake. I ripped the drawers out of the buffet with glass missing from its doors because Helen had wrapped Hannah in a bed sheet and swung her around the room. I ripped the drawers from the kitchen that held the utensils she'd been forced to wash in scalding water. The goddamn pantry door that held the food she was hardly allowed to eat, I kicked in.

I gathered leaves from the tree line, old-ass wood

from the pile next to the small detached garage, threw them in the house, then went back to the garage to find an old can of turpentine. It took half a second for the pile of shit in the house to light up from the drop of a match. My heart continued to pound with rage, and the fire just didn't feel angry enough. It was the only thing I could give Hannah, burning that house and everything in it, and it'd never be enough. She could take my life and it wouldn't atone for me leaving her in that doctor's office.

The front of my truck bared my weight while I bawled like a child for a few minutes. As much as I wanted to watch the house fully burn, I couldn't stay. I had to leave and cover my tracks carefully, and literally. My truck tires were evidence I'd been there. Regardless of my standing in the situation, arson was arson, and it was illegal.

I drove up to Louisville and found a shitty tire store that wouldn't keep records, had my tires flipped out for different ones, had my truck thoroughly washed afterward, then drove up to Kansas City to leave my paper trail. It was going to take me a day or so to reel myself back in.

Chapter 15

Ryan

I smiled. He'd clearly found my note. Granted, I didn't expect Ben to go burn the house down, and I really wished he hadn't, but he found my note... It only cost me a fair sum of my personal savings to hire an out of work B class actor to walk into that prison, bribe Patty for information, then hop a flight to Tennessee, but I had the ancient-ass thumb drive. Tim had told me the FBI occasionally kept tabs on when inmates like Patty were visited. Someone would get a system alert, but only one. So I had used Ben as a blanket to get my guy in undetected, then had Tim hack the prison's computer system to erase the paid actor's visit. Now, I just needed to get back to Seattle to have Tim pull the information off the thumb drive.

The garage door opened and closed, and I quickly shut off the TV. Nelson would find out about the house sooner or later, but I didn't need to make her feel like she might be in some kind of spotlight with Grey around.

"Car's packed up and waiting. You ready?" Grey picked up his phone from the counter and pulled it off the charger.

"Yeah." I grabbed my bag from the couch and slung it over my shoulder.

"Crap. I forgot my one bag downstairs. I'll be right back." Grey touched the back of Nelson's arm before he walked past her. She looked at him but didn't jump; she'd been doing better with her exaggerated responses to touch where Grey was concerned.

"You ready for the big move?" I asked Nelson. If I could gauge her thinking now, there was a chance I could avoid the almost inevitable freak out later.

She held up her shoulders. "I don't know... It's not real yet." She rubbed her hands together and looked over toward the maid who was carrying the cleaning basket into the kitchen.

I nodded toward the door. "Let's go outside."

She nodded and waited for me to get past her before she turned and followed. The only time she walked in front of Grey and I was if we were deemed the lowest threat.

"Are you gonna be okay staying at Grey's house?" I asked her once we were in the car.

She took in a deep breath and held it for a second. "Yeah... I've stayed there before, so this is kinda the same, I guess..."

"Well, you can stay with me if you want to. Tim pretty much never comes out of the basement, and I have an upstairs room and an extra bathroom." I watched her in the rearview mirror as I spoke.

"I appreciate it, but I think it'll be okay." She watched as Grey came through the door from the house. "I think he'd be crushed if I changed plans last minute."

"He'd be fine. He's too afraid of running you off."

She shook her head, looking down at her hands. "He shouldn't be."

162

Grey opened the door. "Alright, let's do this." He passed his laptop bag back to Nelson. "You can sit up front, B."

She shook her head with a small smile. "No. I fit back here better than the two of you."

"Lame excuse. Are you sure you don't want to sit up front?"

I frowned. "Just get your ass in here. We still have to stop at the diner and we're already running late."

"No, I stopped by the diner this morning and said my goodbyes." Nelson handed a bottle of water up front to Grey.

"Thanks," Grey said as he took it and shut the door.

I put the car in reverse and backed out of the garage. It was a huge relief to be going back to Seattle and staying there. Monterey was nice, but Seattle was home.

"This thing's old," Tim said as he started clicking around on his computer. I'd given him the thumb drive to plug into his computer that was completely offline. It was more likely that there was no kind of tracking coded into the thumb drive, but it wasn't a chance I was willing to take. "Okay, looks like you're clear. I'm gonna go take a shower."

"Good, cause I could smell you from upstairs." I shriveled my nose at Tim as he got up.

He gave a sneer and went back toward the bathroom in the basement. Aside from going up to the kitchen, he really had no reason to ever leave the basement, and I found it gross.

I sat down at Tim's computer and grabbed a disinfectant wipe to clean the keyboard, mouse, and desktop before I started picking through anything. I was going to need to call someone to come scrub the basement again because there was no way in *hell* I was doing it after last time. He could sit there embarrassed as someone other than me cleaned up his nastiness. Maybe it would deter him from being such a pig.

The folders on the drive were clearly labeled and organized, and there were more than I expected. I didn't know if this would be a duplicate of the drive that Grey and I had originally gotten our hands on, but I was glad it wasn't. Grey had already decided Nelson was the girl he wanted to marry, and she'd never be able to do it freely if the threat of her past was still looming. And even if Nelson wasn't part of the picture, I'd still take Henry Greer down. If I didn't hate politics so much, I would have taken the offers from the CIA or FBI when I was approached over a year ago. By working alone, rules only applied if I got caught.

I clicked on the "Employee" spreadsheet and raised my eyebrows when it was a fully detailed document. Names, aliases used for work purposes, addresses, phone numbers, social security numbers, a detailing of alive or dead, how they died if they were marked dead, the dates they were employed, where they were working, job description, and a small picture of their faces. Was this the motherload of all records?

I clicked on the "Sales" folder and there were more folders inside named by year up to the year Nelson escaped and Patty had been arrested. I clicked on the first year, the same year she'd been taken. There were spreadsheets labeled by month, so I clicked on the top one. It was just as detailed as the last spreadsheet. There was a date, client name, "servant" name, and the service type. Each name was hyperlinked, so I clicked on the first client name. Geoffrey Phisher. A name I found entirely annoying. Why not just spell shit normally? Jeffery Fisher. Was that so hard!?

The hyperlink brought me to a completely different document. It was an incredibly detailed summary of the client Geoffrey Phisher along with a full and clear picture. Anything that could be known about him was in that summary. Family members' names and addresses, occupation, a record of medical examination, social security number, banking information, transaction lists, and sexual likes and dislikes. The small-town vet was a frequent perv who enjoyed the company of little girls. There were also hyperlinks that went to a single photo to document each visit. The ones I checked were all in the house in Tennessee.

I clicked the back button to go back to the services spreadsheet and clicked Hannah's name. A document, just like the one for Geoffrey, showed up, but I didn't expect the picture to be so explicit. My hand quickly went up to cover the parts of Nelson I really didn't need or want to see. I scrolled past the front, back, and two side view photos so they weren't showing on the screen. My embarrassment for her was so heavy my face and neck burned. I swallowed hard and went back to paying attention to words. There was a family tree diagram for breeding. There had been more children than just Grace. She'd had two boys when she was thirteen and fourteen, both were marked as deceased. I couldn't bring myself to click those hyperlinks, so I scrolled down further.

The page just kept going... There were so many dates; names that were frequent, names that weren't... and it just kept going. If reading Toby's book hadn't disturbed me, this did... profoundly. My eyes burned and watered, and my throat felt tight. For seven years, Hannah Lawrence had been touched, raped, and stared at. I truly couldn't fathom how she chose to stay alive and live with the horrific memories. And for only the second time in my life, my heart felt truly and deeply broken. I didn't give a shit about looking weak for crying...

Grey smiled as I walked into his open-floor kitchen, dining room, and living room. "Tim bugging you already?"

Nelson turned on the stool at the island with a small smile and her hand on the bottom of a wine glass on the counter. I could hardly look at her because all I wanted to do was hug her and tell her I was going to kill every bitch I had to, to get to Henry. I wanted to promise her that I'd never let anyone touch her against her will again...

I nodded. "The house smells like ass, and it's trashed."

Grey scrunched his nose, but his smile didn't leave. "Yeah. It was pretty bad the last time I was there."

I raised my eyebrows and dropped them in a quick expression before I set a jar of Nutella in front of Nelson. My gesture was pathetic, like a stupid jar of hazelnut spread fixed anything in her life, but it was all I could do without raising suspicion.

"What's this for?" She smiled a little.

"Because your boyfriend is ditching you for me. Call us if you need something."

She looked at me slightly confused, but more worried. "Are you okay?"

I shook my head. "Nope." There was no point in lying about it, and Grey wouldn't try to put off the talk I needed to have with him if I was honest. I was also aware that my usual emotionless face was showing anything but.

I looked at Grey. "Drive?"

He nodded and pulled the dish towel off his shoulder from cooking. "Yeah. Let's go." He looked at Nelson. "We'll be back, feel free to anything in the house, and the timer will go off when the fish is done. Everything else is ready."

"I got it," she nodded understandingly, then looked at me.

I pulled back the corner of my mouth, feeling like an asshole for letting her worry about what was going on, and held my fist out just above the counter. Nelson bumped the side of my hand with hers, and I turned to leave. Grey followed me to my truck, then I drove us down to the small park inside the gated community Grey lived in.

166

Grey looked at me. "You're making nervous. What happened?"

I bit the inside of my cheek for a second, knowing this was potentially about to get ugly, and preparing myself to be the toughest beast in the fight. "You know I've got your back in this shit against your dad. I'm still gonna help you put the man on his knees, and you need to believe me and trust me when I say that."

"Yeah, I know." He sounded a little surprised that I would imply otherwise.

"Honestly, if I didn't value you so much as a friend, I'd walk right into his fucking house and stab him until all that was left was hamburger meat and feed it to the damn fish in his office."

"Jesus. What happened?" Obviously, Grey was disgusted by my brutality.

"You need to keep Nelson out of your vendetta against your old man."

"I already told you I wasn't gonna put her in the middle of—"

"No!" My voice was loud and sharp, and I looked at him. "I mean you can't use *anything* against him that even remotely leads to her." I pointed toward the direction of the house. "You'll get her *killed!*"

Grey looked at me like I was crazy. "What?"

"I didn't take you as the deaf or stupid type. If you use anything that is even remotely connected to Nelson, you'll get her *killed.*"

Grey frowned. "Yeah, I'm neither. I'm just trying to draw a view from less than a few pin-picks of information. I'm hearing you, but can you shed some light on why?"

I looked forward out the windshield, feeling the anvil-sized lump in my throat. "No... All I'm gonna say about it is, you have no idea what she's *really* been through—I can only read a paper and make empathetic assumptions—but it's the vilest... existence imaginable..." My voice was quieter because I was desperately trying to hold back tears and vomit again.

"What happened to her?" he asked just as quietly.

I shook my head. "That's not my place... It has to come from her if she wants you to know, but as someone who knows you as well as I do, you don't want to... I sure as shit don't." I rubbed my face hard, the muscles around my eyes felt like they were atrophied in a painful scowl.

"I can't help her or keep her safe if I'm in the dark. I already said I don't want her in the middle of the shit with my dad, and I can't guarantee that if I don't know her involvement with him." Grey spoke easily but was still concerned.

"I'll worry about it. I'm not trying to be a pain in the ass, but as a basic human right, she deserves to have her secret protected, and if I tell you anything then she's not getting the one thing she probably deserves most. That drive you found, I have it, and it doesn't matter who you pay or blackmail, no one knows where it is but me. I know your fight with Roger is important to you, but if you love Nelson as much as you say you do, she has to be more important. If she's not, you have to let her go... It's all or nothing, anything else will end up with her dead. Very literally dead."

Grey took in a deep breath and let it out. "Then it's an easy choice... And fortunate for you, I trust you, otherwise I'd think you were in love with her."

I shook my head and looked at him. "There's things I won't tell you, but I won't lie to you. I'm in the crosshairs of the only two people in my life that I can confidently say I love, but with this one thing, I'm completely on her side. I'm on your side for everything else. I have her back exactly like I have yours, so yes, platonically I love her."

He nodded. "I know... I've got yours too. I'll make sure she's completely out of the crossfire. If I have the choice between you and Bex over MWM, I choose you guys. I'm not my dad." His eyebrows raised with a look of pure honesty.

I nodded. "I know... That's why I pulled you out of the house and not her. She doesn't know I know about her, because she'd bolt if she did. She's as safe as she can be with you." I rubbed my forehead to stretch the muscles again. "If you're done gushing, I need to go home, drink a bottle of scotch or acid—something that gives my guts a reason to feel like shit—and go to bed." I started the truck and backed out of the parking spot as I spoke.

Grey laughed lightly. "Come back to the house, have dinner with us, I'll pour us a drink, and you can head out."

I shook my head. "No... I can't sit in front of Nelson right now. I'm too screwed up over knowing what I know."

"It's that bad?"

"Bad enough for me to puke in my front yard, cry like a bitch, and honest-to-god contemplate a killing spree... The killing spree probably isn't so hard to imagine, but—"

"I remember the last time you cried, so enough said. I just want to know what I can do to help her, besides what's been previously discussed."

I parked in front of Grey's house. "Don't ever ask her, and don't ever make her tell you. Only listen if she does. Otherwise, you're probably already doing what you can." I took in a breath. "Really, I have to go before this headache turns into a full-blown migraine. My skull feels like it's going to implode."

"Alright. Text me when you're home, and don't worry about it. We'll find something else to turn my dad into hamburger with." Grey got out of the truck.

I wasn't waiting for Grey to get into the house before I left, I just needed a minute to keep my vision straight. The mass amount of information I was in possession of had my brain firing on all fronts. There was a loose plan in my head, but it had to be solid and airtight before I could set it in motion. I could leave nothing unthought of.

Nelson was going to be freed, one way or another, but I wanted to leave her with the choice of remaining Nelson or returning to Hannah Lawrence, if at all possible.

Chapter 16

Bexley

Grey came in from his drive with Ryan, took my hands to have me stand, and hugged me. I was uncomfortable, but also more comfortable than I'd been since Toby.

"Everything okay?" I felt nervous to ask.

"Everything's good..." He tipped his head down so his cheek was against mine. "I just want you to know I love you more than anything and everything."

I smiled a little. It'd been a relief when he said it at the party last month. While it'd only been just five months, I felt more in love with him than anyone I'd ever met. For me, it was a profound notion. A hopeful part of me had always held out for Toby, and now there was only Grey in my sight.

I turned my face into his shoulder, reminding myself I was safe to do so because it was my choice, and took in a breath of Grey's pepper and citrus cologne. "I love you too."

"Enough to not be mad at me for buying you a car?" His voice was a whisper in my ear.

I pulled back and looked at him. I was angry! We had an agreement about him spending ridiculous amounts of money on me. If it wasn't something I could afford myself, he wasn't allowed to buy it for me.

Grey held up his hands. "Hear me out before you get completely pissed."

Too late!

"I need you to be able to get around on your own here. You're taking on more responsibilities at MWM, you have school, we have dinners, meetings, and who knows what else. Ryan has a big class load, I've got a lot going on at work, and it's just easier for everyone if you have a car. You won't let me help with the classes and other school expenses MWM doesn't cover, you insist on paying rent, and since I know what you make, I know you can't afford to go get something reasonable to get around in. And I'll have a stroke if you take a bus anywhere. Ever."

I took in a breath so deep it almost hurt, then let it out slowly. I was unsure if it was the strong breath or the anger making me temporarily dizzy.

"You don't owe me anything, don't think of it as a gift, just... try to understand three things. I need to know you're safe unlike on a bus or walking, I want you to always have a way to and from school, and I *really* need to make sure you're able to help me at MWM." He gave an impish smile. "A lot of really selfish intentions going on... I've got mounds on my plate, I don't want to be staring at my watch because you're late, and worrying you got kidnapped or something. So, I'm asking you very kindly to just accept this one thing, for me, and give me the peace of mind that you'll be okay getting to wherever it is you go in a day." He was trying to smile, but it was saturated by honest to god worry.

I'd been ready to fight him tooth and nail until he

threw the word kidnapping into the conversation. That one word stirred a vat of emotions and thoughts. He usually worked so hard to be respectful of me and my wishes, never asking questions about where I came from, why I was the way I was, but at some point, I had to give something back. Did it really have to be a car?

Grey raised his eyebrows, still worried. "Can you say something?"

I pressed my lips together and shook my head. "I don't know what to say, because I don't appreciate being ambushed. If this was so important to you, you could have said the same things, then asked." My voice cracked and broke.

"I didn't want you to say no."

"And it's okay to manipulate and force me to say yes?" I knew he wanted me to bite my tongue and say thank you, but I was offended. "Because I can't be reasoned with?"

He cringed. "No, it's not okay to force your hand, but this is important to me, so I didn't know how else to do it."

My frown cleared, because the only thing I could do was walk away.

"No, B, wait." He caught my hand.

I pulled my hand back from the electric shock that charged up my arm and brought it up to my chest as I turned. I pinched my wrist with my other hand to stop the temporary pain and tried to quickly clear the fact that I'd been about to yelp.

Grey held up his hands for a second, realizing he'd made the mistake of taking my hand when I didn't expect it. "I'm sorry, I forgot." He gently took my hand between his and rubbed it with little pressure. "I didn't mean to grab you to make you stop. I mean, I did, but I forgot I can't and shouldn't." He brought my hand up to his lips and kissed the back of my hand. "And you're right, it wasn't fair of me to manipulate you. I'm sorry. I bought it today, so I can still take it back." He looked at me intently, and his eyebrows raised together when I still didn't say anything. "B, I'm *really* sorry. I promise I'll take it back the second I have a chance tomorrow."

I took in another breath and let it out. "Can I pay for it?" I *did* need a way to get around.

He flashed a quick smile. "A kiss and it's yours. You can drive that baby off the lot tonight."

He wasn't taking me seriously, which irritated me again, so I turned around.

"Ga! No!" Grey slipped past me quickly and stopped in front of me. "I'm sorry. I can't help it. I get stupid when I'm in trouble."

He couldn't help his smile, I knew he couldn't, but I didn't reciprocate.

"Okay, let's see if we can come to an agreeable compromise. I have things I want, you have things you want. Can we sit down and talk about it without anyone walking away, or you looking like you're ready to ditch me and go stay with Ryan?" Just a little of his smile stayed.

"Things?" I raised my eyebrows.

"Yeah... but I want an honest chance to talk about it. Preferably on the couch or somewhere of 'like' comfort... Please? I'm trying to do the right thing here, instead of going behind your back or trying to be sneaky, I'm asking for the chance to talk, and you giving what I have to say some honest thought before you get mad at me."

He was using my words against me, so I had no choice but to nod and agree. "Okay."

Another brilliant smile quickly lit his face. "Okay."

I stepped back and out of the way to let him go toward the living room.

"Uh, wrong direction, because I'm a shameless rat, and I already did something else." He took my hand and led me toward the stairs.

"What?"

"Just follow, you'll see."

174

We went up to the second floor of the house to the French doors at the top of the stairs. Grey's house was three stories, not including the walk-in basement. A basement I still refused to enter, despite the wall of floor-to-ceiling windows that entered the backyard.

"Please, let me just give a blanket apology for being a thoughtless ass who was *trying* instead to be thoughtful." He cringed and opened the door.

I gave a slight frown and looked in the room I usually stayed in when I was at his house. Everything was beautiful... the floor to ceiling windows on the back wall showcased the stunning view of the sound, and new white chiffon curtains made the view even more breathtaking. I could imagine just how beautiful the sunlight would look coming through them in the daylight. The walls were the same color as the apartment I'd had over the summer, and the room was decorated in the same taste. It was spacious enough to pass for a small apartment, complete with a queen-sized bed, a couch, two chairs, a coffee table, and a desk. Just the beauty of it made me want to go in and see more, but I looked at Grey instead.

He nodded inside the room. "Let's talk." Keeping my hand, Grey led me in and we went to sit on the couch. After he sat down, he leaned forward and rested his elbows on his knees with his hands folded in front of him. "I know there's no way in hell you'll agree to stay here without paying something, because you're you," he smiled and reached over to squeeze my hand lightly, "so we can talk about it if you want, but I do wanna say, I don't want you to. What I'd rather you did was take that money and put it in savings, or spoil yourself a little and go on a shopping spree once in a while." A smile crinkled the corners of his eyes. "I don't want to watch you struggle. I want you to go to school, put everything you have into it, and not have to worry about money. You've worried long enough. Time served."

"Why are you doing this?" His generosity was seemingly endless, but it made me worried what the end cost would be. Nothing was ever free; good deeds always needed a reward.

"I already told you... I love you, and I don't wanna watch you struggle trying to balance school and work because you're trying to pay for a place to live, a car, food, and all the other bullshit expenses life brings. School needs to be first. You were robbed of a childhood where you could live freely, so do it *here*. You're smart as hell, more than anyone else I know besides Ryan. You deserve to climb the ladder in front of you, I want to make sure the ladder is secured."

I shook my head. "I can't stay here for nothing, and I can't take a car I know I could never afford on my own."

He nodded. "Okay. What do you want to do? What gets you to stay here and keep the car?"

"I pay rent and I pay for the car."

"Two hundred a month to rent the room, and three hundred for five years for the car. You don't need to pay insurance because I have an account that basically holds money in case something happens, just like an insurance company would. Help me out with getting groceries for the house so I can stop making Harry do it, and let the cleaning ladies in once a week to take care of the house."

I shook my head. "That's too little. Five and six, plus everything else you mentioned. That leaves me about a thousand to put into savings after paying for my classes, books, and other stuff."

Grey chewed on his lip for a second. "Four and four."

I shook my head. "No. Five and six, or I find an apartment and I get a car when I can afford to." Thankfully, I'd already been able to prepare some before moving here, but I still had more of it to do. At least three-quarters of that thousand would go to buying beater cars, finding places to store them, and stashing money in them. The

176

ones I had in Monterey had to stay for anytime I went back, and I had to have at least five ways out of Seattle to feel like I could breathe semi-comfortably.

He laughed a little. "I'm trying to meet you in the middle here."

"I don't want the middle. I already feel like I owe you more than I'll ever be able to repay, and I don't like the feeling."

He reached over, taking my hand again, tilting his head slightly and giving a slightly sympathetic look. "I'm not counting, Beautiful. You shouldn't be either. I have more money than I can reasonably spend in a lifetime. If I stopped working today, my lifestyle wouldn't change—other than being incredibly bored—and there'd still be enough in the pot for two future generations to live and never work. Even your grumpy buddy will tell you I just like sharing what I have. If I have the ability and the means to help people who deserve it, to make them smile or feel good, I do it. I bought Ryan his house, both of his trucks, I pay for his schooling, I employ him so he can have flexible hours and a job that doesn't make him want to become a serial killer. I make sure his brother's medical expenses are taken care of because Ryan already lost one brother... It's what I do, and I love it more than my actual job... The only thing I want in return from you is to go to school and do well. You don't have to have a four-point-O GPA or be the top of your class, just give it what you've got, then go out in life and do something with it. You're smart, B. More than you give yourself credit for." He squeezed my hand again. "Four for rent and six for two years."

"Six for three years."

He laughed again. "Okay. Six for three years if you let me take you clothes shopping tomorrow. We have brunch with my parents Sunday morning, I have two business dinners I want you to sit in on during the week, and the office has a dress code."

I rolled my eyes. "I have enough to do my own clothes shopping. I've been saving for months."

He smiled. "I know, but I want you to save it because I can use your clothes as a tax write off. It's a business expense." He let go of my hand and held it out in front of me. "Deal?"

"Grudgingly." I shook his hand.

"I love you, you know... That has to allow me a little bit of spoiling."

I gently raised an eyebrow. "Spoiling me with money doesn't constitute love."

"Money or not, spoiling or not," he wrapped his arm behind my shoulders and pulled me toward him as he sank back between the arm and the back of the couch, "I love you." He kissed the side of my forehead.

My heart pounded loudly in my ears and I felt like it was harder to breathe. I knew he wasn't going to do anything but sit on the couch with me, but I was still afraid.

"And as much as your inability to accept help drives me absolutely insane, I respect you for being a self-made woman." He took my hand before wrapping his arm around the top of my chest.

"I'd be happier if I accepted far less help." My voice was a little strained, but I was trying not to jump up from the couch and find a wall to put my back to. It was buzzing with electricity.

"Everybody accepts help. Even me... When I broke off from MWM, I went begging to potential clients for an initial investment. My parents paid my way through college, cosigned on a loan for my first house, my first car. My dad taught me how to successfully run not only a business, but an entire corporation. My mom helped me plan client events because I had no clue. There's nothing wrong with help." He rested his chin against the side of my head. "When I was about five, my grandpa told me it was okay to conquer as much success as I wanted, but

178

to make sure I reached back and helped other people do the same... I don't know, that kind of mentality has always stuck with me."

"Your grandpa sounds like a good person."

"He is, and you'll get to meet him Sunday." He rubbed the top of my arm lightly.

"Is Sam gonna be there?" I reached my other hand up to Grey's arm because I felt claustrophobic having his arm around me, but I didn't want to be rude and ask him to move it. We had an agreement that if he did anything that made me uncomfortable, I was supposed to say something, but I always felt like a jerk. He was nothing but kind, and I was nothing but scared.

"No, he's already at Vanderbilt. Did you want to invite Ryan so you feel like you have more than one person you know there?"

I shook my head. "It's okay."

"It's no problem. My parents love him. Probably more than they love me."

"I doubt that."

"Maybe not my mom, but for sure my dad. He'll even tell you so." Grey laughed lightly. "It's funny because Ryan hates him, and my dad has no idea."

"Sounds about right." I took in a deep breath, let it out, and tried to calm my nerves.

<hr/>

The next day, we went around town for a while and Grey took me shopping. He wouldn't let me look at price tags and he gave the lady at the counter his credit card and told her that I wasn't allowed to see or hear the total. I'd frowned and he'd flashed a cheesy grin. We were taken to a private dressing room area and she started bringing me clothes to try on. Grey sat on the couch with his resting smile and patiently waited. There was a particular white dress that made him raise his eyebrows in surprise. He pointed at the mirror for me to look.

I walked over and looked in the mirror. He stood

up and walked over to stand next to me. It was strange. When I looked in the mirror, I saw someone different than the ragged basement girl I usually did. I saw someone I could be. It wasn't just the dress, it was the whole picture. Grey looking at me adoringly, waiting for nothing but me to smile. My hair was pulled back the same way it always was, but it looked different with the dress. I didn't look like a broken person.

"I want to be her." I stared at the mirror and looked at Grey.

His beautiful smile held, and he laughed quietly. He raised his hands to hold the tops of my arms, another thing that was new. "You are."

"No. What I mean, is..." I turned to face him. "You're right. If I don't take the opportunity to work my way up, it may not come again... I've waited long enough for it."

He looked so happy that he had to contain himself. "Mindset is the biggest part of the battle." He reached forward and pulled the paper part of the tag off. "Heather, we'll take this dress and the others she liked."

The lady that'd been helping us nodded. "Yes, Mr. Maslen."

"And she's wearing this one out. Can you get me a pair of scissors for the tag?"

She nodded again and went to the counter and came back with scissors. Grey looked at me, ready to be careful as he snipped the plastic. He handed both the tag and scissors back to her, then turned to look at me through the mirror again.

"I see you had no problem picking out shoes."

I smiled. "They caught my eye."

Grey laughed and looped his arm through mine before taking a picture of the two of us. He held his phone so I could see the picture. "That's who we'll be."

I looked at him. "Thank you."

He nodded. "You're completely worth it, and you're welcome."

When we got home from dinner, Ryan came over for a while and I was glad to see him in a little better spirit than the night before. He'd honestly worried me, because he looked like he was about to put a gun to his head. He also couldn't seem to really look at me and I'd wondered if I'd done something, but Grey had assured me it was nothing to do with me. I assumed it was Ryan having a moment of missing his late brother, but I didn't ask. Instead, I was more than happy to sit on the couch with him and Grey and eat away at a jar of Nutella together while we watched a movie.

———※◈※———

I jumped with a loud yelp and sat up from a fractured nightmare that was partially a memory.

"Hey. What happened?" Grey asked groggily.

I held my hand to my chest tightly, panting from the surge of adrenaline and fear. My brain was scrambled, and I looked around to remember where I was. The living room was full of morning light from the wall of windows at the back of the house.

"Bad dream?" Grey prodded.

I nodded, taking a deeper and more controlled breath.

"I'm sorry, Beautiful." He reached over and rubbed my arm. "Come here. You left a cold spot on my side." He laughed a little.

I shook my head. "Not yet." My voice was for the birds.

I looked at the TV and it was on a low volume, but not low enough that I couldn't hear.

"Just this morning, Texas Judge Donald Lawrence, the father of missing Hannah Lawrence, came out in a press conference to comment on the death of his brother, Patrick, the man convicted of kidnapping young Hannah," a female news reporter said before the screen switched to an image of my father standing in front of a few microphones on a podium.

"Good mornin'," my dad said with a slight nod and dismay on his face. His voice sounded exactly the same as I remembered, calm, gentle, and a deep baritone. "Early this mornin', Patrick Lawrence was found stabbed to death in his cell. At this time, the FBI, and local police are still investigatin' the incident. All security cameras temporarily went down at the time of the occurrence, but the authorities expect to have more information as the day continues." He paused and itched the back of his head for a moment.

"B?"

"Hm?" I looked at Grey. My heart was pounding as hard as it could without giving out, and every part of me was burning.

"I asked if you wanted anything to eat to hold you over before we went to my parents."

I shook my head.

"You seem more rattled than usual, do you wanna talk about it?"

I shook my head again.

"Okay." He pulled back the corner of his mouth and walked around the couch.

I quickly looked at the TV. I shouldn't have been watching the broadcast in front of Grey, but it was the first time I'd heard my father's voice in fourteen years and the man who'd held me captive was dead.

"...ask that everyone be respectful of my family's privacy. There isn't a mornin' my family doesn't wake up missin' Hannah, or spend the day hopin' she'll return to us. That bein' said, I know the main question on everyone's mind is how we feel over Patty's death. Our answer is, he was a man who did unspeakable things, but only the Lord has the right to judge—no matter how hard it might be for us to accept. I *will* say, we're relieved to know he's no longer a threat. That'll be my only comment as far as that goes. I'll start takin' questions, but please keep 'em factual and courteous." My dad had struggled his way through speaking.

An uproar of unseen voices started, and my dad pointed.

"Judge Lawrence, has there been any speculation that this was the work of Henry Greer?" a reporter asked.

"Of course," my dad nodded. "Where Patrick is concerned, there's always suspicion of Henry Greer, but as I stated before, the investigation is still ongoin', and updates will be provided later."

"Is the FBI still making it a priority to find and arrest Henry Greer?" the same reporter asked.

My dad nodded again. "Yes. In fact, there's a two-million-dollar reward being offered to anyone who comes forward with information that leads to Mr. Greer's capture and arrest."

"Judge Lawrence, is your family still offering a reward for anyone who locates your daughter?" another reporter asked quickly.

"Yes. Anyone with information on her whereabouts is encouraged to contact the Dallas FBI offices." He pointed to another person, looking like he wanted nothing more than to be done with the questions. I knew the feeling, and I so badly wanted to hug him and let him know I was okay.

"Thank you, Sir. Is it true that you and Patrick grew up in an abusive home, and that Patrick shot your father?"

My dad rubbed his forehead out of irritation. "Young man, that's a matter of public record, and it's been out there for years. Go do your research and stop wastin' people's time." Again, my father pointed at another person.

"A few days ago, the house that Hannah was held captive in was set on fire, have you been given any further information on that, or been told that it might have been Mr. Greer that set the blaze?"

What? The house had been set on fire? When?

And why hadn't I heard about it?

My dad shook his head. "No. It's speculated that it may've been teenagers, but no one knows."

"Do you believe Hannah may have started the fire?" another person called out.

My dad's eyebrows raised, and he tipped his head to the side for a short moment. "Again, I don't know, but I'd highly doubt it. I can't foresee anyone wantin' to go back to a house they'd been held hostage in." He pointed. "The young lady in the front there."

"Thank you, Judge Lawrence. I know it's believed that Hannah is out there living on her own somewhere. If she's watching this from wherever she is, is there something you want to say to her? And why do you think she hasn't returned home?"

My dad took a breath, held it for a second, and let it out. "Well, with Henry Greer still at large, I don't believe she feels safe enough to, but I also think there's some fear about goin' back to somethin' she probably doesn't remember much of. If she's watchin', I want her to know she's loved, she's got a big support system waitin' on her if she'd like to come home, and we'd keep her safe at all costs if she *did*. The rest, I think I'd rather just wait to say when I see her."

My eyes burned, and my throat felt like there was a tight hand around it.

"You still believe she'll come back?" the same reporter asked.

He nodded. "I know she will. It just takes time." My dad picked up a paper from the podium. "That's all the questions I'm answerin' today. I'll turn ya over to FBI Agent Clarence Minton." He gave a nod. "Thank you."

The crowd of reporters roared with questions again, but my dad ignored them, shook the agent's hand, then walked down the steps of the courthouse while being protected by two police officers.

I sat back in the couch. My brain didn't know what

thought to think. The house was gone. Patty was dead. I missed my dad... There was nothing I could do about missing my dad. Going home wasn't an option, so I had to put it out of my mind and prioritize.

What did the house being burned down mean? Arson wasn't something Henry usually did unless he was trying to dispose of something or send a message. If he was sending a message, it likely wasn't for me. Patty being killed though... that wasn't good. It sounded like a move Henry would make, which meant something serious happened. Patty talked to someone or told something he wasn't supposed to. There was a reason I didn't put myself out there, tell everything and hope the police or other authorities could keep me safe. If there was a dirty cop, Henry would find them and offer a lot of money to get what he wanted. So, what had Patty told? And to whom?

———❈———

I jumped at the knock on my door.

"Nelson, can I come in?" Ryan called from outside the door.

I answered with a, "Yeah," but my voice failed, and I had to do it again.

Ryan opened the door, saw me, looked up toward the third-floor landing, then came in and shut the door. "Hey... You okay?"

I nodded. "Yeah. Why?"

He shrugged. "You look jumpy." He walked further into the room and looked around. "Someone was desperate for you to stay."

I forced a smile and nodded. "Yeah."

"I wanted to catch you alone before we got to the Maslen's. Be careful around Roger. Grey doesn't ask questions, but Roger will ask plenty, so if you have to lie, make sure it's something he can't dig up, and make sure you can remember it."

I frowned. "Why would I need to lie?"

He held up his shoulders. "I'm just trying to help you. He's a shark, and the second he smells fear or blood, he'll attack. Grey and I will try to deflect as much as we can, but obviously, we can't save you from every question."

"I'll be a dolphin then."

Ryan raised an eyebrow and the side of his nose turned up a little.

"Dolphins fend off sharks." I'd read about it once.

He widened his eyes with an otherwise flat expression. "Be a careful dolphin then."

I nodded.

"Do you want me to open the door?" He pointed over his shoulder with his thumb. "You're gonna rub the skin off your damn hands if you keep it up."

I looked down at my hands not even realizing I'd been rubbing them together so hard it was starting to cause pain. "No." I pulled my hands apart and stood up. "We should go though."

Chapter 17

Bexley

The entryway of the Maslen's estate was an experience. A very large and elegant chandelier hung from the tall, sculpted ceiling. The tile on the floor was decorative, but not overdone. There were marble statues along the back wall, and it was incredible how life-like they looked. I'd never seen one in person before, so I really just wanted to go and have a closer look, but I couldn't.

"Oh, my goodness, look at your beautiful face. No wonder Grey is so in love with you." Cynthia, Grey's mother, stepped forward with her hands up to hold my cheeks. Her hair was light blonde and held perfectly in place, but didn't look stiff either. She had blue eyes that were sort of dull in color, but they were still pretty. She was about as tall as I was, slender, and a little younger looking than I would've expected. Her face was diamond shaped, and the apples of her cheeks were soft with smooth lines below them that curved down to her chin.

"Alright. We had this talk already. No touching

people's faces." Grey stopped Cynthia's hands.

She folded her hands together and looked at him stubbornly. "Then don't bring someone with such a sweet face." She looked at me. "It's so good to meet you, Bexley." She held out a hand to me with a bright smile.

"You too." I reached my hand out and held my breath behind a smile.

She took my hand in both of hers and looked at Grey. "She's perfect!" She laughed and dropped my hand.

I let out my breath quietly and balled up my hand at my side. It burned so badly and didn't stop just because she wasn't touching me anymore.

"And you." She stepped over toward Ryan and stood on her toes to hug him. "It's been too long since I've seen your grumpy face around here." She kissed his cheek.

"Probably because you keep calling me grumpy." He gave her a brief hug but looked uncomfortable doing so.

Cynthia stepped back with a brilliant smile. "Then don't look so grumpy." She turned to Grey. "And you," she pinched Grey's cheeks with one hand, making his lips pucker slightly, "didn't call me back last night."

"I was busy, then tired. I didn't want you telling me how tired I look, so I went to bed." Grey smiled at her.

"I suppose I'll accept that." She kissed his cheek. "But you still look tired." She let go of his face. "We'll be eating outside on the terrace. I'll go get your father."

"Tell him to hurry up." Grey took my hand.

"No need. I'm already here. Bexley, it's good to meet you." Roger, his dad, held out a hand to me with a hard and unfriendly look on his face. He must have come from the room off to the right of us, and I hadn't seen him. I'd previously seen pictures of Roger, so I knew what to expect. He was taller than Grey, but a couple inches shorter than Ryan. Roger had a slightly more defined jawline than Grey, and dark eyes. His hair was graying from dark brown, but perfectly combed. Just in stature, he was intimidating.

"You too." I forced a smile and shook his hand.

"Shall we?" Cynthia directed her hand down the hallway after Roger dropped my hand.

Grey put a gentle hand on my back to get me to go first. I forced another smile at Cynthia and stepped forward.

"Did you see the S&P this morning?" Roger asked Grey from behind me.

"I told you it was on its way up."

"Always business with those two," Cynthia laughed quietly as she walked next to me. "I hear you've been helping Grey quite a bit."

"Just paperwork," I shook my head.

"I worked for Roger forever ago. I started out as his secretary and ten months later we were ready to get married."

"Mom." Grey had a warning tone.

She looked back. "I'm not implying anything." She held up her hands. "I was just making conversation." Cynthia looked at me again. "I hope you like quiche. I know it's not that fancy, but Georgia, our cook, does it just excellent."

I shook my head. "I've never had it before." Nor had I heard of it. Grey's habit of finding foods I'd never heard of must have come from his mother.

"Then you're in for a treat. You three didn't eat already this morning, did you?" She looked at Ryan.

He shook his head. "No."

Cynthia raised an eyebrow and looked at me.

"We haven't," I confirmed quietly.

"You have such a lovely voice. Has anybody ever told you that?"

"Stop your gushing, Cynthia," Roger said in a gruff tone. "You're going to drive the poor girl out of her skull."

"Oh hush. This is why the boys never bring anyone over. Bitter old man."

I pressed my lips together to keep from laughing. I hadn't expected her to be so... verbal.

"Just out here, Darling." Cynthia directed her hand through a glass door that went outside.

I cringed a little. I really hated being called Darling, and having to step through the door first to keep up appearances made it worse. I stepped to the side to wait for Grey and Ryan. We sat down at the table and I didn't do anything until everyone else did. It was always my rule.

When I'd first gotten out on my own, I'd been invited to stay in the home of a woman whom I'd helped escape from the house in Tennessee. I was embarrassingly reminded that people didn't often eat with their hands, and sometimes people prayed before they ate. I could remember having normal dinners with my parents and siblings, but the memories had become faded, and didn't come back until after the awkward occurrence of me eating like an animal at the lady's table.

"I hope no one was waiting on me. I'm old and slow."

Everyone looked back toward the house, including myself. Willum Maslen, Grey's grandfather, walked toward us. He was just about as tall as Grey, maybe an inch or two taller, had white hair, a wooden cane, gold-rimmed glasses, and looked like an older version of Grey. Besides age, the only difference in appearance was Willum had brown eyes instead of blue.

"We just sat, Willum," Cynthia said graciously.

Grey took my hand and stood, so I did too, and so did Ryan.

"Good Morning, Pops," Grey said with a slight laugh.

"Morning!? Eleven o'clock is damn near afternoon. Brunch," he scoffed. "Ridiculous. Making me wait this long just for breakfast, skipping lunch and waiting exhausting hours for dinner." He shook Grey and Ryan's hands as he ranted, then turned to me.

"Pops, this is Bex. B, this is my grandpa, Willum."

"Boy oh boy. Look at this beautiful young lady. How are you, Girly?" Willum smiled kindly at me and held out a hand, palm up.

"I'm okay, thank you. It's nice to meet you." I reached out my hand with a polite smile. "I've heard many great things about you."

Instead of shaking my hand, Willum held it between his. "Of course you have. I'm a fairly lovable character." He stepped a little closer. "It's my son you have to watch out for," he mumbled to me as he leaned in, then winked.

"I thought you claimed we were starving you. Sit down so we can eat," Roger grumbled with irritation.

Willum looked past me. "Just go on, prove me right." Willum patted my hand and let go. "Have a seat, dear."

I turned, glancing at Grey who was smiling at me, then sat with him and Ryan. Willum made his way around to the other side of the table and sat beside Cynthia. She nodded at one of the maids that was standing in wait to serve the food.

"So, Bexley, what is it your family does for work?" Roger unfolded his napkin and put it on his lap.

"Dad. Seriously?"

"What?" He frowned at Grey.

"Her parents have passed, Roger. Grey told us that already." Cynthia spoke patiently, passing the cream to Willum. "I'm sorry, Bexley," she gave me a sympathetic smile, "you tell him something, and it goes in one ear and right out the other if it doesn't involve business."

"It's okay." I shook my head and gave a polite smile. I looked at Roger. "My father was a doctor and my mother stayed at home." It was the answer I gave whenever the subject came up, and it was true of the forged records that were available to the public. The person who'd created my identity made sure to create somewhat of a paper trail to go with it. I also made sure the fakes resembled Patty and Helen to some degree because it was easier to remember more truths than lies.

"A doctor, huh? What area of medicine did he specialize in?"

I hadn't been asked that before. It stumped me for a moment because I had to make sure my answer was a safe one.

"Just a general doctor, I guess. He worked at the clinic in the town we lived in."

"So, family medicine then. Was he successful?"

I was stumped again. "I don't know."

"You don't know?" Roger laughed a little. "Well, did he do well at it, or didn't he?"

"Dad, come on." Grey frowned at Roger and shook his head.

"Dear, perhaps more current events are appropriate?" Cynthia looked at Roger expectantly as the maid set a small dish of fruit on top of the beautiful china plate in front of her.

"Alright then." Roger leaned back to let another maid set down his dish of fruit. "Have you decided on a degree yet?"

I nodded. "I'd like to get my law degree." I'd chosen it because of my dad. This morning I'd learned he was now a judge, and maybe that would be the end goal for me, but I didn't know.

"What type of law do you intend on specializing in?"

I shook my head. "I'm not sure yet. I'd like to wait until I get a little closer to law school and use the time to do some research and figure it out."

Roger looked me over for a moment, then picked up his fork. "I think that's wise... You should consider corporate law. There's good money in it."

I nodded. "I'll look into it." I didn't know what else to say. It didn't sound interesting, but I honestly didn't know much about it.

"What day does class start for you, Bexley?" Cynthia asked with a kind smile.

I gave a polite smile. "Next Monday."

"Have you gotten your books already?" Roger removed a piece of pineapple from his dish and set it aside.

I nodded. "I got them when I was in Seattle last."

"How many credits are you taking?"

I looked at Willum, who'd asked. "Just thirteen this semester. Hopefully by next semester, I'll have a better idea of how many classes I can handle."

Cynthia poured a small amount of milk into her tea and asked, "Are your classes online, or at the school?"

"Three are online, one at school." I forced a small smile.

"Can she eat now? She hasn't been allowed to touch her food." Grey's voice was slightly irritated.

"Of course. I'm sorry, Bexley," Cynthia responded gracefully with a smile.

"It's alright."

"Ryan, what's on the agenda for you this semester? And have you finally figured out what you want to do?" Willum smiled across the table at Ryan.

"Outside fork," Grey whispered when he noticed me looking at the setting in front of me.

I gave a barely noticeable nod. It wasn't the fork choice that was confusing me, it was the fruit in the bowl. There were fruits I was unfamiliar with. One was green and was shaped like a star after being cut, another was milky white with tiny black seeds, then one with a dark skin that turned white and had yellow seeds. There were also smaller red translucent seeds that were loose inside the bowl. Only the pineapple, kiwi, and strawberries were familiar to me. I decided to try the milky white piece first.

"Have you had dragon fruit before?" Roger's voice was quiet.

I looked at him to see if it was me he was speaking to, then shook my head. I gave an impish smile out of embarrassment. I should've just eaten instead of taking so long to inspect what was in front of me.

"That's dragon fruit, the one with yellow seeds is passion fruit, the red seeds are pomegranate, then there's star fruit, kiwi, pineapple, and strawberries," Grey said quietly as he pointed each one out.

I nodded. Thankfully Cynthia and Willum were engaged in a conversation with Ryan and didn't notice. There would be no impressing Roger, but I didn't want Cynthia or Willum to think I was an idiot for not knowing what food was in front of me.

I tried each of the foreign fruits—not caring so much for the passion fruit because of the texture—but when I got around to the kiwi, my throat started to feel tight. It felt somewhat like I was about to cry, but I wasn't. I took a deep breath, trying to consciously open my throat, and ate another piece of kiwi. I nearly choked as I swallowed, and my throat felt so tight it was becoming hard to breathe.

"Are you alright, Darling?" Cynthia asked after I held my throat because I couldn't help but cough.

I shook my head and struggled to get a breath through my throat. It made me feel like I was being choked which made my heart race and fear set in.

"What's wrong, B?" Grey pulled the cloth napkin from his lap and set it on the table.

I shook my head again. "I can hardly breathe." I

could hardly speak either.

"Is she having an allergic reaction?" Cynthia asked. "Emil, there's Benadryl in my bathroom. It's behind the mirror on the left."

I hadn't thought of it because I'd never experienced it or witnessed someone with an allergy that wasn't seasonal.

"Benadryl won't cut it," Grey said quickly and looked behind him at Ryan. "There's an EpiPen in my glovebox."

Ryan got up quickly and ran. I grabbed Grey's hand as soon as he looked at me because I couldn't get in a breath and my mind was filled with memories of being choked.

"It's okay." Grey reached his hands up to my jaw. "Tip your head back a little, try as hard as you can to get a breath."

I was already trying and making a terrible wheezing sound.

"What's she allergic to?" Cynthia asked as she got up.

"I don't know. She probably hasn't had half of these fruits before." Grey held my face in place when I tried to look to see where Cynthia was going. "No, keep your head straight, B. Look at me."

I grabbed his wrists because I wanted his hands off of me. My skin was burning, I was honestly terrified I was going to die, and my mind was screaming at me with memories I couldn't get under control.

"You're okay. I know you're scared. Ryan's grabbing the EpiPen and you'll be fine."

I didn't know what an EpiPen was, so Grey trying to reassure me wasn't helping. Tears were filling my eyes as a response from being unable to breathe and the volume of my thoughts became louder.

"I got it!" Ryan yelled from somewhere in the house. Grey turned his head to look, and I turned mine. It was probably two or three seconds before Ryan ran out, but it felt like several minutes.

"Here." Ryan handed Grey something that looked like a marker.

"Thanks." Grey grabbed it quickly and pulled a cap off the top. "Hold still, B." He grabbed my leg, just above the knee and slammed the marker looking thing into my thigh. I didn't realize there was a needle right away until I tried to move my leg away from Grey's hand. "No! Don't move! Three. Four. Five. Six. Seven. Eight. Nine. Ten." Grey pulled whatever he'd stabbed me with away from my leg and let go of my knee. "Keep trying to breathe. It should work fast." He looked at Ryan. "Did you bring the second one?"

Ryan showed another in his hand.

"Oh, I feel awful." Cynthia rubbed the back of my shoulder, and I arched my back forward to get her hand off me.

"No, don't touch her. She has a hard time with it." Grey looked at me like he was scared and worried.

"We need to get her to the hospital." Ryan held out a hand to me. "Come on."

I shook my head and covered my mouth because I was finally able to get in a wheezing breath. There was no way in hell I was going to the hospital, but I also couldn't stand. I was too dizzy, my skin felt charged with electricity, and one more touch would send me out of my mind.

"B, we have to. You could have a second reaction. We have to go." Grey held his hand out in front of me.

"Well, give the girl a damn minute to get breathing again," Willum chided.

Ryan shook his head. "We have a second EpiPen. Just wait a minute."

"Should we just call for an ambulance?" Cynthia asked quietly.

Grey shook his head. "No. It's working, we can take her in." He held his hand out for the other EpiPen and Ryan gave it to him. He looked at me and held the pen out to me. "If you feel like your throat is closing again or it's not getting better in two minutes, you pull this top part off, and stab yourself in the same spot. You want to get the large muscle in your leg. Okay?" He looked saddened more than worried, but both expressions were there.

I took it and nodded. My throat was still tight, and I was trying to catch up on breathing, but there were too many people around me, my skin continued to burn, and I wanted to leave, so I reached out my hand to Ryan. He helped me stand and Grey stood with me, keeping a hand near my elbow in case I fell.

"You guys call later. Let us know everything's okay," Willum said as he extended his hand to me.

I forced a smile and nodded as I gripped his hand lightly out of politeness, but the bones in my arm hurt from the feeling of electrical shock in my hands.

"Make sure they run an allergy panel on her, Grey," Cynthia said as I walked away with Ryan.

"I know. She'll be fine. I'll call later." Grey stepped ahead of Ryan and I and opened one of the French doors to the house.

I waited until we were in the car before I protested going to the hospital again.

"B, you have to. The Epi only lasts so long, and you could have another reaction. All they're gonna do is draw some blood, check your throat, and make you sit there for four hours. If everything's clear, they'll send you home." Grey turned his head briefly to look at me from the driver's seat.

I looked at Ryan wondering if it was true, or if he'd find a compromise or excuse for me not to go.

He pulled back the corner of his mouth. "It's not

something to mess with."

I looked away from him at the back of the passenger seat in front of me while my heart pounded so hard it made me dizzy. In Mexico, I'd still been too desensitized from my childhood to be as terrified as I was now. I'd also been under a cloud of drugs on the days I didn't have a procedure. Now, I was sober and far enough away from the torture to be terrified of it happening again.

When we got to the hospital, I felt like I was walking to my death. For a moment, I considered running until my legs gave out, but Ryan would catch me before I got even five feet from them. The closer we got to the door, the more scared I got, and at a certain point I was ready to fight to not go in.

"I can't do it," I said as I turned. If Grey wouldn't take me home, I'd get a taxi. I didn't care.

"Bex." Grey spoke my name rebukingly as if I'd cussed at someone. "Hey."

I shook my head, wrapping my arms around myself to keep from being grabbed, and didn't stop walking.

"Nelson, we're not gonna let anything happen." I could almost hear Ryan rolling his eyes behind me.

"B, hang on a second." Grey got in front of me and reached toward me to hold my arms.

I stopped, stepped back, and put my hands up. My body was a live wire with a constant pulse of shocks, and I really couldn't take any more.

"Okay. I'm not touching you. Just stop for a second and talk to me." He let out a breath. "What's the problem? Is it just you don't want to be touched? Because we can tell them to keep it to the bare minimum."

I had to tell him something, I just didn't know how much I could say and still convince him.

"Love, we can't help if you won't say anything. I don't know if you don't believe me that this is life threatening and serious, or... What am I missing here?"

As soon as I unclenched my jaw to speak, it trembled with the rest of me. "He was a do—" My voice momentarily froze, and I shook my head—wrapping my arms around me again, but for security this time—and tried again. "He was a doctor..." I shook my head. "I can't go in there."

"Nelson, we won't let anything happen to you. Grey's a black belt and I'm just mean. We'd break someone's neck before we let anyone hurt you." Ryan's voice didn't have its usual bitterness.

I shook my head.

"Not only that, but my dad owns this hospital. If someone did something, they'd be over in a split second. Despite the inability for a normal person to tell, my dad likes you, or he would have been a huge asshole at the table. So, you'll be perfectly safe in there. And if you want Ryan and I to sit there and never leave the room, you got it. But your skin is still splotchy, you could have a second attack, and it can be worse the second time, so we need to go in... Please, trust me."

I closed my eyes because I wanted to cry. It wouldn't help a damn thing, it wouldn't make me feel any better, but I wanted to so I could have one less thing I was trying not to do.

"We won't leave your side. Even if they have some bullshit excuse about not being allowed to go with you. I promise." Grey's voice was less pleading, and quieter.

I felt like I had no choice, so I turned around. Ryan and Grey walked on either side of me like a pair of bodyguards, but it made me feel like I was being escorted to a client's house. It'd only happened four or five times, but Henry had his men fly me to unknown locations to be pimped out to higher profile clients.

"I'll go to the counter, you guys find a place to sit for a second," Grey said quietly once we were inside. "Do you have your insurance card and license, B?"

I let my purse slip off my shoulder and gave him the whole thing.

"Okay. Go sit down. I'll be right there."

Ryan and I turned toward the waiting area and I held onto his arm just because I didn't want him to walk behind me, but my back felt overly exposed.

He put his other hand over mine. "I have to do this with Tim too, so I get it."

We turned and sat down in a corner set of chairs where the rest of the open room was visible.

"You ca-can't le-ave me a-alone." My lungs were in on the same attack of fear running through me.

He shook his head and squeezed my hand tightly. "I won't. I promise."

If Ryan weren't there, I wouldn't do it, no matter how much Grey pushed. Grey was the nonconfrontational kind, and Ryan would beat a person until death was a plea they couldn't utter from their busted jaw. He was like having Ben by my side. In my mind, a hospital was no different than the doctor's office I'd been kidnapped from, and Patty was a doctor... He'd helped me every time Helen, Henry, or a client had injured me, but it came at the cost of being touched. Even though it was all over the news that Patty was dead, I wasn't sure I believed it. He was very clever, and even Henry had underestimated Patty because he was so outwardly messy. For all I knew, he'd already found me, slipped into the Maslen's house as a staff member, poisoned me with something, and was waiting in the nearest hospital for me to be alone.

"Come on. Grey got you the private suite." Ryan slid forward and waited for me to get up.

"What are you talking about?" I asked quietly as we stood.

"When you're a Maslen, you get your own private room and private doctors. No sitting in an ER listening to druggies scream it out and people's bodily smells." He pulled me closer to him as we walked past a homeless-looking woman who was talking to herself and playing with a ball of tin foil.

"People can't help it," I whispered. I could only imagine what he would have said about me as a child. The house had always reeked from the bucket left in the basement for me or other kids to go to the bathroom in. And I was only granted the privilege of a bath or shower when Patty allowed, so I almost always smelled. My clothes had been no better than a homeless person's— when I was allowed to wear them. Being able to wear clothes was a rare treat that usually only happened for a week out of every month while I was on my period. Patty used to call it 'the curse,' and told me I was shameful, and I had to hide my shame from god by wearing clothes. Being shameful for a week was a blessing.

The room we were brought to barely looked like a hospital room at all. The thing that gave it away were the plug-ins for oxygen and whatever else they put on the walls to make things readily available. I was asked to change into a hospital gown, and I refused. There was no amount of convincing that Grey or Ryan could do to change my mind, but surprisingly, neither argued. He simply told the nurse they'd have to cut my dress if something happened. She began to protest and Grey snapped at her harshly. After that, she was agreeable about everything; including letting me place my own IV in. I knew how because of Patty. Ryan cringed as he watched me, and Grey just sat there with guilt on his face. He'd been wearing it since his parent's house, but I didn't understand what he had to be guilty for. I was the one being difficult.

Sitting there for four hours was torture. Ryan and Grey tried to keep a conversation going for a while, but Ryan fell asleep, and Grey had a work phone call. He didn't leave the room, but it left me with no one to distract me from my thoughts. The heart monitor would chime periodically because I would panic about where I was, and my heart rate would jump too high. The doctor offered anti-anxiety medication and I refused it. As much as I wanted to be on anything to take the edge off, I couldn't let myself fall down the rabbit hole again. That only left horrible memories...

7 Years Prior

"You wanna die, bitch!?" The back of Henry's hand struck my cheek with all the force he had. "Huh!?"

I took the hit and just closed my eyes to get through the climax of pain. If I cried, it'd just be worse.

Henry grabbed me by the hair and pulled me against him. "I asked you a question!" His spit hit me in the face, then a gun was shoved into the soft flesh under my jaw. "Here! Do it! Pull the trigger!"

I reached my hand up in a quick motion and I did, but the gun only clicked. At almost the same time, a chair hit Henry in the head from the side and knocked him over. I cried in honest-to-god despair that the gun didn't blow my brains out at the ceiling.

Toby tried to grab the other gun from Henry's jacket holster and Henry hit him, but Toby didn't stop fighting. I pinched my arm as hard as I could to pull my mind back into place, then grabbed the gun from Henry as soon as I could without getting hurt. I was pregnant and due anytime, and while I didn't want the baby, Toby did. It was my only insurance policy if we got out. He felt so guilty having to do what he did, that he swore he'd get me out and take care of me. He was trying to keep the promises he made me, so I had to help.

I pointed the gun and pulled the trigger. Henry

yelled out and grabbed his shoulder.

"Run!" Toby said as he scrambled his way up and grabbed my arm to make me go. He grabbed the gun from me and started shooting at the locks on the door. It took both of us to yank it free, but we ran as hard and as fast as we could once it was.

"Hannah!" Toby yelled just before I was taken down to the ground.

"No!" I slapped and I fought as hard as I could against Patty.

Toby tried to fire Henry's gun, but it just clicked, so he used it to hit Patty in the head. It knocked him off of me, which gave me only enough time to get out of the way before Toby and Patty started pounding on each other. I grabbed Patty around the neck and pulled him back with every bit of strength I had. He was slamming Toby's head into the ground repeatedly.

"STOP IT!" I screamed as hard as I could, trying to save Toby.

As soon as Patty reached back to try and get my arm from around his neck, Toby kicked and got out from under him.

"RUN!" I screamed at him.

A car screeched to a stop on the road about thirty feet ahead of us.

"Hey!" A man yelled as he got out of the truck.

"Get him away from my daughter!" Patty yelled, pointing at Toby. "He raped her! I'll kill him!"

Toby looked horrified and turned to face the man. "Help us! He kidnapped us!"

"Shut your mouth and get in the truck, Son. I'm taking you in."

Toby shook his head and looked at me. He hadn't heard the man because of the wind. His implants made it so he could hear, but he didn't always understand. I knew we weren't both going to get out, but if one of us did, it had to be him.

"Take him!" I yelled at the man. "Have him arrested! He hurt my Daddy!"

"What?" Toby looked shocked and hurt. "No." He looked at the man. "No. He keeps us in the basement! He kidnapped her. She's Hannah Lawrence!"

The man put a hand on the gun holstered on his side. "Get in the truck, Son. Or you're gonna have a world of trouble on your hands."

"Leave, Toby!" I yelled.

Present

It still disgusted me that the person who'd held me captive was also the person who helped me escape. We were in a car with one of Henry's puppets, on our way to a town in Northern Minnesota, and we'd stopped in Des Moines, Iowa. Patty asked the puppet to stop at a restaurant and go in to get us something to eat. When the puppet got out of the car, Patty quickly uncuffed me and took me to the bus station next door.

7 Years Prior

"Come on, keep up, Darlin'. I know you're hurtin'." Patty kept going forward, holding onto my arm to help me keep up with him. "I gotta get ya outta here. You're gettin' too old as is, and now that Toby's out, Henry'll kill ya the second that baby comes out. Now listen to me," he stopped and turned to face me, but looked around nervously first. "Ya can't go home. I know it's all ya ever wanted, but he'll find ya there. And ya can't go stayin' with Toby neither. I'm gonna send ya on a bus to Omaha, you wait somewhere public with lots of people till you can't wait no more. You have that baby, leave it for Toby

204

at the feed store, then ya run, and ya don't stop. Ya don't go back, ya don't call or write. Henry'll be waitin' for you to mess up, so don't. Ya hear me?" Patty was near tears as he spoke. He was sick, but in his sick way, he did love me.

I nodded.

"Alright. You just go along with what I say in there. I'm gonna get ya a bus ticket and see ya off. It's leavin' in just a minute." He looked at his watch, then we went inside.

I didn't know what to do or how to act. I hadn't been in a place with so many people since the day I'd been stolen. It was frightening.

"Mornin', I need a ticket for the next out to Omaha, for my niece here." Patty smiled and pulled out his wallet. He wasn't an ugly looking man, he looked like my dad, except Patty had dark blonde hair and wasn't as lean. He wore thin gold framed glasses and always had clean pressed clothes. Clothes that I pressed.

"Name?" The lady behind the window asked.

"Rebecca Neilson," Patty answered.

"Age?"

"She just turned eighteen. She came out here to spend her birthday with her grandparents and me." Patty looked back at me with a smile.

I forced a quick smile because I knew I was supposed to.

"Alright, next bus is just about ready to leave."

"I know. We were cuttin' it close. Ran into a tractor on the highway for a few minutes." Patty pulled out a twenty from his wallet.

"Okay, fifteen even."

Patty passed the money through the opening in the window. The lady passed a five and a ticket back. "Hun, you can go outside, and it'll be the bus on the side of the building over here." She pointed.

"Thank you, Ma'am." Patty nodded once.

I thought he was going to go outside, but he didn't, instead, he went up to a vending machine. Ben had gone to help Emily with one the day I was taken because it ate her dollar. Patty put the five in, got something out, took the change, got something else, then went to one that had drinks inside. He got a bottle of water out, then we went outside.

"Alright. This is your ticket. Don't lose it. They'll ask ya for it when ya get on."

I took the ticket and looked at it.

"Don't talk to anyone on the bus. If ya get caught for any reason, it's best ya just don't say nothin'. Don't ever tell anyone your real name. I got ya a fake ID, you're eighteen, so ya can't buy alcohol, but ya don't need it anyhow. It's a bad habit." He swallowed hard. "There's ten thousand dollars in this envelope. Don't lose it, and don't spend it all. Use it to get a cheap motel that takes cash, eat cheap, find yourself a job... Keep your head down 'till ya get where you're goin'. Most places got cameras everywhere. Walk as much as ya can, don't try to fly on a plane, and if ya take a bus, only take it for a short distance, just an hour or two."

I nodded, taking the envelope, the water, and odd things he got from the vending machine.

"I shoulda bought ya this stuff when I had ya. I don't know why I didn't." Patty's chin trembled. "I shoulda done it all different." He pulled me against his chest and hugged me tightly, sobbing into the top of my head. "I love ya, Darlin'. I'm so sorry."

I didn't know what to do but stand there. If I was really being given a free pass to get away, I didn't want to ruin it by pushing him off and making him snap.

"Last call for Omaha!" A lady called. "Last call for Omaha!"

"That's you. Anderson Feed. That's where ya gotta

find when ya get there. You'll be safe for a short time, cause they got police watchin' the store. Go on now." He let go of me and gave a gentle push toward the bus.

I went forward and half expected to be shot in the back of the head, but I got on. The lady asked for my ticket, ripped it, and gave me a piece back. I looked out the windows as I walked back to find an open seat, and Patty braved a smile and held up a hand. Instead of waving back, I just took a seat in the middle of the bus. My stomach hurt really bad every fifteen minutes or so, so I knew the baby was coming soon. I just hoped I'd make it to Toby's before that happened.

Chapter 18

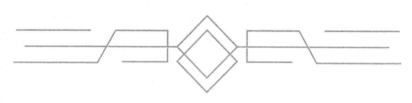

Grey

I knocked quietly on Bex's door and grabbed the handle to open it. She'd been up in her room since we got home from the hospital. I imagined that after spending five hours completely petrified, she was probably exhausted.

"Hey." I saw her and couldn't help the smile on my face. She was sitting on the couch in a cream-colored sweater that made her look warm and comfortable. "I came to see if you were up for going out to dinner with my parents. My mom feels thoroughly cheated after this morning." I sat down on the couch, next to the mess of papers she had around her.

She nodded. "Okay."

"You don't have to. I know you're probably wiped out after sitting there biting your nails at the hospital for most of the afternoon, but I told my mom I'd ask." I picked up a set of papers and looked at them before I put them back. She'd been working.

Bex shook her head. "It's okay." She closed her laptop and started collecting the papers around her. "I need to get over it and stop hiding."

"That's not at *all* why I came up here." Obviously, her father had done something to her, and that made her reaction understandable.

Bex shook her head, setting the stack of papers on the coffee table, and looked at me. "No, I know. It's my own conclusion." She took in a breath and let it out. "I'm sorry for earlier. I don't mean to be difficult, I just..." She let out another breath and shook her head.

I shook my head, moving my arm along the back of the couch so I could touch her shoulder. The sweater was as soft as it made her look. "You were scared, you shouldn't have to apologize for that..." Not only that, it didn't matter how difficult she'd been, I'd done something worse. I'd paid off her doctor to get an extra tube of blood from her. Ryan knew who she was, had all the information locked up, and I wanted to at least know. I wouldn't confront her, or even do anything if there was something to be done, because I believed Ryan when he said she could be killed, but... I needed to know.

She stared at her hands for a moment and the muscle on the side of her neck tensed for just a brief second. "Do you know what Munchhausen syndrome by proxy is?" Bex looked at me again.

I shook my head.

She pulled back the corner of her mouth and traced the edge of her laptop with her finger. "I didn't either until a couple years ago when I saw a movie... It's where a parent or a caregiver makes someone sick or injures them so they can heal them."

I tried not to react, she wouldn't keep talking if I did, but I felt immediately sick to my stomach as I drew conclusions.

"It went on for years." She shook her head. "It wasn't just me, but I got the worst of it... And you seemed really

upset that I stuck to Ryan so closely, and I'm sorry."

I rubbed her shoulder. "No, I was just worried about you. Ryan's an angry giant, so I get why you stick closer to him when you don't feel safe." It was a little hurtful that she didn't trust me as much, but I tried to understand that Ryan had me beat simply because he was an angry hot head. I felt bad for snapping at the nurse and Ryan would have done it regardless of Bex being scared, and without remorse.

"You did a lot he couldn't have though... and I appreciate it." She shrugged and finally mustered up the courage to look at me again. "You also get points for not falling asleep and snoring loudly."

I laughed. "Yeah. He and Tim are both really *loud* sleepers."

She moved over to my side and rested her cheek against the front of my shoulder. It was the first time she'd ever instigate a hug, and I was ready to burst over it but still careful when I wrapped my arms around her.

"Thank you."

"Anytime, Beautiful." I took my chances at hugging her just a little tighter. "Especially if this is the thanks."

"What time do we have to leave?"

"Right now, I don't want to. We could just sit here all night."

"Except I haven't eaten anything but that fruit and I'm hungry."

I'd tried to get her to eat something after we left the hospital, but she'd been too upset. I didn't want to point that out to her though. "They'll be here in a few."

"Okay. I'll get changed then."

"No. We're not going anywhere fancy." My mom might have said something to me because Bex was in jeans, but she looked so soft and warm, I didn't want her to change. I already felt badly that I'd implied the clothes she had weren't good enough for work. She didn't understand being in or near the Maslen family required a dress code.

The next day I kept Bex close. She mostly worked from the couch in my office. I was a little worried at how people would treat her, but also worried about how she'd be in an office setting. She'd never done it before. I wanted her to feel comfortable because I wanted her to do well and stay. I loved her the moment I saw the picture of her, and every day after I loved her more. I hated that I'd only known her five months because I wanted to propose and marry her. It wasn't always there, and it'd taken a lot to bring it out, but when she was content or happy, she just... shined. Her smile was so beautiful, and the personality she kept buried so deep would come out.

Watching her work, she was just radiant. Bex was happy to be doing something meaningful. I'd put her in charge of contract renewals, which pissed Erin off something fierce, but she'd have to meet with each of my clients and bring out her eloquent charm. I'd still be there to seal the deal, but I was throwing her into something she'd thrive at. Her protective wall was thick, but I'd keep pulling back layers.

"You've been staring at me for almost five minutes now." Bex looked at me from her laptop with an expectant look.

I laughed. "Yeah, and you noticed, so you're indirectly staring back." I smiled at her hoping to get one back.

She shook her head with the slightest of a smile and went back to writing her emails. "You're distracting me. Stop staring and work."

"You got it, boss lady." I smiled, shaking my head and turned my chair to look up at my screens on the wall.

My desk-phone rang and I picked it up. Normally, Erin just used the intercom, but this meant I was getting the phone call I'd been waiting all day for.

"Mr. Schaffer is on the phone. Did you wanna step

out?"

"Yes. Thank you." I hung up the phone, grabbed my cell phone, and got up. "I'll be back, B. Do you want tea or anything when I come back?" I quickly set the parameters for the trades I was currently making.

"Only if you're already going down to get coffee. Otherwise, I'm fine."

"Okay. I'll be back. Ask Erin if you need something." I walked across the room and opened the door.

"Okay."

I closed my door behind me. "Do a soft transfer. I need a minute to get down to my car. I have something in there I need," I lied to Erin before going to the elevator.

My dad had been known to bug the building and I wanted to make sure my conversation wasn't heard. I called another computer guy that wasn't Tim—because I couldn't trust Tim with the information—and had him make sure that the call would come through without anyone being able to listen in. As soon as he gave me the go ahead, Erin called and transferred the line.

"Thanks for getting back to me so fast, Aaron," I said when I answered.

"No problem. I got the results for you, but my computer seems to be having an issue."

"Nope. That's just my guy making sure only my eyes see the results. Sorry."

"Oh. Okay. Um... Do you need me for anything then?" Aaron was stumped but seemingly unoffended.

"I may need you for future tasks, but I think this one is wrapped up. You'll have your money by the end of the day." I opened my laptop as I spoke and watched as Justin, my other computer guy, transferred the information directly to me. He assured me that even *he* wouldn't see it.

"Okay. Thanks."

"Mm-hm." I reached over and tapped the screen on my phone to end the call. "Okay. Let's see where you came from, Beautiful," I whispered as I was about to click to open the file. I hesitated and wondered if I should really look. Nothing I could think of could make me love her less. What was stopping me was the devastatingly sad and afraid look she'd have on her face if she knew what I was doing. I didn't want to betray her, but I also didn't want to see anything happen to her or be blindsided later on down the road. I didn't believe her parents were dead. My instinct told me they were still out there and looking for her, and that was why she'd worked so hard to stay hidden.

After a few minutes of fighting myself, I decided her safety was worth the betrayal, so I clicked and opened the file.

"One hundred percent match for Hannah Lawrence, and six familial matches. Mother, Mildred Lawrence, father Donald Lawrence, brother Benjamin, sister Emily... Daughter Grace Anderson?" I frowned. "What?" Did she have a child, or was I reading something wrong? I scrolled a little further. "Uncle Patrick Lawrence..." Where did I hear that name recently? The names meant nothing if I couldn't look them up, so I called Justin.

"Did it not come through?" He asked when he answered.

"No, it did, but I need a ghost browser or something. Is that possible?"

"Everything is possible. Give me just a second. Your screen is gonna go blank for a second, but you'll get it all back."

"Okay. Next question, how do I save this file where no one will ever see it?"

"That would be a long process, and since I don't have access to it, very hard for me to do without having your laptop in front of me."

"That's okay. I shouldn't save it anyway." I let out a breath. "My screen just came back. Are we good?"

"We're good. Just shoot me a message when

you're done, and don't try to send anything out from your computer."

"Got it. Thanks."

"Mm-hm."

I hung up and pulled up the internet browser. I typed in Patrick's name first because I was certain I'd heard it recently. Looking up Bex's real name could be potentially fruitless... Or not.

"Oh shit," I breathed and took my hands away from my laptop. She was *Hannah Lawrence*... *The* Hannah Lawrence. It was such a normal name that I didn't think about it when I read it.

I shoved my hand through my hair and sat there for a minute... The shock of questions, then just the shock of Bex being Hannah, had me in a pause I didn't know what to do with. I couldn't seem to draw any conclusions or a plan of sorts. I didn't know a lot about Hannah Lawrence, because before today, she was just some kidnapped girl that people speculated might still be alive.

I closed my laptop, texted Justin, then texted Ryan to pick Bex up at four o'clock before texting Bex that I had to run to an unexpected meeting. There was nothing I could do with my thoughts running like civilians in an active war zone. I went to the only place I knew I could sort my thoughts and collect my questions.

＝／二◇二＼＝

"Didn't get enough harassment last night, huh?" Pops smiled up from his book.

"No." I walked around the couch and sat down.

"Either that lovely girl stole your smile, or your father did." Pops looked me up and down, losing his own smile. "What happened?" He set his book on the small table next to him.

"I don't know if I can really even talk about it..." I looked over to see if Pops' valet was still standing in the doorway and he was.

Pops raised his wrinkled hand and swatted the air

214

to signal Larry to leave. "Larry, get the doors and tell the staff to keep clear.

"Yes, Mr. Maslen," Larry answered.

I let out a breath and sank back in the couch. Pops didn't care about my posture like my parents. He was the one person in my family I could relax around. I didn't have to watch the words that came out of my mouth, keep up appearances, or anything else that was expected of me because of my name.

"Is a drink gonna make you talk or cry? I can't tell." Pops had sort of a shriveled but stumped look on his face and it was my favorite.

I laughed a little and rubbed at my forehead. "I don't know yet." I let out another breath and shook my head.

"Must be the girl. You've never looked like this over Sticklesworth."

Sticklesworth was what Pops called my dad behind his back because my dad acted like he had a stick up his ass. It was a way to laugh about it instead of wanting to kill him.

"I think it's both," I said quietly. "I told you about finding the money he laundered for that sex trafficking ring. Today, I found out she was a victim of it." Pops already knew how I found Bex. "I think he's had her followed because if it got out, she'd bring everything down..." I looked at him. "MWM would be done. Booting him out of the company wouldn't be enough."

Pops frowned. "You said she doesn't know anything, right?"

"She doesn't know who we are, she doesn't know what Dad did or that he was part of anything, but... if her identity came out, or what he did..." I pressed my lips together and shook my head. "The entire company will be done for."

Pops' frown stayed in place. "Who is she exactly?"

"I don't know if I should tell you that." I could think of a lot of reasons, and I was sure there were a hundred

more.

"Well... nothing's ever left this house before, and I'm ninety-five, so you could put a little poison in my drink, and I'll take it to my grave." Pops smiled at his own joke.

"It's not that." I shook my head. "It's Bex. She'd be humiliated." I trusted my Pops with everything. He was nothing like my father, and his loyalty to me was far greater than the company he built or my dad. "The entire country knows her name. She's been missing since she was little... I don't get it though; if my dad's been having her followed, why didn't he have any kind of reaction when he met her yesterday, or when I told him about her? I mean, he actually *likes* her. It's weird."

"She's a sweet girl, it's not *weird*... I don't know though. If she's got the power to crumble him, there'd be some kind of reaction out of him I'd think."

Something popped into my head. "Shit." My heart pounded. "The fruit." I sat forward immediately. "You don't think he tried to kill her, do you? I mean, he's got medical records on her. He could've known she was allergic to something in there or had something *put* in her food." And I'd left her at the office to be a sitting duck. "I gotta go." I stood up quickly.

"No, now hold on a minute," Pops demanded.

"No, I have to go get her. She's at the office right now."

"Just stop. Your dad's a jackass, but he's not stupid. He wouldn't have tried to kill her in his own house and run the risk of connections being drawn. Think about it. She's young, they'd do an autopsy, her name would get out, and stink would hit the fan. Sit down."

That was true. I didn't believe my dad was incapable, but I did believe he was too smart to get caught. If he wasn't, I would've had Pops' company back already.

"For argument's sake, let's say he doesn't know. You don't know if that drive thingy was really ever in his possession, you can't even prove he knew about that sex trafficking operation." Pops reached up and scratched the side of his forehead with his hand above his head. "Maybe someone else is responsible and they're using MWM as a storage facility."

"I can't think of who that'd be, and we know he knew enough to stop laundering for them." I shrugged. "And Kato Ling doesn't do coding for anybody but my dad. That drive was put together by Kato and my guy already proved that much."

Pop pinched his white goatee with his hand as he stared distantly in thought. "I don't know, Sunny... You took a lot of precautions to make sure he didn't find out you were with her until he met her because we wanted to gauge his reaction. I'm just not convinced he knows who she is."

"I know. Even at dinner last night, I kept waiting for *something*. Ryan too."

"Yep... Guess you're gonna have to decide how important she is to you. If something happens and word gets out, which side of the fence are you gonna be standing on?"

I let out a huff. "That's not fair."

"I think it is. Either you're in it with her, or you aren't."

"No, it's not fair because I *am* in it with her, which means everything you built will be gone. It's not fair, but she deserves to be the one I choose. I built my own company, I've done everything short of telling my dad to piss off to get out from under him and MWM, and I choose me and mine. The crap part is, the expense comes to you."

The corner of Pops' lip turned down and he shook his head. "I made my money and I've been out for damn near fifteen years now. I can't take it with me when I'm dead. I wanted you to have the company and bring some integrity back, but if the rubicon has been reached, then that's all there is, Sunny Boy."

I let out another huff and felt sick over the fact I was

letting my Pops down.

"You can build something just as great, Grey. You're almost twenty-eight and you've already knocked the pants off what I accomplished at that age."

"Because I had a leg up from you. You deserve to see your company stand tall again."

He shook his head. "Seeing my grandson stand from my knee is enough. Just get your brother on track. That I won't budge on." He waved dismissively and started to try to get up.

I laughed and stood to reach over and help him up. "Sam'll be fine. He just has to figure out what he wants first."

"Oh, I know. I just don't want him going through one of those party stages like you see on TV. Life isn't a party, it's a damn funeral that kicks you in the balls and makes you laugh because you can't cry." He shuffled slowly toward his desk.

I laughed. "I'd say it's not true, but I think I got kicked today."

"No. You decided what's important to your life. The ball kicking will happen if Sticklesworth finds out."

I smirked, but it was true.

"I can't see the damn buttons on this thing. Where's my glasses?" Pops was standing in front of his safe and turned to look for his glasses.

"In your shirt pocket."

"Oh, yeah. I hate being old. I thought for sure they'd figure out how to reverse aging by now, or at least make it less insufferable," he grumbled as he put his glasses on and entered the code into his safe.

"It could be worse, you could be sitting in a bed."

"I will be as soon as you leave. It's my nap time."

I looked at my watch. "Well, I think you're in luck. I need to get going." Bex would be leaving the office with Ryan by now.

"Well, just hold on a minute. You can't leave without

this." Pops closed the safe and turned to shuffle his way back to me.

I frowned a little and wondered what he would have been getting out of the safe for me.

"You keep this and give it to that pretty miss when you're both ready, but don't you dare let her lose it." He handed me an old matchbox.

I took it and opened it to find a ring on a cotton square. "You kept Granny's ring in a matchbox?"

"Sure did. When I proposed to that feisty woman, we barely had two pennies to rub together, and I couldn't afford a ring. My first commission check—the whole damn thing—went to that ring." Pops leaned on his cane with both hands and smiled. "The jeweler wouldn't give me a box unless I paid for it. So, she got the ring in a matchbox from my pocket."

I shook my head. "Are you sure? You didn't even give this to dad when he asked."

"It wasn't my choice. Granny hated your mother. She loved the hell out of you though." He gave a beaming smile. "You treat that pretty girl good. She looks at you the way Granny looked at me, so I know she can put up with you."

I raised an eyebrow. "I still plan to wait a little bit. It's only been five months."

"I proposed to Martha after three, I don't care what your excuse is! You find a good, beautiful woman like that and you marry her!"

I laughed. "I will, but I'm still waiting a couple months."

"You kids these days. You're soft. Can't commit to anything and you think you have loads of time." He shook his head with irritation.

"Yeah, well, I am who you raised me to be."

"Damn right, and don't you forget it." He swatted me lightly with the hook of his cane. "Run off to your girl now. Leave me to nap in peace. With any luck, I won't wake up."

I shook my head. "You're shameless, man." I held out my hand. "Thank you."

Pops took my hand but didn't let go. "I meant what I said about being good to her. If she's been through something like that, she's got a lot of fear behind that pretty face. Your Granny didn't have it quite so hard, but her father was a real bastard. It took years before she wasn't afraid, and sometimes it was infuriating. You be patient, and you be good to her." He nodded once.

I nodded. "I know."

"And you can't fix her, so don't try. If she feels loved enough, she'll fix herself."

I smiled a little. "She's not broken, just scared."

Pops smiled and put his hand to my cheek. "You make me proud."

"I'm always working on it. I gotta go."

"Yeah." He popped my cheek. "Just remember, your mom doesn't get Granny's china when I don't wake up. Granny will turn in her grave and I'll have to turn with her."

"Shameless." I shook my head with a smile and turned to the door. "Love ya, Pops. Thanks for the talk and the ring."

"Love you too, Sunny Boy. I'll have someone send the insurance papers for that ring."

Nothing had really been accomplished by seeing Pops, but I felt better. While I was driving, I tried to prioritize my thoughts. I had come to two conclusions. I needed to know more about Hannah so I could help Bex, and the rest didn't matter. I was officially ending the manhunt on my dad. If I exposed him in any way, I ran the risk of Bex getting hurt and I wouldn't do it.

On my way home, I stopped to get Bex some flowers. After getting back in my car, I texted Justin and had him make it so my laptop couldn't be traced again.

Doing research at home or at the office was too much of a risk. I started with whatever articles came up, then came across a book that was written by a guy named Toby Anderson. I would have purchased it, but I couldn't without it being traceable. I settled for a few excerpts and read the reviews people had left. Some of them were so detailed I wasn't sure if I wanted to read the book.

There was a woman named Helen who'd been in the house that Bex was locked in. And when Bex was eight, she was tied up in a bedsheet and put in the dryer while Helen held the door shut. Another excerpt talked about how Henry had beaten her to near unconsciousness at fourteen years old for letting her own baby bleed out from the umbilical cord—to keep it from being sold—then threw her and the dead baby into the basement. It wasn't until two days later that Henry left and Bex's uncle was allowed to go down, treat Bex's wounds, and bury the baby.

She'd been through things I couldn't even stomach to read. She'd had her fingernails peeled off, been tied down while a dog was allowed to attack her, whipped while she was forced to do dishes in scalding water, tied to a metal chair and electrocuted with a car battery, raped almost daily, and forced to kill and bury other children who were no longer of use in the trafficking operation. I sat there in my car as I grieved over the barbarity of what Bex had gone through. It didn't make sense for her to still be alive, both because of the extent to which she'd been continuously tortured, and because people had been through less and killed themselves.

For an hour, I sat there and tried to think of anything I could do, but Ryan's warning kept coming back. I had near endless money, but that didn't make me a match for the evil of Henry or Patrick. Never in my life had I been vindictive, and fighting for Bex could change that, but she didn't need more vindictiveness, she needed safety. I had to give her that, and also take my own father down.

The problem with letting go of my fight to end his reign over MWM was he could keep funding monsters like Henry who hurt little girls like Bex. I'd make the whole Maslen empire fall if I had to.

I texted my personal team of lawyers and scheduled a meeting. Before I made any moves, I had to make sure Bex was taken care of. She deserved every cent of my money and that meant making sure I didn't lose it. I was also going to put fail safes in place to make sure that even if I *did* lose my wealth, there'd be money stashed away for *her*. There would be nothing I could do until I got her to marry me, but I could plan until then.

When I walked into the house, I paused for a minute because of the music being played. It took me a second to figure out if it was the piano or if Bex had the stereo on, but it was the piano in the living room. I quietly let the door close to the garage, then walked next to the bottom of the staircase to peek down the hall into the living room. There she sat, at the piano... Her fingers were moving as if she'd dedicated her life to playing, and I didn't even know she *could*.

I sat at the bottom of the stairs, watching as Bex played Chopin's Harp Study with elegance. Her body swayed while her face seemed to feel the song's emotion. Even if I knew who she was, this was proof that there was far more I *didn't* know. Was this something that came naturally to her? Did someone teach her? How long had she been playing the piano, and why didn't she do it professionally? There was no music in front of her, she barely kept her eyes open to watch her hands... Muscle memory led her fingers along; timing her movements as she tapped the damper peddles.

After Bex was just about done with a second piece, I got up, went to the garage door, waited for the song to end, then opened the door. The alarm would chirp, letting her know I was home. It was likely she hadn't heard it over the piano before.

"B?" I called as I set my keys in the bowl and dropped my laptop bag for a second time, picking up the bouquet of peonies I'd gotten for her on the way home.

"Kitchen," she called back.

"Did you have the stereo on or something? I thought I heard music a minute ago." I walked around to the kitchen wondering if she'd confess.

Bex was sitting at the counter with her laptop in front of her like she hadn't been pouring her soul into the piano a second ago. "Yeah. I realized it was probably too loud."

"You didn't have to turn it off... Where's Ryan?" I kept the flowers behind my back as I stepped up beside her. It didn't make sense that she'd lie about playing the piano, but I wasn't going to embarrass her by forcing a confession.

"I sent him home because his level of grumpy was over the top." She closed her laptop, turned in the chair to face me, and I held out the bouquet of peonies to her. "You're leaving?" Bex looked at me like I was giving her bad news.

I laughed. "No. Did you want me to?" It hadn't occurred to me before, but I'd never given her flowers in person.

She shook her head and took the flowers. "You usually only get me flowers when you're going somewhere."

"I can take them back. Save them for two weeks from now," I teased as I went to take them back.

Bex held them away and smiled. "No. I like them." She stood, set the bouquet of flowers on the counter, and wrapped her arms around me. "Thank you."

I touched her cheek with the back of my fingers to feel the softness. "You're welcome... I'm sorry I left you stranded today. Something came up and I needed to go talk to Pops and clear my head." Now that I knew the truth, I understood why Ryan said he couldn't face her. I wanted to cry just looking at her. It was painful to see her honest eyes, know how incredibly sweet and thoughtful she was, and know she'd been tortured in the worst way. "Is everything okay?" She stepped back and watched my face carefully.

I wanted to tell her I knew and she didn't have to be afraid, that I would never tell her secret or expose her. It had nothing to do with MWM or the family image. I'd previously read about Henry Greer, suspecting it was *him* my father worked with, and he was dangerous.

Bex's face became more concerned when I didn't answer right away. "What happened?"

I shook my head and pulled the corner of my mouth back. "Nothing." I pulled her back into a hug and let out a breath. "But I'm really happy to be home right now, and that you're here." I kissed the top of her head. "I love being able to come home to you." And I wouldn't have to wait two weeks in between.

Bex loosened her arms and pulled back a little so she could look at me. "Don't make plans for Saturday."

I smiled. "What's Saturday?"

"You'll be gone on your birthday, so we're celebrating early." She gave a light smile, but her eyes showed more of her happiness.

"Do I get to know what we're doing, or is it a secret?"

Her smile grew and she shook her head. "You have to wait."

"You realize I'll harass you all week about it, right?" I smiled back, only because I didn't want her happiness to go unanswered.

She repressed her smile. "You realize I'm good at keeping secrets, right?"

I tried to keep as much of my smile as I could, but I felt sick again. "I'll still harass you. It doesn't matter if you tell me or not." I dropped my arms from around her. "There's some vases in the pantry for your flowers. I'm gonna go upstairs and take a shower. I wanna take you out tonight."

Her eyebrows raised a little seeming confused and maybe a little worried too. "Okay. Are you sure you're okay? I know something is wrong, but you look... I don't know, really upset."

I let my smile clear and pulled the corner of my mouth back. "I'm okay. I got some hard news today, and I just wanna let it roll off," I took a deep breath, "take you out for a nice night, and forget about it."

She nodded understandingly. "Okay... Should I change into something else?"

I shook my head, smiling a little more because I was reminded of her kindness in showing concern. "No. You're perfect. I wanna shower because I need a few minutes to regroup and start fresh."

Bex gave a small and loving smile as she nodded. "I'll be ready."

I stepped forward to kiss her forehead, then went upstairs. My chest felt like it was being crushed the whole way. If she knew what I did, she'd be furious, and if she knew why I could barely look at her, her heart would break. The little I'd read had disturbed me to my core because I could picture it. I could see her as a sweet and innocent little girl, kind as she was, fighting to make it through the day. While I'd never seen Bex cry, I could imagine the pain in her eyes when she did. Then I thought about any of the disappointments she'd had recently, being attacked when she went home, Carol chastising her over and over, being so scared to walk into the hospital that she was ready to run... I was so angry thinking about those things I wanted to hit a wall. How did she walk around being so thoughtful of others, so forgiving of people who wronged her? I was so painfully angry I could barely stand.

I took Bex to dinner at an outdoor restaurant with live music that wasn't over the top, danced with her after we ate, then took her to an art gallery after hours—ice

cream included. The manager was the only one who stayed, but he was more than happy to after the amount of money I'd offered. We walked around to different paintings and made up stories about them.

Bex stopped and smiled at one painting, looking at it as if it inspired her.

"Let's hear what you've got," I said as I watched her eyes stare in awe.

She shook her head. "I don't have anything funny for this one."

"It doesn't have to be funny. Give me what you've got." I didn't want to take my eyes off of her to look at the painting, but it was of a little girl sitting on a rock looking up at the trees.

"She's waiting for the trees to whisper to her." The corners of her eyes looked almost as sad as they did happy. "Her mom told her if she ever got lost in the woods, the trees would whisper amongst themselves to find her family and tell them where she was…" Her eyes looked up a little to see the tops of the trees in the tall painting. "She's not lost, just waiting for them to whisper." The corners of her mouth pulled up in the slightest of a smile, looking comforted, before her eyes went melancholy and the smile was forced again as she looked at me. "I used to believe that when I was little. Anytime I was upset or had a secret to share, I could tell them. Nobody would understand their whispers, not even me."

I pulled back the corner of my mouth. "Who do you tell your secrets to now?" It wasn't a backhanded question, I was being entirely genuine because it had to be agonizing to keep everything in.

She took a deep breath, looked at the picture for a moment, then at me again. "I keep them… They don't belong in this world, so I keep them."

I nodded. "That's lonely, Bex… to be the only person holding onto things. People care about you. Anyone who really knows you wants the opportunity to know you and what you hold onto. Whatever your dad did, whatever gives you nightmares, I'd hold it with you. I hate feeling your heart race and not knowing why or how to keep it from happening. I respect that your secrets are yours to share, and I'm not asking or making demands, but I really hope you know you could tell me... I'd never turn you away, or say something to make you feel bad about them, or whatever it is you might be afraid of by telling me. Tell me I'm never allowed to bring it up again, or never allowed to do anything or try to fix it and I won't. I just need you to know I'm always here to hold them with you." I swallowed the lump in my throat.

At first, Bex didn't seem to show a lot of emotion as I spoke but then looked touched as she gave a sympathetic nod. "I know you would... but they don't belong here." She reached forward and took my hand. "I realize my perception of the world is probably different than most, but in my mind, there is the world I came from and the one I share here with you. My secrets don't belong in this one." She smiled a little. "It's you and me. And as long as my secrets stay where I left them, that can stay true. You and me."

I let out a breath, understanding exactly what she was saying but feeling no better about it. All I wanted was to hold her, tell her how loved she was, and promise her life would never be like it was before. I wanted to give her comfort.

"What?" She looked at me analytically, seeming worried as if she'd said or done something wrong.

I shook my head. "You're right... Even if I don't like it because I want to be the one to comfort you, you deserve to have the life you want." I pulled back the corner of my mouth and gave her hand a light squeeze. "Let's go. Onto the next thing."

Her eyebrows raised. "Next thing?"

"Yeah," I pulled her arm through mine and wrapped it around. "And I have a question. Rocks or water?"

"Mm. Water? What are you planning?" She stepped off to the side to put her empty ice cream cup in the trash.

"You'll see."

"I have school in the morning and you have work. How late are you planning on being out?"

"Don't be such an old lady." I pulled her into my side. "You're twenty-three. Live a little." I reached forward to open the door. "Thanks, Mike!" I called before we went out the door.

Chapter 19

Bexley

I didn't know what was wrong with Grey or what hard news he'd received, but he wasn't himself. No matter how much he tried to make jokes or have fun, it was like there was a cloud of doom he couldn't shake. I regretted telling him what my mom had told me about the trees, then my confession of talking to them because it brought his mood down again. When we got on the boat, there wasn't a lot of conversation because of the wind, and I wondered if he'd intended for that, but then he commented about how he didn't think about how loud it would be.

Grey cut the engine to the boat once the house was in view and sat with me under a blanket.

"Do you wanna talk about it?" I asked after we'd been sitting in the quiet for a few minutes.

"What?" He moved a lock of my hair away from my cheek.

"Whatever's bothering you so badly. I'm not sure

I've ever seen you this upset before." I put my hand on his chest in front of my face to feel his heartbeat so I could make mine match. His was always calm and even.

"I'm sorry. I didn't mean to bring you down at the gallery." He put his hand over mine. "I'll be okay."

I tipped my head back to look at him. "It goes both ways... I can help you hold your secrets too."

He looked at me, reaching his hand up to touch my cheek. "My dad has done a lot of shady shit, and I've always known he was a little crooked, but today..." he shook his head, pulling back the corner of his mouth, "I found out it's much worse. He should be in prison, but there's nothing I can do. Taking him down hurts a lot more people than it helps." Grey pulled up his shoulder. "All I can do is make sure my assets are completely separate from his in the event that someone blows the whistle, and I kinda have to hope no one does."

I frowned. "What did he do?"

"The list of what he didn't is shorter, but money laundering, paying off government officials, manipulating the market..." He shook his head. "I can't really talk about it, but I'm done with him. We have some clients we share, so I still have to do business with him in that sense, but otherwise, I'm done. Pops knows, and Ryan knows quite a bit, but not what I found out today, so don't say anything to anyone. Okay?"

I nodded. "Of course." I hated the sadness in his eyes, mostly because I'd never seen it before. It made me want to do anything to fix it, then I realized there was something small I could do. I took my hand from his chest and touched his cheek, waited for him to look at me, then kissed him. His lips were soft, and he was careful as he held one hand against my back. Every ounce of fear I'd shoved away pushed right back, but I kept fighting.

Grey broke the kiss but pressed his lips against my forehead. "I think that's about as far as we better let that one get. Your heart is pounding," he whispered.

My heart was going so fast it hurt and my entire body was trembling. I slid myself down so I could put my ear against the front of his shoulder, hoping to listen to *his* heartbeat and calm my own again. Grey pulled the blanket up and hugged me a little tighter. We sat there for a long while before we finally got off the boat and went into the house.

Harry was inside sitting at the kitchen island. I'd met him a few times before moving to Seattle and liked him. He was in his fifties with a wife and two young kids. Grey had paid for them to come to the fourth of July party.

"You didn't have to wait around," Grey told him when we walked in.

"I figured you'd want someone to secure and cover up the boat." Harry stood and slipped his phone back into his pocket. "And I found this just floating around in your cupholder. You might wanna find a better place for it." He walked toward Grey, handing him a matchbox.

Grey chuckled a little. "Yeah. I forgot about it. Thank you."

"Mm-hm. Did you enjoy your evening, Miss B?" Harry looked at me.

I smiled and nodded. "I did. Thanks for driving the car back."

"Sure thing. I'll see you two for dinner tomorrow night. I'll get the boat covered and leave out the side gate." He pulled the sliding glass door open.

"Thanks, Harry." Grey looked back, then at me. "Are you hungry? Dinner sucked."

I nodded. "Yeah."

He kissed my forehead and walked toward the kitchen.

"What's with the matchbox? I don't understand why he pulled it out of your car or told you to find a better place for it." I followed him and sat in my normal spot at the island.

He set it on the counter in front of me. "Pops gave

it to me today when I went out to see him."

I picked it up and looked at the box. It had a green velvet wrap with a 3D image of a lady dancing and a guy playing a drum. "I don't understand. Is it supposed to have some kind of significance?" It was clearly old, so maybe it was valuable.

"The box? Probably not. The ring inside is worth a small fortune." He opened the fridge and pulled out a container of food.

I pulled the tab on the box to open it, then flipped up the small lid. A large diamond ring and wedding band sat on a small bed of cotton. It was honestly beautiful, but it had to cost a fortune.

"It was my grandma's and highly coveted among Maslens," Grey explained as he put the container in the microwave. "It was supposed to go to my mom, but Granny hated her." He leaned over the counter and looked at the ring.

I frowned a little. "Your mom's nice. Why would she hate her?" Cynthia didn't seem like she was mean-spirited and Grey had never said a bad word against her, so I couldn't understand how someone might hate her. While something seemed off about her, I had no reason to believe there actually was. It was just a feeling.

"She thought my mom was a gold digger and didn't trust her." Grey shrugged. "My mom also tends to be a pushover and jump when my dad says jump, and Granny was a huge feminist, so she hated it."

"I think as long as your mom's nice, it shouldn't matter." I gave the box and ring back.

"Yeah, that's my thought for the most part, but my dad's done a lot of stuff he shouldn't have, and she just kinda stood there and did nothing."

"But your Pops likes your mom, so how come he didn't just give it to her?" It seemed petty not to give someone something just because they didn't argue their husband's decisions, but there must've been more to it because Willum seemed like a reasonable person.

"Because he wants me to give it to you."

I raised my eyebrows and looked at Grey like I hadn't been thinking about it the minute he told me there was a ring in the box.

Grey put the ring back in and slid it closed. "Guess you made an impression on him." He smiled at me, seeming not to notice the look on my face.

I rolled my eyes. "Yeah, anaphylaxis is charming."

"So, what would you think about it anyway? You've never really mentioned anything about wanting to get married someday, have kids, or anything. What're your thoughts?"

"Um... I never planned on either." I held up my shoulders.

Grey's eyebrows raised. "Even kids?"

I shook my head. The only kid I thought about was the tiny baby I'd left in the bathroom of Toby's parents' feed store.

"What were you planning on?"

I held up my shoulders. "No real plan, I guess. Just go to school, get a job that let me sit in a room with no one else around, buy a house outside of a city..." I shrugged. "Just live." Since meeting Grey, that was all slowly changing.

Grey looked at me like I was a little crazy. "That's kinda sad, B. And lonely."

"I'm not good around people, so it sounded kinda perfect."

"What about now...? Is this something you want? You and me? Or is this just passing time?" He held up a hand as soon as I opened my mouth to speak. "I'm not saying I expect something or I'm gonna throw you to the curb if it is. I'm just trying to figure out where we stand."

I nodded. "I know what you meant, and... I'm here. I can't say I'm not gonna struggle sometimes, but... being with you has given me a different perspective. Most people either find me off-putting or get mad because I can't be who they want. Even Ryan can only take so much of me."

His eyebrows raised. "Ryan can only take so much of anyone. And as far as other people go, I don't think anyone tries to understand."

He leaned over the counter on his elbows. "When I was ten, my parents sent me to this camp for the summer. I got bit by a tick and didn't think anything of it because I was a kid. I got a rash for a little while and attributed it to running through plants in the forest and dirty lake water. Then I was sick with the flu, had a fever, and got sent home. The flu and fever went away, but my body just hurt all the time. I had headaches, my neck would be so stiff I felt like I couldn't turn my head, my knees felt like I'd been cramped up in a box for days... and no one believed me. My parents thought I was faking it because I'd raised a stink about going to camp.

"School came around and it took everything I had to get out of bed in the morning. By lunchtime, I couldn't take sitting in those hard chairs anymore, and I'd make the nurse call my mom to come get me. Finally, after literally walking out of school every day for two weeks, my mom took me to the doctor. They asked me a bunch of questions, ran some tests, and found out I had Lyme disease. All of it was real, no one tried to understand, and even after, it didn't matter to my parents. At ten years old, I wanted to kill myself because I was in so much pain, and I didn't have anyone who wanted to try to understand." He shook his head. "I don't wanna do that to someone else. I don't know what you've been through, or how bad it was or wasn't, but I respect that it happened and that it's bad enough to affect your life every day."

I knew about Lyme disease because Patty used to check me for ticks after he'd sent me out into the woods to bury the remains of another child that'd been brought to the house for slaughter.

I shook my head. "It makes my heart hurt to think about you being that sick and no one believing you."

Grey looked like he was drawn back from my words, then shook it off with a shake of his head. "You astound me." He pushed off the counter and went to the microwave to get the food out.

I frowned out of confusion over his statement. "Why? What do you mean?"

He started transferring the food to two plates. "Because people can tell you their menial strives, and you empathize like you don't have anything bigger by comparison."

I shrugged. "If you were in so much pain you didn't want to live, I know that feeling, and it makes me sad you felt that way. Doesn't matter what caused it."

Grey pulled back the corner of his mouth and nodded. "I guess... I know there's like a point-zero-one percent chance you'll tell me, and I'm not supposed to ask, but what happened to you?" He pushed a plate toward me with a fork.

I looked down at the plate—not because I was ashamed or afraid, but because I felt like I could tell him, and I wanted to.

"You don't have to tell me details, the Hollywood trailer version is enough."

I let out a huff at the irony. Another movie about me had just been released, and it was a bunch of bullshit. I twisted the tip of my fork into the salmon on my plate to watch it flake away. "They don't make movies about what happens to people like me. Not really... Movies aren't honest because they skip to the next scene when someone's being tortured to the end of their limit. The general public isn't brave enough to watch the vileness all the way through."

"And it was that bad for you?" Grey's voice was quiet and honest.

I nodded.

"The guy who raised you—I don't wanna call him your dad, because it seems like an insult to the title—but did he..."

I kept my focus on the plate in front of me, peeling back the layers of fish, and nodded before he could find the words. "Frequently... And the worst part of what happened is that I survived, and the second worst is thinking about it... so please don't ask me anymore." My voice didn't falter and my hands didn't shake. There was still a part of Hannah inside me, and she didn't cower and shake the way I did. She was numb from the inside out because being afraid was just another form of exhausting pain.

"I won't... but I want you to know something before we drop it... Will you look at me?"

I forced in a breath, setting down my fork, and looked at him.

Grey's eyebrows were pulled together, showing his empathy. "Your past isn't what defines you and you're not broken, unless it's your choice. I won't ever judge you or think less of you for struggling—because I truly have no concept of what your life was like before me. But I need you to promise me you'll ask for help if you need it. I don't care if it's homework, something at work, money, bending my ear because you can't handle the memories of what you've been through, or needing protection from something or someone—ask me. And I promise you, I will do everything humanly possible to help. Stop thinking you're my charity case, weight around my ankle, or whatever it is you tell yourself that keeps you from asking, because you're so much more to me than that, B..."

Grey swallowed hard and his eyes were red-rimmed and glassy as he looked up for a second then back at me. "I'm afraid every day... You don't tell me a lot of what you're going through—and that's okay—but

I'm afraid you might hit a breaking point and try to hurt yourself." The corners of his lips turned down as he swallowed again, and he gave a slight shrug. "I can't go after you because it scares you, I can't make you sit down and talk to me because you get too afraid to look at me—let alone speak... So please... ask me... I love you more than I've loved anyone, or anything and everything in my life put together, I do want to spend my life with you if you'll let me, and I want you to be okay. I'll be striving for 'good', but I'll settle for just okay if that's all you can manage."

The sincerity in his words matched the emotions on his face. He was in near tears as he pleaded with me for one seemingly simple thing. It was profound to hear a person tell me that they loved me so much. At first thought, it stirred fear. I'd had seven years of other people telling me I was hated, fifteen years of hating myself, and near the end of five months, Grey was telling me he whole-heartedly loved me... So, part of me was afraid to believe him, but I did.

I nodded with a lump in my throat. "I promise."

Grey reached across the counter for my hand, then held it as he walked around the counter to me. I stood up, knowing he wanted to hug me, and I needed it. The part of me that was Hannah could only stand-in so long.

Grey wrapped his arms around me like he was shielding me from something, letting out a breath as the muscles in his back relaxed. "You actually have to uphold that promise, you know."

"I know... I will." I turned my face into his shoulder and closed my eyes. It was the first time I'd hugged anyone that way since hugging my dad the morning I was kidnapped. I'd never trusted Toby enough, but I trusted Grey.

Chapter20

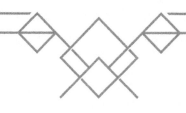

Ben

I stood there in the prison cemetery with my dad, trying like hell not to spit and scream. He asked me to come with him, and if I didn't respect the hell out of the man so much, I would have slapped him senseless for asking. The psychologist in me knew my dad was in a struggle between remembering the older brother who'd shot their drunkard father to save their mother's life, and hating the demon that kidnapped and brutalized his daughter.

"He ain't good enough to be dead," my dad said in a low rumble as he shook his head. "It ain't Christian of me to say so, but I wish our Daddy had killed him that day he tried to run us down in the field."

I looked at my dad wide-eyed because I genuinely couldn't believe he'd ever say something so hateful toward anyone. He'd never done it before. Me, completely different story, but my dad... never.

"If God's actually a parent, I think he gets it, so

you're probably safe."

"Don't talk to me about somethin' you don't believe in." He looked at me.

"I'm not. I'm just saying if there were a god, and he had a son, he'd have to understand if he were any kind of being worth worshiping." I didn't believe there was a god, and if there was, I hated him as deeply as I hated Patty and anyone else that hurt Hannah.

He let out a long sigh. "You make me wanna spit nails. Let's go." My dad turned toward the car.

"You better be talking to your waste-of-a-grave brother," I retorted bitterly.

My dad looked at me with his nose in a scrunch. "You been walkin' around with a stick up your ass for weeks now. What the hell is your problem?" He stopped and turned to face me.

"Wow. Tough question. I haven't seen my sister in fifteen years and the only son-of-a-bitch on the planet who *might* know where she is, is dead. If you'd just gone to see him, he would have told you."

"That's a steamin' pile of cow dung. He didn't know where she ran off to anymore than anybody else."

"The phrase you were looking for is 'bullshit,' and yes, he *did*. There's no way he just let her go. He had *Limerence*, he was *obsessed* with her, he wouldn't just send her off with no idea of where she might go. But it doesn't matter now, he's dead, so let's just go." I turned toward the truck.

"How'd it go?" My mom asked as she wiped her hands on a dish towel.

I shook my head. "I told him I didn't wanna go."

She frowned and gave me a disappointed look. "Ben, you of all people..." She shook her head. "What if it were Hannah? She was your perfect little angel, but what if she came and took Ella? Huh?"

"Wow." I stood up. "You guys are really hell-bent on pissing me off today. Did you hear the stupid that just fell out of your mouth?" I glared at her as I walked toward the basement stairs. "Ella, let's go!"

"Well, you don't know. None of us do. There's just as much of a chance of her growing up to do terrible as there is good."

"Mom, just stop." I shook my head and went for the entryway to get Ella's bag.

"No, you stop," my mom hissed quietly from behind me. "Have some compassion, Ben. It didn't just affect *you*. He lost his daughter *and* his brother—whom he once *loved*."

I looked at her and *really* wanted to explode, but held back. "And I lost my *sister*, and I *have* a daughter, so yeah, I can picture it, but I'm sane enough to hate the guts of a ground-feeder who'd hurt them." I went back to the stairwell and stomped on the floor. "Ella! Let's go!"

"Just leave her and come back later when you're done being angry. You don't need to expose that girl to your bad mood."

I dropped Ella's bag near the stairway. "Yeah. Fine. Because I'm a shit parent that can't keep my shit in check in front of my kid." It was a backhanded stab at my dad, but my mom still looked at me like I'd said it about her. "Stop feeding her so many damn cookies. She's not Hannah and she spent last night puking because you give her too many sweets." I pulled my keys out of my pocket and went toward the front door.

Toby intercepted me in the dining room and asked what the thudding was.

"Do you wanna go get a drink?" I asked as I signed.

He shrugged then nodded.

"Come on." I pushed the buttons on my key-fob to start my truck.

"It was me..." I signed without looking at Toby.

"What are you talking about?"

I let out a long huff before I looked at him and signed that I was the one who burned the house to the ground.

Toby's eyebrows raised. "Why?" He sounded more confused as opposed to asking a question.

"I lost my temper... I saw everything you told me, and I just got pissed... She was there the whole time, she couldn't get out, so I burned it to the ground so there's no chance she could go back."

"That was really dumb." Toby shook his head. "Henry could think it was *her* and with Patty dead, there's no one to stop him."

I rolled my eyes. "There's been nothing to stop him anyway. The pig's been in jail. And who knows if Henry's even alive." I picked up my whiskey and took another drink.

"Until he's not, you have to think like he *is*. He's dangerous."

"I know... Just don't tell anyone. I keep your secrets, you keep mine." There were plenty of things Toby didn't tell anyone about what happened in that house, but he'd told me. Granted, I was bound by doctor-patient confidentiality, but still.

My phone rang next to my glass and it was my mom. I rolled my eyes because she was probably going to hound me into bringing Toby back and bitch at me for taking him to a bar. If he became at all impaired, he'd lose his shit. It'd happened a few times, and I'd had to talk him out of killing himself each time.

Toby's phone flashed and he picked it up to look at the text before he showed it to me. My parents needed us to come home and get our kids because they had to leave.

"Awesome," I grumbled before downing the rest of my drink.

"I'll drive." Toby held out his hand for my keys.

My parents were in the entryway with their jackets on and ready to go.

"Where're you guys going?" I asked as I picked Ella up.

"Cynthia Maslen's in town, and we're gonna go have dinner with her," my mom answered as she handed me a container of food.

"Who?" I gave her a twisted look.

"Remember the lady who came and told us Hannah was in Tennessee just before Toby and Hannah got away? Sends a basket with all that cheese and meat for Christmas."

"Oh."

"Cynthia Maslen," she nodded. "She called and wants to have dinner, so we're goin'. And have Toby drive ya home if that's where you're goin', ya smell like booze."

"No, I wanna go with you guys. Toby can stay here and wait for Emily to get home."

My mom shook her head and put a hand on my arm. "It's just dinner. She doesn't have any more information, honey."

"Yeah, okay, but she *had* information and never said how she got it, so I wanna go."

"I ain't gettin' in a car with you a second time today," my dad said to me as he put a hand on my mom's back. "Come on now. We're gonna be late as it is."

I ground my teeth. "Love you too, Dad."

"I love ya, but you're actin' like a horse's ass and I don't like ya much today," he said before he pulled the door shut.

"Papa said a bad word," Ella said quietly as she picked up her head from my shoulder to look toward the door.

"Yep." I looked at Toby. "You guys wanna come over?"

Toby looked at Grace who looked at me.

"What if that lady knows where my mom is?" Grace's dark brown eyes felt like they were piercing more holes in my heart as she waited for an answer.

I shook my head. "I didn't say we were going straight to my house. We're just giving Grandma and Papa a head start." I nodded toward the door. "Let's get in the truck."

Toby opened the door and we all went out.

I used the family tracking we all had on each other's cell phones and directed Toby where to turn. My parents weren't going to dinner in town if that's what they were really doing. They'd gone to the airport and drove in the entrance for private planes. Toby and I waited to see if my parents would drive back out of the airport, but when the tracking on my parents' phones started to move in a direction they couldn't drive, we knew they were on a plane. I wanted to text them and tell them they were a pair of liars, but I'd catch them in their lie later. They'd eventually land and I'd find out where they were.

Toby drove to my house, and just when I thought my day was done being shit, it wasn't.

"Go drive the girls around until I tell you to come back," I said to Toby.

He frowned and pointed at Beth, who was standing on my porch.

I looked in the back seat at the girls. Ella was asleep, and Grace had her sketchbook and a pencil in hand. I signed to Toby that he needed to keep Ella away until I told him. Toby nodded and I got out of the truck.

"What are you doing here?" I asked after Toby drove away.

"Ben..." Beth's chin quivered.

I shook my head. "You need to go. Your parental rights were terminated, I've got nothing to say to you, and I don't know how you got my address, but lose it and leave."

"I want to see her. I'm her mother."

I raised my eyebrows. "No, you're an egg donor. You gave birth and left. Are you gonna leave, or am I gonna call the cops?"

"Ben..." Beth came down the steps of the porch. "I don't have a good reason," she shook her head, "I wish I did, but I don't. I couldn't handle it. I just... I made a mistake..."

I nodded. "Yeah... and a pretty sucky one. She's an amazing kid. You walked out, so no. No matter what you say, whatever your excuse is, you hurt my kid, you left her, and I'm not gonna let you do it again. You left her to scream in her crib while I was at school. Two days old and she went nine hours without anything to eat or a diaper change! She was so dehydrated she had to spend a day in the hospital. Then *I* was the one who was questioned by social services for child abuse! Who *knows* what you'll do this time!" The more I spoke, the angrier I got. The memory of finding Ella in her bassinet still made me want to physically hurt Beth, but I knew better.

Beth stood there with tears on her face. "I thought you'd be home before she woke up. I didn't—"

"I DON'T CARE!" The words came out in the loudest burst I had. "As far as Ella knows, her mother's *dead*. So, *leave!*" It was wrong of me to tell Ella her mom was dead, but I didn't want to run the risk of her someday trying to find Beth. I couldn't let her get hurt.

"Okay," Beth squeaked as she looked down and wiped at her tears. She kept more than ten feet from me as she went around me to get to her car; her body had a slight cringe as if I might hit her. I'd never hit a woman, so the insinuation of her body language pissed me off.

I walked over to enter the code for the garage door because Toby had my keys. Beth's car made a clicking sound repeatedly but wouldn't start. I stood there gritting my teeth as the garage door opened. If I wanted her to leave, it meant I had to help her get her stupid rattle can of a car started. It was the same car she'd had when we were dating, and it was a headache then too.

As soon as the garage door was open enough, I ducked under the door, grabbed the jumper cables hanging on the wall, started up my fifty-two Chevy pick-up, and backed it down to Beth's car.

"I'm getting a new car, I just had to get some of my student loans paid down," Beth said as I lifted the hood of her car.

I said nothing and hooked up the cables to the terminals.

"I bought a house... I finished my bachelor's last spring, and I got a job as a paralegal in Houston," she continued to prattle from beside me.

"Stop talking." I didn't care if she was finally trying to put her life back together. She was looking for me to give her some kind of acknowledgment that she might've changed, and she could've, but I didn't care. Her second chance was given when she got a summons to appear in court over Ella's custody and she didn't show. Her rights were terminated, and she was nothing to me. I didn't wonder where she was, how she was doing, or think about how much I'd once loved her. There was just nothing.

"I've read your books. They're amazing. All those people you've helped..."

"Go start your car." I reached under the hood of my truck and made it idle higher so she wouldn't kill it when she tried to start her car. As soon as the tin can sputtered to life, I disconnected the cables, but annoyingly, Beth still wasn't leaving.

"Can I please just see her *one time?* You don't have to tell her who I am, you can make up a different name if you want." She held her arms around her chest. "This is probably my last chance and I just want ten minutes with her." A tear shot down her cheek and she wiped it away quickly.

"Your last chance was the day you left." I shook my head.

"No, Ben, I have cancer," she cried and yanked her shirt to the side to show a chemo port and part of a missing breast covered by her shirt. When I didn't say anything, she pulled on her strawberry blonde hair to show it was a wig. "I'm not *lying.* I just wanna see her for ten minutes. I know I hurt you, and I know I hurt *her,* but I just want this one chance to do something right and see her before I'm gone. Three or four more months and you won't be lying to her anymore, but *please,* I'm begging you for this one last *thing.*"

I felt so hatefully angry that my muscles were throbbing to hit something, but I took a breath and made my decision. "You so much as hint at who you are, and you'll wish cancer was your problem. One hour—supervised—and you leave. Don't ask for more, don't ask again."

Beth nodded. "Okay."

I let out an irritated huff. "Turn your car off and go wait on the porch."

Beth wiped another tear from her cheek and turned back to her car. I closed the hood of my truck and backed it up into the garage. After I closed the garage door, I pounded on the punching bag until my bare hands felt like they were going to break, texted Toby to come back, went in the house to seethe for another couple minutes, then let Beth in.

"Living room," I pointed to the right of me. "She'll be

here in a minute."

Beth nodded and pulled off her jacket. It'd been hiding the thinness of her frame. Beth was only five foot two and small to begin with, but now her clothes just hung from bones.

"How long ago?" I watched her as she set her jacket and purse on the bench by the door.

"I got diagnosed almost two years ago. They thought they had it beat last fall, but they did another scan two months later and found tumors everywhere." She pressed her loose hanging shirt against her abdomen and showed a large lump protruding below her ribs on the left side of her body. "Three months is hopeful at this point." She shrugged and looked at me.

"I'm sorry... Despite hating you, I still wouldn't wish it on anyone." I pointed at the living room again so she'd move out of the entryway.

She shook her head as she turned to pick up her coat and purse. "I can't do this again. You win, Ben."

She got the door part-way open and I reached up above her head to push it shut. "You won't get a second chance. You're the one who asked to see her."

She looked at me, tears hanging in her eyes again. "I do wanna see her. It's you I don't wanna see... I left you. I would've taken Ella with me, but you would've killed me, and I was already suffocating, so I left."

I frowned. "Oh please. You didn't wanna be a mom. You chickened out and you left."

"No. Leaving was the bravest thing I did! You're bitter, Ben. It's toxic to be around. One minute you're okay, and the next you hate everyone and everything around you. And the people who're closest to you get the worst of it. You got legitimately pissed off at me because I didn't know how to change a diaper on a newborn and her belly button started bleeding. You stomped around the house for hours, and would barely let me hold her.

I didn't know what to do but leave. And don't tell me I could've taken her with me. I had no money, no job, my parents *still* want nothing to do with me for getting pregnant, and your dad would've made sure I never saw her again anyway! Either I stayed here and let your constant bitterness eat away at me, or I left and had some semblance of air in my lungs."

Shit... She was right, but the only part I saw was her leaving, and I only chalked it up to listening to her tell me—for months—that she wasn't ready to be a mom.

"Can I please leave now? I don't wanna hear whatever you're about to spit at me next, and I literally *am* too sick to get in a tug-of-war match over trying to get the door open." Her hand stayed on the doorknob.

"Just wait," I said quietly as I dropped my hand from the top of the door. My brain was working a million miles an hour to dissect everything and break it down. I wasn't unaware that I could be a bitter asshole, it was my defense mechanism over losing Hannah. "Come in here," I said as I went toward the living room and pulled out my phone to tell Toby to stay in the driveway. I needed to talk to Beth without interruption.

"Ben, I don't wanna fight."

I looked back at her and shook my head. "No fighting. Sit down."

She took in a breath, looking hesitant, but walked into the living room and sat on the couch. I sat at the end of the chaise so I could face her.

I leaned over with my elbows on my legs and shook my head. "I didn't even think about it... I'm sorry." I pulled back the corner of my mouth. "Ella looks so much like Hannah—even when she was born—and the second I saw her, I felt like I had to shield her from everything... I *still* do it, I know it's a problem, but I've never stopped because I don't wanna let it go. And before Ella..." I took in a breath and tried to think of my words. "I was just

248

pissed. I never wanted kids because I didn't wanna sit and worry." I rubbed my forehead to get rid of the tightening ache. "I didn't mean to take it out on you and I'm sorry." She wouldn't look at me and wasn't saying anything, so I reached forward to take her hand. "Beth..."

She let out a huff and shook her head as she pulled her hand back. "You didn't think about it... I'm glad I left."

I felt shocked for a second and realized what I'd said. I hadn't thought about *her*. At no point did I sit down and think of where things went wrong, and now she knew it.

"Yeah... You were probably right for that... I was too angry at you for leaving, and that's all I saw." I looked at her legs and the way her pants sagged around them. "Maybe you did, and I don't remember, but why didn't you say anything to me *then*?"

"Would you've listened?" She looked at me like I'd said something crazy. "Any time someone so much as indirectly implies anything about your sister, you jump off the deep end and you don't hear anything else."

Another true statement, and I nodded. "You're right... but I didn't know I was hurting you and that makes it *really* different. Maybe you still needed to leave—and that's okay—but you should have told me... Regardless of Hannah, or anything else, I don't wanna be someone's monster. I realize I see the extremes in my profession, but things like this are where it starts. I'm not discrediting or diminishing what I did, but I can tell you I never meant to take my anger out on you... I had a ring. I bought it two months before you got pregnant, started planning everything out, and when you found out... I decided to wait. I didn't want you to think I was asking because of the baby, I wanted you to know it was because I loved you." The thought of how much I'd loved her made a lump rise in my throat. "I loved you, Beth..."

She took in a breath and shook her head. "You're such an ass, Ben."

I raised an eyebrow and almost laughed. "That's not the first time I've heard that today."

"Then maybe you should reevaluate yourself. Is she actually coming, or am I sitting here pointlessly?"

I picked up my phone on the edge of the chaise. "She's outside. I'll go get her." I stood up and left her in the living room so I didn't have to sit there while I waited for Toby to bring the girls in. I deserved to sit there and feel like an asshole, but Beth would be there for the next hour to remind me.

"Ella," I said lightly as I rubbed her cheek to wake her up. "Someone's here to see you."

She picked her head up and looked at me with tiredness on her face. I laughed at the lines across her cheek and the flyaway hairs sticking up from her pigtails.

"Can I get out too?" Grace asked.

"Yep. Everybody in. We'll order some food and get you guys fed."

Toby touched my arm to get my attention. He signed asking if everything was okay.

I shrugged. "In the way you mean, yes. Otherwise, no." I signed that Beth had cancer.

Toby's eyebrows raised.

I nodded. "Exactly." I grabbed Ella's bag from the back seat and closed the door. "And I also found out I'm somebody's abusive ex."

"That's easier to believe."

I gave Toby a shitty look. "What?"

Toby smiled a little. "You're a good doctor, but otherwise a dick."

I frowned. "Thanks..."

He shrugged. "As long as Hannah likes you, no one else matters, right?" He walked around the truck and took Grace's hand.

Was that what he really thought? I pushed the button on the door handle to lock my truck and followed him. In the house, I set Ella on her feet, took her hand, and walked into the living room. "Ella, I know I told you your mom was in heaven, but that wasn't true. This is your mom. Can you say hi?"

Ella stepped behind my leg, letting go of my hand so she could hide behind me like I was a tree. "Hi."

Beth smiled and looked like she might cry again. "Hi, sweetie. How are you?"

"She's shy, but if you color with her, she'll talk to you," I said as she set down her bag of stuff on the coffee table. "Come on." I pulled Ella away from my leg and lifted her around to the other side of the coffee table.

"Gosh, Toby, you look so different. How are you?" Beth gave him a smile but looked nervous.

"Better than you, I hear." He stepped forward and hugged her. "I'm sorry."

"Thanks." Beth gave him a sort of grimacing smile with a shrug after stepping back.

"You remember, Gracie." Toby put a hand on Grace's shoulder. "Grace, this is Beth. She knew you until you were three."

"Hi." Grace gave a small wave.

"You're even prettier than the last time I saw you, if that's possible." Beth smiled at her.

She held up her shoulders, said a thanks, then pulled back the corner of her mouth in an almost expectant way as she looked at me. "Can I go upstairs?"

"Knock yourself out. You know where the stash is, just don't let someone else catch you." I had a stash of snacks upstairs where I spent most of my time, and Ella would eat the whole damn lot of it if she wasn't supervised. Grace, on the other hand, would take one thing without leaving a trail of crumbs.

"Daddy, it's broken." Ella tugged on my hand.

I looked down and she held her pencil sharpener out to me.

"I can fix it," Beth said with a kind smile as she sat back down on the couch.

Ella let go of my hand to step over and give the sharpener to Beth.

"I was gonna order something for dinner. Anything sound good?" I watched Beth and the way she smiled at Ella. All I could think was, *what had I done?* Me continuing to be bitter over Hannah had cost Ella having her mother in her life. On a horrible note, maybe it was okay because Ella wouldn't be devastated in three months when Beth wasn't there anymore, but that wasn't a fair thought either.

"I want peet-za," Ella said quietly.

"Peet-za," I repeated with a smile at Beth.

She gave a small smile back for a moment then had a slightly guilty look. "Don't worry about me." She pulled back the corner of her mouth in an almost expectant way. Probably because of the tumor sitting on her stomach.

"I can get you a smoothie, or soup." I scrunched my nose. "I also have a blender."

She shook her head. "You don't have to get me anything."

"I want to. Just tell me what you want."

"A smoothie or milkshake is fine." She shrugged.

"Okay. Just that? No soup or anything?" I knew I was being pushy, but she was so sickly skinny.

"If you can find something decent, but I can't do large portions."

I nodded. "Okay. I'll be in the kitchen."

Chapter 21

Ryan

"Did you find him?" I asked as I sat down in one of the three gaming chairs Tim had.

"Yup. Caught him on a gas station camera in Mackinaw City, Michigan. He was on his way to pick up two girls on a boat from Cleveland. There wasn't enough time to wait for you to get back, so I had to call in the calvary without you." Tim moved to a different set of monitors and pulled up the news.

I was a little proud that my efforts were getting so much attention from the media. Between helping Nelson with school, helping Grey at the office, my own schoolwork, and staging the take-down of Henry Greer, I was exhausted. Some days I was only running on a few hours of sleep and caffeine. Having my efforts applauded by the general public because someone was actually doing something about a monster was gratifying.

"Did you fix the pictures and send them?" I rubbed at my face to help wake myself up.

We had all the proof we needed to send every asshole to jail thanks to the thumb-drive. There were pictures of each person mid-crime. Before they were sent to media outlets, I made Tim blur the faces of the girls. We also tried to avoid the ones involving Nelson. I couldn't get away from them entirely without risking Henry or someone else noticing that the photos never involved her, so we had to send a few, but I tried to keep it to the bare minimum. There was also the fact that they were harder to stomach than the rest. The other kids were equally as important as Nelson, but not to me personally. There were times where I'd look at her and couldn't stop seeing one of the photographs.

"Yeah. Go back upstairs and get some more sleep, man. You look like shit." Tim's fingers clacked against the keys loudly.

"I can't. I have to take Nelson to the doctor. Where are you on that prick, Alan Bain?" I pulled my phone to check the time.

Alan Bain was one of the bastards that had paid for the first baby Nelson had been pregnant with. He'd purchased thirty-seven babies from Henry, and if I didn't have better sense, I would have killed Alan Bain instead of turning him over to the FBI. According to Toby Anderson's book, the first baby Nelson birthed didn't come out alive. The second one, she'd been alone when she birthed him, cut the cord and didn't clamp it. She couldn't stomach another child being hurt and brutally killed. Henry had beaten Nelson near to death for letting the baby die. There were certain people on the list I wanted taken care of before others, and Alan Bain was near the top. I couldn't imagine what it must've done to Nelson mentally to birth a child then let it die just to save it from something worse.

"I have most of his bank statements decrypted. Maybe another hour or two." Tim frowned. "That's weird and not good. Cynthia is calling Mildred Lawrence."

I frowned. "What?" I rolled over to see.

"And Cynthia sent a text to the pilot to get ready to fly to Dallas. You better go before that plane takes off." Tim looked at me.

"Shit." I looked at my watch. "Call Nelson and tell her to reschedule her appointment. I can go with her tomorrow or Monday." I stood up and started toward the stairs. "Call Harry and have him meet me outside the airport. I need him to get me through the gate."

"Yep. I'm on it."

I ran upstairs, grabbed the small bag of necessities I kept packed for emergencies, and ran out to my truck.

Harry met me at the airport and got me to the plane. They were just about to pull up the stairs when I got there.

"Ryan, honey, what are you doing here? Is Grey okay?" Cynthia picked up her phone from the side table to check the screen.

"He's fine, but we need to talk." I dropped my bag on the floor and sat in the chair across from her. "Get me a coffee," I told Ava, Cynthia's personal attendant.

"Yes, Mr. Brae," she answered quietly before glancing at Cynthia with slight concern.

"What's going on?" Cynthia asked quietly. "This isn't like you."

"What are you going to Dallas for?" I wanted to make Cynthia say something before I did.

She frowned. "I'm going to see an old friend. How do you know I'm going to Dallas?"

"I know a lot of things. What friend?"

Her frown held but turned disapproving. "I'd rather not say. What's this about? You're acting strange and it's concerning."

"How do you know Millie Lawrence?" I felt ready to do whatever necessary to protect Nelson. Cynthia could easily expose Nelson by just a phone call.

"No." She shifted in her seat with an expression of anger. "Now you tell me what this is about? Is Roger paying you to keep tabs on me?"

"No. I'm working on something for someone else and you're about to blow everything to shit with what-ever call you just made to Millie Lawrence. What do you know and how much?"

Cynthia looked at me analytically for a moment. "What does Bexley know?"

I raised an eyebrow. "She doesn't know anything, and it better stay that way. Why are you talking to Millie Lawrence?" I was going to keep asking until she gave me a damn answer. I didn't care if Cynthia had been a mother to me longer than my own.

Cynthia took in a breath and let it out as if she were about to admit defeat. "This conversation better never leave this plane."

I shrugged a shoulder. "I'm fine with that."

"You and Grey have taken this further than I in-tended." She shook her head as she crossed her ankles and picked up her wine glass. "You both were supposed to take Roger down, but instead you've gone after ev-eryone else. And Grey was never supposed to seek out Bexley and marry her."

"You're talking in circles. Spit it out." I didn't know if she was implying what I thought she was.

"I've been poisoning Grey against Roger for years, Willum too. I'm sick of being treated like his servant while he philanders about. Just before Bexley escaped her captors seven years ago, I found out what Roger had been participating in. I went to Willum, showed him everything I found about Roger laundering money for Henry Greer and his partners. I can't expose Roger without the whole kingdom coming down, so we began grooming Grey against Roger. Willum had already retired so he couldn't expose Roger without losing everything either. It's been a long game waiting for Grey to officially be on the books, but after it was done last year, I lead you both to a portion of the files, then to the external drive regarding Bexley. She's the link to *everything*, the one detail that ties everything together." Cynthia sat confidently as she spoke.

I frowned. "What's Nelson have to do with anything?"

Cynthia waited for Ava to hand my coffee and go back to the back of the plane before she answered. "She's always been plan B. Bexley knows the inner workings of Henry Greer, his partners, and their disgusting operation. Her uncle, Patrick, shared that information with her so she'd have a weapon if she ever needed it. I was right to keep an eye on her all these years. I couldn't guarantee Henry wouldn't have Patrick killed, even in prison... That's exactly what happened." She took another sip of wine.

"You were the one having her followed?" I honestly didn't expect any of this, but it made sense... Sort of.

Cynthia nodded. "And helping her stay hidden from a distance."

"So, why are you in contact with her mom?" Something stunk, but I had to play on careful lines.

"I befriended her mother years ago. Through a paper trail, I'd found the house Bexley was kept in as a child. I sent some employees to check out the house, only one was able to get close enough without being injured by traps outside the property. Anyway," she waved dismissively, "that's how it was discovered. I went to the Lawrence's to tell them where their daughter was after reporting the findings to the FBI through an anonymous tip, but at that same time, Toby Anderson managed to escape, causing Patrick to flee with Hannah."

"And that's when she was able to escape and disappear," I concluded. No one knew for sure how Nelson had gotten away, only that she did, because she left her daughter with Toby.

Cynthia nodded. "I was rather suspicious of Bexley when I learned of her relationship with Grey, but either she doesn't know what Roger did or she doesn't care."

I shook my head. "She doesn't know. She would've been gone the second Grey showed up if she knew something."

"I suspect so. She's rather skittish."

I frowned. "Wouldn't you be?"

"Anyone would. I simply meant she's the type to run, not fight back."

A bigger part of me felt like Nelson would fight like hell in the right circumstances. She was a chicken-shit over stupid things, but the bigger things she handled better than anyone I knew. I wouldn't put it past her to outwit me.

"Why are you going to see her mother?" She was going to answer the damn question, even if I had to ask a thousand times.

"I want them to know she's alright. I know you lost your little brother, but you can't imagine loss as a parent. It never stops eating away at you."

I let my eyebrow twitch. "Depends on the parent." My mom had clearly moved on, unlike Tim and I. She'd left without us and never came back. "You can't tell her parents where she is. It's not safe. I'm going after Henry, but I have to take his army out first. If I can keep things on schedule, Nelson will be able to spend Christmas with her family next year. Is Roger more than a laundromat for these guys?"

"No. If he was any kind of another participant, I wouldn't have waited. I want him in jail so I can leave him and take his money with me." Her voice was bitter.

I shrugged. "Don't get in the way of what I'm doing, and I'll make it happen."

"I'll agree to that as long as I know what you're planning. I can't imagine Grey knowing about Bexley and not saying anything to her."

I shook my head. "No one knows what I'm doing or what I found. Tim is the only one, and that's only because I need someone with hacking skills to dig and cover my tracks."

"How far down the list are you?" Cynthia seemed uneasy somehow.

I shook my head again. "I'm just getting started. It's a long list. Thankfully, most the work has been done for me, but there's plenty more. There's a few holes." Instinct told me not to share too much information. Cynthia was very much like Grey, never good at sitting on the sideline. She also took child injustices a little more personally than most. I thought it was because of the loss of her daughter, but Grey once told me it was because of what'd happened to Tim, Remy, and I. It didn't matter—keeping her in a controlled state of knowledge did.

I didn't think it was safe enough for Cynthia and the Lawrence's to go to dinner in Dallas, so Cynthia had them meet us on the plane and flew to Oklahoma City. It wasn't ideal for them to be meeting me before planned, but I didn't have much of a choice. I needed to control Cynthia's conversation with them and prepare for damage control.

"My goodness, Cynthia, you haven't aged a bit." Millie smiled and hugged Cynthia after boarding the plane.

"I could say the same for you. I guess we're a couple of the lucky ones." Cynthia stepped back with a smile. "Don, it's good to see you again." Cynthia offered a hand.

He gave a single nod before reaching for her hand. "You as well." His voice was deeper than I expected, even though I'd heard him speak on the news and recorded interviews.

"Millie, Don, this is Ryan, my adopted son of sorts." Cynthia looked at me with an adoring smile.

I smiled and extended a hand to Millie first. "It's nice to meet you. Cynthia has told me a lot about both of you." I reached over to shake Don's hand next. Despite his slender frame, he looked like a man who'd easily kick someone's ass if he was ticked enough.

"It's good to meet ya," Don mumbled in a slow southern drawl.

"Please, both of you have a seat." Cynthia directed a hand to the two chairs across from us, where I'd previously been sitting. "We decided it would be best to go somewhere else for dinner. Oklahoma City is just a short distance—the same as driving somewhere in Dallas—if that's alright?"

Millie looked at Don with hopefulness—looking exactly like her daughter—and Don seemed less than pleased but gave a small nod.

"I think that'll be just fine," Millie agreed with a smile before she stepped over to the window seat.

"Wonderful." Cynthia held up a finger to get Ava's attention. "Can I offer you something to drink? We have a full bar, soda, coffee, hot tea, water..."

Millie's kind smile held. "I think water would be just fine."

"Nothing for me, thank you." Don gave Ava a nod but still held a straight face.

"Mr. Brae, would you like another cup of coffee?" Ava asked.

I nodded. "Please." I looked at my watch before I sat down.

"Nothing for me, dear. I've had enough," Cynthia said politely before she was asked, then sat.

"So, I assume this is just a social call. I didn't get much of a chance to talk to ya on the phone with the grandkids carryin' on." Millie wore a light look of question, another look that Nelson sometimes had. It was easy to see what Nelson would look like in twenty or thirty years.

"Yes, but not entirely." Cynthia glanced at me, then

looked back at Don and Millie. "Mostly, I wanted to let you know Hannah is alright."

The lightness on Millie's face was replaced with heartbroken eyes at the mention of her daughter's name. It was the same damn sad face Nelson got when she was hurt and didn't want anyone to notice. I felt just as guilty as I did when Nelson looked that way.

Don frowned while taking in a deep breath. "And just how do ya know that?"

"To be honest, I located her some time ago." Cynthia spoke with her normal poise, but it was gentler. "My oldest son happened upon the records I'd been keeping on Hannah—thinking they were something else—and after meeting, became taken with her." Cynthia gave more of a smile. "They've been dating for quite a while now. Grey doesn't know anything about her past, and it'll remain that way unless Hannah tells him herself. Ryan," Cynthia directed a hand toward me, "knows, but understands the need for secrecy. You can credit him for the recent string of arrests you may have noticed lately."

Don looked at me with distrust. "How are ya managin' that?"

"A lot of research and lack of sleep." I took the coffee from Ava. "I acquired information about a few individuals, then followed breadcrumbs. Your daughter is my friend, but I'm also paid by Grey to look out for her, what I'm doing is part of that."

Don shook his head. "Well, you'd just better stop. You're gonna get her killed."

"Don, I assure you, we'd never let that happen." Cynthia spoke sympathetically. "She's safe with us, and she's doing very well. She works for Grey, she's in college—"

"She's happy," I interrupted. They didn't care about her accomplishments, they wanted to know she wasn't miserable. Both Don and Millie looked at me like they wanted to believe that more than anything. "She strug-

gles sometimes, and she won't say anything because she won't tell anyone who she is, but more days than not, she's happy." I handed Millie my phone to show her a picture of Grey, Nelson, and I from a few weeks ago. Sam had taken it and sent it to us. It was probably one of the best pictures of Nelson I had because she was actually smiling.

"Oh, my baby," Millie whispered as she touched the screen. Her eyes filled with tears. Don looked at the picture too, but he looked more miserable than relieved.

"She's a lovely young woman," Cynthia reaffirmed with a smile. "Quiet, but she's kind hearted. Grey adores her more than anything, and he's been helping her since they first met. Ryan too. They both helped her get her GED, apply to college, Grey has given her a job she loves and is highly skilled at, they helped her find more suitable housing, and Ryan continues to look after her and help her with schoolwork. She hopes to be a lawyer." She looked at Don, seeking approval.

"How is it there's barely a mark on her?" Don looked at me like I was responsible for hurting his daughter.

"Thousands of dollars in cosmetic surgeries," Cynthia answered. "She spent nearly every dollar she made prior to meeting Grey."

He nodded once as he looked back at the picture. "She sure does look like ya, Mil."

Millie laughed a little, sniffing back her tears. "I'll say. I didn't realize how much I'd aged until seein' this."

Cynthia shared a melodic laugh.

"Do you have any other pictures?" Millie looked at me with hopefulness as she held my phone out to me.

"I might, I'm not sure." I took my phone and opened my messages from Grey. If I had any other pictures, it would've been ones he sent me of the two of them. He was the only one out of the three of us that ever took pictures. I couldn't text him and ask him for more pictures without Grey questioning me, but I wanted to for Millie's sake. She seemed so sweet.

Once dinner was through, Don excused himself to the restroom before we left the restaurant. I waited a minute and did the same so I could catch him before he got back to the table. He was already waiting in the hallway, still looking mad as hell.

"Took ya long enough."

"Cynthia likes people to think she's oblivious, but she's not. I had to wait so it didn't look coordinated." I continued to walk past the door to the bathroom toward the emergency exit.

"You got about two seconds to tell it to me straight before I rain down hell you ain't never seen before," he warned with a tight jaw.

I showed no signs of intimidation because I wasn't. "I don't know how much of Cynthia's side is true or accurate, I can only tell you mine. Hannah's safe, and I'm after anyone who so much as had an idea of what happened to her and didn't do anything. I've got people who've been looking out for you and your family, including Toby and his daughter. I've personally met with Ben but he doesn't know who I am. Hannah's happy, but she's scared of her own shadow, so I'm paying Ben to coach me so I can help her. I need you to make sure you say nothing to no one. The two FBI agents you've been talking to, Slater and Morley, are dirty. Morley has been making sure every raid on a trafficking house turns up empty. Slater has made witnesses disappear on more than one occasion, and he knew where your daughter was the entire time. I have pictures of him at the house she was kept in, with her standing right there. Watch the news tomorrow and I'll prove it."

I handed Don a piece of paper. "This is a number for my brother, Tim. He's contracted with the FBI as a professional computer hacker, and he has good people he trusts. If something happens or you're worried about anything, you can call him. I plan to have this done by Christmas next year. I know I can't promise Hannah's safety, but she got pulled into the lion's den without any of us knowing and this is the only way to make sure she gets out. Grey, whom I work for—not Cynthia or her shit-bag husband—would spend every last cent of his billions to keep your daughter safe. You can take it or leave it, but if you expose me, or expose your daughter, she'll be gone and she'll make sure none of us find her again. She's got ten exits planned for every entrance. She's scared, but she's also incredibly smart."

Don continued to look at me with sternness for a moment before he asked, "Why're ya doin' this? Cynthia said Grey doesn't know anything."

"He doesn't. He's a good guy but he gets ahead of himself and doesn't think twenty steps ahead like me. He knows she comes from something horrible, but not what or who. I told him not to dig and let me handle it. And I'm doing this because your daughter is my best friend and she'd do it for me if the tables were turned." I didn't have some profound statement to make him stop and believe me, just the truth.

Don took in a deep breath and let it out. "You get my girl back to me and the reward money is yours, but anything that happens to my daughter is gonna happen to you. I rightly don't give a horse's ass if I spend the rest of my life in jail. Ya hear me?"

I nodded. "I can live with that, but I don't want your money." I nodded behind him. "You should go before Cynthia suspects something."

Don turned and walked away from me. I respected him for being suspicious.

Five minutes after I finally crawled into bed, my phone rang. Cynthia and I didn't get back until the middle of the night, then I spent the rest of the wee-hours of the morning with Tim so I could properly nail Agent Morley, Slater, and the fifteen other dirty agents who'd been moonlighting for Henry. The director of the FBI was also on that list, which made things a little more complicated. I made sure the media received and ran the story first before internal affairs got what they needed on the off chance that someone tried to cover something up. As much as I hated media outlets, I loved that they could always be counted on as starving sharks when you needed them.

"What?" I answered tiredly.

"Hey, is Bex with you? I haven't been able to get a hold of her since yesterday morning." Grey's voice had mild concern in it.

I rolled over on my back and rubbed at my face. "No, she's probably in class." I held my wrist up to see the time.

"It's Friday, she doesn't have class. Did she say anything when you took her to the doctor yesterday? She seemed really off when I talked to her last, but she wouldn't tell me what was up."

Shit. I forgot to ask Tim if he told her to reschedule her appointment. I pulled my phone away, put Blondie on speaker phone so I could text Tim, and answered, "I didn't take her. Something came up and I couldn't make it, so she was supposed to reschedule."

"Again? She really needs to go in, she's hardly been able to eat without getting sick."

I let out a tired huff. "She didn't tell me that." I got up to put a shirt on. "Tim said she didn't answer back when he texted yesterday. I'll head over to the house and get her to the doctor. Do you have time to call and see if they can get her in today?"

"Yeah, I'll text you with a time. Let me know if I need to come home early."

I rolled my eyes. "You sound like a first-time mom.

She's fine. I'll get her to the doctor, and everyone will live." I pulled on a clean pair of jeans. "Go back to work. I'll call when there's something to call about." I hung up and grabbed my wallet on my way out the door.

Chapter 22

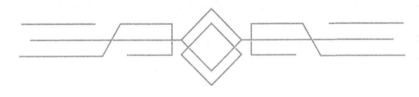

Grey

The second Ryan texted me to come home, I was in a mad-dash, and sitting on a plane for three hours didn't help the sense of urgency I felt. When Bex didn't answer my calls or texts, I knew something was wrong. We hadn't had an argument, I didn't buy her anything expensive, I didn't even say anything about her lying to me about rescheduling her doctor appointment. The doctor's office charged my card twenty-five dollars for every last-minute cancellation, and Ryan had only been responsible for one of them that I knew of. There was no reason I could think of for her to be upset with me, so something was wrong...

I left my stuff at the door and went straight for the stairs. At the landing I heard a quiet whistle and looked over. Ryan had come from the hallway downstairs, so I went back down the short flight.

"Anything?" I asked quietly.

Ryan shook his head. "Not a word, but I found

these." He held out a pill bottle.

I frowned and took it to look at the label. "Xanax?" I looked at Ryan.

"Yeah, and a high dose too."

I looked at the bottle again to see who the prescribing doctor was, then noticed the date. "This is expired; it's from two years ago." I turned the bottle to see how many pills were inside. It was still fairly full, no refills were ordered, which made me wonder if the pills in the bottle matched the label. I knew Bex had abused pills before, and I wondered if she'd fallen back into it and this was her way of trying to hide it. "Did you make sure these are what the bottle says they are?"

"Yeah, the pills match." Ryan scratched the back of his head. "I think we should take her in. She's been asleep this whole time, and she didn't even flinch when I touched her arm to wake her up."

"Just opening the door to her room wakes her up." I let out a breath.

"That's my point. I think we have to take her in."

I shook my head and gave the pill bottle back. "Let me go up and see if she'll talk to me first."

"Godspeed."

I turned and went up to Bex's room, knocking on the door before I went in. It was strange when she didn't so much as roll over. If she was abusing drugs again, I wasn't even mad about it, just worried. If it were anyone else, I would have been far less tolerant, but Bex worked so hard to overcome things. I didn't want to jump to conclusions, and I was trying not to.

"B?" I spoke loudly enough for her to hear me but not to startle her.

She took in a deep breath, her body becoming less relaxed as she opened her eyes, but otherwise, she didn't move.

I got on the bed, laid in front of her, with just a foot between us, and gave a small smile as I tucked a lock of her hair behind her ear. "Hey, Beautiful."

A small frown slowly set in. "What day is it?"

"Friday." I brushed my fingers over her cheek. "Ryan said you weren't doing so great, so I came home early."

She took in a deep breath, moving the pillow out from between us, slid forward to hug me, and buried her face in the center of my chest. I pressed my lips against her forehead and hugged her. There were times I wondered if I'd lose her. Certain things seemed to trigger her differently than most, and I'd seen her depressed, but not like this.

"Did something happen?" I asked quietly against her forehead.

Bex shook her head.

"Just a bad day?"

She nodded.

"Can I stay here with you?"

More times than not, she wanted to be alone when she was in a funk, so I was surprised when she nodded. I wanted to find out exactly what was bothering her, but I knew better than to press her for answers. If she was allowing me to sit with her, she was trusting me not to ask. Usually, if there was something that had the possibility of resolution, she'd talk, but if there was nothing to be resolved, she'd keep everything to herself.

I pulled my phone out and texted Ryan that she was okay and he was free to go. He asked about the pills, and I told him I'd ask her later. She needed someone to sit with her, not make her feel worse. I was worried, but I was there to make sure she was okay so that had to be enough.

Bex slept the evening away, but I stayed next to her as a human body pillow and responded to emails on my phone or did research on stocks. It was a rarity for me not to be running a hundred miles a minute for work or out doing something. In the few months that

Bex had been living with me, I'd only been home a total of two or three weeks. I saw less of her now than when she lived in Monterey. Sitting there made me realize I was doing exactly what I never wanted to do. I was ignoring her for work, just like my dad did to my mom, Sam, and I. She deserved better, so I started looking through my schedule, delegating certain tasks to other people, emailing Erin to reschedule things for different times, and reorganizing how I did everything. I couldn't avoid going out of town, but I could lessen it. I would be gone one week out of every month unless I had to go overseas, and home most evenings.

After I rearranged my schedule, I realized the other problem I had, I was still working outside of work. My career was my hobby, a passing of time, not a means of making a living. I'd already done that. So, instead of sitting there working from my phone, I started doing what anyone else would do. First, I paid a visit to my social media platforms. I had people that maintained them for me, but I personally hadn't checked in for who knows how long. That bored me to no end, so I started reading whatever news articles my phone suggested to me. The problem was right there.

Either Ryan knew and didn't say anything, or it'd gone right under his nose. I wouldn't have caught it if I'd kept on working from my phone. I didn't stay up on current events that didn't contribute to stocks, it was too depressing. This was depressing, and it wasn't even about me. A mother of an abducted child had written a lengthy article attacking Hannah Lawrence, and it was vicious. There was a picture of two girls, one was the writer's three-year-old daughter, and the other girl was Bex. While both faces were blurred in the picture, there was a birthmark that Hannah Lawrence had on the left side of her lower back. It'd since been removed—the only reason I knew was because of the medical records from my dad keeping tabs on her. But the woman of the three-year-old had gone on about how Hannah Lawrence was a "sick little twist" and had obviously been a willing participant in recruiting girls and took pleasure in murdering them. The woman didn't believe her daughter mercifully died to be spared from being sold.

According to Toby Anderson, who'd been present in the house at the same time as the three year old, Bex poisoned certain kids in an attempt to save them from a worse fate than death. He mentions a blonde toddler with golden curls tied in pigtails in a navy-blue dress. It was the writer's daughter. Bex had been especially taken by the toddler and "according to Mr. Anderson, had told the girl to, 'pretend like she likes being touched' to make a client happy." The toddler had become inconsolable, refusing to go with the client, so Bex was dragged in and raped. The woman claimed that Bex had killed her daughter out of malice and revenge instead of mercy.

I looked at Bex, resting against my side, and felt sick to my stomach. This woman didn't know Bex or the first thing about her. She didn't know Bex wouldn't hurt anyone if she had a choice. The beautiful woman next to me didn't have a single bone in her body made for revenge. Bex would turn the other cheek to her death rather than seek revenge, especially on a child. No one could convince me otherwise. That the writer of this article would say differently infuriated me in a way I'd never been before. There were thousands of comments in response to the article, all of them in defense of Hannah Lawrence and other children victimized by sex trafficking operations, but I was still angry. I wanted to make a few phone calls to have the article pulled, but I couldn't without leaving a trail leading straight to Bex. She was hidden here with me; I couldn't jeopardize that more than I already had.

I put my phone on the nightstand and hugged Bex. She startled at my touch.

"You're good, B," I whispered. "I'm just hugging

you."

Her poor heart was pounding—I could feel it against my side—and she was shaking. She couldn't be blamed for her response to an unexpected touch, but it broke my heart every time. I wanted to be able to pull her close without feeling like a monster for accidentally scaring her. I still couldn't get the image of her terrified face out of my head from the night I'd told her about the car I bought her. Usually, I was so careful to never stop her when she walked away, but I'd forgotten for just a second because I was so desperate for her to hear me out. Even with a loose grasp around her hand, she'd looked as if I'd crushed her arm, her mouth opened like she was about to cry out in pain, then she looked at me as though I'd said the most hateful words she'd ever heard. I felt so guilty over it that I could hardly sleep that night... I wanted to be able to touch her and not hurt her.

"I know you don't want to hear it right now, but you have the most beautiful heart out of anyone I've ever met," I whispered near her ear. "You're always kind, considerate of everyone around you, and you fight like hell to always do the right thing." I couldn't tell her I knew about the article, but I could rebut it by telling her she was a good person. "You have no idea how much better you make life and how much I love you for it... I love you more than anything and everything, Beautiful." I kissed her cheek with a deep breath, then hugged her a little closer as I let it out.

Bex's hand moved down from my shoulder, and she wrapped her arm around me as she moved a little closer. Her thin body relaxed against me, but her arm kept me in our tight hug. I wanted to stay there with her for as long as she'd let me. It was killing me not to run straight to my safe, pull out my grandmother's ring, and ask Bex to marry me. I knew she needed time to adjust to all the recent changes in her life, and she was still acclimating to being in a relationship. There was a chance she wouldn't say no if I asked her right now, but I wanted her answer to be resolute because she wasn't giving into fear. It wasn't "want" or the lack thereof that stopped her from things, it was fear.

"I love you too," she whispered quietly after a few seconds. "Thank you for coming home."

I was so damn happy that my profession of love had been reciprocated that I couldn't help my smile. "You got it, Beautiful... Always." I kissed her forehead, closed my eyes, and stayed right there with my beautiful Bex.

My watch vibrated quietly against my wrist with a message, pulling me from sleep. I opened my eyes to see the message and saw the time first. The last time I'd slept past seven in the morning was when I'd come down with a horrible cold a few years back. I never slept in. Ryan was checking in because he hadn't heard anything from me. He also said if Bex wasn't up yet, to coax her out of bed and have her do something simple, like take a shower or eat something. I'd respond to him after I gauged where Bex was at mentally. She was still asleep against my side, but her arms were wrapped around her torso.

"B?" I waited for her breathing to change before I lightly rubbed her arm. "Did you want to get up and we'll go out for a late breakfast?" She needed to take a small step to get herself back on track again, and I'd premeditated my plan to help her last night before I fell asleep.

Her dark eyes opened and observed her surroundings before she looked at me. "I'm not hungry."

I pulled back the corner of my mouth. "I know you're not, but you've got to start somewhere, and I doubt you ate anything yesterday." I rubbed the back of my finger over her cheek. "You can take a shower and we'll go find something to eat."

She rubbed her forehead and looked stressed over the thought, but I knew she wouldn't protest. If she knew she was doing something "socially unacceptable," she'd force herself to correct the issue, no matter the toll it would take on her. It felt like a dirty trick, but it was only to help her.

"I'll turn the shower on for you, then I'm going upstairs to do the same." I pushed myself up to kiss her forehead and got up.

After I went into her bathroom and turned the shower on, I went up to my room and took one too. My brain was still turning over that damn article. I wanted so badly for her to talk to me, but I didn't want to make it seem like she had to either. No one would want to talk about something like what she'd been through. It had to feel unnerving to have someone look at you and wonder if they were thinking about the abuse you'd been through, maybe even feel embarrassed. That wasn't to say she had a reason to be embarrassed, because she didn't, but I wondered if she felt that way.

Adding to that humiliation, there were pictures of her being circulated in the media. Bex's face and certain things of graphic nature were blurred, but did it make a difference? People were still looking. I couldn't ask Ryan if it was him going after Bex's abusers, but I had a strong hunch. The reason I was okay with it was because Ryan was smart enough to handle things without getting caught. It would also lead to Bex being safe from Henry Greer and anyone else who might be out to hurt her. When he started asking for more money to "take care of things," I didn't ask, I told him not to get caught with a teasing smile. Ryan was incredibly loyal, and I trusted him more than anyone. He'd do the right thing. The part I was having a hard time with was what it might do to Bex. Every time another arrest was made, she was a nervous wreck for days after.

After I got out of the shower, I called Bex's doctor to see if I could get her in. She was having a hard time keeping her food down anymore, and losing weight she couldn't afford to as a result. Ryan was supposed to take her, but he kept rescheduling, which ticked me off. I thought it was Bex because she was terrified of doctors, but I found out yesterday it was Ryan. Her doctor told me she'd gone in by herself the other day.

Bex was looking through her nightstand when I went back to her room.

"Are you looking for the pills Ryan found yesterday?" I'd considered playing dumb asking what she was looking for, but it seemed manipulative.

She looked at me for a moment, then shook her head before she pulled an envelope out of the drawer and put a few other things back. I didn't know if she wasn't being verbal because she didn't want to or if she was upset with me because I'd mentioned the pills.

"Anything sound good food wise?" I asked as I sat on the end of the bed.

"I have to take a raincheck." She handed me the envelope with money for rent and the car. "I didn't get any work done yesterday, so I need to go in for a few hours. I'll grab something from the kitchen to eat on the way."

I tried not to seem butt-hurt. I hadn't seen her in three weeks, and I wanted to spend time with her. "It can't wait until Monday?"

She shook her head. "I'm already behind and Erin needs to send out the policy changes Monday morning."

"Okay, well, let's go get something to eat first and we'll go to the office together. I have some stuff for my dad I have to do." That was actually true, but I'd planned to put it off until the last minute.

She shook her head again as she walked over to step into her heels and grab her purse. "I don't have time. My economics professor is going to be in his office at four and if I'm not there early, there'll be a line to see him." Bex grabbed her phone and keys off the top of the dresser. "There's an extra nine hundred in there," she glanced at the envelope in my hand, "because I had to use your card last week when I got my windshield replaced. Please don't tell me not to worry about it."

I frowned a little. "Why are you mad at me?" With the way she was speaking and actively not looking at me, something was up.

She stopped near the door and still didn't look at me. "I'm not a child and I don't appreciate anyone coming in here and taking my pills off the nightstand. They're addictive, but I only take them when I need them—when things are really bad. The side effects are horrible but it's better than feeling out of my mind." She went out the door after she said her peace.

I got up and followed her. "B, I didn't take them off your nightstand, Ryan did. He was worried, and also concerned because they were expired."

Bex stopped halfway down the stairs and put her back against the wall. It wasn't because I was behind her, it was because we were on the stairs. I could only assume she'd been pushed down stairs too many times to trust having someone behind her.

I let out a breath and continued down the rest of the stairs, waiting for her to come down.

She stopped at the bottom of the stairs. "I know they're expired, but I had to take something so I could go to the doctor by myself because Ryan kept telling me to reschedule. The doctor prescribed me new ones, but I was so out of it I barely made it home as it was, so I couldn't pick them up." Her voice got quieter as she spoke because she was so upset. "I know he's busy—he shouldn't even have to come with me—but I needed to go to that appointment. I waited three weeks already, I couldn't anymore. My stomach hurts so bad I barely make it through a single class."

"I didn't know, Bex. You can't be upset with me for something I couldn't know, and we were worried." I planned on having a conversation with Ryan. It would have been one thing if it was a friend helping a friend, but I *paid* him to help her.

She shook her head. "You didn't ask why I took them, neither did Ryan. You both assumed I was using again, and you can't tell me that wasn't it or those pills wouldn't have been taken from my nightstand. And neither of you put them back, so that says to me that neither of you trust me. I know I have my problems—you can't imagine how constantly aware of them I am—but I don't have that problem. I let you and Ryan in my life in a way I haven't let anyone in, I've trusted both of you—even when it terrifies me—so I think it's pretty awful that I'm not trusted. I've done nothing but bust my ass to do and be better. Ryan taking those pills, you knowing he did and not telling him to put them back means it doesn't matter—my efforts to do better don't matter to you. You're holding me to the same low standard you hold any addict at—"

"No. Stop. That's not—"

"Grey," she looked away from me tiredly, "I'm not wrong." Bex looked at me again, "so don't tell me I misunderstood and you both care. If either of you cared, you would've had more faith in me and, at the very least, asked. But it is what it is. It's the residual consequence of my actions, and I'll live with that. I need to go, and you need to let me." She let out a tired breath and went out the garage door.

I stood there for a minute just trying to process the burst of words Bex had unleashed on me. She didn't even give me the chance to tell her I was going to ask her later because I wanted to make sure she was okay first. It didn't really matter though, she was still right. When she moved in, I put any of my prescription pills that might be a problem for her in my safe. It wasn't that I thought she'd go searching the house or steal from me, it was more of not wanting to tell her there was something in my medicine cabinet and having her confronted with

pills when I knew it could be a struggle for her.

I pulled my phone out of my pocket as I turned to go toward the kitchen. I still had a bone to pick with Ryan, but I'd leave out the rest of what Bex had said. It was likely she was more upset with me than Ryan, but if she had something to say to him, it was up to *her* to say it. Also, it wouldn't mean anything coming from me. If Bex chose to say as much to Ryan, he'd probably take it in the gut like I was.

Chapter 23

Bexley

After meeting with my professor and being told I was clearly not suited for college because of the help I constantly asked for, I went to Ryan's house. When he opened the door, he gave me a pissed glare and walked back to the kitchen without a word.

I'd been to Ryan's house a couple times before. It was an older two-story craftsman house, and I only knew because I'd mentioned I liked that type of house and Grey told me what it was. The woodwork inside was all dark in color and the walls were painted dark except for the tan-colored living room. The built-in bookcases in both the living room and dining room were packed tightly with only books. There was also an upstairs room with several more shelves full. But despite all the other places in the house to be, it seemed the kitchen was Ryan's preferred spot.

I sat down at the island in the center of the kitchen and Ryan put a jar of Nutella and a spoon in front of me.

I shook my head. "I don't want any right now."

"Then it's there if you change your mind." He pulled out a bag of coffee beans and poured some into the expensive coffee maker sitting on his counter. It was probably the flashiest thing Ryan owned, but it was because he was serious about his love of coffee. "What kind of tea do you want?"

"I don't want any of that either. Obviously, he texted you, so how much did he tell you?" I crossed my arms on the counter and watched Ryan. He hadn't said anything when he answered the door. All he did was open it and walk back to the kitchen, which meant he was expecting me. If he wasn't, he'd complain about being bothered at home.

Ryan turned around, crossed his arms, and wore a shitty look on his face. "Is there someone in your life that you have to prove something to?"

I frowned because I didn't know where the leading question was going. "What are talking about?"

His eyebrows raised. "You couldn't wait one more fricken day! Tim texted you, I know he did because I saw it. I also saw that you read the damn text, so why the hell didn't you wait? No!" He held up a finger to stop me as soon as I opened my mouth to respond. "Whatever excuse you have is bullshit! You could've waited! So either you thought it would be cool to have a reason to pop some pills and play the petty victim, or you wanted to stick it to me because I had to cancel. I have a fricken life, Nelson, and it doesn't always revolve around you! I had a goddamn emergency that couldn't wait, and if I thought it could've, I would've put it off and taken you."

My anger flared up again, and rather than explode, I decided to leave. Again.

"Sit your tiny ass back down," Ryan barked as I got up.

"No." I continued for the door.

"Yeah, go be an ingrate."

"*Ingrate!?*" I turned around and walked back. "I didn't ask you to go with me, Grey *told* you to, because for some reason, he has to make it your job to take care of me like I can't do it *myself!*" I yelled right back because I hated being screamed at like a child.

He dropped his arms. "Really!? Tell me how well that went *before*? You were homeless, working in crap diner, fishing your dinner out of a dumpster! So tell me, who's the fricken idiot for making sure you're taken care of, because it's sure as *hell* not Blondie!"

"I didn't *ask* for his help! You—"

"Who cares!?" Ryan burst loudly. "He wants to help you, you're dating him, so who gives a shit!"

"I do!" I yelled louder because I was tired of being overpowered. "And you're always advocating for him! 'Nelson, it's a good job,' 'It's a free place to live.' 'Take it and if it doesn't work, drop it and move to the next thing.' You've been a part of it right from the beginning, messing with my head, probably taking pleasure in it like a sociopath."

"Hey! No one forced you to do *shit*. The choices were yours. And who gives a shit how it came about, you got out of the homeless *bullshit* situation you were in, and you're doing something besides wasting away in a diner under two control freaks. And I'm not saying you can't help yourself, but he's made it a hell of a lot easier! The reality is, you weren't doing it on your own, because you're too goddamn pig-headed to do what's good for you without chickening out over every goddamn thing! Where were you going? Huh? Were you gonna be a manager in the Mom and Pop shop? It's not a damn crime to accept a handout, unless you don't do anything with it!

"You think Roger Maslen didn't get a handout from his old man? He got a whole damn, fully built company!

Grey learned the way of business from his dad, got help getting clients from his grandpa, and reached a billion dollars in worth in just two years! No one's frowning on him, are they? No! Because he said thank you, shut his goddamn mouth, swallowed his pride, and built something with it! It's the same thing you're doing! You're building! So, shut up, say thank you, and swallow your goddamn pride! If Grey did anything, if I did anything, it was to help YOU!"

"I didn't ask for it." I spoke my words through my teeth to keep from yelling.

"Because you're too goddamn proud to ask." Ryan over enunciated his words.. "Is there someone out there you have to impress by being entirely self-made? Someone who's gonna tell you you're a fricken idiot because you got a leg up? If there is, you should probably get rid of them because they're oblivious to how life works. You have no one. Sorry to point out the obvious, but you don't. You didn't have parents to teach you the shit they were supposed to. You didn't get to go to school, you didn't have school counselors to talk you through college applications, you didn't have your parents to help pay for college, or at the very least make sure you didn't end up sleeping on a beach with your belongings in a trash bag... You have us.

"Next time, don't be a dumbass and take expired pills unless you're actually trying to kill yourself. Wait. Don't make it Grey's or my responsibility to save you from yourself. Start making choices like you're not on some psychotic bender to screw yourself over because of whatever shitty life you had before. Or because you have to prove that you can be independent. It's not an excuse, it's pathetic! You can let people help you when you actually needed it without it being misjudged as a crutch! You scared the hell out of me! Grey had to fly home because I couldn't get you to fricken wake up! Did you think of anyone else besides yourself before you popped some pills?"

I stood there feeling like I wasn't standing in my own body. No matter what I chose to say in that moment, it wouldn't stop him from yelling or thinking he was right. Maybe he was in certain aspects, but it didn't mean I wanted to stand there and be screamed at.

"Stop walking away, Nelson. You can be a big girl and yell right back," Ryan called as I walked to the front door.

I spent a few hours at the office working and responding to emails I'd missed. Keeping my mind busy didn't stop Ryan's words from turning in my head all day, or my professors. Obviously, I'd messed up, and I knew that, but all I could do was keep walking through it. I hadn't taken an excess of pills, nor had I done it because I had something to prove to anyone. Ryan was overloaded with whatever Grey had him working on. The first few times I rescheduled was because Ryan was dog tired, then after he kept canceling, I went because I needed to and it was one less thing on his plate. Xanax had weird effects on me, but it was better than pissing myself because I was too afraid of going to the doctor for a problem that was getting increasingly worse. Then, when I saw the article that'd Elsie's mom had written, I wasn't in a good state of mind from the xanax and it was furthered by hatefully written words.

After getting caught up with work, I went home. I knew Grey would be waiting to talk to me, so I knocked on the doorway to his office.

"Hey." He pulled the corner of his mouth, not appearing happy, but not upset with me either.

"Hi." I took a breath to calm myself. "I don't know if you ate already, but I stopped at Parsley's."

"No, I've been working all day."

I nodded as I went over to open the sliding glass door on the other side of the room. Home offices scared me, and both the sliding glass door and the regular door had to be open for me to tolerate being in the room.

"I saw all the emails." I sat down on the couch instead of in one of the chairs in front of his desk. "I'm sorry for earlier." I looked down as I twisted my index finger between my thumb and finger on the opposite hand. "It's not wrong for you to assume I might still have a drug problem or fall back into old habits. I'm embarrassed that I had a problem in the past and I took it out on you." My words sounded forced and rehearsed but they weren't.

"You don't have to be sorry or embarrassed. Everybody has a past, and you were right earlier... I don't think you want to talk about whatever has you so bothered, and that's fine, but because I don't know what it is, I can't know it won't pull you into old habits. I know you can take a lot, Beautiful, but I've never seen you the way you were yesterday, and it was scary. You know where you draw your lines, usually I do too, but not yesterday. Ryan showed me the pills as soon as I walked in the door, but I didn't know what to think, so I was gonna ask you after I knew you were okay. And I'm still asking now, only because I don't understand what happened. Did you go to the doctor the other day and it knocked you out of the game? Or was there something else?"

I continued to stare at my hands as he spoke, twisting my finger from side to side, and still didn't look up when I responded. "It was a combination. I took one of the pills before I went to the doctor, and it helped until it didn't..." I swallowed hard. "She looked and pushed around on my back and the pills were out matched by the panic... When I got home, the panic kept growing and growing... I couldn't get a hold of Ryan, and I knew you were sleeping, and I didn't want to take another pill, so the panic built... It gets so bad I don't even know where

284

I am, I hear people and things that aren't there anymore, and I get lost..." My hands were shaking as I spoke. My cheeks were flushed and my forehead hurt from keeping my tears in. "That medication has been the only thing to ground me when I lose touch with what's real, but I was so out of it I didn't know they were right there."

"You can always call me, even if I'm asleep... Is there anything I can do to help? Find a psychiatrist that'll make a house call, or... I don't know—anything?" Grey's voice was gentle.

I shook my head. "No. It doesn't happen that often, and I usually handle it better when it does."

"Okay... The offer is always on the table. Whatever you need, even if it's not *that*, you got it. I'll be around more from now on. Last night, I realized I've been working too much, so I'll be gone one week out of the month and try to be home in the evenings unless we have a client dinner."

"You don't have to do that. I'm okay, it was just a bad day." I looked at him. Ryan's words were in my head again, reminding me that I was making myself other people's problem.

"It's not because of yesterday. I asked you to move here so we could see more of each other, and we've seen less. One Roger Maslen in the world is enough. I think I worry about you a little less here, so it gives my over-driven brain a free pass to be a workaholic." He smiled a little.

I held up a shoulder. "It's not a bad thing to work if that's what you want to do. I'm busy with homework even when I'm home, so..."

"B..." He smiled a little more.. "I like you more than work, I want to be here even if it's to watch you hold a spoonful of Nutella in your mouth while you read." Grey chuckled a little.

I gave a small smile as I looked back down at my

hands. He meant it, and I knew that, but Ryan's words...

Grey took a deep breath. "Okay. You brought up food. My brain and stomach have aligned in a plea for sustenance. Let's go eat."

I nodded and got up to close the sliding glass door.

Chapter 24

Bexley

I was haunted by every child that came to the house. The majority of them left the house alive, either because Patty had saved them just to send them off to their death elsewhere or because they were in holding to be sold. There were a hundred and thirty-three that didn't make it out alive, and I remembered every one of them. I knew why they ended up at the house, how they died, and where they were buried. Until I'd birthed my second, I'd refused to be responsible for the death of any child.

Henry had hammered nails through my hand on five separate occasions, whipped me with straps or chains, even waterboarded me in attempts to make me cooperate. After my second baby had come out alive, I felt like I had no choice. He was so tiny, and regardless of how he was conceived, I couldn't resent him enough to let him suffer from some sick monster abusing him. So, I left his end of the umbilical cord unclamped because I didn't think I had it in me to hold my hand over his mouth. It was fast, he didn't struggle, he just drained of color while I held him and cried hysterically. After that, there were certain children I couldn't see be sold... like Elsie Freely.

Elsie was a cherub three-year-old with golden curls, big blue eyes, pink bow lips, and the cutest nose. She came to the house in a navy-blue eyelet-lace dress, one shoe missing from her foot, and red marks on her legs from being struck with a belt. Henry's goon had snatched her from a toddler pageant at a Nashville mall. The moment Elsie saw me, she reached out for me as she wailed and struggled to get away from the goon. I took her, calmed her down, and brought her to Toby in the basement. It took a little while before she trusted Toby enough to stay in the basement with him and not scream. As soon as she did, I went upstairs to listen. There was a client, number one-four-one, who'd specifically wanted the child. I didn't know all the client numbers, but I knew that one. He was especially vile; I knew from personal experience.

After learning where the girl was supposed to go, Patty chained me in his office, then brought Elsie up and chained her too. It meant there was a visiting client coming to the playroom. I told Elsie she couldn't scream if the man hurt her and she had to do what she was told. Clients that came to the playroom were barely human. There'd been countless kids who'd ended up with broken bones or snapped necks from fighting against the clients. I was terrified for Elsie, and I didn't want her to suffer more than she had to. When Patty came to get her, she screamed, fought, bit, kicked, and headbutted. He took her and threw her down into the basement and I was taken to the playroom. After the client left, I made a cup of rice and two plain potatoes that Elsie, Toby, and I were to split. I let her eat, then put the last of the medicine Patty had given me in Elsie's water. I held her close as she fell asleep, and for an hour after she was gone. I didn't believe in the god my parents told me to pray to, but I still prayed Elsie was somewhere better.

———⋙⋘———

"You okay, B?" Grey's voice was quiet, but it still startled me.

I nodded but kept my head down between my knees. Grey was a light sleeper and probably heard me throwing my guts up. I was embarrassed enough about everything else, this was only adding to it. My mind wasn't straight, and I was struggling so badly that it was hard to keep pushing through. I was tired of drowning in memories I couldn't escape, done with the judgments of those who didn't bother to understand or at least be sympathetic, and sick to death of holding in the flood's worth of tears I refused to let go of. Every time I felt the darkness of the basement, it got hard to keep my promise to Toby.

Grey got down in front of me, but I didn't pick my head up because I was still trying to keep myself from coming completely undone. "I know you don't want to talk about whatever is going on, but I'm worried..." He took my hand that was hanging over the side of my knee. "Can you give me something here?" His thumb rubbed over the back of my hand lightly.

I shook my head. "I'll be okay," I whispered. "I didn't mean to wake you up. I'm sorry."

"Don't apologize, and you didn't wake me. My brain won't shut up because I know something is wrong, but I don't know how to help and I can't get you to talk to me... Whatever it is, I'm not judging, I'm not going to run and tell the first person I find, or whatever you're worried about." His thumb rubbed the back of my hand again. "I'll listen and pretend like I never heard it if that's what you want—or make up a good lie, I won't know the difference—but please say *something*."

I took in a shaky breath, moved my other hand

to my forehead, and let my elbow dig into my knee to support the weight of my head. "I keep trying to move forward and... people keep putting mirrors in front of me, forcing me to see the past..." I took in a slow shaky breath because I was still starving myself of crying. "I have to see what I've done, then try to look myself in the eye and believe the things I tell myself to get through the day... I was forced to do horrible things when I was little, and when I wasn't forced, I was desperate... I desperately wanted to be merciful to people who showed me no mercy, I was desperate to help people who couldn't be helped, and I was desperate to stay sane... I know I did terrible things, I would never say differently, but I didn't do them to hurt other people."

"I know it's not the point, but who's putting mirrors up?" His voice was still quiet and calm.

I shook my head. "Ryan, Carol, Joe, a lot of times. People who don't even know they're doing it."

"What about me?"

I didn't want to answer him because I didn't want to hurt his feelings, but lying seemed just as wrong. "Sometimes... but I know you don't mean to."

"No, I'd never mean to. Can you give me an example?"

I changed the position of my hand on my forehead so I could rub over the area where my head was throbbing. "The automatic assumptions I'm abusing drugs again, Ryan telling me I'm an idiot for going to the doctor by myself, professors telling me I don't belong in their class because I 'clearly didn't pay attention in high school,' or complete strangers automatically assuming the worst of me in untenable situations... I work so hard to be here, to do things normal people don't have to think twice about, learn as much as I can as quickly as possible so I don't irritate people, and be a good person even when it's at an expense I can barely take. I know not everyone means to, but I feel like a dog getting their nose rubbed in their mess on the carpet." The only way I could maintain my voice was to speak just above a whisper.

"You are a good person, B." Grey moved to sit beside me against the wall.

I shook my head. "It doesn't matter. There's a point where being a good person and good intentions don't matter... There's so much you, Ryan, Carol, and Joe don't know... and I don't know if any of you would be here if you found out."

"Try me."

I let out a huff that was more of a failed laugh because nothing was funny. "That's like telling someone to detonate a bomb."

"Maybe I have my bomb suit on and I'm really good at diffusing them."

I looked at him because I couldn't tell if he was being serious. His tone of voice was just light enough that I didn't know if he was telling me he could really handle it.

"You don't have to tell me, but I can handle it if you do. And it'll stay between you and me." He pulled back the corner of his mouth.

I didn't know if I could tell him. Even if he could handle it, could he look at me the same? Then there was making sure I didn't reveal enough for him to find out who I was. Hannah Lawrence was all over the news on a near-constant basis because of whoever was going after Henry. Toby's book was on the best-seller list because of the media coverage. I was the hot topic on talk shows, radio shows, and podcasts. People wanted to know where I was, if I really got out, if I was still alive, what happened... They wanted the truth from the horse's mouth... I wanted to tell one person just enough to feel like I wasn't the only one holding everything. I'd never be able to, and even Toby only knew pieces, but I wanted to feel like I wasn't being crushed by the things I held. And I really wanted someone to understand that I wasn't sitting there in a cloud of depression over petty things like fear of a doctor or my professor being a dick.

Grey knew other things just by observance. It couldn't have been any more evident that I'd been abused in every way possible. He was still here, constantly walking on eggshells, making sure I felt safe, and caring enough to put in the effort where other people stopped. I didn't have a lack of friends because I was unfriendly, too quiet, or an anti-social, it was mostly due to people not wanting to give the effort it took. No one wanted to think about not touching me for fear I'd freak out. No one wanted to sit there and explain basic concepts the rest of the world was privy to... But maybe I would tell Grey this one thing and he'd stop. Could I handle that...?

I turned my head to look at the floor a couple feet in front of me. "I've killed people..." There would come a day where Henry would be gone and I'd be free to say what I wanted. I hoped Grey would still be in my life when that day came, and if he was, he'd be the only person I'd want to tell the truth to. Just by knowing my real name, he'd know what I'd done, and it would be easier if he walked away from me now instead of a max of twenty to thirty years. "One was entirely out of self-defense, and I didn't mean to. My mother didn't die in a car accident..." It felt like holding bile in my mouth by referring to Helen as my mother. And the only reason I could elusively mention her was because no one knew more than her first name, or a couple small references from Toby's book. I'd never told Toby much about her, so it wasn't obtainable information.

"She was a very petty and unstable person, always angry or jealous of something or someone. When my dad would bring me up to the bedroom to do what he did, he'd have to make sure she was passed out drunk first or she'd come after me... She usually waited until he went into town or he wasn't looking, but that day she didn't. She stabbed a kitchen knife into my dad's shoulder, yanked me out of the room by my hair, and threw me over the railing from the second floor." I rubbed my knee at the memory of feeling it break. "While she ran down the stairs, I got myself up and started hobbling for the basement. My dad would lock her down there too, so she usually didn't chance it by going past the door. But she caught up to me before I could get there because my leg was broken from the fall... She kept punching me all over, just pounding and pounding on me. She had too tight of a grip on my arm, I couldn't pull away, so I shoved forward into her as hard as I could, knocking her down the basement stairs... There wasn't a railing on those stairs, so she'd gone off the side, landing just the right way, and it broke her neck. I didn't mean to kill her, I was just trying to make it stop..." I took in a jagged breath. "My dad hated her, so he didn't care. He made me clean and stitch the knife wound on his shoulder, then he re-set my knee, casted it, did what he always did, and left me locked in his office while he buried her under a tree...

"The kids I can't tell about, just that they were small enough to not understand or fend for themselves. They were going to be raped until they were killed, so I wanted to eliminate the worser of the two. There's a lot that happened that I had no control over, couldn't change—it was just everyday life for me—but... then there were the few times I had a choice. I didn't make them lightly. Even as a kid who didn't have someone to teach me to think about the very real consequences, I still did... And I look back, and I still don't know if I chose right." I shook my head again. "Mostly, I think I chose wrong. I wanted so badly to help, to give them what I couldn't have... someone who'd make it stop."

I ran my fingers through my hair. "Sometimes, it was easier being there than out here in the rest of the world... In there, I knew what was expected of me, I knew who'd hurt me or wouldn't. I knew the doors were locked as tightly going in as they were going out. There weren't ups and downs in that house, everything was always the same, and that made it easy to know... When I left, every day was a good one... but when the bad ones came, they felt extra bad. It started to sink in that I didn't know what normal people expected. People out here play these mind-games and assume you know what they want. And I didn't know what was legal or wasn't. I didn't know who I could trust. This one girl, she was really sweet to me, let me sleep in a tipped-over dumpster with her, and the next morning I woke up to find everything gone. My clothes, my money... everything I had... Other people my age are having the time of their lives celebrating being out on their own as adults, looking for that next rush of what the world has to offer, but me...?" I shook my head. "Freedom hasn't offered much. I've had to work three times harder than everyone else—and that's okay, I can handle it, but... I'm tired."

Grey hadn't said a word or made a sound, and it wasn't like him. He *always* had something to say, and because he wasn't, I was sure I knew what was happening.

I let my legs down and rested my head back against the wall behind me. "I understand if you want me to go. You didn't ask to be pulled into my mess." I tugged at my face. Even though I hadn't been crying, my face felt puffy as if I had been.

"You're *insane*."

I looked at him because his voice was a strained whisper. He was pulling his hands away from his face, exposing his red-rimmed eyes. Grey reached his arm toward me, so I moved closer.

"No, come here." His voice was still quiet and strained. He reached his other hand over to lightly pull on my arm. I couldn't get any closer, so I was forced to lean over. He hugged me in front of him and pressed his lips to the back of my cheek. "You are the most innately beautiful person I have ever met... why the hell would I ever let you go?"

"I can think of a few reasons," I whispered.

"Mm. Your Nutella problem *is* expensive, but I'll live with it."

"I wasn't being funny."

"I know." He kissed the back of my jaw, sending a surge of anxiety through me. "I know you did the best you could... For those kids and yourself... I watch you struggle *every* day, and it amazes me that you can hold onto these things and still stand... I don't think you did the wrong thing, I think you did the really *hard* thing and spared innocent little people from a hurt that would never go away if they *had* lived... I can't imagine having to make a choice like that, and don't think I could ever be strong enough to survive what you've gone through." He hugged me tighter and rested his cheek against my forehead. "You didn't deserve that life, B... no one does, but especially not you. Last month, I was a little offended when you said the worst part was that you survived, but I get what you meant now. I don't think anyone would want to after having to make choices like that and seeing it through... Others might see it as sacrificing *their* lives, but you sacrificed the rest of *yours*... You'll never forget."

My throat was burning again and I was afraid to let my lungs breathe. Having Grey know just enough to understand, and be so kind about it... I didn't expect anyone to even remotely understand. Even Toby had been upset with me. Each of the five times, knowing the fate those little kids would suffer, he was still angry. He wanted me to take them and escape from the house. So, having just one person understand that it was the hardest choice I'd ever made, and that it came at the expense of having to live with it the rest of my life, meant everything to me. It didn't make what I did right, I just needed understanding.

"Can I do anything for you?" Grey kissed the side of my forehead and stroked my hair back.

I shook my head.

"Make you a cup of tea, buy you a car faster than

your Volvo, buy you a house, buy the whole Nutella factory, hire a hitman to go hunt some sick assholes down, anything?"

I shook my head. "There's no one to hunt," I lied. If he knew or even thought there was still someone out there who might want to hurt me, he'd start a war if he had to. "And I don't need anything."

"Want, then. Money, diamonds, gold, uh... your very own jet ski?"

"Stop trying to make me laugh."

"I'm sorry." He kissed the side of my forehead again, then rubbed the back of his fingers over my cheek. "I'm serious, though. Can I do anything?"

"You already did... I need to go back to bed, my head is throbbing, and my stomach is killing me."

"Any chance you'll let me stay with you again?"

Part of me wanted to say no because I didn't sleep well with another person in the room, but more of me wanted Grey close. "Yeah."

"Okay... Let's go." He helped me sit upright again.

It was a *long* night full of nightmares. I felt bad for Grey because I woke him every time I shot up in a panic. The third time was the worst of four. The first two were just mixed-up memories of being in the house. The third was long and felt more real than the others. I feared Henry because he would beat the life out of me and it would be a slow death, but there *would* be death. Patty, on the other hand, wouldn't beat me and he wouldn't kill me. He would keep me locked away, somewhere where I couldn't be found, and I wouldn't get out. He was mentally unstable and believed he was in love with me to the point of obsession. I feared him more than anyone, and in my dream, he'd found me. His death at the prison had been faked and he'd come to save me after Henry had captured me. After he'd saved me from Henry's grips, I was drugged and taken to a house in the middle of nowhere, forced to play the role of his "darling" little sister again. The nightmare after that one wasn't as bad by comparison, but enough to wake me.

After getting up in the morning, I showered, got dressed, put my makeup on, and put my hair up. It wasn't my usual routine on a Sunday, but I needed to feel like Bexley Nelson and not Hannah Lawrence. In my mind, they existed as two separate people. Bexley was certainly scarred by Hannah, but she was an entirely different person. The biggest difference between them was Hannah could rough bad weather. She didn't walk around timidly, her skin didn't burn at a harmless touch, and she functioned at a higher level under duress. Hannah could go days without sleep, food, and stretch small amounts of water long enough to stay alive in a state of utter dehydration. She could survive injuries— both mental and physical—that would normally break a sane mind. Bexley was certainly the weaker of the two, but she was always ready to run, and ready to let Hannah take over at a moment's notice. I wasn't crazy, I didn't have multiple personalities, but there was a separation because there had to be. It was how I survived.

"Hey." Grey gave a sympathetic smile. He was sitting at the kitchen counter on his laptop. "Did you sleep any better after I left?"

I shook my head. "No. I told you it wasn't you."

His smile changed a little, making it touch the corners of his eyes. "I would've suggested a day on the couch, but you look like you're ready to go somewhere. Did you have something planned today?"

I nodded once. "Get out of the house and find something to do, a place to be, I don't care, but I need to keep moving."

His eyebrows raised. "Can I tag along?"

I smiled a little. "It's mandatory, but I'm driving."

He laughed. "Okay. Are we staying in the city, going

out of town, going to another town...?"

"Mm..." I thought for a moment and was interrupted by my phone vibrating in my hand. I pushed the volume button to make it stop. "Somewhere with no cell service."

Grey's smile had faded slightly, noticing me ignoring Ryan's call. "He's calling to apologize for yesterday. He called me fifteen minutes ago because you're not answering."

I held up my shoulder, pulling back the corner of my mouth. "I'm not interested."

Grey took in a deep breath, meaning he didn't like my response. "How soon are we going?"

"As soon as you're ready."

Grey looked at his watch. "I can be ready in five minutes or less. Does that work?" His expression was lighter as he looked at me again.

"Yeah. I'm gonna grab a yogurt."

"There's a cold omelet for you in the fridge. Stick it in the microwave and eat something *real*." He stood up and kissed my cheek before he went down the hall.

I went to the fridge and grabbed the omelet, but only because I didn't want to be rude and not eat what he'd made for me. I'd been having a hard time with my stomach because of stress. If I ate anything that was too hard to digest, my stomach would turn into an acid pit, eventually leading me to throw up. Grey had me seeing a nutritionist a week after I'd moved to Seattle, and she was able to help quite a bit, but not completely. I'd spent too many years being starved, drugged, fed poisons, and given bad water. The nutritionist said it would take nearly as long to repair the damage to my gut. I saw her once a week to adjust the supplements I was on, but I wasn't convinced any of it worked that well. Both the nutritionist and Grey said it would take time before I noticed a difference.

Ryan called two more times while I ate. Both times, I ignored the call. Since moving to Seattle, he acted like

I was a constant thorn in his side. Asking for help with homework was pointless because he was always "busy", or he'd tell me, "I have my own damn homework." Then, there'd been four times we'd made dinner plans and he'd cancel last minute. When he came over while I suffered in bed all day, it was the longest I'd seen him in weeks, but I was too out of it to talk, and I didn't want to talk to *him*. I knew if I told him I'd gone to the doctor by myself and past things were stirred up, he'd lose it on me, and I was right. What I didn't expect was *how* right I was. So, I didn't think it was petty to ignore his calls because I was simply done with him. Grey could be friends with him all day long, it made no difference to me, but I was tired of feeling like the pest he couldn't shake.

"Okay. I'm ready if you are." Grey interrupted my thoughtful stare at the floor.

I nodded and put the lid back on the glass container before putting it back in the fridge.

"I was thinking we could drive up the side of Mount Rainier. I think you'd like Paradise Valley Road, and we can come back up through Tacoma and hit up your favorite ice cream place on the way back," Grey said as we walked to the garage. "Unless that's longer than you want to be gone."

"No. It sounds perfect."

Grey opened the garage door. "Pick a car."

I went down the steps into the garage, looking at my pick of six vehicles. Grey's Range Rover and my Volvo were our daily drivers, but at the back of the garage was a burgundy-colored Bugatti, a midnight blue Aston Martin, a musk blue nineteen fifties pickup with a wood tailgate, and a bulletproof black Mercedes car.

"The Aston?" I bit my lip as I looked at Grey with a cringing smile.

He laughed. "You're responsible for your own tickets, Lady." He turned to the lockbox hanging on the wall where the keys were kept to the four extra vehicles.

At the house Grey had before this one, someone had broken into his garage and taken his prized Bugatti out for a joy ride, so he kept the keys locked up instead of in the cars like he used to. "You *cannot* go more than ten over in town."

I scrunched my nose a little. "And you tell me I'm no fun?" I took the keys from him.

"You got lucky I knew the cop."

Grey had taken his Range Rover into the shop for service, ended up needing to go out of town, and took my car, so I'd driven the Aston Martin for two days. I was late for class and not paying attention... then I was *really* late for class. Because I was in jeans and a hoodie, the car wasn't registered to me, and the cop knew Grey but didn't know about *me*, he called Grey. Grey asked for a favor, and I was let go with a lecture and a serious warning. Regardless, I loved to drive fast, even in my Volvo.

"I didn't know I was going that fast." I walked over to the car and touched the handle to make it open.

After Grey backed my car out, I backed out and waited for him to put my car back and get in. Ryan called *again*, so I went to his contact and blocked him. Not answering the first eleven times should have got the message across, so maybe being blocked would.

It'd been a while since Grey and I had spent the day just driving. We'd done it quite a few times in Monterey, but not since I'd been in Seattle. Our conversations were all over the place, one topic morphing into another. While on the topic of religion, voices were raised but it was all in fun. Grey believed in a higher power and I didn't. For every point he made, I had a counterpoint and it frustrated him straight into a volume control issue. I found that more amusing than the actual conversation and poked fun at him for being so overzealous.

Grey had been right about the road up the side of Mount Rainier. Not only were the twists and turns fun, but the thick forest of pine trees hugging the sides of the road were calming to me. We got out at a few of the look-out points for a break outside the car because it was a long drive. Near Reflection Lake, Grey asked about Ryan, wanting to know all that was said. He understood my side of things and wasn't happy with Ryan, but told me to give Ryan some leniency. Grey had been working him like a dog, Tim was in a depressive and therefore needy state, and Ryan was only getting a few hours of sleep a night. Ryan always turned into a grouch when he didn't get his full eight hours of sleep, but I still didn't think it was a good enough reason to be an ass.

When we stopped for ice cream, Grey suggested taking a self-defense class in hopes of easing my anxiety. I was against it because it involved strangers touching me, so we came to a compromise. He would have an instructor come to the house and Grey would be the only person touching me. Grey was a blackbelt in Judo but didn't think it would be as helpful to me as a self-defense class that covered other bases like disarming someone with a weapon. By the time we got back, he'd already hired someone.

Chapter 25

Bexley

After Grey and I got home, I went up to my room to finish the last of my homework. Once that was done, I went to my closet—which was bigger than the room I rented before I met Grey—and started unpacking the last of the boxes I had left and sorted the laundry I'd done Wednesday morning. I hung one of my pencil skirts up and jumped after turning to go back to the laundry basket. Ryan was standing in the doorway of the closet. I had music on and didn't hear him come in.

Ryan raised an eyebrow at me. "I knocked before I came in your room."

"Well, I didn't hear you," I said breathlessly as I dropped my hand from my chest and reached over to turn my music down. "Why are you here? It's almost midnight." I walked back to the pile of clothes sitting on the large ottoman in the middle of the closet.

"Because you didn't answer the phone all day and I couldn't get here until now." He reached over to grab a dark gray sweater hanging off the edge of the box next to the door. "I was looking for this."

"You left it in my car. I washed it for you. And that entire box is yours." Mostly, it was full of books Ryan had lent me.

He didn't bother to look or acknowledge what I said. "I know I owe you an apology, but I want to explain first."

"I don't need either. You wanted to say whatever you thought would hurt me, and you'll be sorry until it happens again. I don't want people like that in my life. You can take your stuff and go." I grabbed a small stack of hangers for my blouses that couldn't be folded without wrinkling.

He walked into the closet and sat down on the ottoman with a sigh. "You scared me... I don't know if Grey has ever told you about what happened when Tim and I were kids, but my dad beat the shit out of us." He looked at his wrist as he twisted his watch closer to his hand. The only reason I wasn't immediately kicking him out was because I was a little shocked by what he'd just said. "My mom just left one day, but she left us kids behind. Roger was working my dad into the ground, so when he was home, he was tired and drunk... Grey was going to camp for the summer, Roger offered to pay for Tim and I to go, neither of us wanted to because Remy, our little brother, wasn't old enough at five years old and we knew he'd get hit while we were gone... It was worse than that.

"It was a six-week camp." Ryan pinched his hand down the stubble on his face to his chin. "Tim and I came home and found Remy in the closet under the stairs. He had cuts and bruises, burn marks, a broken leg, he was laying in his own piss and shit... and he was dead from starvation."

I sat down next to Ryan, not knowing what to say

or how to say it, but my guts felt twisted. And I wanted so badly to hug him or hold his hand—anything to make him feel better—but I didn't know if he'd want me to. I knew Ryan lost his little brother, but I'd never asked how.

He let out a breath, pausing for a minute. "I don't know what you went through, Nelson, but I've seen the scars on your back." He itched at his forehead with a thumb on his temple. "I know you're terrified of basements, and you were starved. You were locked away so no one could help you... You remind me of Remy—quiet, wouldn't hurt anyone... I've never scared easily, but I've watched Tim spend his life terrified to leave the house because we weren't home to save Remy. And I didn't have it as bad as you, but I know what it's like to remember... spend the day in bed and stare at a bottle of pills...

"I couldn't go to the doctor with you because I was out of town, and when I found you in bed and you wouldn't respond, it brought shit up. It's not your fault, you were trying to get through your own shit. I was pissed everything got brought up for *both of us* because you couldn't wait another day to let me go with you to the doctor. When you showed up yesterday, I'd just gotten off the phone with Grey after he chewed my ass, and I took that out on you too..." He messed with the crown on his watch. "It won't happen again... and I'm really sorry."

I could understand the compilation of past things adding up with current ones. It was enough to make a person lose their mind once in a while. Ryan had just lost his in a different way than me.

"Can I be your friend again?" Ryan looked at me.

"As long as you don't ever talk to me like that again."

He shook his head. "I won't. I promise."

"Okay."

His eyebrows raised just slightly. "Are you okay after the other day?"

I held up a shoulder, pulling the corner of my mouth

back. "Better, but not there yet. What about you? You don't seem like your usual bitter self."

He looked down at his hands with a smirk. "I'm plenty bitter, don't worry." He looked at me, seriousness back on his face. "I've just been worried about you. He didn't tell me what was going on, but Blondie said you had a pretty rough night last night too."

"Yeah. There's a lot of past stuff lingering, then I told Grey some things I wish I hadn't." I shook my head, looking down at my hands. "Not because he reacted badly or anything like that, just... It makes me nervous having anyone know certain specifics about my life. It's that constant paranoia of waiting for the other shoe to drop."

"Yeah. Be careful what you tell him though, he's one of those 'sensitive' people. He's also one of those people who'll do something if there's something to be done, especially for you."

I nodded. "I know... I'm careful about what I tell anybody. There's not many people who could handle it." I wasn't even sure Ryan would handle it well. I was fairly sure if he knew the entire truth, he'd be hunting Henry down just for sport. Grey would put Henry in jail, but Ryan would go for the kill.

"Yeah..."

"Can I ask what happened to your dad?" I looked at him to gauge his reaction. He'd chosen to tell me about his brother, but I didn't know if he'd talk if he was asked.

"He's in jail. He wasn't home when we got there, and I called Roger before the police because Tim was losing his shit and I didn't know what to do." He shook his head. "I remember parts and pieces after we found Remy, but I know Roger sent his guys out to find my dad because he wasn't at work. They beat the shit out of him before they took him to the police... He's up for parole next year, but he already got a slap on the wrist with twenty years, so I plan to make sure he serves every second of it, because it'll only be thirteen years by the time he's up for parole."

"Have you ever gone to see him?"

"Nope. Last time I saw him face to face was before we left for camp. He better pray it stays that way." Ryan's watch chimed and he looked at it. "I gotta get going." He dropped his wrist and looked at me. "Are we good?"

I nodded, pulling the corner of my mouth back. "Don't forget your books." I pointed near the door.

"Keep 'em. I'm already playing Tetris with books. But if you get rid of them, don't tell me."

I laughed quietly as I stood up with him to walk him out. "I don't know what that is, but you have a book problem." Ryan couldn't get rid of a book. He could loan them out, give them to someone who he thought would enjoy them, but he couldn't donate or sell them. Every shelf in his house was stuffed with books.

He looked at me wryly. "Tetris?"

I shook my head and opened the bedroom door.

He sighed, shaking his head. Ryan looked at Grey who was coming down the stairs from his room. "She doesn't know what Tetris is." He stared down the stairs.

"Really?" Grey looked at me with raised eyebrows and a smile.

"And apparently I won't until I find a dictionary." Ryan could've just said what it was instead of making a big deal about it.

Grey went down behind Ryan. "Your house or mine?"

"Mine. I'll make dinner. Normal time."

"Are either of you going to tell me what it is?" I waited until Grey was a few steps down before I followed.

"It's a video game," Grey answered.

"No. I don't want to go over just to watch you two and Tim play video games all night while you verbally bash each other."

Grey and Ryan laughed.

"It's not just a video game, it's a classic. You'll actually like this one." Grey looked at me with a smile from the landing.

"It's basically putting puzzle pieces together to clear as many lines as you can before it reaches the top. It's stupid and addicting." Ryan stopped in front of the door and turned.

I scrunched my nose. "I don't like puzzles."

Grey's smile was still in place. "Just trust us, you'll like it."

I was still against it, I hated video games. "We're taking separate cars. I'll stay for dinner."

Ryan rolled his eyes, then looked at Grey. "Thank you." He held out a hand.

Grey shook Ryan's hand with sort of appreciative-adoring type of smile. "Anytime. You know that."

I wondered what the exchange was about. It wasn't their normal goodbye.

Ryan looked at me and held out his wrist. "Don't ever bring anything up with Tim, okay?"

I shook my head and bumped his wrist with mine. "Of course not."

Grey opened the door for Ryan.

"See you tomorrow. Have a good night." Ryan turned out the door.

"You too," Grey and I responded.

Grey waited a minute for Ryan to be out of sight before he closed the door.

"What was he thanking you for?" I asked lightly as if I weren't being nosey.

"He needs some time off and some stuff taken off his plate for a while because he can't balance everything he's got. I didn't realize how much he had been doing at one time, so we did some reorganizing."

I nodded. "Good. He's been looking worn down for weeks now."

"Yeah." He pulled back the corner of his mouth with a partial smile. "What aren't you supposed to mention to Tim?"

"Remy. He told me what happened."

Grey's eyebrows raised. "Really?"

I nodded and walked over to make sure the garage door was locked.

"Wow... I'm surprised he told you." Grey itched the back of his head, seeming almost confused.

"He doesn't talk about it?" I guessed.

"You're probably the first person he's ever told. The only reason I know is because I was in his life at the time. Mostly, my dad told me. It's a pretty untouchable subject with Ryan and Tim."

My brain sort of paused at the thought of something and I went straight out the front door. Ryan turned with a confused frown when he heard me. "Are you okay?" I took a few steps closer so he didn't have to speak loud enough for someone else to hear.

"Yeah, why?" His frown stayed in place.

"Because remembering isn't usually as short lived as the memory." He'd obviously been stuck in the memory of his brother the past few days, or he wouldn't have mentioned it to me. Normally, Ryan didn't give personal details about himself, even when he was asked. I would deflect or lie when asked, but he wouldn't answer at all. It made me wonder if he felt like me, where it was becoming harder to hold on to the longer it was held, and having any part of it come up made it throb uncontrollably. "I also know what it's like to have that little control over a situation—to feel like it might be your fault in some way because you weren't big enough to be able to do something."

His eyebrows raised. "I was big enough to do

something. I could have told anybody what my dad did behind closed doors and it would've been taken care of. And I'll straight up blow a gasket if you tell me I was just a kid and didn't know better."

I shook my head. "It's rarely about knowing better and more about caring for someone you know you shouldn't. I think you loved your dad... You hated him when he hurt you, but you knew he had a disease. Nothing wipes away your brother's death or makes it easier to live with, but you weren't wrong for ever loving your dad..." I held up a shoulder. "I can only speak for myself here, but for me, the hardest part is letting someone else be responsible for their actions. I have to chip at myself because I need someone to take accountability, and I know the people responsible won't. The other problem is, even if they did, nothing is changed... Remy probably loved his dad too, and if the tables were turned, I can't see you ever blaming Remy. I think you'd be angry if he did. Little kids just want someone to love them and care, and you do. *Still*... Let that matter more than feeling guilty."

Ryan's jaw was tight as he stood there silently for a moment. He turned to face his truck, then leaned over the hood on his forearms. We could be very different, but sometimes, Ryan and I were exactly the same. Silence was our cry. I stood next to him and looped my arm through his because I didn't want him to be in the silence alone.

His voice was nearly a whisper. "I don't know how you don't walk around in a cloud of anger, Nelson." He shook his head. "There's days I lock the door because I know I'll break the first skull I see."

"My dad used to say, 'Misery likes company, and anger is a mask made to cover something else'... I'm not angry... just hurt. And I don't hate anybody because hate is what caused people to hurt me. I'm too tired to perpetuate it... I'm hurt, and I'm tired."

Ryan reached over and put his hand on my arm but didn't say anything. We stood there in front of the truck with our silence while the breeze whispered through the trees. I didn't lose my brother and sister or my parents in the same way as Ryan had lost his, but I did lose them. I understood the regret that came with it. If I'd just told my dad what had happened at Emily's birthday party instead of being angry and petty, everything would've been different. If I'd told him instead of begging him to take me to the doctor, I wouldn't have left him with a life of guilt, my mom wouldn't regret asking her teenage son to take me so she could catch up on sleep, Emily wouldn't feel bad about getting a dollar stuck in the vending machine, and Ben wouldn't blame himself for leaving the room to get Emily her dollar back...

I put my other hand over Ryan's because I was thinking too much again and the pain of it was becoming excruciating. My chest felt physically heavy from simply missing my family. When I'd been locked away in that house, I used to think about them obsessively because I was terrified of forgetting them, but after being set free it was too painful. I tried not to think about them now, to wonder what they were doing, who they'd become in my absence... Thinking about them felt like a worser torture than Henry, Patty, any employee, or client could impose.

"What's your favorite classical piece?"

I looked at Ryan with confusion at the randomness of the question.

"We're distracting ourselves," he answered without me actually asking.

I looked above Ryan's truck at the tall hill of houses and trees. "Beethoven's seventh symphony."

"Why?"

Chapter26

Bexley

Time was a funny thing. If you paid attention to it, it would punish you by dragging along in a tormenting taunt, and if you paid no mind, it punished you by passing too quickly. There was no winning with time; there was either too much or not enough. Lately, there hadn't been enough. I'd made it through my first year of college, saved a nice little nest egg, went to my first concert, first opera, Switzerland for Christmas, New Zealand for spring break, and now we were in the Hamptons for a two-week summer break with Grey's parents.

For the most part, things were good. Living with Grey was easier than I'd expected. Part of me had been sure I'd move out after a few months, but it never happened. I enjoyed whatever time I got to spend with him between work and school. He was easy to be around, didn't pry about my past, gave me space when I needed it, and made me feel like there was more to look forward to than just surviving another day. The weeks he was gone on business were the only dreaded days I had.

While everything with Grey was good, I still couldn't forget about the past. Someone was for sure going after Henry. It'd started with the house being burned down, Patty being killed, then continued with a series of arrests that seemed to come in waves. At least a hundred or more of Henry's most frequent clients had been arrested. All the evidence the FBI needed had been provided to them from anonymous tips. Someone had found the hidden thumb drive in the house, and I wondered if that someone was Toby. He was the only one besides me who would have known Patty kept pristine records. Henry would've killed Patty on the spot if he'd known Patty was keeping those kinds of records on anyone, let alone everyone.

I stared at the screen on my phone, seeing a face I hoped to never see again—just like the rest. Earnest York, a man who was nearly as twisted as Henry, had finally been arrested after evading the FBI's first attempt a month ago. He'd been spotted at a grocery store in a small town in Arizona, and someone had recognized him from the near constant stream of media coverage. The entire US was keeping up with the takedowns tied to Henry, rooting the FBI on like a bunch of cheerleaders. Granted, I wanted all guilty parties behind bars or dead, but I also knew my life was more at risk now than it had ever been.

"You allergic to the pool or something? We've been here a week and I haven't seen you get in once." Sam draped his towel over the sun lounger to the left of me.

"Sam, don't be a pest. She doesn't have to get in if she doesn't want to." Cynthia spoke in a monotone as she continued to hold the arts and leisure section of the newspaper in front of her.

"I don't like being in bodies of water larger than a tub," I responded politely with a smile. There were still thick scars on my back I couldn't yet afford to have removed, they required surgery before laser removal would work. My dental implants had costed more than anticipated, then there were the seven surgeries to rebreak various bones to have them set properly so I'd have less pain. By the time I got through it all, not only was I heavily addicted to painkillers, but I was out of money. My priority had been to take care of the scars clothing couldn't cover, and I'd done that, but some remained hidden.

"Are you afraid or you just don't like it?" He sat down facing me on his sun lounger.

"Sam," Cynthia warned.

He turned his head to look at her. "Dude, I'm asking a legit question, not cracking jokes." He shook his head, looking at me. "Jeez."

"Too much exposure," I answered quietly. "Where'd Katie run off to?"

Katie was Sam's new summer-time girlfriend. I thought Grey was kidding when he said Sam had a new girlfriend for every season, but found it wasn't a joke.

"Sailing with her family or something. I don't know." Sam reclined back on the lounger and put his sunglasses down before he crossed his hands behind his head.

"Bexley, may I have a word?" Roger's stern voice came from behind us.

I looked back at Roger, forcing a smile. "Sure." Roger had been seemingly nice to me, but I didn't trust him. Grey hardly spoke a word to him since the brunch. Because Grey wanted nothing to do with him and Ryan didn't like him, I was cautious. Grey was a good judge of character, and while Ryan was an antisocial who didn't like people, he'd known Roger most his life, so he must've had a good reason.

Cynthia looked back at Roger. "Is everything alright, Dear?"

Roger gave a single nod. "Just fine. You should start getting ready for dinner. We don't want to be late."

"I'll be ready." Cynthia looked at her watch, then back at her newspaper. "Bexley, Sweetheart, come see me after you've gotten dressed."

"Okay," I answered before walking over toward Roger. I forced another polite smile at him while putting my phone in my back pocket. "I spoke with Grey earlier, he said he'd meet us at the restaurant."

Roger nodded once. "Yes, a message was relayed to me already."

I bit the inside of my lip, not knowing what else to say. Roger was full of awkward silences when he wasn't entertaining someone. We walked up to the doors that went to his office inside the house and he directed a hand for me to go in ahead of him after opening the door. I'd worked on going through doors with someone behind me, but it still made my back sting. It didn't stop once I was through the door because I didn't know what Roger wanted to talk to me about, and I didn't have Grey or Ryan to buffer. Both of them were in New York City.

"Please, have a seat." Roger walked behind his desk and sat in his chair after I was seated. "I rather hope this conversation will remain between the two of us. Grey is already upset with me over a myriad of reasons and I'm not looking to add to it."

I nodded but I didn't like being asked to keep anything from Grey.

He nodded once. "I also want you to know this conversation isn't meant to intimidate, dissuade, or create further disputes. You'll have to forgive my elusiveness, but I have knowledge of unrelated matters that can't be shared at this time."

I frowned a little, wondering what he was getting at.

"You've managed to win the hearts of our family, which isn't an easy feat. While we have many friends, we Maslen's tend to keep closed ranks to keep out problems and phonies. Any number of people could use us to seek financial gain and social status. You seem to seek neither... I've been skeptical of you for some time, but it would seem your intentions have been honest throughout." He took in a deep breath. "I think you're a very lovely young woman and you've been good for Grey, but I still have concern over your seemingly non-existent past. There are detailed paper trails, but there seems to be no other trace of you until you ended up in Monterey. Whomever you paid to keep your past concealed did a rather impressive job. However, my private investigator hasn't been able to find one live person who's heard of you." Roger's expression didn't seem to be one of suspicion, threat, or even judgment. "It's obvious by your habits that wherever you came from wasn't a good place. My question to you is, should I be concerned your past may become a future problem?"

My heart was pounding so hard I could feel it in every inch of my body. Did he know more than he was saying? Was he trying to run me off? I looked toward the windows, wondering if I should just run now. If I could wait until we went to the city, I could excuse myself to the bathroom without suspicion and disappear. New York City was a big place with endless ways to evade Grey or anyone he might send to find me.

"Bexley, I'm not threatening you, I'm offering my assistance."

I looked at Roger again. How would he know I needed help? I felt like I did need help, but I didn't know for sure. I didn't know who was going after Henry and everyone associated with him. Because the house had been burned down, and because of the knowledge I had, Henry would easily assume it was me going after him. There was no real way for him to find me, so my safest option was to stay put and be vigilant, but still... I didn't know if I was safe or if I needed help.

"Is there anyone out there who may potentially pose a threat to you or our family?" Roger continued to watch me with a gentle but concerned expression.

Regardless of what Roger potentially knew, my best option was to lie. If he knew any part of the truth, I had to assume he didn't and keep to my lie. It was safer for everyone.

I shook my head. "I didn't grow up under normal circumstances. The people who raised me were cruel. No one's heard of me because I wasn't allowed out of the house." I paused a moment to gauge Roger's reaction. "When my parents died, I ran and stayed hidden. I didn't know if there was other family who might try to take me in or reach out. Given how I was treated by my parents, I didn't stick around to find out."

Roger took in a deep breath as he nodded. "Alright... Should something arise, I hope you'll come to me. While Grey is resourceful, he's been sheltered to an extent. He doesn't have the experience to handle matters that may take a certain kind of discretion or finesse—if you will. While involving the law may be applicable to many matters, you've obviously learned somewhere along the line it's not applicable to *all*."

I nodded, knowing that better than anyone. What I didn't understand was why Roger was offering to help. "Can I ask where this is coming from? Why we're having this conversation?"

He gave a small, kind-eyed smile. "I can't divulge all of my reasoning at the moment, but I believe you have a very bright future ahead of you. In the year I've known you, you've achieved a great deal—both personally and professionally—and managed excellent grades in school. I'd truly hate to see your efforts go to waste over past matters."

I pulled back the corner of my mouth. "Me too."

Roger took in a deep breath as his eyebrows raised. "You have a dinner to get ready for, my dear. You'd better go before Cynthia hunts us both."

I forced a smile with a nod and stood up. "Yeah."

"Bexley?"

I turned around at the door.

"I meant what I said. If ever you need help, please come to me. I *will* help you... You have my word."

"I will." If it came to the point of needing help, I'd be gone. I couldn't let Grey or his family become entangled with Henry in any way. Part of never telling Grey about me was to keep him safe. If he didn't know anything, Henry would have no use for him.

I turned and left Roger's office to go to my room.

After dinner, Ryan, Sam, Grey, and I went to a Broadway show. Grey and Sam enjoyed the show, but I sided with Ryan about being thoroughly uninterested. I didn't care for the music, the over-the-top acting, or the painted sets. I realized it wasn't supposed to be like watching a movie, but I simply didn't enjoy it.

Once the show was over, we boarded a yacht that would take us back to the Hamptons. The four of us sat up on the deck with a few drinks. Ryan made fun of the show we'd watched while Grey and Sam tried to defend. As per usual, I was lightly teased for not joining in on their banter. It didn't bother me though, I enjoyed their dynamic.

"Mr. Maslen, you asked for a reminder when it was time," an attendant of the yacht said when there was a break in the boys' rantings.

Grey looked at his watch briefly, then smiled at the man. "Yes, thank you."

Sam and Ryan both put their beers down on the coffee table between the four of us.

"It's about damn time." Sam stood up and rubbed his hands together like he couldn't wait for whatever was coming.

"Are we stopping somewhere?" I asked Grey as he took my drink from me.

"Nope." He flashed a grin that told me he was up to

something. I knew that look.

I took his offered hand to let him help me stand. "What did you buy now?"

Ryan let out a short bark of a laugh. "Ha!"

"I didn't buy anything," Grey laughed. "Come on. We can't miss it." He led me to the front of the boat.

I looked back at Ryan for some indication of what we were doing, but his face gave no clues.

"Are you ready?" Grey wore a beautiful smile.

I shook my head. "I don't know what we're doing."

All the lights on the boat went dark, leaving only the city lights. Spots of light in the sky instantly coordinated by at least a hundred drones hanging in the air. Music began to play from the boat's speakers.

"Did you do this?" I looked at him.

"Of course he did." Ryan leaned over the railing on his arms as he watched.

"Look up. You'll miss it."

I gave a slight laugh and looked at the sky. "Are you really that bored on a boat?"

He laughed. "I might be if this doesn't go well."

The lights danced in an array of patterns with the montage of music playing. It was mesmerizing but dizzying because we were moving along the water. The drones moved about forming hearts, then words appeared in the sky. "Beautiful Bexley, will you marry me?"

I was stumped for a second until I saw Grey move beside me and the lights on the boat started to raise. I looked at him in disbelief, seeing him get down on one knee, holding a ring in one hand and my hand in the other.

"I know you probably wanted some kind of fore-warning, but I thought this was only fair. The first time I saw you, I was blindsided." He laughed a little, making the corners of his eyes crinkle with his beautiful smile. "I wanted to marry you about twenty minutes after I first saw you at the diner. You care about people, expecting nothing in return, and you'll do it to the point of sacrifice..." He pulled back the corner of his mouth in a gentle expression. "That's the kind of person I want by my side. I love· you more than anything and everything, B. Will you marry me?"

I was still in a state of disbelief. We were very obviously more than friends, and the thought of a life with Grey was a dream, but part of me always expected him to be done with me at some point. He was spontaneous and fun, and I was predictable and quiet. We were just about as opposite as we could be, and I expected him to be bored with me. While I'd managed to pull my life together, most of it was done on his dime with his advice, and that never seemed fair. I expected him to see me as a weight around his ankle more than a partner in life. But for whatever reason, he clearly didn't feel that way. Grey could make fast and loose decisions all day long, but I knew this wasn't one of them. To him, marriage was too sacred of a commitment to be suggested without a great deal of contemplation. Because I knew that, I knew my answer.

I nodded. "Yes." My voice was quiet because I felt embarrassed to have him on one knee in front of me.

Grey flashed a quick grin. "Are you sure? I could be broke tomorrow. We might have to sell the cars and move into a cardboard box."

"Stop talking about money."

He laughed and slipped the ring over my finger before he stood up. I felt a little self-conscious when he kissed me, then near mortified when all the staff on the yacht started clapping and the horn sounded. My cheeks were burning as we pulled away. The drones were flashing "she said yes". In the distance, there were cheers, whistles, and car horns from on land.

Grey chuckled lightly. "Should have done this at home on the couch, huh?"

"I would've thrown you a party if you *had*." The

public display of being proposed to was something I didn't know what to do with. I knew Grey couldn't help himself, and I wasn't upset about it, I just didn't know what to do.

"Selfishly, I think I got the better end of the stick this way."

"You and Sam owe me a hundred each." Ryan handed me a glass of champagne from the waiter who'd come with a tray.

I looked at him with confusion, wondering why I would owe him money, then saw he was talking to Grey. "I was expected to say no?" I guessed.

"No, Sam said you'd get teary-eyed, and I said Ryan wouldn't be able to keep his mouth shut about all of this." Grey took a glass of champagne from the tray. "I'm still not convinced Ryan didn't say something though."

"He didn't, and I'll extract my revenge accordingly." I looked at Ryan disapprovingly.

Ryan rolled his eyes. "You can be a big girl and deal with an in the moment decision."

I gave a small, but not so friendly smile. "I'm aware. I'm making decisions as we speak. I think Tim will enjoy what I have planned."

Ryan shook his head. "No. You leave my house out of this."

I raised an eyebrow. "I didn't say anything about your house." I looked at Grey and held my glass up between us. He laughed and clinked glasses with me before we took a sip.

It was a couple hours before we were back at the house in the Hamptons. Roger and Cynthia were waiting up to congratulate us, Sam went with his girlfriend to a bonfire party. I thought everyone went to bed, but when I was sitting out on one of the back patios lost in a daze of thought, Ryan came out. My brain was on overdrive, so I hadn't bothered with trying to sleep.

"I don't think anyone's expecting you to run around excited, but you don't seem like you're very happy about being engaged." Ryan sat down in the chair next to mine and lit up a cigarette.

"I am, I just... didn't expect it." I still couldn't wrap my mind around it.

"And...?"

"And, what?"

He blew out a line of smoke. "I could've gone fishing on the boat." Ryan looked at me. "What's the problem? You're acting like you said yes and you didn't want to."

I shook my head and looked out toward the ocean. "I wouldn't have said yes if I didn't want to... but I don't feel like I deserve it." I let out a breath. "And I don't need a lecture right now, so keep it to yourself."

"I'm too drunk to lecture. Why don't you deserve it?" He continued to look at me while I continued to stare at the water.

I shook my head. "I don't know," I answered quietly. "I know it's not completely true, but I still feel like a mess of a person... I could have a decent job pretty much anywhere, I can afford the payments on my car, rent on an apartment, school... but the second he asked me to marry him, I felt like a homeless diner-waitress again."

"You're past that... Grey might put a lot of emphasis on your achievements, but it's not how he measures you." Ryan took another drag of his cigarette.

I nodded. "I know... It's how I measure myself though." I looked at him. "I don't have any family, I'm not fun like him, my skin still burns if I'm touched unexpect-edly—and I can't even tell him why..." I shook my head. "I don't understand why he wants to marry someone who can't even tell him the truth."

He stared at me for a second with a frown of concern. "What is the truth?"

I pulled the corner of my mouth back as I shook my head again and looked out at the waves. "Even if I could say, no one would want to hear it, and no one could begin to understand... And that's the other thing, Grey has always been kind enough not to ask, but how long will that last? What happens when he does and I can't give him an answer? How long is he going to put up with the panic attacks and paranoia before he's tired of it...?" My throat was burning at the heartbreaking thought of Grey walking away because he was sick of dealing with me.

"He wouldn't marry you if he wasn't prepared to deal with it." Ryan's voice was quiet. "He might ask, and you might not be able to answer, but I think he loves you enough to let it go... As long as he knows you're okay, or you're going to be, that'll be enough."

"I don't know... I think I'm not being fair to him." I swallowed against the lump in my throat, honestly contemplating my answer. Grey didn't deserve someone like me, he deserved better.

"Do you love him?"

I glanced at Ryan for a moment. "Of course I do, but it's not enough to just love someone."

"Yeah, it is. If you love him enough that walking away feels like the worst thing you'll ever do, it's enough. No matter what someone else did, no matter what you did in response, out of survival, or lack of knowing better, you've changed. You've busted your ass to be here, and you've earned it. If you let people from the past take that from you, they win, and you let them... Don't do it."

I chewed on the inside of my cheek for a moment. "He still shouldn't have to deal with it."

"Maybe, but who gave you the right to decide that for him?"

I looked at Ryan, feeling as though I'd been verbally slapped.

His eyebrows raised. "He's a big boy, Nelson. He's also honest. If there's something he doesn't like, he'll tell you, and you know that. If you back out, it's because of you, not because Grey can't handle whatever the hell you're dealing with."

Ryan didn't know my past could easily come back, and I couldn't say that without raising a problem—in so, *making* my past come back.

"You guys will figure it out." He put his cigarette out in the grass. "If you're really that worried about it, talk to him, but I doubt he'll have anything different to say."

I already knew Grey wouldn't have something different to say. He'd tell me he loved me more than anything and everything and the rest doesn't matter.

"Incoming," Ryan said quietly after looking behind us. "I don't want to hear it," he said as Grey approached. Ryan was supposed to quit smoking, but he struggled with it.

"I wasn't going to say anything. You already know." Grey came up beside me and touched my cheek. "Can't sleep again?" His eyes were light-hearted.

"No," I answered quietly, giving the smallest of a smile.

"I can. I'm turning in." Ryan stood up as Grey sat down in the chair on the other side of me. "What time are we doing stuff tomorrow?"

Grey shook his head. "I don't have anything planned."

"I'm sleeping in then. Don't wake me up." Ryan turned to the house and went inside.

"What's going on, Beautiful? You've been off tonight." Grey sat leaning forward with his arms on his thighs to support himself. His lightness didn't change with his question.

"I'm okay." I forced a small smile.

"Naw, come on." He smiled a little. "A big life changing decision happened and you're squirming over it. I know you. What's on your mind?"

I took in a breath and let it out. "Why have you never continued to press me about my childhood?"

He seemed surprised by my question and his eyebrows raised with concern. "Was I supposed to? The last time I asked, you said never to ask again."

I shook my head. "No, but I don't know why you never asked after the one time. Other people would pry until their fingers bled but you let it go. Doesn't it bother you?"

Grey pursed his lips to the side. "Sometimes... and I do want to know, but I respect that you don't want to tell me." He held up his shoulders. "Where's this coming from?"

I looked down at my hands, tracing the edge of my fingernail with my thumbnail out of nervous habit. "I'm not sure you'd want to marry me if you knew."

"Are you secretly a serial killer?"

I looked at him with a frown.

Grey's eyebrows raised again. "B, you have a past but I know what I need to. You're a good person, you work hard at everything, you're constantly putting an effort forward to do better, and you were doing those things long before you met me. I love you and I know you love me."

I looked down at my hands again. It wasn't the answer I wanted to hear, but I wouldn't hear what I was looking for because he didn't know the truth.

Grey reached over to take my hand. "I care about who you are right now... I know the past weighs on you, but all I have with you is right now. You'll tell me what happened if you want to, but either way, tomorrow looks the same because the past is the past." He squeezed my hand lightly. "This isn't to say I'm not here for you, but those are your struggles, not mine. I don't struggle with who you are or where you've been. I love you more than anything and everything, and I want to be in your life... I want you to look back on your life when you're old and think it was a good one, despite the rough start."

The last of his words struck me so hard I could barely breathe. I didn't even know if it'd ever be possible for the lifetime of good to outweigh the seven years of horrendousness. The thought that seven years could weigh enough to ruin all the other years of my life was nearly as devastating as those seven years had been. I wanted to step out of my life right at that moment. I wanted to break my promise to Toby and be done with all of it... But then there was Grey. The thought of leaving him behind, of not taking in every single second with him, was more than devastating. And it was enough to make me stay.

I stood and pulled on Grey's hand to have him stand. As soon as he did, I buried my face in his shoulder as I hugged him. I hadn't felt safe since the day I'd been kidnapped, and despite anyone saying it, I hadn't felt loved in as long, but I felt both right there in Grey's arms. I knew he loved me, but I'd never allowed myself to feel it.

"I love you too," I whispered.

I could feel his cheek pull back with a smile. "I know."

Chapter 27

Bexley

"Bex?" Grey called from the entryway.

I quickly changed the channel on the TV with a shaky hand. The FBI was on a hunt to find me again. Everyone was sure I was behind the obvious attacks against Henry's operation. My family seemed to be keeping their head down in the media storm, which I was thankful for. One good look at my sister and Grey and his family would easily know who I was. I was damn near identical to her, only with brown hair and brown eyes as opposed to her blonde hair. Also, she wasn't as sickly skinny as me. Either way, things were becoming worse for me. One wrong move and I was dead. If the FBI found me, that would mean Henry had found me. Just because a bunch of people in the FBI had been busted as double agents didn't mean there weren't more to follow suit.

Today was especially bad for me because a client of Roger's had been taken down. The reason I knew he was a client was because I'd spotted him walking into a meeting with Roger last month. I hadn't even known the man's name. To me, he was client three-ten, but to the rest of the world, his name was John Clyde. He was the CEO of a security software company, now known to pro- vide Henry with a covering on the dark web. John, and a select number of people who worked for him, had set up the infrastructure for Henry to be able to market and sell humans like the average product, stream footage of child pornography, schedule sessions at houses like the one I grew up in, and a myriad of other illicit activities. John Clyde being handed over to the FBI meant a war was being staged in a very head-on way. It also meant I couldn't continue to lay low and go about my days ignor- ing what was happening. Henry would use any means necessary to draw me out, and I couldn't say I wouldn't go if the right string was pulled. I'd protect my family, even if I had to spend the rest of my life in the clutches of Henry.

"I'm in the living room," I called back weakly. I shut the TV off all together and started picking up the mess of papers around me. Our wedding was three days away and I'd been hashing out final details. I had zero idea what Cynthia was paying the wedding planner for when I seemed to be the one doing everything on top of making preparations in case I had to run over the situation with Henry.

Grey laughed. "There's a lot of tables in the house, desks even. What's with the mess?" He leaned over the back of the couch for a quick kiss.

I tipped my head back, kissed him, then looked at the papers. "Serena does nothing."

"Don't tell that to my mother."

"Oh, I'm aware. Serena walks on water. She's the best wedding planner in the country. Blah. Blah." I let out a huff and scooped the papers up; I didn't give a monkey's hide if they were organized. Serena could do some kind of work. "I'm still up for just signing papers.

No dress, no ceremony, no vows, just sign the papers and go home."

Grey laughed again. "My mom would hurl herself off the tallest building she could find, and we'd go down for murder. Three more days." He wrapped his arms around me from behind the couch. "I have some not-so-great news."

I shook my head. "Take me with you."

"Why do you automatically assume I'm going somewhere?"

I tipped my head back to his shoulder. "Aren't you?"

"Yes, but how do you *know*?"

"Because that's what I expect at the mention of bad news. Take me with you. It ensures everyone's safety." I closed my eyes and let out a breath.

"I have to go meet with Conway Freeman. Still wanna go?"

I scrunched my nose. If it were anyone else, I would. An idea quickly sprung to light. "No, but I still want out of here. No grumpy Ryan, no phone, no wedding plans, no Cynthia or Serena. I've been running like a horse at the triple crown since we left the Hamptons almost three months ago."

"I know. What do you want to do?" he asked quietly with his lips against my cheek.

"I don't know. Wing it. Go rent a beach house across the country, get a cabin in the woods."

"Make it happen. My treat."

I smiled a little. "No escort?"

"Mm. I don't know if I can do that. There's a lot going on with MWM right now, and we've worked really hard to keep the wedding quiet, but there's still jealous weirdos out there who want to be you." He chuckled lightly but it was grossly the truth.

"No. I don't want anyone following me around or driving me places. I want complete solitude. Shack in the middle of the woods, no electricity, lake water, fire."

He laughed. "Sounds like you want to be a cavewoman."

"If that's what gets me five minutes of no human interaction, yes."

Grey took in a deep breath and held it as he thought about it. "Okay." He let out his breath. "I'm grudgingly agreeing. Find a place and put it on my card." He kissed my cheek and pulled his lips away but didn't let go of me. "Can I take you out for dinner tonight?"

"Nope. We have to go to your parents' for dinner, remember?"

He dropped his face on my shoulder and let out a soundless whimper.

"I know." I ran my fingers through his soft golden hair. "But I'm all for getting a stomachache from the appetizer and finding something after we leave because I'm dying."

He chuckled quietly. "Deal. I need to go take a shower. Find yourself somewhere weird to stay."

"You know I will."

"Love you, pretty lady." He kissed my cheek quickly and let go of me.

"I love you too." I pulled my laptop onto my lap. I had to make my lie believable and find someplace to go that I could easily ditch.

My first stop was the cabin I'd rented at Trout Lake in Colorado. It put me fairly close to where I needed to be, but not too close. I spread my stuff out around the cabin as if I were actually staying there, turned on the bedroom light, closed the curtains, and left. On the off chance that Grey showed up or sent Ryan, I wanted to look like I'd been staying there. If I got back and someone was there, I could make up a lie about getting lost on a hike. I'd make sure my hair and clothes were a little disheveled before I returned. There was even a lie in place for the junky, untraceable car I paid for in cash.

Marvel, Colorado was about two hours south of Trout Lake. It was a nothing town with a handful of run-down houses and each with about five or more dead cars in the yard. I passed through, about ten miles south of town, on a gravel road until I saw the mailbox with a bear statue made out of wood. My stomach was in knots, and I felt about two seconds away from puking. What I was doing was dangerous for so many reasons, but sitting quietly while the edges of my world crumbled wouldn't work for much longer. I had to be prepared for whatever came instead of hoping I survived the unexpected.

The land around was relatively flat and ugly. The only reason I liked it was because I could see a couple miles out if someone was coming, or if I'd been followed. There hadn't been a car in sight for at least the last thirty minutes of my drive. The dirt had a reddish hue and there were small patches of desert plants around the posts of the barbed wire fences on either side of the road. I drove over the cattle guard, my heart continuing to pound harder as I looked at the curtains on the house. They were closed and the front porch light was on, even though it was daytime. It meant the house was safe.

When I neared the back corner of the small brown house, there was a silver car parked in the grass. I let out a slow breath, parked beside it, and got out. The air was as quiet as it had been described to me. There were nothing but empty fields for miles around. I continued to listen for just a minute to make sure there was no other sound that didn't belong, like a car or plane. My entire body felt like an electric nerve, every part of me was hyper aware of my surroundings. I pulled the sleeve of my sweater down over my watch. It was off, but I could easily turn it on to activate the SOS feature if needed. It would send Grey and Ryan a message with my location. Ryan would be smart enough to figure out where I was, who I was, and start searching from there if something went wrong.

The back door of the house opened with no urgency and Toby stepped out onto the top of the crumbling concrete stairs. He looked sad or worried at first, but then a loving smile appeared on his face. He looked so different without his clothes and face stained with dirt. His strawberry blonde hair glinted in the sunlight, and it was still a little overgrown to hide his cochlear implants, but not as much as when we'd been locked away. He'd grown only another inch or so, just a couple taller than me, and he wasn't sickly thin anymore. Toby had been seventeen when he was captured and nineteen when he escaped, so he was twenty-seven now. The four-year difference didn't seem as big as it once did, but eight years passing had aged us. It felt like a near lifetime had passed.

Toby jogged down the stairs casually with his smile and I walked toward him. As soon as we were within range, he hugged me tightly. I wanted to love that hug, I wanted it to be a happy reunion, but I felt like the dirty basement child. It felt like my hair wasn't up, my clothes weren't clean, my teeth were missing or chipped, and I was covered in scars.

"I missed you so *much*," he whispered before kissing my cheek and stepping back. "Look at you." Toby held my cheek with one hand and loving eyes. "You're even more beautiful."

I pulled back the corner of my mouth because I didn't know what to say. Being beautiful didn't hold a lot of value to me.

I signed, asking him how he was because I didn't know what else to do or say. It would've been rude to jump straight into business.

His smile stayed but his hand dropped from my cheek. "You can talk to me normally. I can hear you."

I nodded. I knew that, I just felt too embarrassed to speak. It'd never been safe for me to send him so much as a letter, but things were coming to a head, so I didn't have a choice.

"I'm okay. What about you?" His smile changed to concern. "I assume this isn't because you miss me."

I shook my head. "I need to know if it's you going after Henry." I still signed as I spoke because I wanted there to be no mistake. It would be exactly like Toby to lie about something like this.

He shook his head, looking at me like I was slightly crazy. "No. I don't even know who half these people are that are being arrested. I thought maybe it was you, but then some woman, Cynthia Maslen, came to see your parents last year. Ben said she was the one who knew where we were in Tennessee. She told them where to find you, but I got out first, then you the next day. And I left messages for you here, hoping you'd at least check them because you've been here before, but they've been untouched."

The earth felt like it was shaking under me. I'd wondered if Roger knew something, but never suspected Cynthia... Maybe it was both of them? That didn't make sense either because Cynthia didn't like me.

"Do you know her?" Toby asked when I stood there in shock, saying nothing.

I nodded. "Yeah..." I looked at him again. "Whatever you know about any of this, you have to tell me."

Toby nodded. "I will, but there's something else you need to know first." The corner of his mouth pulled back. "Patty's not dead. I think someone staged the prison death, but I can't prove it. I haven't seen him, but I know he's not dead."

"I've never believed he was." I held my hand to my forehead. My brain was trying to sort too many things at one time.

"And I wanted to see if you know this guy. He's probably no one, but he's been visiting Ben like once a month. And last month I saw him talking to your dad. Maybe it's nothing, but I'm just..." He let out a breath of exhaustion and handed me a paper with a picture of Ryan.

I bit the inside of my cheek and nodded. There was no fear, just anger. "Have you ever seen a blonde guy with him?"

Toby shook his head. "No."

"Okay..." I knew it didn't mean anything. Ryan worked for Grey, so he had to be behind everything, which was the exact reason I'd never wanted him to know.

"What's going on? Who are these people? They're going to get us killed."

"The less you know, the better. I'll take care of it." I itched under a pin in my hair, reminding myself I had to stay calm. The side of me that was Hannah was taking over; it was my survival instinct, and I had to keep a mind free from panic to hear her.

"No. I have a daughter to protect. What's going on?" Toby looked at me angrily.

"She's my daughter too, and I'd never let anything happen to either of you. You know that." It hurt that he didn't trust me more, but then again, it was my fault that we were meeting for any other reason than Henry being dead. "I'll handle this. I promise."

"Daddy?"

I froze, feeling like I'd been electrocuted by just the sound of a little girl's voice. Toby held up a finger to her, but I didn't move because I didn't want her to see me. I shoved his other arm and signed, "why" in front of my body.

He held up his shoulders, looking at me as if he were tired and disappointed in me in some way as he shook his head. "Because you came here without knowing what's going on around you, and that means you don't have a handle on anything. It's not your fault, I know you've done the best you could to protect everyone, but this was always bigger than both of us. We both know

Grace will be a casualty, so after I show you the house, you meet Grace, and you leave, I'm taking her and we're hiding."

I shook my head. "You're acting like I'm the monster here."

He frowned, looking more hurt than angry by my words. "Your daughter is in the house behind you, and you're mad."

"Because it's not *safe*! And what happens if she tells someone about this house, or that she saw me? She can easily recognize me, Toby. I look just like my sister."

"The fact that *that's* what you're worried about is the problem..." He pressed his lips together.

I felt like he'd slapped me. How was I wrong to be worried for Grace's safety? I'd done so much to protect both of them and my family, lived in complete squalor at times because it was more important to me than eating.

"*Nothing* about having a kid is convenient, and we couldn't help bringing her into this world any more than *she* could. None of us asked for it, but she's *here*, she *loves* you, and she's waited her *entire* life to meet you. So, I don't care if you have to go in there and fake it, but this might be the last time she sees you... Don't hurt her just because you're scared. We all are." Toby's mouth was quivering as he spoke. His hazel-green eyes had been boring into me with every word.

It felt like a different kind of fight to keep from bawling my eyes out and raging at Toby for his words, but I fought. "How dare you... Leaving her behind felt worse than most anything that happened in that house, especially after you went running to my family when I couldn't. You've been in a protected little bubble because Henry doesn't give a damn about you, and that is because of me. I'm the one who made sure you stayed inconsequential in all of this. I'm the one who'd made deals with *literal gangs* while you sat there and built your cute little campouts thinking it has *EVER* been enough! I've been getting ready to fight, while you've been plotting to hide. *That is why I'm here!* Hiding isn't enough, and if I can hope for any kind of a good outcome here, it'll be that my daughter doesn't have to walk out the door and fear being taken! That she won't have to *hide!* Don't pretend like you know a damn thing about me, Toby Anderson. *No one does...* I give small pieces of myself to any one person because I trust no one, and you should be grateful or both of you would already be dead."

I turned, taking in a deep breath, and looking at my daughter behind the screen door as I walked toward her. It would never be how I dreamed of meeting her, but meeting her was the real dream. Grace smiled as she pushed the door open, her beautiful dimples showing, and she ran out to me. I got down on my knees to be at her level so I could hug her as tightly as I wanted to.

"I knew it was you! I knew you'd come back for me," Grace said after she threw her arms around my neck.

"Even if it kills me," I whispered. "I love love *love* you."

"I love you too. Do you get to come home now?"

I shook my head. "I wish I could, but not yet." Her hair felt like silk as I combed my fingers through it.

She nodded. "Daddy said there's bad people that'll hurt you if they find you."

"That's right." I pulled back so I could look at her beautiful face again. She looked so much like Toby, but had my mom's eyes. "I'm gonna do everything I can to come back to you, but I need you to know if I can't, it's not because I don't love you. I love you so so much."

"I love you too." Grace picked up my necklace to look at it.

I reached up and combed her hair back behind her ear. "I'm so sorry I haven't been here for you, Gracie. I hope one day it'll be different."

"Me too." She looked at me with sullen eyes. "Do you have to leave right *now?*"

I gave her a smile and shook my head. "Not yet. You and I have some catching up to do first."

Grace's smile came back in a flash and she hugged me again. "Yay! I want to show you my paintings. In November, they get to be in a gallery because Aunt Emily's friend loves them so much she sent one to a guy in New York. A whole bunch of people are gonna come see them and buy them. I already sell a lot online, but this is like a store where they can see it in person." She pulled back, her eyes gleaming with happiness as she looked at me.

"That's amazing. I'm so proud of you." I touched the dimple on the side of her cheek, understanding for the first time why everyone often commented on mine. On Gracie, they were beautiful.

I got up and followed Grace into the house. She showed me some of the smaller paintings she'd been allowed to bring with her, and pictures of others. They were incredible and full of color. She painted portraits of animals' faces using dabbled strokes and rainbow colors. There was one of a calf I wanted for a room in my new house, but didn't tell her because I didn't know if I'd even make it there. I didn't want to get her hopes up.

After spending a couple hours with Grace, she ended up falling asleep on my lap. I sat there quietly, just stroking her hair and staring at her. It was the last time I was going to see her because the odds of me coming out alive were next to nothing, so I was just sitting there...

Toby came into the near barren living room and sat in the recliner next to the couch. "I'm sorry, Hannah... I made an assumption and I shouldn't have." His voice was quiet, but it always was.

I nodded. "People are full of them."

"I'm sorry, I didn't hear you."

I looked at him and signed, "People are full of them," as I spoke the words again.

He pulled back the corner of his mouth, looking

guilty. "Which is why I should know better..." He looked down at my hand, then at me again. "That's a hell of a ring."

I nodded. "He's a really good person."

"Does he know?"

I shook my head. "I didn't think so, but after what you told me earlier, he might."

He raised an eyebrow. "You're married to a guy and you haven't told him who you are?"

"We're not married yet, and he knows enough." I nodded once.

"Does he know you have a daughter?"

As sweet as Toby was, he could also push my buttons.

"It's not a loaded question." He held up his shoulders. "I'd want to know if I were in his shoes. Your identity is already a kicker."

"Which is why I don't tell him anything that could lead back to it, so no, he doesn't know. If it's anything that's been made public, I haven't told him."

Toby reached up and itched at his eyebrow with a wince. "I can explain the book. It's not a good one, but—"

"It wasn't a stab at your book, and I know why you wrote it."

Toby loved me and he didn't want to be called a rapist because it wasn't the truth. Henry wanted another baby he could sell, Toby refused to impregnate me, so Henry started slicing me open on Patty's surgical table to get Toby to agree and cooperate by manipulation. As I screamed from the pain, I begged Toby to help me, to not let me die. I signed with my hand that was strapped at the wrist. I knew if I died, Toby would be dead too, and I couldn't stand the thought.

"I *am* curious why you've made yourself close to my family though. You knew I had no intention of ever going back." I tried to keep the hostility from my voice this time. The situation was frustrating, my nerves were still burning, and it was hard to keep everything from showing in the form of misdirected anger.

Toby gripped the back of his neck for a second. "My parents told me to drop Grace at the fire station and forget about her. I told them 'no,' and they told me to get out because I was an embarrassment to them... I told them what happened, that I didn't rape you, and they didn't believe me. My siblings went spreading lies around town until I was beaten out in the street with six-week-old Grace in my arms. The only thing I could do was try to find a safe place for Grace, so I went to your parents in hopes that they'd be the good people you remembered them to be. Even still, even after explaining to the world with that book, I still get death threats, my car still gets vandalized, my house—with my daughter inside—still gets set on fire. We just moved again—this time out in the country—so hopefully people will leave us alone."

I felt awful for him. I also wondered how Grace must have been affected. School was a faint memory for me, but I still knew kids could be just as cruel.

"I'm sorry," I said quietly as I brushed Grace's hair back again.

He frowned the way he usually did when he didn't catch what someone said, so I signed the apology. Toby shook his head, but with a disapproving frown this time. "It's not your fault."

"I'm the one who begged you to do it." I traced the side of my finger over Grace's cheek after signing.

"That doesn't make it your fault." Toby was quiet for a minute before he said, "She writes you a letter almost every day... She's always been curious about you, but last year, she started to have a really hard time, so I told her to write you a letter. Now, she has a book. A few of them actually."

I pulled back the corner of my mouth in acknowledgment but didn't know what to say.

"And my parents?" I looked at him again.

"Your mom is even nicer than you said. Grace is her little pet." His small smile faded a little. "She does okay for the most part, but she'll close the door to her sewing room when she misses you. And your dad, he's not at all like you described. He'll talk to your mom, but otherwise, he pretty much keeps to himself. He sits in his office a lot... Emily, I swear, I can hear her even if I don't have my implants on." He chuckled a little and looked down. "She's sweet though. And she still irritates the hell out of Ben. They fight like dogs."

"So, nothing's changed." I watched him because there was something he wasn't telling me. "Ben doesn't sit there and blame himself, does he?"

"Every minute of every day. The way he misses you, you'd think he lost more than a sister..." Toby rubbed his hands together in a nervous manner and looked at me. "He's a good guy, but he's got one hell of a mean streak when it comes to you. He even ran off the mother of his own child over you."

I frowned. "What do you mean?"

Toby shook his head, looking down at his hands again. "He has a daughter—who could be more your identical twin than Emily—and when she was a baby, her mom, Beth, would do something not quite right and Ben would lose his temper. He's terrified of losing Ella the way he lost you. Anyway, Beth left when Ella was three days old because she couldn't take it. She came back last year to see Ella, and she and Ben worked things out and got back together, but... she died last week. She had cancer, and she lived a lot longer than they expected her to, but..." He shrugged his shoulders.

"Poor Ben." I was crushed for him. The only comparison I had would be losing Grey, and that would be something that *literally* killed me.

Toby nodded. "Yeah. He's taking it better than anyone expected but... Beth was really sick when she showed up, every extra minute he had went to her and Ella."

"Are you married or seeing anyone?" I turned my ring on my finger.

He laughed weakly. "I was hoping you wouldn't ask."

I looked at him with a confused smile. "Why?"

"Because you know her, and you don't like her." He sounded like he was posing a question.

I frowned, still confused.

"Emily," he nodded once.

I let my eyebrows raise, completely unsure how I felt about Toby with my sister.

"I asked her to marry me back in June..." The corner of his mouth pulled back. "She's done a lot for me over the years... She's been there."

I shook my head and looked down. "You don't have to explain. It's your business."

"She's your sister and she'll be Grace's step-mom, so it's kind of your business."

I felt like I was going to puke again. It wasn't that I wanted Toby, or even that I was jealous of Emily, really, I was just upset that I didn't grow up the way she did. She wasn't kidnapped, she didn't live the horrors I did, and she had our family in her life; she could be around Toby, and raise my daughter when I couldn't. I would never wish to trade places with my sister, I just wanted to be free the way she was. She didn't have to worry about anyone coming for her, she could marry and not feel guilty because she was in a hornet's nest of problems, and she wasn't hiding half of her life from someone.

"You didn't come back. I know you can't be around your family, but I thought you'd—"

"I'm not upset about it," I said quietly as I signed. I knew my voice was too quiet. I took in a breath to shove any emotion back down. "I have a good life. I'm getting married in a few days, we're moving into a beautiful house after the wedding, I work for him, I'm in college, I have good friends, most of his family is really nice... Other than some skeletons in the closet, things are good." Everything I said was true, but I didn't feel it because I was still missing my family. They wouldn't be at my wedding or be part of the life I'd been working so hard to have.

He smirked. "Some? There's an entire graveyard bigger than Arlington."

"Pretty much..." I took a deep breath. "Okay. Help me up without waking her. We need to get started."

"Yep." Toby got up from the chair and helped me move Grace to a pillow.

The house used to be Toby's uncle's who was estranged from the rest of his family but not Toby. When he passed from a heart attack, he left Toby everything he had. Before we escaped, the plan had been to meet at this house. He was going to make it a sort of fortress for us if we needed, but not the kind anyone would expect.

Toby showed me the well-hidden escape doors in each room, where guns and knives were hidden, food, first aid supplies, the instructions for chemical mixes to make gas bombs, where the chemicals were stashed, and both under the house and up in the attic were burner phones and a machine that would send out an SOS signal. He'd thought of far more than I expected, and I teased him for being paranoid. We'd both taken a lesson from Patty, though. He'd booby-trapped the house we were kept in ten ways to hell and back. Things were hidden in places people wouldn't even think of. Patty had even drilled holes down the center of chair legs to hide rolled-up papers from Henry.

After he showed me around, I gave him lists of things I'd done, where to find cars, money, and people to call depending on what situation was occurring. As soon as Patty was labeled as dead, I knew I needed to be prepared in the biggest ways I could. I made use of nearly every trip Grey took, disappearing for a few hours to find certain people or buying another car, guns, or stash money. The only way to survive Henry coming for me was to have backup plans in every direction possible, for both me and anyone affiliated with me. I'd even befriended high-level members of two different gangs in Seattle—on top of the ones in Texas and California. Toby needed to know everything I could tell him to keep Grace and himself safe. Saying goodbye to her was even harder the second time around. Grace cried and it killed me inside.

Chapter 28

Bexley

Once I left Toby, I went back to the cabin and turned my phone on. A single text from Grey showed up saying he hoped I was enjoying my "unabomber" time. I responded with something bland because I was headed to Dallas but wasn't ready to tell him yet. I needed to see my family at least once before I died. They would need it as much as I did.

Between seven hours of driving and flight time, I landed in Dallas in the late evening. Toby told me I would be able to catch Emily at the arena because she was training for a barrel racing show. I put my stuff in the back of her truck, then laid down in the bed parallel to the cab. My flight had been late and I'd been cutting it close on time because she was out within just a minute or two. The drive home was a little shorter than I expected, but I sat there smiling when she pulled into the garage. It smelled the same as I remembered; a mixture of timber, motor oil, and a faint hint of my dad's cologne.

Because I didn't want to scare the life out of Emily, I waited for her to go in the house before I sat up and got out of the bed of the truck. My hand was shaking as I reached for the doorknob to go into the house. I'd waited for sixteen years—to the date—to come home, and I finally was. Quietly, I opened the door and peeked in the kitchen. It felt like a waking dream; meaningless things had changed, but everything was the same. The kitchen was cranberry red with apple wallpaper underneath the cabinets. The counters were tidied up but there was still a little clutter to them. New appliances sat in place of the old ones, but otherwise, it still looked like the home I remembered.

After passing through the dining room, I entered the entryway and looked at the coat rack I'd helped Ben and my dad build. It had years more of wear on it, but seemed to be standing as sturdily as it did before. The hall light from upstairs didn't creep very far into the living room, but I didn't mind because I wanted to see my parents. I was going to go upstairs, but then I saw the light coming from under the door to my dad's office. My heart pounded so hard I felt like the whole house could hear. I was both excited and terrified, but took even breaths as I walked down the hallway and knocked on the door.

"Come in." My dad's voice felt like enough of a reassurance to allow me to open the door and not run away with fear. "How'd ya do tonight?" he asked without looking away from the papers on his desk.

"I don't think I'm the person you're expecting." I kept my voice quiet.

"Who—" My dad turned in his chair, saw me, and froze for a moment. "Hannah."

I tried to let myself smile, but I felt an overwhelming need to cry, so I just nodded.

"Oh, my Sweet Girl." He got up instantly, and we both walked quickly toward each other. I held my breath as I buried my face in his shoulder because tears had

344

never been closer. "My *girl*. Thank you, Lord... for bringin' my *sweet* girl home." His voice was as shaken as the rest of him.

I stood there with my eyes closed, holding my breath, unable to say anything because I felt mentally paralyzed. The emotional hit kept pounding me in waves. It was all I had to stand there and not break.

"I think this is just 'bout the best damn hug of my life right now," my dad whispered sweetly after a few minutes. His voice was broken, but he sounded happy. "I missed ya so damn bad I didn't even know how, and I can't begin to tell ya how sorry I am. I'm sorry I didn't stay home, I'm sorry 'bout the birthday party, and I'm sorry I didn't have Patty locked up when he shoulda been. My sweet girl, I love ya with all I got and I couldn't be more sorry."

I shook my head because I didn't want to hear it. "It's not your fault. You can't know what you didn't know."

He held the back of my head and a quiet cry shook out of him.

"And I missed you too... just *more*."

He let out a slight chuckle. "I'll bet ya *did*. Let me look at ya a minute."

I pulled back because he'd already started to. It felt hard to look him in the eye, but I knew I had to.

My dad smiled tearfully. "By god, just look at ya. You're more beautiful than your mama." He put a hand against my cheek. "I suppose ya wanna see her too, huh?"

I nodded. "I do, and Ben, if you wouldn't mind calling him. You can't tell him I'm here because your phones are likely tapped, but tell him you had a pipe burst in the basement or something."

My dad smiled. "Well, we got codes just for this. He'll come a-runnin'." He stepped back to get his phone off his desk. "You can go on up and see your ma. She's in bed, but she'll be happy to get woken up by you."

I shook my head. "I'll go up in a minute. I need to talk to you first, and I don't have a lot of time, so I need you to call Ben before we talk."

My dad's smile didn't falter, and he already had the phone up to his ear. "Son, there's a whole mess a glitter in my truck and the damn thing won't start. Get yourself over here and help me." He winked at me.

My cheeks burned from the instant recall of embarrassment. When I was five, I'd had the bright idea to dump glitter all over the inside of my dad's truck and especially in the vents, so it'd be a birthday snow globe when he turned it on.

He chuckled quietly. "Yep. I think your girl got in there, but I need some help... Alright. Drive safe and I love ya." My dad set the phone down on his desk. "Glitter. That's our word for ya."

I nodded, still partially embarrassed. "I caught that."

He shook his head again. "I just can't believe it. I can't believe how beautiful ya are, I can't believe you're here..."

I forced another nod as I glanced at the floor. "I shouldn't be, but I had to..." It felt so cruel to say anything that'd take his smile away, but I didn't have a choice. "I need to know where Patty is."

My dad frowned like he was confused. "He's dead, honey. For 'bout a year now."

I shook my head. "Please, don't lie to me. We both know he isn't, and I won't tell anyone, but I need to know where he is."

My dad went to open his mouth, but paused as he looked at the door behind me. Out of instinct, I turned to look. Emily was standing there with a mouthful of food and what appeared to be a burrito in her hand.

Her eyes went wide at the sight of me and her hand went up to her mouth as she nearly choked to swallow. "Oh my god!" She threw the burrito in the trash and darted toward me.

"No. Please!" I'd quickly backed up to put the chair in front of my dad's desk between us and held out a hand.

Emily stopped and looked at me like I was nuts. "I was just gonna hug you. Am I missing something here?" She looked at our dad, who just looked confused.

"No. I just—" I rubbed the back of my stinging neck as I tried to come up with a good reason for my reaction. "I have a really hard time with being touched, and..." My brain wasn't turning fast enough in the direction I needed it to, so I was struggling for words.

"Oh, that makes sense. I'm sorry." She looked at me and shook her head, seeming pretty hurt. "I thought maybe you thought I was going to hit you or something."

That's *exactly* what I thought.

I shook my head and stepped around the chair. "Just slow and careful, please. My nerves are already on fire because I'm here when I shouldn't be." I hugged Emily and begged my brain not to send shooting currents through my body.

"Well, I should know better because of Toby, but I just got excited." Emily was careful as she wrapped her arms around me. "Hi, Sissy."

"Hi."

"Oh my gosh. I can't believe this. Toby kept saying you were out there, but I just never believed it." She let out a breath.

"Yeah, well, unfortunately, he's gonna be gone for a little bit now too. That's partly why I'm here."

Emily pulled back and looked at me as if I'd called her a terrible name from out of nowhere.

"He and Grace aren't safe here, so he's taken her and they're gonna hide out until Henry is out of the picture." I pulled a letter from my back pocket and handed it to her. "He asked me to give you this."

She looked as angry as she did hurt.

"He's not being paranoid," I told her, continuing to hold out the letter. "Grace is *especially* unsafe here, but

I'm gonna do everything humanly possible to make sure they can come back safely."

Emily took the letter, looking more angry. "Do you know where he is?"

I shook my head. "I can't tell you. I'm sorry."

Her eyebrow arched with an expectant look.

"It's not safe for anyone to know, and the only reason I know is because of my daughter."

Her other eyebrow shot up. "You mean the daughter I've raised? That one?"

"Emily," my dad warned.

I glanced at my dad and looked back at Emily unapologetically. "I'm sorry this is so difficult for you, Emily. It must've been such a challenge growing up here in this nice house, having your family around, not being forced to have a kid at fifteen, and being forced to give her up because it's constant hunting season and you're the game. What a pity. Oh, wait, no, you wanted a thanks. That's right." I pulled my hand away from my head like I was having a realization. "Yeah. Thanks for going to the vending machine. I very deeply enjoy that it's ruined your life so much."

"Hannah. Both of you. Come on now." My dad let out a huff and scratched the back of his head.

I continued staring at Emily, unwilling to back down from my position. If Ryan had taught me anything, it was to hold ground while watching the opponent crumble, and she did.

"They're both safe while I deal with this. Have a good night, Emily." I nodded toward the door.

"I'm sorry, Hannah," she said before turning to leave.

I followed behind her, but only to shut the door.

"Honey, you got every right to be upset, but she was just a kid too. Ya shouldn't've said that to her," my dad said quietly.

"I'm done rolling over to bullies." I crossed my arms.

"Cynthia Maslen is one of them, so why have you and Mom been talking to her?" I leaned back against the door.

He shook his head. "I don't trust that woman as far as I can throw her. What are you doin' with her son?"

"I'm not here to explain what I know, I'm here to find out what you know. You can let me walk out of here as blind as I came or give me a better chance at fighting."

My dad took in a deep breath and directed a hand to the chairs in front of his desk as he went to sit.

I shook my head. "I can't sit over there."

He looked at his chair, seeming to realize why that was, and walked over to one of the two loveseats in the room. My nerves were screaming at me, but I sat in the corner of the loveseat that was next to the door as a compromise.

"I don't trust Cynthia, but I been loosely trustin' a guy named Ryan Brae who says he's your friend. He don't trust Cynthia or her husband, but he says their son Grey wouldn't hurt ya. I ain't met him, so I can't speak to that. And both Ryan and Cynthia say he doesn't know what they've been up to. The only reason I even *half* trust Ryan is cause he's been goin' hard after Henry. I figure an enemy of my enemy is a friend... to a certain point, that is."

I nodded, trying to yet again accept the betrayal from Ryan. "And Patty?"

He shook his head. "He's dead. Saw his body my-self." My dad rubbed the center of his lips like he was scratching them, but looked at me meaningfully.

"Okay... Well... trust Ryan unless I personally tell you not to, and don't trust Cynthia. Grey would say oth-erwise, but she doesn't like me, and she's reserved about it until no one is within earshot." I rubbed my forehead, still wondering how I was going to deal with anything.

"What about her son? You're supposed to be mar-ryin' him aren't ya?"

I nodded. "Grey would never hurt me, and I wouldn't

marry him if I had any doubt. While I'm not happy to find out what's been done behind my back, I know it's because he cares." That wasn't exactly true anymore, but I wanted to believe it. Either way, I had to go through with the wedding.

My dad itched the back of his head. "I guess I don't understand how he'd be payin' Ryan without knowin' where the money's goin'. Assumin' Ryan's tellin' the truth about that."

I smiled a little. "Grey doesn't care too much about money. He likes working, he likes making it, and he likes spending it on other people. Ryan works really hard, he's incredibly loyal, honest, and Grey trusts him more than anyone else in the world. More than his own family."

"I'm assumin' since ya saw Toby already, every-thing he's had to say is true?" My dad looked worried as he asked.

"His side of the story is a little naïve, but the truth." I nodded once. "I needed to save *his* life, not mine. He would've been killed, and I couldn't let it happen just because he was hell-bent on doing the right thing." I shook my head. "I don't expect anyone to understand, but Toby is..." I tried to think of the right words. "He is very much a part of me in a way I don't have words to explain, but... I'd rather be caught by Henry again than lose Toby... There's precious little I wouldn't do for him."

My dad nodded. "He says the same about you. You okay with him endin' up with Emily?"

I smiled and nodded. "I'm happy to see him happy. I just hope she's nicer to him than she was to me."

"She is. She's still Emily, but he doesn't put up with it too much."

I shook my head. "I don't imagine he would. He's fairly patient, but he's never tolerated attitudes. He used to give me this look, this calm, irritated stare." I laughed quietly. "That look is probably the reason I didn't walk out of that house with the mindset of an eight-year-old."

He shook his head. "You were hardly ever eight. You turned thirty right around your sixth birthday."

My shoulders raised. "Because I hung around you and Ben, and I didn't want to be like Emily."

He raised his eyebrows with a slight eye roll. "You think she was bad, you should meet her oldest."

I smiled. "That's a terrible thing to say."

He snorted with a slight smile. "Not if it's true. Good hell, that boy is crusin' for a bruisin' most days." He shook his head with a huff. "I love 'im, but I'd also like to give him a swift kick."

I looked at the clock on the shelf. "I better go up and say hi to Mom."

"Yep. She's already gonna be sore she didn't get a hug first. Her and Ben." My dad stood and opened the door.

I got up and followed him. "I can't believe how much things still look the same here in the house."

"Yeah... That was a little intentional. Your ma wanted ya to come home to the house ya remembered, and I'd rather spend my hard-earned dollars on my kids than some fancy old two-by-fours." He gave me a crinkly-eyed smile and stopped at the bottom of the stairs to let me go first.

I smiled back and pointed up the stairs. "You go ahead. Someone behind me on the stairs is like nails on a chalkboard in my brain."

He nodded and went up. "Cynthia and Ryan said you were in college."

"Yep. My first semester I took a light load, but after that, it's been sixteen credits a semester and working full time. I've got a little bit of a lighter schedule this coming semester, but after that, I'll hit the ground running again."

"Goodness, you sound like Ben. That boy barely slept. He had his doctorate in less than seven years. What's got ya slowin' down this comin' semester?"

"I have a surgery coming up in October. All my

classes will be online, so it shouldn't put me behind."

"Surgery for what?" He turned at the top of the stairs to wait for me.

I itched under a bobby pin in my hair. "A double hip replacement."

"Hip replacement?" He looked at me with a wry expression. "You're just turnin' twenty-four in a few days."

I raised my eyebrows, hoping he'd catch on so I wouldn't have to say it. He let out a breath and shook his head when it finally came to him.

"I'm sorry, honey. You got insurance to pay for it?"

I nodded. "It's already taken care of."

"Alright, but if it ain't, you just let me know. We got a trust set aside for ya."

I shook my head. "I'm really okay. Put it aside for Grace or split it between Ben and Emily." I opened the door to my parents' room quietly. My mom was asleep on her side, the way she always slept.

I smiled at my dad as I slipped off my heels, then walked over and crawled up through the center of the bed the way I used to. My mom's hand came up to rub my arm when I wrapped it around her.

"Hi, baby... You alright?" she asked tiredly without opening her eyes.

"I'm alright, but I could use a hug."

Her eyes opened in an instant and she turned her head to look at me.

I smiled and laughed a little. "Hi, Mama."

"Oh my god." She quickly turned herself to sit up. "Is this real right now?"

My dad chuckled as he turned the light on at her bedside table. "Well, ya ain't dead if that's what you're askin'."

My mom looked at him as innocently as a child with tears in her eyes, then looked at me. "You're home? Oh, my baby girl. Come here." She opened her arms.

I smiled and leaned forward to hug her. It was the

best feeling in the world to know how happy she was, but also the worst because I knew it was temporary.

"No. You get your tiny butt on my lap. I wanna hold ya." She started pulling me over to her lap before I had a chance to move myself.

"I love you," I whispered as I hugged her. My mom was as soft and warm as I remembered, and I didn't realize just how much I missed her until right then in her arms.

"I love love *love* you," she whispered back, then kissed my cheek. "My god... you don't got any idea how much."

"I do." Holding Grace earlier had given me a very good perspective.

"Well, I told her 'bout Ryan and Cynthia. So we're just down to small talk now." My dad sat on his side of the bed, then slid in under my legs.

"Did ya call Ben? Is Emily home?"

"Yes, and yes. Ben'll be here any minute now, and Emily's in her room poutin' cause Toby's hiddin' with Grace. I don't like it, but I don't think it's the worst idea since Ryan's gettin' ready to wrap this stuff up." My dad turned my foot to look at a scar that wrapped around from the bottom to the top. It was a faint surgical scar, but once had looked as grizzly as the procedure had been. I found it strange that my parents could act so normally, hugging me and touching me, and it didn't instill fear. Instead, it was comforting...

"Ryan's out of his league on this one and doesn't know it yet, so if I call and tell you guys to go, you need to. Henry and the rest of them will use whatever means necessary to get to me. I know all their identities and where Patty hid every ounce of proof." I spoke quietly because I was just resting there in my mom's arms, but also knew I didn't have much time with them.

"I ain't accusin' ya of nothin', or sayin' ya did any-thing wrong, but how come ya know this stuff and ain't ever done nothin' with it?" My dad looked at me with a gentle expression.

"Donny, don't be puttin' this on her. It ain't her responsibility." My mom combed her fingers through my hair.

I shook my head. "He's not. I understand what you're asking, and the main reason has been I simply haven't possessed the money or resources until now. I'm sure you've seen the news—they're everywhere. It's government officials, police, FBI, doctors, lawyers, farmers, gas station attendants. Anyone that'll take money. It's never been something I could do on my own... not before now. I've been trying to figure out exactly who's after them so I can join in and make sure it ends."

"Honey, I think you're best to let Ryan handle it and just lay low. Tell him what ya know, and let him handle it." He patted the side of my leg. "He's got a solid plan, and so far he's managed to keep ya from gettin' hurt."

I nodded. "I know." I couldn't begin to explain to my parents how under-equipped Ryan was. He'd obviously been able to acquire the flash drive in the top compartment of the banister, but nothing else, which meant he couldn't actually get to Henry or anyone else.

"Sounds like Ben's here. I'll go get Ella." He patted my leg again before he got up and left the room.

"Well, your daddy hasn't changed much. It's always business. How are ya, honey? Have ya found some happiness in your life?" My mom continued to stroke her nails through the side of my hair.

"Yeah... more than I thought I'd ever have." I took in a breath because my mom's calming effect was about to put me to sleep. "I love my job, where I live, my friends, and Grey... I'm mad at him and Ryan after finding out what they've been up to, but... they've been the best thing to ever happen to me."

"I know I shouldn't put nothin' in your head, but how are ya so sure you can trust 'em?"

"Because they've both worked too hard to earn it... Grey especially... He's so careful, with everything he says and does. If I'm having a day where my skin feels like it's on fire from being touched too many times, he'll make sure not to touch me, and he's never bothered by it. He never makes me feel guilty about anything. I'm afraid to go in the kitchen, so he cooks every night, or makes sure something is delivered to the house. He constantly checks on me to make sure I'm okay, and will find the sweetest words to say when I'm not... The new house he had built as our wedding present doesn't have many stairs because my body aches so much of the time, there's no basement, and three panic rooms... That's too much work to put into a person you don't care for. He cares every minute of the day, and he's never shown anything less."

My mom let out a breath like she was relieved. "Well, that's good... I hope I get to meet him sometime soon."

I nodded. "Me too..."

"I know your daddy's been havin' a real hard time trustin' Ryan to keep his word, but I told him... there wasn't much left to *lose*. Either things stayed the same, or they get better. Cause you not being home has been the worst." She hugged me a little tighter.

"I'm sorry."

"Don't you ever apologize to me, Hannah. Ain't a damn thing of this is your fault, and I don't wanna hear it. You got the right to be where ya want to, and keep yourself safe. We *all* understand that."

I heard the front door open and shut for the second time and felt my heart lift a little more.

"Well, that'll be your brother. You better get up." My mom patted my hip.

"I'll be back to snuggle some more," I told her as I got off the bed.

"I'm not countin' on it," she called as I bolted out of

the room.

I stopped briefly at the top of the stairs just to make sure it was my brother, and when I saw his tearful smile, I ran down as fast as I could and threw my arms around his neck when he was close enough to catch me. It was something I'd always done when I was little, but would never dare do as an adult. However, I couldn't help it this one time. If there was anyone I'd ever felt desperate to see again, besides Grace, it was Ben.

Ben laughed a little, wrapping his long arms around me tightly while I stood two stairs up from the bottom. "Hannah Bean," he whispered as he held the back of my head, then kissed my cheek.

My heart felt as full as it could be. I couldn't remember a day when I hadn't been glued to Ben when I was little. Anywhere he went, I'd always gone with. He was my best friend and I was his. I used to sleep on the floor in his room if I didn't crawl into bed with my parents. There hadn't been a day in that god-forsaken house in Tennessee that I didn't wish Ben would come rescue me. I used to sit by the window, staring out into the trees, and imagine how I would've latched onto him with a hug, feeling like I might never let him go. My heart was broken every day when I didn't see him come through those trees to save me. I wanted him to hold me all the way home, then run through the house to my parents.

"I'm so sorry," he whispered after a few seconds.

I shook my head. "You better be apologizing for the weather."

He let out a weak laugh. "No. I shouldn't have left you alone in that room."

"I don't accept your apology because it's dumb."

He smirked, then laughed.

I smiled a little, mostly to keep myself from bawling, and pulled back from the embrace. "It was never your fault, and it would've happened regardless."

The majority of his smile was gone. "I know, but I can still be sorry regardless of fault."

Chapter 29

Bexley

I stayed at my parents' house visiting with them, Ben, and eventually Emily. We all sat on my parents' bed while I was peppered with questions about my life. Thankfully, they all stayed away from the harder questions. I'd imagined going home so many times, but it was better than anything my imagination had come up with. There was so much laughter we woke the kids up a couple times.

Around two in the morning, I had to tell my parents and Emily goodbye because I knew Grey, Ryan, Roger, and Willum would be getting back to the hotel. Ben drove me downtown while I asked him about his visits with Ryan. He hadn't known it was me he was indirectly helping, but didn't seem terribly upset about it. It actually made things easier because he was able to talk to me about different things, like Grey spending irritating amounts of money on me, and why it bothered me so badly. I'd never thought about it before, but Ben pointed out that I was used to being manipulated by Patty or Henry anytime something was given to me. Things as simple as food, clothes, or even using the bathroom always came at a high cost, so I was subconsciously waiting for Grey to set a cost.

Ben put the truck in park and let out a breath. "I know I have to, but I don't know how to say goodbye. Even if it's temporary." He looked at me.

"Me either. I keep wanting to say, 'screw it,' but I really can't. I've already put everyone at risk just by sneaking around to come see you."

He shook his head. "We'll take whatever comes, Hannah. At a certain point... it'll start costing you more to stay away. I'm sure you know, but Mom and Dad aren't gonna live forever. Every day you spend hiding is one less day with them... You're finally in a position where you can do something, so I think it's time. Use the resources you've built around you and fight back. I'll drop everything to help, so would Dad, Mom, even Emily... We're all tired, and we wanna see you come home."

I nodded. "I know... I have to talk to Ryan and Grey, see where they're at and what they've been up to, and I'll find a way to reach out to you tomorrow."

"I'm here. And if you walk in there and things don't go the way you want, or in a direction you're comfortable with, call my office number. It's a secured line. My answering service will answer, but you tell them your name is Ann, you're feeling suicidal, and you want to talk to me. They'll transfer you, no questions asked." He pulled a paper out of his shirt pocket. "And if all hell breaks loose and you need somewhere to go, this is the address to a cabin. Legally, it's under Luke Wheaton's name, but Mom and Dad paid for it. I don't know if you remember Luke."

I smiled and nodded. "I do. How is he?"

Ben returned the smile, the way he'd been doing

all night. "He's good. Still living out on the farm behind the ranch house, which is another place you can go if you need. Luke will help you in a split second, and not just because Dad pays for him to take care of the horses when we're not there. Anyhow, this is the address, but when you get there, you won't find anything but a post with a wooden plaque. If it's facing the street, no one is at the house, if it's facing away from the street, one or all of us are there. There's ribbons stapled to the trees, you'll follow them about a half mile back and there's a shed with a couple four wheelers and UTVs. The trail going back to the house is behind the shed. It'll be about a mile in. There's no electricity, but there's food storage in the pantry, a hand pump for water, and money buried on the North facing side against the clothesline post closest to the house."

I nodded and took the paper.

He reached into his pocket and pulled something out. It was a bracelet I'd made him from a bead set I'd gotten for Christmas. It had blue plastic beads, then three white ones with the letters B, E, N. The black paint had been rubbed off the impression of the letters.

I smiled and picked it up from his open hand. "Oh gosh. You still have this?"

"I've had it in my pocket every day. Dad has his too."

I looked at him with a wincing smile. "It's sweet, but a little sappy." I handed it back to him.

Ben laughed. "Yeah, well, you've been missed."

I nodded. "I know."

He kept a semi-light expression and held out an arm to me. I leaned over and hugged him.

"You're welcome to my house, or anything in it, anytime you need, okay?" Ben put a hand on top of my head the way he used to. "The garage code is your birthday backward."

I nodded.

"And I'm happy you're okay, and *really* damn proud

of you."

"I haven't done anything," I said quietly. I was still embarrassed by the lack of things I'd done since escaping.

"You have. Trust me... I have a lot of patients who've been through less and can barely manage to put their socks on in the morning. You are an anomaly... and I'm grateful and *really* proud." His voice was straining. It was a Lawrence family trait to lose our voice when emotions were too high.

I didn't know what to say in response, so I sat there quietly and absorbed the hug.

"Be safe, okay?"

"You too." I pulled away.

Ben kept his hand on top of my head. "I love you a hell of a lot more than you know." He smiled. "More than ice cream."

I gave a small smile. "More than ice cream," I agreed.

"Be safe, best wishes on your wedding day, and happy birthday on Saturday." He took his hand off my head.

"Thank you, and I love you too. No more blaming yourself." I gripped his arm lightly, then got out of the truck because I was too afraid I'd cry trying to say goodbye.

I pulled my bag out of the bed of the truck, then went down the sidewalk to catch a taxi. Ben didn't pull away from the curb until the taxi did. It was only a few blocks to the hotel, so I turned on my phone and checked to see where Grey was. They were only ten minutes away. By the time I got a key card from the front desk and went up to the room he was only a few minutes behind me. No matter where Grey went, he always put my name down at the front desk in case I decided to show up for whatever reason, and I always appreciated it. Typically, I had no need, but the few times I'd needed to meet him somewhere, it'd been convenient.

After putting my bag next to the couch and using

the bathroom, I finally heard Grey and Ryan come in. They were laughing about Conway, the client they'd been with. He was a flamboyant party animal and always did something ridiculous, which was why I didn't usually partake in his parties.

"Hey," Grey laughed but also looked a little concerned. "I didn't know you were here. Everything okay?" He walked toward me but stopped when I shook my head.

"No. It's not. Both of you are going to sit down while we have a sobering conversation." I nodded in the direction of the couch.

Grey looked hurt and confused while Ryan seemed to be amused.

"The jig is up. She found out about the car." Ryan plopped down in the corner of the couch.

"Beautiful, it's just a car. I know I promised no big-ticket items, but it's a wedding gift, and you love that Superleggera," Grey explained with a sympathetic smile as I picked up the phone on the end table next to the opposing couch.

"Room service," someone answered.

"Yes, could you bring up some fresh coffee and some baked goods to sober up two drunken men, please." My voice was as cold as my stare. "Room fourteen-twelve."

Grey frowned, appearing hurt again.

"Sure. It'll be about ten minutes," the guy responded.

"Thank you." I hung up the phone. "This isn't about a car. Sit down." I nodded in the direction of the couch behind him.

"What happened, B? I'm lost here." Grey looked behind him before he sat in the center seat of the couch.

I crossed my arms over my chest, still not knowing how to address things after the hours it'd been turning in my head. My temper wanted to roar out of me, but it wouldn't do any good.

"She's crossing her arms. She's pissed about

something," Ryan laughed. "Seriously, Nelson, can this wait until tomorrow? Conway was all but pouring drinks down our throats. Grey and I just had to carry Willum to bed."

I shook my head, biting the inside of my cheek because I felt like I was about to cry. "It can't. The two of you..." I cleared my throat and looked toward the windows because my eyes were watering.

"Bex, hey, what happened?" Grey got up to come toward me and stumbled a little.

"For the love of god, Grey. Just sit down," I snapped with nearly no voice.

He held up a hand. "Okay. Just say something. You're scaring me."

"Agreed."

I rubbed my arms and looked at Ryan. "How did you get the flash drive? Who told you where it was?" I already knew the answer because only two people knew of its existence, and I was one of them.

Ryan looked at me like I wasn't making sense. "I don't know what you're talking about."

I looked down at my bag beside the couch. I was tired... It'd been sixteen years of exhaustion, fighting to stay alive, actively planning for the worst, and missing my family with my every breath. I didn't want to fight, I didn't want to keep hiding, I wanted to stop.

I picked up my bag and went toward the door.

"Nelson, wait."

"Bex, what happened?"

Ryan and Grey both got up.

"Nelson, stop." Ryan pulled my arm back.

My brain snapped right then. I dropped my bag, grabbed Ryan's arm, twisted it, leveraged his weight over mine, and dropped him to the floor. "Don't grab me!" My voice didn't work as I tried to yell.

"Shit. Bex, Stop." Grey quickly stepped over Ryan to block the door. "Hey, I won't touch you, I promise. Just talk to me. What flash drive? I don't know what you're talking about. Give me a chance here." He looked at me fearfully.

I shook my head. "Don't lie to me. You know who I am, and I don't know how, but you've somehow decided that lying to me while you try to clean everything up is okay. You don't understand the very *real* danger I'm in, and I don't know if I can fix it before everyone gets *hurt*. I have a family I've been trying to protect. I have a daughter who's devastated because she's not safe enough to stay in her own home or go to school with her friends. Her *friends* aren't even safe by association. My nephews and niece." My voice was choked because I was fighting tears.

Grey shook his head. "Okay. Yes, I know who you are. I know you're Hannah, but I swear I haven't done anything. As soon as I made my dirtbag move of finding out who you were, I did nothing. I haven't even read that guy Toby's book. All I've done is pay to keep you safe. I swear on my life—on *Sam's* life." His hands were shaking as he continued to hold them up like someone had a gun on him.

"You've been paying for Ryan to do it so you could plead your innocence, and that's no better." I looked at Ryan who was already up from the floor. "Who told you where the flash drive was?"

"I told you to keep her safe. I *never* told you to go after anyone, and I asked you if you were," Grey snapped.

"Yeah, well doing nothing was never an option." Ryan was quick to explode back. "The second you decided you couldn't wait to meet her, it was done. I told you to wait, and you refused because you were too caught up in a pretty face. There's been no choice here. You wanted her safe, this was the only way."

"Couldn't wait to meet me?" I looked at Grey.

"We found an external hard drive in the records building for MWM—"

Ryan held up a finger to stop Grey. "No. You don't know the half of it." He looked at me. "Cynthia left it for me to find. On that hard drive, we found you and a bunch of random pieces surrounding you. Warehouses Henry used, pictures of the house in Tennessee, and everything about you since LA. Cynthia has been manipulating you for years so she could keep tabs on you, I just don't know why. You can be pissed all you want, but you're dead center in a hurricane you can't fight off, and if you step one toe out, we're all screwed. So, whatever you're planning, whatever you're trying to plan, don't. I'm sorry for lying to you, but I've been trying to keep you from bolting and getting people killed, because you're right, Henry will come for all of us. He's already tried twice and failed. And I can smell your brother's cologne on you, are you trying to get yourself killed?"

I stood there angry, scared, and tired. "No. I wanted to see my family before I end up dead. There are more than just Henry and my uncle Patty, and every last one of them knows about me and the risk I pose to them. I have all the keys to bring them down, but I can't get a step toward the door without being killed. All I've been able to do is stay off the map."

Ryan shook his head. "You were never off the map. The second you were spotted running drugs at the border, there were eyes on you. You moving to Monterey, do you remember who suggested it? That little roommate friend of yours, Evie? Paid by Cynthia. You were in this a long time ago. I'm doing everything I can to help you. I've even been playing along with Cynthia and taking her money because Grey cut me off, but I am helping you. So, you can tell me what you know, I'll tell you what I know, and we work together to make sure we all live, or you can try running and see if you get lucky a second time."

Grey shook his head. "I don't understand. How does my mom have anything to do with this? My dad's the one who was laundering the money." He looked at me. "That's why we were digging through the records. I found a bunch of stuff, crimes my dad committed, and I wanted to bring him down. When Ryan came to me and said I had to choose you or that, I chose you. Hands down, B. I'll always choose you over business, and I didn't know Ryan was doing anything."

I could tell just by the tone of his voice that he wasn't lying. Grey had very subtle but distinct tells when he lied.

"I don't know what she has to do with it, but from what I've been able to gather just in the last couple weeks, and today while we were at the office, your dad got ambushed with this. Mine too. My dad was framed for killing Remy, and my mom was killed by Nelson's uncle." Ryan's breathing changed at the mention of his mom and brother.

My eyes went wide. "What?"

Ryan looked at me and shook his head. "My dad was an accountant at MWM, he found money that was being funneled, tried to take what he found to the SEC, but he didn't make it. They took him and my mom to the house you were in, but only my dad came back. That's when the drinking and the beating started. I needed access to the servers down here so Tim could decode a bunch of files in the system, and we found encrypted emails about my dad. He didn't kill Remy, there were guys sent to the house, they locked Remy in the closet, took my dad, and left Tim and I to point fingers at him. He got locked up on a murder charge and his credibility was shot."

My ears were ringing and my heart was pounding. While it wasn't my fault, I felt like it was. And I was also terrified of what I might know about Ryan's parents. I'd never seen so much as a picture of them, and had never asked because they were such a sore subject.

"Do you have a picture of them?" I asked.

He shook his head. "It doesn't matter anymore,

Nelson... She's dead, and he still beat the shit out of us."

"Was her name Patricia? They're really the only couple I ever saw come into the house." I remembered her very well. Both her and her husband.

"Oh my god. How is everything this twisted?" Grey leaned back against the door and shoved his hand through his hair.

"I don't wanna hear it, Nelson. Please."

I held up my shoulders. "If that's her name, she's still alive. She helped me after I had Grace, my daughter."

Ryan's eyebrows raised. "What? How?"

"It's a long story, but your dad didn't do what he was supposed to when they brought him to the house, so the puppets—Hen-Henry's guys," I shook my head, realizing they didn't know my common terminology, "they told my uncle Patty to kill your mom. He didn't do it because your dad was nice to me on a day when I *really* needed some kindness. Your mom was sent to the basement with me for a couple days, she was so kind. She wanted to get me out, kept asking my name, asked who my parents were... I didn't tell her anything because I knew she'd be killed for trying to save me. When it was burial day, I wrapped her up in my tarp, put her in the wheelbarrow, and took her out to the graveyard. She tried to get me to go with her, but I knew I couldn't. I told her how to get past the traps, and before she left, she told me she was going down to Mount Dora, Florida and to come find her if I ever got out and needed help." I nodded. "I did that after I left my daughter. I went to the First Baptist Church like she told me to, and she was there. Obviously, this was nine years ago, but she lived on Sullivan Street, owned a tea store on Donnelly, and went by the name Laura Whittaker. I stayed with her for about a month to recover, then I left in the middle of the night because I was too afraid she'd get hurt because of me."

Ryan stood there with glassy eyes for a moment.

"I'm too fricken drunk for this shit." He pulled his hand over his mouth. "I know you probably feel like you're in a tailspin with this shit, but there's no immediate threat, so can we please talk about it tomorrow?"

"Yes, but there's one thing I need to know first. I know Patty's still alive, but I don't know where he is. Do you?"

Ryan frowned and shook his head. "No. Why do you think he's still alive?"

"Because there's people and places going down that were never on that thumb drive from the house. Ramos Escarra was killed with insulin and cut up with a buck knife. That's Patty." I watched Ryan carefully, trying to spot even the faintest signal he might be lying.

He ran the butt of his hand up his forehead and grabbed a tuft of his hair as he closed his eyes and let out a huff. "That sums that up. Dammit... Is there any way to find out where he'd go next?"

I shook my head. "No, and we can't do anything to stop him either. Patty is too smart, he's always ten steps ahead, and he'll be my only micro chance of survival. I do need to find him, but not to stop him."

"Stop saying you're gonna die. You're here, and if we have to have a full security detail on you twenty-four-seven, that's what'll happen. The pig can run around squealing and picking up slop all it wants, he's not getting near you, and you better not think we're letting him help us from anywhere but an extreme distance." Ryan let out another huff. "Tomorrow, Nelson. I'm too damn drunk, and I'm about to puke if I don't get some damn sleep. And don't go see your family again, not until this is done."

Chapter30

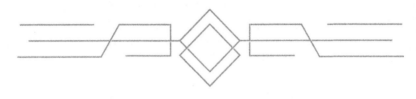

Grey

Ryan went out the door and I stood there not knowing what to do. Bex had every right to be upset, and I was terrified she was upset enough to call off the wedding and leave.

"I didn't know what he was doing, and I didn't know who you were until after you moved to Seattle. That doesn't make anything right, I know it doesn't, but I don't want you to think I've pulled you into something for any other reason than loving you and wanting to keep you safe." I watched her as she continued to stand there with her arms wrapped around her torso.

"How did you find out?"

The worst question she could ask...

"In about the most dishonest way possible. When you had that allergic reaction to the kumquat, I paid the phlebotomist to take an extra vile of blood for a DNA sample. It was done in a lab I own, and the results were seen by no one but me. Ryan had already warned me that if you were found by the wrong people you'd be dead, so I took every precaution possible. And the only reason I did it was so I could know what you were facing and keep you safe. Again, it wasn't right, I know that, and I'm sorry for betraying your trust."

She shrugged a shoulder. "You didn't. I expected you'd go searching for answers, I just wasn't prepared for how you'd get them." Bex picked up her bag from the floor and went to the bedroom.

Her words hurt because I knew they were true. While I wanted to be upset because she didn't have more faith in me, I couldn't be...

I opened the door to hang the Do Not Disturb sign and jumped when there was a person there with a cart.

"I forgot she called down. Sorry." I reached into my pocket and pulled out my wallet. "We're actually headed to bed, so you can take it back and still charge me for it." I handed him a twenty. "Thanks, man."

"Are you sure?" The guy looked confused.

I nodded. "Yeah. Thanks." I forced a smile, closed the door, and locked it.

Bex was in the bathroom when I went into the bedroom, so I sat on the bed, sent a few messages to Harry about upping security around Bex, then tried to think of what I could say to let her know how sorry I was.

I rolled over and the pounding in my head woke me up. "Crap," I whispered as soon as I realized I'd fallen asleep. Bex wasn't beside me, so I got up. Her bags were still in the corner so I wasn't completely worried, but I was when she wasn't anywhere in the suite. I checked everywhere, and there was no sign of her. After texting her and hearing her phone chime from her bags, I texted Ryan. There'd been no response from him after I was done puking from my hangover, so I tried to call him, but still got nothing.

I picked up the hotel phone on the nightstand and

dialed Ryan's room number.

"What!?" Ryan snapped tiredly after the fourth ring.

"I can't find Bex."

"Check her phone."

"Her phone is here in the room." I held my head because it was pounding. My phone vibrated in my pocket. "My dad's calling me. Can you call down to the front desk and see if anyone saw her leave?"

"No. There's hundreds of people coming and going, no one would've noticed her." Ryan hung up.

"Yeah," I answered my dad's call.

"You and Ryan need to come over." His voice was dark, meaning he was pissed about something.

"Ryan's refusing to get up and I need to find Bex."

"Now, Grey!"

I hung up on him because I wasn't going to give him a response after he yelled. He'd been fairly decent over the last year, but I'd still heavily ignored him as much as possible. After grabbing a couple ibuprofens, I walked across the hall, got Ryan, and went to my dad's shared suite with Pops.

Pops opened the door and looked displeased with me.

"What's going on?" I frowned a little because I didn't understand why Pops would be upset.

He pointed into the room. "Just go have a seat."

I walked in knowing whatever it was, it was bad. Anything that brought Pops down to a normal person's level of enthusiasm usually meant something serious happened. I let out a slight breath of relief when I saw Bex sitting at the table with my dad. There was a spread of food laid out and Bex looked despondent. I took the seat next to her, Ryan sat on the other side of me, and Pops took the seat between Bex and my dad.

"What's going on?" I asked my dad without showing intimidation.

My dad rubbed his jaw with his thumb and fingers.

At first glance, I thought he looked angry, but I couldn't tell if that was it either. "Bexley, I'm terminating your employment with MWM effective immediately."

"What?" I looked at my dad with disbelief, then at Bex who looked flushed and confused.

"Grey, please stop." He held up a hand as he looked at me patiently, then looked at Bex again. "I've been very patient with your vendetta, I've even shown support for it, but it's caught attention now. The wrong attention; and you have put my family and our business in grave jeopardy. To my knowledge, Grey is unaware of what you've been trying to accomplish, and since this could directly affect him and *his* business as well, I would advise honesty."

"Bex, stop." I held up a finger as she went to say something and looked at my dad. "What exactly are we talking about here? If it's what I think it is, you've got it all wrong."

"She's been using our company to go after some very dangerous criminals—and while I would love nothing more than to see them go, in the last twenty-four hours she has not proceeded as cautiously." He looked at her again. "I sympathize with your situation, I really do, but understand that I cannot risk my children."

"We're talking about Henry Greer? Is that correct?" He was tiptoeing around the subject, and I was sick of it.

"Grey, you were aware of what she was doing?" Pops asked.

I shook my head. "Bex has nothing to do with it. *I'm* the one going after him. She had no idea until literally hours ago. What I still can't figure out is what the hell you've been doing with these guys, and why the hell you would condone it by laundering money for these sick assholes." Ryan would understand why I lied, but I hoped Bex would continue to stay silent and let me explain later.

My dad's eyebrows raised. "Please don't cover

for her. There's no possible way you could've known where hundreds of sex dungeons were or the people associated with them. Bexley—also known as Hannah Lawrence—on the other hand, *would*." He looked at her.

"Yeah. Grey, I appreciate it, but I'll take my strike." Ryan cleared his throat. "Grey and Nelson haven't known about a damn thing until about three this morning. It's been *me*. I found a hard drive in MWM records, that's how we found Nelson, and after some digging, I found out who she was and decided to go after every bastard responsible for hurting her. I paid someone to talk to Patrick Lawrence in prison, then obtained a comprehensive set of files he left behind in the house in Tennessee. Maybe you'll recall it caught fire mysteriously last year?" He crossed his arms.

Bex looked at Ryan like she was either hurt or thankful, it was hard to tell. My dad noticed her face, then looked at Ryan.

"If that's true, you've put us all in danger. I've already lost one child to this." My dad was angry, but seemed scared too.

"What are you talking about?" I asked.

My dad looked at me. "The baby your mother lost when you were five, she didn't die, she was taken by Henry Greer after I attempted to do the very same thing Ryan claims to be doing."

I felt shocked. "Does... does Mom know?"

He shook his head. "No. I paid the doctors to tell her our daughter had passed of SIDS in the nursery. The casket we buried was empty."

My stomach was instantly sour and not because I was hungover.

"Why were you laundering money for them to begin with?" Ryan reached forward and grabbed a muffin.

My dad shook his head. "Thirty years ago, MWM was hanging on by a thread. I needed a big account to balance the scales. A man named Issak Weinrab had a booming tech company in Germany. I don't remember who suggested him, but I pursued the lead. Seven months later, he put me in touch with a man named Alex Vaughters who owned a small financial institution of which MWM was able to acquire due to Isaak's financial backing."

"Alex Vaughters is Henry Greer's adopted brother. Henry's real name is Klaus Ockert-Vaughters," Bex said quietly as she stared at a plate of pastries in front of her.

"Nelson, not here."

Her eyes shot over at Ryan in a heat of anger. "No, you don't dictate what I say or to whom. You have *no idea* what you've done! You didn't even know these names. You've been going after a single person think-ing he was the only one and clearly unaware of how they're affiliated all around. You're pumping Roger for information you should've obtained before you even contemplated something like this. You were unaware of your own *father's* position in this! You've spoken enough for me by starting something *no one asked you to!*" I'd never heard Bex raise her voice before, and it worried me. "Grey didn't ask you, *I* sure as hell didn't. You thought this was some sweet little gesture of friendship but it's a *death sentence.*"

"Really? Can you see the future? Getting more infor-mation is how we reach a resolution, *Nelson*. Information doesn't just fall in someone's lap all at once, and at least I haven't just been sitting on it for *years* when I could've been doing something!" Ryan barked right back. "You knew where that thumb drive was, apparently know all the important names. Have you tried to do *anything* with it? You have a near-limitless bank sitting next to you, did you ever consider doing something?"

Pops stood up and pointed his cane at Ryan with an angry stare and a shake in his hands. "That's enough out of you. You're out of line."

"Seconded." I looked at Ryan with a glare.

"I've heard enough." Pops put his cane down. "It's obvious we've reached the Rubicon, doing nothing would hang us *all*, so we're going to work together to bring these bastards down. If I hear one more barb or raised voice, I'll knock *all* of you in the head." He looked at Bex. "Not you, Girly. You've been knocked around enough for one life."

"Really, Pops?" I was disgusted by his insensitivity. Bex apparently wasn't because she gave him the smallest of a smile.

"I'm quite fond of you. We'll figure this out *together*." He gave a single nod, looking at her sweetly.

Bex nodded and went back to looking at the plate in front of her.

"I'm sorry, Nelson. I feel like shit, and I didn't mean that. You've been outnumbered from the beginning, and you *couldn't* do anything." Ryan spoke with sincerity.

"We need to find Patty." She didn't move her eyes from her plate, the hurt in them was making my heart break for her. "He holds all the cards, and we don't have a chance without him."

"I thought he was killed last year." Pops put a tart on her plate.

"Nelson has good reason to believe he might still be alive. And now, thanks to Roger, I think we know why Cynthia's been manipulating Nelson and anyone else she can. She must've found out about the baby being taken and wants these assholes taken out too." Ryan nudged my arm and pointed at the glass pitcher of water in front of me. I picked it up and gave it to him.

"I don't understand what that would have to do with Bex though." Something wasn't sitting right with me about the entire situation.

My dad looked at me. "Have you not been listening? Bexley has information we all need to put these criminals to bed."

"Yeah, I'm not dense, I just don't understand why

Bex would be the person everyone is betting on." I looked at her. "And I don't mean that offensively, I just don't understand why you have information no one else supposedly knows."

She nodded. "I know what you meant. Patty is acutely paranoid, among other things. He's also incredibly sly and intelligent. Those put together with his strong obsession over me led him to do whatever it took to ensure I stayed alive. If anyone hurt me, he could bring them down. If anyone tried to hurt me and he wasn't there to bring them down, he made sure I was equipped for that too. I know all the hiding spots, where to look depending on the category. The thumb drive Ryan acquired is the mass bottom spread. The equivalent would be taking down all the employees of MWM, but not you, your father, Willum, the board, etcetera. I know where everything on the mid-level players is, and the top. The thing that makes me trusted with that information is, I've already endured excruciating amounts of torture, so I won't fall prey to it. It either dies with me, or I use it at my discretion."

"So, you're holding out on us then?" Ryan sounded like he was in disbelief.

Bex looked at him, no sign of emotion on her face. "Until I find Patty, yes."

"Bexley, I can assure you, no one at this table has ill intent." My dad looked at her as if she'd said something to hurt his feelings. "I apologize for jumping to incorrect conclusions and coming on too strongly. We would like to help you, and hopefully, in the process, I might learn exactly what happened to my daughter."

"If Grey was only five when she was born, that would have occurred before Patty's time with Henry. It's not impossible, but there may not be a record. I'll do my best to help though." Bex was looking at her plate again.

"Even still, we're all committed to helping you and putting those bastards where they belong." Pops went to pat the top of her hand and Bex nearly jumped out of her skin. She continued to sit there rigidly while her cheeks pinkened.

"I hate to be the one to pose the question, but are we still expecting a wedding this weekend?" My dad was looking at Bex as he asked, then his eyes turned to me.

"We haven't had a chance to talk. Like we've already said, this all came to light as of us coming back to the hotel this morning," I responded, hoping to take some of the pressure off Bex.

My dad took a deep breath and moved his chair back from the table. "Then we'll leave you to talk. Bexley, I hope you'll consider my sincere apology. I think it would be a terrible loss for all of us if you no longer wished to join our family, however, I would understand and still offer our assistance. That said, for the time being, I would advise against seeing your family again while you're here. I'm sure it's not unknown to you, but it's incredibly dangerous." He looked at Pops. "Shall we?"

"We shall." Pops grabbed his cane and stood. "Don't blow it, Sunny Boy."

I expressed my irritation with his comment by raising an eyebrow at him. Ryan nudged my arm, then nodded in the direction of his room after I looked at him. I nodded, knowing he was wondering if he should go too. Bex and I sat quietly as everyone left. Last night, I'd mildly had some words in order, but as I sat there I realized nothing could express how sorry I was.

"We don't have to get married, B... I know I broke your trust, violated you in a way I can't take back, and if I could let you know how sorry I am... I would." It was a struggle to get my words out because I already knew what her decision would be. "When Ryan came to me, knowing who you were—in near tears and afraid for you—he refused to tell me... I became desperate to know because I didn't want to pull you into something that could hurt you. Inadvertently, and regardless, I did... but I never wanted to, and I really hope you can believe me on at least that."

"Why am I here?" Her eyes hadn't moved from her plate, and she was sitting just as rigidly as before.

It took me a second before I said, "I don't understand what you mean."

"Why did you make Ryan come find me? Why did you come to the diner? Why did you ask me to dinner?" The muscles in her neck tensed for a split second.

"The sadness in your eyes haunted me... I saw a picture of you on that hard drive, and you were the most beautiful person I'd ever seen, in a way I can't fully explain. I desperately wanted to know you, so I sent Ryan because I wasn't trying to create a tidal wave by going to meet you less prepared than I already was. I didn't know if my dad had wronged you in some way—this was before finding out my mother was the one having you followed, obviously, but... Ryan described you as smart, quiet, and incredibly scared. When I came down there, met you in person, saw you put your tip money down to replace what'd been stolen from Ann... it made me want to know you even more. Loving you has never been a lie, B... Not a single second of it."

"Were you ever going to tell me you knew who I was?" She finally looked at me, but I couldn't read her expression. It was either hurt or anger, but indistinguishable.

I nodded. "Yeah... I wanted to tell you on the plane to Germany because there'd be no one to overhear, I'd have time to explain myself, and tell you I don't want anything from you other than what we already have. I have a whole letter in my laptop bag already because I wanted to be very clear about what I mean by that, and I know you like letters because you never get them. I've never wanted you to think I've expected something from you. The only thing I want is you. Finding out who you were was just to know how I could keep you safe—what

I needed to do to make that happen—but I've never asked you or pushed you to tell me things because I don't want to know if you don't want to tell me. Other than my one—massive—slip up, I've tried to do nothing that would ever take from you." My hands were shaking under the table because I was so afraid to lose her.

"Why didn't you just ask me who I was?" Her expression had softened some but was still unreadable.

It was such a simple thing, but I never had. I'd never even tried asking her. "I was afraid to... Afraid you wouldn't tell me, afraid you'd be mad at me just for asking, or that you'd run because you might be afraid of me because I knew enough to ask. I'm terrified of losing you or doing anything that might cause that. But I should have asked, and I'm sorry for being too cowardice to try."

She nodded and looked at the table in front of her again. "Please, don't ever keep anything like this from me again... if you do, it'll be the last time. You can't begin to understand—" she stopped as her chin quivered and her eyes filled with tears, "how tired I am." Bex took in a deep breath, trying to push her emotions back down. "I have fought so hard just to get through minutes of my life, to survive them... please don't be one of them." Her eyes closed as she shook her head. "I'm so tired."

I wanted to say I understood, but I didn't. "Never again, Beautiful. I swear on Sam's life. Sam's because I feel like swearing on my own isn't good enough of a promise." I reached my hand over the table to see if she'd take it. "And I'll do whatever it takes to make things right, and not behind your back. All this stuff with Henry, I won't make a move you haven't okayed first because I don't know what you're up against. I trust whatever decisions you make, even if it's just to walk away."

She looked at me, seeming confused.

"I won't ask you to stay to help us fight what may or may not be coming. It wasn't right of Ryan to start this, I should've done more to confirm he wasn't, but you don't deserve to be pulled into another mess you didn't ask for. So, if you need to run to save yourself, then I want you to do what's best for you." I felt like I was going to throw up saying the words. "I can't promise you safety, I can only promise to do my best, and I don't know if that's enough, so I'm leaving it for you to decide. If you need money, if you need me to buy you some time so you can slip out unnoticed, you got it. Whatever you need, you got it. Anything and everything." My heart was breaking just at the thought of saying goodbye to her, and my chest physically hurt from it.

Bex shook her head. "I don't *want* to... I wanna stay, but I'm not sure *if* or how long I can."

I nodded. "I understand, all I ask is that you tell me before you go. You don't have to tell me where, I won't stop you, just *please* tell me."

She took my hand and nodded. "I promise."

"Thank you."

Bex stood up and pulled on my hand to get me to stand so she could hug me. "I know Ryan thinks I'm crazy, but you need to know there is a very *real* possibility that something might happen to me. If that happens before I find Patty, you *have* to find him. Other than being gross, he won't hurt me, and he'll do anything to get me back. The fastest way to pull him out of the woodwork will be to kidnap my dad. Leave something behind to clue him on where to find you and he *will*. Please promise me you'll do it."

I wrapped my hand around the back of her head and nodded. "Anything and everything, Beautiful. I promise."

"And I don't trust your parents. It has to be you and me. I'll tell Ryan whatever I want him to know, but you can't tell him anything I tell you in private unless I'm missing."

I smiled just a little right then because for the first

time, I had her trust. *Real* trust. "I'll follow your lead." I kissed her cheek and hugged her tighter.

Chapter 31

Ryan

"Thank you for calling The Tea Cup. How may I help you?"

I hadn't heard my mother's voice in fifteen years...

"Hello?" she sang.

I hung up and set my phone down. The thought had never crossed my mind that my mother hadn't chosen to leave. Even before my dad started knocking us around, he was a stressed-out asshole who came home and bitched about everything. In my mind, it'd always made sense that she wanted to leave. My dad was a dick, and us boys were a pain in the ass to deal with most days.

There was a knock on the door, so I got up and walked over to open it. Nelson and Grey were both standing there, but I couldn't tell from their faces whether or not they came with good news. I stepped back so they could come in, then followed them to go sit at the table.

"Do you have access to what was on that thumb

drive?" Nelson asked as she sat.

I nodded. "Yeah."

"Can you please pull it up?"

"Hold on, I have to call Tim. Don't say anything about our parents, he doesn't know." I picked up my phone, called Tim, and put it on speakerphone.

He answered after the first ring, but I waited for the beep, signaling the line was secured.

"I need you to pull up everything on my computer. Nelson wants to see it," I told him.

"Yeah. How much shit are we in?"

"A lot more than you think," Grey answered as he crossed his arms.

"Uh, hi, Grey. Please don't pull my funding for my side projects."

Pathetic.

"That'll depend on how this 'side project' out." Grey looked at me with the same level of irritation that he had earlier.

"Tim, just quit groveling and get it all pulled up." I hung up the call.

"Who else knows?" Nelson asked quietly.

I shook my head. "It's just been Tim and I. Cynthia came into it later, but I've been careful not to give her usable information. I don't trust her, and especially because of how she treats you."

"What're you talking about?" Grey frowned, looking at me, then Bex.

"Thanks for that." Nelson gave me a flat expression, then let out a huff as she looked at Grey. "The second you're not around, I may as well be gum on the bottom of her shoe."

"What? Why didn't you tell me?" Grey looked her over like it'd left some kind of visible mark on her somewhere.

"Because you're a mama's boy and everyone knows it." I clicked to open the file on the desktop after

my screen blanked and refreshed.

"Ryan," Nelson warned.

"It doesn't matter right now. Figuring this shit out does. Here." I turned my laptop toward her.

Nelson sat forward, then looked over at Grey. "You may not want to see what comes up. There are lots of pictures on here."

"Take that under serious advisement. I've honestly puked a few times." I wished I'd never looked at certain pictures, but had no choice.

Grey looked at me, again with irritation, then looked at Bex. "Unless you don't want me to see something, then I'm okay."

Nelson looked at me, seeming a little nervous, but gazed back at the computer. "Do you remember the month and day?"

"Um, it was June. I'm not sure of the day." He shook his head. "It was toward the end of the month."

"What are you looking for?" I picked up my coffee and took a drink.

"I'm gonna see if I can find Grey's sister. I doubt she would've come through the house given that she was taken as a baby, but I'll try."

Babies didn't live very long after they were taken. Toddlers sometimes lived another year or two, and everyone else just depended on who they were sold to.

I got up and moved so I could sit on the other side of Nelson. About twenty names came up when she searched the birth year, and three of those were in June. She clicked on one before I even had a chance to read the name.

"Holy shit," I whispered after seeing the picture of the girl who looked undeniably like Grey and Sam. She had the same blonde hair, blue eyes, and eye shape, but she had Cynthia's cheekbones and chin. Her name was Charlotte Vaughters.

"Vaughters. Didn't you mention that name earlier?"

Grey asked her.

Nelson nodded. "Yep. And I've met her... I don't understand how your mom could know that though."

"How do we find her? We have to get her out of this." Grey shook his head.

"She's not in it." Nelson rubbed her forehead, letting out a breath. "At least not in the way you're thinking. She's Alex's daughter, and both he and his wife treat her like a princess." She let out a breath and sat back in her chair. "How does this keep getting more and more twisted?"

"That's what I keep asking." Grey reached forward to the laptop. "Who's in the picture with her?"

"No, don't," Nelson said quickly, but it was too late.

"Oh my god," Grey whispered, then looked at her like the injuries from the picture were still there on her.

"Please don't say whatever you're about to say." She reached forward to minimize the picture to just Charlotte. Her cheeks, neck, and part of her chest were turning red from embarrassment.

"Why was that picture posed when the others weren't?" I asked. It wasn't the first time I'd seen it, and I'd already noticed it was different from all the others. Nelson also had clothes on, even though they were too big and fairly dirty.

Nelson shook her head. "Patty told us to. Charlotte didn't know anything strange was going on in that house. She believed she was visiting her aunt's husband and stepdaughter. Helen Vaughters is the woman I accidentally killed by pushing her down the stairs. The only people who know that are Patty and I, and now the two of you. Patty made it look like she disappeared by forging letters. Alex and his wife came to see if they could find her, leaving Charlotte at the house while they searched. During that time, I stayed in the bedroom upstairs, was allowed to wear clothes, and was expected to act like a normal kid." She was pulling up the names of other people while she spoke.

"How were you supposed to act like a normal kid? You were beat to *hell*." Grey's voice was partially strained as he continued to look at her pathetically.

"Patty was too. Charlotte was told we were in a car accident." Nelson kept her eyes on the computer, just pulling up different people in separate windows. "Ryan, every person I'm pulling up is either someone you haven't gotten to or have missed. You need to take care of them before Grey and I leave for Germany after the wedding."

"Some of them I haven't been able to find, and three of those are employed by MWM. I was waiting until after the wedding until I took them down because it's not safe for you." I pulled my phone out to start messaging Tim so he could get on it.

"We're already legally married. My dad signed off on it and had it recorded to record about ten minutes before we walked in. The wedding will go on as normal, and if it doesn't, we don't care." She didn't even pause at what she was doing.

"*What?* Are you kidding me right now? That was incredibly stupid. You just tied your fake identity to your *real* one." What was she thinking?

"I'm aware, and that was the point. We're doing things my way from now on. You should also know that your contract with Grey has been sold to me, along with Tim's for the time being."

"You're trying to draw Henry out by making it look like it *is* you. Nelson, I've been trying to keep you out of the line of fire." I shoved my hand through my hair and held it there because I was trying not to violently explode.

"Henry, among others, yes. And I have no intention of sitting idly while you go after people you know little about. We do this my way and you can be the co-pilot, or I still do it my way and exclude you from everything by using your contract against you. The choice is yours."

She looked at me, stopping what she was doing.

I already knew she was angry with me, and I deserved every ounce of it. "I wanna help you, Nelson. Contracts have nothing to do with it, you're my friend."

"Then please trust me to know what I'm doing."

I nodded. "Okay."

She pointed back at the laptop screen while still looking at me. "These are all people that need to be gone as soon as humanly possible. I know it's going to make a nightmare for Roger, and I'm counting on it. We need the distraction. If at all possible, make it look like this came from Patty and not you. Having a honeymoon in Germany was never a coincidence. I have certain things that need to make it to the German BKA, and now we have to find Charlotte on top of it all. These people aren't as insignificant as Patty's records make it appear, and I can move around easier if I know they can't show up. Roger will be landlocked in the US, and Henry will be waiting for me when our empty plane lands in Germany while I obtain certain things here. After he finds our empty plane, he'll be forced to come stateside, but Grey and I will be on a different flight under different names. We'll deliver what I have to the BKA, hopefully, be able to locate Charlotte, and pop off the grid until D-Day has ended. My family is already under a very heavy blanket of protection from my own means. I've ensured that they're untouchable without an all-out ugly gun war in a public display. As I'm sure you've gathered, Henry avoids public displays. And it's Maslen now, not Nelson."

I laughed a little because of the sheer irony that my very quiet and timid friend was really neither of those things. "I'm sorry..." I rubbed my forehead, trying to keep from laughing further. "I'm proud to have underestimated you."

She took in a deep breath. "Don't be proud yet. I'm just hoping I haven't underestimated Henry."

I nodded. "I think you've got a fairly solid plan, and

I can make this look like it came from Patty. Dare I ask what your protection plan around your family is?"

"The gang in LA I was running drugs for is based here in Dallas. I went to school with a boy named Juan. His father is Oscar Reyes, the king of the Three Kings. It takes an army to fight an army, and the enemy of my enemy is my friend, and has been since my first bible camp."

"Oh my god," I shook my head. "I feel like I should bow at your feet right now. You've been ready for this for a long ass time."

She pulled back the corner of her mouth. "Since I got out of the house."

"And you're sure Toby and Grace will be safe?"

"As safe as I can make them." She held up her shoulders. "I need you and Tim to do your part. Grey and I are gonna head home, but we need you to stay here with Roger and Willum until tomorrow morning. You're no longer meeting with my brother tomorrow, I've canceled that. If I want his help, I'll ask for it."

I nodded. "You understand why I did it, don't you?"

She nodded. "I do, and I appreciate it."

I nodded again. "What do I say to Cynthia in the midst of all this?"

"Not the truth. I'm not trusting anyone outside of you, Tim, and Grey."

"Okay. What about the pig? Where do we look for him?" If she was leaving, I wanted to get as much information as I could.

She shook her head. "Right now, we don't. He'll come to me."

"Why do you want him to?" I couldn't understand how she'd trust him for even a second. "He's sick."

"I have my reasons."

"It's a lot harder to keep you safe the more you leave me in the dark." It was frustrating to know she didn't trust me with all the cards.

"Leaving the right gaps allows the right people to appear when I'm ready for them. Please trust me." She looked at Grey. "We should go."

He nodded, gave her an appreciative smile, and offered a hand after standing. "Yep."

I wondered if she was marrying Grey for other reasons than loving him, or if she was just that quick to forgive. I still didn't know how he found out who she was without me knowing.

"Hey." I watched her as she stood. "Best wishes, Maslen." I held out my wrist.

She smiled and bumped my wrist. "Thank you."

I nodded once and looked at Grey. "Congrats, man."

Blondie's eyebrows raised and dropped before he turned without a word. It seemed I finally did something that pissed him off enough to stop talking to me.

Chapter 32

Bexley

Grey and I were testing a plan, and the bright side of that was being able to see my family again and spend the day with them. I smiled when we pulled up to Luke Wheaton's family farm. I had so many of the best memories spending summers at our Ranch house and the Wheaton's farm just up and over the hill behind it.

"Everything always looks so much smaller than I remember. It's weird," I said to Grey as he parked next to Ben's truck.

"You were smaller, so everything seemed bigger."

"Yeah. I can't believe I'm here again. It feels like a dream." I looked at the old farmhouse with a smile. There was nothing special about it other than it felt like a piece of home. The siding was dirty from years of dusty fields being plowed around it. The clothesline looked like it was on its last leg, and the porch needed a coat of paint again. From the looks of it, the last time it was painted was the summer Luke, his sister Amy, Ben, Emily, and I had painted it. It'd been my last summer home.

"Hey, you good?" Grey asked.

I looked at him with a smile and nodded. "Nostalgic."

He smiled. "Good. Let's go."

I leaned in for a quick kiss before we got out. It'd become something we did before leaving the car.

Luke came down the porch steps, pulled his baseball cap off, and held it over his heart with a happy smile that made him look near tears. "By god, I thought I'd never see the day. And you're even prettier than the last time I saw you, little lady. Can I hug you?"

"You better." I stepped forward and hugged him tightly.

"Good grief, you're still tiny." Luke squeezed me and let out a breath like he was relieved. "How have you been, honey?" he asked in a whisper, not ready to let go.

"If I knew how to answer that, I would. Life's a roller coaster, but I'm okay."

"Well, I think that's just about as good as we can ask for." He pulled back and looked at me. "Man alive, you look like Emily, just prettier."

I gave a slightly embarrassed smile. "So everyone keeps telling me." I took another step back and directed a hand. "This is my husband, Grey. Grey, this is Luke. He and my brother have been best friends since they were born."

"Yep, sorry about that. Hannah's probably more my sister than my own." Luke reached out a hand. "It's good to meet you."

"You too, and no apologies necessary." Grey smiled and shook Luke's hand.

"I appreciate that. You never know with a guy hugging another man's wife." Luke chuckled a little and bopped my nose lightly with the top of his hat. "And telling her she's pretty cause it still makes her blush."

Grey laughed.

"I've got a surprise for you." Luke stepped to the

side. "Send him out!" he called loudly.

I turned, wondering what in the world was going on, and what he'd be surprising me with. My jaw dropped a little when I saw my mammoth of a horse start galloping, then running toward me. I smiled at the sight of Cletus. He had a smooth buckskin coat with a mane and tail that were dark brown and trimmed perfectly. I couldn't believe he was still as lean and healthy looking as he was, but it made sense because my dad was particular about the keep of the horses.

Luke laughed. "Here he comes."

I held out my hand. "Whoa there."

He snorted and vocalized himself as he walked up to me with a bobbing head. I reached up for Cletus' halter, but it made no difference. He walked straight into me and put the length of his head against the front of me. He snorted and breathed in heavily as he rubbed the top of his head against me.

I laughed a little as I hugged his giant head. "You didn't miss me at all, did you?"

"I think that poor horse is so happy he's crying," Luke laughed as he pet Cletus' muscular neck.

Cletus scored the ground with his hoof and kept rubbing his head into the front of me while he made the saddest sounds a horse could make.

"I missed you too, buddy. Take it easy." I rubbed my hand down his slick coat on his neck while hugging his big head with my other arm.

"He's beautiful. Is he a Draft?" Grey walked up on the other side to pet Cletus.

"I think he's Draft and Gypsy Vanner," Luke answered. Despite having a horse and my family loving horses, I didn't know the first thing about breeds.

"What are they talking about?" I asked Cletus. "Say, 'I'm just a horse. Does it matter?'" I pulled up his giant head to look at him. "I'm more impressed you're still alive and that you remember me."

"He's still healthy as can be. Your dad's got a vet out here every six months to make sure of it." Luke smiled at me like he was proud of me for something. "You can ride him down the hill if you want. Everyone's down there waiting on us."

I looked at Grey. "Are you up for it?" He was still hungover and had little sleep. I was on *no* sleep, but not hungover.

"Let's do it." Grey smiled with one of his beautiful smiles; like he was more in love with me than a minute ago.

"I don't know if you remember the way or not, but this guy does. He's up here more than he's down *there* anymore." Luke held Cletus' halter.

"I remember." I looked at Grey again. "You first."

Grey grabbed the horn on the saddle and put a foot in the stirrup. I knew Cletus was going to try to nip, so I blocked his head.

"You be nice," I told Cletus as I pushed his face back.

Luke laughed. "If you weren't any taller, I'd think no time had passed."

"I keep pinching myself because I feel like I'm making everything up in my head; it's been so long." I put my foot in the stirrup and took Grey's hand to pull myself up.

"Well, you're right where you're meant to be." Luke gave a small smile, seeming like he was thinking of something else. "I'll be down in just a few. I gotta get my farm hand his check and feed the dogs."

"Uh, you're not letting them come down, are you? I'm terrified of dogs."

He gave a single nod. "Ben told me. That's why they're inside."

"Thank you."

"Yep. Happy trails." He smiled again.

I gave a smile back and clicked my tongue as I bumped Cletus' side. "Let's go home, big guy."

Grey wrapped his arms around me as we entered

the trees. "You look happy," he whispered into my shoulder.

I let out a breath. "I'm trying not to be scared shit-less. Everything in me is telling me I'm gonna get caught, but even if I do, I just want this one good day."

"We'll have lots of them, and there's no reason our plan shouldn't work." He kissed the top of my shoulder, then the side of my neck.

"I need to talk to you about something, and I've been avoiding it for weeks because it makes me nervous as hell."

He laughed a little. "Yeah, I think after this morning, admitting that I stole your blood, you're good."

"You didn't beat me in order to steal it, so I'm not too worried about it. And the nervousness is more just hav-ing an awkward conversation as opposed to admitting to something."

Grey rubbed my arms. "You're good. Take a deep breath and give it your best."

I took a deep breath and let it out in a huff. "Um... I know this is going to sound super weird, but my brother is a psychologist, so I kinda talked to him about it be-cause it's super hard to talk about. And I thought I'd have a couple more days to work up a better time to talk about it, but we unexpectedly got married today, so the clock is out."

"I'm going out on a limb here, but you're giving me a whole back story, so I'm assuming this is about sex?" His voice was easy and non-judgmental.

I nodded.

"Don't worry about it, B. I'm not racing to cross the finish line. I had to wait a few weeks just to hold your hand, and that made me aware that it's a privilege to be allowed to. It was three months before I could hug you, six months before we kissed, and I wanna make it very clear that I hold no timeline on anything beyond that, regardless of us getting married. I knew who you were when I asked you to marry me, I knew you had a daughter who might be in the picture someday, and I knew there was a possibility you might never be ready or okay... I'm okay with that. No, it's not always easy to hold back, but you knowing you're safe and that I'll never do anything you're not ready for is far more important. So, please believe me when I say I'm not sitting here checking my watch. Okay?" He rubbed my arms lightly.

"I appreciate that. And that's definitely been on my mind, but not the only thing. It's kind of hard to explain, so forgive me if it doesn't come out making complete sense." My heart was pounding because I felt like a gross ball of slime.

"Do your best, we'll get there," he reassured.

"I think a lot of the fear for me comes from not know-ing what to do. Um... I've—" I cleared my throat because my throat was tightening and making my voice crack. "I dealt with pe-people who had fetishes, and... um... I know I can't trust movies or books to tell me what's right or n-n-not..." I reached up to my neck because I felt like I was about to come out of my own skin.

"Hey." Grey dropped his hand. "I'm catching what you're telling me. Just take a couple breaths and reset. You're good, and it's a good conversation to have."

I nodded as I took a breath and held it before my lungs took over and threw me into a hyperventilating mess.

"I'll tell you right now, I'm pretty boring," he chuckled a little. "Kinks and fetishes aren't my thing as much as being comfortable with each other. That's what makes it for me. I don't know that I've ever said 'no' to much, but bland love is my favorite. For the most part, I'm pretty aware of what kind of touching is off-limits with you, but if there's more, I'd definitely like to know before that time comes. It doesn't have to be now. Just whenever you feel comfortable telling me."

I let out the breath I'd been holding and rested my

head back on his shoulder. "Do you just sit here and rehearse this stuff in your head all day? Why do you always say the perfect thing?"

He wrapped his arms around me. "Not all day, but I try to think about how hard it has to be to trust someone, who for the first time, isn't out to hurt you, isn't forcing you, and think about what I'd expect from the person I'd want to trust. Then I try to one-up that because you deserve better." He kissed my cheek. "I think more times than not, you need peace of mind over reassurance. I want to have both... My heart breaks every day, Bex. Not because I see you as this pitiful and injured person, but because I see you as the most honestly kind and beautiful one, and I can't understand why anyone would ever hurt you." He hugged me tighter.

"I love you too," I whispered back.

"More than anything and everything."

I smiled as he kissed my cheek, and picked up my head because I could hear the laughter of my family through the trees. There were a lot more people than I expected.

"Oh my gosh. That is so much more than family."

"I know. Surprise." Grey patted my hips.

I turned to look at his face. "What do you mean surprise?"

Grey smiled. "I may have faxed an additional paper."

I raised my eyebrows. "Now you're in trouble."

Grey laughed. "Yeah? I'll be in trouble for this. Worth it."

"Did you honestly learn nothing from my birthday? I don't like big parties."

"Nope. Didn't learn a thing." He held a charismatic smile.

"I'm taking the Aston Martin back."

He shrugged. "Can't. It's special order."

I reached back and pinched his side.

Grey laughed. "Just enjoy it. It's a welcome-home-happy-birthday-wedding party." He kissed my shoulder again. "I love you."

"I love you too. I want a month-long trip to Switzerland, Iceland, and Norway and you're not allowed to work. Not one email. Not one phone call. That's your punishment."

He laughed. "Yeah? No work, huh?"

"Yep." It was painful for Grey not to work.

"You got it, Beautiful," he chuckled.

"I'm being serious." I looked at him with a raised eyebrow.

"I know, I am too." He reached up to hold my chin and kissed me quickly. "No work for a month. Just you and me."

"You need a faster horse! Hurry up!" Emily called.

I looked up in the attic window and saw exactly who I hoped to. I knew my dad had lied to me...

Chapter 33

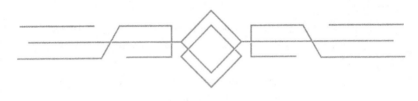

Grey

There were probably twenty people or better clapping as we came down the hill through the tree line that circled the house. Bex's brother, sister, and Toby jogged toward us.

"Surprise!" Emily clapped before a terrible squeal.

"What are you doing here?" Bex signed as she spoke. I felt stumped because I didn't know she knew Sign Language.

"I'm staying at Luke's. He told me." Toby reached up for her hand, along with Ben.

"Mom!" A little girl ran from the back porch.

I held my hands up to make sure Bex didn't slip as Ben and Toby helped her down, then got down myself.

"I'm Ben, Hannah's older brother." Ben reached his hand out to me with a smile.

"Grey. It's nice to finally meet you." I shook his hand with a polite smile.

"Yeah. I've been hearing about you for a year without knowing you, so it's nice to put a face to the right name." He put a hand on Toby's shoulder. "This is Emily, and Toby, Grace's dad."

"I'm not sure how much you know about anything, but Toby's family too, and that's that," Emily said as she shook my hand.

"Noted." I nodded once, then forced myself to give a convincing and polite smile as I shook the hand of someone I couldn't understand. "It's nice to meet you."

"You too and congratulations." Toby nodded with a seemingly genuine smile.

I nodded once. "Thank you."

"Are you my stepdad?"

I looked at Grace as she stood in front of Bex, wrapped in her mom's arms. The question caught me off guard.

"Uh." I raised my eyebrows and looked at Bex to see if she was as thrown as I was, but she wasn't. "Technically, I guess." I looked at Grace. "I didn't think about it that way until just now."

"Cool. Emily's gonna be my stepmom soon, so I'll have a stepmom and a stepdad." She smiled brightly at me. I didn't expect her to look as much like Toby as she did like Bex.

"Take it easy on him, Grace," Bex laughed. I'd never seen her around a child before and didn't expect her to seem so maternal right off the bat.

"The party's down here, Hannah Banana," an older man called from the porch.

Just like that, Bex's smile was gone as she looked at Ben with irritation.

"Yep. I know. I told Mom not to invite them," he mumbled.

Toby touched Bex's arm and signed something with a concerned look.

"No," Ben shook his head. "Royce and Carla."

Toby rolled his eyes. "Say no more." He held out a

hand to Grace. "Hey, don't hang on your mom too much, okay? We'll get to spend more time with her after everyone else leaves." I was a little surprised that he was fairly easy to understand when he spoke. It was obvious that he couldn't hear well from the way he formed words, but he wasn't unclear when he spoke.

"Royce, the guy that just called her Banana. Avoid him and his wife at *all* costs," Emily cautioned before she followed Toby and Grace.

"Who are they?" I asked Bex.

"Carla is our mom's sister, and she's okay, but Royce is a loud dumbass. Don't give him *any* information about *anything*. Don't tell him your last name, don't tell him what you do, because he'll act like he knows more about it than you do. Just," Ben held up a hand, "for once, Emily's right, steer clear."

"Don't let him touch me. I will seriously go spastic," Bex said to Ben with a slightly heated look.

"I already told everyone not to hug you or crowd around, but I'll intercept if need be." He put a hand on top of her head with a small smile. "Don't be grouchy, Beans. You're loved and you were missed."

"I know."

He dropped his hand, and she reached out to me. "Seriously, break Royce's hand if you have to, don't let him touch me," she whispered as she looped her hand around my arm. "My parents hate him too. Just be nice to Carla, we like her."

I nodded. "Got it."

"And you're about to meet the world's best parents," she said quickly before she let go of my arm and went to hug Donald and Mildred.

There were a lot of introductions to get through, and that felt slightly tedious, which was sort of humbling because I now understood the overwhelm Bex constantly felt around me. Royce was certainly a loud-mouthed dumbass like Ben said. He thought everything was a joke, and constantly kept reaching out to touch Bex's arm or would come up behind her to startle her from behind. The second time he came up to scare her, I walked right up to him, got uncomfortably close, and told him to knock it off. It wasn't funny or cute to scare someone who was legitimately afraid of being touched just to get a laugh. Thankfully, Don didn't see it as an overaggressive move, because he stood next to me and told Royce he'd take him out in the field and shoot him in the ass for a laugh if he did it again. I didn't know Don well, but I was pretty sure he wasn't kidding based on his tone.

After that, I got to talking with Don. I expected him to hate me, but it didn't seem that way at all. He was incredibly nice, and interesting to talk to. I loved the way he was sweet to his kids, especially Bex. I would've pegged her for a mama's girl, but she was both. Bex sat between them with her head on her mom's shoulder and held her dad's hand. If I could've taken a picture of the happiness in her eyes, I would've.

When the aunts, uncles, cousins, and grandparents left, it was just her immediate family and Luke left. I finally got to talk to Ben and Emily for a little bit because they weren't occupied trying to entertain the masses. It took about an hour for Bex to relax after the extra people were gone, but once she was, I went inside to go to the bathroom. When I came out, Toby was waiting at the bottom of the stairs.

"Can we talk for a minute?" He looked at me nervously.

I forced myself to smile the way I normally would. "Yeah. What's up?"

"Let's go out front." He pointed at the front door, then went out.

I didn't know what he was about to say, but I tried not to overthink it and followed.

"I want to clear the air with you. If Hannah does what she says, we'll probably be seeing a lot more of each other, so..." He held up his shoulder with an impish expression. "If you have questions or something you want to say—I don't know—but I don't want there to be problems."

I shook my head. "I don't either, and I don't know the details of the situation you and Bex were in." I held up my shoulders. "The reality is, you were both kids. I wouldn't understand that so much from your perspective if I didn't have a brother who is eighteen. He's a great kid, but totally unequipped to handle something that serious. So, I'd rather choose to try to understand than judge." I pulled the corner of my mouth back.

Toby stood there like I'd called him a monster. "She begged me... I couldn't end her life. I watched her get beat every time Henry came to that house, saw her go from room to room, walking out without a tear—even when they hurt her, and all she wanted was to come home. *Here.*" He directed a hand at the house. "If it'd been my life, I would've been dead years ago. If I didn't have Grace to take care of, I'd still be dead because I'm sick of what lives in my head... Hannah deserved to get out, to come home. She puts everyone first. Always. If there's not enough food, she won't eat. If someone's hurt, she'll take care of them no matter how broken her bones are. In a house where kindness didn't exist, she made it exist... no matter how scared, sick, starving, or hurt she was..." He lifted his shoulder to wipe a tear off his cheek. "She just wanted to come home... and I couldn't be the reason she didn't." He swallowed hard, the corners of his mouth trembling while he looked as tortured as a person could. It was hard to watch, hard to hear, and made me realize just how much more I didn't understand.

I nodded. "Then I think you did the right thing... as hard as it was. We as men can be prideful in our commitment to never hurting women, but we forget that not every situation is black and white." I nodded once. "It seems like you did the best you could, and what was best for Bex. You didn't owe it to me, so thank you for explaining... I mean that." I reached out a hand as a peace offering.

Toby looked at my hand but didn't reach out. "Please, don't hurt her... I don't understand everything that's going on because she won't tell me, and I can never tell if she's being honest, but please don't hurt her."

I shook my head. "I won't. You have my word."

He took in a deep breath and stepped forward to shake my hand.

Ben opened the door. "Hey, we're getting ready to do presents." He looked at Toby, noticing he was upset. "Everything okay?"

"Yeah. I have to run out to the car." Toby immediately turned down the steps.

I pulled back the corner of my mouth and nodded as I turned to go inside. Ben backed up but seemed like he was waiting for an explanation, so I told him, "He wanted to clear the air. Everything's okay, just a difficult subject."

Ben nodded. "He's not like Hannah who holds everything back." He looked out the window. "And he's always teetering on a fine edge with mortality, so be careful what you say to him. I haven't gotten much out of Hannah other than confirming his accounts are true, but I can tell you they're tightly bound in what they share. Accepting one means accepting the other." He looked at me like he might be a little irritated with me in some way.

I pulled back the corner of my mouth. "I caught that. I'm not judging, and I know Bex needs him in her life for more than Grace's sake." I held up my shoulders. "Seems like that's mutual, and it doesn't bother me."

"What about Hannah and Ryan? I haven't seen them together, but I've heard them talk about each other." He watched me like he was suspicious of me now.

I smiled. "They got matching tattoos on their wrists two months ago and I sat there while they got them done. Ryan would cut off his hand before he'd stab me in the back, and Bex is just too honest. I'm also not the jealous kind, and I think people should be free to have the friends they want to have."

"Are you trying to say whatever you think will impress me?"

I laughed a little at his directness and shook my head. "I don't need to impress anyone unless they're a potential business prospect. I come as I am, and people either like me or they don't." I held up my shoulders. "I'm good either way."

"Grey, honey, come on. Ben, did you find Toby?" Millie called from the kitchen. "Oh, never mind, he just walked around. Come on you two."

"You good?" I asked with raised eyebrows and an inoffensive expression.

"Yeah." Ben went past the stairs to the back door, and I followed behind.

Bex smiled at me when I came outside and moved over for me to sit next to her. After a year and a half, I'd finally witnessed the first whole-hearted smile. It radiated from her. I could see there was nothing else on her mind, no negative thoughts making her hold something back, she was there in the present with her family, and filled with true happiness.

"What's with the look?" A halo of evening light shined on Bex's shoulders from behind her while she smiled at me questioningly.

I shook my head with a smile. "You're beautiful."

"Okay. This is a gift, but it's not for your birthday." Millie came over with a large flat box and set it on Bex's lap. "I asked Ryan for your measurements some months back. He was supposed to pick this up from me tomorrow and bring it to ya on your weddin' day, but since you're *here*, I wanted to see your face while ya opened it." She smiled beautifully at Bex.

"Okay." Bex laughed quietly and pulled the lid up. I took it from her because it was a fairly large box and she needed both hands to keep it from tipping. Her smile fell and shock took its place. "Mom... Oh my gosh."

"Now, I know I promised ya Grammy's dress, but it got stained after the attic had a leak in the roof. So, I made this one myself, and hopefully, you'll be able to pass it down." Millie continued to watch Bex lovingly as Bex pulled the dress up.

"I can't believe this. It's so beautiful." She stood up with the dress as I moved the box to the floor in an attempt to keep the bottom protected. "Thank you so much." Bex looked from the elegant dress to her mom with the most grateful smile I'd probably ever seen.

"You're very welcome, baby. Just make sure I get every picture." Millie touched Bex's cheek and pulled her into a hug.

"I think you just made me excited for the wedding just because I get to wear this dress," Bex laughed.

Millie stepped back and looked at her daughter like she'd said something crazy. "I hope you're excited for more than that."

Bex realized instantly how that could've been mis-construed and turned to look at me with fear in her eyes. "No, I didn't mean it like that. I just—"

I was already laughing and shaking my head be-fore she could finish her words. "I know exactly what you meant." I looked at Millie. "Bex wanted a small wedding with just close family and friends. She hasn't been looking forward to the three hundred people she doesn't know coming to gawk."

"Well, this dress will give 'em somethin' to gawk at, that's for sure. But there ain't nothin' at the weddin' gon-na be prettier than you." Don smiled at Bex and pinched the end of her nose lightly as he passed her to sit in his chair.

"That's right." Millie agreed.

"Me next." Emily smiled with a child-like grin and held out a small box.

"Here, I'll put this back. You open gifts." Millie took the dress from Bex.

"I'm afraid to open this. The last time you gave me something, I ended up with a rash." Bex looked at Emily suspiciously.

Emily laughed. "Why do you remember literally every bad thing?"

Ben snorted. "There weren't a lot of good ones with you."

Bex glanced at Ben with a small smile. "Be nice. We were kids." She opened the box and closed it immediately. "Really?" She raised her eyebrows at Emily.

Emily held up her shoulders. "It'll help spice things up. You're married now."

"What is it?" Ben went to pick up the box, but Bex pulled it back quickly and stuffed it under her leg so no one could grab it.

"Don't worry about it." Bex picked up another box from the side table, her cheeks flushed with red and her smile gone.

"Oh, come on, Hannah. I didn't mean anything by it." Emily looked honestly worried that she'd upset Bex.

"What'd you put in there?" Don asked with a frown.

"Everyone, just let it go, please." Bex kept her eyes on the box she'd picked up as she slid her finger under the tape on the sides.

"Hannah, I'm sorry. It was meant to be a funny, normal bachelorette party kind of gift. I didn't mean to be insensitive. *Really*." Emily continued to look at her like she was crushed.

"It's okay."

Ben looked at me and gave a slight nod toward the box under Bex's leg. I frowned and shook my head. If Bex didn't want anyone to know, I wasn't going to press the issue.

"Inside Emily," Don demanded as he took her arm and pulled her into the house.

"Luke, you composed this?" Bex looked up at him with a bright smile as she pulled out sheet music.

"Yep. Probably about a year after you were gone, I think." He took off his hat and scratched the top of his head. "It's published and all that, but I thought you should have the original pages."

"That's sweet." Bex looked down at the papers in her hand with a touched smile before she looked at me. "Luke plays the cello beautifully, and I used to play the piano for him at all his recitals. He's been composing since you were, what—" she looked at him, "five or six?"

He nodded. "Somewhere around there."

"That's incredible. And you said this was published?" I looked at him, but glanced at Don as he came toward Bex and I.

"Excuse my reach," Don said as he leaned in to grab the box under Bex's leg.

"Dad, let it go. It's fine." Bex put her hand down to stop him.

"No, it ain't, and I'm throwin' it away." He took the box and walked back inside.

"Uh, yeah," Luke turned his attention back to me, "it's published and the Dallas Symphony Orchestra recorded it with some of my other works." He pointed at the papers. "All you gotta do is search for it on whatever music platform you listen on."

"This is really special. Thank you so much." Bex hugged the pages to her chest.

He nodded once with a heartfelt smile. "You were terribly missed, little lady."

Bex returned his smile. "I missed you too."

"Can I go next?" Grace asked sweetly as she kicked her dangling legs and leaned on her hands at the edge of the chair she was on.

"Absolutely. What've you got there?" Bex smiled at Grace in a way she never smiled at anyone, but it was the way Millie smiled at Bex.

Grace got off her chair. "I have two presents. The first one I painted this last year after Ben got me a new set of paints for my birthday." She picked up a canvas that had a sheet over it. "Grey, can you help me?"

"Yep." I stood up and took it from the back the way she handed it to me.

"It's not the cow you liked, so don't be disappointed, okay?" Grace looked at Bex, slightly worried.

Bex continued to smile. "If you painted it, I'll love it just the same."

Grace pulled the sheet off and looked at her mom. "It's you and me, but you can't see our faces because I didn't want to paint you wrong without a picture to look at. Dad told me your hair was super long and curly, and I gave us matching white dresses because blue wouldn't look as good with all the greens. I was going to paint us in a field like the one at our house, but dad said you loved trees."

"Gracie, this is..." Bex reached for the canvas as she shook her head. "Oh my gosh. This is so beautiful. Thank you, sweetie." She pulled Grace in and hugged her tightly.

It was beautiful, and somehow perfectly captured Bex from the back. Her hair flowed down her back in large soft curls, the shape of her body was almost exact, and there was even the detail of a scar on the back of her right shoulder, though faint. Grace and Bex walked hand in hand through a small patch of green grass in a thicket of trees.

"This'll go great in your alcove," I told Bex as I took the painting so she could keep hugging Grace.

"What's an alcove?" Grace looked at me earnestly.

"It's a small room off of a larger one," I explained.

"Oh. Well, maybe you can put these in there too."

She pulled back and handed Bex a couple hardcover notebooks. "It's all the letters I wrote you while you were gone."

"Oh, thank you." Bex rubbed her back. "I promise I'll respond."

"Okay, but send it to Grandma and Papa's house so I get it faster."

Bex laughed. "I'll do that."

Chapter 34

Bexley

Saying goodbye to my family the second time was even harder than the first. The car ride to the airport in Oklahoma was insufferable because all I wanted to do was turn around and go back. It'd been the best day I'd ever had, and it felt as gone as the day I'd been taken. The feeling settled a bit once we were home, but it would never be gone.

"Can I do anything for you, Beautiful?" Grey asked quietly after we laid down. It was early morning, but I hadn't slept since I was home last, and Grey was only on a few hours.

"No, I'll be okay." I rolled into his side and tucked myself against him. He felt like the only comfort I had left.

"It won't be long before this is over, right?" He rubbed my shoulder. "As soon as Henry's out of the way, you can go see them as much as you want."

"Except I don't wanna be Hannah." I closed my eyes because tears felt like they were too close.

"What do you mean?"

"I don't want the media storm, or for people to know who I really am. It's hard enough with the people who already know. The looks of pity, the questions, and the tiptoeing. That's not how I wanna be known in the world."

Grey shifted under me. "You don't think that's how I view you, do you?"

"Not usually, but sometimes... It's not your fault, and I understand intrusive thoughts better than most, but that's why I don't wanna be her. Hannah's a part of me that I don't want to exist anymore."

"Mm," he rubbed my shoulder, "you're not. You're my beautiful wife, Grace's amazing mom, Ryan's best friend, your parents' pride and joy, Ben and Emily's sister... None of that has to do with a name." Grey kissed my forehead. "You're loved, no matter what you call yourself."

He was being sweet, but it didn't make me feel any better. All I could think about was how a gift meant to be a funny gag was a complete insult because of my past. Emily had given me a vibrator, and I'd been so instantly horrified and petrified all at once. In the moment, I couldn't even think beyond the mental snap to keep my mouth shut. I should've laughed it off as intended, or better concealed my horror at the very least. Then my dad had to make it worse by taking Emily in the house to demand answers and yell at her.

After getting some sleep, Grey and I went to our rehearsal dinner. I dreaded it far more than the wedding because of the people Cynthia had invited. In the world of the Maslen's the rehearsal dinner wasn't for family and close friends, it was for special clients and Cynthia's odious friends.

"Bexley, where's your dress? There're guests here already." Cynthia looked like I was about to be arrested for something.

I gave a polite smile. "This is my dress. I decided against the other one."

"It's our night, Mom. She can wear what she'd like," Grey said calmly before she could say anything further. He leaned forward to kiss her cheek. "You look beautiful."

"I know it's your night, but that gold dress was perfect."

Except I didn't like the gold dress! After learning Cynthia had been meddling behind my back, I'd decided I was going to trust my instincts about her. Something had always been off, and I didn't find her to be as wonderful as everyone else seemed to. Other people feared Roger—I didn't—but Cynthia was very crafty about concealing her nasty side, whereas Roger wasn't. What you saw with him was generally what you got.

Willum walked up and gave a low whistle as he looked me over. "Boy oh boy, if I was sixty years younger, I'd steal you away, Girly. Grey wouldn't know what hit him."

"Your cane is about to hit you." Roger looked at Grey expectantly. "Grey, a word, please?"

"Roger, I swear. Now is not the time for business," Cynthia chided quietly.

"It's not about business, and it doesn't concern you. Go worry about your centerpieces."

I took the squabble as my opportunity to get away from Cynthia. Tonight was going to be a headache without Ryan to be an outcast with. He'd called to tell me he and Tim needed a little more time to get through the list of people I'd given him. Carol, Joe, and Ann couldn't make it because the restaurant was booming with the end of the season tourists. Grey would be occupied with making sure he spoke to everyone that came, and Willum wasn't an ideal wingman at any kind of function because he was a social butterfly. People looked at me when I walked in the room, then went back to talking

412

to whomever they were speaking to. Sam was over in the corner talking to people close to his age that I didn't recognize. Really, I didn't recognize anyone except for Cynthia's best friend, but I'd only briefly met her once.

I walked over to the bar, got myself a glass of white wine, let Willum introduce me to his brother Willard, and spent a few minutes talking to them before Cynthia pulled me away to introduce me to Roger's five sisters. They were all sort of rude, sweetly delivering back-handed comments about how upsetting it was that my friends couldn't make it, or saying they would have just had a small wedding if it were them. Having a big wed-ding had never been my idea, but Cynthia couldn't help herself, so I'd kept my wants to myself for the most part. The comments didn't bother me that much because far worse things had been said to me in life.

Dinner was loud. Nearly everyone had too much to drink, the men were all shop talk, and the women were all heckling someone. Once most everyone had finished eating, the storytelling and toasts began. It was funny to hear about Grey as a child. He'd been a little prankster, so there were plenty of laughs around. Ryan unexpectedly arrived when Willard was speaking. I was so happy he was there, I couldn't even be upset with him for all that'd transpired in the previous days.

Just after Willum began his toast, a staff member came to give me a small piece of paper. I opened it while everyone was laughing at whatever Willum said. My heart stopped for a minute, and it felt like the air had van-ished from my lungs. I sat there feeling like the room was silent, but knowing it wasn't. My stomach was churning, and I wasn't sure if I was going to be sick or not, but just in case, I excused myself from the table quietly.

"Nelson. What's up?" Ryan called quietly behind me when we were out of the room and in the lobby.

I turned around because Ryan could help me. "Do you have your phone?" I held out my hand.

He reached into his pocket. "Yeah. What's up?"

I shook my hand in impatience. "Just give me your phone."

"Here." He put it in my hand.

I tapped the phone icon and hurriedly dialed Ann's number. Ryan took the paper from between my fingers as I put the phone to my ear.

"What!?" Ryan sounded almost hurt.

My stomach twisted over itself three times before Ann answered.

"Hello?"

"It's Bex. What happened?"

Ryan pulled the phone out of my hand and put it on speakerphone.

"—guy came through the back door and shot her. Carol was in the back changing out one of the syrup boxes and we heard a loud pop and Joe ran back. We didn't even know what happened." Ann let out a short cry. "I was in front talking to a customer, I thought something got dropped or, I don't know. Joe went around to where she was and yelled her name, and he was panicked, so I ran in back." She let out another cry, but it was longer this time.

I didn't know what to say right away because I was just trying to process. "Um, where are you right now?" I was fighting to stay sane.

"I'm at the diner still. The police are doing *nothing*! You're all just leaving her on the floor like she doesn't mean anything!"

"Ann, calm down. I know you're upset, but making a scene isn't gonna help. Where's Rowen?" I knew he'd be at the babysitter's, but I needed to get her to focus on something else.

"He's at the babysitter's house. Oh god, what am I gonna tell him?" she cried in devastation.

"Tonight, you don't tell him anything. Take some time, breathe a little, hold Rowen while he sleeps, and tomorrow when you've had a chance to calm down and process, you explain to him as simply as you can. But right now, you need to take care of *yourself.* Do you need me to call the babysitter and ask them to keep Rowen longer?"

"No. I'll text her." Her voice was marred by her grief, but she was calming down.

"Okay. Is there anything I can do for you? Find you a ride home, call Derrick maybe?"

"No. I have to stay here. They're questioning Joe and I'm waiting for *him.*"

I rubbed at my throat and pressed my tongue to the roof of my mouth for a moment to keep the vomit down. "How is he?"

"I don't know. God, I've never seen a man cry like that. Shit—I have to go. They wanna talk to me again."

"Okay. Call me back when you can." I felt slightly relieved because I didn't know what to say or do. I was good at doing things, not comforting people.

"I will. Bye." She hung up before I could say anything back.

I held the phone out to Ryan.

"What do you need, Nelson?" He asked as he took his phone.

I shook my head because I didn't know. My brain felt like it was stuck, and I rubbed my forehead while just trying to think of anything at all. It almost felt like my body wasn't real, that nothing was.

"Nelson?"

"What's going on? Pops was in the middle of a speech. Mostly for you, Bex." Grey sounded slightly offended.

"Grey, just shut up. Nelson, look at me." Ryan reached for my arm.

I looked around me because I was trying to figure out if things were real. My body, where I was, Ryan in front of me, Grey standing a few steps behind and to the side of Ryan—it felt like a dream or a hallucination. Did any of the last five minutes happen? Had I dozed off on the plane or in the car?

"What's going on?" Grey looked me over with worry.

"I think I'm gonna pass out." I heard my voice, but I didn't feel myself speaking.

"Okay. Come on. I'm taking your arm." Ryan took my arm first, then put his arm behind my back. The sense of touch was delayed, and so was the sensation of walking as we approached the small couch and chairs. "Sit down and take a few slow breaths."

I sat, closed my eyes, and leaned forward to hold my head up with my hands. My brain was doing that funny thing where it made my body feel like it was moving even though it wasn't.

"Bex, you've been around more people than this before, and the doors have been open the whole time."

The couch sank beside me on the side that Ryan had been on.

"Will you shut up? She's not having a panic attack, she's in shock. Carol was killed. They don't know what happened, some guy came in the back of the restaurant and shot her."

Shock. Why didn't I think of it? That's why I felt like nothing was real.

"What? Carol McKernan?" Grey sounded confused.

"Is there another Carol she'd be upset over?"

"Stop being a dick. It's just unexpected." The couch sank beside me on the other side. "I'm sorry, B."

"I need to leave," I whispered. Someone had died, and my rule allowed the tears, but I still fought them as I stood and walked away. I knew either Grey or Ryan was following me, and I made it just about to the exit before I stopped. "Catch up or stop walking behind me."

Ryan came up beside me and offered his arm. I looped mine through his, and we continued out into the parking garage to his truck. It was a silent ride back to the house, and after he parked, we sat there for a minute.

"Do you have your laptop?" My voice was for the birds.

"Yeah." Ryan reached to the back seat to grab it. It was a rare day when he didn't have his laptop with him. He put his finger over the sensor to unlock it and handed it to me. I opened the internet browser and went to the website for the security cameras at Joe and Carol's restaurant. It was me who'd set it all up for them over two years ago, so I knew the login information.

"Nelson, don't," Ryan said quietly.

I did it anyway. The live feed showed police walking all around the restaurant, and Carol was still there in the back with a wool blanket to cover her body. I clicked on the little button to move the footage backward, and prayed to the god I didn't believe in that I was wrong about my suspicions. The camera outside, in the back of the restaurant, wasn't working, so I couldn't see if someone had walked up to the backdoor. The only working cameras were in the hallway between the walk-in fridge and freezer, and the one that faced the open space where the syrup boxes, CO_2 tanks, and dry storage.

Just as Ann had said, Carol walked in back and opened a syrup box for the soda. Sunshine came in as the back door opened, and she was shaking her head and saying something before she was shot. I looked at the hand holding the gun and paused the footage. The hand was completely scarred and had no thumbnail. It was twenty seconds before Joe walked back from the line to the back room. I logged off the website, closed Ryan's laptop, and sat there for a minute.

"I'll see if Tim can pull anything else from neighboring cameras," Ryan's voice was raspy.

I nodded.

"You don't think she was some kind of warning, do you?"

I nodded again. "I think that's exactly what she was... I'm certain if I scrolled back further, those other cameras would be working."

"I'm so sorry, Maslen... This is my fault. I thought Joe and Carol would be left out of this because you don't have much to do with them anymore. I should've taken more precautions with them."

I shook my head. "Anyone I've ever come in contact with is in danger." I cleared my throat quietly. "I need you to get some of Grey's guys down there to look after Joe, Ann, and Rowen. I'll tell Ann that Grey sent them because he's worried." My lungs felt heavy, so I took a slow deep breath and let it out.

"Okay... Can I do anything else? Do you want me to stick around?"

I shook my head. "I'll be okay, just make sure you and Tim stay vigilant."

"Don't worry about us, Tim's too paranoid to take his eyes off his screens..." Ryan took a breath and let it out in a huff. "I didn't start all this to hurt you, Maslen. I hope you know that..."

"I know you didn't... and after finding out what we did yesterday, I'd probably be worse off if you hadn't." I sat there listening to the stillness of the night. The breeze outside was quiet and a cricket chirped from somewhere in the grass.

"I don't know how Blondie found out, but I was trying to keep both of you out of it. Blondie because he'd want to do something. What I said yesterday at the table, I really didn't mean it, and I'm sorry... When I found out who you were, I wanted to make sure you didn't have to combat this again. Then I got that thumb drive from the house... One picture of you, and it was Remy... someone who was scared, alone, and trapped... You and all the other kids on there... I had to do something."

I nodded and held out my hand over the center console because he was struggling and I was too. Ryan took my hand and we gripped tightly while we sat there with our soundless, tearless cries. After about ten or fifteen minutes, Harry and Grey pulled into the driveway beside us.

"Are you sure you don't want me to stick around?" Ryan asked quietly.

I shook my head and pushed the door open. "No, I'll be okay... Can you be here at seven tomorrow?"

"Yeah."

"Thanks for bringing me home." I got out of the truck.

Ryan looked rigid but nodded.

"Goodnight." I closed the door, turned, and walked around the front of Harry's car to get to the keypad for the garage door. I entered the code while Grey got out of Harry's car.

"Nelson, wait."

I turned, praying Ryan wouldn't say something to shake my fragile emotional state.

He held out a paper to me. "I asked Carol, Joe, and Ann to write something for the toasts tonight. I was gonna read it after my toast."

I took the paper and opened it. Carol's handwriting covered half the page. My throat closed and tears pricked at my eyes. It didn't matter what she'd written, it was that she'd taken the time to do it.

"Thank you." The words were straining as I folded the paper.

"Yeah... Call me if you need to." He held out his wrist.

I bumped his wrist with our matching tattoos and nodded before I turned to go in the house. Grey was waiting for me, looking guilty and hurt. We went inside and I stepped out of my heels.

"I need to change, then I need to call Ann again," I said quietly before going toward the stairs.

Grey caught my hand. "Hold on a minute."

I stopped to look at him, and he pulled me into a

hug.

"I'm sorry," he whispered against the side of my forehead.

"I know. I need a minute though. Let me go change out of this dress." It was hard to speak because I was still trying not to cry.

"Okay. Do you want anything? Tea, crackers, something to settle your stomach? You didn't touch your plate at dinner."

"Because I didn't like anything your mom picked." The petty jab at Cynthia came out without thinking about it, and I put my hand up to my head. "I'm sorry, I shouldn't have said that. Um... not right now. I can't."

"Okay..." Grey touched the back of my shoulder, then partially unzipped the back of my dress for me. "I'm gonna check on a couple things, then I'll be up."

I nodded and started up the stairs. My hips and knees were aching from all the walking around and standing.

Chapter 35

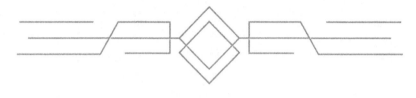

Grey

I stopped my alarm before it went off and woke Bex. She'd gotten more sleep than she had the last three nights, but it still wasn't enough. I wanted to give her whatever extra time I could. Today was going to be a hard day for her. There'd be more people than she could plausibly keep track of, all eyes on her, lots of brief hugs and handshakes, being introduced to people she didn't know, having no family or friends of her own to talk to, and thinking about Carol and Joe. Part of me wondered if she wasn't going through with the wedding because she knew how much money had been poured into it. I didn't care if it all went to waste, I just wanted to be married to her, and I was.

Last night was already awful without Carol's death. My extended family was *the worst*. My mom's friends were catty gossips, and they took shots at Bex like they were soldiers in a war. I expected my mom would have shut them up, but until Bex said something last night,

I hadn't realized that my mom was being so awful to her. I'd heard and defended the comment about Bex's dress, but I didn't notice the food choice until Bex said something last night. After she said it, I thought about other things lately. My mom was kind of being a bully, and publicly, so I wondered what was being said when I wasn't around.

Carol... I didn't love her, but she was a good lady. Bex saw her as somewhat of a mom and talked to her every Sunday at two o'clock. After Bex had been here a couple months and was doing well with school and work, Carol relaxed and wasn't so hard on her. We'd gone down there four times in the last year so Bex could see her and Joe. Poor Joe. He and Carol had celebrated their thirty-fifth wedding anniversary in June. I couldn't imagine his life right now, losing a spouse after that many years together. More than half of his life had just been taken from him.

I looked at Bex and wondered if I was going to end up like Joe. Would I even get a year with her? A month? These bastards clearly knew where she was, and I could only guess that they had killed Carol because they couldn't get to Bex. My dad was a powerful man, people didn't dare mess with him, so it was likely that her association to our family was the only thing keeping her alive. My dad adored Bex. He saw her as a daughter of his own, so I could only think he might be the one keeping her safe...

Today, August sixteenth, was Bex's real birthday. Last year, I hadn't yet learned who she was in time and I'd missed it by days, but not this year. I reached into my nightstand and pulled out the velvet box with her gift. She didn't much care for gifts or surprises, but this one she would love. It broke no rules. It was something she could afford herself, and it was nothing ostentatious. The rules didn't apply anymore anyway. We had a deal that getting married gave me a free pass to spoil her as I pleased. Actually, she'd never agreed to it, I just told her it was happening.

"Hey, Beautiful, we have to get up," I said quietly.

She took in a slow deep breath and her eyes opened. She looked so tired, but as beautiful as always. It still amazed me that someone could be as naturally stunning as she was. I smiled and touched her cheek. It was rare for her to sleep in my room. Unless we were out of town or she was having a hard time over something, there'd only been a few times we slept in the same bed at home. The exception for out of town was because she didn't do well in strange places. It was especially nerve-racking for her if there were other people in the house—any house. I didn't know if yesterday and last night were because we were already married, but I liked having her close.

"How'd I get so lucky?" I lightly brushed the back of my finger over her cheekbone. "I know you don't think so, but you're perfect. The first time I saw you, I hoped you were as beautiful as you looked... then you were. This whole package of perfection, right there in front of me. I was nervous to even speak to you." I brushed her hair back. "I was pretty sure you were gonna think I was just another rich asshole chasing tail."

She pushed herself up enough to move up in front me. "I did."

"I have something for you before you get up and leave me until two o'clock." I reached back to grab the velvet box and gave it to her.

She looked at me. "You already got me a wedding gift, and don't say it's 'part two'."

"It's not a wedding gift, it's a birthday present."

Bex still didn't look pleased as she took in a breath and looked at the box to open it. Her expression changed, then changed again, and a gentle smile appeared. "You bought me pearls."

"I bought you pearls." The smile was worth it. Her

smile was worth all of it and then some.

"Thank you."

"You're welcome... I want you to know you're appreciated and loved just a little bit more every day... Even with what's going on, I'm glad you're here in the world... I know it hasn't always been easy for you, but I'm very grateful to have you in my life and be in yours." I brushed her hair back and leaned in to kiss the side of her forehead. "I love you."

She looked at the string of pearls and moved her thumb over a few of them. Some of her smile came back to the corners of her mouth, but it went deeper than that. "I love you too... I appreciate the words and the necklace." She looked at me again, her smile still in place.

"You got it." I leaned over and kissed her. "We need to get moving. Ryan is gonna be here in forty minutes to pick you up."

"Are you gonna forgive him? You haven't said a word to him that you didn't have to."

I shook my head. "Today is 'you and me'. No heavy stuff, just you and me." I was so blindingly angry with Ryan I couldn't even begin to think about forgiving him. What he'd been doing was beyond dangerous for everyone. He'd overstepped too far and lied to me on multiple occasions. I'd also told him not to do anything and he'd betrayed me.

I got up out of bed, put my watch on, and grabbed my phone.

"Grey, where have you been? We have to leave in ten minutes." My mom looked at me like I was covered in mud. "You're not even dressed."

"It takes five minutes to put my tux on. What's going on with you and Bex? Why was she going hungry last night when I paid almost ten thousand dollars to the caterers?" I was being demanding because it was the only way to get a response out of my mom. If I ap-

424

proached her sweetly, I'd get sweet bullshit. If I pissed her off, she'd usually give an honest answer.

"She's a picky eater. We couldn't serve our family and close friends yogurt and soda crackers."

I raised my eyebrows. "She's not that picky, and you could've found something appropriate that she could eat. You wanted fish, you could've picked about any other kind. Vegetables? Any other kind. And I don't even like arugula with fermented beets. You had a fit over her dress! She didn't like the one you bought, and before you bought it, she told you she had one already. I was right there. So, what's your deal? Are you jealous? You don't get attention from me anymore? You're losing your precious baby? Did she piss you off? What?"

"Lower your voice. This family has standards, Grey. You know that. And if Bexley has a problem with something, she can come to me. It's high time that girl learns to speak up. You don't get to where we are by imitating meek vermin. She—"

"VERMIN!?" She was lucky I didn't hit women; I wanted to smack her so hard her teeth bled.

"I'm not calling her vermin—"

"NO. You stop and listen." I was so angry I was shaking. "She's not marrying into this family to take over tea party luncheons, host fundraisers, or whatever else bored-house-wife-crap you do to entertain yourself. That's not the life she wants, so stop trying to groom her for it. Neither Bex or I wanted this big wedding, we were doing it for you, and we're more than happy to cancel the whole damn thing, take Sam, and elope." She and my dad didn't know we already had or I would've heard about it.

"Don't you threaten me! I have worked tirelessly to make this wedding the affair of—"

"Stop," I warned her again. "You're listening, not talking. Be nice. No heel nipping, no going around to guests making backhanded comments in jest. Tell your friends to keep their fat mouths shut. I so much as see one icy stare in her direction, and I will have you and your friends escorted out and write you off. She's done nothing but be kind, patient, and help you in every way possible. You will show the same courtesy." I looked at my dad who was standing at the edge of the hall. "I need to talk to you. Can we go in the same car?"

He nodded once.

"No. I'm not arriving there by myself," my mom chided.

I looked at her. "You'll be fine. You're an adult, not a child." I looked at my dad again. "Are you ready?"

He nodded and walked toward the door without a word to my mother. It was probably the only time I empathized with how frustrated he constantly was with her. They forever threw daggers at one another; this was the first time I'd ever had my mom throw them at me.

Harry stood outside of the back car door with a hand over his wrist until my dad and I were close enough. I normally didn't require him to act like an obedient servant, but he had to in front of my parents, or they'd complain. There were days Harry had to pick his kids up from school and I was more than happy to sit in the car with them. I liked being the person my employees felt comfortable around. Anyone who worked for my dad cowered in his presence and I found it disgusting.

"Good afternoon, Mr. Maslen," Harry greeted my dad before he opened the door for him.

"It's good to see you, Harry." My dad gave a polite nod before getting in.

Harry looked at me and I looked at him. My dad usually ignored employees who greeted him unless they made him money. I held up my shoulders in sort of an "I don't know" gesture and got in.

"Your mother doesn't believe Bexley is good enough for you. She expected you would part ways." My dad's voice was quiet as he fixed the cuff of his shirt. "She's also jaded over Pops giving you my mother's rings."

"She might've had them if she didn't act like *that*." I shook my head.

"Why is your driver standing there? We'll be late." He looked at his watch.

"Because I need to talk to you. How did you hear about those guys? Did someone refer them, or what? Because they clearly needed MWM, and it doesn't make sense that you randomly found them." It'd been bugging me since after the sit down at the table yesterday morning.

He shook his head. "I've been wondering the same for years. It wasn't until about four years after that I realized they were a band of crooks." He looked at me. "I truly can't recall, but I swear to you, I didn't enter this knowingly. It's devastated me for years, and not just because I lost my daughter to it."

My dad was being genuine, and the hurt in his eyes made me want to tell him we were sure we'd found my sister, but I couldn't. I promised Bex I wouldn't say anything, and if I wanted to keep whatever trust she had left, I couldn't betray her again. "Was it maybe another client or someone in the office?"

"I don't know. If I could, I believe I'd have more answers. Bexley wasn't as forthcoming as I'd hoped. I've known what Ryan was doing for some time now. Yesterday was a ruse staged to force everyone into admitting what they know so we can work together. There's another person operating this thing at the top, and I can't tell if Bexley is unaware or won't say for one reason or another. Before you proposed, I spoke with her and alluded to knowing who she was, offered her my assistance, but she's continued to keep her silence."

I nodded. "I know... She's scared because she doesn't know who she can trust."

He took a deep breath. "I know the feeling all too well. I won't even trust your mother with what I know.

You and Pops are it. Ryan's a ticking time bomb. While he's intelligent, his temper gets the better of him. I don't understand his position in this."

I frowned. "Are you not aware of what these guys did to his dad?"

"I heard Bexley mention something when she snapped at Ryan yesterday, but otherwise, no." A slight smile turned up the corners of his mouth. "She's unexpectedly intimidating when she's angry.

I raised my eyebrows with a slight smirk, then cleared my smile. "They framed Craig for Remy's death. Craig tried to go to the SEC with everything."

My dad took in a deep breath again and shook his head with an exasperated expression. "I had no idea... and I pushed that DA to prosecute him."

"Well, just because he was innocent for that doesn't mean he was innocent." I remembered Craig and his drunken screams.

My dad rubbed his forehead.

"Bex still trusts Ryan, and I do too. He might lie to me to fulfill his own agenda, but he'd never hurt me, and he really wouldn't hurt Bex."

My dad nodded. "She's very secretive, but also smart. As are you. I don't foresee either of you taking unnecessary risks, so I believe you're right."

"I have to ask, if you knew who Bex was this whole time, why have you been so accepting of her? I mean, she could bring everything down if she wanted to."

He nodded. "You stand to lose more than myself or Pops should this turn badly, and I didn't raise you to be an idiot. You are far more careful in business than I ever was, so if you're confident marrying Bexley won't cost what we've built, I trust you."

Huh? "You trust me," I repeated doubtfully.

"You act as though I don't possess the ability to be human or have compassion for a person." He looked at me with a flat but angered expression.

I raised an eyebrow. "You don't usually show a lot of it, no."

He took in a breath and let it out in a huff. "I have told you since you were born, to do better than me."

I gave a frown of confusion.

"I chose money. I chose a wife who held the proper etiquette to help me make more money, someone whom I have never loved. She bore my children whom I ignored until they were of age to learn the ways of business because I couldn't otherwise be bothered with them..." The corners of his mouth were tight and his eyes were bloodshot. "Everything I have done has been for more money. I have a wife who detests me, and whom is detested. I have two sons who haven't spoken to me in more than a year if it wasn't essential to business, and a father who is embarrassed of me because I shook the hands of evil men for more money..." The muscles in his neck were tense as he swallowed hard. "I told you to do better than me, and thus far you have. You've earned your living honestly, you've chosen friends who are loyal and honest, you've chosen a wife who is a woman driven toward family as much as success in business. And should you have children, I believe they'll be happy when you call... You know what you stand to lose, and because of me, you learned early on, money is not the most important loss."

I didn't know what to say... He was right, I *did* do everything different because I only wanted certain parts of his life. I wanted work to be a hobby, to be excellent at what I did, but not let it be the *only* thing I did. Since I was old enough to grasp the concept, I wanted a family that showed love instead of numbers in a bank account. And for years, I wished my father a rude awakening, for him to feel the loneliness he left the rest of us with because money was more important to him, and now he was... I just didn't expect to feel so badly for him.

"You also taught me things can change," I said

quietly after a moment of thought. "You can change how you treat people and stop being focused on money. Treat Mom like she's a person, talk to Sam about baseball instead of what classes are more conducive to running a fortune five-hundred... Call me because you want to, not because you need something. It's really that simple."

He nodded once. "That's why I came over last night to check on you and Bexley."

I held up a shoulder. "Then the door is open." Last night, I was instantly irritated when the guard shack called to say my dad was coming through. I'd gone downstairs, fully prepared to tell him to piss off, but when I opened the door, he said he and Pops were there to check on Bex. He'd even asked if there was anything he could do to help. "But you have to stop doing bad business because I don't want to get wrapped up in your mess. You should be in *jail* for some of the shit you've done."

He nodded again. "I'm working on that too... Pops is going to come in and hopefully, we can clean up the company before it's too late."

"Well... I'm here too." I had no problem cleaning house, I'd been waiting to do it since I walked in the doors of MWM.

My dad shook his head. "I'll clean my own messes. You give your time to Bexley right now. Your mother was wondering if the two of you were canceling the honey-moon because of Mrs. McKernan's passing?"

I shook my head. "No, we're still going to Germany."

"Good." He nodded once. "I'd wish you good luck today, but I believe you've already been provided luck, so congratulations. Bexley is a wonderful young woman." He knocked on the window to signal Harry that we were ready.

I smiled a little. Getting a congratulations from my dad was his way of saying he was proud.

Chapter 36

Bexley

Ryan opened the curtain to the tent and came in. "Are you ready?"

I nodded. "Almost."

"What do you have left?"

I picked up a gift box from the table. "Just this." I gave a small smile. "I realize this is a little more than a normal gift for a man of honor, but you're a lot more, and it's my day so you can't say anything." I pulled the lid off the box and showed him the watch. "Grey pays you to do a lot of stuff for me, but I know you'd do most of it anyway, and I appreciate it. I wouldn't be here, and I wouldn't have Grey without you."

Ryan smiled a little. "You're right."

I let out a huff in place of a laugh.

"Thanks, Maslen."

I nodded and pulled the watch out of the box to put it on him. "And I tried to talk to him this morning. He's still mad but he'll come around. I took over your contract because he was going to fire you."

"I don't care. Blondie's a pain in my ass."

I looked up at Ryan sternly. "He's your family before anything else and you broke his trust. It won't be today, but I expect you to fix things with him."

"Hello? Are you two coming? Everyone's waiting," Serena, the wedding coordinator, sneered as she poked her head into the tent.

Ryan turned his head and held out his wrist to me. "She's the bride. She can walk when she's ready. Go squawk up a tree."

"Ryan," I whispered disapprovingly as I fastened the watch.

"My job is to coordinate, your job is to walk her down the aisle. Walk her down the aisle." Serena held the curtain open and directed a hand.

"Your job doesn't include being rude," I said as if it were a simple reminder. "It's my wedding, I'll do as I please, and you'll wait patiently outside."

Serena took in a breath like she was forcing patience. "I'll be outside then."

"Thank you." I pulled Ryan's cuff down and turned his cufflink the right direction.

"Are you feeling okay?" Ryan let out a short chuckle.

"I'm a little thin on tolerance." I set the box back on the table near Ryan's other stuff.

"Which is weird, hence the question." He looked at me expectantly. "Have you talked to Joe yet?"

I nodded. "I'm okay, and I did this morning."

"If you're gonna have a meltdown, do it now."

I shook my head with a sigh. "Come on. If we're late, Grey will think I ran."

"You're already married, so hold on. There's more tradition shit."

I stopped and raised an eyebrow. "Are we supposed to do a rain dance?"

He rolled his eyes at me and pulled something out

the inside breast pocket of his tux jacket. "Left wrist."

I frowned. "What is that?"

"Press on tattoo of a blue sparrow. It's your something blue, but also a symbol of true love according to Greek mythology." He held out a hand. "Wrist."

"I already have a tattoo and when did you get all sentimental?" I held out my wrist.

He stuck the paper to the side of my wrist and put a damp napkin over it. "Don't be a pain in the ass. I'm trying to be nice."

I smiled a little but didn't say anything.

"Are we taking bets on whether Blondie is gonna cry like a girl when he sees you?"

"No. Firstly because it's mean, and second because he won't. He's seen the dress already, and seen me in dresses tons of times. This is no different." I'd already told Ryan that Grey and I had spent the day with my parents the other day. He and Tim hadn't known, and I knew from Grey that Roger hadn't either, which was exactly what I wanted. Moving under the radar after tonight meant everyone's radar.

"You're wrong. He's been waiting for this since he met you. Ten bucks and I don't have to dance with you if he cries."

"You're not required to dance with me, and no bucks because I'm not making bets. It's rude."

"Come on. I'm already on a roll today. Cynthia and Roger are fighting, twenty bucks from Grey. You didn't have a panic attack and run, twenty bucks from Tim. And twenty bucks from Sam because he said I wouldn't walk you down the aisle without bitching about it. I haven't bitched once." There was a slight self-satisfactory tone in his voice.

"You're an ass. And why *is it* you haven't complained since I asked? You hate all of this in its entirety."

He frowned. "No, I hate the guest list and show. I'm not against marriage, and I'm definitely not against *this* marriage." He carefully pulled the paper away from my wrist. "I'm glad I get to walk you down the aisle."

"Me too." If my dad couldn't be here to walk with me, I was glad it was Ryan. When Joe and Carol said they couldn't make it, Ryan volunteered, but I didn't realize it was because he wanted to. I just thought it was because he felt bad that I had no one. I was pretty sure it bothered Grey and Ryan more than it bothered me. If my parents could've been at my wedding, nothing would have stopped them. Knowing that was enough for me.

"Okay." Ryan pulled a pen from his pocket and stuck it in my flowers. "Borrowed and old. Don't lose it. My grandpa gave it to me." He pulled out his sage green pocket square, then a small white, lace-trimmed handkerchief. "I saw this online and thought it was great." He smiled as he showed what was embroidered.

I read it, raised my eyebrows at him, then laughed. It said, "Keep your shit together."

"Something new."

"You're an ass. *Nothing* new," I laughed. "And the dress is new." I still couldn't believe the gorgeous dress my mom had made me. The top was all cream-colored lace appliques that crept down to the soft champagne tulle skirt, with appliques edged around the bottom. It had to have taken her months of work.

He laughed. "Stuff it somewhere and let's go."

I took the handkerchief and his pocket square and put them back in his pocket. "It won't look right if I'm digging down the front of my dress, so you have to hold onto it."

"God, please don't cry. In Dallas you just had tears in your eyes, but I almost threw up. Too sad."

"All bets are off today," I sighed as I picked up my bouquet from the table. I made sure Ryan's fountain pen from his grandpa was securely stuck in the center so it wouldn't fall out.

"No, I'm still putting ten bucks on Grey crying." Ryan

held out his arm.

I shook my head and looped my arm through his before walking out of the tent with him. Ryan and I followed the designated pathway to a veil of green garlands with tiny white flowers that were hanging down. Two men drew them back and everyone stood from their chairs. I took a deep breath and looked at Grey. His smile was the best one I'd seen yet. He had the gentleness he always had, but also appeared to be in a bit of disbelief and awe.

I smiled at him, then glanced up at Ryan to see if we were actually going to move. Ryan put a hand over mine on his arm and we started walking. Sam mouthed the word, "Wow," and I struggled not to laugh. Grey had a light khaki tux on, and it made him look even better than he usually did. The sun was peeking over the mountain and through the trees to the side of us, touching his sandy-colored hair. He was absolutely perfect.

Ryan squeezed my hand before he reached out to shake Grey's hand. "She was my friend exactly three weeks before she was yours, be good to her or I'll kill you," he said quietly as he gripped Grey's hand.

Grey chuckled without a sound and nodded. "Always."

Ryan nodded once and turned to face me. "I walked you down the aisle and now you're gonna make me hug you." He shook his head and smiled. "You owe me."

I laughed a little and hugged him carefully.

"Love ya, Maslen." He patted the back of my shoulder, let go of me, and gave my hand to Grey before he stepped behind me to his spot.

Grey smiled at me lovingly before we stepped forward toward the pastor and turned to face one another.

"Before these two begin their vows, I'd like to say a few words about the bride and groom," the pastor held a small smile as he spoke loudly to everyone. "I've known Grey nearly his entire life. He's always been known for his generosity, infectious—and almost permanent—

smile, but also as the bachelor that no one could quite pin down."

Grey smiled but shook his head at the pastor as everyone shared a quiet laugh.

"Over a year ago, I turned the ripe old age of thirty times three, and Grey was there at my birthday party. I asked him how he was doing, and we started talking a little bit. I asked him if he had a girl yet, and he told me about Miss Bexley. And he said, 'She's beautiful from the outside in, but I have a problem.' So, naturally, I replied, 'What's that? You just said she's beautiful...'" The pastor paused for a brief chuckle from everyone. "Grey's next response caught me off guard just a bit, maybe because it was an instant red flag in my mind. He said, 'She doesn't smile. If she does, it's because she thinks it's expected.'"

I felt a little embarrassed at what was being said. It wasn't a lie, but it wasn't something I felt should be shared, and I also felt guilty.

"There was only one explanation I could think of... *She's not interested, man!*" Pastor Bill waited for another pause of laughter. "And I told him that, and I saw him get mad—I think for the first time. He said, 'She wants to, but she's afraid.' So, I asked, 'Well, did you introduce her to Roger? He'd cause anyone to second guess a smile.'"

Everyone broke out into laughter, and even I laughed a little and looked over in Roger's direction with a kind-hearted smile. He winked at me with the smallest trace of a grin.

"At any rate, I said, 'She's hanging out with the most annoyingly smiley person I know. She'll catch on. If all else fails, start making faces at her until she cracks up.' And I checked in with Grey a few weeks later, asked him how things were going, and if he got that smile he wanted. He said he was working on it, and I'm sitting there thinking, how hard is it to crack a fart joke?"

Everyone laughed, and I gave a slight look of disapproval at the pastor. He gave an oops kind of smile.

"I waited a couple more weeks and asked again. Grey looked at me and said, 'Actually, I was wrong. She smiles a lot, just not the way everyone else does. If you watch her, you'll see her heart smile. She gets really calm, and you can see nothing else is bothering her.' Grey had Cynthia yoo-hoo-ing him in the background, so he walked away from me. I stood there thinking to myself, 'man, that kid just grew up ten years and made me old.'"

Everyone laughed again.

"The first time I had the pleasure of meeting Bexley, we were at Cynthia and Roger's for a luncheon held for church members. I caught her alone for a moment and asked her what she liked about Grey. She looked over at him for a moment, and by God, if Grey wasn't right." Pastor Bill shook his head with a smile. "Not a smile on her face, but she had this instant peace that took over in her eyes, and she said, 'He means it... Everything he says and does, he means it.' Then she looked at me, and the tiniest smile appeared, and she said, 'And he's always happy...'" Pastor Bill paused for a second, but I couldn't see why because I gave Grey a small smile. "Man... I have married two-hundred and thirty-seven couples, and not a single one like these two. They see each other far deeper than the surface.

"There's a difference between loving someone and loving the things that make them who they are. It's easy to love a gift, but it's completely different to appreciate everything that went into that gift. For instance, just the packaging. You have the trees that grew for several years, the loggers that cut the tree and loaded it on a truck, the hands at the sawmill that touched the wood, the driver that transported the sawdust to the boxing company, the water that was added to make a paste, the stamping machine that formed the cardboard, the hands that folded and taped it when it got to the store... And that's just the box...

"I believe both of these people before us today have everything they need for a long, blessed, and happy marriage, and everything we believe for love to hold... And now, we'll witness as both Bexley and Grey share their hearts with their vows." The pastor nodded at me. "Bexley."

I nodded, then looked at Grey and took a deep breath to calm myself. "I don't have a lot of words, but I have a lot of gratitude..." I swallowed hard and squeezed his hands because I was nervous. "When we met, I had this small list of things that I wanted for my life. I wanted to have a job that wouldn't be looked down on, I wanted to buy a house away from people, and I wanted to be alone...

"On our first date, my list grew with one more item. I wanted to be able to hold a conversation the way you do—with confidence. On our second date," I smiled, "my list grew one more item. I wanted to be as passionate at a job as you were with yours. On our third date, I wanted to go to school and do as well as you thought I'd do. The fourth date, I wanted to learn how to be a good friend the way you are. My list kept growing with all the things I wanted for my life, and the ones I started with, started to fall away...

"I didn't know to ask for someone like you... I felt like I couldn't, and I didn't deserve to." I nodded and looked down at my hand for a moment, embracing the burn in my throat. I looked at him again. "I don't have words for love the way you do, but I feel it. And you have an incredible amount of love you share with me, and I promise it'll never go to waste or—" my voice broke and I had to pause to get it back, "or be taken for granted... And I promise you'll never feel like there isn't enough in return. I'll love you with everything I have."

Grey looked at me sweetly. "That's a lot more than you think."

I smiled a little out of nervousness and took in a

deep breath as I nodded.

"My turn." Grey squeezed my hands a few times and seemed like he was trying to have courage. He wasn't usually nervous, which made me question what he might be about to say.

He smiled with what seemed like a small struggle. "There were clearly people who didn't treat you with love and kindness, and they should have... I don't know what you went through in life before me, but I know you never deserved it... You're too whole-heartedly good, and you didn't deserve to be hurt, or feel scared..." He took in a deep breath the way I would have. "You have my word, I will never contribute to what isn't good in your life. I'll spend every day telling you you're beautiful and kind until you believe me. I'll never leave you or let you feel alone. I'll help you smile when you feel like you can't... I'll spend the rest of my life making up for whatever it was that happened—things I didn't do—so you can look back at your life when you're eighty, and say you had the best life." His hands shook as he held mine. "For every hateful thing someone said, I'll say ten beautiful things. When you feel small, I'll get on my knees so you feel tall again. I'll love you more..."

I bit the inside corner of my lip and struggled for composure.

"You are beautiful, by its entire definition, and I won't let you forget it." He shook his head. "Not ever... I'll stand by you, I'll be kind to you, I'll love you, protect you, and I will never... hurt you. I love you more than everything and anything, and I'm not sure you understand what I mean when I say that, but you will."

I sniffed and looked away to blink and make sure tears didn't surface.

Grey squeezed my hand. "I love you, B."

I gave a small smile. "I love you too."

The pastor cleared his throat quietly. "Do you have the rings?"

Sam, Ryan, and the pastor were choked up. I was close, but I had to keep myself together. It was a beautiful day, but it was also heartbreaking. My dad wasn't there to walk me down the aisle, my mom wasn't tearing up in the front row, Ben wasn't there to make faces at me, Emily wasn't standing behind me, and Toby wasn't tearing up next to my mom because he's a softy. Joe was sitting at home, grieving his beloved wife, with no idea it was because they'd taken me in three years ago. I had a list of the things that were, and the things that weren't, and they were weighing against each other. One toss in the right direction and the things that weren't could break me.

Sam pulled out the ring he had, and I turned and looked at Ryan as he pulled out the ring for Grey. He smiled at me as he put it in my palm, and I gave a returning one.

The pastor cleared his throat again. "I think Grey's vows make the exchange of I do's feel insignificant." He wiped under his eye with a chuckle.

Grey and I both laughed, along with everyone else.

"Do you, Grey Maslen, take Bexley Ann Nelson to be your lawfully wedded wife? To have and hold, in sickness and in health, for richer or poor, from now through eternity?"

Grey flashed a grin. "Hell yeah, I do."

I laughed and held up my hand. Grey slid the ring onto my finger, then kissed my hand.

"Do you, Bexley Ann Nelson, take Grey Maslen to be your lawfully wedded husband? To have and hold, in sickness and in health, for richer or poor, from now through eternity?"

"I do." I took Grey's hand and slipped the ring over his finger, feeling a little sad that the rest of my life didn't feel like it was long enough.

"By the power vested in me by God and the state of Washington, I now pronounce you husband and wife.

You may kiss your bride."

Grey smiled brightly, reaching a hand up to my cheek, and kissed me. "You are so damn beautiful. And smart. And Pretty. And *mine*." He laughed and hugged me tightly.

"You act like you're the lucky one," I said quietly as I hugged him.

"I am." He kissed my cheek quickly. "C'mon."

We let go of each other, but kept holding hands, and turned to face everyone.

"Ladies and Gentleman, it's my great pleasure to introduce to you for the first time, Mr. and Mrs. Grey Maslen."

Everyone stood and clapped. I held a reserved smile as I looked over a crowd of faces, knowing only a few. Grey took a small step forward and looked at me. We walked forward down the aisle while people tossed white petals into the air. At the end of the aisle, Grey quickly scooped me up into his arms and carried me through the curtain of garlands.

"Oh gosh. Why?" I wrapped my arms around his neck loosely.

"Because otherwise we can't kiss and walk."

I laughed and kissed him. "You'll regret it by the time you get to the car. My dress weighs as much as I do."

"Naw." He kissed me again.

I smiled and hugged him. "I love you."

"I love you more, Beautiful." He turned his head and kissed my cheek.

Right then, I felt like something shifted in the world. I couldn't explain it, but it felt like I'd been brought through a veil that led to a different path in life. The disappointing thing was, I knew it was false. I was getting ready to re-face every fear I'd ever had.

Chapter 37

Bexley

The reception was astonishing. There was a large patio of pavers centered in an open field of grass, surrounded by trees with hanging lanterns. Dripping crystal chandeliers hung over each table while green eucalyptus leaves laid under cream-tinted pillar candles. A short bouquet of white peonies sat in the center of the candles, their petals lit with dim light from underneath. It was simple but elegant, and people continued to comment on the beauty of it all.

Roger cleared his throat into the microphone as he moved the cord. "Can I have everyone's attention, please?"

I looked around just to see what people would do, and why he might be about to make an announcement. There was nothing visibly wrong that I could tell.

"I want to thank you all for coming tonight. It's been a wonderful evening being gathered around friends and family members. I especially want to thank everyone for helping us welcome Bexley to the family. She's a very bright and lovely young woman, and Cynthia and I are exceptionally pleased to have her as our daughter-in-law."

I smiled a little, in appreciation of the kind words.

Roger cleared his throat again. "Years ago, unfortunate circumstances with Bexley's family prevented them from being in attendance in her life. Even though Bexley is remarkably well-composed, I can only imagine how difficult it must be on such a significant occasion as this. So, I'm hoping I can do one small thing. Bexley, while I'm only a father to you by marriage, I would be very honored if you might join me for a father-daughter dance."

"Oh, that's so sweet," a woman next to me crooned.

I smiled—knowing all eyes were on me—and nodded as I started toward the dance floor. A slower song started as I neared the edge of the wooden dance floor that was laid over the grass.

Roger smiled as I approached and held up his hands, waiting for me to step in. I gave a smile of my own and forced my nerves to stop burning. Roger had been nothing but kind to me, but still, my skin stung.

"How are you fairing with so many people around? I believe Cynthia invited far more than you ever intended," Roger said quietly as he started leading me to the steps of the slow jazzy song being played.

I smiled. "Yes, but it's alright. Grey deserves to have his friends and family here."

"As do you, my dear. I'm rather embarrassed by our guests' comments about your absent family, both tonight and last."

"It doesn't bother me. I don't need an audience to know I have family and friends."

Roger gave a soft chuckle. "I suppose you don't. Here comes the spin." He twirled me slowly and put his hand back on the back of my shoulder blade. "You and Grey are much the same in that aspect. He loves being around people—socializing—but he's never bore much weight of thought on the opinions of others. As a Maslen, you'll find yourself subject to certain ridicules and expectations others are unaccustomed to. After a certain number of years, one might become overrun with decisions made in defense of such ridicule and make the fool's choice." He twirled me again, and I wondered where he was going with his line of conversation. "As you now know, I've made many decisions that have affected my family—and a number of others—in a number of ways I'm not proud of. It's only as of recent I've become aware of the larger impact. While I hold no right to ask you, I'm hoping you might help me where Grey is concerned."

I shook my head. "I'm doing everything I can to keep him safe. He doesn't deserve to be pulled into this, but he's not safe if I just leave. He's not vigilant enough."

Roger shook his head. "I know why..." He stepped back and twirled me out again. "The heart would like us to believe that love and marriage aren't conditional, but they are. If not respected and honored, both will leave... What I'd like to ask of you is, honor your love before making decisions. Very soon, Grey will need you, and you'll be faced with difficult decisions. Please think about your love for Grey before you make your choices, because he'll need you."

I looked at Roger and tried to figure out if he was warning me of something he currently knew of, or if he'd just been looking back on his own life and was feeding me experience.

"Please keep smiling or our guests will become concerned."

I smiled as if he'd said something kind and made it convincing. "Are you warning me of something you already know, or speaking from experience?" The only way to find out was to ask, then gauge his facial expressions.

"Both." He formed a smile but looked afraid somehow. "All I can tell you safely is to trust those you've already come to trust, and not a single person more. No matter what someone might tell you. There will be one who speaks of innocence and is the least of it. Another spin, my dear. Please remember to smile." Roger looked at me like a proud father as he spun me outward and back in. His dark eyes still showed fear as he pulled me back in. "The last thing I must tell you is that I have done something that could be misconstrued as a betrayal against you but isn't. I've taken many precautions to protect you, and he is one."

My back stiffened, but I tried to show no fear. "Patty?"

Roger nodded once with a smile he didn't mean. "Be cautious. Many eyes are on us. One could read if they were looking for the right words."

It took me a second to understand, but I was good at riddles because of Patty. There were two answers given in what Roger had said. The first was a confirmation that he'd been the one to get Patty out, the second was to warn me we were being watched, even as we danced.

"Is someone here, or you suspect there is?"

Roger turned me again, and when he pulled me back, he was briefly facing the band while I faced the crowd. "I suspect someone is not who they say, and if that's true, I'm in as much danger as you are, my dear." His voice was quieter as he spoke. "I cannot risk an inaccurate assumption."

I looked up at him with a faked tender smile. "I can't help if I'm not sure."

He chuckled as if I'd said something amusing. "We are each responsible for our own demons, Bexley. You have a great share on your plate, one that was never yours, so I will pilot my own should I find I'm right, but I will still assist you in whatever you need."

I understood what he was saying, but I didn't like it. Being unknowing of anything was dangerous. Whomever he suspected was at the wedding and potentially watching us. "Thank you for the dance," I said quietly as the song ended. "It means a lot." I gave a small but genuine smile this time.

He continued to hold the hand used for dancing and placed his other on top. "Welcome to the family, Bexley. I can't say you've married into a family as wholesome as your own, but perhaps you and Grey will do better than Cynthia and myself. I truly do wish you the best. I couldn't have asked for a better or brighter daughter-in-law." He gave me a smile I didn't often see from Roger.

"Thank you." I appreciated his kindness, though I wasn't sure I'd done anything to earn it.

Roger smiled behind me. "I assume you'd like the next dance?"

I turned to see who was approaching and smiled when I saw Grey.

Grey smiled at me. "Yep. I've only gotten one dance so far." He held out a hand to me.

I looked at Roger with a kind smile. "Thank you again. It means a lot."

Roger smiled at me, nodding once. "To me as well. Best wishes, my dear." He stepped away and Grey stepped in.

"I thought you might need saving. Everything okay?" Grey asked quietly as we moved in a slow circle.

I nodded, holding my gentle smile. "Yeah. It was all friendly conversation."

"Was he drilling you with questions?" Grey didn't have the smile he'd been wearing all night, but didn't look upset.

"Not at all. It was just a dance and a nice conversation. I wasn't paying attention to my face," I lied and smiled a little more to cover it. "Will you stop being so suspicious of him and just dance with me?"

"You sure? You usually don't smile that much unless you're trying to keep up a façade." Grey gave a smile that held concern.

"Not this time." I stepped forward and rested my cheek against his shoulder. "He thinks someone here can't be trusted." I smiled as I spoke to minimize the movement of my lips. "I'll tell you about it later."

"You got it." He turned his head and kissed my forehead. "Are you having a good night? I know there's been a lot of handshaking, hugging strangers, and people coming up behind you."

I let out a huff of slight irritation. "You have a problem.

I know you think you're going to have to send someone up a tree to go get me, but I'm fine. Stop worrying so much."

He laughed a little. "A tree? Is that your master plan?"

I shrugged. "Figured I might test my abilities as a flying squirrel."

Grey laughed. "I can't even picture you climbing a tree."

"I used to do it all the time." Trees were a good place to hide if they were thick enough.

Glasses started clinking all around us again.

I let out a breath. "Why is this a thing? Are we supposed to be attached at the face?"

He chuckled lightly. "You're the only one with a problem with it." He smiled, putting his forehead against mine. "And I'm dipping you back for this one." He kissed me and twisted me backward until it was only him holding me up.

"Okay, you're done," I said after a second. It was a horribly awkward position and made me feel like I couldn't get out of it.

Grey tipped me back up and kissed me quickly. "I've always wanted to do that."

"And now you have." I wrapped my arms around him and rested against the front of him as we went back to dancing in a slow circle. "What time is it?"

I felt Grey turn his wrist behind my back before he answered, "Almost eight-thirty. Did you want to head out?"

"Yeah. I'm gonna go find Ryan and get changed."

"Okay. I'll let my mom know we're ready to go." He kissed my forehead but then held me tighter. "I don't want to let go of you, I'm on cloud nine." Grey let out a breath. "My beautiful wife... I can't believe it."

"It is strange," I agreed. "But a good strange."

"I always thought you would bolt on me. Even today, I kept sending Sam to make sure you were still here and it was happening."

I pulled back and looked at him. "Why?" It seemed like a strange thing for him to say since we were already married and I'd promised him not to run without telling him first.

Grey smiled, but there was a slight sadness, or something like it, in his eyes. "I don't know... I always thought you'd get scared, or worry you were making a mistake. Losing you is the only thing that's ever *really* scared me."

I shook my head. "I wouldn't leave you... Do you remember that night we sat on the beach and the ocean made the algae light up?" I waited for him to nod, then I nodded too. "That was the first time in years I could breathe around another person since I was a small child. I didn't know it was possible to feel that way after what I *narrowly* survived, and I hardly knew you... Then two weeks later when you took me to recreate the one 'perfect day' I told you about," I smiled at the memory, "that was the day I became grateful I *did* survive." I reached up to hold onto the lapels of his suit jacket and smiled. "I can't leave a person who makes me feel that way."

Grey had never been wrong to worry—I'd often worried he'd leave me too—but I didn't want him to. He repeatedly told me all the reasons why he loved me, but it wasn't something I told him often enough, so I felt like he should hear it and know I never had any intention of leaving him.

Grey backed up, biting his bottom lip with two of his upper teeth and a big grin on his face. "Hold that thought." He turned and walked to the closest table.

I couldn't figure out what the heck he was doing until he took a glass from someone and started hitting it with a fork. He waited for it to catch on before he put the glass down and used his hands to signal everyone to keep it up.

I laughed as he ran back to me. "I think you just like the attention."

Grey raised his eyebrows and dropped them with his big smile. He was being a show-off, but he looked so handsome I didn't care.

"Menace." I grabbed his lapel, pulled him a step closer, and kissed him. He laughed as he kissed me.

"Why in the hell are you wearing this thing?" Ryan griped as he strained to pull my girdle together enough to unhook it. I'd struggled to get it undone by myself for twenty minutes and couldn't, but I also couldn't do it back up enough to go find Grey. Thankfully, Ryan showed up.

"Because it kept me from going insane every time someone touched me. Which one did you want to deal with?" I'd gotten a nude-colored girdle that not only hid my scars through the see-through parts of the lace and fabric of my dress, but also acted as a barrier from people's hands.

"Neither. And what the hell do you have on under this?"

My other dilemma had been having someone see the scars while fastening the girdle. "It's a shirt I cut. Don't let it fall down." I reached back to hold it at the top of the girdle.

"But why did you need it so tight?"

"It's what the lady gave me."

With another tight pull, Ryan freed me. "You're done. Go."

"Thank you." I held the back of my dress and walked into the bathroom. "Do you know if Grey's ready?" I asked through the door as I stepped out of my dress.

"No. Cynthia said you were looking for me, so I came to find you."

"Yeah, where have you been all night?" I lifted my dress up to the hanger on the door, hung it, then pulled my other dress down.

"Mostly on the phone making sure we got every-one out of the way. Cynthia told Grey that she and Roger were sending you to New Zealand for your honeymoon, so he told her you were still going to Germany and you'd go to New Zealand after."

I checked the lining of my dress to make sure the

things I'd sewn into it were still there and found a note from Patty. It felt like a massive relief, and I let out a breath before I said, "Yeah, I know."

"Maslen, I feel like you're not telling me something and it's making me nervous."

"I've told you what you need to know." I pulled on the dress I was leaving in and zipped it up before I opened the door. "I need you to take this dress to your house with the rest of my stuff, please. Hang it up, don't just drop it somewhere." I zipped up the bag my dress was in and gave it to Ryan.

He nodded. "How am I supposed to get a hold of you if something goes wrong?"

"You're not. The second we leave here, your only responsibility is keeping you and Tim safe. When you get to the house, park in the garage only, close the garage door before you get out of your truck. Tim has my instructions, follow them to the letter. Don't deviate." I grabbed the EpiPens out of my purse, uncapped them, then stood in the mirror to carefully push them into my pinned hair.

"What are you doing?" Ryan asked as if I were insane.

"Getting ready for the inevitable. I don't provoke fights unarmed or unequipped."

He frowned. "Are you planning on giving someone a heart attack with those? It's not gonna work, and leaving them uncapped like that is dangerous, what if Grey bumps your hair."

I turned and looked at him. "He won't. He knows not to touch my hair, and they're not normal EpiPens. They're filled with concentrated cyanide." I took in a deep breath and turned to look at Ryan. "Please promise me you won't do anything other than what I instructed you to. I know who I'm up against, and while you might think you do, you're entirely unprepared. I'll call you when my end is done."

He nodded.

"I have one more thing." I stepped forward and

reached my arms up around his neck to pull him into a hug. "Roger said there was someone here he couldn't trust," I whispered next to his ear. "He said if he was right, he'd be in danger. You have to be careful leaving here. If Patty comes to you for any reason, you need to do what he tells you. I've already made indirect contact with him. He'll protect you."

"You better make sure he gets locked up with the rest of them or I'll take the pig to slaughter. I mean it."

I hugged Ryan a little tighter and put my face down in his shoulder. "Thank you for today... As much as I might've wanted my dad to walk me down the aisle, it meant so much more to have you. You've changed my life and you're so much more than family to me. I truly don't know where I'd be without you, even if I had Grey, it would... never be the same. So, please, trust me, and be safe." My throat was burning as I spoke because I was trying not to cry.

"You better not be saying goodbye to me, Maslen." Ryan's voice was quiet, but also strained and angry.

I shook my head. "No... I'm saying thank you for being a better friend than I thought I could have, and I love you."

Ryan hugged me tightly. "If you don't come back alive, I'll never forgive you."

I nodded. "I know."

"Okay... Let's go." He let out a breath, kissed my cheek, then let go of me.

I grabbed my purse and Ryan took the rest of my stuff that was going with me. My security team was waiting outside my door when we walked out. Ryan passed my things off to them, then gave me his arm as we went toward Grey. While Ryan didn't want to believe me, it was more than likely the last time I'd ever see him and it was killing me the closer we got to the door. He meant as much to me as Grey did, just in a different way. To deflect my heartbreak, I took in a deep breath and let Hannah take over. I needed the numbness she brought with her.

Chapter 38

Ryan

Maslen had said goodbye to me... She'd tried to make it seem like she wasn't, but I felt it from her. There wasn't a lot Maslen was ever wrong about. With all her knowledge, being hyper-aware of her surroundings, experience in the darkest corners of the world, and having a true sense of who a person was just by looking at them... she was rarely wrong. Letting her leave while all of that was eating me from the inside. I didn't know what I'd do without having her as a friend. She listened even when I couldn't speak, said everything I needed to hear without a word, and filled the place where silence usually sat. Losing a friend like her felt like losing the sun.

Tim and I were out of the house within twenty minutes, and in the car Maslen left behind after another hour. She had a whole binder of what to do, where to go, and how long to stay before moving to the next place with a different car. I knew she had escape routes, but I had no idea how meticulously she'd worked on them.

There were drive times, alternate routes, places to stop depending on the needed situation. It was no wonder why she was constantly broke, every extra penny would've had to have gone into her evacuation plans.

"What do we know about Cynthia?" I finally broke the hours-long silence between Tim and I. He knew about our dad being wrongfully accused of Remy's murder, and had a different opinion about it than me, so he hadn't spoke to me since we left the house.

"That she's two-faced and bossy." Tim let out a huff. "I can't wait for her to stop calling me."

"No, I mean what do we really know about her? This thing with her trying to get Maslen and Blondie to go somewhere else for their honeymoon isn't sitting right with me and I can't let it go."

"Cynthia Maslen doesn't sit right with anybody." Tim looked up, put his head back against the headrest, and rubbed the bridge of his nose vigorously. "Uh... I don't know. She does a bunch of parties for Roger that suck, uh..."

"She used to work for Roger. That's how they met." I rubbed my forehead. "She was his secretary which would've given her access to literally anything in MWM. She grew up an only child, her parents died in a house fire after she left home." I stared at the road like it was going to show me the answer.

"Wait. Henry's parents died in a fire."

I looked at Tim with a frown. "What?"

"Yeah. Klaus Ockert. When I looked him up in Germany, there was a paper that said his parents died in a fire. Let me dig some more." Tim looked at his computer.

"You don't think Cynthia's related to Henry, do you?"

"At this point, there is no god, and nothing is out of reach." Tim's fingers jabbed at his keyboard quickly. "Okay... translate page... Herbert and Herta Ockert died from a house fire set by Helena Vaughters, daughter of Otto and Charlotte Vaughters. Herbert and Herta's two children, Klaus and Catrine, survived... uh... The families were friends and their kids played together... Um... the Vaughters took Klaus and Catrine in after the fire... Catrine found evidence that Helena had started the fire and told police. Helena was taken to a mental hospital where she continued to plead innocent... After a visit from her brother, Alexander Vaughters, Helena confessed to the premeditated murder of the Ockert's. She claimed Klaus Ockert had sexually assaulted her, and when she told Herbert and Herta, they dismissed her."

"Good grief. Search Catrine Ockert, and if that doesn't work, search Catrine Vaughters. Have you been able to find a picture of any of them?"

"Not yet. I'm trying not to break laws in Germany."

"Okay. Focus on this, not finding Henry's plane. If Cynthia is Catrine Ockert, this just got a whole lot worse. We need to know before Maslen heads to Germany, and we've only got," I glanced at the clock, "maybe six hours."

"I'm on it. Are we stopping anytime soon? Because Wi-Fi would be preferable over this satellite BS."

"Two more hours, and she probably picked somewhere without internet." I didn't know what to do. Keeping Tim safe was my priority, which meant following Maslen's instructions, but I couldn't let Maslen walk into a trap unknowingly.

"Dude, I can't get anything done if it takes minutes to load a single page. I need real internet."

"Yeah. I'll stop off at the next town. Just keep working on it until then." My brain was in a frenzy trying to think out a plan. We needed to be near an airport, so I slowed down and turned around to go to Bellingham.

"Wow, that is for sure Cynthia because she looks just like her daughter." Tim held out his laptop.

I glanced at the picture. There was a family of six standing in front of a bank. Tim was right, she looked a lot like the picture of her daughter. "Who's all in that picture?"

"Uh, Otto and Charlotte Vaughters with their four children, Helena, Alexander, Klaus, and Catrine. Are we seriously supposed to believe that Cynthia's adopted brother kidnapped her daughter, named it after his mother, and she just spent years not knowing where her kid was? None of this makes sense." Tim looked at me.

"It does if Cynthia had nothing to do with her brother's operation but found out they used her to infiltrate MWM. She might've tried to go after them the same time Roger did and they took their daughter to shut them up. If Cynthia knew they took her daughter, but knew she wasn't being sold or killed, they could've used her daughter to get Cynthia to do whatever they wanted. Feed them information, poke Roger in the background..."

He took in a deep breath and let it out. "Yeah. How are we gonna tell Bex? I mean, she and Grey couldn't be any more off the grid. The second they left the wedding reception, I lost them. I haven't even gotten a ping on Harry's car."

"I know where to find her. We just have to get there on time."

Chapter 39

Bexley

My plan was still working. The note I'd slipped under the attic door at my parents' ranch house had been received. The note in my dress had told me to go to the cabin at Trout Lake in Colorado. I didn't know how Patty knew about me going there, but I wasn't shocked either. When we got to Colorado, there were tickets from Denver to Atlanta, Atlanta to Nova Scotia, and Nova Scotia to Germany. There were also directions on where to go and how, once I got to Germany. Patty was helping me, but from a distance. I'd asked him to purchase the tickets and told him where to meet me, but he wasn't at the cabin when Grey and I got there. We were being sent to Charlotte only, and Patty was making sure all the evidence he had was going to the BKA. It wasn't ideal, but I understood exactly why. He was giving me instruc-tions so he could stay a step ahead of everything I did. If I was taken, Patty would know, and he would find me.

Grey and I got through airport security with no issues, took the flights we were supposed to, and passed through customs easily. The thing that scared the crap out of me was when our alias names were called over the intercom in Germany. Grey said we were being asked to go to a specific airline desk. We were supposed to fly to another airport, but Patty hadn't left tickets, so I wondered if he'd found a way to arrange it and found he had. When Grey went up to the counter, they told him someone had found our tickets. He showed his fake passport and we were on our way to another terminal to fly from Dusseldorf to Hamburg. It was more of a risk than I normally would've allowed for, but I had to trust Patty would keep me alive.

In Hamburg, I gave Grey a new passport and ID to get the rental car. It was at that point that he started asking how many fake IDs I had for him, how I got them, and to what extent I'd been making plans over the last year and a half. Even while we were right in the center of it all, he couldn't understand the very real danger we were in and how necessary my preparations were. He began to question why Ryan's mom could sit there in the same place in Florida with no one coming for her, and my answer was simple—Patty and I had been the only ones who knew she was alive.

"I'm not saying I don't trust your judgment, but I still don't understand anything surrounding your uncle. How did he get into this, why, and why is he trying to help you get out of it after years of keeping you locked up in it...? None of it makes sense." Grey's blue eyes glanced away from the road to look at me.

I looked forward and realized I had no reason not to tell him everything. Grey was already in the vortex of the storm with me, so I decided it was finally time to say something. "Alex Vaughters' sister, Helen, was being kept in the US in a mental hospital after it was claimed she killed her husband and twin children in a house fire.

She was certainly evil and crazy, but I really don't think she did it. She was too devastated and broken over it... Anyway, Patty's always struggled with his mental state after he killed my grandma and aunt by accident when he was only trying to kill my biological grandpa. His dad was a drunkard that beat them all, and Patty got sick of it. My dad got adopted and Patty went into the system. He was about seven, I think. Patty met Helen at the mental hospital. She would tell anyone who'd listen that she was being framed for the murder of her family, and Patty didn't know if he believed her but didn't care since he'd murdered his sister and parents.

"Henry would go visit Helen every other month at the mental hospital, and that's how he and Patty met. Henry needed a doctor and promised Patty his own practice, a house, supplies, and everything."

"He already had his own practice in Dallas, I don't understand why that was appealing to him." Grey glanced at me again, this time with a frown of confusion.

I nodded. "You're right, and at first, it wasn't. Patty declined the offer and told Henry he couldn't leave Dallas because his family was there, specifically me. He's always believed I was a reincarnate of his sister Rebecca—to the point of a literal obsession over me. So, Henry sweetened the deal and told him he could bring me with and no one would be able to find us. He'd give Patty a new identity and no one would know. Patty still said no, and that night, he was refused his medications by the nurses at the hospital. Then he was locked in a padded cell for days on end. Henry went in every day to 'visit Helen', but was there to ask Patty until he finally agreed. Initially, Patty took me because Henry had threatened to kill me. We were caught in Arkansas by Henry and his puppets, then brought to the house in Tennessee. Patty had stupidly trusted Helen and told her his plan, then Henry bribed her with a house and having Patty for herself..."

I took a deep breath because it felt closer than it had in years. My hands were shaking while the memory of my cries filled my mind. "Patty did what he was told because they would kill me if he didn't... From that point on, he either had to be subservient and gain trust so he could get us out, or let us die."

Grey looked at me. "You're making him sound guiltless."

I shook my head. "He's not guiltless... just less guilty than most make him out to be. Toby painted him as this evil madman, and he's not. Patty is mentally ill... but will go to any length to keep me alive, and always has."

"B... I'm not trying to make you feel a certain way about things because I wasn't there and I don't know, but I feel like I need to point out that mental illness isn't always a good enough excuse. People who do these things, they're *all* mentally ill, but it's not a free pass that dismisses their actions."

"You're patronizing me. There are no free passes in this world. I hold Patty responsible for plenty." I wanted to scream right then.

"No, hey, I'm sorry." Grey reached over and took my hand. "That wasn't my intention. We've never talked about this stuff, and you don't often express a lot of opinion, so I didn't know where you stood. I didn't mean to make you feel patronized. I'm really sorry."

My hand was stinging for the first time as Grey held it. My mind was screaming at me to pull my hand away, so with my other hand at my side, I began tapping my leg to expel the nervous energy. It wasn't enough, the screaming in my head was louder than anything else, so I pulled my hand away and ground it over my thigh to make the stinging stop.

"*Hannah... I have to be Hannah,*" I reminded myself.

"What?" Grey looked at my hand as I rubbed it vigorously. "Don't do that. You're going to hurt yourself." He pulled my arm away.

I sucked in a fast breath and closed my eyes as I held it. Being in the air for too many hours had allowed me to revert back to Bexley. The only thing I had to fear on the plane was it going down, but I wasn't afraid of death. Now that I was on the ground again, I needed to bring my survival instincts back to the forefront of my mind and be Hannah. I should've done it at the airport when I got the surge of adrenaline from hearing my name being called.

"B, we don't have to talk about this. It's okay. I was thinking about the Switzerland trip. We could go over Christmas break, and I was thinking maybe we could get a couple of chalets and invite your family for a week. We'll do a two-week Christmas break with a no-work policy, then go again in the summer. What do you think?"

I shook my head. "Ask me when this is over. I can't feel anything right now."

"What do you mean?"

"I'm Hannah... When I'm Hannah, I can't feel emotion. I just exist to survive. My body won't respond to pain the way it wants to, it responds the way I control it to. I don't get angry, show or feel fear, and sadness is non-existent because all three stunt my thinking and cloud my judgment. Neither of those are allowed because they won't serve me in surviving."

Grey looked at me, but I kept my eyes forward because the right expression on his face would force me to lose focus. "Okay... We don't have to talk right now."

"Thank you. I think this is it." I pointed toward the town house on the left side of the road while my eyes studied everything they could. My brain was absorbing the sets of windows on all three floors, the surrounding trees that looked stable enough to support my weight, the slope of the roof, the placement of the chimney, and the number of stairs going up. All in just seconds, I had several different exit strategies. "Circle the block, I need to know the lay of the land before we stop."

"Okay."

I was checking cars and house windows for anyone who might be watching. At least two houses had dogs, but neither of them next to the house we were going to. My brain felt instantly tired trying to take in everything and imprint it in case I needed to recall something later.

"You good, or do you want me to go around again or stretch out further?" Grey asked as we came up to the house again.

I shook my head. "You can park. If I itch my eyebrow casually, we need to leave. If we need to go out the back of the house, run straight between the other sets of houses on the opposite side. If we're being chased, we'll just keep running. If we're not, we'll find a safe place to call for a car. Regardless of how we leave here, as soon as we do, we need to get rid of this car, disappear for a couple hours minimum, then find another car to leave the city in. Whatever you do, don't tell Charlotte who you are. I'll introduce you as Christopher, like your passport, after I've gotten her to remember me."

"You said she didn't speak English."

"Much, and what she did know wasn't that great, but she was being taught English in school. I'll try speaking to her first, if she doesn't understand me, then you can translate. You cannot tell her anything more than what I say. She doesn't know Henry as we know him, she knows him as her uncle Klaus. And no matter what, do not mention the name Helen. You know nothing, you've never heard of her, and I've never so much as spoken her name to you. My life depends on it. Charlotte was a sweet and innocent little girl, but I have no idea who she is now."

Grey nodded. "I understand. I won't say more than hi."

I nodded once and opened the door.

"Hey, no kiss?"

I paused and remembered that was something I

was supposed to do, so I turned my head and kissed him quickly. We got out of the car and I reminded myself I was only allowed to look around casually.

"Grey, don't look around so much. Blend," I told him quietly as I walked up beside him.

"Right. Sorry." He held out an arm for me to hold. I looped my arm through his before approaching the short gate.

"Leave the gate unlatched," I whispered as we went through. "Think 'exit strategy' at all times. If she leaves one of us to close the door, make sure it's not fully latched. We need to get out as fast as we can."

"Breathe, B." He rubbed the top of my hand. "Right now, we're okay."

Grey would never understand how or why my brain worked the way it did... It was incredibly hard to let him see this side of myself because I'd never shown it to anyone who couldn't understand. Toby understood true and brutal survival. Feeling the insignificance told me I needed to do a better job at being fully Hannah. The part of me that was Bexley kept trying to surface because I cared so much about Grey.

I reached forward and pressed the button for the doorbell. My heart rate was even as we waited and didn't change a beat when the door opened. Charlotte gave a confused expression right away.

I pushed my sunglasses up and smiled. "Hi Charlotte, I don't know if you remember me, but my dad was married to your aunt Helen. We met when you were in the US after she disappeared. I'm Hannah."

Charlotte's face lit up. "Oh my gosh! I remember. Hi. How are you?" She stepped forward and hugged me.

"I'm alright. I hope it's okay that I'm here." I placed a hand on her back carefully.

"Yes, yes. I'm so happy to see you." She pulled back and looked at me. "And you look so different without all the injuries. You are so *beautiful*." Her smile didn't change as she looked at Grey.

"Thank you. This is my husband, Christopher," I introduced.

Grey held out a hand with a smile. "It's nice to meet you, Charlotte."

"You too." She shook Grey's hand. "Please, come in. Can I get you some tea, or coffee?" Charlotte glanced back before stepping into the house and out of the way so we could come in.

"Oh, no, thank you. We had a lot on the plane," I lied with a smile.

Charlotte directed a hand toward the living room off to the right side. "What brings you to Germany?"

"Just a vacation. Helen always spoke so fondly of it, so it's been on my list of places to see." I walked into the living room and toward the spot that would give me the fullest view of the rest of the house. There was a dining room behind the living room and I could see the front door and the windows at the front of the house.

"Oh, yes. You should come in the late spring next time though. How is your father?" Charlotte said in a chair across from me, while Grey took a seat next to me.

"He's well, thank you." I gave a polite nod. "How are your parents?"

She held up her shoulders. "I don't talk to them much. My father is... uh, what's the word," she shook her head, "unmöglich."

"Impossible," Grey responded.

"Yes. Impossible. You speak German?" She held a hopeful smile.

Grey nodded. "Yeah. I learned in school." That wasn't true. He'd told me he'd learned from Cynthia as a kid. She'd also taught him French because she used to bring him to Paris a lot.

"Oh, wonderful. I learned English in school as well. Now, I work at a bank, and I talk to Americans all day long, so I'm much more fluent than when Hannah and I met." She smiled at me again. "I still can't believe you're *here*. How did you find me?"

"Uh, my dad asked Klaus, I think."

Her smile seemed forced. "Klaus knows where I live?"

Crap. "Oh, I don't know," I said quickly. "I'm not sure who my dad talked to, that was just a guess."

She laughed nervously. "Oh, okay. Uh, I'm sorry, I don't have anything to do with my family anymore. I don't want them contacting me. We don't even live in the same city."

I nodded with a sympathetic expression. "Oh. I'm sorry. I didn't know that."

"Don't be sorry. They..." she shook her head, "they are not good people. I think Helen was smart for running away. I'm still waiting on an American visa so I can too."

"At least you know when it's time to cut ties. It's a hard thing to do," Grey gave a supportive smile.

"Yes, especially with my parents. My father is very controlling. I'm hoping, by going to a different country, he will leave me alone." Charlotte was trying a little harder to hold her smile, but I could see she was growing uncomfortable.

Changing countries wasn't going to help her. I stood up because I heard something outside.

"What was that?" Charlotte got up too and followed me to the window.

"We need to leave. It's not safe here," I said calmly as I turned from the window after seeing four guys outside of the rental car.

"Oh my gosh. Is that your car? I'm sorry. My father is crazy." Charlotte continued to stand by the window.

"I'm very aware of what your father is. You need to come with us. We're not safe," I told her quickly.

"No—what?" She looked at me, miffed over something I'd said. "What do you mean you're aware of what my father is? What do you know?"

"Likely more than you. Please, we need to go now." I pulled on her arm to make her go to the back of the house. "We'll come back later when they're gone," I lied as I checked out in the backyard to make sure no one was there.

We went out the door and ran through the yard, and in between the next set of houses.

"Over here, we can go to my friend's house," Charlotte said as she turned her head and looked back.

"No, we can't go anywhere predictable." I looked down the row of backyards and saw a shed on the other side of the fence. "This way."

We ran for the fence and I wasted no time getting down to give Charlotte a leg up over the fence. "Get in the shed," I told her as I looked around. "Grey, go ahead. I can get myself over."

"Are you sure?"

"Yes. Go." I pushed Charlotte to help her the rest of the way over, then hurriedly pulled myself up and over.

"It's locked," Charlotte whispered quickly.

A guy yelled in German down the way.

I was already reaching into my hair and pulling out two pins. It was quick work to pick the lock. "Get inside. Be quiet," I whispered as I opened the door. I got in behind Charlotte and Grey, pulled the door closed, and looked for a way to lock the door from the inside.

"Hey, listen," Grey whispered. "There's sirens."

I nodded.

"They think the police are after them," Charlotte panted.

"We just have to stay here." I looked around the shed, identifying what I could use as quick weapons. A helicopter was flying overhead, and the police were yelling in German through bullhorns. "It'll be a while." I pulled down three lawn chairs from the wall.

"Hannah, what is going on? What do you know about my father?"

"I know he's not *really* your father." I looked at her to see how she would accept the information.

There was hurt in her blue eyes. "They never told me I was adopted. I found out when my mother needed blood for surgery. How do you know this?"

"You were kidnapped like me. I was much older when I was taken, you were just born." I stood to the side of the small window in the shed and peered out carefully. The police were still yelling. Patty was obviously watching me because there was no way the police would've gotten to those guys so fast otherwise.

"'Kidnapped'? Entführen?"

I looked at her because she sounded confused. Charlotte was looking at Grey for confirmation.

He nodded and looked at me. I could see he really wanted to tell her, so I nodded and looked back out the window. Grey began explaining to her quietly in German. The sound of his voice, when he gently explained something, always comforted me. He had this soft quality that was kind and loving. There were times I wanted to record him when he was speaking that way just so I could listen to it whenever I wanted. German wasn't a very appealing language to listen to, but it was when Grey spoke.

Charlotte began to cry as she conversed with Grey and I didn't let it get to me because I couldn't. My eyes were focused out the window to make sure no one was coming. I wasn't unaware of the cruelty of it, I just couldn't let it cloud my mind.

Once it was dark outside, I didn't see any flashing lights, the neighborhood was quiet, and when we could make it out of the shed quietly, we ran again. Grey went into a convenience store, got a disposable phone, and we walked while he quickly set it up. He told us the news had been on in the store and police were looking for Charlotte. We weren't going to be able to sneak her out of the country like I'd originally planned, but thankfully, Patty had a Plan B.

After calling a car, we went to a house Patty had reserved for us. Grey and Charlotte got some sleep, but I didn't dare because I knew Patty was close. If he hadn't come to see me already, it probably meant he was still on his pills and in control of himself, but I would never take the risk. Grey told me we could sleep in shifts, but he had no idea what Patty was capable of. The proof of that came in the morning when Charlotte and Grey woke up. There was a letter taped on the outside of the kitchen window. I opened it, read the instructions, and understood them, but didn't understand why it was necessary. All I could do was trust that Patty knew what he was doing.

Patty wanted Charlotte to deliver the evidence. He'd left a wig, temporary cheek implants, colored contacts, and clothes. There was a car in the garage with keys on the seat, so we drove for five hours to Frankfurt, the city I'd been hoping to avoid. I went through the box that'd been left on the front seat, took pictures of everything on the disposable phone, and hid it under the seat.

Before the edge of the city, Grey pulled over and Charlotte moved up to the driver's seat. She drove the rest of the way while Grey and I hid in the back of the car. We told her to park down a block, put all the *real* documents in my purse, and gave her that to walk with. Between Patty and I, Charlotte didn't look anything like herself, but I was still praying it was enough. After giving her the final instructions, I gave her the keycard that would let her in through the back of the building and hoped Patty wasn't putting trust in the wrong person.

Grey and I waited about five minutes before we climbed up in the front of the car and drove around to the other side of the building. I'd already told him we were about to be taken, but he refused to let me go alone. If he hadn't been driving, I would've stuck him with one of the tranquilizer syringes I had just to keep him safe. Patty had instructed me to stay with Grey for now though, so I was just trying to trust we'd be okay.

Right as we were turning the corner into the parking lot from the street, an oncoming car swerved and stopped in front of us.

"Shit!" Grey slammed on the breaks.

I looked behind us as another car got right up behind us and two more got on either side to pin us in completely.

"I love you," I told Grey weakly.

"No. Get down, get down, get down." Grey pulled me over toward him, then pushed my butt off the seat.

I'd expected the gunfire, but I still jumped and gasped from the initial startle. Shots fired all around us, glass broke, and there were loud cracks like rocks being thrown at metal. It all stopped almost as suddenly as it started.

"Okay. Get out. Let's go. Hurry." Grey pulled on my arm to get me to move.

I would question what we were doing later because we needed to get out. After grabbing the phone under the seat, I opened the door to a nearly dead body on the ground. The guy was shot all over, including in the head, and still gasping like a fish out of water. I scooped up his gun and ran with Grey to get in the car that was at the back. The car was already running, so he threw it in reverse before we even had our doors closed.

"That was my team and good planning." Grey let out a breath. "Holy crap."

I started picking the pieces of glass out of my hair.

He shook his head. "Casey went in, talked to the Chief of the BKA. It was all arranged on the up and up. The BKA was up there on the roof with my guys."

And Charlotte would be just fine because Harry was waiting inside for her with a lawyer Grey had hired. He thought he was going behind my back, but he forgot I saw in more directions than others. I knew who would be more loyal to me, even if they lost their job for betraying Grey. Being generously kind could pay more than money was capable of buying. It was like Ryan, no amount of money would ever allow him to betray me.

"Charlotte will be fine. Harry will take care of her." Grey turned into a parking garage. "Okay. In and out as fast as you can."

Art and Justin, two guys from Grey's security team, were standing outside of a black Mercedes. Art ran around to my side as Grey was pulling in, and they both got us safely into the car like we were still under fire. I thought they were going to come with us, but they didn't. Grey backed up quickly, and both guys went to get in the car we'd just come from.

"Hey," Grey took my hand, "you okay? You haven't said anything." He looked at me with worry.

I nodded and took in a breath. "Yeah. It's not the first time I've been surrounded by gunfire..." I took a deep breath and let it out. "There's two less to worry about. Isaak and Heinrich were on the ground." Unfortunately, they were the less lethal of the four.

Grey looked at me questioningly. "Really? I don't understand why they'd risk coming personally."

I shook my head. "There weren't many guys left to help them. I had Ryan do that big wipe-out, and not all of it was in the US. Yesterday, Patty cleared out more. Someone already knew I was in Germany, or Alex's guys wouldn't have been outside Charlotte's to slash our tires. Patty knows there's a hole in the boat somewhere between our side and Henry's. I've been bait since I got here. Everyone wants me dead, and they'll all come out to get me. Patty knows it's the fastest way to handle this. Just like I know you didn't ask me about your guys coming here or talking to the BKA. Or that you had Harry and a lawyer ready for Charlotte, you, or me in case any of us ended up inside. I'm sure you'll recall you left out the detail of the lawyer in your quick explanation before," I looked at him, "meaning, I already knew what you had planned."

Grey let out a huff and smiled a little. "Nothing gets past you, huh?"

"Lots of things get past me, but I do what I can to limit them."

"Then you already know I have a plane waiting?"

I nodded.

Chapter 40

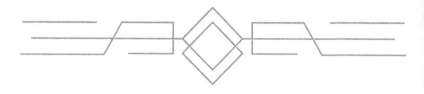

Grey

Bex didn't seem as upset about my plan as I thought she might. It made me crazy that she thought her only option was being taken when I knew I could prevent it. Whatever side of Bex had come out in all this, I didn't like. She was cold, calculated, and devoid of anything that resembled the beautiful person she was a few days ago. It also disgusted me how much trust she was putting into the man single-handedly responsible for her situation. I trusted Bex because it was undoubtedly obvious she was far more prepared than anyone could've thought, but I still felt like she was blinded to the fact that there was another way.

When we got on the tarmac, everything was routine until we walked onto the plane. Bex stopped and immediately looked at the floor after turning to go in the cabin. A man with silver hair in a blue, fitted suit was sitting with a gun on his lap. There were three others with him, but only one other in a suit. He had dark hair and an angry stare. Bex hadn't been blinded at all, she'd been right. It was my plane, but my pilot and staff were missing.

"Hello, Hannah," the silver-haired man looked at her apathetically. "Sit on the floor. There'll be another joining us."

Bex grabbed the wrist of my sleeve and stepped over to sit on the floor in the front corner. I sat beside her closest to them because it was the only protection I could offer her. Obviously, she'd been right.

"Where are the documents?" the silver-haired guy asked, still staring at her.

"I don't have them." Bex kept her eyes on the floor but showed no other signs of fear.

"Empty your pockets and give me your bag."

Bex rose to her knees and gave the guy her bag without looking at him.

"Empty your pockets," Bex whispered quickly as she turned her pockets inside out.

I pulled out my wallet and passport because it was all I had. One of the other two goons standing at the back of the plane walked up and took everything from Bex and me. The silver-haired guy trifled through Bex's purse, handed it to the goon, and the goon threw it out of the plane.

"Where is Charlotte?" the other man in the suit asked.

Bex shook her head. "I don't know. She evaded us when your guys showed up at her house."

"Why were you at her house?" Henry looked at me.

"Because she's my sister," I answered.

Bex bumped my hip with her hand.

Henry chuckled with barely a smile. "And I'm your uncle. Your parents got in our way, and that comes at a cost." He waved dismissively. "Don't speak again, you'll know when I ask you a question directly."

Control freak... I had a lot of experience with them.

I looked over at the door because someone was coming up into the plane.

"Du bist spät." The silver-haired guy looked at his watch.

"Sie bekamen keine Antworten. Ich habe ihnen gesagt, dass Sie es tun würden." The man walked in and sat down after telling Henry they didn't have answers.

The flight was short, not even long enough to get fully up in the air. When the door was open again and the stairs were down, Henry told us to get off the plane. The thing I found so odd about it was no one had bound our hands or legs to keep us from running. It was disgusting that a person could have that much control over another. Bex walked down the stairs quickly, then sidestepped to the right of them once she was on the ground. When I got down, I turned to face the goons as they came down, but Bex yanked me back.

"Just do what I do, and don't speak, especially if they're hurting me. Say nothing," she whispered quickly.

I took her hand because it was all I could do.

"Go." The silver-haired guy lit a cigarette. He wasn't threatening about the way he said anything which somehow seemed worse.

Bex let go of my hand and walked forward, so I walked behind her. It was one more thing I could do for her, to keep her back from being exposed to them. She walked up to the garage about sixty feet from the plane, opened the door, and both of us stopped for a second. Ryan and Tim were in a cage in the corner, both of them beaten and bloody.

"Long time no see, Stupid." A guy stood up from a broken and torn-up office chair. He looked more like the skeevy criminal I'd expected. His creepy lizard eyes that were set too far apart watched Bex as she walked up to the cage door.

"Shut up. Put them both in the cage and let's go,"

one of the other goons snapped.

"You know what they say... save dessert for last." He pulled a set of keys out of his pocket and turned to the cage.

Never had I wanted to hurt someone so violently in all my life. For a brief moment, I contemplated taking his gun and shooting him in the head. The only problem was, I wasn't sure I'd be quick enough to shoot the guys behind us without them shooting me first.

"What are you doing? I didn't tell you to put them in the cage," the silver-haired guy snapped as he walked in.

"I did, Henry. That was my fault," the other goon responded.

Henry pointed at the beat-up metal folding chair. "Tie her up, and put him in the cage."

"Don't make a sound," Bex said quickly as she turned around and walked to the chair.

I looked back at her as I stepped into the cage, then went straight to Ryan and Tim. They looked even worse up close. Tim was asleep, sitting in front of Ryan, resting back against him, and cut up the worst.

"You can't do anything, just sit," Ryan whispered.

I sat on the floor next to him. Ryan's arms were cut up like he'd been slashed at dozens of times. He was shaking as he held Tim.

"He's dead," he whispered.

"What?" Out of instinct, I reached over to touch Tim's arm. His skin was colder than what was natural and beginning to stiffen.

"She'll never forgive me." Ryan starred forward with tears hanging in his eyes.

"Who? Bex?" I looked forward to see her being chained to the chair.

"My mom... They're both dead." Ryan put his face down in Tim's mop of curls.

I felt like I was being gutted. Tim and Ryan were as

much my brothers as Sam was.

"It's not your fault." I kept my eyes on Bex, praying she wasn't next to die.

"No... it's your piece of shit mother's."

I looked at Ryan. "That's not fair. Her daughter was taken."

Ryan looked at me with his bruised face and red-rimmed eyes. "She's Henry's sister. Your mom's name is Catrine Ockert."

I shook my head. "That's not possible. My mom's family is dead."

"No, just her parents. They died in a fire Alex's sister, Helena, set because Henry raped her. Your mother is the reason these pieces of shit got into MWM, and the reason my brothers are dead."

I didn't even know how to process what he was telling me, mostly because I wondered if he was partially losing his mind. Losing Tim could've easily caused a mental snap. But then I remembered what Henry said on the plane. Was he my uncle...? The very thought made me want to puke.

"What did Catrine offer you?" Henry asked Bex as he sat in a chair directly in front of her.

"I don't know who that is." Bex kept her eyes down.

"Cynthia Maslen. What did she offer you in exchange for wiping out billions of dollars in business?" He spoke clearly like he was conversing with an idiot.

"Nothing. Cynthia hates me, and I only found out about her daughter two days ago." Bex closed her eyes, and I didn't understand why until Henry smacked her straight across the face.

"Don't lie to me, Hannah," he sang coldly. "Nothing is free. I left you alone, and I know there had to be an incentive for you to come after me."

Bex shook her head and said something too quiet for me to hear. Henry leaned in with a livid expression and muttered something back before he punched her in the thigh with an incredible amount of force. She let out a short scream before she clamped her mouth shut and breathed heavily through her nose. I didn't know what to do, screaming at him would only make him hurt her more, but sitting there silently was nothing but pure torture.

"Where are the documents?" Henry seethed.

Bex shook her head with the saddest pout on her face. "I don't know. I don't have them."

"Then *WHO DOES!?*" he shouted in her face.

"I don't know. I only had an electronic copy on the phone in my purse. I don't have the physical papers."

Henry shot up, stood there for just a second like he was even more angry, then kicked the seat of the chair between Bex's tied up legs so hard she tipped backwards.

"Call someone," he shouted at one of the goons. "Get that purse before someone else does!"

"Sie nahmen das auto auseinander. Sie fanden nichts," Alex said to Henry. He was telling him a car had been taken apart but nothing was found. "Ich muss Charlotte finden." Alex walked over to Bex, grabbed her by the arm, and pulled her upright again. "Where is Charlotte?"

Bex shook her head. "I don't know. She ran out the back door as soon as your guys showed up at her house. We tried to catch up to her but we couldn't find her." It was incredible how convincingly she could lie. I just didn't understand why she was lying. If Alex cared so much about Charlotte, then he likely wasn't out to hurt her.

"Umzug!" Henry pushed Alex away then grabbed Bex by the back of the head. He let out a scream as he pulled his hand away.

"Was war das?" Alex asked.

"Stupid bitch!" Henry backhanded Bex to the side of the head, but then stumbled and fell over.

"Was ist passiert?" Alex looked at Henry with

confusion, and I was confused too. "What did you do!?" He shouted at Bex as he got down on his knees next to Henry. "Klaus, sprich mit mir!"

Henry started convulsing as his skin turned bright red. Bex kept her face turned away, looking fearfully at the floor as if she could somehow see what was going on behind her.

"Helft ihm, Idioten!" Alex looked back at the three goons by the door. They were standing there like a bunch of idiots, just spectating. So was the one in front of the cage door.

Two goons ran over to help, while the third stayed by the door. I looked at Bex again, waiting for her to look at me, then jumped from a series of deafening bangs. My instinct was to pull Ryan over to protect him because I'd been thinking about it before. I couldn't hardly cover him before another cluster of shots went off. When it stopped I looked around wildly, just trying to collect the important information to understand. Bex was alive, I didn't see blood on her, the goon by the door put his gun down and opened the door.

"Let's move!" he yelled, then ran over to grab the guns off the pile of bodies. He was the one who'd been late to get on the plane.

I looked over at the perv by the cage door because he was groaning. My heart was racing, I was shaking, and I couldn't really feel my body until Ryan moved behind me. I got out of the way quickly, sure that I'd probably hurt him in the process of trying to shield him.

"I don't know what the hell just happened, but holy shit it worked," the guy said as he came over and grabbed the gun and keys off the cage door.

"I put cyanide sodium and water in an EpiPen," Bex responded. "He always grabs my hair, without fail."

The guy laughed, unlocking the cage door, and walked over to her. "Well, goddamn, lady. You just made this a thousand times easier. Let me find the bolt cutters.

I don't know what key goes to what around here."

"Can you walk?" I asked Ryan. "I can carry Tim."

"Yeah."

I got up and crouched in front of Tim. Ryan pushed against his back while I pulled him forward over my shoulder. The pressure against Tim's stomach made his bowels evacuate, and Ryan looked like he was about to cry. I had Tim balanced enough to reach a hand down to Ryan to help stabilize him.

"Dad?" Bex's voice was broken, but I couldn't look because I was helping Ryan.

"Oh, shit," Ryan breathed as he leaned against the wall.

"The plane is outside. It's not that far." I turned to look and saw Bex's dad and Ben. Her dad was trying to help get the chains off and Ben was coming toward the cage.

"Shit." Ben jogged when he looked from Bex to us. "Hold on. Let me help you." Ben turned himself to get under Ryan's arm.

"Grey, are you okay?" Ben looked me up and down for any observable injuries.

"Yeah."

"Son of a bitch! I'LL KILL YOU!" Ryan shouted hatefully.

It took me a second to find who he was screaming at, then I saw Patty. He looked different than his mug shot, but it was him.

"I'll fricken help you, but right now he's helping us. Just keep going." Ben walked slowly out of the cage with Ryan. His back was almost as bloody as his arms.

"Ryan?" Bex squeaked. She grabbed her dad's arm and limped forward to get to Ryan.

"Don't, Maslen. Just take care of yourself." He sounded almost angry with her.

She looked at Tim, then me.

I shook my head, "He's gone. Let your dad help

you."

Her eyes turned even sadder as she reached for Tim's arm and her chin quivered.

"Come on, honey. We gotta get ya out," Don said gently.

Chapter 41

Bexley

Grey flew us back to Frankfurt and called for medical assistance while we were in the air. It was a bit of a fight with my brother and Dad because they didn't want to let Patty drive off by himself, but I threw somewhat of a guilt trip on them. Even with Henry, Alex, Isaak, and Heinrich dead, I didn't trust that it was over because Patty wasn't acting like it was. He looked too nervous.

Patty had left plane tickets and a note for my dad to find, which was how he and Ben ended up in Germany trying to help. None of them knew Ryan and Tim had been captured, and when I tried to ask Ryan, he didn't say a word. I knew he was sitting there suffering, so I didn't push. He kept his eyes out the window when I took his hand, but he was squeezing my hand tightly so I knew he still wanted me there.

After we landed, it was a full storm of medics, police, and agents from the BKA. They took Ryan and Tim off the plane on stretchers, and they tried to get me on one, but there was no way in *hell* I was leaving Ryan's side. Ben insisted on coming with Ryan and I, so Grey and my dad went with Tim. The BKA followed us to the hospital but didn't try to question me or Ryan. He had to go into surgery for minor internal bleeding and an unstable rib fracture. After lots of protest on my end, I was taken back for an x-ray and MRI. My injuries from Henry were superficial for once. I was still shocked Alex or someone else hadn't tried digging through my pinned-up hair to find the three EpiPens I'd stuffed in there. I'd tried to place them in a direction that would trigger them if Henry grabbed my hair. It was more of a prayer, hoping it worked, rather than expecting it to.

Brian, the guy who'd shot everyone else, was someone from the Tres Reyes gang posing as one of Henry's guys. The second he'd come on the plane, I knew we had a fighting chance of making it out, we were both just waiting for the opportunity. I just wished it'd all happened before Tim was killed...

"Miss Lawrence?"

I opened my eyes and picked my head up from Grey's shoulder. Both he and Ben were still sitting next to me, holding my hands. The sleep deprivation had obviously caught up to me because it wasn't like me to fall asleep in a hospital, even in a waiting room.

Four guys in suits showed me their badges.

"I'm Agent Chris Moore with the FBI. These are Agents Marks, Willmer, and Petosky. May we ask you some questions?" the first guy in the lineup asked kindly.

"Can this wait? We're waiting for our friend to get out of surgery, she's barely slept in seventy-something hours, and we're out of energy." Grey's voice was raspy.

Agent Moore gave a sympathetic look. "The majority of our questions can wait, but we have a few we need answers to. We'll do our best to be brief." He handed me a business card.

"It's okay," I told Grey as I sat myself up from my slump, "but I want my dad here while you ask questions." I looked at Ben.

He nodded and got up. "I think he's just down the hall. I'll be right back."

The three agents gave him a polite smile, but Agent Moore shook Ben's hand before he passed by. The four of them sat in the row of chairs across from us.

"Is your leg okay?" Agent Moore asked as he directed a hand toward my thigh.

I nodded. "Yeah. It's a compression wrap with an ice pack. I didn't get hit hard enough to break anything, but it'll be a little bit with a cane." I pointed my finger toward the wall.

Agent Moore smiled. "I think I'm just impressed you're alive at *all*. I've been on your case since the day you went missing. I was fresh out of school back then."

"That's what the handshake was for then?" I gave an upward nod in the direction Ben had gone.

He nodded. "Yeah, I've known your family for as long as you've been gone. They're wonderful people."

"They *are*. Thank you."

"Why are you *thanking* him?" Grey's voice was quiet but a little raspy.

I looked at him with confusion.

"He just told you he failed you for seventeen years and you thanked him."

I shook my head. "Grey, that's rude. It's not his fault." I couldn't believe he was outwardly acting in such a way. It was so unlike him, I wondered if he was having some kind of snap.

"He's not wrong, Miss Lawrence. We did fail to bring you home."

"Maslen. Her name is *Mrs. Maslen*. And you did a hell of a lot more than fail to bring her home. You failed to—"

"Grey!" My snap was sharp and made him stop

abruptly. "Take a walk. Ben and my dad will be back in just a second." I rubbed his arm.

He pulled his hand over the dark blonde stubble on his face. "Yeah." Grey got up and left.

"I'm sorry. We haven't had a lot of sleep, and one of us didn't come back, so he's having a hard time," I said kindly after Grey was gone.

"Hey, it's alright. I doubt he'd say anything I haven't said to myself over the years." Agent Moore gave a cringing smile. "We all have cases that get to us a little more than others, and yours has always been *mine*. Your mother put a picture of you on my desk," he smiled a little more. "She was madder than I've ever seen her. It was about a month after you were gone. Anyway, she slammed a picture frame on my desk, pointed at your face, and told me it was going to stay there until I found you. There were some other words too, but," he laughed a little, "that picture has been on my desk ever since. Even when I upgraded desks and offices."

I smiled. "That sounds exactly like my mom." It seemed a little strange to have a picture of a little girl he'd never met on his desk, but I was trying not to read into it the way the paranoid side of me wanted to.

"Well, I wasn't sure you'd get permission for a vacation," my dad said as he came in.

The four agents stood and smiled.

Agent Moore laughed. "Yeah, I don't know about vacation with the BKA involved."

My dad smiled and shook the agent's hand with somewhat of an admiring smile. "You're likely right about that, but I'm glad you were able to come in person. It wasn't a guarantee, but man I had a feelin'." He patted Agent Moore's hand before letting go. "And ya brought the whole crew with ya." My dad stepped over and started shaking hands.

Ben sat next to me in the spot Grey had previously been in, leaving his old seat for our dad.

"Where's Grey?" Ben whispered.

"He needed to cool off. I think things are getting to him." I felt guilty over telling Grey to take a walk.

"Do you want me to go talk to him?"

I shook my head. "No, give him some time to reel and grieve. Tim meant a lot to him, so I think he just needs to let it out for a minute."

"Tim Brae is the one who didn't make it back alive, correct?" Agent Moore asked, having already sat back down.

I looked at my dad as he sat.

"Just be honest, honey. Ain't nobody here to charge ya of anythin'." My dad gave me a loving smile and took my hand. He looked so much happier, like the world was finally off his shoulders.

I gave my dad the smallest of a smile before I looked at the agents. "Yeah. I think Tim had already passed before we got to that garage. I can't be sure though, you'd have to speak to his brother Ryan or my husband. I was kept separated from them while we were there."

Agent Moore nodded. "That's okay. How do you know Tim and Ryan Brae."

"Ryan is my best friend, and he and my husband have been friends since they were kids." I had to be careful about what I said. With Cynthia being related to Henry, I understood what Roger had cautioned me about at the wedding. He'd asked me to consider Grey, and I was. Just because she was related to Henry, it didn't make her a monster like him. She'd obviously been away from them for many years or she would've known Alex had her daughter.

"And how did you meet them?"

"These are the questions that couldn't wait?" Ben asked.

Agent Moore looked at Ben. "It seems there's some involvement between the Maslens, the Breas, and this whole operation."

"I'll give you the simple run down. Roger Maslen didn't know who he was signing as a client until it was too late. They took his daughter when he attempted to notify the FBI. As for Craig Brae, it was worse for him. They kidnapped his wife and killed his youngest son. Neither family was ever a willing participant in anything other than bringing this operation down." I held a slightly irritated expression because I was pissed over the implication that Ryan could be in on something.

Agent Moore nodded. "That's what we've been able to uncover so far. But were you also aware Cynthia Maslen is actually Catrine Ockert, Henry Greer's—AKA Klaus Ockert's—biological sister?"

"I'm aware. Relation does not a monster make, or we'd all be like my uncle. If Cynthia had any contact with her brother or the Vaughters, she would've known where her daughter was." I didn't know how he already had that information. Had my dad slipped up even though I told him not to say anything?

He looked at me with confusion. "I'm not sure I follow. Why would she have known where her daughter was if she had spoken with them?"

"Because Alex Vaughters raised her as his own. Her name is Charlotte Vaughters. We had her walk into the BKA with all the proof of who everyone was, DNA samples, everything. I've already confirmed that it was received."

"If you had such evidence, why did you send it to the BKA instead of the FBI?" Agent Petosky asked.

I smiled questioningly. "I can't tell if that was a serious question."

Agent Petosky looked down the line of his colleagues looking for reassurance, then looked back at me. "It's a serious question. That information is gonna be nearly impossible for us to obtain from the BKA in a timely manner."

"Then you'll be happy to know I have digital copies

of all documents. As for the DNA, you'll have to get a warrant for a DNA sample from Cynthia Maslen. If you can get me access to a computer, I can transfer the documents whenever you'd like." I hoped giving them what they were ultimately after would keep me from answering the original question and most that were likely to follow.

It worked because Agent Moore had someone get a computer and bring it up to me. I had them saved to a cloud server, so all I had to do was log-in and drop everything on the desktop. That seemed to satisfy them enough to get them to leave. I sat there talking to my dad, trying to tell him as much as I could about everything so he could guide me the next time I was questioned.

Grey came back to tell us Ryan was out of surgery, awake, and asking to see me. He apologized as he walked me to Ryan's room. It was still hurting my brain to see Ryan so beat up because it was supposed to be me that looked like a post-slasher film. When we'd first walked into the garage and I saw him, I nearly cried seeing him so broken.

"Hey, are you okay?" he asked as he picked up a hand to reach for me.

I nodded. "Yeah. Superficial. How are you feeling?" I walked around the bed to the other side so I could sit with him and not have to strain my hurt leg to get it up.

"I can't feel shit. I'm just tired." Ryan moved the IV line out of the way so I could sit.

"Can I get anything for you?" Grey asked quietly with his hands in his pockets.

"No, I need a few minutes alone with Maslen though."

Grey nodded and looked at me like he needed confirmation, so I gave a small nod. "Holler if you need something."

"Yep." Ryan tugged on my arm to get me to move closer, then lifted his arm.

"You have a bunch of stitches, I don't want to put pressure on them," I told him.

"Keep your head on my shoulder. You'll be fine."

I slid over more, rested my head against his shoulder, and he draped his arm along my back. If I knew I could hug him without hurting him, I would've.

"I didn't mean to snap at you before... Tim dying isn't your fault... and I don't want you to think that. I was in a ton of pain."

I moved my hand up by my cheek since it seemed to be a semi-safe place on his shoulder. "I know, I didn't take it personally. It's hard to manage that much at once, and I'm very familiar with it." It wasn't just the physical pain or the emotional toll of losing a loved one, it was the damaging wreckage of having no control, knowing there was no help, and the suffocation of near death.

"I know, but still... I'm sorry... I went about everything wrong... I should've trusted you the way you trust me. I messed up so bad." His voice was just above a whisper.

"You did what made sense. You didn't know I wouldn't run this time... and if I didn't have so much to lose, I still might've. I might make you write a few essays for me or guilt you into bringing me lunch, but I already forgave you."

"Write your own damn papers, and you have a phone to get your own lunch."

I smiled. "Okay, you have to make me banana bread on request."

"I don't wanna smile."

"I'm afraid you'll cry if you don't." It sounded like I was teasing, but I was mostly serious.

"Are you that allergic to tears?" His tone was flat, so there was likely an eye-roll with his words.

"I'm not allergic... I'm afraid... I might do it too, and I'm afraid of how hard it might be to stop."

He let out a huff. "You'll stop... You'll either get dehydrated or you'll fall asleep."

"You know what I mean," I whispered.

"Yeah... We were coming to warn you about Cynthia. They caught up to us on the plane to Germany, but we don't know *how*. Tim was being so careful to make sure we didn't leave a trail."

"No, there's been a leak between sides. I already know that. Alex and Henry clearly knew I was here before they were supposed to. This stays between you and me, and you can't tell anyone, but I think it's Cynthia."

"I do too, I'm just not sure how we prove it." Ryan moved his arm away from my back. "Can you grab me that cup of water?"

"Yeah." I sat up, grabbed the cup and handed it to him. "Even if we could prove it, I'm not sure we *should*. It'll devastate Grey. I think for now, we keep it to ourselves, don't let on that we know anything, and see how things go once she and Roger have Charlotte back. As a mom, I can say with confidence that I would do *all* the shady shit to get my daughter back."

"It's gonna be a lot harder to keep tabs on her without Tim. You know that, right?" Ryan didn't look at me, but I could see the heartbreak on his face just from the mention of his brother's name.

I pulled back the corner of my mouth. "I don't think she's in the business of selling kids off, so... if she's not hurting anyone, we leave it alone."

"I don't know why you're like this." He stared into his cup angrily.

I frowned. "I don't understand."

"You never get pissed... You won't hate people that deserve to be hated."

I held up my shoulders. "I told you... hate is what got me here. My grandpa beat Patty and my dad, Patty lost his mind after retaliating, Henry was a hateful psychopath, and I don't want to be like them. I want to be different, even if it's hard."

"Yeah, it's okay to be pissed off once in a while." His

eyebrow raised.

I shook my head. "It doesn't serve what I want out of life."

"I think you'd feel differently if you actually *lost* your family. I'm not wishing it on you, but I think you can see it differently because you didn't lose anyone."

"I've lost plenty I'll never get back. Your insinuation that I didn't lose enough because I still choose to do better is petty, rude, and insulting." I stood up and grabbed my cane.

"Maslen, that's not what I meant. I just meant none of your family died. It's *different*, not less."

"And I buried over a hundred children, two of whom I birthed. Remy and Tim are most certainly tragedies. Tim was my friend. I've missed out on raising my daughter, I wasn't there when my nephews and niece were born, I didn't get to go to prom or graduate high school. Loss is loss, and I've known plenty of it, but I would never be so bitter as to say someone else's losses didn't compare just because they didn't feel the same way about it that I did." I opened the door and left. Ryan could sit there and be pissed off by himself. While I realized it was part of grieving, I didn't feel mentally stable enough to withstand getting run over by his words.

Ben was the only person in the waiting room. He sat with a tablet, reading something, and looking much older than when I was little. I'd lost so much time with him and it hurt to know I could never get it back.

He looked up from his tablet with a questioning smile. "You okay?"

I pulled back the corner of my mouth and shook my head. "No... Can we get out of here?"

His eyebrows raised. "Yeah. Grey and Dad went to the cafeteria. I'll text them." He grabbed his jacket and laptop bag.

Chapter 42

Ben

The moment I looked at Hannah when she came back to the waiting room, I knew she was struggling. I was surprised she didn't lie when I asked her if she was okay, but it killed me for the hour she sat silently without saying a word. It was normal for a person to take an emotional dive once the storm cleared, but I needed her to come to me with it and not pry or suggest. I'd warned her it would come when we were at the ranch house because I didn't want her to feel like she was losing her mind for no reason. My hope was that she'd want to come to me with it.

Because it was the middle of the night, we'd gone to the house Grey rented for everyone and sat in the garden. He told me he'd chosen it because she liked sitting outside a lot. I knew Hannah was doing what reminded her of home. Our parents always sat outside on the deck in the evenings if it was warm enough. When Hannah was little, she used to ask if it was time to sit outside as soon as dinner was over and cleaned up.

Hannah's eyes were tracking from side to side like she was watching something, but her brain was over-processing as she grew more upset. "I'm so tired," she squeaked quietly with tears hanging in her eyes.

I rubbed the top of her hand and waited to see if she'd continue and explain. Sometimes a prompt only made the pressure worsen.

"I'm suffering *all* the *time*... Suffering over hundreds of things at *once*... and I'm so tired."

I nodded with understanding. "Give me a list."

Her eyes grew tired, her shoulders relaxed, and she released a breath. "I barely know where to start... I'm suffering because my friend is hurt and I can't fix it. Tim was my friend. He was agoraphobic, but I can't tell you how many times he would fight his fear and come sit on the porch with me just to make sure I was okay. I lost my friend, it's killing me, but I feel like I'm not allowed to be upset. He wasn't my brother or this lifelong friend. And I know you're going to tell me that's crazy and I'm not thinking right, but..."

I shook my head. "I'm listening, not judging. How you feel is just *that*, and you have reasons for those feelings." Hannah had years of never being able to say anything; she needed someone she trusted to hear her and acknowledge her thoughts, not immediately correct her. For certain things, Hannah would require a direct answer or solution, but there was a whole lot more she'd have to be inconspicuously led to because she'd openly challenge a solution. She either felt responsible for Tim's death, or she truly didn't feel like she meant enough to him to justify grieving.

"A friend of mine in California died the night before my wedding. She was shot in her restaurant—not because she had to do with anything, but *simply* because she knew me. Anywhere I went, I tried to never let people get close to me. I knew it was dangerous for them.

Carol and Joe broke the rules. They were like parents to me, and I needed that so bad, but it cost Carol her *life*, and Joe the rest of his. He'll never be the same without her." Her chin quivered. "I shouldn't be *allowed* to grieve someone when I'm the reason they're dead."

"Did you know someone would hurt her?"

"No one has ever been safe for knowing me. I'm a walking time bomb with no clock. Henry didn't care who he hurt or killed, he wasn't capable of it, so if he simply didn't like the way someone looked, addressed him, whatever—he'd just pull his gun and shoot. If he killed them or injured them, he didn't care, just as long as they knew they'd irritated him. Allowing anyone to know me beyond a business transaction was a *death* sentence, and I've *always* known that. So, yes, I knew someone would hurt her."

She had me in a bit of a mental check. Not because I thought her logic was right, but because it was hard to refute without the typical verbiage of telling her it wasn't.

"I know this only adds to the powerlessness that you're already feeling, but Hannah, you were *powerless* to him. Tim and Carol were not within your power to save or you would've done it. Forgiving ourselves for what we can't control is incredibly hard, some people aren't ever able to achieve it, but I think you need to do your best to try."

Hannah's chin was quivering again.

I gave her some time to see if she'd say something, but she didn't, so I asked, "What's going through your mind right now?"

"I know... you're right, but... If I'm not responsible, then there's *nothing* for them. Tim and Carol have no one responsible for their death because Henry didn't *care*."

"Do you feel like someone needs to take account- ability by being guilt-ridden? I can't imagine any person wanting that for someone they cared about. Would you want Grey or Ryan to feel guilty if you had died?"

"Of course not, but they didn't do anything."

"Neither did you, Bean. You didn't hurt Tim and Carol, that was Henry and the people who worked for him. Listen..." I leaned forward to look at her because she was focused on the garden again. "You do not hold the role of gatekeeper and are not responsible for all occurrences in the world. You can only do what's within your own sphere of influence and reasonable knowing. Do you understand what I mean by that?"

She nodded, her bruised face looking even sadder. "I understand, but I still feel so guilty. They shouldn't have died... There's so many people that shouldn't have died." Her chest moved forward like she'd received a blow to the gut, and her face pitched up. Hannah's hand came up to cover her mouth and stifle a sob. I wanted to grab her in a tight hug the second it happened, but I knew she may not have wanted it.

Hannah took in a deep breath, forcing her emotions back down, and looked up toward the sky to let her eyes dry naturally.

"You should really let that out... As badly as it hurts, it's so much worse keeping it in."

She shook her head. "I can't... It triggers the depression, and I don't have time or space for it."

I didn't like her response, and I wanted to tell her to make time, but I couldn't. She needed to feel ready to grieve and she clearly wasn't.

The sliding glass door opened behind us, and I turned my head to see my dad and Grey coming out. While I'd had many suspicions about Grey, I couldn't find a reason to not like him. After he'd told me he didn't need to impress me, and showed every sign of meaning it, I was impressed. There was also the fact that Hannah just went calm around him. It was like watching her go from limited oxygen to breathing freely.

"Hey, Beautiful." Grey touched her cheek lightly as he smiled lovingly at her.

"Ryan kicked you out?" Hannah looked up at him like she was disappointed somehow.

"Yep. It's okay though. Harry's posted outside his door."

Hannah frowned. "Then where's Charlotte?"

He nodded toward the house. "She's inside." Grey looked at her again. "You up for a little bit, or have you been waiting for me?"

She shook her head and got up. "Not waiting, but I am ready for sleep."

"'Night, Bean," I told her quietly.

Hannah looked at me appreciatively. "Good night. Thanks for listening."

I nodded with a smile. "Any time."

She turned and took her cane from Grey. "Are those mom's cookies?"

I looked back to see my dad chewing and a cookie in his hand.

"Mm-hm." He pointed with his thumb over his shoulder toward the house. "Whole container in the kitchen for ya."

I chuckled quietly. "They were supposed to be all for you," I told her with a smile.

She narrowed her eyes at Dad as she walked up to him. "Eating your sweet little girl's cookies."

Dad put the remainder of his cookie in Hannah's mouth. "Guiltin' me like that over cookies ain't sweet, but ya sure are cute."

She took a bite and pulled the cookie away. "Eat my cookies again and I won't be so cute either."

The three of us laughed, then our dad tapped Hannah's nose. "Yeah, you will. You can't help bein' cute."

"Good night, Dad." She gave a polite nod with a smile. I'd noticed she didn't like people calling her pretty, cute, or beautiful. Hannah didn't seem to mind when Grey called her Beautiful as a pet name, but otherwise, she seemed almost irritated by it.

494

"Night-night, Sweet Girl. I love ya." He stepped forward to give her a careful hug around the shoulders and kissed the side of her forehead.

"I love you too."

Hannah and Grey walked inside, and my dad came around and sat next to me where Hannah had been.

"You wanna cookie?" He pulled two out of his jacket pocket.

I shook my head with a slight laugh. "You're terrible. She missed those cookies almost as bad as she missed us."

"Oh, you and I know your ma's makin' her more already."

"Doesn't matter. She loves those and you're mean."

He laughed and shook his head. "Alright, I'm a terrible person then. You want one or not?"

I laughed. "No."

"Good." He took a bite out of both cookies at the same time. "Just in case ya thought you were gonna change your mind," my dad said after he chewed.

I shook my head.

"She alright?"

I held up my shoulders. "Yes and no... I think she's having a harder time keeping composure than before, but that's not entirely bad... She's still scared, like Toby used to be." Hannah and Toby weren't allowed to show certain emotions without serious repercussions. "Too... I don't think she's accepted that it's over."

"Course not. She let that dumbass go." My dad shook his head. "Goddammit... I trust she knows what she's doin', but I don't trust *him*. Who's to say he ain't gonna come for her again?"

I shook my head. "According to Hannah, he never really wanted to in the first place."

"Yeah, what, he tell her that?" He raised an eyebrow at me. "It's a bunch of bullshit."

I held up my shoulders. "She hasn't been wrong

about much else."

"I think she's still brainwashed by him. She wadn't even the least bit scared or bothered when he walked in today. She looked relieved." He shook his head.

"Because she knows he's not out to kill her. Too, if he hadn't conditioned her the way he did, she would've been dead years ago. I'm not saying it's right, I'm certainly not defending him, but I do understand why he did it, and why she still lives by it."

"Well, ya need to get to work and start fixin' it. That girl is gonna keep throwin' herself on top of fires for the sake of everybody else, and she's been burned up enough." He took another bite of a cookie.

"It's not that simple... She's not ready to accept that it's even over. That alone is gonna take a while. Hannah has to feel safe in her life again, then she'll start to realize that her systems aren't serving her anymore. It took sixteen years to create the damage, it's gonna take even longer for her to be able to face it and repair what she can."

He let out a huff. "I'm too tired for this conversation."

I nodded and got up to offer him a hand. "I'm just tired."

"That too." He took my hand, and I pulled him up to his feet.

We went inside and there was a young blonde girl about Hannah's age in the kitchen. Her resemblance to Grey was uncanny.

"Miss Charlotte, this here is my son, Ben. Hannah's brother," my dad said to her.

Charlotte appeared to force a smile. Her blue eyes were red-rimmed and her face was puffy like she'd been crying. "Good to meet you." She reached a hand over the counter.

"You too." I gave a polite smile back and stepped closer to shake her hand.

"Your sister is a wonderful girl. I'm so sorry for all

my f—" She stopped herself, and itched the side of her head like she was pained and confused by a thought. "He's not my father, I guess, but I'm sorry for what Alex did to Hannah. I *really* didn't know."

I gave her a warm and sincere smile. "It's not yours to apologize for, but I appreciate the sentiment." Her English was surprisingly clear, so I hoped I wasn't throwing an unknown word her way.

"If you're lookin' for somethin' to eat, there's makin's for a sandwich in the fridge," my dad offered.

Charlotte shook her head. "No, thank you. I was looking for tea. Hannah said there was some in here."

"Oh, it's up here." I walked around the counter to the cupboard above the range. "Looks like there's mint, black, green, or hibiscus."

"Mint, please."

I grabbed it down for her.

"Well, I'm off to bed. You kids have a good night." My dad gave a nod.

"You too, Mr. Lawrence." Charlotte forced another smile.

"Night, Dad. Love you."

"I love ya too, son." He gave a smile like he was proud of me, but he usually did when we were on peaceable terms. Now that Hannah was back, he was more lighthearted again.

"I know you don't know me, and it's not really my business to ask, but are you okay? I imagine it's been a very long and difficult twenty-four hours." I looked at Charlotte empathetically after lighting the burner.

She shook her head. "You're kind for asking, but..." Charlotte fidgeted with the box of tea in her hands, "I think I'd be crying to the wrong people." She looked up and forced another smile, looking exactly like Grey.

I shook my head. "You wouldn't be. As it was told to me, you didn't know what Alex or Henry were doing, you were also taken and lied to about it, and if Alex wasn't a terrible father to you, then I'd imagine part of you might be upset over his death."

As soon as I mentioned death, Charlotte seemed to struggle a little more. "But he was a liar, a murderer, and horrible to other people. He doesn't deserve to be missed."

I nodded once, understanding what she was trying to convey and convince herself of. "You might be right, except you deserve to miss what you lost. He was the only father you knew, you probably had good memories with him, and loved him. While Alex may not have deserved it, you do. Those things ended and you're allowed to miss them."

Charlotte's kind face pinched up with tears and she covered her mouth to quiet a sob. "I'm sorry." She turned her head off to the side and wiped her tears away.

"Don't be sorry. I didn't mean to make you cry; I meant to let you know it's okay to grieve your losses without being afraid of hurting someone else's feelings around here. I'm not so sure about Grey, but the rest of us understand. My dad's brother, Patty, was part of it. While I never liked him, my dad once loved him, so did Hannah... It's incredibly hard to just stop caring about someone you love."

Charlotte shook her head. "I don't love him, I'm angry."

I nodded gently. "You're angry because you did once. If he was no one to you, you'd think he was an ass for what he did, but you wouldn't feel so hurt and angry."

She seemed to chew on that for a second. "You're very smart."

I smiled. "I have an advantage. I'm a psychologist."

"Psychologe? A doctor?"

I laughed a little. "Is that how you say it in German? It sounds far less intimidating than in English somehow."

Charlotte nodded. "Sy-show-low-guh. This is the masculine name. For female, it would end in 'in'. I, N."

"Hm. Cool."

"What is?" Grey came into the kitchen.

"I was telling Ben how to say psychologe." Charlotte smiled.

Grey gave an upward nod, then asked her something quietly in German.

Charlotte winced a little and pushed her hand downward as if to suppress something. "Please, I don't like to speak German when someone can't understand. It's not polite. I'm okay."

He nodded again. "You're right." He looked at me. "Can I talk to you for a minute?"

I pushed away from the counter and followed him to the dining room at the front of the house.

"I'm not trying to start anything, but I need to know if you said something to Bex. She's out of it—like sitting on the bed with her head between her knees, shaking, and completely unresponsive to sound or touch."

I shook my head. "No. Nothing of consequence. I know she was extremely upset when she left Ryan's room, that's why we came here. I promised her all of our conversations would stay between her and I, but she's likely trying to stop and process the overload she's been through. Rest and low stress will probably help, but I can try to talk to her again if you're really worried."

He seemed dismayed by my answer and shook his head. "Maybe in the morning if there's no improvement. Thanks." He shoved his hand through his hair. "Was Charlotte crying again?"

I nodded. "Yeah. She feels guilty for being upset that Alex died, and I told her she shouldn't. As hard as it is for us to make the separation to look at it empathetically, she lost the person she knew as her dad."

Grey nodded. "You're right... it's hard to look at it empathetically." He shook his head. "I need to go back. Bex won't be able to sleep otherwise."

"Yeah. Before you go, I do have a question. I don't

know if you've asked her or if she's mentioned it, but do you know what she prefers to be called?"

"I did ask, she wants to keep the name Bex because Hannah is someone else to her, but for people who already know her as Hannah, she doesn't plan to ask anyone to change it."

I nodded once. "Okay. Thanks."

Chapter 43

Bexley

"Oh, Mom..." Gracie looked at me with a broken-hearted pout. "Are you okay?"

I smiled at her lovingly and opened my arms to her. "I'm okay, sweetie."

"I don't want to hurt you if I hug you." She looked me over, seeming like she might cry.

I shook my head. "You won't. I look worse than I am, I promise."

Grace sat beside me and was careful to hug me.

"I missed you, pretty girl," I whispered.

"I missed you too. Are you sure I'm not hurting you?"

"I'm sure. It's just my face and my one leg, and it really isn't that bad." I hugged her a little tighter.

"What happened to you?" She pulled away and looked at me with the same saddened face. I finally understood what everyone meant about my sad face because Grace's pout was breaking my heart.

"I'll tell you about it another day when you're older."

I smiled at her.

"Hannah," Toby shook his head, "I don't do that with her. We're honest about things." He looked at Grace. "The man who hurt Mom and me when we were kids, he found your mom again, and he hurt her."

Grace looked at him fearfully.

I rubbed the top of her hand. "He did, but the good news is, we don't have to worry about him anymore."

"Oh... Was it Patty?" She looked between Toby and I for an answer.

"No. Patty wouldn't do this, it was Henry." I combed my nails through her hair. "They're gone now, and they can't hurt us ever again. Okay?"

Grace didn't look entirely convinced but nodded. "Okay." She leaned in for another hug. "I'm glad you're okay."

"Me too. And I'm glad I get to spend more than a day with you." I squished her and kissed the top of her head. "Why don't you go find Grey and ask him to show you where your room is."

"Okay." She got up and walked around the couch.

Toby sat next to me and we hugged each other immediately without a word. The last couple weeks without him had been some of the worst because no one could understand but Toby. Neither of us thought I would ever live to see the day when Henry was no longer a threat to my life. The moment almost felt sad instead of happy. It had nothing to do with those who died in the process, but I felt a grief I couldn't explain.

As much as I didn't want to, I pulled back to look at Toby and started signing to him. I had to figure out how to find out more about Cynthia. Helen *hated* her. She used to talk about Henry's sister being nearly as bad as he was. Helen wished his entire family had died in the fire because they were horrible people who ruined her life over and over again. She would plead with Patty to call Alex and make him believe her.

Toby looked over when I was explaining what I could because Grey and Grace were walking by. He pushed my hands down to keep Grace from seeing something, then looked at me when they were both upstairs.

"Do you know where Patty is?" Toby asked quietly.

I shook my head. "I had to let him go. Everyone was there and wouldn't leave me alone with him to talk, and Ryan was severely injured. So, I didn't have time either. He was staying at my parents' ranch house, but I don't think he'll go back there because it's the first place my dad will look."

Toby nodded. "What about the house he grew up in?"

I shook my head. "Too obvious. My dad won't admit it, but I'm almost dead sure he knew Patty was out this whole time. Roger, Grey's father, was the one who helped him get out to keep me safe."

"Then we should ask *him*." Toby looked around cautiously for a second. "These guys have too much money and power to just let Patty walk free with no insurance or backup plan."

I rubbed my forehead. "Of course. I should've thought of that. I'm sorry."

Toby touched my arm to get my attention, then shook his head. "Don't be sorry. You've been operating on overdrive for months now."

I picked up my phone because it vibrated. Ryan was awake and couldn't find the refills on his medications Grey picked up.

"Come with me. I want you to meet Ryan." I slid myself to the edge of the couch to get up carefully, but Toby was already up and helping me.

We went to the kitchen to grab the pharmacy bag, then down the hall to what was supposed to be our workout room. Grey had the movers come back, clear out the room, then set up a bed and nightstand for Ryan. He was staying with us while he recovered, then moving into our old house because he didn't want to go back to his house without Tim. Currently, my family was staying in our old house while they were in Seattle because I couldn't handle having so many people in our house with no break from it. If it'd been just my parents and siblings, it would have been okay, but the kids made it too much.

I knocked on the door and opened it. Ryan was sitting up on the mound of pillows that kept him propped enough to keep his ribs from hurting so badly while he slept.

"Hey, Toby's here. Is it okay if he comes in for a minute?" I asked Ryan before we both just walked in on him.

"Yeah." Ryan pushed the button on the remote to make the blinds raise.

"I told Grey not to bring these in while you were asleep." I held the bag out to Ryan.

"I appreciate it. That's probably the most decent I've slept in weeks."

I nodded with a partial smile. "I told you the weighted blanket helps." I angled myself so I was partially facing Toby. "Ryan, this is Toby. Toby, this is Ryan."

Toby stepped forward and reached out a hand. "It's nice to finally meet you. Thank you for everything you've done."

Ryan shook Toby's hand with a single nod. "Yeah. Glad I could help." I already knew Toby hadn't understood him because Ryan was mumbling and too quiet, so I signed for Toby.

"Would you mind if I used you for some thoughts?" I asked Ryan.

"It's better than sitting here doing nothing." He handed me a pill bottle. "Can you get this? My wrists are throbbing."

I took the bottle and opened it.

"Did he hang your wrists with cable?" Toby asked.

Ryan nodded, taking the bottle back from me.

"It's worse than chain. If you stretch out your pinkies

504

and thumbs, make a Y with your hand, extend them as far as you can, rotate them, then move them side to side, it'll help. It hurts like hell the first few times, but it helps break up the atrophy better." Toby glanced at me, almost like he wasn't sure he was supposed to say anything.

Ryan raised his eyebrows, seeming a little surprised somehow. "Thanks. I'll do anything that helps. I'm sick of asking for help for everything."

I sat on the side of the bed. "It's good for you to be humbled once in a while." I gave a small smile.

He raised an eyebrow with a flat expression. "What do you want, Maslen?"

"I need to find Patty. Roger is the one who helped him escape prison, do you think he'd be keeping tabs on him?"

Ryan frowned. "How do you know that?"

"Roger told me at the wedding."

His eyebrows went straight up. "And you didn't tell me?"

"No. Do you think he'd keep close tabs on Patty or not?"

He let out a huff of frustration. "Yeah, I'd be surprised if he didn't."

I nodded once. "And if Roger were to hide someone from Cynthia in Seattle, where would one look?"

Ryan shook his head. "I'm not letting you go off on your own."

"You're laid up in bed, and I'm not." I directed a hand at Toby.

"No offense," Ryan looked from Toby to me, "Toby going with you isn't good enough. You go with Grey, your dad, or Ben too. Hell, take Harry and Casey with Toby. I'm not telling you unless you promise me you bring two additional people who can kick his ass."

I could still make it work, so I nodded. "Okay, I promise."

"And no one sits in the car while you go in." I was

given another flat expression because Ryan knew me too well.

"I will have two additional people within a five-foot radius of me at all times, I promise."

Ryan looked at Toby expectantly.

He nodded. "I'll make her keep her word."

"The most likely place is Willum's."

"Really? I don't think Willum would agree to that." It seemed like a far stretch.

"Cynthia isn't allowed over there because Willum doesn't like her, there's security, and it'd be the last place anyone looked. If he's not there, then he's probably on the seventeenth floor of tower two at MWM. It's been unexplainably vacant since before you got here."

"And if those are a bust?" I asked.

"Then I'd talk to Roger because it'd be a needle in a haystack. He owns twenty percent of the city. What are you trying to find him for? I mean, I understand before, but not now. Henry's dead. The pig needs to be put back in his pen." Ryan put a handful of pills in his mouth and chased them with water.

"Because I need information from him about Cynthia and I can't go to Tennessee with the FBI watching me."

He raised his eyebrows. "You could if you told them where the bodies are buried."

I let out a breath and shook my head. "They're not gonna let me go off in the woods by myself while they're there. And the field I have to go to, I don't want anyone going there."

Ryan seemed confused. "If you're gonna dig up evidence you're just going to hand over, I don't understand why it would be an issue."

I itched at a pin in my hair trying to find a delicate selection of words.

"The second field she's talking about is where the two babies are. Hannah doesn't want anyone disturbing them," Toby said quietly.

"Oh. I'm sorry, Maslen. I didn't think about it. I thought that was maybe why you didn't want them digging around out there to begin with." Ryan pulled back the corner of his mouth with an apologetic expression.

I shook my head. "No... I'm going to bring them out to the first field eventually, I just... need some time."

He nodded. "I'm not judging, and they can wait or find their way through the traps themselves. It was just a thought."

I nodded. "I know."

"When are you planning on going to find Patty?"

"Now. I'm gonna tell Grey, but tell everyone else Toby and I are going for a drive to talk." I picked up Ryan's laptop and the book he was reading from the nightstand and put them on the bed next to him. "Do you need anything before I go, or while I'm out?"

"If you have time, can you stop at my house? I'll text you the list."

I nodded. "Sure. I don't imagine we'll be more than an hour or two."

Ryan held out his wrist. "Don't forget to bring someone."

I nodded again and bumped his wrist. "I know."

———※◈◈※———

"Well hiya, Girly." Willum smiled at me. "What do I owe this visit?" He set his book down on the table next to the couch he always sat on when he was reading in his study. "And who are these two?"

I smiled at him. "This is my brother, Ben, and my friend Toby."

"Oh. Well, I'm not quite put together for company. You boys will have to excuse an old man." Willum got up and grabbed his cane.

"I apologize for the unannounced visit. Roger told me he was the one to turn a certain someone loose, and I was wondering if that person might be *here* since it'd be about the last place someone would suspect."

Willum chuckled and reached his hand out to Ben. "This girl is too smart for her britches. Good to meet you, boy. I'm Willum, but everybody who's anybody calls me Pops."

Ben smiled. "It's nice to meet you, Sir."

Willum looked at Toby without a smile, then looked at me expectantly with raised eyebrows. "And before I shake hands with this one, I want you to look me in the eye and tell me why I shouldn't have Frank drop-kick him."

I mirrored his expression. "Because he means every bit as much to me as Grey and Ryan. If you're rude to him again, you'll wish you were only drop-kicked."

Willum smirked, then laughed. "Alright, Girly. I'll trust your word." He looked at Toby. "My apologies, young man. This little lady is the most forgiving-to-a-fault person I've ever met, so I'm wary of whom she chooses to trust at times."

Toby gave a nod as he shook Willum's hand, but I could see that he was still hurt. It made me sick that no one saw Toby for the hero he was.

"Your reason wasn't an excuse to be rude. You could've greeted him the same as anyone else and addressed me in private. I hope—"

"Hannah." Toby put a hand against the back of my arm as he interrupted me. "It's okay. Let it go."

"No," Willum shook his head and looked at me, "she's right. It was rude, sweetheart. I'm sorry to both of you. I have no business judging a situation I don't know anything about, and I'm terribly sorry." He looked at me meaningfully, then Toby after I nodded.

"Thank you, Sir," Toby said quietly.

"Alright." Willum took a deep breath. "Now, say I know where this person you're looking for is, what do you want with him?"

I glanced at Larry and Frank over by the door because I didn't know what either of them did or didn't know, which meant I needed to choose words carefully. "I need to get information from him, and if he doesn't have it, I need to send him to obtain it. Doing it myself is too much of a risk because the FBI and someone else could find out."

He took another deep breath with a nod as he seemed to mull my words over. "Okay. I'm assuming this other someone is the one Roger suspects."

I nodded.

He nodded again. "And you've considered how this may affect Grey?"

"That's why I need to speak to *him*. I don't know how this will affect any of us until I know everything there is to know. Grey will be made aware of whatever I learn, and the decision will be ours."

Willum shook his head. "I think you misunderstood what Roger was asking, Girly. You can't let Grey make a decision like that, it'll destroy him. I know you wanna do the right thing here, and I respect the hell out of that, but... think about it with the shoe on the other foot. Could you choose between him and a person of the same nature to you?"

Thinking about turning my mother in was a form of torture I couldn't explain. I loved her more than I could express to *anyone*, and time had only made that love stronger.

"There's a distinct difference between a villainous person and a person who's done villainous things. We *will* respect your right to choose, with no animosity whatsoever—you have my word on that—but I beg of you to treat this as if it were your own beloved. Do you understand what I'm getting at?" Willum was looking at me with an almost saddened expression.

I nodded. "I understand. This is about risk, not vengeance or justice, I assure you."

"Very well then. Frank will see you to where you're going, and he's not to leave your side." He looked over at

Frank. "You hear that? One eye on her, and one eye on *him* at all times. You'll lose more than your job if anything happens to these three."

Frank nodded. "Yes, Sir."

"Alright. Off with ya's. I got my reading and a nap to get to. Tell Sunny I'll be by your house tomorrow like I'm supposed to be. That is, unless I don't wake up from my nap, of course."

I shook my head with a smile because it was typical of Willum to make jokes about dying in his sleep. "Thank you, Willum. I appreciate your help and the perspective."

He gave a smile back. "Anytime, Girly. Just be sure these types of visits don't become regular, someone might notice."

I nodded. "I know. Thank you." I turned and walked with Ben and Toby toward Frank.

"It's been a while since I've seen you, Mrs. Maslen. How was the wedding?" Frank asked with a kind smile as he pulled the door closed behind us.

"A few glimmering moments, but otherwise a regular Maslen affair. How was your vacation with Nancy and the kids?" I followed him down the hall.

Frank was incredibly nice, just like Harry. He was usually present for bigger events, but he'd been on vacation with his family.

"It was great. If Grey hasn't taken you to Bali yet, put it on your list."

I chuckled a little. "He's already planning on it. And I'd really prefer if you still called me Bex or Bexley."

"Of course. If I'm being honest, I wasn't sure which first name you might prefer to go by, now that the cat is partially exposed."

I nodded. "I figured. I still prefer my chosen name. But those who already knew me as Hannah can continue to call me that."

Ben chuckled a little. "I've been too afraid to ask. I love your name too much to call you anything else."

I smiled at him. "I know. You are the only reason I'm not asking everyone to adapt to my new name." Ben was the one who suggested my name to our parents after I was born, and he'd always been proud of it. I didn't have the heart to ask him to forsake that by calling me Bexley.

"You could call her B, like Grey does. Short for Beans." Toby chuckled a little.

I held up a finger. "No one is allowed to call me that but Grey."

"And your security team," Frank reminded.

"Grudgingly," I agreed.

He laughed.

"Why his security team? I don't get it." Ben looked at me with a questioning smile.

"They call me Queen Bee, or the queen. Grey thought it was a clever code name, but it's ridiculous." I shook my head with a quiet sigh.

"And Harry, his head of security, calls her Miss B, which is personally my favorite." Frank chuckled and pointed to another hallway down to the left.

"That one I do like. Willum calls me Girly, Roger will only refer to me as Bexley or 'my dear', Sam calls me Bexy, and Ryan calls me Maslen." I shook my head. "At this rate, I think I have more names than I can keep up with."

"Yeah, and I call you Beans, Dad calls you Sweet Girl, Mom calls you Baby, and Em calls you Banana. I think Toby's the only one without a nickname for you." Ben laughed a little.

"Nope. He's got one too." I looked at Toby.

He smiled at me and signed the word "sweetheart" by tapping the tips of his four fingers on his chin, pulling downward twice. That was the sign he'd given me for my name in Sign Language.

"I didn't know that." Ben looked at him almost as if he'd lied about something.

Toby shrugged. "It's between me and Hannah."

Frank stopped at the last bedroom door before the backdoor that went out to the car stables. The building used to be for horses, but Willum loved his old collector cars.

I took Toby's arm because my heart was starting to pound. Facing Patty was still painfully terrifying, just not as bad as facing Henry.

"Do you need a minute?" Ben asked in a whisper.

Frank stopped his hand before he knocked and looked at me.

I shook my head. "I'm okay." My head was spinning, making me feel like I might fall sideways, but I had Toby's arm for at least a minute. "Frank, I haven't been in this room before. Is there a door to the outside like the others?" I kept my voice at a whisper.

He nodded, seeming confused.

"Then I need you to go in first and open the door for me. Stand there near the door the entire time, but don't block it. Just like my security, if something happens, stay beside me, never behind me. My brother or Toby are the only ones allowed to follow behind."

Frank nodded. "Understood."

"Go ahead." I took in a breath, reminding myself to be Hannah and not Bexley. My confidence was too shaky, so I needed to stop having emotions or fear. I let my eyes close, took another deep breath, and opened them.

Chapter 44

Bexley

"Mr. Lawrence, you have visitors," Frank said coldly as he walked in ahead of us. He went straight to the doors and opened them as I'd asked. It wasn't until they were fully ajar that I walked in with Ben and Toby.

Patty's eyebrows raised a little as he looked up from his computer and saw it was me. "You ain't supposed to know I'm here," he said quietly as he closed the lid of the laptop.

"You haven't given me very much choice but to find you." I walked forward, though I felt like I was physically forcing my body to do so. He was sitting at a small table, but it was being used as a desk and that made me feel like a child again. "Will you please move from the table? I'd like to stand near the open doors." I spoke plainly because it was hard to maintain anything that didn't sound cowardice.

Patty looked at me calmly, then set his pen down and stood. "You can have a seat if you'd like." He directed a hand toward the couch and chairs.

I shook my head walking forward toward the doors. Frank moved to the other side of the doorway when he realized he'd be behind me if he stayed where he was. I turned to face the rest of the room. Toby and Ben stood in front of the couch with hateful stares toward Patty.

"Did you always know about Catrine?" I asked stiffly. Using Cynthia's real name was a way for me to ask without Frank knowing whom I was speaking of.

Patty nodded. "Yeah." He reached up and itched the top of his head as he looked toward the floor. "Back when I met Helen in the hospital, Catrine'd come'n visited her." He shook his head. "She started hollerin' at the orderlies to get Catrine away from her. She was sayin' 'that's Catrine! She's Catrine, get her away from me! She's gonna kill me.'"

"I've heard it all from *her*," I reminded with a hint of bitterness. "And you saw her there? Catrine?"

Patty nodded. "Yeah. But that wadn't the name she signed in with, if you're catchin' my drift."

I nodded. "Tell me what I need to know."

He took in a deep breath. "You gotta know why I started all this *first*. I found out who you'd been hangin' round, and I had to do somethin'. Ben came'n saw me there in prison, I told 'im 'bout the flash drive. I'm gettin' back to my cell, and I'm told I got another visitor. Some guy is tellin' me *you* sent 'im to go fetch what was in that house. I sure didn't trust 'im 'til he showed me a picture of you with that friend of yours. So, I told 'im I *would*, if he gave me his name."

"Brae," I mumbled in conclusion.

Patty nodded. "That's right. Looks just like his old man. Couple a computer clicks, found he was hangin' round that Maslen boy, then there ya were... I called up Roger, cause I already knew Roger wadn't ever wantin' to be part of all it. I told 'im I had to keep ya safe and get rid of anybody 'for you and his boy got *killed*." He let out a breath. "I just don't know what you were *thinkin'* Darlin'. I told ya to *hide*, not go and put yourself in front of public cameras under a different *name*. You were playin' with fire and I told ya, you don't know who's out there in the world."

"Stop." Ben's voice boomed threateningly.

I looked at him feeling surprised because I didn't know what Patty might've done wrong.

"You do not lecture her or perpetuate your need to assert dominance by shaming her. Facts. You state the facts only. Your personal opinions or feelings will not be spoken to her. I will kill you right here and not a damn person in this house will stop me." Ben sounded like our dad, and it was hard not to smile.

Patty nodded and had a slight wince as he held up a hand and looked at the floor again. "You're right. Eyes on the floor and facts."

I looked at Ben again because I was both confused and stunned. Had Ben been doing psychological work with Patty previously? How had he picked up on something so subtle? Why did Patty just submit like that? What else did I miss? I didn't see what Patty was doing until Ben stated it.

"I called Roger, told 'im 'bout your friend Brae, told 'im what that boy was there for, and told 'im I needed out so I could help ya stay safe when everybody went down. Next thing I know, I'm gettin' attacked outside my cell. I found out Mr. Brae wadn't workin' for you. You were off makin' all your own plans cause you were scared, so I knew ya didn't know you were up to your nose in shit." Patty looked at me.

"Eyes," Ben warned sharply.

Patty nodded once, looking down.

"What I want to know is if Catrine knowingly participated in her family's business," I said quietly but with the same even tone. Ben's loud snaps made me feel like I had to counter with a quieter volume to restore the balance in the room.

"Yes. She knew what she was doin' when she entered the office. She's the one who started it. Henry was doin' stuff, gettin' in trouble with the law, and she got real good at cleanin' it up. She wadn't but seventeen when that 'cleanin' up' involved her workin' for the original founders of the operation. Henry found out, killed those guys, and he and Catrine took it all over. He liked what he liked, and she liked the money. The Vaughters were broke at that point. Alex joined in for the money, took over his father's bank. They ran like that 'til they could get their hands on a bigger bank."

"What do I do?" This time I sounded like a child because I felt entirely thrown. He'd just told me Cynthia not only knew about it all, but she'd started it.

"Why did Alex take from Catrine then?" Toby asked.

"Because she started keepin' all the money. She had all the money she wanted without the business. Catrine was tryin' to starve the rest of 'em out to let the business die. She's as selfish as they come. She got a new name, she got all the money to back it up, and she put herself in a place where she thought Henry couldn't come after her. She was mad at 'im for ruinin' their lives and gettin' their parents killed. Helen did set that fire that killed the Okcerts. She didn't set the fire that killed her husband and kids."

"Catrine did?" I couldn't believe it.

Patty nodded. "Yeah. Henry raped Helen, and Catrine was just terrible to her, so Helen set the house on fire. Henry and Catrine survived, Catrine couldn't take her revenge and ended up broke and orphaned, but she was the youngest with the longest to wait. Helen got married, had the twins, and Catrine struck. After Catrine started keepin' all the money, Alex struck back and took her kid."

I shook my head. My god... "It was an eye for an eye."

"'Til everyone is blind."

I rubbed my forehead. "So, what do I do?"

"Let me handle it. That's what I'm still doin' here."

"Okay. How long is this gonna take, and what should I be careful or aware of?"

He shook his head. "Just keep watchin' your back. Don't think you're safe. 'Bout a week, this'll be over." He gave a single nod.

I didn't like his answer, but I could risk exposing him more than I had. He was my ally against a ruthless woman who'd stop at nothing to take what she believed was hers.

"There's one thing I don't understand though, if there's no business and she has what was taken from her, then why would there still be an issue? If she's willing to live and let go, then I'd prefer it."

"She already made an attempt on your life once. You hold the potential to take away everythin' she's worked for." He nodded once. "She ain't gonna let ya be, even if ya left here and didn't stay with your husband."

"What if I told him everything and had him talk to her and handle it? She listens to him." He'd know I was talking about Grey.

"Darlin'... you got no reason to trust me, but ya got no choice. It's past time this stopped." Patty itched the top of his head.

"I'm not going to trust you, but I'm also not gonna stop you until I think you're about to overstep. I'll be very clear that I don't want any more people dead unnecessarily." I looked at Toby and Ben, nodding them toward the door. As soon as they started walking, I did too.

"Hannah, it's less than water to ya, I know, but I'm sorry. None of this should've—"

"Stop," Ben snapped again. "Hannah, come on." He held out his hand to wave me toward the door.

I shook my head and turned to face Patty. "I think if you had to do it over again, you would only change certain things, but not that it happened. You destroyed countless lives and contributed to the destruction of countless more. What's worse is you made me contribute as well. You might be capable of remorse, but I don't believe you're capable of understanding the very real suffering you inflicted. You can't apologize for that. You couldn't even begin to conceptualize it. If you were capable of something requiring so much responsibility, you would end yourself after just Rebecca. I don't need to forgive you. Forgiving you is as much a waste of my time as living in that piece of shit house with you. My forgiveness is for myself. I hold it for me, because you are a person who's lost the luxury of being capable of forgiving yourself. You're a special kind of monster—one who's committed too many unforgivable acts. You have to live with it, it's your punishment for what you took. I don't believe in god, but I wish I could so I could pray for pathetic weaknesses such as you to stop existing in the world. I would pray for him to send souls like yours straight to hell without ever passing through this earth." I turned and walked out the door.

Frank followed us to the car and opened the door for me. "Please let me tell Willum. I'm not allowed to tell him any part of your exchange because it was his orders, but let me just tell him you gave that creep one hell of a speech."

I raised my eyebrows. "My words aren't something to boast over. Too many people died who never got to say them, and I've suffered for sixteen years to be able to say them." I shook my head. "I didn't want to suffer and grow to be the person who said them, I would've liked to have stayed home with my family... grow up never knowing what evil really lives in this world." I got in the car and pulled the door closed because I didn't want to hear whatever apology he might utter. He didn't need to apologize for something he couldn't have understood, he just needed someone to tell him so he could.

"You *have* to feel a little better after *that*," Ben turned his head to look back at me.

I shook my head. "It doesn't make it all go away... Things like that in there are just temporary... Temporarily said, temporarily considered, and temporarily remembered. It changes nothing."

Toby pulled forward around the roundabout and toward the end of the gate. I expected him to say something, but he didn't. His hands were shaking, there was a sheen of sweat on his forehead, and the veins in his neck were bulged. Just a mile away from Willum's house, he stopped on the side of the road, got out of the car, and threw up in the ditch. When it seemed like he was done, I got out with the bottle of water from my purse and a pack of tissues. He was struggling to breathe while he kept a hand on the back of the car to stabilize himself.

"I'm sorry," Toby rasped as he took the water.

"For puking? I think we've done worse." I let him rinse his mouth before holding out a tissue.

Toby shook his head and signed that he couldn't stop hearing the screaming. Anyone else would've asked what he was talking about, but I didn't have to. Seeing Patty mixed up our minds. We were so used to being in a powerless position in front of him, used to the manic screaming, used to having something thrown at us as he yelled... the list would go on forever. He didn't hear as much of the screaming as I did because his implants didn't always have batteries, but he was still affected by the times they did.

"The person who caused him to act that way is dead. It doesn't mean he isn't still capable, but it means we only have *him* to fight if it were to come to that. I'm not afraid of Patty because I know how to play his emotions." Maybe letting Toby think I had a handle on everything would reassure him enough to let him keep moving forward. It used to work that way, but things were different now.

Toby shook his head. "It's not about fearing him... it's remembering... I don't wanna remember anymore." His eyes stayed focused on the trees in front of us on the side of the road.

"Then look around yourself," Ben said quietly as he leaned against the back of the car. "The past only exists in your mind, so look at what's around you in the present." He crossed his arms loosely. "These trees are different, you have me, we have Hannah, you have the keys to a car that'll take you wherever you want to go. What you remember does not have the control to matter in this moment unless you let it."

I looked at Ben because I didn't like what he was telling Toby. "Just because something lives in the past doesn't mean it doesn't hurt now. You'd hit someone for telling you to get over what happened to me."

Ben shook his head. "I'm not telling anyone to get over it, I'm telling him to change the subject so it doesn't feel so overwhelming."

"He's right, Hannah." Toby leaned back against the car next to Ben.

I looked at Toby because I didn't understand.

"Listen, I'm not telling him how to feel. Toby's done a lot of work with me to overcome, you haven't yet. Just like two people could share a private joke, Toby and I share certain phrases or views that help him process things in the moment. I'm reminding him that his conscious mind is in control of his subconscious mind. A better analogy would be, Toby is driving the car, I'm just the GPS giving him step-by-step directions to help him get where he wants to go." Ben spoke calmly, but I could see he was concerned about me not understanding.

I crossed my arms. "I understand what you were doing, but I don't like it because you can't understand. Hearing something and experiencing it firsthand are different things. We can't always will something away because we want to."

Toby pulled me against his side. "Easy, Han. You don't have to snarl at every person who says something to me that you don't like." He chuckled a little. "We're okay, and I can speak for myself. Okay?"

I stood there still feeling irritated but tried to let it go with a deep breath in and out. "I wish Ryan was here," I said after a minute. "I need a cigarette."

Ben reached into his pocket, pulled out a pack of cigarettes and a lighter, and handed them to me.

I leaned forward as I took them. "You smoke?"

"Sometimes. And if you tell anyone, I'll tell Dad you were the one who broke that dog on his shelf in his office."

"And I'll tell Mom you were the one who mowed down her begonias." I pulled a cigarette out and lit it.

"How do you *remember* this shit," Ben laughed. "Seriously. The pettiest shit, and you remember."

I took a deep drag, enough to give me a temporary buzz, and let it out. "I was afraid to forget, so all I thought about was everything I remembered."

"Yeah, I guess..." He shook his head.

Toby held out his fingers for the cigarette so I passed it to him. "So, for the sake of a subject change, and something we need to talk about, what did you want to do about Grace?" He looked at me cautiously. "I know we discussed what would happen if something happened to me, but we haven't discussed what'll happen now that nothing is happening to either one of us."

I felt a little blindsided because I wasn't prepared for the conversation. "Um... to be honest, I haven't thought about it because I didn't expect to survive Henry."

He nodded. "I know. And I'm not saying anything has to change if you don't want it to. We can explain to her that you'll be in her life a little more, when you come for holidays or birthdays, but otherwise nothing changes. Or, if you *do* want more, I wanna talk about what that looks like."

"I want more," I nodded, "but I don't know how that's gonna work. I'm not in a position to be able to move, I don't want to take her from you, and I could never ask you to uproot your life. I think we'll just have to schedule visits because we can't just toss her back and forth."

Toby nodded. "We can do that. I just want to be clear that there's no pressure, and I'm not judging if you tell me you can't or don't want to. The only thing I'm asking is that you don't just disappear from her life."

I shook my head and took the cigarette back from him. "Will you please stop thinking that me giving her up meant I didn't want her? I never wanted to leave her behind, I didn't have a choice." I took another strong drag from the cigarette.

"I'm trying to be considerate, not offend you. I know you love her, and I'm not questioning that. All I'm saying is, I don't want you to feel trapped into something. I *did* choose to keep her. The second you were pregnant, I made that choice, but you had no choice in anything so I'm trying to give you that now. If you want the occasional visit, that's okay. If you want something more permanent and shared, then I'm willing to try to work that out. I'll sell my house and move up here if that's what it takes."

I rolled my eyes. "Yeah, Emily would go for *that*."

Toby leaned forward and looked at me with raised eyebrows. "This isn't about Emily, this is about Grace. Grace comes first and Emily knows that. She needs her mom, and Emily *would* never and *will* never be able to fill that spot. Stop being combative with me and tell me what you want because we," he moved his finger between us, "have a daughter together. Not me and Emily, you and me."

It didn't occur to me that I kept snapping at Toby anytime the conversation was about Grace. She was the touchiest subject I had because I loved her more than I could explain to anyone. Other people didn't have to explain their love for their child because they weren't forced to have them or die.

I took in a deep drag from the cigarette and looked at the trees because I felt like I was about to cry.

"Beans, you can say whatever is on your mind right now. Neither of us would ever judge you for what you're feeling. Being a parent is the hardest and most complicated part of life for anyone, myself included. I have days where I feel like I couldn't breathe without Ella, and I have other days where I wish she was someone else's kid because I can't handle it anymore." Ben reached his fingers over for the cigarette.

"I'm terrified of messing her up... I'm okay a lot of the time, but I still have days where..." I shook my head, unable to finish my words.

Toby turned and stood in front of me with an empathetic expression. "Me too. I have bad days all the time... There's days I can't even get out of bed to get her breakfast or take her to school. I'm not a bad parent for it, I'm just a person who deals with more than others. She understands that. She sees that life is hard and complicated. She sees that life and people aren't perfect. All Gracie needs to know is that she's loved, and that she's more important to us than anything else."

"And if ever you run into one of those days, and you need someone to come help with Grace, you can call any of us. Mom, Dad, me, Toby, Emily, we'll all drop everything and come help out." Ben reached over and took my hand. "You've got your family. It's a five-hour flight, and none of us will ever mind. Hell, if you want one of us there the first few times she visits, consider it done. We're all here to support you."

My brain still couldn't grasp that I had my family to lean on. I was so used to being alone, doing everything by myself, and the "all or nothing" mentality that it was hard to snap out of it.

I nodded. "You're right... I think I do need help for a little bit." I glanced at Ben. "I love her, and I don't want to fail her again."

Toby took my face in his hands. "You've never failed her... She's here, alive, and happy because of you, and I've never let her forget it. You saved us, and she's as proud about that as I am. She *loves* you, Hannah. She knows you sacrificed *everything* so she could have a good life, and she knows you'll never stop because that's who you are. I *told* her. I told her everything good about you."

I stared at Toby's eyes feeling like we were kids again. Even though he'd been in my life for the last few weeks, time felt like it'd driven a wedge between us that I didn't know how to remove. I was worried about being disloyal to Grey, ticking my sister off, or making Toby think I was still holding hope of the future we used to dream for ourselves.

"I need you in my life." The words blurted out of my mouth. "I need you and Grace, but not the way we..." I stopped myself because I was desperately trying not to cry.

Toby nodded. "I know... I don't think we really wanted it when we said it, I think we just wanted the freedom we knew came with that life... You're the love of my life, but not the way I love Emily or the way you love Grey. You're the sweet and caring girl that risked her life every day for me, you're the mother of our beautiful and loving daughter, you're the woman who just risked everything *again* to keep our daughter safe, so I love you, and not even *death* could stop it... You have me. You will *always* have me, and I will still keep that promise no matter what. I'll haunt you from beyond the grave when my day comes, because we stay together. Do you hear me?"

I nodded as my chin quivered. Toby pulled me into a tight but comforting hug. Leaving Toby had been every bit as hard as leaving Grace the day she was born. I'd spent years telling myself I'd done the right thing, but it'd never stopped hurting me. There was also the voice in my head telling me I still wasn't allowed to be anywhere near him, not because it was unsafe but because I felt undeserving of him.

"If no one understands us, we're not gonna ask them to," he whispered in my ear. "Only we know, and better us than the people we love. We don't want them to understand."

I nodded. "I know... I just feel unforgivable... for leaving. I left you and you wouldn't have done that."

Toby kissed my cheek. "I let you go, Sweetheart. I watched you leave the store, and I let you go because I already knew."

I pulled back to look at him to see if he was lying.

He traced my bangs back behind my ear. "You were wearing a blue dress and Patty's white jacket over it."

He couldn't have known that if he hadn't seen me...

"You're not unforgivable because you didn't do anything wrong... Hard doesn't make it wrong." He shook his head with tearful eyes.

Dammit...

My face pinched up and I stepped forward to put my face in his shoulder because I couldn't keep holding tears back. Pain kept coming in overwhelming waves and I was growing more tired every time it happened. In Germany, I couldn't even find the strength to move, let alone speak. It scared the hell out of Grey, but I was just fighting.

"It's okay... You're okay." Toby held the back of my head while holding me tightly in his arms. The horrible cries that came out were as physically painful as they were mentally relieving. It'd been nearly nine years since I'd allowed them. Toby was the only person I could trust with them because he was the only person I trusted to catch me as I fell.

Chapter 45

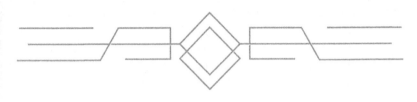

Grey

"Grey?" Grace walked down the long hall to my office.

"What's up, Ace?" I smiled at her.

"Someone is calling you." She held out my phone to me. I'd given it to her so she could shop for some of her favorite books to put in her room upstairs.

"Oh. Thank you." I took the phone and swiped to answer even though I didn't recognize the number. "Hello?" I lifted my shoulder to hold the phone because I needed to finish the email I was working on.

"Hi, this is Officer Lasloe with Washington State Patrol, is this Mr. Grey Maslen?"

My heart stopped. I looked at Grace and tried not to show it. "Yeah, one second." I moved the phone away a little. "Ace, can you go find your Papa and send him in here for me?" I smiled at her.

She nodded and turned.

I waited until she was down the hallway before I

resumed the phone call. "Yes, this is Grey. What's this about?"

"I was asked to call you by a Mister Ben Lawrence. He's currently on his way to St. Catharine's Hospital by ambulance. There was a hit-and-run accident and he said your wife was in the backseat and was captured by the two men who hit them. Given the state he's in, we're not entirely sure there was a third person in the vehicle with him and the other gentleman."

I coughed as soon as he said Bex had been taken because my body felt like it'd been hit. "She was in the car. Um—shit." What was I supposed to do or say? The FBI knew her identity, but the general population didn't. She didn't want everyone to know who she was.

"Okay. And her name is Bexley Maslen, correct?"

I stood up and looked around because I couldn't think. Sitting there felt like a hindrance, but standing didn't seem to help either.

"Sir? Mr. Lawrence lost consciousness before we could get more information, but he told me her name is Bexley Maslen, is that information correct?"

"Y-yes. Um... She was taken? Are you *sure*?"

"That's what Mr. Lawrence claims, yes. We haven't found anything in the backseat to indicate another person was in the car, but she may not have sustained injuries since it was a head-on collision. Can you give me a description of your wife? What she was wearing, height, age, hair color?"

"Um. S-she's five-seven, twenty-four, brown hair, and she was wearing a white skirt with a tan blouse. She has a small tattoo on her wrist of a triangle and a bunch of scars on her back." As I spoke, I felt like I wasn't in my body or the person blurting out words. "Um, I'm sorry. Don Lawrence, Ben's dad is here, you have to talk to him." I held out the phone to Don. "I have to call the FBI. Bex was taken. They were in an accident and Ben's on his way to the hospital. I don't know about Toby."

Toby, I had to ask about Toby. Grace was here and Bex would never forgive me if I let anything happen to him or didn't take care of him like the rest of her family. "Toby Anderson, he was in the car with them. Is he on the way to the hospital too?" I asked the officer as I looked at Don. His eyes were filled with fear.

"No. I'm sorry, but Mr. Anderson was killed upon impact."

I put the phone down and put my hands down on the desk because I wasn't sure I could stand on my own. My ears were ringing, my brain was firing in too many directions, and I felt like I was literally going to drop dead at any moment.

"Hello, this is Don Lawrence. I'm Ben's father and Toby's just about my son too. Will ya tell me again what happened?"

Ryan.

I walked around my desk, then ran through the house.

"Grey, honey, is everything okay?" Millie called when she saw me run past.

I couldn't answer her, my mind could only do one thing at a time, and in the moment that was running to the only person I knew could help me. Ryan was sitting up in bed with a book and looked at me with a frown after I burst in.

"She's gone. Someone took her. Toby's dead, Ben's hurt and on the way to the hospital, and the guys who hit their car took her. What should I do? Where do I even start? Do we tell the police her real name, do I call the FBI and just let them handle it? Did I already screw up by confirming that she was in the car? I can't. I can't lose her. We have to find her. We have to get her back because I can't lose her." I grabbed the collar of my shirt and pulled it away because I felt like it was choking me as I struggled to breathe.

"Stop. Just sit and calm down before you pass out."

Ryan picked up his phone from the nightstand. "Where were they?"

I shook my head. "I don't know. I don't know. Shit. I didn't ask."

"Okay, well, she was going to Pops' house then MWM, so did the state police call you or metro?"

"State." I sat down in the chair and put my head between my knees.

"Okay. I'm gonna call what's-his-face with the FBI, just calm down because panicking doesn't help her." Ryan didn't speak as harshly to me as he normally did. "What did they tell you?"

I shook my head. "They said there was no sign of her in the car. Ben told them she was in the back seat, a car hit them head-on, and two guys pulled her out of the car and took off. Toby's dead. That's all I know."

"Toby's dead?" Emily squeaked.

I looked over, not knowing she was standing there in the doorway.

"That's what Grey was told, but you have to keep yourself together." Ryan looked at her as he put his phone to his ear. "You can't say anything to Grace right now. Come in here and sit down for a minute. Grey, shut the door."

I realized that I had to pull myself together the way Bex would. She was always good at snapping out of her own head and into helping. I had to be and think like her if I had any chance of finding her, so I got up, closed the door, then hugged Emily as she let out a pained cry. Emily certainly wasn't my favorite out of Bex's family, but I could understand her loss because I was suffering my own.

"Hi, this is Ryan Brae. We just found out that Hannah was taken. Washington State Police are on the scene. Toby Anderson is dead, and Ben Lawrence is on his way to the hospital. I think they're probably going to take him to St. Catharine's because it's the closest." Ryan

looked at me. "Do you remember who you talked to?"

"Uh, Lasloe. Officer Lasloe."

Ryan repeated it back then started telling our contact at the FBI to investigate leads on my parents, Pops' house for Patty, and everything else he could think of. He told them we still wanted to conceal Bex's identity, if at all possible, but to put out her real name if it would truly help.

"Pops," I whispered. She'd gone there because she thought Patty was there; Pops would tell me whatever he knew if Bex was missing. He'd clearly been keeping lots of secrets lately, but I knew he'd still have more loyalty to me than anyone else. "I'm sorry, Emily." I rubbed her back. "I have to go make a call. Bex is missing. I have to try to find her. Just stay in here and sit with Ryan."

"Oh my god. This can't be happening again. You have to find her, we can't do this again, and I can't do it without Toby." She pulled away, trying her best to quit crying.

"Yeah. I can't do this without *her*, so..." I turned out the door and went into my room. Bex had burner phones in her closet still, and since Don had my phone, it was my only option. I dialed the number for Pops' house so I was sure to get an answer.

"Maslen residence, this is Frank."

"Frank," I let out a breath. "It's Grey. Bex has been taken, I need to talk to Pops."

"I'll find him. Taken? She was just here about thirty minutes ago."

I shoved my hand through my hair. "I know. What I need to know is if Patty is there. The FBI is going to be there probably within the hour."

"Yes. He's here. I'm telling you that because she's missing."

What!? "He's actually *there*? Right now?" I couldn't believe my Pops had in fact been harboring that shit-for-brains bastard.

"He's been staying here, yes. I'm walking to his room now to check, Sir."

"Yeah. Okay." I needed to think. "If he's there, I need to talk to him. He's probably the only person who can find her." I was thinking out loud because it was really the only way to think. Bex's favorite sweater was on the large ottoman in the middle of her closet. I picked it up and put it to my face to smell her perfume. The scent of her, and the possibility of losing the wonderful scent of her hair made me break down for just a minute. I truly didn't know what I'd do without her. There wasn't anything else in this world that could be taken from me and cause as much heartache. Even losing Sam wouldn't compare, and the thought felt like a crime against him.

"Oh shit. Search the property! He's gone!" Frank yelled. "Mr. Maslen, he's not here, Sir. I'll call you if we find him."

"Yes! Right away! I'm gonna tell the FBI to look for him in the area."

"Okay. I'll let your grandfather know." I could hear him running as he spoke.

"Yes. Thank you. Bye." I hung up quickly so Frank could do his job without distraction. My grandpa would likely call soon anyway.

I looked around at all the things I'd bought for Bex. Anything she ever gave a second glance to, I bought for her. She'd learned to stop looking twice, but I could always see the twinkle in her eye when she could see herself in a beautiful dress, a new pair of heels, or even in a car. It was such a privilege to me to buy her everything she could ever dream of. She didn't often smile when I handed her another gift, she'd frequently scold me for it, but she was always grateful, and nothing beat watching her feel like a normal person because she was wearing a skirt she loved. She relaxed behind the wheel of her car because driving brought her peace. The first bracelet I bought her became something to fidget with while she reminded herself she was safe around me... The things I bought her didn't make her feel rich or more beautiful like they would other people, they brought her away from her past. Little by little, by flowers, by a simple cup of ice cream, those things I bought her made her terrible childhood slip away so she could keep going forward... but it wasn't enough. I wasn't done giving that to her.

I got up and walked out into the living room. Millie was crying into Don's chest as he hugged her. She was the sweetest person and it broke my heart—more than seemed reasonable—to hear her cry.

Don cleared his throat quietly. "I told 'im he had to call the FBI, gave 'im the number, cause we just gotta hope they can handle it. I know Patty's gone and done it again. I knew I shoulda killed 'im the second Henry was dead." His face pinched up and he hid it in the top of Millie's head.

"I'm not sure you're right, but he is missing," I said quietly. "Where's Grace?"

Millie sniffed and stepped back from Don. "She's upstairs with the kids. God, I don't know how we're gonna tell her." She put her hand up to her head and let her face pinch but didn't let out the cry.

I wanted to tell them they should wait, but it wasn't my place. The only thing I could do was make sure they didn't have to tell Grace her mom was dead too.

"I'm going out to my parents' house. I'll call if I find something out." I grabbed my phone off the table near Don and Millie, then went out to the garage. I grabbed the keys for my Mercedes Guard just in case someone decided to come after me.

Pops called me on the way out to my parents' house. He lived on the same road as them, just a little further down. I wasn't prepared to see the site of the accident. The car Toby had arrived in was flipped upside down, and the front was smashed completely in. How

Ben had even managed to live was beyond me. The county coroner was putting Toby's body into the back of the van. If Bex did survive, I wasn't sure how she'd take Toby's death. Ben had already warned me that Toby was an essential part of her survival. He was the reason she kept herself alive.

I didn't stop to talk to the police because it was unlikely they knew anything more, and the FBI was already there questioning them and setting up. When I got to my parents' house, I found my parents in the back living room with Charlotte and Sam. I asked my dad to come talk to me, told him what happened, and told him my plan. My mother wasn't going to talk, we weren't going to cause a scene to make her talk, just to make her think I wasn't onto her so she wouldn't take extra precautions. Even though Patty was gone and he was a likely option, my gut told me my mother had something to do with it.

"Dad, stop! Just because they're related doesn't mean she was ever part of it!" I yelled after him as he marched back to the living room.

"Cynthia! Where is she!?" My dad's voice boomed so loudly it echoed from the ceiling.

Both Charlotte and Sam looked at me with worry and confusion, but my mom looked at my dad with a frown.

"Why are you yelling, Roger? Where's who?" She closed the photo album on her lap.

"Bexley! Someone's taken her and you're the only one left of those criminals. That girl has suffered enough, so where is she?" My dad's face was red, making his faked rage seem more believable.

"Dad, this is crazy. Mom has no reason to hurt Bex. It's not her, I just need help finding who it *is*." I stepped forward to look at him.

"Grey, your mother never liked her, and now that we have Charlotte back, there's no reason for your mother to allow Bexley to continue being here." He looked at her.

"What have you done with her?"

"Nothing! Of course I've done nothing. Roger, this is preposterous." My mom acting apathetically was how we knew she was lying. If and when she *hadn't* done something she was accused of, she'd become genuinely offended.

"Why don't you like Hannah?" Charlotte shook her head, appearing hurt. "She's the sweetest person and she saved me from terrible things. Her uncle came into my room in the middle of the night, and she stopped him by offering herself. She's a kind and wonderful person."

"No, Charlotte, my dad's being crazy. Mom would never hurt Bex, they just don't see eye to eye on everything," I explained quickly.

"Your mother tried to kill Bexley with star fruit!" My dad burst as he directed a hand out toward the patio where it happened. "Open your eyes, son."

"That's *insane!* Do you hear yourself? That was just an accident. Even if Mom knew who she was, she couldn't have known about Bex's allergy. Bex didn't even know," I defended. It was only then I realized what my dad had just stated wasn't a lie. Previously, I'd believed it was *him* but had forgotten about the incident the moment everything came out and I learned he was trying to help her.

"Both of you stop yelling." My mother stood. "Bexley goes off on her own all the time, I'm sure she'll return as she always does, but we'll help you search for her if you'd like."

"I *know* you have something to do with this, and I will prove it. When I do, I will ruin you far beyond what your psychopathic brother was even capable of." My dad glared at her with every ounce of hatred he had, but it was no act.

My mom raised an eyebrow. "It seems you've fallen in love with another one of your pets, Roger." She looked at me. "Grey, I assure you, I've done nothing to harm

Bexley. While I don't particularly care for the girl, I know you do, and I would like to see her home for your sake. I'm going to call some of my contacts to see if they're able to locate her." My mom glanced at my dad with an arched eyebrow and walked out of the room.

"Sam, I need you to come with me and help take care of Ryan," I said calmly.

"Yeah. I'll grab my stuff."

"May I come with you?" Charlotte asked.

I put a finger to my lips. "No, it's best if you stay here at Mom and Dad's. It's safer."

She glanced between me and our dad. "Okay..."

"Trust only Dad," I whispered to her.

She nodded. Charlotte and I already had an understanding, and because I knew how loyal to Bex she was, I trusted her not to betray me.

"I'm going to make some calls myself," my dad said quietly before he waved Charlotte to come with him.

I walked back to the kitchen to find my mom. She didn't start speaking until I walked into the kitchen, and pretended to be in the middle of a conversation.

"That's right. You'll need to check all highways and back roads in the area. Call me as soon as you hear something... Okay, Bye." She put her phone on the counter, but the screen was just the regular photo of flowers, even when she had it to her ear. "Your father is arrogant."

"Yeah... I know you wouldn't do something like this, I just came to ask him for help. I'm sorry he blew up at you."

She shook her head. "It's just who he is. He thinks brute force wins all."

"Yeah... Call me if your guys come up with something because I'm at a complete loss here. To my knowledge, there was no one left, but..." I raised my shoulders, "I don't know because she's not here to ask... I just know I need her back because I don't want a life that doesn't have her in it."

"Don't say that. I'm sure she's fine. Bexley disappears all the time to run off on her errands, that's probably all that's happened. Call the airports, check her credit cards, and we'll find her somewhere." My mom was still apathetic as she spoke.

I pulled the corner of my mouth back. "Thanks for being on my side. I know you understand because of losing Charlotte, so I know you're trying to help." My words were to see if I could stir any emotion from her at all, and as soon as she nodded and I saw it didn't. I walked away.

Chapter46

Bexley

A horrible twinge in my nose made me gasp and open my eyes. In the same moment, I became aware of the pain in my body. My hands instinctively pulled toward my face but were held back. I looked around me because I didn't know where I was or how I got there. The disorientation was so bad I felt like I was moving when I wasn't.

"Welcome back."

I looked at the man in front of me and felt my heart start to pound. He was tall, bald, had dark beady eyes, had scarring that made the left side of his face droop, and I had no idea who he was. While I'd seen many faces in my life, his was one I would have remembered.

"We have some questions for you, and you can answer them truthfully the first time you're asked and nothing happens, or we go about this a different way." He wiped a knife with a white towel. While he had a slight German accent, his English was crystal clear and the accent could've been easily missed if I didn't know it so well.

I looked around again, trying to figure out where I was or if there was anyone else around. My brain didn't feel like it was working the way it was supposed to. I felt like I'd been drugged, but my body was aching, so it could have been from an injury too. I seemed to be in some kind of garage or shed with piles of old tools and equipment that hadn't been touched for a very long time. The wood planks that made up the walls were half-rotted and letting sunlight through. I was tied to a chair, but I leaned to the side to look through a larger hole between the planks. Toby's uncle's house... Toby.

"Toby?" I looked around frantically. Toby and Ben had been in the car with me. We'd been hit. "TOBY! BEN!" My voice was hoarse and hardly sounded like me.

The man laughed. "There's no one else here. Not another person for miles."

"Where are they?"

"You're not the one asking questions. Where's Helena?" The man set the knife down and picked up a small strip of thin chain.

"She's dead. She's been dead for years," I panted as I looked around for my brother and Toby.

He shook his head and walked toward me. "You're only going to get this one free pass. Alex has been receiving letters from her for years, so she's clearly not dead. Given who you are and what you know about everything else, we know you're aware of her location." As he approached me, I saw scars covering his hands. He had no nails, and just from that, I knew he was the man who'd killed Carol.

"Those letters were written by Patty to cover up her death. She died when I was nine. She was pushed down the stairs and broke her neck. Patty buried her under a willow tree on the property in Tennessee."

Even after telling the truth, the man violently lashed

me several times with the chain. I clenched my teeth together as hard as I could to fight the screams of pain that wanted to come out.

"Lie to me again, I dare you," the man seethed. "Her letters are sent from all over the country even while Patty was in prison."

All I could do was breathe through my nose and wait for the climax of pain to end.

"Where is she?"

"I told you... the truth." I did my best to control my breathing through the pain.

"And I don't believe you. Patty said she's alive and you know where she is."

I didn't even know who this guy was or how he seemed to know anything at all, but he was badly scarred from burns, so I had to assume he was either a victim of Helen or Cynthia.

"Armin," I whispered as I looked at him.

His eyes narrowed at me. "Where is she?"

"She's dead. You're her husband, those burns are from the fire," I concluded.

"Yes! Where is she!?" he burst.

"She's dead. There's a second field to the Northeast of the house in Tennessee. She's buried under the willow tree there. I can show you on a map exactly where it is."

Armin took several more lashes at me with the chain, one of them hitting my cheek, which hurt a hell of a lot worse. I stayed cringed off to the side, doing everything I could to keep my sanity.

"You wanna watch your little girl die the way I watched mine!? Where's Helena!?"

"I told you! It's not my fault you don't believe me! And Helen didn't set that fire, Cynthia did! Catrine Ockert! Klaus raped Helen, she wouldn't shut up about it and Catrine set the house on fire to kill you and the girls so Helen would be blamed and locked up! But Helen's dead. She was pushed down the stairs and she broke her neck!" Being hit when I was telling the truth was far more infuriating than being hit for a lie, so I yelled just to make myself feel better.

"Who pushed her?" He stared at me hatefully.

"I did. She threw me over the stairs, I ran to get back in the basement because she wouldn't go down there, she caught me in the kitchen, and I snapped. She had a hold of me, and I pushed against her as hard as I could. She went down the basement stairs backward, fell off the side, and landed on her head. It snapped her neck. Patty brought her up, took her out to the second field so she'd never be found, and buried her under the willow tree." I spoke quickly and gave details so he'd believe me. Most people couldn't spout an elaborate lie that fast.

"Where are the documents you were given?"

"Charlotte took them to the BKA. They have everything I was given."

"No. Where are the documents for *Catrine?*"

I shook my head. "I don't know. Patty probably has them."

Again, he violently whipped me.

"GODDAMMIT! I DON'T HAVE ANYTHING! I NEVER DID!" I screamed angrily, fighting against the chair, trying to control what part of my body the chain was striking.

"*BULLSHIT! WHERE ARE THEY!?*" he screamed right back and kept whipping me.

I just screamed as hard as I could because it was all I had.

"*SHUT UUUP!*" he screamed in my face.

I stopped and gasped for breaths because I'd ran myself out of air and the pain was numbing up because there was enough of it.

"Where are the documents for Catrine?" he snapped again.

"I don't *have* them... I never *did.* I only had what Patty... gave me. He had Charlotte take them to the BKA."

540

"We'll see about that when I come back." He turned and dropped the chain on the decrepit workbench, then picked up a metal bucket.

I was able to turn my cheek to the water he threw at me when I realized what he was doing.

"There's your water while I'm gone," he spat.

"Oh wow. I've never been deprived of water before. I'm really panicked about dying. I've enjoyed life so much, I'm too afraid to die," I retorted bitterly.

He glared at me like he hated me more than anyone on earth, so I smiled at him.

"I'll see you when you're back, honey. Guten tag." I continued to hold my smile, not caring that it hurt my face.

His mouth twitched with anger. "Fick dich."

I laughed. "Couldn't figure that one out in English, baldy? Oh, shit. Was that a low blow? I mean, you couldn't help that your hair got burned off."

"I have cancer, you little shit!"

If he was screaming at me instead of killing me, then he wasn't in charge. There was someone else pulling the strings.

"Hm. I'd say I'd trade you, but where I'm sitting is probably a quicker death and I'm selfish. So, good luck with that." I flashed another smile. Death was far easier than continuing to get beaten by the monsters that kept seeping through the dark corners.

Armin went out the door, closed it, and locked it. I let out a breath, then let my stomach retch. It had been sour the entire time, and having the chance to actually think about it made me puke almost instantly. I'd already soiled myself at some point before being woken up.

After taking several minutes to recoup, I started looking around to see if there was any way to get myself free. The chair I was in was reinforced with concrete inside cinderblocks, so I couldn't tip it over. The chains around my legs, wrists, and elbows weren't something

I'd be able to cut through. Armin was clearly as good at his job as Henry. I couldn't believe he was still alive, and I wondered if Patty knew about it.

⸻⸻⸻✦⸻⸻⸻

The night was cold and miserable. My bones ached and I kept wishing I could just put my hair down to keep myself warm, but I couldn't do anything. I had another two EpiPens filled with cyanide in my hair, and I needed them to stay there. With Patty still walking around, I kept them hidden there. Spending another seven years stuck in a house with him wasn't an option for me.

The next day I was in and out of sleep. My body still ached from sitting in one spot, but it wasn't the ache from the cold. Staying awake at night to let myself shiver was necessary, but I still fell asleep the early morning of the second night. My mind was lost in the wonderful memories of my family to help me keep my sanity. I revisited the conversations with Grace, walked through the streets of San Francisco with Grey, snuggled up against my mom, held my dad's hand with my head on his shoulder while we sat on the bench swing, laughed with my brother, and got to know my sister as a friend instead of foe. The memory of all of them gave me company.

⸻⸻⸻✦⸻⸻⸻

"Hannah, wake up."

Toby's quiet whisper was a relief I couldn't describe. It felt like home, somewhere comfortable and warm. I smiled at him. "I knew you'd find me."

"You have to get out of here. Grace is counting on you to come home. She needs you." Toby took my hand. "You promised me you wouldn't give up and you'd take care of her."

I shook my head. "I didn't break my promise. She has you."

"But she needs you now. Look around you. I prepared this entire place for us to be able to get out." He

542

pointed behind me.

I turned my head to look. There was a grinder hung low on a support beam. The cord was already plugged in; part of Toby's preparations.

"Go cut the chains."

I looked at Toby. "I can't move. Go grab it." I glanced down to bring his attention to the fact that I was tied down to a chair locked in concrete blocks.

"No, you have to get yourself out of this. Look down."

I looked down, but didn't understand why he wouldn't just go grab the grinder and get me free. "Stop wasting time. We have to get out of here."

"I'm already out, Han. Look at me. You haven't even noticed."

My eyes went back to Toby, trying to figure out what the heck he was talking about. He took his base-ball cap off and pulled back his strawberry blonde hair to show that there was nothing there. His implants were gone. Then I realized he hadn't sounded the same when he spoke to me.

"I'm dead," I whispered.

Toby shook his head. "Not yet... That's why you have to wake up and get out of here. Grace needs you, your family, and your husband... You can't give up. You have to keep your promise to me."

My eyes started to water as I looked at him. "You have to keep yours too. You promised you wouldn't leave me."

He shook his head. "And I won't. I'm here, you just have to wake up and keep fighting. I won't leave you." Toby got on his knees and put his forehead against mine. "I'll never leave you, Hannah. I promise. Grace is half of me and half of you."

I started to cry because I knew I was hallucinating. He wasn't there to save me.

"Hannah, stop. You have to look down. You can still

get out of this, but if you wait any longer, it'll be too late. Just look down. See what you missed."

<hr/>

I jumped after another painful twinge in my nose, then coughed and sneezed.

"Where's the documents?"

My body hurt, my mind felt clouded on top of the brain fog. It was hard to understand what was going on or where I was. I closed my eyes because I was tired and Armin was going to hit me regardless of what I told him.

"Hey. Wake up." He snapped his fingers.

A cold bucket of water was thrown at me again. It should have been an insult, but it felt relieving to the open sores on my skin.

"Drink this." Armin grabbed my chin and poured water into my mouth. Part of me hoped it was filled with poison, but that was something Patty did. Most everyone else would shoot, beat, or leave someone for dead.

"Where are the documents?" he asked again.

I shook my head. "I don't know." My voice was so dry it barely made a sound.

"You tell me where they are and you get out of here alive."

"Then I'm not getting out of here because I don't know." I closed my eyes out of tiredness and Armin pushed my head back with a hand on my forehead. I didn't have time to register what he was doing until he was dumping water down my airways so I choked and coughed. There was a thick wood plank set on two sawhorses. Around it were gallon jugs filled with water. I was going to be waterboarded for information, just like after Helen had died.

"Where's Helena?"

"Fertilizing a tree." I croaked with my eyes closed again.

"Why are you protecting her?"

I almost laughed. "Protecting the person who locked

544

me in the dryer...? The one who branded my back with an iron rod?" I looked at him when he didn't respond. Armin was staring at me hatefully, and I started to wonder if he was asking because he still cared about her. "I sat on the floor with her while she suffocated to death. She couldn't breathe because her neck was broken. I put her head on my lap and pet her hair. She was terrified, and she couldn't fight because she was paralyzed... It was slow and she suffered." I didn't speak in a way that made me sound like I was gloating because I wasn't. Helen's death disturbed me as much as anyone else's.

In a sudden burst of rage, Armin grabbed my neck to stop me from breathing. "You should die the same way. The same as my Marlena and Julia couldn't breathe from smoke." His mouth twitched from his anguish as he stared into my eyes. "My Helena..."

He cared, and I did too. I didn't fight to break his grasp, as much as my mind screamed at me by instinct. I consciously focused my thoughts on choosing to hold my breath. My soul was ready to gracefully slip through the memories of those I loved for a final goodbye before I took refuge in death...

Chapter 47

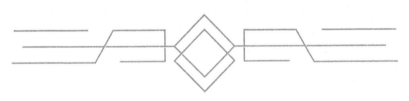

Grey

The burner phone rang from the cupholder, so I pushed the button on the steering wheel. I'd been driving for hours. Texas, Tennessee, Alabama, Louisiana, Michigan, Minnesota, Nebraska, I'd looked everywhere for Bex. Sam and I were in California, checking every one of Bex's hiding spots, places where she had cars parked to see if any of them were missing. It'd been more than a week and I couldn't find her.

"Yeah," I answered quietly and looked over at Sam while he slept.

"Colorado." Ryan sounded as tired as me.

"Why Colorado?"

"She went there before the wedding before she flew into Dallas."

I rubbed my face. "You're right, but I don't know where. That cabin was just a decoy."

"Yeah, that's why I've been digging and making calls for hours. Then I got smart and asked your little buddy. Toby has a house in Marvel, Colorado." Ryan cleared his throat quietly.

"Okay. I'm just outside San Jose. Can you get me a flight out?" I looked to the right because I needed to exit instead of continuing north. I was going to stop at my dad's condo in San Francisco to sleep. I'd only been sleeping on flights and the exhaustion was catching up to me.

"Yeah. I'm doing that now."

"Tell him he has to look for the bear statue when he gets there," Grace prompted in the background. "It's a really big statue of a bear at the end of the driveway."

I looked at the clock. "What is she still doing up? It's almost midnight."

"I couldn't sleep, and I heard Ryan, so I came to sit with him so he wasn't lonely," Grace answered back.

I chuckled a little. "Hey, Ace. You need to go to bed, kiddo. You can turn the TV on if you want."

"No, I wanna help find my mom." There was a pout in her voice, and I could easily picture the face that went with it.

"I'm here for it, but I'm in California right now and I have to fly into Colorado, so let's catch a few hours of sleep and Ryan will wake you up when I'm ready for directions. Does that work?" It was funny how Grace had only been in my life for a couple weeks and I loved her like crazy. She was just as sweet as Bex, and all she wanted to do was help. Grace called me at least twice a day since I'd been out looking for Bex, just to keep me company while I was driving and tell me about her day. I thought it was the sweetest thing, but every time she called, my heart was broken. It only reminded me how much I needed to find Bex. Grace was doing her best to keep a good head on her shoulders about Toby dying, but there'd been a phone call two days ago where she just cried and cried. I listened and tried to say the things Bex would have to comfort her. It made me feel so guilty

I nearly flew home just to hug her. I didn't want to put her in danger by bringing her with me, but I felt so bad for leaving her too.

"Can I stay in here with Ryan? I don't want to sleep by myself and Uncle Ben snores and Ella kicks in her sleep."

I laughed a little. "You're gonna have to work that out with Ryan, but I think you should go back in my room, turn on a movie, and crash."

"Dude, stop giving me that face. You look like your mom, and I already told you your mom wouldn't want you sleeping in here," Ryan grumped at her.

I pressed my lips together to keep from laughing.

"My dad's not here. He always sits with me when I can't sleep."

I laughed because I couldn't help it. "Ace, that's dirty manipulation. Ryan's right, your mom wouldn't want you sleeping in his room. You can hang out with him for a few more minutes, then you need to either go up to your room upstairs or stay in your mom's and my room. You don't have to sleep, but you can't stay in Ryan's room. Okay?"

"You can chill in here, but the second your eyes close, I'm booting you out. Don't cry," Ryan told her in a gentler tone.

I took in a deep breath while I mentally kicked my-self. The poor girl had to feel like she had no one, even with Ben staying at the house, it had to be so hard for her and I just made her cry.

"I'm sorry, Aces. I'm not trying to hurt your feelings, I just know your Mom wouldn't like it, so we're trying to respect her wishes until she's here to say something. Okay?" I rubbed my forehead, then shoved my hand through my hair.

"I know," Grace whimpered. "I just don't wanna be alone anymore. I miss my dad, and I don't think my mom is coming home."

"You're not alone, Pal," Ryan told her quietly. "You can stay in here, and I'll fight it out with your mom when we find her, and we *will* find her. I promise."

I wiped the tear off my cheek because I felt about the same as Grace. Finding Bex felt impossible after the first twenty-four hours.

"Me too, Grace. I'll talk to your mom if she has a problem with it, and I promise we'll find her. I'll never stop looking. Okay?" I wiped under my nose, then took the next exit to the airport.

"A plane will be ready for you in twenty minutes from the South gate. You'll fly into Durango, then drive thirty minutes to Marvel. Use your fake ID and keep your head down from any cameras." Ryan's voice was still quiet.

"I know. What's the status on my mom?" She'd been in Tennessee which was part of a designed plan. I sent Charlotte and my dad with my phone to Bell Buckle to let my mom think I'd gone there. Ryan was tracking my mom to make sure she didn't catch up to Charlotte and my dad. Once Frank told me Patty was trying to take my mom down too, I wondered if he had proof of things my mother had done. That would be a good reason for her to take Bex. The fact that she'd gone straight down there after my phone was leading me to think I was right.

"Her plane is currently over Missouri. It's set to land back in Seattle, but I'm still keeping a close eye for any touchdowns. I'll let you know if anything changes."

"Okay. I'm coming up on the gate, so I'll check in when I land." I was only looking forward to the flight because it meant sleep, otherwise, it felt like more time being wasted. "We're moving to a smaller country after this."

Ryan chuckled darkly. "Yeah. Now you know how *my* life has been for the last year. I'll talk to you later."

"Yep. Bye, Ace."

"Bye. Be safe."

"I will." I smiled a little. "Have a good night." I hung up the call and let out a sigh. "Sam, wake up. We're getting on another flight."

<hr />

Two hours of sleep wasn't enough, but I didn't care because the second I landed, I had a text from Ryan saying my mom had landed nearly an hour before me. I called him as soon as I had a truck, and he gave me directions to a property he found under Toby's uncle's name in the county records. When we got on the dirt road the house was on, I turned the lights off and drove until I could see the house in the distance.

"We got lights," I told Ryan.

"It looks like there are two cars, but I can't tell from this far," Sam said quietly.

"Then you guys are gonna have to stake out until they leave, or until the FBI can get there. It's gonna take them at least a couple hours to show up in that remote of a place."

I shook my head, staring at the house. "I'm not sure we should call the FBI yet. If she's not there, then my mom is gonna know we're on to her and we'll never find Bex."

"I hear you, but if your mom is trespassing on Toby's property, Ben can press charges on Maslen's behalf and they can hold the bitch for interrogation."

"Is Grace still awake?" I looked around for another road or house.

"No, do you want me to wake her up?"

"No, it's not worth it, and I'm pretty sure I know the answer. If Toby and Bex went to lengths to make sure no one knew about this house, then Toby probably didn't make friends with any neighbors. It's flat land out here, so I was thinking it'd be easier if I could park on a neighbor's property to keep an eye out without being exposed on the side of the road." I shoved my hand through my hair.

"We should go back into town and get supplies,"

Sam said quietly. "If she is here, she's probably gonna need food and water."

"Toby will have everything in that house. Just stay there. I mean, we know your mom is there, so we just need her to leave. You guys have to be ready to run in. There aren't any trees or anything you can get the truck behind?" I could hear Ryan typing on his laptop as he spoke.

"Way in the distance, but we probably wouldn't be able to see from that far." Sam pointed further down the road.

"No. It's flat as flat can get out here. And Sam's right, the only trees out there are too far. I'm not even sure those are trees." I squinted as I tried to focus my eyes in the darkness.

"There's another road you could loop around to, I'm sending you a screenshot. Since she came in the way you did, I imagine she'd leave the same way. This would put you in a position to go in behind her."

I picked up the phone to see what Ryan was talking about. "Yeah. That looks like a better option, and it puts me closer to the house than I am now. I don't dare get closer from this side." I set the phone down and turned the truck around, letting out a breath. "God, I hope she's here. I don't know how much more of this I can take."

"Same. I'm so tired I'd rather suffer from my injuries than stay awake another five minutes." Ryan let out a breath.

"I offered to drive." Sam grabbed another energy drink and opened it for me.

Ryan snorted. "Street drifting doesn't qualify you for defensive driving."

"I'm a good driver."

"Stop. Both of you. I'm not in the mood." I crept up to the stop sign, then turned right.

"Could we call the local police? Like for a well check or something?" Sam suggested.

I shook my head. "No. We're not calling anyone until we have Bex. And we definitely can't trust local police. Mom could've paid them off."

"Right..."

I picked up the phone again to look at the screenshot. We were making a larger loop than I really wanted, but Ryan was likely right. My mom wasn't as careful as she thought she was, and Ryan had spent the last year keeping close tabs on her, so he knew her patterns.

It took about ten minutes to get to the spot Ryan suggested. Sam had been right, there were two vehicles outside the house, but the lights were coming from a shed or small barn that looked like it needed to be torn down. We rolled the windows down and I shut the truck off. The stupid crickets chirped in the empty fields around.

"I can't believe Mom's been lying to us for all these years," Sam whispered as we both stared at the house.

"Yeah... I always thought Granny was crazy for hating her so much... for insisting there was something wrong with her." The more I thought about it, the more I *could* believe what my mother was capable of. What I couldn't believe was how blind I'd been.

Sam shook his head. "How did Dad really not know?"

"Sh!" I grabbed Sam's arm and listened harder because I'd heard something. It took another second, but there was another scream followed by a loud clamor.

"Holy shit. Look, look, look!" Sam whispered hurriedly.

Patty was crouched over as he ran from behind a propane tank to the side of the house.

"Son of a bitch. Okay. Call Ryan. Do not under any circumstances get out of the truck. Get in the driver's seat, keep the windows cracked open so you can hear me but not all the way down," I said quickly as I grabbed the bag out of the back seat. "If anyone but me or Bex

552

comes toward you, gun it and go wherever Ryan tells you. Don't come back for me, just tell Ryan I said to send the FBI. No local police. No matter what. Do you understand?" I looked at him, praying he'd be okay on his own without me.

"Yeah. Go. Hurry."

"There's another gun in the bag. Only shoot if you don't have another choice." I hit the button to make sure the dome lights stayed off before I got out of the truck. As soon as Sam moved over, I very quietly closed the door, then hunched down to look before I ran across the road over to the ditch in front of the house. Patty was straightening up, and walked right into the shed like he was supposed to be there.

Chapter 48

Bexley

"As soon as I have the papers, your daughter goes free, Bexley." Cynthia looked at me simplistically.

I just sat there in the chair. Armin hadn't even tied me up after the third round of waterboarding because I was too weak. He said something to her in German.

"That doesn't mean she doesn't know where he hid them," she snapped back, then looked at me. "Grey was in Tennessee. Does he have them? Did you tell him where they were?"

I sat there silently. Nothing I said would make a difference. They didn't believe me, but now that Cynthia had come, there was a chance Patty was right behind. Giving her no information meant the smallest chance of getting out. Every time I fell asleep or passed out, I had a dream that Toby was there telling me I had to stay alive for Grace because he was dead. Now Cynthia was claiming to have taken Grace, offering no proof, but I still had to assume it might be true. Grace's only chance relied on me staying alive. Giving Cynthia information, or even the suggestion of it would mean she'd have no reason for me to stay alive.

"ANSWER ME!" she screamed.

Armin kicked the chair I was in, knocking both me and the chair to the ground. Thankfully, I'd figured out what Toby had been trying to point out in the first dream when he told me to look down. The concrete hadn't fully set. I'd been able to break the chair legs free, but Armin had returned before I could get to the grinder on the wall to cut the chains.

"Where are they!?" Cynthia yelled again.

I didn't move.

"Don't shoot. It's me." Patty's voice came from outside before the door opened. I used the brief moment when both Armin and Cynthia looked toward the door to grab an EpiPen from my hair.

"Where have you been? We had a deal!" Cynthia raged.

Patty looked down at me and back at her. "And it didn't involve you kickin' the shit outta my girl."

"That's exactly right, *Patrick*. I was supposed to get my papers *and* Charlotte, not just Charlotte. You only half delivered, so she's not leaving with you until I have the rest of what's mine. The house is ready, but you don't get her until I get my papers." She stared at him heatedly.

Patty's fists balled up at his sides and his eyes were crazed. "You hurt my girl. You want me to come for *yours*?"

"Don't threaten me," Cynthia spat.

Armin pulled a gun on Patty, and like a strike of lightning, Patty leaned back, grabbed Armin's arm, and slammed him against the beam nearest them. The gun went off at the ground, Cynthia let out a scream, and at the same time, I scrambled to get up and help Patty.

"NO!" Cynthia hooked her arm around my throat to pull me backward. I grabbed her arm, leveraging her weight over mine, and flipped her to the ground. No matter how much I wanted to take her out, I couldn't. She was Grey's mom, and she knew where Grace was.

"Hannah!" Patty yelled as he kept straining to fight Armin over the gun.

As soon as I stepped forward to stab Armin with the EpiPen, Cynthia grabbed my ankle and took me down again. She rolled over to drag me back, then grabbed my arm to pull me over so she could roll on top of me. I pushed, clawed, and fought to keep her hands away from my throat while bucking my hips to knock her off. She was no bigger than me, but she was more nimble. In their brawl, either Patty or Armin kicked me in the head before they went crashing to the floor beside us.

"GET OFF ME!" I screamed out of frustration and pain to push someone's leg off my face. Cynthia got her hands around my throat, but I threw my arm over to break her grip. She finally fell off to the side but grabbed a plank of wood on the ground to hit me. I rolled quickly, expecting the hit from the side of the board, but still stabbed Armin's ankle with the EpiPen.

There was a single gunshot right before the plank came down on my upper arm, then Cynthia dropped herself on top of me again.

"NO!" I grabbed at the post near my head to pull myself away from her, and another shot was fired.

"Dammit!" Patty yelled.

After pulling myself out from under Cynthia, I realized something wasn't quite right. She wasn't grabbing at me, so I stopped to look. My eyes went wide when I saw squirts of blood pumping out from the top of her head, and her lifeless blue eyes looking at me. I quickly pushed myself back with a panicked cry and looked over at Patty. He was on the ground, holding his arm as he groaned loudly in pain.

"Don't move or I'll kill you!"

My head snapped to the side so fast it made me

dizzy. Grey's voice was angry, and I hadn't even known he was there. Instantly, my brain made me cower against the pole, thinking it was me he was threatening. Did he think I shot his mother? Had I trusted him when I shouldn't have?

Grey ran in with a gun in his hand, but he wasn't looking at me. I folded my hands behind my head, covering my ears, and cringed as he went right by me and kicked something away from Patty, just two feet in front of me. Whatever it was, hit the back of the shed wall loudly, making me jump. I closed my eyes because whatever was going to happen to Patty, I didn't want to watch.

"SAM! HELP!" Grey yelled so loud I could feel it. "Stay down, you piece of shit!"

I opened one eye just a little, staying in my fetal position against the support beam. Grey was dragging Patty toward me.

"B, look out." He leaned Patty against the post and grabbed a piece of chain.

I shoved myself back against the lawnmower behind me and sat there cowering as Grey chained Patty to the post.

"You move and I kill you," Grey threatened before he sidestepped over to me. "Bex, can you walk?"

I looked up at him, watching as he kept the gun pointed at Patty.

He glanced over when I didn't respond. "B," he looked at me for another second longer, "it's okay. I'm trying to get you out of here. Can you walk?" He looked at me again.

I nodded, then realized I needed to actually get up and do it.

"Okay. Come on." He reached out a hand to me but kept the gun pointed at Patty with the other.

I got up without taking his hand because I was filthy. A used rag with twenty years of mold on it was cleaner than me. My back stung as I walked out of the shed followed by Grey. I was blinded by lights from a truck just after stepping outside into the night. Instinct told me to run toward the house. All I had to do was get inside, wait for whoever it was to come inside, and blow the place three ways to hell. It would take me just seconds to detonate.

"Bex! Stop!" Grey yelled. "It's Sam! Stop!"

My legs burned so badly as I ran. They shouldn't have felt so strained from such a short distance, but I hadn't eaten and barely had any water. The fatigue was so bad my ears were ringing, but I didn't have far to go so I had to keep pushing.

"Bex! It's okay!" Sam yelled at the same time Grey yelled at me to stop again and caught me.

My focus was only on taking out whoever had just pulled up to the house in the truck, so I fought to break Grey's grip from around me.

"Bex, stop! I'm not here to hurt you! There's no one left. It's just me and Sam!" Grey lifted me, despite me dropping my weight to break his grip.

"I have to stop them! Let me go!" I yelled as I tried to kick to get my feet back on the ground again.

"There's no one to stop. Just look at me." He allowed me to stand again but turned me to face him. "Look at me. It's over. You're okay. I'm here and you're safe. Look at me." Grey's ocean-blue eyes were desperate as he tried to keep a grip on me and make me look at him at the same time.

I looked behind him and saw Sam standing on the running board of the truck... Sam was in the truck...

My eyes darted around to spot any remaining threats. House, curtains, flat fields of desert, no lights, no sounds of planes, just crickets.

"Bex, look at me." Grey's voice was quiet.

I looked at him again, seeing nothing but fear in his eyes.

"You're safe. It's over." He nodded. "We have to go. Okay?"

I shook my head.

"Why not?"

I looked at the house. "Toby..." My voice was only a whisper.

"He's not here, Beautiful. We *really* need to leave."

I looked at Grey, feeling my heart begin to break in my chest. "He's dead...? Right?"

Grey took in a breath, relaxing his grip on me but didn't say anything.

"Gracie?" My voice broke.

"She's at home with Ryan. She's okay." He nodded.

"And Toby's dead?"

Grey nodded. "I'm so sorry... He died in the accident when they took you. Ben's a little beat up, but he's at home with Ryan and Grace."

I grabbed my chest as I looked at the house. The amount of pain that came with realizing my hope had died was the worst I'd ever experienced. No beating, no form of torture, no state of mental exhaustion could compare. I was looking at the very house that Toby had described to me in long conversations as we sat in the dark basement. He couldn't even hear himself speaking the words, but he'd promised me hope of a life without a basement. We were going to have horses, cattle, chickens... I would read books while Grace took naps, and Toby would farm the acres of field behind the house. We would turn every light on in the house to starve out the darkness through the night, and he'd watch out for me as I slept, making sure no one and nothing ever touched me against my will.

"B... I'm so sorry. We have to go. You have to walk or I'm gonna carry you."

Grey's voice broke the trance of a future that never existed outside of my mind, and I looked at him for a moment. Could I live in a world with only Grey and no

Toby? I didn't know how long I'd been locked in the shed, but in that time, I'd forgotten what my future looked like because I'd only looked back on the past.

He stepped forward and carefully reached up a hand to my cheek. "Bex... What do you need? What can I do?"

I couldn't answer that because I could barely feel my own body. There was the numbing throb of pain, the sting from sitting in my soiled underwear for too long, and the tiredness that never ended, but what did I need?

"I need my mom."

Grey nodded. "You got it, Beautiful. Let's go." He partially turned, keeping his eyes on me out of worry.

Sam was walking toward the truck from the doorway of the shed with his hand over his mouth. He hugged me just before I got in the truck, but I could only take it for a few seconds before I had to step back. I felt so gross that I didn't want to be touched by anyone until I scrubbed myself clean.

"Sam, you drive. I need to help Bex," Grey said quietly as he opened the back door of the truck. "Turn the rearview mirror up and keep your eyes forward."

"Hannah! Don't leave me like this! Kill me! *Please!*" Patty yelled from inside the shed.

"Don't worry about him. The FBI is on the way," Grey whispered as he caught my hand.

I nodded and let him hold my hand until I got in the truck, then let go. Sam closed the door behind me, then got in.

"I brought a bag for you." Grey pulled up my old backpack from the floor. He started pulling out clothes, baby wipes, a bottle of water, and some protein bars.

"I need to call Ryan before he freaks out," Sam said as he pulled out of the driveway.

"Go ahead." Grey handed me a pair of scissors. "I thought this might be easier to get your clothes off."

I nodded and took the scissors. I cut my shirt first,

and Grey put it in a plastic bag, followed by my skirt and undergarments when I had them off.

"Please, tell me you have her," Ryan answered tiredly.

"We have her, but we need directions to the closest hospital. I don't know where I'm going," Sam responded somberly.

"Durango. That's the closest. How bad is she?"

"Not bad enough. I'm not going to the hospital. Get me a flight to wherever my mom is." My voice was half gone.

"Maslen." Ryan let out a breath, sounding relieved.

"B, you have to go to the hospital first. We have to wait for the FBI. I just shot two people, and I can only justify leaving the scene if you go to the hospital." Grey spoke loudly enough that Ryan could hear while keeping his eyes forward as he handed me wet wipes as I needed.

"He's right, but who did you shoot?"

"My mom and Patty. I don't know what happened to the other guy." He closed his eyes and shook his head. "She was about to kill Bex, I didn't have a choice."

"I'll try to hold my shitty comments. Everyone is dead then? I need to give Agent Moore a heads-up. He's flying out, but the guys from Grand Junction are already on their way."

"Patty's not. I left him chained up." Grey held out another wipe to me.

"That was dumb."

It wasn't. I still needed Patty alive. Clearly, after encountering Armin, there were still more people coming out of the woodwork. But a trip to prison, where I could find him, wouldn't hurt anything.

"Can you check on Grace? I need to know she's there and okay." I threw the last wipe I'd used in the bag and grabbed the sweater off the seat between Grey and I.

"She's asleep next to me. And I know you're probably pissed that she's in my room, but she started crying because she didn't want to be alone when Grey and I told her she needed to go back to her room."

"I trust you... As long as she's okay." I slipped my feet through a clean pair of underwear and winced as I stood just enough to pull them up. Hannah was back in the basement of my mind, which meant I felt all the pain my body was in. It wasn't muted anymore.

"She's okay. Did you want me to wake her up so you can talk to her?"

"No, let her sleep. She's probably struggling because Toby isn't there. She's used to having him next to her at night." I slid the sweatpants on and tried not to cry from the aches in my body.

"I was trying to avoid the topic. I take it you remember the accident?"

"I remember being in one, then nothing, but I know because I know." I didn't want to tell anyone about my dreams of Toby because they were mine. They were the last I had of him. "I don't wanna talk anymore. I don't feel good. Make your calls and we'll see you when we see you." I wiped a tear off my cheek and regretted it because of the terrible cut. It frustrated me that I'd worked so hard to pay for scar removal surgeries and therapies to only have to do it again. That made more tears form in my eyes.

Grey handed me a bottle of water with a saddened expression on his face. I took it and leaned against the door.

"Okay... I love ya, Maslen. I'm glad you're okay, and I'm sorry about Toby. I'll text you guys with updates, just keep me posted, please."

"We will. Later, man." Sam ended the call.

"Come here." Grey held out an arm.

I shook my head. It didn't matter if I'd wiped myself down and changed my clothes, I was still filthy. I couldn't have been more humiliated. Grey had seen the basement child, a part of me I never wanted him to know.

Chapter 49

Bexley

The hospital was filled with embarrassing moments, people touching me, FBI men interviewing me while parts of my body were exposed and being cleaned, and Grey snapping at everyone because I just wanted a shower alone. He stood outside the bathroom door while telling everyone exactly what I was a victim of and how they needed to treat me with dignity. It wasn't his fault, and he was helping me when I needed it, but he didn't understand that there was no dignity left. Everything that had happened to me was to humiliate me into compliance because I wasn't worth anything to those who didn't know me or care. The FBI agent who took pictures of the wounds on my exposed body didn't care, she was just doing her job in the name of justice that could never be given.

After my cuts were cleaned and I'd received two bags of fluid to rehydrate me, Grey got me checked out of the hospital. All I wanted was to go home to my mom, so Ryan and my family flew there just before us. Everyone was waiting in the entryway when we got to my parents' house, waiting to hug me, and I felt like I was suffering through it. I didn't want to talk, I didn't want to hear how much anyone loved me or how they were glad I was okay, I just wanted to go upstairs and sit with my mom. Annoyingly, Emily came upstairs with us, laid on the other side of my mom, and bawled her eyes out. As badly as I wanted to comfort her, I didn't have it in me. The only person I could muster anything for was Gracie when she came in to tuck herself in between my mom and I.

Eventually, Grace and Emily got tired of laying there with me, but my mom didn't. She stayed, combing her nails through my hair, letting me fall in and out of sleep, tear up on her shoulder, and feeding me the occasional chocolate chip cookie. While I didn't want to eat anything, I was grateful for her sitting there with me. After the sun had gone down, my mom ran a bath for me, then helped redress some of the deeper wounds that needed to stay covered. Unlike the hospital staff, she was respectful and only exposed each of the wounds individually to dress them. When we were done, my dad was sitting in bed with a book. He didn't say anything, he just set the book down, moved over, and patted the side of the bed. I sat next to him and rested against his side for a while.

The next few days were about the same, but the day of Toby's funeral, I had to get out of bed, then out of the house. Toby had most of his wants listed in his will, and Emily decided the rest because I asked her to. She'd been a little hurt that Toby had left everything to me and Grace. The houses and land were mine, the vehicles, all the money went to Grace to be put in her trust fund. They weren't married yet, so he hadn't changed his will. Poor Emily felt left out, and she wanted to make all the arrangements for him but felt like she couldn't ask, so I asked her.

I hadn't been in my parents' church since the Sunday before I was taken, but nothing had changed. It looked the same, smelled the same, and the hymnals were still old. My family stood in the entryway to greet people coming in, but I didn't want to. I sat up front with Grace, Ryan, and Grey, avoided looking around too much to show my face, and just hugged my brokenhearted daughter. My grandma and my aunt came to sit behind me, to shoo away anyone who tried to stop to talk to me, and there were a lot. The whole room was whispering behind my back, speculating about my life, where I'd been, things they'd heard, things they wondered... I wanted to scream at them because they should've been talking about Toby and all that he was.

It made me so angry to sit there and hear some of the things people were saying that I leaned over and whispered to Ryan with a plan. He was a little shocked, but in true Ryan fashion he loved making people uncomfortable. I sat quietly and waited for my turn to get up and say something, and Ryan came up and hooked his computer up to the large screen that'd previously been displaying pictures of Toby. Grey took all the kids out of the chapel, and I stood at the podium silently until they were out.

I hadn't planned my speech like everyone else and it was hard to find the words to begin. "Toby deserved so much better than what he got in life... He was born to a family that didn't give a damn about him because they saw his hearing-loss as an insurmountable handicap. He was taken from that same family at seventeen because my uncle thought he'd be the right person to make me stop trying to kill myself when he wasn't looking... Then when he got out of an impossible situation, most everyone called him a pedophile and a rapist." My eyes were on the podium as I spoke because I was too angry to look at the guilty faces. "I'm disgusted by the number of people who think they know enough of what happened to judge a situation they didn't experience or witness. So today, for Toby, I'm going to set the record straight. Those of you with small children or weak minds are strongly encouraged to leave the chapel for the next five minutes while I allow everyone to witness what really happened in small part."

I looked up to see just a few mothers I didn't know get up and leave with their kids. As soon as the door closed, I looked over at Ryan. He gave me a slightly worried expression because I wouldn't be able to take back what I was about to do, but I didn't care. What happened would forever be my reality, so I nodded and Ryan played the video footage from Patty's office.

I took a deep breath just before the sound of my cries from more than nine years prior filled the room. My wrists and ankles were strapped to the examination table in Patty's office, Toby was chained in the corner, Patty sat behind his desk with his ears covered, and Henry stood over me with a knife in hand. He screamed at me to shut up and stabbed the knife into my abdomen before he yelled that he was going to sell me for body parts for refusing to produce children. I cried, screamed, and fought the restraints, begging for my life. I screamed, "don't let me die," at Toby frantically as Henry walked over to open the beer cooler filled with ice. Patty tried to get up from his desk to help me, but Henry's puppets pointed their guns at him and yelled at him to sit back down, so he did. With my right hand, I signed "save me," in individual letters, then screamed and cried when Henry came back with a scalpel and a bone saw.

A few people got up and walked out of the chapel, but I didn't blame them. It was hard to take, even as the person it'd happened to. I looked back at the screen, watching Henry draw the scalpel up my stomach, hearing myself scream, and watching the devastation on Toby's face as he made the hardest choice he could've made.

"I'll do it! Stop!" he screamed before crying in devastation, "I'll do it."

Henry turned to Patty with a satisfied smile. "Awe, see? I told you I could make them comply... You are weak."

A tear slipped down my cheek watching Toby sit on his hands and knees crying. I hadn't seen it the day it happened because my focus had been on the ceiling. It'd taken all I had to convince Toby to save me when I had *really* wanted to die.

Henry grabbed a towel and told the puppets to take Toby and I upstairs, and that's when I gave Ryan a second nod to stop the video. The room was dead silent, and I let it sit for a moment because I was trying to form words again.

"Toby was the only boy his age who came into that house and didn't hurt me, didn't try to trick me, didn't eat my food when I was called upstairs... He took care of me as if I were his own sister, and I couldn't let him die for that. I begged him to save me because if I died, he would be next. Boys his age were more difficult to sell because they didn't comply as easily as girls. It took more to restrain them, more to drug them, more to feed... Henry knew he couldn't convince Toby to join ranks, so that would've made him useless for anything but black-market body parts. I needed him to save me because I needed to save *him*... I wanted him to go back out in the world and do all the things he talked about. He wanted to get away from his family, move across the country, own a farm, get married, have four kids, and sit on the porch while he watched them play and listened to the windchimes... After the hours of listening to the horror stories of his parents' neglect and abuse, I wanted that for him."

I bit my lip for a moment. "I was fortunate to come from a loving home, to have parents who did their best turning the world inside and out to try and find me. I was fortunate to have a mind full of beautiful memories to focus on when I was alone and locked away with literally nothing. Those memories were my company, they were my safe haven, my greatest blessing, and the very reason I survived..." I shook my head. "Toby didn't have that. He went from a bad home to a worse one..."

I took in a deep breath because my grief was becoming too heavy to hold. "I don't believe any person should die in a world where they didn't know happiness, joy, or love... He deserved everything I could give him, and our daughter was just the first of that." I closed my eyes for just a second, struggling to keep my composure, then looked over at my parents. "I couldn't be more grateful to my parents and my brother and sister for helping me give Toby all the wonderful things they gave me, for making his life something he'd miss if it were taken. You are exactly the wonderful people I described to him, and he and I are so blessed to have the gifts your love brings. Thank you for being the kind of people who choose love instead of judgment, who chose to speak from their hearts instead of gossip. Toby, Grace, and I wouldn't have had good in our lives without you." I shook my head. "He would've died alone and miserable, and I wouldn't have been able to bear letting him go that way."

I swallowed hard and wiped the tears off my cheeks. "Toby Anderson saved my life... he was a hero to me and anyone who gave him the time of day. So for anyone left in this room with doubt or question of that, then you didn't know him, how abundantly he loved, and I pity you. You were deprived of knowing one of the most honorable men in my life, and that's a tragedy of your own doing... Please don't offer my family any more condolences for our loss; instead, honor the kindness they spread in this world by letting it spread to those who need it most... people like Toby." I stepped down the stairs quietly, paused for a moment to put my hand on top of Toby's casket, then walked back to my family. Emily took my hand tightly as our Dad walked up to the podium.

He took a deep breath, looking at the paper in front of him for a long moment. "Well, I had these closin' words written, but... I just don't think they're enough... I got me four of the best kids a man could ask for... and I lost one." His chin quivered as he looked over to the casket. "Toby was my boy... my beautiful boy. And goddammit if I don't miss him like hell right now. I wanna hug 'im, keep tellin' him how proud I am of the man he is..." My dad pulled his thumb and finger over his tears to wipe them away. "I'll always be grateful for those few weeks when our family was whole, but without Toby... it just won't be that way again. We lost our tender-hearted boy..." He continued to stare at the casket tearfully. "Y'all go on and sing hymn one-sixty-two. I'm gonna hug what I got left of my family cause I don't know how long I got 'em for."

My dad came down the three steps and made a straight line for me and Emily. He pulled us both into a hug, then my mom, and Ben took up the back. I held on for just a minute before I couldn't take it anymore. There was something in me breaking that I couldn't fight off, and I was almost jogging to get out of the chapel. Grey was in the entryway with the kids and other moms but stood as soon as he saw me, following me into the hall. As soon as I felt like I was far enough back for no one to hear, I turned into Grey and felt like I was being murder- ously tortured. I didn't know how to lose Toby, and with Henry out of the picture, I truly hadn't expected I would.

"Mom?" Grace's voice was behind me and full of worry.

"It's okay, Ace. Come here." Grey moved a hand

away from my back to reach out to her.

I held my breath to fight the tears because I didn't want to scare Grace or make her feel like she had to be the strong one. She'd lost her dad, and that was far worse a loss than mine. If there was any glimmer of light where I was, it was from Grey...

<hr>

After the burial, there was a catered luncheon, but I didn't stay long. I got sick of people coming up to hug me, talk about me and my life, where I'd been, why I didn't come home, and how much I was missed. No matter how much my family asked people to leave me alone, they just didn't listen, so Grey, Grace, and I went back to my parents' house. My family came home about an hour later, and we all sat outside on the front porch. Austin wanted to ride the lawnmower with my dad, so my dad took him to mow the lawn. Ella and Grace painted, Kylan sat on his phone, my mom and Ben sat there talking, and I sat against Grey's side while he, Ryan, and Sam talked. The windchimes hanging from the corner of the porch rang out quietly in the soft breeze. Toby should have been there... Times like this were all he ever wanted.

Everyone was sitting there trying to enjoy the rest of a sunny day and move forward. But why? Why were we forced to just move on? Why couldn't we go back to experience the good parts of our life again? Why weren't we allowed to go back and fix anything? Why did we have to keep moving forward like the past wasn't a blessing or a curse? Why were we forced to move forward without people, but instead with guilt and regret?

I became so angry that I got up.

"Bex?"

"Han?" Ben watched as I went inside.

I went through the house, out the back door, across the long backyard, and behind the old shed where my dad hid the wood piles. I moved a log onto a large stump, grabbed my dad's ax, brought it up over my head, and threw it down as hard as I could. The ax split through in one hit, so I moved more logs onto the stump and split them all. My muscles burned and it felt like I was getting stronger and angrier with every split.

"Han, are you okay?" Ben asked as he came up.

"No, but I'm doing something productive." I slammed the ax down again.

"Yeah," he chuckled. "In a dress no less. Cut that out before you get hurt. You don't even have shoes or gloves on."

"I don't *CARE!*" I burst while the ax came down as hard as I could make it, through another log. "I don't care if I get hurt! I don't care if I'm not in appropriate attire to split wood in! I'm still fricken *HERE!* I'm still in this body for some reason only a god could explain! It doesn't make sense! I should be dead. For the amount of times life has kicked the shit out of me, I should be DEAD, not *TOBY!*" I gasped in a loud jagged breath because I was out of air.

"I know you miss him, Han, but... You can't control who lives and who doesn't, no one can." He held up his shoulders.

"That's bullshit! Henry could, Patty could, Grey's mom could choose! They did whatever they wanted and got away with it for the entirety of their lives. They got rewarded with a quick way out that they don't have to live with. They don't have to stay here on this sadistic earth and keep living with pain and *suffering!*" I lifted the ax up and started chopping pieces that didn't need to be chopped.

"They didn't get away with it, they paid with their lives for it. Death to those people was something they all fought against, not welcomed. Otherwise, they would've ended themselves. Hannah, you could not control the actions of others, and you don't need to fix anything because it was never your mistake or responsibility. There's nothing for you to fix."

"So I'm just supposed to be a chicken shit who didn't tell her dad that her uncle touched her under the table, then took her upstairs and had his way? How is that not my mistake? Huh? I knew better, I knew I was supposed to tell Mom and Dad or you if someone hurt me. I didn't! I gave one halfhearted attempt, then decided to be petty and not talk to any of you because I was *pissed!* I was pissed that you all ignored me, pissed that dad told him to take me upstairs when he could clearly see I was losing my *shit!!* He practically served me up on a golden platter for Patty. But I *knew* I was supposed to say something, and I wanted to be petty instead! What a freaking nightmare of a lesson I got for being petty! I got a goddamn life sentence of being screwed in the head! Keep staring at me!" I yelled at my entire family as they watched from a distance with concern. "Take a picture! Hannah's lost her fricken mind! You've all been waiting for it, so here it is!" I let out the most gutted scream I had. It took so much energy from my muscles that it folded me in half.

"Will you all go inside and mind your own business!" Ben yelled at them.

I pressed my wrist into my thighs to keep my balance as my scream turned into a dead silent cry. My lungs got stuck for a moment because they were out of air for a long time, and I felt like I was going to die right there. Just as the panic set in over the lack of being able to breathe, I gasped loudly before letting out a cry that brought me to my hands and knees in the pile of bark.

"Okay, come here." Ben pulled me up to sit on the stump next to him and held me sideways in front of him. "Let it out... Let it out with all you've got."

I hugged his arm as my lungs got stuck again before another hideous cry came.

"I've got it. Just leave us alone," Ben said as Ryan

and Grey walked up.

I shook my head and reached for Grey, trying to get up when my body felt legitimately too weak from crying so hard. Neither he or Ryan listened to Ben, and Grey pulled me up into a hug. I grabbed Ryan's hand and squeezed as hard as I could while I stood there bawling into Grey's shoulder like a child. Years of pure anguish flooded out so heavily I felt out of my mind. It made my body ache and sting, my nervous system didn't know what to do with it all at once. My heart hurt... from sixteen years of secrets, memories, and excruciating pain.

"Breathe, B," Grey said quickly as he rubbed my back after I'd been stuck in a cry so hard I was beginning to panic again. I couldn't draw a breath, and as soon as he figured that out, Grey popped me hard against the back. A loud gasp reinflated my lungs, but I'd been so out of breath I needed more air. The panting cries turned into a fit of hyperventilation.

"Thumb on your nose and hand over your mouth," Ryan and Ben said almost in unison as Ryan pushed my own hand up to my face.

"Maslen," he leaned down to be at face level with me, "remember that morning on the beach?" Ryan put a hand on my cheek. "You told me you loved hearing the ocean because it made you remember how to breathe. Focus on that. Just for a minute... The waves coming in and out."

I closed my eyes, still hugging myself as close as I could to Grey, and tried to think about the sound of the ocean. Everything in me wanted to be on the beach, hear the roar of the night's tide, and see the heavy mist that was mysteriously lit over the darkness of the ocean. Grey rubbed my back more lightly as I began to calm, and Ryan kept his hand on my cheek.

"I wanna go to Monterey," I whispered.

"You got it, B. We can leave whenever you want."

Grey kissed the back of my head.

"You guys can't go. You're supposed to meet with the FBI tomorrow because Patty is still missing," Ben said quietly.

Ryan looked back at Ben. "You're the psychologist. Write her a note. Mental health."

"She doesn't need a note. She's the one doing them a favor, so they can wait and be thankful they get one at all after the shit job they've done." Grey hugged me tighter. "We'll go wherever you wanna go, whenever you're ready."

"Now... Ryan, will you ask my mom if she'll keep Grace for a few days?" I wiped another tear from my cheek.

He gave a small cringe. "She doesn't wanna stay here. She already asked Grey if we could go home early. Sam and I can take her back to Seattle with us? I'll see if Emily can come with."

I nodded. "Yeah. I just need a day or two."

Ryan shook his head. "Take your time. Surprisingly, I like that pip-squeak, and she loves Sam, so she'll be fine."

I nodded. "Thank you."

Chapter50

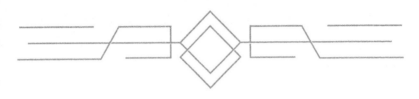

Grey

As soon as Ryan had mentioned the ocean, Bex was fixated. We landed in Monterey late at night, and she didn't even want to drop off our bags at the house, she just wanted to sit on the beach. I don't know how I managed to stay awake, let alone Bex. She was severely sleep deprived, having a night terror every time she went to sleep if she wasn't laying next to her mom. It was incredibly hard to watch her suffer the way she had been since finding her. I wanted to be there for her, but up until Toby's funeral, she hadn't seemed to want me. Normally, it wouldn't have bothered me, but because of what my mother had done and the fact that I didn't know what happened to Bex during that week she was missing, my mind was racing with the worst. She'd asked me to leave the room when the FBI questioned her. I didn't even know Patty was still running free until Don told me when we first got to Dallas.

The first day in Monterey, Bex slept up against my

side. I'd opened all the doors in the bedroom so she could listen to the waves crash against the bluff below the house. Whatever it was about the sound, it seemed to keep her from waking up absolutely petrified every two hours. Then in the late evening, Joe came by to see Bex. She cried again the moment she saw him, and hugged him for the first time—or at least that I'd ever seen. The look on Joe's face as he held her was the worst. He was trying so hard not to break. I was so fortunate to not be in his shoes, but part of me didn't feel as if I deserved it. I'd been dumb enough to look in every direction my mother pointed so she could do something terrible right under my nose.

The next morning, I got up early, packed the Aston Martin, then woke Bex. We drove down Highway One through the rainy weather just past Cambria to her favorite one-lane road that came out in Morro Bay. It wasn't until we were on that road winding through the trees and vineyards that she finally started to talk. Bex told me about the accident, not remembering anything past being ripped out of the car by Armin. He'd drugged her with something. When she told me she'd been waterboarded, I started to understand why she'd been so out of sorts. She said she was having a hard time knowing what was real, and the night terrors were memories she couldn't get out of. Seeing her suffer, then hearing how deep it ran made me feel as helpless as finding out she'd been taken.

On the drive back to Pebble Beach, I tried to come up with a list of things we could do in the coming months that might help take some stress off her, but she refused nearly everything including the trip to Switzerland she'd requested before her birthday. She wanted to go home and find her new normal, so we talked about schooling options for Grace, her work schedule, how much time she needed with Ben and how frequently, and the laundry list she had with the FBI. They'd asked her to show

them where every body was buried, where any more papers that might've been hidden, and needed her to sit down and identify as many people as she could. People who had been found dead over the years or were sitting in prison.

After we showed up to the house, we dressed up, and went out for dinner while we continued to lay plans for the next six months. When everything had been planned as far as it could be, we went for another shorter drive. I found a remote road that led to a cliff near the ocean, and it was one of those rare nights when the sky wasn't overcast over the water. It was simple, probably lacking in creativity, but I left the doors open on the car while music played and danced with her. There were only trees, stars, and the ocean. She wasn't able to dance for all that long without pain in her hips, so we laid on the hood of the car and stared at the sky for a while.

"I'm not sure if I'm still not supposed to ask, or if I can now that it's over, but you said something to Ben that keeps running through my head." I kept my eyes up at the stars because the memory of her breaking down felt heavy.

"You can ask." Her soft voice was a little distant, likely because I'd pulled her from her own thoughts.

"You said Patty touched you under the table, and your dad let him take you upstairs. I'm assuming the context made sense to Ben and your family, but not to me or Ryan. Did you parents know something happened before you were taken and not do anything?"

She shook her head. "No. They didn't know. That was the point. I didn't say anything..." Bex drew in a deep breath. "Emily's birthday is a couple weeks before mine. That year, she didn't want to have a shared party with me, so she had her own the weekend after. Patty was there..." Her breaths sounded like they were taking a little more energy from her than they normally did. "He asked me to sit on his lap, and I did because nothing had ever happened before. Patty was always my favorite; I had no reason not to trust him. We sitting there at the table outside, family, friends, church members all around, and his hand worked it's way up my dress." She took a deep breath and let it out calmly. "I started to squirm to get down, and he didn't let me, he just kept on. I finally yelled that I wanted to go play. He let me down and I ran for the tree house to go cry to Ben, but he was up there smoking weed with his friends and yelled at me to get down. I went in the house and my mom shewed me out of the kitchen because she was getting the food ready with the ladies from church.

Bex rubbed at her throat as she took another deep breath. "When I ran to my dad, he was in his office with the door locked because he was on a business call. I cried and banged on the door, trying to get him to open it as Patty came down the hall. My dad opened the door, madder than hell that I was wailing. Patty told him he caught me trying to open Emily's gifts and that's why I was running to him. My dad was pissed because he'd previously told me this party wasn't for me and I'd have my own in a couple weeks."

I wiped a tear from the side of her eye as it rolled back toward her hair.

"My dad told me to go sit up in my room, I started screaming and saying 'no,' so he asked Patty to take me upstairs." Her eyes shifted from side to side as if she were watching it all happen right in front of her. "Everyone was just downstairs," she whispered.

I pressed my lips together and looked up at the sky again because I was trying not to bawl. Picturing Bex as a little girl was the easiest thing in the world after having met Ella and Grace. There was so much rage over hearing what happened that I could barely sit there with it, but I had no choice.

"Um... I was grounded for the first time over it, and I was mad, so I didn't say anything. Not to Ben, my mom,

Dad... and of course Emily." She shook her head. "I didn't talk to any of them for more than a week. And I got really sick—some terrible cold from my cousins—and my mom was up all night with me. In the morning, she asked my dad to take me to Patty's office because I couldn't breathe very well, I had a terrible fever and a rash... He said no because he had court and couldn't reschedule, so he asked Ben. I started howling again, begging him not to go to work, not to let Ben take me to Patty's office, and to stay home with me. I told him he could take all my presents back for my birthday if he just stayed home. And while I was crying and begging, he was holding me, but he got irritated with me because I wouldn't let go of him. He didn't know I was terrified."

"B..." I rubbed her arm. "You don't have to tell me if—"

"No. I want to. I've never told it, and I don't want to hold it anymore. I know you're worried because I'm doing a bad job of holding myself together, but I can't hold this anymore." Her voice was breathy as she spoke.

"You don't have to hold yourself together, I just don't want you hurting yourself just because I asked." I brushed her hair back because it was sticking to her skin from the tears. "You can keep going, but only for you. I'll gladly listen to whatever you need to get off your chest." It was painful to watch her suffer through the words, and more so to feel it as an outsider who loved her, but I would listen even if it killed me. Whatever made it easier for her to breathe, I would do.

Bex took another breath to recompose herself a little more before she spoke again. "My dad yelled at me because I wouldn't let go of him. He told me there would be no party if I didn't stop, and I didn't, so he said he was taking everything back and canceling the party. My mom chimed in, and he was resolute, saying I'd been nothing but disrespectful the prior week, and now I was acting like an animal instead of a little girl. I got away from Ben just as he was going out the door, grabbed his brief case to try and stop him... He yanked it back so hard I couldn't keep my balance. I was so dizzy and weak, but I was desperate to stop him from leaving..." She swallowed. "He left me there on the floor and slammed the door shut on his way out. I stayed on the floor, crying my eyes out, and Ben picked me up. He took me to the doctor so my mom could get some sleep. Emily threw a fit because she didn't want to go to school when Ben and I weren't, so he didn't make her.

"At Patty's office, we were taken back to a room to wait for him. Emily left to get something from the vending machine, and that was okay because I still had Ben..." Her eyes closed for a moment as she shook her head. "She came back and asked him to help her because the machine ate her dollar, and I cried, and begged... He promised to be right back. Patty came in just as Ben was leaving, told him they'd be right back, and... Ben heard me screaming as Patty ran out with me. I watched him run down the hallway for me. He even grabbed my arm, but I had a dumb bracelet on... He lost his grip." She shook her head again. "I keep telling myself that I was little and I didn't know, but... I'm still just mad that I was so petty."

I hugged her closer. "I don't think you were being petty. You were hurt because no one listened the first time, and scared to tell them after the fact. And I could be wrong, but from the sounds of it, you were pretty calm as a kid too, so I feel like your family should've known something was wrong when you started screaming and crying like that." My shoulder raised under her head a little. "And I've been a step-dad for about two whole minutes, but if Grace carried on the way you're describing, I think I'd have to stop—no matter how frustrated I might be. Kids wear their heart out on their sleeves, and there's always a reason, even if it doesn't seem that important to an adult... I'm so sorry they didn't hear you, Beautiful." I kissed her forehead, then held my lips there just to smell her hair. "And thank you for trusting me enough to tell me... I promise it'll stay with me unless you ask me to tell someone."

I held her for a long while before she finally went back to laying on her back and watched the stars. Her hands were sitting palm up on her legs and she took controlled breaths. Ben would tell her to do it every now and then, but I didn't know what for or if it was something that was actually helpful. I didn't like all of his approaches to things with Bex. He was either too strict or too relaxed and there didn't seem to be a balance as far as I saw.

"Are you okay with Ben being the person you work with?

She held up her shoulder. "I don't want to do it with anyone else... He knows a lot because of Toby and being part of it, so there's less for me to explain. It's been a little frustrating that he won't let me walk away when I need to. You know me, I don't often blurt things out, just to go back and clean it up after. But, Ben was always the person I hoped would come save me and hug me while I cried, and part of me still wishes for it so I don't want anyone else unless he doesn't want to hear it."

Bex's relationship with Ben was interesting. While she was more comfortable around her family than I expected her to be, she was still careful around them with the exception of Ben. It was like they didn't have those years of separation. And Ben was more aware of Bex than his own daughter. He watched her like a fragile doll, taking in every word she said, responding to anything of concern with great consideration. I assumed he must've always been that way because Bex did the same thing with everyone else. She'd know if Ryan or I were having a bad day before we did. Much of her personality was a direct reflection of her parents and brother who'd only spent eight years with her. And while I still wasn't sure I entirely liked Ben, I was relieved that Bex had just one person she could talk to and get help from. I could feel the sense of content that radiated off of her when he was around, and it brought me my own sense of peace.

"I'm sure Ben has his reasons, but if you need to walk away, he needs let you. Tell him you'll be back in five minutes." I turned my head to look at her. "You're allowed to have your own set of rules." She wasn't paying her brother, but regardless, he should have a little clemency for his sister. "No one has the right to make you stay somewhere you don't wanna be, and if you need me to say something, I will.."

"I can handle it. I don't know how I'm gonna sit there with my life as an open book. The thought of sitting in a pile of my own filth, just on display... makes it feel formidable." She shook her head and looked at me. "But I wanted to ask if you'd be able to stay home the next couple weeks. It's easier when I know you're in the next room if I need to take a break, or..."

I nodded and offered a small smile. "You got it, Beautiful." I rubbed a finger down her arm. "I know what happened made you feel dirty and used, but somehow... it makes you a little purer of heart. You've withstood expanses of pain people can't understand, then you choose to keep persevering, and you don't let it make you bitter." I shook my head. "You're inspiring, and most when you least feel like it."

She let out a breath and was quiet for a minute before she asked, "You don't feel like I don't trust you, do you?" She looked at me again.

I couldn't help it, her face was so damn beautiful and I had to touch her soft cheek again. "What makes you ask?"

"Something Ryan said."

I pulled up a shoulder. "I think you trust me a lot more than other people." She didn't fully trust anyone, so I tried never to take it personally.

She shook her head. "That's not good enough. I do

trust you, it's everyone else I don't trust. When I have a bad reaction, it's me I don't trust, and when I can't tell you something, it's because I either can't stomach saying it or I knew it was too dangerous for you to know... I've wanted to tell you everything so many times, but it's other people I couldn't trust." She held up her shoulder. "I know that sounds like a bunch of excuses, but it's the truth. I do trust you, you make me feel safe."

There'd been a few times her lack of trust made me want to give up, but I didn't. In marrying me, I had an unspoken hope that it would make her know I was someone she could trust. I didn't want to know things to fix them, I wanted to understand, and I didn't want to hear things she didn't tell me herself.

Bex's eyebrows raised. "You're not saying anything."

I shook my head. "I was letting it sink in... I'm not always sure with you, and I needed to hear that."

She rolled on her side to lay against me with the smallest amount of lightness in her eyes as she touched my cheek. "I chose to trust you the day I accepted that free condo for the summer." A smile grew on her face and she leaned down to kiss me. "Convenient timing, a safe neighborhood, an adorable fur-creature so I wasn't completely alone, and sea-glass colored walls..." She kissed me a little deeper than she normally did, so I carefully made sure my hand on her arm was only resting there and not holding her. "I suspected it was you, Ryan confirmed it, and thought I'd run if it didn't work out. Then a month later, Carol told me, but I trusted you most when you finally told me because you were too guilty to keep your own secret."

I nodded. "I wanted to help."

She nodded. "And I needed it... Thank you."

My hand felt like a magnet being drawn to the rose-silk softness of her cheek. "Always."

Bex leaned down and her soft lips touched mine as she started to unbutton my shirt. I let her, because I felt like it was an insult to her to stop her, but I was afraid for her. She'd get moments of bravery, and with seemingly no trigger, she'd become so paralyzed with fear that I couldn't be within ten feet of her. It wasn't such a big deal when we were in the confines of a house or a hotel suite, but we were in the middle of the woods with a cliff thirty feet ahead.

I broke the kissing just enough to say, "Promise me you won't run."

"It's your turn to trust me."

I wanted to trust her, but I was so afraid of scaring her. Every time her fragile heart broke, I felt like it was going to make me have a mental snap. I was afraid if I held her too tight, she'd disappear, like she was never real to begin with... But I couldn't ask her to trust me or trust herself if I couldn't. So, I moved my hand from her arm to her side, then down to her hip to start pulling up the water-like silk of her dress until I could touch the skin on the outside of her thigh. I rubbed the back of my fingers lightly down to the outside of her knee, testing to see if she was really okay. She'd never mentioned it as a place I couldn't touch her, but I was still worried. It had nearly an opposite effect; she pressed herself closer to me, so I embraced it.

While we kissed, I slowly slid my hand back up to her side and around to her back to unzip her dress, appreciating the velvet feel of her skin. Her shoulder was somehow softer than her dress as I moved it out of the way. I sat up with her so she could finish getting my shirt off and I could get the other half of her dress off her shoulder, but also because I didn't want her to feel trapped under me by rolling on top of her. She seemed to have no fear as I unclasped her bra, but I could feel her pulse under my lips when I kissed her neck. The warmth of her in combination with the cold air of the night made her even more desirable to touch.

I wasn't a promiscuous person before Bex, but I wasn't abstinent... and no one and nothing compared... Whole heartedly loving someone and feeling it right back changed everything. I already knew I'd never loved the partners I'd had before—so much so, I never bothered to say it—but I didn't realize the way it would change something as simple as sex. The only thing bothering me now was the twenty minutes of complete stillness from the astoundingly beautiful woman laying against my side under her blue silk dress. There'd been no shaking, she didn't hold her breath, and she'd never stopped or signaled that she wanted to... And even now, she didn't startle when I ran my fingers down from her shoulder to her elbow... Bex was just still.

I took in a breath for courage, telling myself if the moment ended in her having a panic attack, then I'd just have to take it and help her as best as I could. She still didn't startle or move when I touched her cheek, and I looked down, but only had a view of her brown waterfall curls twisting down toward her opposite shoulder. I hadn't felt any tears on my chest, but that didn't mean they weren't hanging in her eyes like they usually did when she was upset.

"How you doin', Beautiful?" I asked in a soft whisper, caressing her cheek lightly again.

She took in a deeper breath than the ones before. "I'm good."

"Yeah...? You're pretty quiet."

She shook her head a little. "Sorry."

"Don't be sorry." I touched her hair, which was another test, but I also loved her hair and wished she'd leave it down more than just at night. "I just don't want you sitting there suffering in silence."

I felt her cheek pull back on my chest. "I'm good..." She laughed a little, but it only had the sound of her breath. "I think I'm just in a little bit of shock... but the good kind."

I laughed a little. "Yeah... I'm kinda there with you. We pushed a lot of boundaries, which is why I'm sweating it out."

"Mm... You might be sweating it out, but I'm starting to get cold, and a little tired." She took in a breath and sat up as she let it out. "Can I have your jacket?"

I reached behind my head for my suit jacket and gave it to her before I sat up. She wasn't asking because she was cold, she wanted to cover the wounds and scars while she put her dress back on. I put on my white undershirt, then focused on buttoning my dress shirt so she'd have her privacy, but I wanted to stare at the beauty she couldn't see.

"What'd you do with my pins?" she asked as she checked the pockets of my jacket.

I laughed. "I threw them on the ground so you couldn't put your hair back up."

"Are you serious?"

I slid off the hood of the car with another laugh and shook my head. "No." I reached into my pocket. "I wouldn't do that to you." I pulled out the wad of pins and handed them to her. "But I thought about it."

She shook her head. "I don't understand your obsession with my hair."

I moved her hair over her shoulders and smiled at the way the large curls touched the sides of her neck. "It makes you look warmer." I wanted to stare at her for hours. Her dress was on, but she was still wearing my jacket, and with her hair down in front of her shoulders, she was just... gorgeous.

Her eyebrows raised a little. "I look like I'm twelve."

I shook my head, running my finger under her chin. "You look your age, but you look thirty when you put your hair up."

She smiled at me. "I'll leave it down if you let me drive back."

I laughed. "You can drive if you want to anyway.

Maybe it'll inspire you to drive your new car more when we get back."

"Let's go. It's cold." She tucked her arms closer into her sides.

I chuckled a little at how she ignored my comment and grabbed the lapel of the jacket to hold her off. "Hang on a second."

Bex looked up at me with honest eyes. The way her long lashes flared out, along with the innocence on her face, had me a little dumbfounded for a second, but all I could do was give her a gentle smile and hold her face for a moment.

"What changed... You've panicked over me kissing your hand before, you've recently been through hell, and you can be really convincing at hiding something from me. So I'm concerned, and I'm asking." I didn't let go of her face because I was afraid she'd look down, and I wanted to know that the answer she gave me was honest.

"I let it be different..." Her shoulders raised just a little. "There's no one around us for miles. It's just you and me... There's no one watching, no one forcing me, no expectations. It was just you and me, because we love each other... I focused on that. At least seven or eight times, I got scared but... I thought about you." She held up her shoulders still looking innocent. "The way you smile at me, the way you stare at me from across the room because you can, and the way you're really careful about how you touch me because you don't wanna cause me pain... All of it was different because I trust what I know." She didn't look away from me. And while her voice held a quiet confidence, there was a stray tear on her cheek.

There were so many things in her words I wanted to respond to. I wondered if I'd have to find places where she'd know no one else was close, I wanted to rage over the fact that anyone had ever forced her while others watched, then I wanted to reaffirm that I was always careful because I was scared shitless of hurting her.

"I love you." I wiped the tear off her cheek, being careful of the cut there.

She gave a small smile and nodded. "That's what I know... It made it different."

"And what about now? After, I mean." It wasn't just the tear, it was a deep-rooted fear in her eyes that she was fighting.

"I'm struggling a little bit... My mind has a hard time processing, but I keep sticking to what I know." she shook her head. "If this gets taken from me, it won't be their fault this time."

I kissed her forehead and put my forehead against hers with a smile. "You zigged, zigged again, zagged, spun in a circle, barked like a llama, and threw the cat a piece of bacon."

She laughed. "What?"

I laughed with her. "You keep throwing me off. I think it's gonna be one way, and you go off in a direction I didn't think of."

"You're insane," she laughed.

"Naw." I wrapped my arms around her and let out a breath of relief. "Just had to make us laugh before I dropped into a puddle at your feet. You're goddamn crazy-beautiful, and I don't know how to love you more right now." I hugged her tightly and took in the feeling of her body against mine. She was right there, safely in my arms, as beautiful as she could possibly be, and alive... I'd had such little hope that I'd find her again, so holding her closely was more for me than her.

"I love you too." She turned her face into my arm and her small body relaxed into me.

"More than anything and everything." I rested my cheek on top of her head, smelling the warm scent of her shampoo.

Chapter 51

Bexley

6 Years Later

I looked around the house and didn't expect it to appear so normal. There were couches, a recliner, a TV, paintings on the walls, and books on the shelves. The kitchen was just a plain design from the sixties, right down to the grocery list on the freezer door. Every gun I'd found was in the garbage can except for the one I left on the table with a pad of paper and a pen. I'd been careful to leave no trace of myself while collecting the stacks of hidden papers and putting them in an easier place for the FBI to locate. Their questions were never-ending, even six years after the fact, and I was tired of being asked. I no longer wished to make space in my life for the past, so I was doing everything I could to make it end.

Grey and Ryan didn't know where I was because they were on their flight back from Oslo with Roger, Sam, Charlotte, and Pops. Grace was safe in Dallas with my family, all of whom believed I was still in Seattle. I'd left my phone at home, brought nothing electronic with me, and used fake IDs I hadn't turned over to the FBI upon request. I was using ones I'd never used before, so there was nothing associating them to me.

I listened as a car pulled up outside, but didn't allow myself to feel afraid. This would be the last time I ever allowed myself to be Hannah and feel the numbness she brought. I looked at the gun, praying it would be the last time I ever saw one while I waited for the sound of the front door.

"What—Hannah... What're you doin' here? How'd ya find me?" Patty had stopped short in the doorway to the kitchen with a bag of groceries in his arm.

I shook my head and looked at a picture on the wall of Patty, my dad, and their sister Rebecca. "I've always known where you were. Colorado up to Michigan, down to Florida, back to Tennessee, then... Texas." I looked at him. "This is the house Cynthia bought for you to keep me in after you fulfilled your end of the deal. I told Dad years ago about what was said in that shed at Toby's, and he told me the two of you, along with Roger, were playing Cynthia right from the time you were first arrested... But neither of them knew she already bought this house."

He looked at me for a long moment before asking, "How come ya haven't had me arrested?"

I shook my head. "I couldn't trust that no one else wouldn't come out of the woodwork. I know you killed Luisa Vaughters."

Patty nodded and set down the bag of groceries he carried in. "I ain't buggin' nobody, and I'm still on my medications."

"I know. I've made sure of it. Your friend Alan that checks in everyday," I shook my head, "he's nothing more than an employee for a dummy corp. that leads to another dummy corp., and on, until there's nothing but an empty lot and a cash start up on a name that doesn't exist."

Patty frowned, and I could see the betrayal in his

eyes for just a moment before he cleared it. "Well... alright then. What'r'ya here for?"

"It's been over twenty years, there's no one else left, and I need peace. The police are already on their way, so you're faced with an option." I directed my gloved hand to the handgun on the table with a single bullet in it. "You can go to prison and be sentenced to death, or you can go by your own hand." I kept my eyes on him while watching him realize what gun it was.

"How'd you get that?" He looked at me fearfully.

A cold-hearted part of me wanted to tell him Rebecca told me, but I didn't. I pulled the pen and notepad down next to the gun and stood as I directed a hand for him to sit.

"I ain't bothered ya, and I always been sorry. I did everythin' I could to save ya, and I'm sorry Toby got killed in the process, but you been free for six years. What more do ya want?" He looked at me with so much hurt and betrayal in his eyes, but I couldn't feel it. I was Hannah Lawrence.

"You haven't bothered me...?" I shook my head. "I'll always have that moment of terror right before someone shakes my hand, I'll always wake up in physical pain, and I will never scrub the blood off the walls of my mind. That more than bothers me." My voice was as cold as I felt. "You're not sorry, you're sick, and I deserve to be rid of you." The words came seething through my teeth.

Patty looked at me for a moment while he breathed from the top of his chest due to stress, then nodded. "Alright..." He sat down. His hand shook as he picked up the pen.

"Write it out to me so they know it's real." My voice was quieter because I wasn't delighted by his choice, or mine.

Patty paused for just a second, then wrote my name at the top of the page, followed by whatever waste of words that followed.

"Ya can't stand in here. You'll get blood on ya." His voice was a shaken whisper as he looked at the gun.

I walked around to the side of the table, near the wall I was about to stand behind. "I want you to know, as much as I wanna hate you, I don't. I'm full of pain over what you did to me, but... I'm grateful you helped take the whole operation down, that you kept me alive... but I'm most grateful you manipulated Cynthia into leaving that hard drive for Ryan and Grey to find... My life is made better because of them."

Patty nodded, keeping his eyes on the notebook. "How'd you find out about that?"

"Ryan obtained the records of who visited you in prison... Catrine Ockert. It didn't make sense that she'd sit around and wait to find out where her daughter was, then one day decide she had enough... "

He nodded, his eyes still down. "It had to end... You weren't supposed to be one of them kids..." His shoulders slumped and he shook his head. Patty sat there in silence for a moment, tears hanging in his eyes. "I never meant to hurt ya... Every time I brought ya in that room—after—I'd swear I was never gonna do it again... but I couldn't stop." His chin trembled. "I'm sick in the head, and Henry understood that. He didn't make me feel bad 'bout it or nothin'... He was the only one. I wanted just one person who didn't hate me, who didn't see me like a monster... You were too young and sweet to hate anybody. At your sister's birthday party, you came up to the table with that smile just like Rebecca's... She didn't hate nobody neither." Patty let out a quiet cry, tipping his head down so his face would be covered behind his hand.

I stood there trying not to be provoked by his emotion, but it was hard. For me, knowing as much pain as I did, it made me sympathetic to anyone's pain. It didn't matter who it was or the terrible things they'd done. People didn't lose their mind over happiness, they didn't retaliate because something felt good, it was pain, suffering, and anger that made them act so hatefully.

"Patty, I know you wanted things to be different. You've been suffering your whole life, you wanted to be loved, but I've never been the person who was going to fix that for you... I saw you just three weeks ago outside of Grace's school, she did too, and she told me she saw you on her field trip that day... I have to protect my daughter... I found all the pictures you hid of her, Ella, me... You can't help it, and I know that, but it doesn't mean I can leave you here and hope you're still taking your meds. And you and I both know they're barely helping. Alan told me you got too close to a neighbor girl, she was here in this house alone with you. She's fourteen, Patty..."

He shook his head, still sobbing quietly. "I know it. I swear to God, I didn't..."

I took a deeper breath, shook my head and let out a quiet huff. "I know you didn't... but you would have if Alan hadn't caught on. I tried... I tried letting you live out the rest of your days without being behind bars or locked in a hospital because I didn't wanna do what you did to me." My throat was aching from the emotion I was holding back. "I can't be responsible for one more child. So, as much as I don't want to ask you, I am asking you to end this... Because if you don't, I have to. I'm tired."

He nodded, picked up the pen, and shakily signed his name at the bottom of the note he'd written. "Ya gotta go, Hannah."

I nodded and walked around to the corner hall that went to the small half bath or outside to the backyard. The sound of the hammer cocking back felt like the loudest noise I'd ever heard. I held my breath and plugged my ears just before the short blast. I could see the blood splatter back against the kitchen cabinets before feeling the soft thud of the gun falling to the floor through my shoes.

"I'm sorry," I whispered as I closed my eyes and

stood there for a moment. Experiencing death wasn't something new to me, but I'd forgotten how cold it was. The air would tangibly change because there was less energy in the room. It made my skin prickle and my legs grow numb. I knew what it felt like every time I'd witnessed it... it was just cold.

⬦⬦⬦

"Mom." Grace ran across the living room and hugged me as soon as she saw me. "What are you doing here? Are you okay?" She continued to hug me.

I closed my eyes as I embraced her. She was fifteen now and still stuck to me like glue, but I adored every second. Her friends' parents couldn't understand how Grace didn't hate Grey and I, like most teens hated their parents, but her friends hadn't lost a parent at nine years old. "I missed you and I was getting lonely in Seattle all by myself."

"I missed you too. Are you sure you're okay?" She stepped back and looked at me just like Toby would have. She was a straight combination of the two of us in looks, but I only ever saw Toby. Because of Grace, Toby was always with me. She was the best of him.

I smiled and touched her cheek. "I'm good. I promise. Are Grandma and Papa here?"

"Uh, I think Grandma's in her sewing room with Uncle Ben, and I know for sure Papa's in his study. Is Dad here too, or did you come by yourself?"

"Grey and Ryan just landed in Seattle about thirty minutes ago. You and I are gonna go back in a couple hours, but you are coming back after Ryan and Emily's wedding." They'd been dating since a year after Toby's funeral and were getting married next weekend. My graduation ceremony from law school was in two days, so Emily wanted the wedding the following weekend to make it easy on our parents. "And I say it grudgingly because I'll miss you, but you're staying for the summer like you wanted." I cringed as I spoke because I *really* didn't want to be without her for that long. Since she'd moved to Seattle with me, I'd never been away from her for more than three days. I'd gotten the hip replacement surgery I needed, but otherwise, Grace had gone everywhere with Grey and I.

Grace squealed and hugged me again. "Thank you, thank you, thank you!"

"You're welcome, but if you don't call me every day, you're seriously going to make me cry." I kissed her cheek and pulled back.

"I will. I *promise*."

I nodded. "Okay. I need to go find my dad."

"Yep. Can I call Dad and thank him?"

"Of course." I touched her arm as I passed in front of her to go down the hall. My dad's door was closed so I knocked before I opened it.

He turned in his chair with a questioning look, then his face lit up. "Well, what're you doin' here? We're supposed to be coming up your way in the mornin'."

"I know, but I missed Grace." I gave a slight pout.

"You forgot she had that registration for her art class next year, didn't ya?" He chuckled as he stood and took off his glasses.

"I *did*." I'd forgotten until he'd mentioned it, and thankfully it contributed to my lie. "Did Grace mention it?"

He nodded and hugged me. "She did, but she thought you were just gonna call 'em and take care of it." He rubbed my back. "It's good to see ya, Sweet Girl. I've been missin' ya."

"I missed you too." I let out a breath and closed my eyes while I absorbed the hug. We saw each other at least once a month, but it never felt like enough. My parents had become vital to my everyday life. I called my mom every morning and my dad on my way home in the evening. A larger part of me had expected to have a falling out with them because of all I'd been through and their tendency to hover, but we all seemed to find the right balance after the first few months.

The doorbell rang, telling me my timing was spot on, though I was a little dismayed it was interrupting the long hug I needed from my dad. Before I'd walked in the house, I had to let go of Hannah and my emotions had returned. There was a pit in my stomach over what I'd done earlier in the morning, and the guilt was biting at me in the worst way.

"I got it," Grace called.

"You okay, honey?" My dad rubbed my back.

"Yeah." I stepped back and gave a small smile. "Just needed a hug. It's been a long time since I've been by myself, and I've come to realize I don't like it."

He chuckled and tapped my nose. "Ya never did."

"Papa? It's for you," Grace called.

My dad frowned and looked at his watch. "I wonder who that could be?"

I followed him out of the room to the entryway. Agent Moore and his new partner Agent Finch were standing there asking Grace how Seattle was treating her.

"Gracie, will you run up and ask your uncle to come down?" I gave her a tender smile as I reached a hand toward her. While Agent Moore hadn't shown himself to be untrustworthy in any way, I was still very careful when it came to Grace. It would be the death of me if anything happened to her.

"Yeah." Grace gave my hand a squeeze and ran upstairs.

"I can't believe how much she's grown. It's crazy." Agent Moore gave me a polite smile. "And she's looking more like you by the day." He reached out a hand to my dad.

I held up my shoulders with a polite smile of my own. "So I'm told."

"You guys just stoppin' to say hi? Or'd you catch wind of Hannah bein' in town and come to pester her with more questions?" My dad laughed a little, but I knew he was irritated by just how much the FBI *didn't* leave me alone.

"No, not this time. After the treasure trove we've obtained, I think we may not have to anymore." Agent Moore took a deep breath. "Would you mind if we sat?"

"Not at all. Come on in." My dad directed a hand to the living room.

I looked up at the top of the stairs and saw Ben. He signed to ask me what they were here for and I held up my shoulders as I waited for him to come down. My dad sat in his chair, the agents took my usual couch, so I went over to the one across from them.

"Ben, how are ya?" Agent Moore reached out a hand to him.

"Oh, not too bad. You?" Ben shook his hand and sat next to me, putting an arm around my shoulders to pull me into a side hug. "Hey, Bean," he whispered.

"I'll tell you after I've said what I'm here for." Agent Moore pulled on his chin with his hand. "I'm not entirely sure how this news will be taken, but Patty was found dead in a house just outside of Texarkana. He shot himself in the head with an old Luger. We have some testing and record digging to do, but we believe it was the same gun he used to kill your sister and parents. If it *is* the same gun, we're not sure how he obtained it." He looked at my dad nervously. "We also found stacks of papers and computer drives hidden around the house that seem to document just about his whole life, his dealings with Henry Greer, and things we weren't even aware of."

"Do you have pictures?" I asked quietly.

Both agents looked at me wryly.

"I want proof that he's dead because it's not the first time I've heard it," I clarified.

Agent Finch nodded, opened the folder on his lap, and handed me a small stack of printed photos. I took them and didn't need to memorize them because I'd seen it all first hand, but I had to act like I hadn't. They'd be suspicious if I didn't question everything the way I normally did.

"There's a photo of a note he left at the bottom. It was addressed to you," Finch told me quietly.

I nodded, flipping to the next page. "I still want to see his body in person, and I want to watch him be cremated." I sat there with a cold demeanor because I could've easily cried.

"It'll be a couple weeks, but I promise you, he's dead. They've already run a DNA test on him, and I waited until I had the results before coming here," Agent Moore responded.

"Like I said, I've been told this before." I handed Ben the last page because I didn't want to read the note. I knew he'd not only want to, but he'd also tell me what it said when I felt ready to hear it.

"I'll make sure it's arranged and give you a call when we release his body." Agent Moore looked at my dad who was sitting in his chair silently.

My stomach sank seeing my dad's expression. He looked disappointed as he stared at the papers in Ben's hand.

"Dad?" I couldn't sit there and watch him and pretend not to notice. Whatever he felt was my fault.

"I'm alright, Sweet Girl." He took a deep breath, then let out a humorless chuckle. "I think I feel bad 'cause I don't feel bad at all." He scratched the top of his head and looked at Agent Moore. "How'd y'all find 'im?"

"Local PD got a call from his neighbor, one of the officers recognized him and called us." Finch looked at me. "You were correct with your assumptions years ago. He was only in places he knew or near you. Our team located several pictures of you, your daughter, and your husband." He looked at Ben. "And your daughter as well." He looked at me again. "It would also seem he planned on attending your graduation this weekend. We found bus tickets to Seattle and a printout of the ceremony location and time. The FBI and I, personally, owe you an apology for dismissing you and your concerns. I'm sure your brother could tell you, but psychology isn't an exact science, our profiler got it wrong."

"Don't deflect your wrongdoing with the instabilities of psychology, it was your arrogance and nothing less. You don't like it when people tell you to do your job. I imagine that's why you were partnered with Agent Moore, so he could rid you of your insolence." I stared at him with a strong backbone. It'd also been my stab at Finch to place the bus tickets and itinerary in the house. I'd placed a few other things as well, but they weren't for retaliation of any kind, they were for the FBI to discover; to help more children with stolen voices.

"Hannah," my dad muttered with slight disapproval.

I looked at my dad with a calm expression. "I said nothing untrue."

"You didn't." Agent Finch agreed as he rubbed his hands together nervously. "You were right, Mrs. Maslen. It was inexcusable—both the failure to investigate and my behavior."

"And the reason why he was partnered with me." Agent Moore crossed his arms. "You couldn't have possibly known that."

I smirked. "Please, don't ask me to show my hand now." I glanced at my dad and looked back at Finch casually.

He looked confused for just a short second, but then I could see the realization before he laughed. "You're gonna make a real fine lawyer." He shook his head and looked at my dad. "She's too smart for her britches."

My dad winked at me. "Don't I know it."

I forced a convincing smile like I was grateful, but I couldn't be. He wouldn't be proud of what I'd done, he'd be forced to see the monster I hid away. I wanted to cry. No part of me regretted my choice, I only felt guilty because of my dad. Guilt was easier than fear, but it still hurt.

"Well, I don't want to monopolize your time, and I have work piling up as we speak. Do any of you have questions about anything?" Agent Moore looked from my dad to Ben, then me.

I looked at Ben to see if he had anything, but he shook his head and handed the papers back to Agent Finch. "Nope. I hope it's him, and I hope there's no god to save him."

I elbowed Ben with a frown. It wasn't that I believed in god, but our dad did. I didn't like it when Ben insulted their beliefs.

"Sorry, Dad." Ben looked over at him.

"Well, I think hell ain't good enough for 'im, so I get what you're sayin'." My dad pushed himself up from his chair. "And I thank you two for comin' out here to give us the good news. I'm glad this'll finally be put to bed."

"Of course," Agent Finch shook my dad's hand first because he was closest. "We're doing our best to keep the press away from this too. The name Hannah Lawrence is slowly becoming forgotten in the manner we hoped."

I chuckled. "There you go again, crediting yourself for another failure. My husband's lawyers and PR manager have made people forget me. I could send you the bill and the documentation to prove it."

My dad looked at me with raised eyebrows. "Ya made your point, now move on."

I shook my head, crossing my arms. "I have the right to defend my husband's hard work that paid for it, and his team of people that have seen it through." I looked at Agent Finch. "You should understand that while I may seem harsh, I find it unlikely that you have a view as to why your prior actions were beyond insulting. It's not that you didn't listen, it's that men like you were the exact reason why I was taken, why I was tortured, and why I was never found. The commonality in all of them was arrogance. So, the next time you feel intimidated by a woman contradicting your subjectable intel, listen to the woman with facts and more experience than you would ever want to have. You and the way you conduct your investigations are the number two reason most kids don't come home. Being second to pedophiles and exploiters is surely not a place you should want to be."

"No..." He nodded. "You're right and I'm very sorry."

I shook my head. "I don't accept your apology, I accept change." I uncrossed my arms and looked at my dad. "Ben and I will be out back for a minute." My dad nodded once, then I looked at Agent Moore. "Thank you, and it was good to see you without being questioned to death." I gave him a smile.

He nodded. "I've been trying not to. Congrats on law school. Send me a new picture from graduation for my desk."

I laughed a little. "I'll have Mom bring it for you."

Agent Moore laughed. "You think you're being cute, but I'm terrified of that woman."

"I don't know what you're talking about, she's as sweet as can be." I walked with them toward the entryway.

"'Til she's mad," my dad chuckled, "then she's as sweet as a cat gettin' pet backwards."

We all laughed, but Ben and I continued through to the kitchen, then out the backdoor.

I let my smile end almost immediately as I turned to face Ben. "I had you read the letter because I eventually want to know, but not right now." My body felt overly tired from the tense state it'd been in.

"I figured. Take a few deep breaths and let things roll off. Tell me what's left."

I took a quick deep breath, looking at the wooden bench to the side of Ben. "I think Dad summed it up best, I feel guilty for not feeling guilty. I don't know why I feel like I lost something important, but I do, and that's really disturbing me. Mostly, I'm relieved to know there isn't another basement with my name on it." I crossed my arms.

Ben pulled on my arm. "Don't close yourself off, and look at me for a second."

I looked at him.

His eyebrows pulled up a little. "You know I would never judge you for your feelings because you have a right to them. Explain to me what you mean by feeling a loss. Do you mean you lost someone you cared about?"

I shook my head. "No. I don't know exactly how to explain it... It's like a void where there used to be a threat and my brain doesn't know what to do without it. I feel exposed by this gaping hole where my paranoia was perched comfortably."

He laughed. "I like it when someone pisses you off, your vocabulary and descriptions become more clever." Ben tried to shake the rest of his laugh and smile. "Okay, I get what you're saying now. And yes, this is going to be one of your bigger adjustments. You're not gonna be able to justify certain ticks or compulsions, like having getaway cars stashed, because your basis has been removed. That makes your life look a little different now. We can talk about this through the week while I'm in Seattle because this is going to be a multi-layered feeling."

I nodded. "Yeah... I feel so bad for Dad." I looked at Ben and pulled back the corner of my mouth. "If his shoes were on my feet and it was you... I just don't think I'd feel any kind of good or relieved. I'd be angry, but not happy you weren't a problem anymore."

Ben put a hand on top of my head. "Apples and oranges, Bean. You're not Dad, you don't have his experiences with Patty. You're a mother, not a father, and you and I have a very strong relationship that doesn't allow you to see without prejudice. I know you have a soft spot for Dad, but he can take care of his own feelings. You need to focus on your own and not add to it with someone else's when they haven't said anything or asked. I'm not saying you can't care about him, just... in a healthy way. Okay?"

I nodded. I understood what he was telling me and why, but this situation was different. It was my fault my dad was upset, however, I still couldn't bring myself to be sorry for putting the gun in front of Patty.

Chapter 52

Bexley

My house felt like a circus with so many people. It was big enough to handle it, but I wasn't sure I'd ever get used to the noise level of my family plus Grey's. Thankfully, as the kids got older, there was less running and screaming, but they were still loudly playing video games in the living room. I was more than grateful that it was warm enough outside so we could sit at the table on the back deck, it meant the loud booms of laughter weren't ricocheting back. We'd already gotten through dinner but everyone was still around the table just talking. Sometimes it was small groups, and sometimes it was everyone all at once.

"So, Girly, are you taking Sampson and Harris up on their offer to join ranks?" Pops asked from across the table.

I shook my head. "No. They want me to come in at entry level."

"Well, honey," my dad scratched his head, "that's

how ya work your way up."

I shook my head. "I started working my way up before I was even in law school. I have offers from four other firms to walk in at or above where I am now."

Roger looked at me with a frown. "Sampson told me you'd be walking in doing the same thing you're doing now. Are you sure he knew who you were?"

"My last name is Maslen, he knew who I was. He gave me some speech about how they promote from within based on merit, so he can't let me skip ahead of guys who've been waiting for their shot. It was an utter waste of my time, and especially after watching some of the people in the office act like a band of monkeys, I'm not taking the job." I picked up my water glass and took a sip. "Right now, I don't want to leave where I am."

"What's your input on this?" Pops looked at Grey.

He shrugged. "Why are you asking me? It's not my decision, and if I have to make one, I want her to stay simply because I can't replace her. Bex is formidable without a law degree, now that she has one, even better." Grey leaned over and kissed the side of my forehead.

"I'd have to agree." Roger shrugged. "Congratulations, my dear." He held out his glass to me.

"Thank you." I picked up my water glass and clinked glasses with him.

"What about you?" Pops turned his attention to Ryan. "Are you ever gonna get a real job?"

"I did." Ryan spat a piece of ice back into his glass. "I'm Maslen's paralegal and whatever else I'm assigned to." He looked at me with the smallest expression of happiness in his eyes. Ryan loved that it bugged people that he had a law degree but chose to be my right-hand instead.

"There's nothing wrong with the job he has, Willum," Patricia defended before she reached over to comb her fingers through the front tuft of Ryan's hair. She loved him with every fiber of her being and it showed. After he'd gone to Florida to find her, she'd packed up and moved straight back to Seattle. She lived in his old house since he'd moved into our old one. I love Patricia as much as I always had, and felt utterly blessed to have her so close. She was another grandma to Grace, and like a mom to Grey, Sam, and Charlotte. While we were sure nothing would ever be officially declared, Patricia and Roger had also become close. They spent lots of time together, and Patricia seemed to win out the best in Roger. He was easier to be around than he'd ever been. Craig Brae was released from prison, but Ryan and Patricia had both refused contact with him.

My dad got up when the conversation morphed into a different topic, and he lightly pinched the end of my nose on his way inside. I got up so I could take the opportunity to get him alone. He seemed perfectly fine, but I was still worried about him.

"I think it's funny how Roger and Willum can't figure Ryan out," my dad chuckled as he went into the kitchen.

"It's always been that way. Sometimes I wonder if Ryan does things just to mess with them." I walked up the long breakfast counter that served as a clear separation from the kitchen. Grey had it designed almost the same as the one in our old house because I felt most comfortable with that style. It was all open, with two ways out, but there was no walk-in pantry, just large cabinets instead. Grey had designed an absolutely perfect house for us in every way. I loved being home more than anywhere else.

"I know cowboys don't cry, but are you alright after yesterday?" I asked my dad with a sympathetic look.

A grin pulled back the corner of his mouth. "I got my girl back, didn't I?"

"Yeah, but it doesn't mean you can't be upset about Patty."

He gave a slight upward nod in an acknowledgment of understanding. "Honey, I ain't upset he's gone,

I'm *relieved*. He ain't stopped bein' a noose around my neck from the time he turned eighteen. It's hard seein' past those gentler sides, but he was owned by his compulsions, and that made him dangerous to everyone. Especially for you and the girls."

I nodded. While I'd planted the bus tickets and the itinerary to my graduation, I hadn't planted the pictures of Grace and I, or Ella. Those were something Patty had actually done, and I'd been spotting him around more frequently.

My dad walked around the counter and took my hands after he stopped in front of me. "My sweet girl... I know it's hard to stop lookin' when it's the one thing that took the most from your life, but I need ya to try." He leaned a little closer and whispered, "You put the last of it to bed yesterday... Now be done with it."

I looked at my dad fearfully. Did he know what I did?

He reached up and touched my cheek. "I ain't mad. You gave a cautious chance to someone who didn't deserve it, but you saw it wasn't goin' the way ya hoped. Someone was gonna get hurt, and you got the right to do whatever it takes to protect your child. You ain't done nothin' I didn't, or *wouldn't* do. Ya understand me?"

Tears welled up in my eyes. He *did* know. "I'm sorry, Dad... I couldn't keep fighting this fight anymore and he wasn't stopping."

"Oh, honey," he pulled me into a hug, holding the back of my head, "I know it. I ain't mad at ya." My dad rubbed my back. "You gave 'im more of a chance than I would've. The state would've done the same thing, but they would've made a political show about it. I think you showed a lot of courage, humility, and forgiveness where no one else would've bothered."

I shook my head. "I don't know how you can see it that way." I stepped back and wiped under my eyes.

My dad put a hand on my cheek and leaned down

to look me in the eyes. "Did ya do it cause you were angry?"

"No," I shook my head again.

He nodded. "That's right, honey... So, I don't wanna hear another word about it. You got a beautiful girl, you got yourself a good husband, loyal friends, and your family who loves you just as much as we know how." He smiled sweetly. "Alright?"

I nodded and tried to smile. My dad was one of the most fair people I knew. He might've seemed like he saw the world in black and white, but he didn't; he saw in full color with every angle he could catch a glimpse of. "Thank you."

He smiled even more. "I love you, Sweet Girl. I'm always on your side."

I nodded and looked down for a second because now I was starting to care. "Does the FBI know what I did?" I looked at him.

He snorted with an eye roll. "Them dummies wouldn't know it if ya told 'em yourself." He pinched my nose. "Quit your worryin', we're supposed to be celebratin'. Where's the champagne?"

I rolled my eyes a little. "Yeah. There's some in the wine cooler in the kitchen. Just—if you're gonna make a mess, do it outside where it can be easily cleaned."

"Te-he!" He was already pretending to slow jog to it. "Ya gotta do somethin' 'bout that stick up your rear, honey. Ya ain't no fun! Kids! Get down here! We're havin' a party!"

"Oh god," I laughed quietly as I went to go outside. Ever since he retired from being a judge, he'd been enjoying life.

Grey looked at me like he was worried for me when I came out.

"You okay?" Charlotte asked from the chair beside Grey's.

I nodded. "Yeah. I'm good." I sat on Grey's lap and

hugged him. It wasn't normally something I did when the entire family was around, but I wanted a hug from him and didn't want to make him stand up.

"You're beautiful," Grey whispered before he kissed my cheek.

"Alright! Listen up and pass these around," my dad came out with a bottle of champagne under his arm, and a bunch of glasses crammed between his fingers. He walked up to Ben to have him help pull them out.

"Donny, have you lost your mind?" My mom shook her head.

"No, but you have if ya ain't the proud ma of this here young lady." He held out his other handful of glasses to Ben and grinned at me.

"Stop spoiling the fun. I like Dad like this." Emily started setting the glasses in a group for my dad to fill them.

"Of course you do. It's another opportunity for you to drink and walk around talking about how drunk you are like you're at a high school party." Ben rolled his eyes.

Ryan, Grey, Sam, Charlotte, and I laughed because it was painfully true. One night, we'd made it a drinking game.

Emily scoffed and rolled her eyes.

"What's going on?" Grace walked out, followed by her cousins.

"Come on, Ace." Grey reached out an arm to Grace so she'd come sit with us.

"That's enough you two." My dad popped the cork out of the champagne bottle and started pouring into each glass. "We're celebratin' your sister graduatin' law school, we're celebratin' her future that is free and clear of Patty and Henry. Lord, I never thought I'd see the day, and I can die a happy man."

"Not for thirty more years, buster." My mom gave my dad a narrow-eyed smile.

My dad grinned at her. "Yes, honey." He handed

Grey and I a glass of champagne. Everyone else either grabbed one or waited for one to be passed to them. My dad smiled at me proudly. "My sweet girl... goddammit if I ain't the luckiest dad in the whole world. You, Emily, and Ben turned out better than I ever could've thought... All your smiles and sweetness, it just fills up my heart fuller than I got words for. I'm never gonna understand where ya get so much strength from without havin' a mean bone in your body, but I'm a grateful man. You make me so damn proud." He was smiling with tears in his eyes. "You are a self-made young woman with a big heart, a beautiful smile, and a bright and free future, and I can't wait to see more of it. To my very smart and beautiful girl with her self-made name, *Bexley*. I love ya, babygirl." He smiled lovingly and held up his glass.

"To Bex." Grey smiled and clinked my glass.

"To Bex," everyone else chimed.

I sat there on Grey's lap with Grace on the other side, just smiling as everyone took a drink. Moments like this one made my freedom feel real... and I soaked them in when they came.

"B, it's bad luck not to drink after a toast," Grey chuckled.

I looked at him and smiled. "Then drink up. You're drinking for two now." I held my glass for him to take.

"What?" He laughed. "Are you taking a break or something?" His smile had a slight bit of concern in it.

"Yeah. For six more months. I'm sad too, because that case of wine you ordered me from Italy is going to sit there untouched." I shook my head with a nostalgic sigh.

"Wait. Are you pregnant?" Grace's face lit up like a Christmas tree.

I looked at her, then at Grey with a smile.

"*Really?*" Grey looked like he wanted to be happy but wasn't entirely sure. "Are you okay?"

I laughed a little. "Well, I'm not dying." I laughed

again, but also knew he was genuinely concerned and trying not to spoil anyone's fun. "I'm okay. Are you?"

"Oh my god. How are you not freaking out right now?" Grace sat forward and hugged me. "Yay! I'm so stinking excited!"

I laughed and hugged her while trying not to spill champagne on her. Charlotte stood up and took the glass from me.

"I can't believe it! Do you know what you're having?" Grace pulled back and looked at me with bright eyes.

I looked at Grey because I didn't expect him to be silent. He didn't look upset, just in a state of blissful disbelief. I raised my eyebrows at him. "It's a *girl*. You said you always wanted a girl."

He laughed a little but looked like he was going to cry too. "I do. I'm speechless right now." Grey hugged both Grace and I and kissed my cheek.

"As long as I have you, it'll be okay," I whispered next to his ear as I hugged him. He always worried about me and I didn't want him to.

"Always. It's you, me, and Ace." He kissed Grace's cheek. "Don't be getting jealous on me, okay? You're always my ace of hearts. Got it?"

Grace smiled at me. "Can I do it now? It's *killing* me."

I nodded with a small smile. "Yeah. Go get it. You know where it is."

"Stay here. Nobody move." Grace got up and ran into the house like a bolt of lightning.

Grey laughed. "What's that about?"

"She has a gift she's been waiting to give you."

"Yeah? Did she change her mind about this summer?" He rubbed his forehead with a slight nervous laugh. She and Grey had been best buddies since Toby died, and probably loved her as much as he did me.

"Sadly, no." I let out another sigh.

"Well, the good news is, after this summer, you won't have to worry about it anymore." My dad leaned back in his chair and put a hand on my mom's back. "Your ma and I are goin' house shopping up here on Monday."

"What? Really?" Emily looked pleasantly surprised.

"Yeah. Only reason we're waitin' is cause Ben's got some stuff he's gotta wrap up 'fore he comes up too."

My jaw dropped as I looked at Ben. "Really?"

He laughed. "Yeah, you finally sold me over on this place. I'm keeping my practice, just opening a new one here. I'm looking at office parks and houses Monday."

I got up and squealed. Ben laughed and got up to hug me. I threw my arms around his neck and squished him. My heart was so happy I was about to explode.

"Hey, how come I didn't get that reaction when I told you I was moving here?" Emily laughed.

I looked at her from over the back of Ben's shoulder. "Because you texted me and you were still in Dallas, then you didn't move for another two years after."

"What she means is, you're not me." Ben laughed.

Emily stuck her tongue out at him like a child.

"I'll say, we're sittin' over here feelin' like chopped liver," my mom teased with a wink.

"Are you kidding?" I laughed and let go of Ben to walk over to her and my dad. "I'm so happy I'm trying not to cry."

"Oh, you got them cute tears. What're you afraid of?" My mom didn't get up but patted her lap and opened her arms.

I sat down on my mom's lap and hugged her. "Nothing." I closed my eyes and hugged my mom. Her perfume and warm hug made my brain quiet to the chatter in the background of Grey offering Ben one of the many office buildings he owned in town.

"Good." She held a hand over my cheek. "I love love love you."

"I love love love you too," I whispered.

"Okay," Grace sang as she came out with the box for Grey.

"Ryan, a hundred bucks." I nodded toward the box. He knew what it was because he'd helped me draw them up.

He shook his head. "Oh for *sure.*"

I laughed.

"Is that what I think it is?" my dad asked.

I nodded with a smile. "Yep."

Grey laughed. "I thought I knew what it was, now I'm not sure." He glanced at Grace as he pulled the lid off the box.

"Read the card out loud," I told him.

"Okay." He pulled it off the top of the manila envelope inside the box and opened it. "'To the world's best bonus dad.'" He turned to the inside of the card. "'You've wiped every tear, been my best friend, been my guard and shield, and loved me like your own. Let's face it, you've been so much more than a bonus, so let's make it official. Will yous—" He stopped and looked up at Grace with the happiest tear-filled smile.

Grace held up her shoulders. "You're the greatest dad in the world next to my other dad, and he set a high bar." Grace looked at him with hopefulness. "Will you adopt me?"

Grey looked into the box for a second, likely realizing what was in the envelope, and looked at her again. "You got it, Ace." He stood up and hugged her tightly.

I smiled and looked around at everyone's smiling faces. My dad was the only one looking at *me*; he gave a wink before he stood up and took the pen from his pocket to set on top of the papers. He came back and held out a hand to me.

"Seein' him hug his girl makes me wanna hug mine," my dad said as he hugged me tightly. "You spread kindness and love wherever you go, and it just bleeds out from the people who know ya. Just look at that beautiful girl you and Toby made. If she didn't have you, she'd still be dyin' inside from missin' 'im."

I looked at Grey and Grace as they sat there while he signed the papers. It was the best experience watching Grace have everything I didn't have in the years of my life where I hadn't had it. Some of the void was filled by watching them, and the rest was filled by my own sweet dad. "Life didn't go the way we wanted it to, but I'm glad I'm still here. And I'm here because you loved me enough to make me want to stay. So, thank you." I hugged him tighter. "And don't forget to tell your other two favorites how proud you are, because you raised two of my best friends."

He chuckled quietly. "Feelin' guilty cause you're gettin' all the spotlight today?"

I shook my head. "No... I'm feeling grateful for being alive." I wiped a straggling tear.

"Donny, stop smotherin' that girl with your sweetness. You're makin' her cry." My mom tugged on the side of my dress. "And you come back here. I wadn't done holdin' my baby."

I laughed and let go of my dad. "Will you ever be?" She'd keep holding me until the day she died.

"No. I'll be ninety years old, sittin' in an old folks home, still holdin' my babies. I don't care what anybody's got to say 'bout it," she responded back with stubbornness in her voice.

I laughed a little. "No. You'll be here with me when you're ninety, and I'll still sit on your lap."

"It's a deal." She tapped the end of my nose.

Grey and I sat on our private patio that overlooked the lake below, under a shared blanket. Everyone was home or in bed for the night, and Grey and I were enjoying the quietness of the wind through the trees. It'd been a little tough to say goodbye to the last house we lived in, but this one had become my patch of heaven once we were settled in. Grace had her two rooms upstairs, one for a bedroom, and the other for her paintings. Grey had used a few connections to get her in art galleries all over the country. She never wanted to know how much they sold for, which I thought was funny, but we had a trust set up for her that the money went into. I had my alcove off the side of our bedroom for days when leaving my haven was too much. It had all the sunshine and a breathtaking view. Grey had his home office that had only one actual wall, the rest were glass, along with the hallway that led to it. He'd had trees planted all around the house. At first, I thought he'd had so many windows because he loved the outdoors and being able to see the weather, but I found out he'd done it so I never felt trapped.

"You okay? You're a little more quiet than usual." Grey rubbed my arm slowly with the back of his fingers and kissed the top of my head rested on his shoulder.

"Yeah... I'm just enjoying the quiet... The world feels still."

"That's because our family is *loud*." He chuckled quietly. "A concert would feel quiet in comparison."

I shook my head. "You're right, but that's not what I meant... It'll probably feel fleeting after a while, but right now, I'm not worried about anything. I don't feel like someone's watching me, or lurking around a corner I haven't checked. I'm not sure what to do with not needing to keep an eye over my shoulder, but right now it's nice."

Grey hugged me a little tighter. "You deserve it... I don't think I've ever seen you as happy and content as you were today. I could get used to it."

"Me too. It was a perfect day." A thought ran through my head and made me laugh a little. "I don't know why, but when Grace gave you those papers, I wanted to marry you all over again."

He chuckled quietly. "I seriously wasn't expecting that... Was it her idea, or something you suggested? I know you and I have had our talks behind closed doors."

I shook my head. "Nope. It was all *her*. She came to

me a couple weeks ago and asked. I told her I was fine with it, but I wanted her to talk to Ben, just to make sure there wasn't some underlying reason that..." I shrugged a shoulder, "I don't know, wasn't the right reason to want it. They talked, and Ben said she just wanted to feel like she had something real and provable between you... She's really afraid of losing you in some way. Which isn't a great reason, but it's understandable."

"Mm. I know she is, and it makes me sad that she feels that way. I don't know what else I could do to reassure her I'm not going anywhere." He took in a deep breath and let it out.

"That's the thing. Aside from adopting her, you *have*. She needed it so she could feel like it was real and less of a fairytale. I knew you've been wanting it since the first day of her living with us, so I thought it'd be a good surprise." I smiled as I thought about the look on his face again.

"Second best I've ever had." He kissed my head, then moved to reposition me so he could see my face. "You marrying me was the first."

I raised my eyebrow. "That wasn't a surprise."

He laughed. "Yes, it was. I was dead sure you were gonna bolt. Either well before the wedding or the day of. But looking back at it now, other than the night I proposed, you were resolute..." He smiled at me with appreciation and love in his eyes. "Even after the wedding, I didn't see that you still had your feet planted firmly on the ground because I was sure you were still angry with me, but... you were still there because you were fighting to stay where you were. In Germany, when you asked to go home and not to your parents, I got it then."

I nodded. "I wasn't as mad about being lied to as I was afraid that I'd never make it back home with *you*."

He nodded once. "And here you are... Now that it's all *really* over, I'm gonna have to come up with a better incentive besides guaranteed safety to keep you here."

"Hm. You're right. I was thinking about that earlier. My Superleggera is getting old. I need something new and faster. Also, getting a new Volvo every two years is bull, I want a new one every year. Maybe even six months. My shoe collection is for the birds. I've worn everything at least twice, so I need tickets to Paris and the fashion show by tomorrow. And we're about to outgrow this house, so I'm gonna need a bigger one. Lastly, the fact that you haven't already hired a nanny to help me grow this baby, then take care of it for the next twenty years is appalling. If you think being insanely handsome, perfectly sweet, giving me all the freedom in the world, understanding my quirks, and being loving is going to keep me here, you're out of your mind. Step it up. I deserve more." I looked at him flatly through the duration of my rant.

He laughed.

"That's how stupid your last statement sounded to me." I reached up and pinched the front of his shoulder.

"It was a joke," he laughed as he brushed back my hair. "I promised you anything and everything, and I meant it." Grey was looking at me more seriously now. "I will love you more than everything I've ever known, and more than anything my heart has ever known. Anything and everything I have is yours, Beautiful."

I shook my head. "On our wedding day, you said someday I'd know what you meant by, 'anything and everything,' but you change the meaning just about every time you tell me."

He shrugged with a smile. "Because it's anything and everything. It covers all the bases; nothing is off limits because I'll give you it all... whatever it is you want."

I nodded, finally understanding. "I've had it for eight incredible years." I reached my hand up to touch the dimple on the side of his chin while he smiled contently.

"Me too..." He moved his hand over my stomach as he looked down for a moment. "I love you, Beautiful."

"It's my turn to love you *more.*" I pulled lightly against his face until his lips touched mine.

I never stopped loving him more, but if I was honest, I still think Grey loved us most. Our daughter Noel was born in December, on a snowy night at home. Grey had been the proudest man in the world welcoming his second daughter. He poured everything he had into his girls, teaching them everything he could, being fully present in their lives—whether they *needed* him or *wanted* him—and giving them all the unconditional love he could; myself included. Grey never complained about my anxiety never fully going away, or the need to keep an eye over my shoulder. He understood every time a touch bothered me, or a kiss was too close, and he was happy to still be that person who stuck it out with me.

My situation was different from anyone's, and I'd always known that. Plenty would state that marrying a billionaire gave me an unfair advantage, but Grey's money didn't save my life, I did; along with those willing to risk their lives to help. And money didn't make living with the past any easier. Remembering made life harder. Most children who were taken never returned home alive, and if they did, they could never see beyond what happened to them. Their lives were laid in shambles.

I was also different because I was never taken to be trafficked, I was a reward for my uncle who was labor trafficked. I hadn't even been aware of such a thing until Ben informed me. With all I knew of my situation, it was several years before I understood all the facets. Patty was a victim who was groomed by Henry to become a monster. I'd always known how trapped he felt, how Henry often went against Patty's wishes in many ways that weren't outright obvious, but it took me a long time to understand why he didn't fight back sooner.

Patty was chosen because of his mental illness, and that was used against him constantly. If one were brave enough to make the comparison, they might note that Toby and Patty had certain things in common, but a person's view of good and evil lied with the angle in which a story is told. Both were taken because they were an easy catch, both were taken because they had a disability that could be used to gain an advantage, both were forced to commit a heinous act to save another, but only one had the mental capacity to stop when it was time to stop...

Reframing my own story in my mind was always important. Being angry couldn't be an option because it would inevitably lead to revenge. I felt I'd already dug too many graves in one lifetime to dig one more for myself when I was done retaliating, so I chose a path of understanding, grace, and eventually forgiveness. All three came to me in one night when I realized why I'd gone so long saying nothing. I didn't know how to say something without anger. Fear for my family's safety had certainly been one of my reasons, but not being angry was the biggest one. Anger would've kept me in the life I'd been so desperate to get out of. I needed a better reason than myself to dislodge me from the freeze hold I'd been in; Grey had been the best reason, followed by my girls.

Grey kept his promise. Every day, when I looked behind me, those years of hell mattered a little less each time.

Ready for more?

Visit www.ellymagdaluyo.com for cut scenes from Say Nothing, the Spotify Playlist, in-depth character descriptions, see which actor/actress would be cast for each character, and other books by Elly Magdaluyo.

www.ellymagdaluyo.com

ACKNOWLEDGEMENTS

First, I have to thank my wonderful readers! You make it possible for me to continue sharing my stories with the world. I appreciate every thoughtful comment and message I get.
Thank you!

To my beta readers, Kc, Lily, Tricia, Lashelle, Ashley T, Ashley N, and my editor, Leilani Dewindt, I owe a big thanks. It's always so much fun to hear your thoughts and suggestions. It's the best part of the publishing process for me.

Thank you to my husband who gives me the best, most harsh, critiques. You helped me make this book so much better. I love you, and thank you for 13 wonderful years and counting.

For my two littles, thank you for being such good sleepers so I could work at night and being patient when I work through the day. Please always remember to spread your kindness and love wherever you go. I'll always aspire to be the "Millie Lawrence" kind of mom, but I'm still so proud to be *your* mom. I love love *love you*.

Forever, I will always have the utmost gratitude for my fourth grade teacher, Ms. Moschkau. My love for reading was inspired from her great pick in books, and my love for writing came from her eagerness to teach me.
Eight hugs a day!

Lastly, to "Mama Totsy," thank you for being my best friend/sister and helping me take care of my household. You are so very loved by all of us. I don't ever want a life without you in it. Your constant thoughtfulness and generosity inspires me to be better everyday.

It's estimated 1 person out of every 100 is rescued from human trafficking...
Statistics are only that, so if the math were done according to the statistics, that means of the 6.3 million taken in 2021 for sexual exploitation, 6.2 million never returned home.

If you see something, please say something.

For free resources, please visit the National Human Trafficking Hotline:
https://www.thehotline.org
Call: 888-373-7888 (Available 24/7)
or
Text: 233733

Stay vigilant, stay safe!

ABOUT THE AUTHOR

Author of **Your Life Will Have You Back**, Elly Magdaluyo currently lives in Las Vegas with her husband and two young children. When she's not wrangling her toddlers or writing, Elly enjoys playing the piano or finding beautiful back roads to drive through in her beloved Volvo-with the music turned up.

Made in the USA
Las Vegas, NV
24 November 2024

12529287R00364